# Single Wife

# Single Wife

A NOVEL BY NINA SOLOMON

ALGONQUIN BOOKS
OF CHAPEL HILL
2003

Published by
Algonquin Books of Chapel Hill
Post Office Box 2225
Chapel Hill, North Carolina 27515-2225

a division of
Workman Publishing
708 Broadway
New York, New York 10003

Library of Congress Cataloging-in-Publication Data
Solomon, Nina, 1961–
    Single wife : a novel / by Nina Solomon.—1st ed.
       p. cm.
    ISBN 1-56512-382-4
       1. Married women—Fiction.    2. Runaway husbands—Fiction.
    3. Missing persons—Fiction.    4. New York (N.Y.)—Fiction.
    5. Deception—Fiction.    I. Title.
    PS3619.O437S57 2003
    813'.6—dc21                                          2003040406

*For Nathaniel*

# ACKNOWLEDGMENTS

I owe a debt of gratitude to those people in my life—my angels, mentors, and friends—who gave me the courage to stay on the path. To my stellar editors, Andra Olenik and Elisabeth Scharlatt, for their inspired vision and dedication to this book. To Patricia Bozza, for her keen attention to detail. To my agent, Irene Skolnick, for making this all happen. With admiration and respect to Kaylie Jones, for her unswerving faith and insight. And to Betsy Crane, for her friendship and example.

Many thanks to my constant readers and advisors: Tim McLoughlin, Renette Zimmerly, Janine Veto, Pamela Brandt Jackson, Adam Levin, Christopher Rothko, and Thane Rosenbaum. To Betsy and Richard Shuster, the truest of friends, for allowing me to bring Grace with me everywhere, even to poker night. To Michael Fleisher, for helping me see what I couldn't. To John Lippert, Jennifer Reicher, Carole Ridley, and Richard Zabel, for always being there.

And with love to my mother and father.

# Single Wife

# 1

# THE DURO-LITES

When Grace and Laz got married, her parents gave them twelve Duro-Lite lightbulbs for their dining room fixture. "They'll last till your twenty-fifth wedding anniversary," her mother had promised, kissing her cheek. Grace shrank at these unscripted tender moments. Her father added with a wink, "I'll put my money on the bulbs." This, Grace knew, had more to do with her father's utter and complete faith in the Duro-Lites than lack thereof in their union.

November would mark their fifth anniversary. They had been one of those presumptuous couples who get married on Thanksgiving weekend, forcing all their closest friends and relatives to wear black tie after gorging the night before on chestnut stuffing and pecan pie. "Just roll me home," Laz's oldest friend, Kane, had joked as he adjusted his cummerbund, but even he got into the spirit after a few cosmopolitans. At the very least, their anniversary was easy to remember. Only three more weeks.

Laz had been gone since Halloween. It wasn't the first time he'd left with no explanation, but then only for a night, a couple of days, a week at the most.

She remembered the day he left—how intently he had been studying his cereal as if reading tea leaves. "Gracie, I'll be back in a little while." He left as if he were going to the bank or to buy the Sunday *Times* (although they had it delivered) or to walk the dog (but they had none). An ordinary good-bye.

"S EÑOR  B ROOKMAN  IS  AWAY ?" Marisol, their house-keeper, had asked Grace the Friday after he left.

"Yes," Grace responded. She'd covered for him before—calling his editor, rescheduling his Tuesday squash game, turning down the invitations that seemed to come with more ferocity whenever he was gone. She once even edited one of his articles, which his editor later told him was some of his best work. Laz was always so grateful when he returned, lifting her in his arms into the bedroom and making her forget his absence. And without hesitation, Grace added, "But he'll be back on Sunday."

"So I'll make some of his favorite custard for him before I leave."

"I'm sure he'll love that," Grace said automatically. Marisol made the most perfect caramelized custard. Laz liked to eat it warm right out of the serving bowl, one heaping spoon at a time.

"I can die now," he would tell Marisol and kiss her hand.

G RACE  HADN ' T  INTENDED for the deception to continue this long. She'd assumed he'd be back in a matter of days and everything would return to normal.

And yet Sunday arrived, and Laz did not. Grace went into the living room, carrying a ramekin of Marisol's custard and a large spoon, and played one of Laz's favorite CDs. She blasted it just as he would have done until the coffee table vibrated and the doorman called up to say the neighbors had complained. Just as if he were home. Grace's father once gave Laz a pair of headphones, thinking he'd solved the problem, but Laz never used them. He said he preferred to be surrounded by the music as if in the eye of a tornado.

It began with these small things. Monday, she left a knife with peanut butter and an empty orange juice glass by the sink. Tuesday, his unedited manuscript on the coffee table. Wednesday, a bouquet of sweet peas on the windowsill behind the baby grand, some loose change on the hall table. Thursday, a cigarette butt in a seashell from their honeymoon in Belize, his rumpled tuxedo shirt over the side of an armchair.

"It's nice to have him home again—the house is filled with joy," Marisol commented, as she swept the remains of the ashes with a soft rag.

Laz's presence began to feel tangible. It was easier than Grace had expected. Easier than telling everyone that Laz had left and she didn't know where he was or when he was coming back. It was all in the details. She began to see Laz as an accumulation of habits and idiosyncrasies, things left out, half done, out of order.

Grace put a pair of his socks and underwear in the laundry basket each night. Sometimes she'd sleep in his undershirts to give them a semblance of having been inhabited by a warm body. And each morning she'd take out one of his button-down shirts from the closet, slit open the plastic cellophane from the dry cleaner's that he said kept the shirts crease-free but which Grace thought didn't allow the fabric to breathe, apply some Old Spice to the underarms, and throw the paper collar in the garbage. One of the hardest things to do was learning to leave the toilet seat up in the second bathroom, but that, too, eventually became habitual. She found she could be quite meticulously unruly if she put her mind to it.

Laz was often out late, coming home long after the night doorman was off duty, usually leaving before José came on in the morning. Sleep was at times inconsequential to him; he was fond of saying it could never be too late or too hot, but there were those times when he'd sleep for almost two days straight and nothing could wake him. Grace now began to get up early—a practice against her nature, as she needed a lot of sleep in order to feel like herself, and then not fully until around midday—so that she could run to the deli and get José the cup of coffee that Laz always left him on the concierge desk.

She had a growing feeling of being overwhelmed by these details, but continued with a strong sense of purpose. In order to streamline her morning routine, she bought a supply of the coffee cups they used at the deli with the Greek motif *We Are Happy to Serve You*, and prepared the coffee herself. She worried that José would notice the difference, so she made inquiries after the first couple of days.

"How's the coffee?" she asked.

"Just the way I like it," he answered. "Mr. Brookman is so thoughtful."

EVERYONE LIKED LAZ. Not just in a superficial way, either —they each considered him among their closest friends. At Grace's ten-year high school reunion, at least a dozen people had come up to him, certain that he had graduated with them. When he said that he was just accompanying Grace, they looked at her as if trying to place her. *Didn't you leave after tenth grade?* or *Weren't you a grade below?* or *You used to be blond, right?* After some awkward attempts at small talk, they turned back to Laz. It may have been the way he listened, so people felt understood, or how he seemed to be sharing his soul with them, or the way he remembered minute details, or how he always made them laugh.

One rainy, waterlogged Sunday, after a week of not hearing from him, she discovered his hammered-gold wedding band—the one they'd had made in Florence—behind a rusting can of shaving cream. She had been on a rare cleaning binge that morning, having just finished polishing the silver and wiping the dust from the moldings, and thought the medicine cabinet could use a bit of reorganization. She didn't expect to find Laz's wedding band off his finger. She sat down on the edge of the bathtub. Grace remembered how Laz had haggled with the Florentine merchant until they not only reached a fair price but also were invited to his house for a lunch of bruschetta and veal shank, along with receiving three bottles of Chianti Classico and a private tour of San Gimignano the following day.

It was conceivable that the ring might have been there for months. Grace did not consider herself to be the most observant person (sometimes it took her weeks to notice that a particular store had closed on their block, having been replaced by a Pinky's nail salon or a Starbucks coffee shop). But the ring? She knew better. Laz had abandoned the ring as sure as he had abandoned her—at least for the time being. She steadied herself on the edge of the tub. Her thoughts spiraled, caught between longing for his return and the desire for its deferral. She held the ring in her palm, the light glinting off its uneven surfaces. How could something so light carry so much weight? A symbolic circle of gold now marooned beside an aerosol can.

As she placed the ring back in the medicine cabinet, she ruefully acknowledged, after wiping away a smudge on the mirror, that Laz was going to be gone longer than she had anticipated.

ON HIS BIRTHDAY, twelve days after he left, Grace had a Greenberg cake delivered and two bottles of Veuve Clicquot and cassis for kir royales as usual, and she found it not too difficult to polish off almost an entire bottle by herself. All major events for Laz seemed to occur in November—his birthday, the publication of his first book, the signing of the movie deal, their wedding day. He always called it his lucky month. They may have even met in November, although it was still up for debate. It was at a Halloween party, and Laz swore it was just minutes after midnight.

Grace set the cake on the small glass table by the window and lit the candles, letting them burn just long enough for tiny drips of blue and yellow wax to adhere to the mirrorlike dark chocolate icing. She had fielded phone calls from friends and family all afternoon. She thought that she would most certainly be discovered in her charade when his mother called with birthday wishes, but Mrs. Brookman hadn't heard from him, either, which was not that unusual, so Grace just said he'd call her soon. Grace insisted the doormen take the remains of the birthday cake. Even though she'd always said the cake was too rich for her, she'd eaten two slices, just as Laz would have done.

That night, in one of his dove-gray Calvin Klein T-shirts, she felt strangely closer to him than she ever had before.

THE DAY AFTER Laz's birthday, one of the Duro-Lites burned out. Grace wasn't sure whether to take it as a sign of fate, a dimming glimpse of the future, or the futility of a modern warranty. She stared at the bulb long and hard, and rubbed her eyes as if she might still be dreaming. Laz had seemed so close the night before—almost there. She thought of the trick candles they'd had at his thirty-seventh birthday last year—twenty friends, a pot of Grace's vegetarian chili, and the chocolate cake.

"Make a wish, Laz," Kane had prodded.

"Why? I have everything I could possibly want," he said, squeezing Grace's hand. He'd meant it, too, she was sure of that. But that night, as on numerous others, she had dismissed the signs that something was amiss. When the candles began to flicker and rekindle, Laz's expression changed. A look flashed across his face that she'd never seen before. He suddenly seemed absent or like a stranger, as if in that unguarded moment a glimmer of someone else had surfaced. Grace kissed him on the cheek, and just as quickly, he was back to his old self—everything as always.

Grace found she was holding her breath, waiting for the Duro-Lite to reignite as the candles had. Then the phone rang, and she heard her father's voice on the answering machine. Fitting. Her father had won the bet—Laz had left before the bulb had given out —but she wouldn't let her father know that. Instead, there was a big commotion and a heated discussion about whether to sue the company for selling them defective bulbs or the possibility that they had bought a case of pirated bulbs. Conspiracy theories were very popular in Grace's family. Nothing like a good plot to keep the family united.

"What does Laz think?" her father asked.

"He thinks the wiring was faulty, so he said we should call in an electrician to check it out," she said.

"He's such a levelheaded fellow, that Laz is," her mother added from the extension. Grace's mother was usually listening in on the extension, for some reason, perhaps having to do with wanting to hear what people said when she wasn't around. She pretended not to be eavesdropping, but that was pointless; as much as she tried to be unobtrusive, she couldn't help but interject.

"I think we bought bum bulbs," her father said, exhaling slowly. He sighed often, especially over the telephone. Grace could picture him in his worn leather chair, looking as if he might deflate like one of those surrealist Edvard Munch *Scream* balloons they sell at party stores. "Not even five years. I told you we should have gotten the Satcos."

"Laz said he'll take care of it. Write some sort of letter to the company," Grace added. "As soon as he gets back from London." Grace found that sending him on a trip now and then served her purposes well. It gave her a chance to refuel the energy necessary to sustain two lives and provided a break from her new reality, which was quite time-consuming. "He'll be back the day after tomorrow," she said. She suddenly felt like a character in one of Roald Dahl's dark tales, in particular the one about the landlady who stuffs her boarders so they'll never leave. Grace hadn't realized how accessible her own dark side was, and she found a degree of comfort in following the dictates of her new role as if it lay already mapped out for her.

THE FOLLOWING EVENING, the night of their weekly Scrabble-cum-potluck dinner at her parents' house, was the first true test for Grace. The week before, to her relief, the game had been called due to the imminent approach of Tropical Storm Irene, even though it had still been miles off the coast of the Carolinas.

Weather was of vital importance in her family. The telephone number for the National Weather Service was on speed-dial and was consulted each morning. It was important to get the most up-to-date weather report, so calling a few minutes after the hour was best, and only then could plans be finalized. Otherwise it was "We'll have to see."

When Grace was a child, her father used to give her "rain showers" in the bathtub. Grace, her Mary Poppins umbrella poised above her, would wait for the approaching squall as her father flashed the lights on and off to simulate lightning. In the sixth grade, she had been kept home from school for a total of eighteen days because of wind, rain, ice, snow, or bitter cold. "You never know when the picture windows from one of those skyscrapers will fly out," her father would say. Grace knew then not to question it, and even now on exceptionally windy days found herself looking up, just in case.

GRACE'S PARENTS HAD moved to an Upper East Side building from Stuyvesant Town when Grace was thirteen years old. Her parents loved the building for all its amenities, most notably the in-house dry-cleaning service, their glass-enclosed terrace, and the sleek, ultramodern kitchen. Space-age, her mother still said when referring to the now twenty-year-old interior design, which included white leather chairs and a chrome banquette.

White-brick buildings were just coming into vogue at that time, with no thought whatsoever to how emissions or other things in the air might eventually sully the pristine exterior. But her parents chose instead the only blue-brick building in existence at the time, which her father thought blended perfectly with a clear blue sky. Grace thought it more closely resembled the tube of her mother's creamy cerulean-blue eye shadow that she'd once mistook for a crayon when she was a child, and which her mother still wore for special occasions.

As Grace walked into her parents' building, she saw the usual cluster of elderly widows wearing their best outfits as they lounged in the lobby, and she was struck by a wave of recognition, as if they, too, were just filling the time since they'd lost their husbands. It's just that theirs were dead, and hers was simply missing. And yet there was a finality to both. As she passed by them, she felt sorry that their husbands, unlike Laz, would not soon return.

THE SUGARMANS HADN'T yet arrived, although they lived less than five blocks away. Grace's parents and the Sugarmans had been neighbors in Stuyvesant Town, and both couples had long ago decided to stay no farther than a zip-code distance from each other, whether it be in Manhattan or Delray Beach, Florida, where they had adjacent condos. It would have been easier if Grace and Laz had opted for the same proximity to her parents, but Laz preferred the West Side, and Grace's family had had to come to terms with that.

"By the way, how did he like the sweater we sent him for his birthday?" her mother asked as she set out the Scrabble board. She was petite, dressed in what she called her uniform, which consisted of a knee-length skirt, sweater set, a gold pendant, sheer stockings, and low-heeled shoes. Her hair was swept up off her forehead, accentuating what she considered to be her best features—her large, deep-brown eyes and small, straight nose. She had been a brunette, like Grace, but now her hair was golden-honey blond, from a tube of Loving Care. Other than her hair color, Grace had inherited only her mother's eyes. The rest of her features, including her height, her slightly off-center nose, and her wide smile, were from her father.

"He loves the sweater," Grace answered. Until now, she had rarely found it necessary to lie, even by omission. Her mother had always told Grace when she was growing up that when Grace wasn't being honest, a red splotch the size of a thumbprint would appear right above the bridge of her nose between her eyebrows. Grace thought she was beginning to detect a furrow line right in that same location.

Grace had forgotten to wear the special Scrabble shirt her mother had had printed. It was a black shirt with white lettering arranged in a crossword pattern: Grace's name interlocked with the first *A* in Lazarus, along with Milton and Paulette, and Bert and Francine Sugarman in connecting block letters, complete with a small registered trademark symbol at the bottom.

"Not to worry, Laz left his last time he played. Why don't you wear it?" Her mother said this so reassuringly that Grace wished, as she slipped the shirt over her head, that she could believe this would somehow make everything all right.

"SWEETIE, TELL LAZ that they're predicting a bad storm for late tomorrow. Is he flying into Kennedy?" her father asked.

"I think so," Grace answered.

"Could be long delays. He may even have a layover. Tell him to call ahead to make sure the flight hasn't been canceled." As she listened, Grace thought the three of them made a good, if unwitting, team.

By the time the Sugarmans arrived, her father had printed out two copies of the five-day local forecast from the National Weather Service.

Francine Sugarman was a renowned cook among their circle of friends, and these Sunday Scrabble games were often more about food than etymology, although Bert always faithfully lugged his *Oxford English Dictionary* from their apartment on East Sixty-fifth Street in case of any disputes, which he clearly relished. Bert and Laz shared a love of words. For Bert, his dictionary was like a thirty-pound, two-volume security blanket, while for Laz, words were the source of some greater understanding, as if when the roots of a word were traced back to its source, there was order at last.

"Your mother tells me Laz isn't going to be joining us," Francine said to Grace in the kitchen. Francine's silvery white hair had recently been cut severely short, further accentuating her pale blue eyes and her distinctive nose, which Grace's mother suspected had been "done." "And I made my famous sweet-and-sour meatballs just for him," she added. And they *were* for Laz. Certainly not for Bert, who was diabetic and for whom the meatballs were supposedly off-limits (although he was known to sneak a few when Francine's back was turned), or for Grace, who was a vegetarian. "You know you can freeze them and then thaw them out when he gets back. I'll send you home with a container of them."

Francine's containers had her name embossed both on the lids and the bottoms, and with masking tape, their contents labeled in indelible ink. As Grace looked at the assortment of containers on the kitchen counter, she wondered when this meal had actually been prepared. In Francine's skilled hands, thawing had been elevated to an art form.

"Your microwave heats much more evenly than mine," Francine commented as she and Paulette watched a serving bowl turning inside the microwave oven.

"Paulette," Milton called from the dining room, where he was arranging the tiles upside down and in a diamond pattern, "remember what the doctor told you about your eyes."

"What?" Francine asked.

"Oh, nothing, just something about microwaves causing cataracts," Grace's mother answered, dismissing him as if she were shooing a fly. She opened the door to the microwave and gave the meatballs a stir.

"You could always try smoking marijuana," Bert chimed in from the dining room.

Grace had heard this exact exchange dozens of times, and she could predict what Francine would utter next with more accuracy than the National Weather Service could predict tomorrow's weather.

"Honey, I told you before—that's for glaucoma," Francine called back from the kitchen.

THE GAME PROCEEDED uneventfully, at least in terms of Grace and her dissembling. Her husband was mentioned throughout the game in statements such as *Laz would have gotten the triple-*

*word score,* or *Milt, save some meatballs for Grace to take to Laz,* or *Doesn't Laz's shirt look cute on Gracie?* Bert won the game, which he attributed to the fact that Laz was not there. In the final round, Grace had a *q, y, x, r,* blank, *m,* and *w,* but she was challenged by Bert when she put down *quim,* which would have been her highest score of the game.

"That's not a word," her mother said. "Don't you have a *t* or something?"

"It's a word all right," Bert said, with a customary downward swivel of his head, which looked more like he was trying to suppress a burp than an illegitimate word.

"What does it mean?" her father asked.

"Oh, never mind," Grace said, snatching the tiles off the board. She felt as if she had been caught by the principal kissing a boy in the stairwell at a high school dance. Laz often read aloud to Grace from obscure nineteenth-century volumes he found at the Strand bookstore downtown. Some of the books were on the racy side. *Quim* was one of their favorite words. Like *buzz* or *gargle,* it sounded as it felt. Grace wondered if Bert's dictionary contained the archaic word for G-spot as well.

"It is a word. But it's slang and therefore not permitted," Bert said officially.

"Good, honey," her mother said. Grace looked at her mother, who obviously thought she had bestowed upon her daughter the most lavish of compliments. "Next time you'll get it right."

THAT EVENING, WHEN Grace returned home, she put the container of Francine Sugarman's sweet-and-sour meatballs in the freezer. Francine said the meatballs would keep for over a year. Hopefully, that wouldn't be necessary, Grace thought, as she drifted off.

# 2

## JANE MEETS THE
## INVISIBLE MAN

The dimness in the dining room was bothersome to Grace. So in order to compensate for the burned-out Duro-Lite, the next morning, after leaving coffee for José, she carried in a standing lamp with a pink bulb that she found especially pleasing. When she plugged it in, she discovered that the outlet was not near enough to the table, and went into the pantry to find an extension cord. Grace was absolutely certain that there was one in the utility cabinet above the broom closet. The cabinet smelled of old rubber cement and lemon oil as she pushed aside rolls of duct tape, tins of shoe polish, and old rags.

After several minutes of searching to no avail, she began to grow testy and felt a sudden craving for Saltines that she attributed to having had two cups of tea on an empty stomach, which often left her queasy. She reached farther in the cabinet, thinking the cord might have been shoved to the back. Laz referred to the cabinet as the black hole of household products, and now Grace understood why. She was trying to think of other likely places an extension cord might be when the telephone rang.

"Grace?" It was Kane. "You sound out of breath. Something wrong?"

"Hi, Kane," she answered, brushing the hair off her face. "I was just looking for an extension cord."

"Literal or figurative?"

"Kane, really." She was not in the mood for his playfulness. "I've turned the apartment upside down looking for it."

"You lost it?" he inquired.

Grace could practically hear the wheels in his head turning. "What are you implying?"

"Just that maybe it's time that you cut the cord."

"Kane, I'm talking about an extension cord."

"So am I."

"And anyway, I didn't lose it, I misplaced it," she said.

"My point exactly, but you'll never admit it. I'm just calling to let Laz know hockey's canceled this week because of the Peewees."

"I'll tell him as soon as he gets back."

After Grace hung up the phone, she returned to the cabinet, rummaging around a little, but still unable to locate the missing cord. She did find several odd items and miscellany, like a beaded evening bag with a broken strap, several remote controls with no batteries, a pumpkin carving kit, and a mismatched glove she thought she might someday make finger puppets out of.

Just as she was about to close the cabinet and step down, she caught sight of a photograph. She'd never been fond of the picture. Kane had copied it for them. It was taken seven years ago at the Halloween party at which Grace had first met Laz. They were all in costume. She was standing next to Kane, and Laz had his arm around Grace's friend Chloe. There was a layer of dust over the plastic frame, and Grace removed the picture to look at it more closely. Laz had joked that he wouldn't show up on film since he was, after all, dressed as the Invisible Man. But he was quite visible then.

GRACE HAD MET Kane before she met Laz. Technically, she and Kane had been dating, although it was laughed off as a non-event for both of them. As with all such events, it was often funnier in the retelling.

Once Laz and Grace laid eyes on each other, of course, it was a fait accompli to Grace—she knew that they would be together, despite the fact that she was dating his best friend. After the party, Laz simply took Kane aside and told him that he was going to steal his girlfriend from him, to which Kane responded, "Be my guest." It wasn't until much later that Grace even questioned the sequence of events. Mostly, her ego was a bit bruised that Kane hadn't put up more of a fight, but she wouldn't have changed a thing. She might not have married Laz otherwise.

Grace and Kane had had friends in common and were introduced to each other the summer before the party at a group house in Great Barrington. It was the Fourth of July. Kane had been playing blow pong, and in between sips of beer and Louis Armstrong–like exhalations that sent the Ping-Pong ball sailing across the table, he'd flirted with Grace. They shelled peas into a large glass bowl for dinner, decorated shortcakes in patriotic splendor with blueberries, strawberries, and whipped cream, and by the end of the weekend had formed a certain bond. Over dinner one night, Grace heard numerous references to Kane's friend Laz, his name invoked as if he were some sort of legend. Once back in the city, she and Kane went to a few movies together and kissed only once. He brought her a bouquet of yellow roses, which Grace later interpreted as a friendly, rather than amorous, gesture.

That Halloween, Kane had invited Grace to a costume party, and she'd asked if he had a friend for Chloe, her oldest friend, who was in town from Chicago. Grace dressed carefully, pulling her wavy brown hair up into a Wilma Flintstone–like hairdo and adjusting her strapless bra under the off-the-shoulder leopard outfit she had dug up in the back of her closet. She wore a pair of faux-lizard sandals even though it was raining, and she had to jump over puddles to hail a taxi. Chloe was less than enthusiastic—she hated costumes—but with a little prodding, she succumbed to wearing a peasant blouse and a white kerchief. With her tattooed ankle, spiky black hair, rhinestone cross, and blue Doc Martens, she looked like a punk rock milkmaid.

It was almost eleven-thirty by the time they arrived at 120th Street and Riverside Drive at an unlived-in mansion belonging to a friend of Kane's. The mansion was the perfect setting for a Halloween party. It was legendary for its underground tunnels and passageways that led to the river for unspecified purposes, which were the subject of much speculation during the evening. Kane had opted for an S-and-M Tarzan, complete with a leather whip and a wild black wig, to complement Grace's Jane. Halloween was not Grace's favorite holiday. While walking on the streets of Manhattan around Halloween, she often couldn't tell who was in costume and who wasn't, and it unnerved her.

The moment Grace first saw Laz standing in the darkened vestibule, something about him struck a chord in her, in spite of the fact that his face was wrapped in gauze and he was wearing a hat and mirrored sunglasses. She said hello and then proceeded to spill beer on him when she nervously tried to shake his gloved hand.

"You, I won't forget," he said with a smile as he dried his hands with a cocktail napkin. She knew that first impressions could be misleading—she had been misled before—but this was different.

When Laz asked Chloe if she'd like a tour of the mansion, Grace thought it was very gracious of him to entertain her friend, but then she remembered that Kane was her date and she turned to him.

"I know," Kane said. "Women and dogs—it's like he casts a spell on them."

It wasn't just women and dogs, though, it was everyone. People seemed drawn to him, like a long-lost friend.

Grace was amazed that by the end of the evening Laz, who had undone the gauze but kept on his sunglasses and gloves in deference to H. G. Wells, knew intimate details about everyone present. Of course, they knew of him, too, from the articles he wrote for *Esquire* and his appearances on public television, but mostly for the Amnesty International award for his book on Kosovo, from where he had just returned. His book, entitled *Waking the Ghosts*, documented the six weeks he had spent impersonating a mute Muslim prisoner in a Serbian concentration camp, which he had done in order to write firsthand about the atrocities there. The account was deemed groundbreaking and courageous, catapulting him to almost rock-star status among other journalists. The book had done remarkably well—it was a sensation, actually, and it led to a two-book deal. There was even a Pulitzer nomination. Grace had read an excerpt in *Vanity Fair*. It didn't hurt that Laz was also photogenic and well spoken, and gave the impression that none of the money or acclaim mattered to him, which only seemed to earn him that much more respect.

As Laz talked animatedly about the impact on children orphaned by war, Grace tried to listen attentively, but all she knew was that when he looked at her, which he did often, her cheeks flushed as if he could tell she was busy unwrapping the rest of him in her mind.

After the party, the four of them walked north on Riverside

Drive past Grant's Tomb to where Laz's Saab was parked. The rain had stopped, but the weather had grown colder. Laz put his jacket over Grace's shoulders and took her arm. Even their strides matched.

*The Invisible Man* had terrified Grace when she saw it as a child on Creature Feature. Her parents had left her with a new baby-sitter who made Jiffy Pop then turned out all the lights and closed the curtains in order to create the proper mood for watching the film. For months and even years afterwards, Grace had the distinct feeling that she was being followed on her way to school and that when she showered, she could feel the Invisible Man's fingers tickling her back. But with Laz, none of those old associations applied.

Laz drove them back to Grace's building to her one-bedroom apartment on the top floor of a brownstone. Grace made hot chocolate and the four of them played a game of *Trivial Pursuit*. After they all left, Grace took off her costume and picked up the gauze Laz had left on the coffee table, wrapping it loosely around her hands and up her forearms as she sat on the windowsill and finished her cup of cocoa.

GRACE SLID THE photograph back into the frame. She and Chloe had since drifted apart, but she couldn't remember why. When had they last spoken? It had very likely been nearly a year. Their lives had taken such different turns, and, in truth, Chloe and Laz had never really warmed to each other.

She considered what it would mean to see him walk through the door right now. He could, she knew, at any moment. He had done so before. There was no reason to believe he wouldn't again. Grace never questioned why he was with her. For her, the answer was plain. She had witnessed the lulls, which often turned into dark sieges, when he'd crawl into himself, sometimes not calling for days. She gave him room to breathe, always welcoming him back, no questions asked and demanding no answers. He felt safe with her. Safe to withdraw because he knew she'd always be there to fill in the gaps.

The first time he'd left like this, he was gone for two days, sending Grace into a hysterical frenzy. The night before, they'd talked until dawn and had never seemed closer. He told her about his father's abandoning him when he was three and said that he could never bear to lose her, too. When he finally fell asleep, he looked like a small child. The next day, when he didn't come home for dinner, Grace telephoned friends and family, then eventually the police and hospitals.

Francine Sugarman brought over platters to feed the dozens or so people keeping vigil in Grace's apartment. She even offered to spend the night, having arrived equipped with an overnight bag and her electric blanket, which then blew a fuse. Kane brought bagels and whitefish salad; Grace's mother, a noodle kugel and a package of generic English muffins she'd found at a two-for-one special. Relatives from New Haven, whom Grace hadn't seen for years, dropped by for a few hours, lining up on the sectional couch as if for a matinee. Bert Sugarman took one look at the assortment of people and food and joked, "Who died?"

Grace still remembered the expression on Laz's face when he walked through the door to a roomful of anxious people, all clamoring for an explanation from him, although he had hidden his displeasure well.

"Where on earth have you been?" Grace's mother demanded.

"Where were you?" Milton asked.

"We were worried sick about you," Francine said.

"You couldn't have just picked up the phone?" Bert asked.

Laz shrugged his shoulders and kissed Grace on the cheek.

"If I'd known I'd be getting such a big reception, I would have shaved," he said and laughed, but underneath his smile was an icy look that still made Grace shiver, as if she were the one who should apologize for causing such a stir.

Everyone present sat back and gave a collective sigh of relief. "Thank God you're all right."

The second time Laz disappeared, she called only Kane. "Don't worry, I'll find him," he told her. "I think I know where he might be."

Four hours later, Kane and Laz walked through the door. Laz had gotten in the car and just kept driving until he reached Kane's lake house. When Kane found him, Laz was sitting on the front porch. Grace helped him off with his shoes and put him into bed, watching him until he fell asleep.

"Next time, don't get anyone involved, Gracie," he said when he finally emerged two days later. "No one understands me like you do. Not even Kane. I'll always come back. I promise. You have to trust that."

The third time he left was longer, although she couldn't remember exactly how much longer. Grace vowed to tell no one, waiting each night for Laz to return and occupy an apartment that he apparently had decided not to live in.

The next few times after that were even less distinguishable, and it began to matter less and less to her. Grace knew that any attempts at questioning him would be fruitless. He would provide no answers for her. And while she tried in earnest to feel her way around the perimeter of his defenses for a way in, he'd already slipped out the back.

For Grace, the wedding vows would always fall short. Even if Laz had taken a vow to be physically present along with the vows to love, honor and cherish, it could not have kept him home. Laz was not a conventional missing man. He wasn't out with the boys, carousing the town, slumped over a drink in a smoke-filled, mildewy bar, or playing poker or bowling until all hours with his buddies, or even hanging out at a strip club. That would have been easier to accept. Boys will be boys, after all. But Laz wasn't acting out. He was simply unlocatable.

Eventually, Grace settled into the rhythm of his abandonment and return, the ebb and flow of the tidal shifts in his appearances. She began to prepare herself for each leaving, holding down the fort with a force equal to his withdrawal, so that by the time Laz handed her the final pink slip, she would have already filled his position.

SHE PUT THE photograph into the cabinet and closed the door. With the dust and fingerprints on the plastic obscuring the image underneath, it looked as if Laz were really fading.

# 3

# A PERFECT MATCH

Tuesday was Marisol's day off, so Grace could get ready at a more leisurely pace, rather than rushing around in an attempt to leave evidence of two lives. Actually, editing herself was becoming more of an issue, as she was often leaving too many things out and felt that this, in and of itself, could lead to suspicions.

When she and Laz were first married, it had taken Grace some time to get used to the idea of having someone in the house doing the cleaning. Her father had always been the one to do the dishes and the vacuuming in her family. And Laz, not one to pitch in with the household chores, had found Grace too disorganized for his liking. Disorder rattled his nerves. After returning from vacations, Grace would habitually leave her suitcase on the floor for weeks until she eventually ran out of clean clothes. She was lucky if her clothes were right side out in the closet or if they were on hangers at all.

Laz was the type of person who liked the food in the cabinets lined up according to size, and his neckties hung on an automated rack, arranged in a color spectrum. Once he realized that Grace would not adopt his organized ways, he suggested that they hire someone full time. Having Marisol around had made Grace feel self-conscious at first, and she used to dust and do the dishes before Marisol arrived. But eventually she, too, came to rely on this externally imposed order, until she felt she couldn't get along any other way.

TUESDAY MORNING, AS she used a lipstick brush to scrape a small amount of her favorite lipstick out of its tube, leaving only enough for one more day, she decided it was time to restock. She'd been wearing the same color of lipstick for years—when Laz had first kissed her, when he proposed, and when they were married. She usually bought makeup in triplicate in order to avoid the scrutiny of the makeup artists at the department stores; she felt that they looked at her as if she had no idea whatsoever how to apply foundation or eyeliner, let alone mascara, poor clueless dear.

When Grace went off to college, her mother took a part-time job at the Estée Lauder counter at Bonwit's in order to fill the void in her life due to what she referred to as her empty nest, even though Grace lived at home and commuted daily to Barnard. Known to make surprise appearances in Grace's room with Q-Tips or sponges, Grace's mother reminded her of a bird of prey swooping down with a ten-pound vanity case. Her lesson: It's all in the application, a matter of having the proper tools; the art of creating another self comes with practice. Her mother hadn't spent nearly as much time trying to teach her to contemplate what she was trying to conceal, as she did trying to perfect her ability to do so.

Mid-November was almost peak season for shopping. As soon as Grace entered the bustling world of Bloomingdale's, where her mother had first espoused her most intransigent myths, she was transported back to childhood with the accompanying full range of insecurities. She rarely went to department stores, always feeling lost in the shuffle without the guidance of a weathered shopper such as her mother, who could assuredly negotiate the aisles. The first floor, with its gleaming black-and-white tiled floor, was hallowed ground for Paulette—a place for transformation and the hope of redemption in every department. Just beyond the revolving doors, where shoppers and fragrances competed for air space, anything was possible. And if need be, it could always be exchanged.

As Grace stood in front of the glossy white Clinique counter, listening to the cosmetologist—with her *chocolate* lip liner and white lab coat—explain that they no longer carried Grace's shade, she was confronted with the dismal possibility that there was no perfect lipstick, no perfect husband, except in memory, like the Bonne Belle Lip Smackers she and Chloe had mailed away for in seventh grade—*Cherry 7-Up*. Just the perfect lipstick for the moment like that Heraclitean river that you can't step into twice.

HER EXPERIENCE AT the cosmetics counter was considerably more upsetting than Grace had anticipated. As she walked up Lexington Avenue, she began to feel what she could only identify as a modicum of panic, so she decided to hail a cab and go directly home.

She turned on the television and switched the channel to CNN. Just as she was putting on the kettle for tea, she heard a headline that caught her attention and went into the living room: *Kosovo Controversy—Fact or Fiction?* The voice of the reporter droned on like an annoying buzz from a fluorescent bulb. *A journalistic account of his harrowing experience in a Muslim concentration camp has come under scrutiny, as new evidence is mounting against* . . .

Grace heard the title of Laz's book and reached again for the remote control. Laz had always said there would be people out to discredit him. But now, locked in her own mercy mission of self-preservation caused by his disappearance, she couldn't afford to become distracted by Laz's misery—self-inflicted or otherwise. She didn't want to feel sorry for him. In order to orchestrate his absence, and evaluate their marriage and her place in it, she found it necessary to maintain complete focus and a measured stance. She would tune out news reports and avoid the papers. Laz's troubles may now involve a national scandal, but in her home everything would be preserved, even Laz's reputation.

As she pointed the remote control at the television to switch the station, she thought of her mother, who had read an article in *Prevention* magazine about the dangers of infrared rays. She had seen her mother duck and weave, accusing her husband of zapping her on purpose when he was changing channels, to avoid being caught in the line of fire.

On the next channel was a holiday fluff story about a company called Heaven Scent that could re-create any fragrance. Grace rarely wore perfume and was reminded of the Little Kiddle perfumery she'd received as a hand-me-down from an older cousin. She recalled using the medicine dropper that came in the kit and working with the precision of a scientist to create the perfect balance of apple blossom, lilac, and lily of the valley. When she'd gotten it just right, she spilled it all over the kitchen floor, and her father was forced to take his dinner into his study for weeks because of his highly developed olfactory sensitivity. Once in a while, Grace would catch a whiff of that same fragrance when she was in the unlikeliest places, such as the Port Authority Bus Terminal, and feel a childlike sense of disappointment that her perfume had not been unique at all.

The television program then gave the name of a company that

could match your lipstick color to your outfit or to your poinsettia, if you so desired, by your sending in a sample of the color—even a swatch of fabric—to a cosmetic lab. Sunblock, shimmer, or flavor could be added to achieve an individual lipstick that could even bear the user's personally chosen name.

Grace scrambled for a pencil and wrote down all the information for the lipstick company along with the Web site address: www.perfectmatch.com. The fortuitousness of the sequence of events surprised her. All was not lost, as her father would say, and she went into the bathroom to get the tube of Velvet. She rolled it up, hoping there was enough left. Perhaps it was possible that everything past could be recaptured.

Grace went into the study, sat down at Laz's desk, and turned on the computer. She liked the musical tone emitted as she logged on. Laz had insisted they buy the most up-to-date model, the newest progeny loaded with the latest software, but somehow it was considerably slower in booting up than her old black-and-white PowerBook, which she rarely used and at which she was only semi-proficient. Grace much preferred pen and paper, preferably pink paper, which always lifted her mood. It reminded her of her high school days, most of which were not all that memorable, but as was Grace's tendency, she looked back at most things with a generous quantity of nostalgia.

Actually, she preferred pink to just about any color. She once inquired at her gynecologist's whether her brand of IUD came in pink instead of the generic-looking white—a pink shimmery material would have done quite nicely.

Once the computer booted up, she typed in the password. It was easy to remember—their wedding anniversary, now only eleven days away. As she waited for the modem to connect, she thought about the night before Laz had left. Grace had felt him stirring in the middle of the night and she'd put her hand on his shoulder. He had turned to her with what she had construed as desire at the time —but now saw as urgency—and had pushed himself inside her until she knew he'd come not once or twice, but at least three times in rapid-fire succession. She was used to his high level of desire, but in retrospect she wondered if he had been making up for lost time in advance.

*Invalid password. Please enter the password again.* Grace thought she must have typed it in too hastily. Then she noticed the problem. Instead of their own screen name, it read *GUEST*. Grace thought back to the last occasion when someone else may have used their account, but drew a blank. She must have pressed the wrong command. She switched the name to *gingko*. The first time Laz had kissed her, the gingko trees that lined the street she lived on were like a bright carpet of yellow paper fans strewn across the pavement. Only a few weeks later, the street would smell rancid from the tree's overripe seeds littering the sidewalk.

She heard the whirring off-key notes as she was connected to the Internet. She typed in the Web site address of the lipstick company and waited for the page to appear. She hadn't received a single e-mail, not even a weather update from her father, Miltonfyi@ yahoo.com, who sent group e-mails and newsletters frequently; they concerned such topics as the shortage of rain in the South that might send the price of orange juice skyrocketing or the threat of global warming.

The lack of mail was disheartening, and Grace suddenly felt like running out and joining FriendsoftheFriendless.com. She was comforted by the thought that it would not be long before she would once again have her lipstick, along with an e-mail confirmation to boot.

She watched the screen as the images popped into view like paper flowers opening when dropped in water. She read the heading utterly confused by what she saw. *What do you desire in a perfect match?* A questionnaire followed, along with information on how to register, in flowing pink script. It was a dating service. Grace looked at the address, realizing she had inadvertently typed the letter *a* before *perfectmatch.* She found her mistake only mildly humorous and was about to log off when one of the questions caught her eye. *Can you describe your perfect match in three sentences? If so, then he or she is only steps away.*

Grace was curious to see if she could describe Laz with such precision. She began to type and found that rendering Laz was easier than breathing. "He would read *Oblomov* aloud in bed with champagne and many breaks." *Why get out of bed, if Oblomov doesn't?* he had said, and how could Grace argue? She remembered the breaks more clearly than she remembered any of Goncharov's words— mostly the sound of Laz's voice, the rumple of warm white sheets. She continued typing: "When he smiles, there is no hunger for anything else. And when he leaves, he always comes back."

Three sentences. Succinct and to the point. She was pleased with herself, as if the sheer act of accomplishing the task would somehow bring him back. But as she reread her words, she found herself growing uncertain. Maybe three sentences were not enough. She attempted to type another line, but stopped. Did these three sentences say it all? She rubbed her eyes. She felt the beginnings of a headache. The screen grew fuzzy. No words came.

She selected the lines she had written and pressed the delete key, when suddenly her session was interrupted. She ran to the wall jack, plugged in the phone cord, and picked up the receiver. It was Kane.

"Me, again," he said.

Grace noticed the receiver was sticky and held it away from her ear. Laz liked to eat while he was talking on the phone; this was probably honey from a peanut butter sandwich. She'd tell Marisol tomorrow.

"Hi, Kane. How are you?"

"I'm getting fed up with your husband. He hasn't answered a single one of my e-mails."

"I don't think he got any e-mails. I was just on-line. Maybe you sent them to the wrong address. She had a passing thought about the unexplained "guest" she'd found on her computer and quickly dismissed it from her mind. She was about to relay the whole story about aperfectmatch.com to Kane, partly because she knew he would get a kick out of it, but mostly as a diversion from the subject at hand, when she got another call and told Kane to hold on.

Grace pushed the talk button on the handset and heard a dial tone. She pressed the button again, and in the split second while she waited for the connection, she thought that she might have just missed Laz and cut off Kane as well, but then she heard Kane's voice singing to the radio in the background.

"In a cheery mood, Kane?"

"Always when I talk with you, sweetie."

"Careful, Laz might get jealous," she said, but even she knew how preposterous that was. Laz had never once shown even the slightest amount of jealousy. Kane became silent—a rare occurrence for him. She wished the call-waiting would beep again.

"So, are you going to go up to the lake for Christmas?" Grace asked, suddenly noticing that she was sweating even though she hadn't been warm a moment ago.

"No, my sister's having the clan over," Kane answered. "But I'll be up at the lake for New Year's."

Each year, Kane drove them up to the mountains to a Christmas tree farm near his cabin. Grace loved Christmas—she would get so caught up in the festive decorations around the city that she wished they could keep them up all year long. Her parents and the Sugarmans had always celebrated Christmas, even though they were Jewish—a nonsectarian, watered-down version, with potato pancakes just to hedge their bets—but they drew the line at having a tree, which they thought was somehow sacrilegious. But to Grace, the lights and the smell of pine were the most special parts of all.

Her first Christmas together with Laz, he'd insisted on a nine-foot Douglas fir that was too large to fit inside Kane's Jeep and that had to be tied onto the roof. It had taken a long time to cut down, and Grace's fingers had gone numb from the cold even though Laz had given her his sheepskin gloves, which were too large for her and so well-worn that they'd assumed the contours of his hands.

Kane's house was a mile away from the tree farm, and when they returned to the house, he lit a huge fire. They were ravenous, but the only thing to eat in the house was a box of stale Wheat Thins, some crisp apples, and two cans of salmon. Everything else, including a six-pack of Moosehead beer, had iced over.

"How about we all go skating?" Laz suggested, after their meager lunch. He stood up, wiped his hands on his jeans, and looked out the window.

"It hasn't been cold enough," Kane said. "It still needs a few more weeks."

"Come on. Let's test it." Laz didn't wait for an answer; he was already pulling on his boots. "Who's coming?"

Kane shook his head.

"You guys worry too much," Laz said as he walked out the door.

Grace watched from the frost-covered window, pressing her fingertips to the glass as Laz walked along the perimeter of the lake then ventured out farther onto the ice. Finally, Kane followed him out and stood by the side, calling him back. Laz stopped walking and began to stomp on the ice with the heel of his boot as if to indicate that it *was* ready. Kane walked partway onto the ice and pointed to the window at which Grace was standing. Laz turned and waved. Grace waved back, but in her head she was thinking over and over again: *please don't fall.* When Laz and Kane returned to the house, Laz wrapped his arms around her.

"See, Gracie believes in me," he said. As he lifted her into the air, Grace watched her handprint melting on the frosted windowpane.

On the ride home, Grace took off her boots and curled up under a woolen blanket that Kane kept in the backseat, and closed her eyes. Laz was in the front with Kane. Every so often, Grace felt Laz's hand rubbing the soles of her feet, which would clear away her mental image of the ice cracking beneath him. The sensation of having the soles of her feet stroked made her nose tickle—becoming one of Grace's time-tested signs of true happiness.

So WE'LL SEE YOU Saturday, right?" she asked Kane.

Still holding on to the hope that Laz would soon return, Grace had planned a small gathering at Sky Rink on Saturday, the week before their fifth anniversary, for thirty or so of their friends and family. Nothing fancy, just pizza and a hero from Ralph's.

"I wouldn't miss it," he answered. "Five years. Unbelievable. Tell Laz to call me when he gets in."

"I will."

"Grace?"

"Yes?"

"You know you don't even need to ask. I'll always be there for you." Grace knew there were missing links in the conversation. She had intentionally dropped them like a stitch in needlepoint, to achieve the desired pattern. She knew Kane wouldn't press her further than she was willing to go.

"Actually, I'd love it if you'd make a toast."

"Anything for you, Grace."

Her nose began to tickle as if she were about to sneeze.

# 4

## INNOCENTS ABROAD

Grace was not in the right frame of mind to teach her class, but it was Wednesday, the night Chimera Books, a used bookstore in the west eighties, had been generous enough to allow Grace to use their back room to teach her ten-week course on bookbinding. Laz had done a reading there when his book first came out, the room filled beyond capacity, some people sitting on the windowsills or the stairs. Bookbinding was a term Grace used loosely in the course description that she placed in *The Westsider*. She believed that most of the students came for the swirling, marbleized endpapers and especially for the gold leaf, which was as magical as butterfly wings for Grace. She had learned the art of bookbinding from her father, mostly creating blank books, to be given as gifts. Occasionally, someone would bring in a flaking family heirloom to class, which would require more guidance than Grace could provide. In those cases, Milton was called in for a consultation.

The bookbinding course pleased Grace's father to no end, and this in turn pleased her. Laz called it her "little notions thing," which Grace took as sweet rather than demeaning. She knew how much he valued her insights into his own work, not to mention her editorial and proofreading skills, which usually involved her sitting on his lap, with some form of stroking or removal of items of clothing going on while she tried to work. She thought someday she might actually fill one of her little notions books with more than just notions, and maybe Laz would sit next to her while he proofread her words—as soon as she wrote anything and when he came back, of course.

GRACE'S FATHER HAD learned bookbinding from his father but never went into the family business, instead finding his calling in podiatry. There wasn't a single book in her parents' apartment that was not beautifully bound, often in embossed leather, with hand-sewn folios, a tenderly repaired spine, and sometimes even a dust jacket.

Her mother's cookbooks were wiped clean with appropriate solvents and dusted carefully so as not to cause any damage; they were covered in a clear laminate material for protection from the elements or spills. "People keep their cigars under better conditions than their books," Milton often grumbled. "I have some cigars older than you, Gracie, and they're as good as the day I bought them," he'd say as he refilled the humidor with water, even though he had given up smoking when Grace was a freshman in college. Her parents had recently installed a dehumidifier and ionizer to help keep the apartment dust-free. If her father could just control the climate outside, he'd be a happy man.

He was also a stickler for detail and was never satisfied with any job unless he'd done it himself. More than a few house painters had quit after completing only half the job, refusing to return his phone calls, frustrated by his insistence that they repaint a room one too many times because of barely detectable drips or streaks. Grace had always secretly thought her father should have gone into plastic surgery instead of podiatry, but she kept this to herself, realizing that she and her mother would then have been prey to his inexorable desire to preserve and restore.

During the first year that she and Laz dated, Laz had a book-binding workshop set up for Grace's father in an empty storeroom in the basement of her parents' building. After befriending the super, Laz was even permitted to break through to an adjacent washroom so that Milton wouldn't have to run upstairs to wash his supplies. Her father subsequently spent much of his free time in the basement, emerging from time to time to check on the weather.

"Still snowing out?" he'd ask, surfacing for air or a light snack. Except for going to his office, which was across the street, he might never have ventured out at all. The workshop had been a gesture worthy of a lifetime of appreciation, but Laz thought it was never enough. To him, Milton was the father he'd never known.

The following spring, at Grace and Laz's engagement party with the Sugarmans over Peking duck at Shun Lee, her father gave Laz a present wrapped in brown butcher paper. As Laz opened it, Grace's father had been simply bursting with pride. Inside was Laz's two-volume first edition of Mark Twain's *The Innocents Abroad*—pristinely restored—along with two plane tickets. *For a pleasure trip,* her father had written on a note card. Grace told her parents that they shouldn't have done it, and she'd really meant it, too, because she knew that the value of the book was now quite compromised. She didn't know how her father had even gotten hold of the books.

"Didn't he do a beautiful job?" Grace's mother beamed. "He

even relettered the title in gold with a tiny hammer. And look at the new endpaper. Milton never comes out of that workshop. He's like a little cobbler."

"Blueberry or peach?" Bert asked.

"Bert!" Francine said, slapping him on the shoulder as she leaned over to admire the books.

"Surprised?" Grace's father asked.

Laz turned the books over in his hands, raising his eyebrows and opening his eyes wide in disbelief. Grace expected him to be polite as always, but when he addressed her father and said solemnly, "Mark Twain would have been honored," Grace realized that he was not just being polite, but was truly touched by her father's kindness. The books were displayed behind glass among his other first editions like precious wax flowers.

It was after her and Laz's return from six weeks abroad, loosely following Twain's peripatetic inclinations, that Laz wrote a journal article entitled *The Disintegration of Words,* and Grace's class was first conceived.

THE PAST TWO DAYS had been unusually rainy, and Grace had been vigilant about leaving two wet umbrellas in the vestibule and then removing one of them, to indicate Laz's absence. She also left a pair of Laz's tan-colored Docksiders that she had held under the faucet until they were soaked through and had turned a mucky dark brown. Marisol arrived on Wednesday with a bunch of eucalyptus cuttings arranged with purple asters, which she had brought especially for Laz, who liked the fragrance.

"Feels like a holiday," Marisol announced after she hung up her coat and went into the kitchen to fill a vase with water.

"Good morning, Marisol. Thank you for the flowers."

"My pleasure, Señora Grace." Grace was sitting at the dining room table, which was still rather dimly lit, as she had not remembered to pick up another extension cord.

She had decided after the previous day's mishap that she was better off contacting the custom lipstick company by mail. She wrote the address on an envelope and filled out the appropriate information, such as how many tubes she would like, and settled on three. There was a two-week wait after the company received the lipstick color sample, sometimes longer if it was a difficult match.

As instructed, she made a streak on a sheet of white paper and covered it with Scotch tape. Grace thought better of having them add a flavor, aware of the olfactory power that fragrances had on her. Even essence of vanilla, innocuous as it might sound, could conjure up for Grace a trail of memories that invariably led back to some unwanted locale she had hoped never to revisit. She couldn't go wrong with fragrance-free. Sunscreen seemed a sensible addition, but she decided against adding frost or glossiness. All she wanted was an exact duplication, a seemingly simple enough request. Grace sealed the envelope and got up from the table.

"Marisol, could you give the telephone receiver in the bedroom a wipe? It's a little sticky."

"Certainly, Señora Grace."

But no sooner had Grace uttered the words than she had misgivings. The thought of wiping away the stickiness, Laz's fingerprints along with it, made her feel a disproportionate sense of loss.

THAT EVENING, SHE arrived slightly late at the bookstore with her supplies due to her feeling preoccupied and a little bit on the sluggish side. Her students were already waiting. The bookstore had been decorated with tiny icicle lights around the windowsills as well as with red, purple, and yellow dreidel lanterns that had been strung along the shelves, as Hanukkah was early this year. Grace's family had never celebrated Hanukkah when she was growing up, which she thought nothing of until recently. Her mother had become obsessed with celebrating every Jewish holiday, usually with a roast of some sort and noodle kugel, suitable for every occasion.

"It's traditional," Paulette would insist, even on Passover, when noodles are not permitted. But then Francine Sugarman's honey-glazed pork chops with bread crumbs and Parmesan cheese violated every law of kashrut known to mankind.

The store looked so festive that Grace perked up and began to feel festive herself. She even accepted a glittery holiday crown, which all the salespeople were wearing. As she set up the materials—small-gauge needles, white PVA glue, and a ream of rice paper, she looked up quickly and noticed a young man, probably not yet of legal drinking age, watching her. He was dressed in jeans and a snowboarding sweater—the generic style typical of people in that zone somewhere between college and work. In his hands he held a volume that was clearly in need of repair. He seemed interested in the proceedings but reticent about interrupting.

As she looked at him, he glanced down at the book in his hands and flushed slightly. Grace couldn't help but stare. Everything about him—his eyes, his messy brown hair and delicate eyebrows, his almost beardless complexion, even the way he held himself, half slouching—reminded her so much of Laz it was uncanny, and she found herself drawn to him.

She started off her students with the sewing of the pages, having them first thread their needles with the nearly transparent thread, then she went over to speak to the young man. As she walked toward him, she imagined a few silver hairs sprouting at his temples, as if every step she took were measured in years, not feet, and that by the time she reached him he would be Laz.

"Can I help you?" she asked. She looked more closely at the book in his hand. The spine was cracked and warped, the binding fraying. She gestured toward it. "Are you interested in repairing that book?" He turned the book over and Grace read the title. It was Twain's *Innocents Abroad*. She was thrown by the coincidence.

"I'd like to sign up for the bookbinding course," he began, and Grace heard in his voice a confidence that was belied by the flush in his cheeks. She couldn't help but notice that he was staring at her; then she remembered the crown on her head, and she removed it.

"The next session doesn't begin until January and runs for ten weeks," Grace explained. "You can sign up at the front desk, if you like." She smiled and explained that the course was really an introduction to bookbinding, all the while trying to place his accent, which was vaguely Southern. She discounted her initial reaction as rooted purely in magical thinking.

Her mother had always said she had quite an imagination, though it had never been tested as it was now. He did remind her of Laz, but only in the most superficial ways. And the book he was holding was not in fact a first edition, but rather part of a specially bound collection of literary classics. He thanked her, and Grace figured that the chances of his actually signing up were slight, as he'd probably be back in college by then. She returned to her students, who had sewn their books backward while she was talking to the young man. Her mind was still off on its own peregrinations, not unlike Twain's, but with the added advantage of never having to physically go anywhere.

WHEN GRACE RETURNED home that evening, she turned on the computer on the chance that Laz had sent her an e-mail. The icon indicated she had mail, and she felt instantly buoyed. Grace was utterly amazed at the number of letters she'd received since she last logged on. Suddenly, the world made sense to her again. All the letters that Laz had been sending her must have gotten jammed or lost somehow and now were miraculously retrieved. There were at least fifty unread e-mails. However, as she scrolled down, she saw that not one of the e-mail addresses was familiar. Then she saw one from aperfectmatch.com and understood immediately what had happened. In her haste the night before, she must have hit the wrong command and sent, rather than deleted, her meanderings about *Oblomov* and her description of Laz.

*Click here to sign up for your one-month free trial membership. We are so sure you'll be satisfied, we have sent you a sampling of responses.* Grace was stunned. Here were fifty-some-odd strangers—*odd* being the operative word—who wanted to read aloud to her in some way, shape, or form.

A kind of grotesque curiosity overcame her, and although her first instinct was to delete each and every one of the e-mails, she found herself unable to do so. Oblomov, himself, might have even contemplated leaving the safety of his bedroom, throwing off his dressing gown, and hightailing it out of there. Grace felt a morbid impulse to continue and began to read. The respondents ranged from a lawyer from Montclair, New Jersey, who listened to books on tape while commuting, to a student of Russian literature, to one man who said he liked to watch the Turner Movie Classics station in his pajamas, to a few widowers and even some who Grace suspected were e-mailing from behind prison walls.

She scrolled up and down several times, thinking she must have missed the one from Laz, then signed off. She tried to erase the image of the pajama-clad gentleman from her mind and felt fortunate that she was not single and alone in what seemed a very uninviting abyss.

# 5
# THE MAGIC 8-BALL

Until recently, Grace had been unaware of how simple it was to deceive. Not to *be* deceived—she'd always known that it was easy to let oneself be fooled. That was a personal choice people made. Grace was not gullible. Rather, she chose—and this was a great distinction for her—to have faith. Deception was her new hobby. What she found most disconcerting was how much she liked it.

JUST AS SHE was about to leave the house for her anniversary party at Sky Rink, José called up and said there was a UPS deliveryman who needed her signature. A few moments later, Grace opened the door to the deliveryman, who was holding a large carton with the word FRAGILE taped along the sides, and THIS WAY UP on the top. If only everything came with such clear instructions.

"What's this?" Grace asked, knowing that the question didn't even warrant a response. She signed the slip of paper and closed the door. The carton was light and filled with bubble wrap, tissue paper, and Styrofoam peanuts, and it took many minutes of unwrapping until the contents were revealed. Inside the box were six Duro-Lite bulbs, each nestled in an individual gold-colored cardboard sleeve, like a honeycomb. Grace thought her father must have written to the company and they were replacing the defective bulb, which to Grace meant that she no longer had to mourn the bulb's premature demise. She left for the party, thinking that the other bulbs had another twenty good years left in them still. Not to worry, as her father would say.

Laz was an expert skater, captain of his Wednesday night ice hockey team. Kane was the goalie, but he hadn't played since injuring his wrist four weeks ago. They played at odd times, sometimes from three to five in the morning, practicing on Sundays before dawn when the ice was free. Kane usually brought some Coronas and limes.

The first time Laz took Grace skating, he'd arranged for the ice to be empty, still shining from the Zamboni. She had felt the warmth of the peppermint schnapps radiating through her chest as he stood behind her on the ice and taught her how to shoot a hockey puck.

The temperature was unusually mild for November—almost seventy degrees. Her father mentioned something about a jet stream from the Gulf of Mexico. It was strange weather. Grace was not against the warmth, but she preferred the weather to fit the season and felt out of sorts when it didn't. She liked cool temperatures when it was supposed to be cool, warm ones when it was supposed to be warm. Just as she didn't like hot fudge on her ice cream, or, worse still, whipped cream, which had no discernible temperature at all.

THE NIGHT'S DECEPTION was easier than Grace had expected. She showed up as planned at eight, dressed in jeans and an ivory turtleneck and carrying her white figure skates. When Laz didn't arrive, she made a small fuss and hobbled over on her ice skates to the pay phone in a feigned attempt to reach him.

"He must have missed his train," she told Kane. "He spent the day fishing in New Hope and I haven't heard from him. Will you please make sure everyone has fun, in spite of this?"

"My pleasure, Gracie. But he's going to have to come up with a good one this time." Kane kissed her on the forehead, a not unpleasant sensation. "Tell Laz he doesn't deserve you—I'd tell him myself if I ever saw him."

Grace skated across the ice to greet some late arrivals. As she did, she closed her eyes and imagined that Laz was leading her. The feeling was close to elation, but when she opened her eyes, she found herself about to career right into a woman she'd never seen before. Grace veered off to the side, banging into the plastic railing. The woman was dressed in a short black skirt and stockings, with a red hat on her head, her hair tucked underneath the collar of her fitted black down jacket. Grace looked down at the woman's feet and saw that she was wearing brown hockey skates, identical to Laz's, only smaller. Before Grace had a chance to say she was sorry, the woman darted off, disappearing in the crowd.

GRACE HAD BEEN a skater in her youth, although her mother had insisted she skate only at indoor rinks for fear of thin ice. Grace, herself, was similarly uncomfortable with depths—two dimensions were more preferable to her. Grace learned to skate at an East Side indoor rink that was enclosed in glass like a giant fish tank. It wasn't until Grace was a teenager and had been invited to her best friend's sweet-sixteen party that she even ventured to step onto the ice at Wollman Rink in Central Park.

"There's concrete underneath," she'd told her mother, trying to reassure her.

"You never know, dear," her mother answered. Grace remembered how hard she had tried to think light as she skated along with her girlfriends that day.

Grace was a reasonably good skater still, and as she twirled around on the ice, she was overcome by a feeling of optimism, a feeling she attributed partly to the 3/4-time *Skater's Waltz* and the synthesized winter chill, but mostly to the belief that Laz would soon return.

AROUND TEN THAT evening, a bouquet of two dozen sterling roses, a case of champagne, and a scaled-down replica of Grace and Laz's wedding cake—a chocolate confection embellished with colorful frosting to rival van Gogh's sunflowers—arrived along with apologies "from Laz." Grace had only remembered ordering one dozen roses, but Laz was such a good customer at the florist that they must have thrown in another for good measure. Grace had also struggled over how to word the card—how to make it sincere without effusion. She had finally decided that less was more and had written, *From your loving husband, who will make it up to you when I get home.*

Kane made a toast, which began "In absentia" and ended with "To my best friend, wherever he may be, we're not saving him any cake, and if he doesn't get here soon, I'm taking Gracie. Just kidding, Milt. Love you, Paulette, and you too, Laz." Everyone laughed and clapped. Grace could always count on Kane to fill these social gaps until Laz showed up—better late than never, he'd always say. All the guests remarked on the exquisite flowers, claiming that the cake was too beautiful to eat, but then all except Bert Sugarman proceeded to devour it and to comment about how truly blessed she and Laz were to have each other.

As she looked around at her and Laz's friends and family, Grace was aware that just the pretense of Laz was enough for them to feel they were part of his life. And people wanted to know her, his wife, because by virtue of being near her, they were close to him. But as little as they knew her, they knew Laz even less.

AFTER THE PARTY, Kane carried the shopping bags filled with anniversary presents down the elevator and through the parking lot to his car. Most of the presents were useless gifts: an array of tacky bottle openers, which Laz collected from around the world; an electronic drum set with matching headphones; and his-and-her Lladró figurines, from the Sugarmans. It didn't matter that the presents were ludicrous, the more ludicrous the better. Laz would have loved them.

Kane opened the passenger-side door for Grace and put the bags in the back. He got in, buckled his seat belt, and reached under the seat. Grace saw that he was holding a square white box that was wrapped with a gold elastic ribbon diagonally around it.

The box looked so familiar. Grace tried to place where she might have seen it before, then she remembered boxes identical to this one that Laz used to bring home for her from the novelty store on Amsterdam Avenue, each filled with some vestige from her childhood.

"Oh, you shouldn't have," she had exclaimed one time, kissing Laz as she opened a box containing two spinning pups. When she was a child, her father used to enchant her by insisting that the miniature magnetic dogs could move by themselves. Laz had set the pups up on the dining room table and sent the black and white Scotties flying across the glossy surface, making them do figure eights around the salt shakers.

Kane stopped at a light and handed her the box.

"Open it when you get home." Grace looked at Kane and realized that even though he was smiling, his eyes looked far away, sad even. She tried to brush away the feeling that she was in part responsible for his disappointment, that he missed his friend, too, and she was deceiving him. Grace held the box on her lap, and they rode home in almost complete silence until they stopped at a light a block from her building.

"Laz missed a great party. You know he loves you, right, Gracie?"

"Of course, I do."

UPSTAIRS, GRACE PULLED off the ribbon and lifted the lid from the white box. She unfurled the tissue paper and took out a shiny black globe. A Magic 8-Ball. Kane had written a note: *To Grace and Laz. For when there are no answers.* Grace wondered if Kane knew, but she remembered how he'd looked in the car, and she knew that he couldn't possibly. Then she noticed the carton of Duro-Lites by the front door. She'd forgotten to thank her father.

"Will Laz come home before another bulb burns out?" she asked, closing her eyes. She turned the 8-Ball over and waited for an answer to appear. *Ask again later.* But Grace could not wait. She shook the ball until there were bubbles in the inky blue liquid. Finally she got the answer she was waiting for. *You may rely on it.*

# 6

## IT'S A MYSTERY

The day after the anniversary party, Grace awoke with a dull ache in her temples, which she suspected was from the champagne. She'd had a fitful night's sleep. At three in the morning, she had awakened from a dream about Laz. His voice had vibrated in her ears and she had heard the faint tinkle of pocket change. *I hope you liked the flowers, Gracie.* It had seemed so real; she'd even felt the warmth of his breath on the back of her neck as he spoke. In the morning, she found Laz's gold-knot cufflinks on the night table. A nice touch, she congratulated herself, not that she recalled having put them there. Next time she'd go easier on the champagne.

She wasn't looking forward to the Scrabble game that evening. The thought of trying to put two words together, let alone more than two letters, seemed overwhelming. She wanted to float in a tub of warm water—sprinkling in twice the recommended amount of Dead Sea salts so that the water turned a deep sky blue, which had a strongly soporific effect. Her morning cup of mint tea did little to revive her.

She contemplated returning to bed, but then remembered the carton of Duro-Lites that had been delivered the day before and decided to replace the burned-out bulb. If changing the bulb didn't serve to brighten her spirits, then at least it would brighten the room. She stood on the stepladder with a new Duro-Lite in her hand, steadied herself, and screwed the bulb in. It was too bright now, so she tried adjusting the dimmer. After several tries with no noticeable dimming, and a phosphorescent tint to everything she looked at, she decided to call the building's handyman.

Before the handyman arrived, Grace closed the bedroom door and slung Laz's favorite yellow Hermès tie over the doorknob. They had won the tie in a raffle last May at a diabetes ball chaired by Laz's mother. It had a striking pattern, but right now Grace thought its motif looked more like squiggly sperm on lily pads rather than green tomatoes.

She recalled many nights when Laz had come home late—too late, he'd said, to call—not wanting to wake her. But the truth was, he knew she would be up waiting for him. After one of those late nights, Laz would usually sleep till noon. Grace had continued the tradition, asking Marisol to forgo the vacuum so as not to wake him, and even Grace found herself trying to be extra quiet. Sometimes, with the shades drawn and the bed slightly rumpled, she could almost fool even herself.

"You have a big problem, Mrs. Brookman," the handyman said as he removed the light plate. She caught herself before she said she knew. He was in his stockinged feet as if he, too, were trying not to disturb Laz, having left his work boots by the door, a detail that Grace found somewhat disagreeable.

Whenever anyone called her Mrs. Brookman, Grace would turn around, half expecting to see Laz's mother in a teal blue leather pants suit, waiting for the driver to take her to Zabar's and

announcing to whoever was within earshot how exquisite their octopus salad was. Laz called his mother a dame. Grace didn't call her
anything. Just a casual, "Oh, hi," when she called.

"I'm gonna have to take the whole thing out—the wires are
crossed," the handyman said, clearly losing his patience. "But I can't
do it today." Grace nodded. "I'll be back tomorrow with the right
splitter. Whoever put this in did a lousy job."

Grace knew full well who had done it. She remembered how Laz
had twisted the red and blue wires together, snipping them with the
wire cutter. He'd tested the dimmer, artfully ignoring the few snaps
and sparks that shot out from the switch, then lifted her up onto
the three-leaf table.

"Keep the lights off until I come back. You could short out the
whole line," the handyman said. Grace imagined the entire West
Side going dark because of an accidental flip of the light switch. She
gave the handyman a ten-dollar bill and closed the door after him.

WITH THANKSGIVING LESS than a week away, Grace de-
cided it was wise to thaw out the cranberries in advance for the relish she was going to make. She found the cranberries in the freezer
behind two Ziploc bags of bagels and the container of Francine
Sugarman's meatballs. Grace's mother had purchased the cranberries last year, a week after Thanksgiving, when they went on sale.
"Only fifty-nine cents," her mother had beamed. As Grace reached
for the bag, she saw the frosted glass fishbowl she and Laz had
put in there three years ago. Frozen in the ice was a key to his old
apartment.

They had argued about his not giving up the apartment, eventually agreeing to put the matter on hold, at least symbolically.
They would thaw the key out and deal with it later. Grace had read
about this technique in an article about relationships, and it

seemed to work—except that they had never thawed the key out or spoken of it again. In the top drawer of Laz's dresser, however, there was a spare key, and Laz still went to his old apartment occasionally to write or listen to his old records.

The fishbowl had once contained a goldfish and a Japanese fighting fish. On one of the previous occasions when Laz had left, Grace neglected to feed the fish or to change the water in the bowl. Every time she passed the bowl, she told herself she would feed them later. By the time Laz returned, the water had become so clouded that Grace couldn't even see the fish, who were by then floating belly-up on the water's surface.

GRACE WAS STILL holding the fishbowl in her hands when the phone rang. Her fingers had frozen to the glass. She ran the bowl under warm water, dried her hands, and put the bowl back in the freezer. The machine picked up. *Hi, Gracie, it's Dad. I didn't send the bulbs.* He paused, sighing deeply. *It's a mystery. Give a call.* Normally, Grace liked her father's expressions, such as *Give a call.* Or *Greetings!* instead of hello. But *It's a mystery* was one she'd never liked.

She had mentioned the bulbs to her mother on the phone last night. Her father had already gone to bed. Now a mystery was at hand, and the family was mobilizing like ants marching to a sugar cube. Mysteries were common in Grace's family. There had been the mystery of the disappearance of the roll of quarters, still unsolved to date.

"I don't know," her father would say. "I guess it's a mystery." And the subject would be dropped until the item was located weeks, maybe months, later in her father's sock drawer, where it had been all along.

And then there was the mystery of the gas-guzzling car, which eventually turned into a conspiracy theory about someone from the garage driving their car. Or the mystery of the Electrolux vacuum, still a sore subject in their family; it was discovered inexplicably years later in the linen closet concealed like a body inside Grace's blue nylon camp sleeping bag. The method was never questioned, or its purpose analyzed. *It's a mystery.* That catchall phrase was used by her parents as liberally as salt for all unexplainable occurrences, the equivalent of *poof* to prestidigitators.

Grace hated mysteries. She wanted an immediate answer to where the roll of quarters could have gone. She would search all over until she was exhausted and nauseated. When the item was still not located, she felt as if some supernatural power was at work. Extension cords could disappear without a trace, and things could happen without warning, like bulbs arriving with no explanation.

Laz's absence at that night's Scrabble game was one mystery that everyone seemed eager to let slide, for now.

"Laz is where?" Bert asked, swallowing a stuffed grape leaf in one bite.

"Utica," Grace answered. "He's giving a lecture at Hamilton College."

"Utica? Really, there's quite a storm expected for the day after tomorrow," her father interjected. "A nor'easter," he said, as if he were a Long Island fisherman. "Could dump a foot and a half of snow."

"Tell him to pick up some sheets while he's there," her mother said.

"What are you talking about, Paulette?" Milton asked.

"You know—J.P. Stevens. The sheet company."

"He's probably too busy to pick up sheets, dear."

"Well, he might feel like browsing."

"Why didn't you go with him, Gracie?" Francine asked.

Grace's mother nudged Francine and whispered, "You know, Laz says she's becoming agoraphobic."

"Agora-what?" Bert asked.

"I'm not agoraphobic, I'm *acrophobic*," Grace said, remembering the onset of her fear on a trip across the Continental Divide. "And this was just supposed to be a quick trip."

"Agoraphobia. Is that a fear of sweaters?" Bert asked, flipping through his *O.E.D.*

"Sweaters?" Francine asked.

"You know, like angora." Grace's father joked. "Gracie's afraid of fuzzy sweaters."

"Did you see that movie *Arachnophobia*?" Paulette asked Francine. "I go weak in the knees when I see a daddy longlegs. Gracie hates spiders, too. Right, sweetheart?"

Actually, Grace didn't mind spiders. It was moths that made her uneasy. The way they got into her drawers and ate through her sweaters, leaving tiny holes even when the drawers were closed tight, or the way they found their way into sealed garment bags. Worst of all was when she found a dead moth on the windowsill and how the moth turned to dust when she touched it, as if it had never been quite real at all. She could not tolerate the smell of mothballs, so theoretically Bert was correct—whenever she could avoid it, she did not wear wool.

"Could you just go already?" Bert snapped.

"Whose turn is it anyway?" Grace's mother asked, passing the grape leaves.

GRACE TUNED OUT the bantering and bickering. She thought about the nor'easter. It was still unseasonably warm out. The thought of snow when it was nearly sixty degrees outside seemed utterly improbable. Still, when she returned home, she turned on the Weather Channel. The swirls of clouds and jet streams captivated her.

As she watched, she began to see the dramatic tension and even a narrative drive to the gathering clouds and high-pressure systems —a testament to the underlying forces of nature. She began to see her father's obsession with weather as almost poetic, noble even. There was a dirgelike pattern and rhythm, a mournful tone. Laz might not make it back for the holiday. It was an unusual thing to wish for, but a nor'easter might just be the answer to her Thanksgiving prayers.

# 7
## WOODSTOCK

The snow arrived in huge drifts all along the eastern seaboard, making air travel impossible, causing long delays on Amtrak's service, but somehow bypassing the tristate metropolitan area and reconfirming Grace's faith in the National Weather Service. Laz would no doubt miss the holiday, and everyone, especially Grace, felt the loss.

THE AMARYLLIS HAD begun to bloom. Laz had brought the plant home just before he left—a wooden crate containing three bulbs covered with sphagnum moss.

This morning, Grace noticed a tight red blossom on one stalk. After she had come up from bringing José his coffee, the blossom had begun to open. Grace usually left the tending of all plants to Marisol, who fertilized them, trimmed off dry leaves, and knew exactly how moist to keep the soil. Grace either overwatered or neglected the plants altogether. When Laz gave her the amaryllis, he told her that it would bloom for six weeks (which she now took as some sort of sign), and then would need to be cut at the stem and kept in a cold, dark place for six months. His words resonated, and she wanted to tell the amaryllis that there was no need to rush.

Grace looked out the window, marveling at the sight of families gathering on both sides of the street more than two hours before the start of the Macy's Thanksgiving Day Parade, some carrying stepladders and planks of wood to contrive curbside seats. It was an unspoken assumption that Grace and Laz would host a brunch every Thanksgiving for all their friends and relatives who had small children so they could enjoy the spectacle of the parade without obstruction or exposure to the elements.

The parade was still a wonder for Grace and for Laz, the two of them bundling up each year to watch the balloons being inflated the night before. The year that the remake of *Miracle on 34th Street* was filmed, they had been able to watch the parade over and over as they drank their morning coffee, like a perpetual Thanksgiving.

Grace's family was small, or rather, there were only a handful of relatives she and her immediate family kept in touch with. Grace had been a teenager when she'd finally realized that Francine and Bert weren't her aunt and uncle.

She knew her cousins in a fleeting way; they generally came out of the woodwork just before the holidays. She didn't know all of their names, so when a group of them arrived at nine that morning to watch the parade, Grace just said a general, "Come on in," which she was afraid sounded insincere and flat. She led her guests into the living room, where they assembled themselves on the window seat like sparrows at the boccie court in Central Park.

MARISOL HAD PREPARED the batter for the Dutch Baby the previous day, which she told Grace to bake in a preheated oven for twenty minutes before serving. Grace placed a half stick of butter in the hot pan, watching it sizzle and melt. Then, as per Marisol's instructions, she poured the mixture into the center of the roasting pan. After placing it in the oven, she sat on her knees to watch the batter bubbling and rising along the sides of the pan, something she remembered having done as a child. She still found it utterly amazing that the end product would turn out so perfect— a giant popover, hollow and steaming. And it worked every time.

The doorbell rang, and as Grace stood up she felt disoriented and wondered if the daily routine of putting on an act was catching up with her. When she saw Kane standing in the doorway, holding a white box, she suddenly felt an overwhelming urge to tell him everything.

"Happy Thanksgiving, Grace."

"You, too, Kane," Grace said, taking the box from his hands. "Another Eight-Ball?" she asked, smiling.

"I think one's enough, unless it's not working."

"No, I think it's been quite accurate thus far." Kane unwrapped the knitted scarf from around his neck, and Grace could see his skin was blotchy and red as if he, too, had an aversion to wool. He followed her into the kitchen, where the Dutch Baby was rising nicely, and he opened drawers to look for a pair of scissors. He cut the string from the box and removed one of the almond croissants that Laz was so fond of. He broke it in half, handing a piece to Grace.

"We might as well," Kane prodded her. She accepted, aware that the tightness she was feeling around the waist of her skirt was due in part to her sudden affinity for all the sweet things that Laz liked to eat, which she no longer could resist in his absence. It was also due to her sudden, unexplainable urges for foods such as the quesadilla grande *with* sour cream she'd ordered the night before, when she'd always been perfectly satisfied with a whole wheat spinach wrap.

The almond croissant was completely unsatisfying and she immediately wanted another.

"Nice Baby, Gracie," Kane commented.

"What baby?" she asked.

"The one in the oven, of course. Is there another one?" Grace felt her cheeks flush, and she laughed nervously, then began to cough from the second croissant she was still chewing. She gave Kane a playful nudge on the shoulder.

"Thank you, it's Laz's favorite," she said finally, after the coughing had subsided and before the hiccups began. Grace always got the hiccups whenever she coughed. According to her mother, Grace did nothing but hiccup in utero, like an embryonic call for help emitted in code. She went to the sink to drink a glass of water from the opposite rim, the only cure for her hiccups, which could sometimes be known to last for an entire day.

THE DUTCH BABY made a beautiful presentation on the buffet. Since the dining room fixture had still not been rewired, Grace lit candles instead.

"Very Martha Stewart," Kane commented, admiring the outlines of leaves that Grace had stenciled with powdered sugar over the popover. Grace ladled raspberry purée onto everyone's plates except those of the children, who preferred maple syrup, and whose sticky handprints she later found smudged along the windows. Kane took his plate and whispered into Grace's ear as he pointed to a serving dish of a creamy-white mixture.

"And that is?"

"Francine Sugarman's famous artichoke dip, of course—circa 1997, although carbon dating can be inaccurate," she whispered. "And if anyone offers you a round orange ball, don't take it. It's a sweet-potato-and-shrimp dumpling from last New Year's brunch."

"Pity Laz isn't here to enjoy this," Kane said. Grace busied herself rearranging the serving platters, consolidating and shifting food as Kane spoke. "He never missed a Thanksgiving before." Grace found herself literally unable to look at him, and she realized how odd she must appear performing these tasks.

"Grace?"

"Just a second, Kane, I think I left the oven on," she said, and quickly left the room. She found some solitude in the kitchen until she heard a commotion from the living room and came out to see what was happening. The yellow tip of Woodstock's crown, then his beak and eyes were pressed against Grace's window, peering in, his body slamming back and forth in the strong gusts of wind as the balloonists tried to right him. Grace thought the window would surely break. She felt the need to brace herself against the nearest, sturdiest object, which happened to be Bert Sugarman.

"Look, he wants to try some artichoke dip," Kane joked, luckily not within earshot of Francine. Grace let go of Bert and ran to the window to pull down the Roman shades in case the glass shattered, just as Woodstock was pulled back under control to the sound of cheers from the street below.

"Never a dull moment at the Brookmans'," Kane said.

HOPING TO BEAT the holiday traffic most of the guests left before Santa Claus passed by on his sleigh. Kane was one of the last to go besides Grace's mother and Francine, who were busy packing up the leftovers. Grace handed Kane his coat and scarf at the door and he kissed her on the cheek.

"I'm counting on you for tonight," he said. "We'll just have to do it without the creep this year." Grace had completely forgotten about their post-Thanksgiving tradition of going out and playing drinking games, their way to decompress after an overload of stuffing and family. The thought of Kane alone made her feel awful.

"I wouldn't miss it. We'll have just as much fun without him."

"That's the spirit, Gracie," he said, kissing her on the other cheek. "Nine o'clock. Tap A Keg."

"It's a date," Grace said. As she closed the door behind him, she could hear her mother and Francine talking in the kitchen.

"Half a Dutch Baby. Such a waste!" Francine said.

"It doesn't freeze well," Grace's mother explained. "It gets mealy."

"It's a crime," Francine sighed.

"I told her to do the waffles. You never have a problem reheating waffles."

GRACE TIDIED UP the pillows on the window seat and felt a chill from the casement windows. She pressed her palm to the glass. It felt like snow. She didn't need to watch the Weather Channel; she could feel it in her bones.

# 8

# THE BUTTERBALL

Grace chopped up two cups of walnuts on the butcher block countertop and added them to the cranberry relish. The walnuts gave the mixture a more substantial look, which was necessary because she'd neglected to buy another bag of cranberries. After the holidays, things would be much less hectic, or maybe more so, depending on whether or not Laz was home by then.

She dressed in the tan-colored leather pants Laz's mother had given her, thinking it was only polite since the elder Mrs. Brookman would be joining them for Thanksgiving. Grace had some trouble lacing up the front of the pants, sucking in her breath as she tied a bow. They were a little snug, but it was the first time she'd worn them, and she assumed that they would loosen over the course of the day.

The first time Grace's parents met Nancy Brookman, they had acted as if they were preparing for royalty. Grace's mother had her hair and makeup done by Phaedra at Frédéric Fekkai, instead of by

Renatta at her usual salon down the block, and she bought a new outfit. She even hired Marisol to help serve, tying a starched white apron around Marisol's waist. Grace's father broke out a bottle of cognac from 1917, which was served out of the Baccarat snifters they'd received for opening an account at Apple Bank. Bert affected a strange, quasi-European accent all evening, as if he'd been schooled in Bombay. The only one who had not acted impressed with Nancy Brookman was Francine, who snubbed her all evening.

"I know a girl from the 'Coops' when I see one," she told Grace's mother after Laz's mother left, not realizing that Laz was standing in the doorway behind her.

The Coops was a progressive apartment complex, built in the 1920s, north of Allerton Avenue, where Francine and Bert had met as teenagers. Grace had always wondered about Nancy Brookman's hybrid accent, which switched depending on the situation, going from upper-crust diction to practically street slang, when she spoke to the garage attendants in her building.

"She's not from the Bronx; she's from Newport," Bert corrected Francine.

"And that outfit—a knockoff of a knockoff! Who does she think she is, anyway? The Queen Mother?" Francine continued, sealing a Ziploc bag.

"No," Laz answered, sneaking up from behind and taking a bite of leftover spinach pie. "That job's already been filled."

WHEN GRACE LEFT her apartment building, snow was falling like powdered sugar being sifted over the city. It seemed to defy gravity, flurrying upwards and sideways, and Grace couldn't imagine how it managed to stick to the pavement. The first Valentine's Day she and Laz were together, snow had piled up on her windowsills overnight. Laz had rung her buzzer at six in the morning, running up the stairs while carrying two pairs of skis under his arms. It had been strangely light out; even though it was not yet dawn, the sky glowed pink through the shutters.

"Get dressed. We're going skiing," he said. He was wearing an orange stocking cap with a pom-pom on the end. He looked like a jester.

"You're nuts. It's Sunday—and just barely," she said, turning to go into the kitchen. "Come on—I'll make us breakfast."

"I got you the day off tomorrow. The car's still running," he said. "The mountain awaits us." Grace stopped and threw her arms around him. She had never so much as taken a personal day before.

Grace taught ceramics at a private school in Manhattan. She got immense pleasure from watching her students work, forgetting everything else as they transformed the clay and themselves. Once she and Laz married, she gave up the job without so much as a word of protest after Laz pointed out that it was just glorified babysitting and that she should focus on her own work. But after she resigned, sculpting became less of a priority, somehow. At the time, it hadn't occurred to her to put her job, along with the key, in the frozen fishbowl.

On the drive up to the mountain that Valentine's Day, they talked nonstop, as if they needed to get caught up after decades, and not days, of not seeing each other. Laz told her about one of the two times he'd seen his father since he left, at a diner near his prep school.

"I had a grilled cheese with tomato and a milk shake. I remember he kept taking out his pocket watch to look at it, but it wasn't even wound up. And he didn't offer me a ride back to school," Laz told her, swallowing hard and clearing his throat. "But he gave me his broken watch. He asked me if I had enough change for the bus, and then he put his hands in his pockets as if he was afraid I might ask him for something else. I only saw him once more, at my college graduation, and afterwards he disappeared into the parking lot, without even saying good-bye."

Grace and Laz arrived at Belleayre before it opened and got the first lift tickets of the day. BE MY VALENTINE was printed on the tickets. On the ski lift, Laz told her that he wanted to marry her. His lips warmed her cheek. As Grace's skis alighted on the snow, Laz blazed the trail ahead of her. This pattern had seemed so simple then, desirable even. All she'd had to do was follow.

WHEN SHE ARRIVED at her parents' apartment in the afternoon for Thanksgiving dinner, her mother had already set out a large selection of bowls and platters for Grace to choose from in which to put her contribution to the feast. There were bowls made of leaded crystal, stainless steel, porcelain, wood, even huge melamine ones in neon colors from her mother's modern period. Most of the bowls were actually for Francine Sugarman, who would empty the contents of her plastic containers into the appropriate receptacles, but only after a lengthy discussion of the serving situation — into the middle of which Grace had just entered.

"The asparagus need an oblong platter," Francine complained. "You can't serve asparagus bent like that."

"Francine, I don't think I appreciate your tone," Grace's mother said, grabbing the asparagus as though they were a bunch of weeds and dumping them onto another platter. "There, is that better?" In Paulette's haste, a few of the spears had snapped in half like twigs, still partly frozen from Francine's Sub-Zero. Francine's jaw clenched but she didn't say a word. Bert, still wearing his wool coat and galoshes, walked into the room carrying bakery boxes.

"Here are the Sacher tortes from our trip to Vienna last spring.

You're going to die when you taste them." He put the boxes down on the sideboard and surveyed the proceedings. "Everything looks beautiful, Paulette," he said, dipping his finger into the sweet-potato purée. "Needs a touch more in the microwave, though." And then, as if on cue, he added, "Where ever did you find baby asparagus this time of year?"

Francine and Paulette suddenly burst out laughing and put their arms around each other, admiring the table as if it were a piece of art.

"What?" Bert asked quizzically. "What did I do now?"

GRACE'S FATHER WAS busying himself in his study, as was his habit. He'd invariably appear just in time to perform his appointed tasks, which, for Thanksgiving dinner, involved answering the doorbell when guests arrived, serving drinks, and carving the turkey. He thought it wiser to stay clear of the combat zone until the last possible moment. If Laz were here, he'd have been in the study as well, while Grace's father proudly showed off his latest high-tech gadget, such as the paper shredder, which he used to shred everything from junk mail to newspapers.

Grace's mother and Francine went into the kitchen to check on Francine's sweet-and-sour meatballs. Grace sat down at the kitchen table and began filling the turkey-shaped salt cellars and rolling the linen napkins into the minipumpkin napkin rings. The pilgrim centerpiece she'd made in the fourth grade had only recently been relegated to the hall closet after having adorned the Thanksgiving table for two decades.

"It's times like this I wish I had a second microwave," Grace's mother sighed.

"Did I mention I'm going to Paris in two weeks?" Francine announced.

"Really? On a tour?" Grace's mother took the meatballs from the microwave and poured them into an orange melamine bowl.

"Don't waste the sauce," Francine said, using a plastic spatula to wipe around the inside of the bowl until it was so clean that it looked as if it had just come out of the dishwasher. "Too bad Laz is missing my meatballs again," Francine said. "Grace, should I pack up another container for him?" Grace looked up from the table, thinking about the other containers still in the freezer at home.

"You really don't need to go to any trouble," she answered.

"Don't be silly, it's my pleasure. Just bring back my containers this time." Even if Grace weren't a vegetarian, there was no possible way she could have consumed that many meatballs before the next Scrabble game.

"Why don't you give her the recipe, for goodness' sake?" Grace's mother asked, for what could easily have been the hundredth time. Francine bristled.

"You know *real* cooks don't follow recipes," she responded, with a quick toss of her head. "Anyway, I'm off to Le Cordon Bleu soon," Francine continued. "Two weeks with the world's most renowned chefs—what could be better?"

Bert walked into the kitchen and sat at the table, his coat off, but still wearing his galoshes.

"Those frogs won't be able to improve on these," he said, spearing a meatball with a plastic toothpick. "How much would you pay for these meatballs in a restaurant?" he asked, while making a second attempt at spearing another meatball, which was swiftly intercepted by Francine. "And I'm losing my dancing partner."

"Bert, really, I think you of all people can make some sacrifices for once," Francine said, shooing him away from the table.

"And who will take care of my butterflies?" he asked.

"Oh, right," Francine said, "The lepidopterist. A plastic butterfly garden and he thinks he's Vladimir Nabokov. All they need is a little sugar water. I think you can manage."

"You need a dancing partner, Bert?" Grace's mother asked, shooting Grace a look that made her want to crawl under the table.

"Mom, no, please."

"You can dance? How's two weeks from next Tuesday? It's Mambo Night at Hadassah," Bert said. Then he grumbled, "That is if Laz doesn't mind, although I wouldn't blame him for laying low while the press is swarming. It's been a veritable hotbed of controversy over his book. Everyone is—"

Grace's mother's mouth fell open. "Why, Grace is a fabulous dancer!" she shouted with enthusiasm in an effort to drown out Bert. "She would love to join you at the Hadassah dance."

Grace fumbled with the napkin she was holding. While part of her wanted to engage in the conversation with Bert, she allowed herself to be waltzed away by her mother's well-choreographed intentions. She thought about the dance classes at the Barclay School of Dance she'd taken as a child. Everything from the powdery insides of her white gloves to the squeak of her Mary Janes felt immediate and tangible. She'd won second prize in the dance competition—a disappointment that her mother was never able to let go of—taking home a ballpoint pen that could perform the times tables and division, instead of garnering the silver ballet slipper trophy.

"Yes, Mambo Night at Hadassah," Bert said. "You don't want to miss that."

"I'll have to let you know."

"Fine, but don't wait too long, I might be snapped up by some twinkle-toed chippie while Francine's away."

THE BUTTERBALL TURKEY was taking longer to pop than expected and was causing some concern. Even Grace's father found himself drawn unwittingly into the drama that was ensuing in the kitchen.

"It's been in since eleven. I had it on a timer so it would start while we were over at Gracie's," her mother said.

"Don't get yourself all worked up, Paulette," Grace's father said, stroking her hair with his oven-mitted hand. "I'm sure it just needs a few more minutes. It's very scientific, you know."

"I think we should try to unpop it, in case it's stuck," Francine suggested. "I just have a sense about these things. This would never happen in a microwave."

"I hate turkey," Bert said, peering into the oven. "It's so dry." As he stood up, he caught Francine's eye. "But yours is delicious!"

"Nancy will be here any minute," Paulette said, wiping her hands on an orange-and-yellow checkered dish towel. "And I'm not even dressed."

"Not to worry, dear," her husband reassured her, tying an apron around his waist. "Your turkey is in good hands."

NANCY BROOKMAN WALKED into the kitchen just as the popper was unstuck with a set of pliers. It shot off like a missile, hitting the ceiling and landing in the dish drain. "I knew it was done," Milton said triumphantly.

"I let myself in," Nancy announced. Grace's father rushed over, wiping his hands on his apron.

"You look wonderful, as always," he said, taking her shorn mink coat.

"Naturally," she answered, removing her sunglasses. She handed him her gloves and her tan-and-white Prada bowling bag, which she'd picked up in Milan the previous summer, months before the waiting lists started forming at the Madison Avenue boutique. Of course, *bowling bag* was a misnomer since it probably contained little more than some tissues and a pair of leather riding gloves. "I understand my good-for-nothing son won't be *gracing* us with his presence—no pun intended," she said, but accentuating the word nonetheless.

"He sends his love," Grace said.

"We got an e-mail from him. He was so sorry to be missing the holiday," her father added.

"You got an e-mail from Laz?" Grace asked.

"From my favorite son-in-law. Just this morning."

"What did he say?"

"He said to save him some leftovers," he answered. Grace felt like running to the computer to see if he'd sent her one, too.

"Just like his father," Laz's mother said. She looked Grace up and down. "I see you're wearing the outfit I bought you. They love me at that thrift shop. I know the good stuff when I see it."

"It's secondhand?" Bert inquired, having spent so many hours waiting for Francine to emerge from the Loehmann's dressing room that he considered himself an authority on women's fashions. He felt Grace's pants. "Like butter."

"I knew Gracie would appreciate that the money went to a worthy cause. Lung cancer or juvenile diabetes, I can't remember which. It doesn't really matter. Just so she feels she's making a contribution."

Grace's father returned from the front hall and began the carving process, sharpening the electric carving knife on a flint stone before determining the exact direction of the grain, as if following a topographical map, and giving out samples as he went along. By the time they sat down, they were already fairly full.

"The stuffing is wonderful, Paulette," Francine said, spooning gravy over her plate.

"Thank you. I used matzoh meal this year instead of bread

crumbs." The stuffing and turkey, along with Grace's cranberry relish, were the only things not from one of Francine's containers.

"Makes all the difference," Francine agreed.

Grace got up from the table to refill the water pitcher.

"Looking a little thick, Grace," Bert said. "Around the middle."

"Bert!" Francine snapped at him. "I knew you shouldn't have had that second Campari. Grace is like a feather! Very willowy."

Grace returned with the pitcher and placed it on the table. The leather pants had not yet stretched out. The two helpings of stuffing she'd had, which were not technically vegetarian, along with a generous serving of sweet potatoes, had not helped the situation. She hadn't had any appetite whatsoever for the soy turkey loaf her mother had prepared for her. She excused herself, saying she needed to check her messages. What she really needed was to lie down. It wasn't so much the stress of having to pretend in front of everyone, it was that just sitting upright was cutting off her circulation.

She walked down the hall to her childhood bedroom and closed the door. Everything in the room—from the green-and-pink checkered curtains and bedspread, to the grassy-green carpet and pink ceiling—could not have been better preserved. On the walls were posters by Peter Max and Degas. Even the pink terry cloth robe on a brass hook by the door was in its proper place, as if Grace had just come home for a snack after junior varsity volleyball practice.

Grace looked at herself in the mirror. She turned sideways, inhaling and holding in her stomach. Bert was right, the pants were not all that flattering. In fact, from the right angle, there was a striking resemblance between herself and the pale underside of her mother's Butterball, trussed and laced and about to burst.

As she was standing before the mirror, she had a flash of Laz wearing the pink terry cloth robe the first time he'd met her parents. Grace and Laz had been walking across the park on their way to the Metropolitan when they were caught in a sudden downpour. Grace had suggested they dry off at her parents' apartment, which was only a few blocks from the museum.

No one was home when they arrived, and Grace and Laz dripped all over the floor by the back door as they toweled off. Grace put everything in the drier and changed into a pair of old hip-hugger jeans with heart pockets on the back and a baseball shirt that were hanging in her closet. She offered Laz the robe to wear while his clothes dried. She suppressed giggles, although he seemed to be completely comfortable, sashaying around, as if he might seduce her.

A few minutes later, they heard sounds from the front hall. Laz quickly retied the robe, Grace tucked in her shirt, and they went out to greet her parents.

"Nice to finally have the pleasure, Laz," her father said, as he shook Laz's hand, seemingly oblivious to the fact that his daughter's new boyfriend was wearing women's clothing. "It's torrential out there."

Grace's mother nudged her in the ribs and whispered, "I like him. We're not going to let this one get away. Nice legs, too," and then went off to make a pot of coffee, which they drank out on the glass-enclosed terrace as they watched the rain.

Grace sat down on the bed. It was a white captain's bed with two deep drawers underneath. She hadn't opened the drawers in years. They contained that part of her life that she referred to as pre-Lazarus, but which she really thought of as pre-Grace. Whatever was in the drawers was now obsolete, or beside the point.

Grace unlaced her pants and rested her head on the bolster.

She'd never really liked her room, but as she gazed up at the pink ceiling, snow falling lightly outside, the sounds of plates and silverware being cleared in the dining room, she wished she could stay there forever.

"WHO WANTS SOME Muscato in honor of Laz?" Grace heard her father say as she returned to the dining room table and sat down.

"Would you like a glass?" her father inquired, offering her a fluted glass filled almost to the top.

"None for me, thanks," Grace answered.

"How about an espresso macchiato? Or a latte?" Her father had recently purchased a deluxe cappuccino maker from Zabar's. She shook her head.

"Any word from Laz?" he asked.

"He says he'll be home by midnight."

"Glad to hear it," her father said. "Tell him he was missed."

"Pie?" Grace's mother asked, displaying a pecan pie in front of her as if she were on *Let's Make a Deal*. Grace looked at the caramelized pecans and the dark syrupy center. Normally, she wouldn't have been able to resist. She glanced over at Bert who was spooning pineapple sections and melon balls onto his plate.

"I think I'll pass," she said, trying to take a deep breath. She couldn't wait to get home, check her e-mail, and change into something elastic and comfortable. And then she remembered she'd promised to meet Kane later.

"More for us," her father said. Grace looked at her watch and then at those assembled around the oval table. There was little changed or missing from previous years, except for Laz, and his absence seemed hardly to make a difference.

"I have to get going. I'm meeting Kane in an hour," Grace said after dessert was finished. Grace's mother ran to the kitchen and returned with a shopping bag filled with leftovers. Laz's mother put out her cigarette in the remains of her pie and turned to Grace.

"I'll give you a ride. The car's downstairs." Grace's mother gave Francine Sugarman a knowing look.

Even if Grace had stayed another five hours, it still wouldn't have been enough. She stood up from the table and gave her mother a quick kiss on the cheek.

"Call us when you get home to let us know you're okay," her father said.

"And don't forget about Mambo Night," Bert reminded her. "Polish up your dancing shoes."

"I won't," she said, looking at her father. "I mean, I will, Dad."


ON THE RIDE HOME Grace stared out the window, running her finger over the fogged-up window in squiggles. Laz's mother lit a cigarette and turned to Grace. "Word has it Kane's in a relationship," she said, taking a long drag of her cigarette. "Someone named Greg."

Grace found it astonishing how casually Laz's mother was relaying this information, as if she were telling her instead that Kane had just changed his address and not his sexual orientation.

"Greg?" Grace asked, incredulous. Kane had dated many women off and on over the course of the years, and the idea that Kane was gay was unimaginable to Grace.

"His mother told me at the conservancy luncheon last week. It sounds serious. Heaven knows how long he's been keeping this one from us," she said, blowing a stream of smoke out of her lips.

"He didn't mention anything to me," Grace said.

"Well, he's not exactly forthcoming in matters of the heart, you know."

Grace's mind raced, shuffling information around in her head and trying to piece it back together. The yellow roses and the lack of amorousness on Kane's part toward her when they were dating now made more sense, but nothing else did. Grace wondered whether Laz knew. Certainly he would have said something to her if he did. The ride through the park was suddenly making her feel queasy. The car stopped in front of Grace's building. As she was getting out, Laz's mother put her hand to her mouth and blew Grace a kiss.

"Kisses, darling. And I'm counting on you for the origami tomorrow at ten. I'll meet you at our usual spot. By the way, we need you to head up the solicitations for the auction at the Historical Society again. I told them you'd love to do it."

Laz's mother was a docent at the American Museum of Natural History, along with her other charitable duties for which she was always volunteering Grace. She had once overheard Laz's mother tell someone, "Oh, Grace will do it—she has nothing else to do." Every Christmas, Grace helped with the origami tree ornaments because she was, as Laz's mother said, *so good with paper.* Between her bookbinding class and cochairing of various committees, Grace "did nothing" for more than twenty-five hours a week.

"Much love to Lazarus," she said, tilting her head. Grace touched her hand to her mouth and watched as the darkened window closed. It might be quite some time before Laz's mother realized her son was gone.

Upstairs, as she put the container of meatballs next to the other containers of meatballs in the freezer, Grace wished she'd had that glass of Muscato after all.

# 9
# BOTTOMS UP

The carpet was barely visible through the clothes that Grace had flung around the bedroom, and it looked as if a giant pressure cooker of blouses and pants and skirts had exploded on the plum-colored Einstein Moomjy. The leather pants were inside out on the floor, having put up quite a fight. Grace wondered what the statute of limitations was on returning things to a thrift shop.

She had given Marisol the following day off, which she now sorely regretted. The room was in a state of complete disarray. She'd quickly checked to see if there was an e-mail from Laz when she got home, but her mailbox was empty. Now nothing she put on felt comfortable. Even her standby outfits, like the clingy Vivian Tam midnight-blue netted dress that came to her ankles and always made her feel just right, looked as if it had hung too long on the wrong hanger, misshapen and suffering from low self-esteem because it had just awakened in a stranger's bed and didn't have the cab fare home.

Kane didn't care about how she looked, she knew that, and Tap A Keg was a dark, smoky bar even in daylight, but Grace was in a frenzy. She gathered the clothes, stuffed them into her walk-in closet, and closed the louvered doors. Then she opened Laz's closet and pulled out a pair of his most worn jeans along with a pale gray cashmere sweater.

The closet was getting dusty. Where the dust was coming from, Grace had no idea, but it was beginning to settle on the tops of the wooden hangers, the collars of Laz's fine wool suits, and his shoes. Laz was asthmatic and could not tolerate dust, an affliction that exempted him from serving jury duty, but which didn't stop him from smoking, often a pack or two a day. Sometimes Grace found herself taking labored, shallow breaths in synchrony with his.

The jeans felt good as she pulled them over her hips and fastened the button fly. They were too large for her, soft and frayed from many washings—in some places almost white.

As soon as Grace buttoned the sweater, she felt immediately calm. She could smell Laz faintly through the knitted cashmere. She brushed her hair and pulled it back, fastening it with a clip. Then grabbing Laz's favorite leather jacket, she left to meet Kane, amazed that she was nearly on time—a sign that everything was still somewhat under control. The mess in the closet was now quite out of sight, soon out of mind. Now if only she could just shove Kane back into the closet as well.

KANE WAS SITTING at the bar, impeccably dressed as always in flat-placket pants and a navy roll-neck sweater, chatting amiably with the bartender. He smiled when he saw her and put his arms around her.

"Grace," Kane said, looking her up and down, "is it Halloween? Or are you just in drag as Laz? I don't miss him *that* much." Grace felt Kane's clean-shaven cheek against hers as he kissed her, inhaling his citrusy smell and all the while gauging her reaction to him now that she had the new information about him. Her reaction was the same as it had been when they'd been quasi-dating. Nice, but no jolt. She thought she must have a sense about these things.

"The usual?" he asked. Grace nodded. Kane reached into his pocket and took out a folded cocktail napkin that he'd picked up in Nantucket at a bar where he swore they made the best cosmopolitans. On it was written exact instructions for making the drink. Kane placed the napkin on the bar for Pete, the bartender. Grace watched as the bartender went through each step ceremoniously: wetting the rim of two chilled cocktail glasses with cranberry juice, then dipping them in granulated sugar; adding ice in the shaker; pouring in the measured amounts of vodka, cranberry juice, lime, and a dash of Cointreau; then shaking it twice and straining it into the martini glasses.

The bartender placed two napkins on the bar and, with a great flourish, presented them with two sparkling-pink cocktails. He looked like a kid, wearing baggy jeans and a backwards baseball cap, the antithesis of how neatly Kane was dressed. Kane's hair was cut considerably shorter than at the anniversary party, brushed forward. It looked so shiny and soft, almost velvety, and Grace had an urge to pet him.

"What'll it be this year?" he asked. "Quarters? Whales, Tales, Prince of Wales? Flotsam and Jetsam?" Grace glanced around the room. The jukebox was playing "Monkey in Your Soul." Laz loved Steely Dan. Grace took a deep breath before answering. She did not want to get drunk. She'd play a couple of rounds and then make some excuse for going home early.

"How about I've Never?" she suggested, mostly because it was a game that involved sips, not shots.

"A lightweight, huh? We'll just see about that," Kane said, motioning to the bartender that they were ready for their second round, even though they hadn't touched their first drinks. The bartender agreed to join them, although he preferred club soda. The three of them clinked glasses and Grace did her best to drink down to the bottom. The bartender waited for the verdict. "Perfection," Kane announced. It was their ritual to start all drinking games after one preliminary drink; Grace could nurse the next one if she played well. Laz was known to be ruthless in these games, but Kane would take it easy on her. If she got drunk, she wasn't sure whether she'd be able to do the same for him.

"I'll start," Kane offered, rubbing his chin with his hand. He was pretending to be deep in thought as if the weight of the next few words he uttered could alter the universe as they knew it. "I know," he started slowly. "I've never snuck into a movie."

Grace lifted her glass to her mouth and took a sip, as did the bartender. Kane feigned a state of shock, leaving his glass on the cocktail napkin.

"Why, Gracie, I'd never have guessed," he teased, finally picking up his glass.

Usually, Grace was the only one left semisober after this game, because she was not the type to overstep bounds. Now nothing was out of bounds.

"You got lucky that time," Grace admitted. She thought for a moment, and then said, "I've never read someone else's mail." Kane laughed.

"This game's rigged," he said, taking a large gulp. "Do you have surveillance equipment set up at my mailbox?"

"I just had a feeling you were the type." Kane looked from Grace to the bartender who left his glass untouched as did Grace.

"It was only a Christmas card, for goodness' sake. And it was an accident," he muttered, pretending to be hurt. It was the bartender's turn.

"I've never told someone I loved them to get them to sleep with me," he said with a grin.

"Now we're getting somewhere." Kane seemed amused, taking another sip of his cosmopolitan. "But I thought I meant it at the time," he added.

Grace left her glass on the bar, shooting Kane what she hoped was her most penetrating and punishing glare, but the more she looked at him, the more disconcerted she began to feel. Images darted through her mind like dragonflies. It wasn't the idea of Kane with a man that was hard to accept, but rather the realization that the person to her right, whom she considered one of her closest friends, and who was now tossing mixed nuts into his mouth willy-nilly, had kept something this vital from her. He seemed like a virtual stranger. That fact was indeed harder for Grace to swallow than the triple sec. In one smooth motion, she lifted her glass, closed her eyes, and drank the contents down. Kane's jaw dropped open.

"Tell me it isn't so," he said.

"Maybe I was just thirsty," she said coyly.

"That's not in the rules," he protested. Grace felt the radiating heat in her chest from the alcohol, penetrating her mother's usually impervious stuffing.

"Okay, so I'm guilty," she said. Any images of Kane and Greg that Grace may have been entertaining in her mind were now significantly dulled. Pete refilled their glasses and topped his off as well. Grace hadn't bothered to keep tabs on whether the bartender— *Pete,* as he had to continually remind her, as she seemed to show a preference for calling him Larry—had drunk on that last round. It was of little concern to Grace. In fact, surprisingly, little at that moment went beyond the *Oh, well. Who cares?* level of importance.

They played a couple of more rounds with statements ranging from "I've never slept with my eye doctor," to "I've never cheated on anyone," and even, "I've never had sex in a department store," until Grace's glass was almost empty for the third time. She hadn't counted on the bartender being such a wild card. It was her turn again. She couldn't think of anything. Her hair clip had come undone, her hair falling across her face in the style of an Afghan hound. She tossed her head and realized for the first time that she was getting drunk. Her head bobbed like a marionette whose puppeteer was absent, and it took a while for the room to reorient itself.

Grace began to feel warm and took off Laz's jacket, hanging it on the back of the bar stool next to her. The sight of the jacket casually flung over the back of the stool in just the insouciant manner that Laz would have done gave Grace a start. She half-believed, for an instant, that he had just gone to get gumballs from the dispenser in the men's room.

"She's plastered," she heard Pete comment, the words muffled as if she had cotton in her ears. Grace stared at him through her hair.

"Yup, she's looped, all right," Kane agreed.

"Why are you talking about me in the third person?" Grace interjected. "Didn't anyone ever tell you that's very rude?" Pete and Kane exchanged glances. "Anyway," Grace continued, "she's not plastered, she's just a little bit tipsy, and she needs to go to the ladies' room."

"I stand corrected." Kane brushed her hair from her eyes, tucking the ends behind her ears. "Gracie, maybe it's time to . . ." Grace looked up at him, and for some reason, reached toward him and ran her hand over his head.

"It's so bristly," she said, making an attempt at standing up. She placed her hand on Kane's shoulder to steady herself. His sweater was so soft, the feel of his shoulder so solid and warm under her hand—she wanted to keep her hand there. "I don't think I've ever felt this material before."

Kane looked at her. "Grace, it's wool."

"Oh," she said, trying to laugh it off. Then she stood up, holding onto the bar. Her legs felt rubbery, like one of those Flatsy dolls she had so coveted as a child. She felt unable to make the journey to the bathroom right then, so she eased herself back onto the stool. She hadn't thought about Flatsies in years, and had a sudden recollection of a cold, gray day when she'd gone to visit a friend for an afternoon. Grace had once asked her mother for a Flatsy when they were in a toy store, but was steered to the paper dolls, which, in her mother's view, had more instructional value. While her friend was out of the room, Grace hid her friend's Flatsy underneath her Danskin shirt. It was a simple task because Flatsies, true to their name, were soft vinyl dolls that looked three-dimensional from the front but which practically disappeared when turned to the side.

She remembered looking at the Flatsy when she got home. The experience of sheer pleasure quickly turned to resentment because she felt too guilty to ever actually play with it but confession was out of the question. She kept the doll in her pocket for days, until her mother washed her pants without checking the pockets—the heat of the drier melting the Flatsy into an indistinguishable marshmallow mass.

As she held on to the bar stool, in a cosmopolitan cloud, Grace wondered which side of herself she'd chosen to neglect. Even under the influence, the question should have been rhetorical.

"I NEED CHANGE for the gumball machine," Grace announced, reaching into the pocket of Laz's jacket and rummaging around. She had decided not to bring a purse, placing her keys and some money in the zippered pocket. She felt the empty pocket, then searched the other one, pulling out a roll of Life Savers and a pocket organizer that Laz had been missing. She remembered how frantically he'd been looking for it.

"Here, Grace," Kane offered, handing her two quarters. Grace shook her head.

"No. My keys," she said. "They're not here."

"Are you sure you didn't put them in the pockets of your cardigan sweater? I mean, Laz's cardigan," Kane asked. Grace was beginning to feel as if she had cotton not just in her ears, but in her mouth as well. She nodded her head.

"Don't worry, Grace. We'll find them," Kane said, in a voice that was immediately soothing in a tell-me-another-story sort of way. She hadn't remembered his voice ever having had that effect on her before, and she felt as if she were in a trance. Kane removed the jacket from the stool and shook it. Grace heard a jingling sound and let out a huge sigh of relief, her shoulders relaxing. "There's a hole in the lining, Grace," Kane said. "Here are your keys and your lipstick as well. Oh, and ticket stubs to *Don Giovanni*," he added, which he tossed into the ashtray on the bar.

Grace reached for the lipstick and then drew back her hand. The tube was unfamiliar. Though she tried to disguise her reaction, Kane obviously caught the look of confusion on her face.

"Well, I assume it's not Laz's," he teased. "It's not his shade." Grace shot him another look.

"No, it's mine," she said quickly, taking the keys and the lipstick from him. "I just didn't remember it was there. Thanks."

She looked at the silver tube, turning it over in her hands. She must have bought the lipstick and not remembered it. Or it might be one of the free samples her mother was always giving her. The more she looked at it, the more it did begin to look familiar, until she was certain that it was indeed hers. She examined the tickets. Laz didn't care for opera, and Grace was positive they'd never gone.

She looked at the date: October 14, seven-thirty P.M. She picked up the keys and the ticket stubs and put them into her back pocket. When she got home, she'd check her calendar. He'd probably mentioned it and she'd just forgotten. Francine was always claiming that blueberries could improve short-term memory. Grace made a mental note to buy some in the morning, although they were out of season and probably imported from somewhere like Chile, costing five dollars for a half pint, but she knew she'd likely forget anyway.

Grace stood up, this time more slowly, took the quarters and the lipstick, and excused herself, walking to the ladies' room with a hypersteady gait as if she had just been asked to walk a straight white line.

THE BATHROOMS WERE demarcated with etchings: the men's room with a picture of two buoys, for *boys*; the ladies' room with gulls. There was a urinal in the ladies' room for reasons unknown, always a startling sight for Grace. She recalled one post-Thanksgiving night with Kane and Laz when she had mistakenly gone into the men's room, and seeing no noticeable difference, she had been totally unaware of her error until she exited to a standing ovation from the amused patrons, Laz leading the cheer with, "Gracie thinks she's one of the buoys."

Tap A Keg had gone all out for the holiday season with garlands and pumpkin lights hung from the stalls. And in the urinal was a chocolate turkey with a huge red plaid ribbon around its neck.

The bathroom lighting was harsh. After washing her hands and splashing her face with cool water, Grace applied a light layer of lipstick. Turning the lipstick over to read the name, she tried to focus. She squinted, not allowing for the possibility that the reason she couldn't remember this tube had nothing to do with her lack of phytochemicals. Grace was just able to make out the name—Opal. Of course. How could she have forgotten?

The wind whistled at the window, disturbing a light layer of soot on the sill. The chocolate turkey peered back at her from its ice-packed perch with its off-center candy corn eyes and vacant expression, as if to say stranger things than this had happened here. She had the impulse to flush the urinal in an attempt to send the turkey to an icy end.

She took one of the quarters that Kane had given her and inserted it in the gumball machine, cranking the handle. She waited until she heard the sound of the gumball hitting the metal hatch, then opened it. Pink. She inserted another quarter into the slot— pink again. Just what she had hoped for.

GRACE SAT BACK down at the bar and held the gumballs in the air as if she'd just landed a sea bass in the gulls' room. After not getting the reaction she had wanted, she put them in the pocket of Laz's jacket. She insisted on playing a few more rounds of the drinking game, to Kane's—and even Pete's—protests.

"I've got one," Grace announced, after finishing her cosmopolitan. "But I'd like a glass of white wine for this round, please." Pete placed a glass of wine in front of her, staring at her in what Grace found to be a strange sort of way, and left the bottle uncorked. "I've never . . ." Grace began, feeling fortified with an uncommon sense of abandon. Kane was her friend, or so she thought, and she couldn't help but be angry at him for keeping something of such magnitude from her.

"I've never kept something from my best friend in order to protect him," she said, finally. It hadn't come out quite the way Grace had imagined it would, having just formulated the words perfectly in her head only seconds before, but it was adequate.

Kane's expression turned grave and he hung his head slightly as he picked up his glass and chugged. Grace felt awful. She hadn't intended for him to take this badly. She put her hand on his shoulder to let him know that all was forgiven, and then she realized that she was guilty as well. She reached for the open wine bottle, stuck one of the red-and-white striped straws from Pete's station into the neck, and began to drink. As soon as Kane realized what she was doing, he turned to her, took the bottle from her hands, and touched her lightly on the chin.

"Come on, Grace, let's get you home."

"Not yet, I'm just getting started," she said, as if possessed. Grace reached out for the bottle once more. Kane took her wrist before she could grab the wine. She braced herself up on both elbows and turned to face him. "I've never had a same-sex affair," she said, finally. Kane was silent. The words bounced back and forth like Ping-Pong balls in her head, but it wasn't entirely clear to her whether they'd actually left her lips. The only thing she knew for certain was that her head was now in Kane's lap.

"Time to go, Grace," Kane said, gently lifting her like a rag doll to an almost-standing position. "And we have to get up for the tree tomorrow." Grace thought it sweet the way Kane used the collective pronoun. It was just like him to remember that she had the origami in the morning.

On the way out the door, Grace slipped and lost her balance, landing smack on the sidewalk, leaving a well-defined imprint of her bottom in the snow. Kane helped her up, brushed her off, and hailed a taxi. They didn't speak at all on the ride home. The cold air cleared her head. It was after midnight. She turned to him, wishing she could take back everything she'd said at the bar. For the first time all evening, no words would come.

"You don't need to say anything," Kane said finally. And Grace knew everything would be all right.

• • •

Upstairs, she removed the ticket stubs from her purse and placed them in the silver tulip bowl on the dining room table. Out of habit, she turned on the light switch and watched with horror as another Duro-Lite burned out with a hiss.

As she reached her hand out to turn it off, she caught sight of her reflection in the antique mirror on the far wall. What she saw shocked her. Her lips were the color of orange sherbet—a caricature. No wonder Pete and Kane had looked at her so strangely when she had come out of the ladies' room. She looked again at the bottom of the tube. Her vision was clear now, the lettering even clearer: Coral. Fish lips. Never in her life would she have even contemplated buying that shade. It was worse than wearing frosted blue eye shadow. She wiped furiously at her mouth and lay down on the couch in the living room, as images of chocolate turkeys with orange lips drinking out of bottles with straws spun in her head.

# 10

# THE UGLY DUCKLING

The next morning, just before dawn, Grace found herself covered with the afghan that her grandmother had crocheted for her when she was in college. Grandma Dolly had stopped crocheting long ago, once arthritis had settled into the joints in her fingers. Now she was in a nursing home, after having suffered her third stroke. Grace rarely used the afghan anymore for fear that the whole thing would unravel in an unfathomable acrylic heap. Her toes were poking through one of the many holes that had recently begun to grow larger, no longer able to be held at bay with a strategically placed knot here or there.

The afghan was a diamond-patterned, multicolored throw made out of that type of variegated yarn that switches from one vibrant rainbow shade to the next without the knitter's having to deal with the nuisance of continually ending off. It was machine washable, although Grace's mother had sewn in a label that read DRY CLEAN ONLY. What puzzled Grace now was how she had managed to

get it out of the hall closet and cover herself without a flicker of recollection—or falling over a single piece of furniture.

As she pulled her foot out of the hole in the violet-fuchsia section, and watched a loose thread disappear like a sand crab, Grace
was slightly tempted to use clear packing tape to mend it. Once, in
a rush to get to Laz's book party, she'd used Krazy Glue to adhere
a button on a silk skirt. It had seemed sensible at the time and had
actually held quite well during the party until Laz's editor came up
to her and asked, "So, what do *you* do?" Just as she was about to answer, the button on her skirt popped off. Laz was by her side like a
shot, grabbing her by the small of her back, a ploy to hold up her
quickly descending skirt.

"We keep each other together," he said. Then he turned to Grace.
"Please try to keep your skirt on," he whispered.

SHE HAD SLEPT in Laz's clothes, and as she lay still, gazing
at the smooth white ceiling, she was overcome by a sense of peace,
as if she had merely dreamt the last few weeks and that Laz was actually just out picking up some scones for breakfast. She could have
sworn she smelled coffee. As she began to grow more fully conscious, the reality—along with the events at the bar with Kane—
came flooding into her mind, replacing the peace and calm with a
dull thumping in her temples. She had definitely overindulged. She
wanted to call Kane and reprimand him for neglecting to inform
her that her lips had been the color of clementines.

She got up slowly and managed a slow wobble into the kitchen
to put the kettle on and to start the coffee for José. For herself, she
selected an Earl Grey tea bag. As she opened the paper sleeve, the
tea bag tore open. The tea leaves spilled out over the countertop
and tiled floor in a mess, only made worse by the application of a
damp sponge. The only thing these leaves portended was a difficult

morning. She opened another tea bag, thankful that it was still dark out. Even so, the thought of putting on sunglasses crossed her mind. She poured the coffee for José into the cardboard cup, added two spoons of sugar, a splash of hazelnut creamer, and pressed the lid on tightly.

The lobby was deserted when she got downstairs. A stack of newspapers on the floor was the only sign that it would soon be daylight. Grace was surprised to see a cup of coffee already on the concierge desk, along with a cinnamon cruller wrapped loosely in wax paper. Farther down the hall, she saw a man with a bicycle coming out of the bike room, dressed in plain black warm-up pants and a hooded windbreaker. He adjusted the seat of his bicycle and headed toward the door, not looking up. As he passed Grace, she noticed he was wearing shiny black dress shoes with white socks, an anomaly she chalked up to New York quirkiness. She put the cup of coffee she had made next to the other one on José's desk, grabbed her newspaper from the pile, and went back upstairs.

GRACE SAT DOWN at the dining room table and took a sip of her now tepid tea from her butterfly mug. The white tips of the *Don Giovanni* ticket stubs poked out from the silver bowl and bore an uncanny resemblance to moth wings. She tried to ignore the tickets for the time being. There was obviously some reasonable explanation, which she was convinced she would discover later when she put her mind to it or deployed her imagination in another dimension.

Suddenly she heard the sound of Laz's voice, as if in a dream, and she realized that the answering machine had clicked on without her knowing the phone had rung, and she was listening to Laz's greeting: *You have reached the Brookmans. We'll call you back later when we get a chance.* Grace ran over to the phone. She must have turned the ringer off, although, again, with no recollection of having done so. However, in the state she had been in the previous night, nothing was inconceivable.

Before she could get to the phone, the person had already hung up. Grace convinced herself that it could only have been Laz. She waited for him to call back. When the phone rang again a few seconds later, she realized that her breathing had been tight and uneven until then. She let the phone ring a second time, savoring the sensation of calm, like the first smell of lilacs, then she picked up the receiver.

"Grace. Thank God." It was her father. "We called you all night and you didn't answer. We're calling from our new cell phone. It's the latest model. Our old one's like a dinosaur. How's the reception?" Grace's parents had been the first of their friends to get a cell phone, but it was of little use as it was usually not charged up, left at home, or locked in the glove compartment by accident.

"Fine," she answered. "Loud and clear. Are you out?"

"No, we're home, just testing it out. We were starting to get worried about you. Laz get in all right?"

Grace looked at the message light. Seventeen calls. She'd forgotten to call her father to tell him she had gotten home safely. It was a ritual they still practiced, however outdated.

Laz had thought it quaint at first, but eventually found it a burden, especially during the many fruitless searches for telephones during their travels through uncharted territory. Sometimes, the search itself became the whole purpose of the trip, like their unending hunt through the Judaean hills until, out of nowhere, a telephone booth had appeared as if it were an apparition on the outskirts of a Bedouin village, right beside a Coke machine. Grace's father had given her a beeper three years ago for her thirtieth birthday, which Laz claimed must have accidentally dropped out of her unclasped backpack into the surf off Grenada during a boating expedition. His explanation put to rest Milton's suspicions of foul play.

"Dad, I'm sorry. I was rushing to meet Kane and I completely forgot. I didn't mean to worry you." Grace could hear a muffled sniffle on the other end and then a high-pitched blow, which signaled her mother's presence. "Tell Mom I'll call her later," she said.

"I will," her father assured her. "And Laz really must come over and see the new Canon copier. Fifty pages a minute—unbelievable. And it collates. He's going to get a real kick out of it."

"Milton, leave the lovebirds alone," Grace's mother blurted out. "I'm sure they have plenty to catch up on."

"Mom's right, sorry. Enjoy. Bundle up—the temperature's dropping. And don't be a stranger."

SHE HUNG UP the phone, suddenly remembering the e-mail her parents had received from Laz the night before. She ran to the computer and turned it on. Laz surely had e-mailed her, too. She clicked on the incoming mailbox. There were several from Laz's editor, one from Miltonfyi@yahoo.com, and a confirmation from the lipstick company. Then she saw one with an unfamiliar address: *Oblomov*. It was Laz! She was delighted beyond belief. Not only had Laz contacted her, but his reference hearkened back to one of their sweetest times. She opened the mail and read: *I think we should meet. How's tomorrow at eight at the Pink Tea Cup? Bring Oblomov.* It was unsigned. Tomorrow? She looked at the date. It had been sent before midnight. *Tomorrow* meant tonight.

The tone was so formal and unlike Laz. Was this Laz, or someone else? And who did she really want to show up? Maybe a stranger would be better. At least for now, while she sorted through things. In place of the marriage, there would be mystery men—the one she had married, and perhaps new ones as well.

Grace stared at the clock on the computer. Nearly an hour had passed. She must have been daydreaming, although about what she had no clue. She could go blank, almost at will, turning off her mind when convenient, such as when she had been on hold with the UPS tracker, trying to trace the mysterious bulbs to no avail, or when she was stuck in traffic or just feeling overwhelmed. Kane was one of the few people who ever inquired about her "absences."

"Grace, you can't just go blank," Kane once said, while they watched the Super Bowl at his apartment.

"Yes I can," she countered.

"You have to be thinking about something. Or trying not to. Like what are you thinking about this instant?"

"I don't know. Nothing, really."

"Come on, don't play dumb."

"I'm not playing dumb—I'm trying to tune you out."

"Okay, but I'm going to ask you every two seconds from now on."

"Just watch the game and leave me alone," Grace said.

Kane leaned over and kissed her on the cheek. "Never," he said. "That, you can count on."

GRACE TURNED OFF the computer. She dressed and then went into the bathroom to wash up. As she was putting away her toothbrush, she saw a flash of gold on the top shelf of the medicine cabinet. Reflexively, she adjusted the can of shaving cream until the ring was concealed to her satisfaction, and closed the cabinet door. Then, hoping to clear her mind, she turned on the water full blast and washed her face a little more vigorously than usual, but the doubts she had about her rendezvous at the Pink Tea Cup still remained. After drying her face, she brushed her hair and pulled it back. Before leaving the bathroom, she checked the medicine cabinet once more to make certain that Laz's ring was still out of sight.

Grace's bedside clock read nine-thirty. If she didn't hurry, she was going to be late for Laz's mother. She ran to get her coat. As soon as she opened the closet door, she knew that something was missing. Where Laz's leather jacket had hung last night was now a bare wooden hanger. One by one, she pushed aside each coat in the closet, even working her way through to the second rod in the back, until she realized that she must have left it at the bar. Tap A Keg probably didn't open until noon. She decided to go there after the museum, pledging never to have another cosmopolitan —ever—as she slipped her arms into the silk-lined sleeves of her pink cashmere princess coat, a present from Laz for her last birthday.

The Museum of Natural History was busy, even at this early hour, filling up quickly with families and tourists. Grace stood under the prow of the Native American canoe in the Great Hall and waited nearly twenty minutes for Laz's mother to arrive. As she came around the bend, Nancy was easy to spot in her winter whites, as she liked to call them, and her thigh-high lizard-skin boots. She gestured as if annoyed that Grace was late, instead of it being the other way around.

"Come on, darling, everything's already set up. No time to waste." Nancy led her through the hall of reptiles, past the Eskimo exhibit, and into a room that featured a life-size diorama of Native Americans presenting maple syrup to the pilgrims. The origami tree loomed in the background, unadorned. There were two long tables set up with stacks of colored origami paper and metal folding chairs for the volunteers.

Grace sat down and got right to work. It was easier than making chitchat with Laz's mother, especially after the little talk they'd had about Kane the night before. She preferred to concentrate on folding paper. She soon became so immersed that she practically forgot

that Laz wasn't actually at home, catching up on sleep or watching
football, as she'd told her mother-in-law.

Grace's hands had formed these creases so many times before,
the paper seemed to fold itself. She created the usual array of animals, lanterns, and stars, choosing the iridescent sheets over the
plain colors. Unfortunately, Laz's mother was not so well occupied,
and as was her usual propensity, she began to gossip with anyone at
the table who would listen. Grace was in the middle of making a silver swan when Nancy began talking about Kane.

"He's quite a catch for anyone, you know. We'll see if this one can
hold his interest."

"He seems happy," Grace said absently as she folded the swan's
tail into the center. She was about to create the wings when Laz's
mother turned to her.

"You look a little puffy. Anything you're keeping from me? You
better not be planning on making me a grandmother. Are you?"
Grace looked at Laz's mother. She was about to speak when she
realized that she had inadvertently decapitated the swan she was
working on, its tiny silver head crushed between her thumb and
forefinger.

"We can't be wasteful, Grace," Laz's mother chided. "Try to concentrate." Grace left the headless swan on the table and reached automatically for another piece of paper. She began folding but felt all
thumbs.

She thought back to the last time she'd gotten her period. It was
still second nature for her to mark the date in her calendar. It
couldn't have been more than four weeks ago, four and a half at
the most, but she couldn't be certain of it. Her cycles used to be so
regular.

The possibility that she might be pregnant was not an unpleasant prospect. She allowed herself to entertain the idea, imagining

the scene that night at the Pink Tea Cup. Laz would be seated at a small table by the window. She'd enter, her skin aglow. When he saw her, he'd get up and approach her, and without needing to utter a word, he would take her in his arms, hold his fingers to his lips, and tell her that this is what he'd wanted all along.

Grace replayed this scene in her head several times, fine-tuning the lighting, the wardrobe, and the dialogue, until the realization that the scene would go nothing like that in reality crashed down on her. Her IUD was purportedly ninety-nine percent fail-safe, and, moreover, Laz had never wanted to have children.

After making a few final folds, Grace regarded her swan for the first time. She had chosen a piece of paper in an unfortunate mustard brown. The wings were lopsided, the body on the squat side; it was not at all graceful. The head looked twice the normal size and was turned down slightly as if ashamed of itself. Grace was about to throw it in the garbage, trying to be as inconspicuous as possible, when a little girl who'd been sitting at the far end of the table ran over and snatched the swan out of Grace's hand.

"Look, Mom," she cried, as she held the mutant swan in the air for her mother and all present to see, "it's the Ugly Duckling."

Seventeen swans later, Grace exited the museum and stood on the street in front of a pretzel vendor. It was just after eleven. She'd have to wait outside Tap A Keg for nearly an hour. A puff of steam emerged from an open manhole, obscuring the pretzel man's cart from sight as she started for home.

The metal stands were still up from yesterday's parade, laced with puckered frost. Her father was right; the temperature was dropping. Each breath made her head pound as if she'd eaten ice cream too quickly. Grace had always found something appealing and romantic about the bleachers, each year eventually convincing

Laz to sit on the top tier the night before the parade with a thermos of hot chocolate. But today, as she passed a couple nuzzled together on the bleachers with their hands in each others' pockets, she felt a vast sense of deprivation and wished the city would hurry up and dismantle them.

JOSÉ GREETED HER as she walked into the lobby. "Señor Brookman always knows when I'm doing a double. He leaves two cups of coffee for me. And he knows I can't resist sweets. My wife says I'm getting fat. Tell him no more crullers, though, I need to go on a diet." Grace assured him she would.

When she got upstairs, she found a stack of mail waiting in the vestibule and picked it up, glancing quickly at the letter on top of the pile as she reached for her key. She had to read it twice. *To Our Single Friend.* Her initial reaction was that it had been delivered to her by mistake. She was not single. But as she looked again, she saw her name on the envelope. Instinctively, she touched her wedding band. Her head began to pound again. The more she tried to reconcile all the opposing thoughts, the more she felt as if she were losing hold. She wished she could go blank—blanker than blank—but instead her head was spinning with no off switch.

# 11
## Past Due

Inside, Grace ripped the envelope addressed to *Our Single Friend* in half and was about to throw it in the garbage when she caught sight of the familiar logo and began to read: "We at A Perfect Match are thrilled to have you as a member. . . ."

This was too much. Grace felt invaded as if by some obsessive, matchmaking stalker.

She'd received other odd solicitations before in the mail and over the phone—even an offer to buy flavored condoms from an Orthodox prochoice organization, whose products came in flavors such as Cookies and Cream, Baked Apple, and Peppermint Stick. They were all glatt kosher and no-cal, just in case. Grace had politely declined, explaining that she and her husband had already purchased a supply elsewhere. She tried to suppress the image of Laz in a minty-flavored, candy-striped prophylactic, the whole episode arousing in Grace a queasy feeling akin to the time she stumbled upon a caterpillar-shaped vibrator on Francine Sugarman's nightstand.

THE BILLS WERE beginning to accumulate like leaves from some deciduous tree. Laz had always taken care of the finances, writing checks in between mouthfuls of Marisol's sweet concoctions. Grace straightened the pile, dismayed that there was still nothing from the lipstick company, and noticed one envelope with the words *Past Due* in red letters on it. Just as she was about to open it, the intercom rang. She stuffed the bill underneath the latest issue of *New York* magazine and pressed the button.

"Mr. Kane to see you," José announced.

She had no recollection of having made plans with Kane the night before, although he could be known to drop by on a whim. Moments later, the doorbell rang. When Grace opened the door, there stood Kane, looking like he'd just tumbled out of bed, which wasn't an unlikely scenario considering he owned his own software company and could work from home.

"Feeling a little bedraggled this morning, Kane?"

"Just a little. Thanks for your concern. I had an early doctor's appointment." Grace noticed that Kane's arm was no longer in a sling, but supported by an air cast made of clear plastic.

"Your arm's better?" she inquired in a sympathetic tone, but the concern was more about how to get Laz out of his Wednesday night hockey games now that Kane would soon be playing again. Maybe Laz's elbow would flare up with an acute case of tendinitis.

"The doctor says a few more weeks."

"By the way, I'm never going out with you again," she said. "Thanks for telling me my lips were bright orange."

"You looked quite fetching, actually." Kane checked his watch. "My car's double-parked. Tell Laz he better hurry if he wants to get back before dark."

Grace was at a loss. Back from where? She stared at him, trying to find some thread in the conversation that would help her understand what he was referring to. Did he and Laz have a game that Grace had forgotten about?

"Don't tell me Laz isn't up yet. I thought you said he was all excited about going upstate for the tree." Then she remembered talking with Kane at the bar about the tree.

She found herself faltering. She fumbled with the buttons on her cardigan sweater. "Laz had to go to this . . . thing," she said, finally.

"He had to go to a *thing?*" Kane asked. "What kind of thing?"

"He tried get out of it. Really. But he just couldn't," she said, trying to sound firm but appropriately apologetic.

"If I didn't know Laz better, I'd take it personally."

"It's not that, Kane, really. He just couldn't get out of this . . ." Grace paused, trying to find the right word.

"I know—that *thing,*" he said, looking down at his hiking boots. Grace noticed that they were brand new. He looked like a small boy dressed up for the first day of camp.

"I'm sorry." Grace hoped Kane didn't think that Laz had bailed out because of the Greg situation. Kane picked up *Time Out* and began flipping through the magazine distractedly. Grace looked at his unshaven face and his hair, which was somehow disheveled despite its short length. It was out of character for him to be even the least bit unkempt, but in a strange way, it made him look more masculine. She shook the thought from her mind. Laz's mother *could* be wrong. After all, Kane wouldn't keep something like this from her.

"Well, I'm up for it, if you are," he said stoically. "Why let him ruin a perfectly glorious day?" He put down the magazine. Grace thought about the tickets and the bills, about her seemingly not-forthcoming period and the jacket at Tap A Keg, and with the precision of a bug zapper on an August night, she decimated these thoughts from her consciousness. The thing she wanted most of all right then was to not think, so she agreed to go. And depending on how things went at the Pink Tea Cup, a tree would serve as either a nice homecoming or a comforting consolation prize.

"I'll just be a minute," she said as she left the room to put on a pair of old boots and to locate Laz's sheepskin gloves. When she returned, Kane was on the phone, speaking quietly.

"Around six, I think. Depending on traffic." He paused. "I know," he said, in a tone unfamiliar to Grace, "I wish you could come, too." Grace noticed a folded piece of paper on the front table that looked like it had been torn out of a magazine, and she opened it. It was part of the classifieds. On one side was the weekly horoscope and on the other side a section from the personal ads.

Grace read: *Men Seeking Men*. It was one thing for Kane to be dating someone named Greg, quite another for him to be browsing the personals! Was he looking to cheat on Greg? She'd always known him to be faithful, and this possible indiscretion upset her more than anything. When she heard Kane hang up the telephone, she folded the page quickly and pretended to be busy sorting through the mail when he walked in.

"Ready?" he asked.

"As ready as I'll ever be," she answered, trying to appear casual, but her voice was noticeably higher in pitch. "How long a trip is it again?"

"If you don't want to go—" he started.

"No, I do. I just need to be back. Laz and I have plans later. It takes about an hour, right?"

"Closer to two, but you guys always fall asleep, so it must seem shorter. It's like driving with two lumps."

"Laz doesn't always fall asleep."

"I beg to differ." Grace thought back to the ride home that first year, and the feeling of Laz rubbing her feet.

"Well, maybe he just rests," she said. She handed Kane the folded piece of paper. "Is this yours?"

"I hope you don't mind. I tore it out of one of your magazines. Just some stuff I'm interested in." Grace found his tone uncharacteristically flippant. So now they were swingers, no less! She looked at him, trying to pick up any traces of his having been found out. He seemed as regular as ever.

"Not at all," she said. "I certainly have no need for it."

THE DRIVE UP the Taconic was more scenic than Grace had remembered. She and Kane chatted as usual, the only difference was Grace's painful self-consciousness about her choice of topics.

"Where are you going with Laz tonight?" Kane inquired.

"Il Duomo," she answered. Grace had slipped up. She didn't know why she hadn't just told him she was meeting Laz at the Pink Tea Cup.

"Il Duomo?" Kane asked. "Isn't that the place Laz calls the Old-Age Home?"

Grace remembered one meal there with her parents. Laz, after scanning the room, which was filled to capacity with white-haired gentlemen and their "blond," coifed companions, had asked the waiter if he recommended the gnocchi.

"It's not one of our *zippier* dishes," the waiter replied, suggesting instead the spinach ravioli and the shrimp diavolo, both of which turned out to be bland, saltless, and utterly flavorless, leaving the blood pressure and cholesterol levels of Il Duomo's patrons uncompromised. Grace's father had salted his dish as if he were salting the city streets after an ice storm. After that, *zippier* turned into one of Laz and Grace's standard expressions.

"This is another Il Duomo," Grace covered.

"Maybe we—I mean I, could join you."

"We?" Grace asked. She couldn't help herself. "Kane, I know about Greg." A look of complete surprise came across Kane's face.

"You do?"

"Laz's mother told me yesterday at Thanksgiving." Grace tried to keep her tone light. She fiddled with the latch on the glove compartment.

He turned to her as if having figured out something vitally important. "Oh, that explains why you were acting so weird last night."

"What are you talking about? I wasn't acting weird. I'm fine with it. I just wish you had told me yourself."

"It's all so new, Grace. I'm just sort of taking it all in. But we couldn't be happier. I can't wait for you guys to meet." Grace was not overly pleased to be included under the heading *guys.* Kane began talking animatedly, as if relieved to finally be able to speak freely. "You're going to love each other," he assured her. "You're so alike."

"Really?" Just then, the glove compartment flew open and a stack of dog-eared AAA guides and a tire-pressure gauge tumbled onto Grace's lap. She attempted to push them back in, but no matter how hard she tried, the door wouldn't stay shut.

"And we understand each other so well," he continued. Grace suppressed the urge to say, *I can imagine,* taking this time to re-arrange the travel guides. She slipped one unusually thick guide-book into the side pocket on the door, and with a firm shove, managed to shut the door.

"I'm happy for you," Grace said. Then, more quietly, "Laz will be, too."

"You haven't mentioned it to him?"

"I thought he'd like to hear it from you," she answered. She kept one foot planted firmly on the glove compartment door, eyeing it warily just in case it flew open again, like some unpredictable, menacing jack-in-the-box.

"I'd be glad to, if I ever get ahold of him," he said, sighing.

KANE GOT OFF the highway and turned onto a two-lane back road. They saw a sign that indicated the way to the Christmas tree farm, and proceeded up the gravel driveway. Grace was glad she'd worn boots, as the snow was starting to melt and get slushy. She followed Kane down a dirt road, slipping her hands into Laz's gloves.

As she walked behind Kane into the thickening woods, Grace was reminded of being knee-deep in snow in Central Park with Chloe. They couldn't have been more than ten at the time and had been sledding all morning. Grace had followed Chloe, pulling her sled reluctantly behind her in search of a hill that Chloe insisted was just beyond the bend. They circled around what looked like the same circuitous, snow-covered paths until they were clearly lost. Grace became panicked but, to her own amazement and relief, she somehow found the way back before Chloe's mother realized they were missing. Grace now suddenly noticed that she'd taken the lead once more—Kane behind her, walking in her deep footprints.

"How tall?" Kane asked, inspecting the branches of a moss-green Scotch pine. It was about a foot taller than Laz. Grace told him it was perfect. Kane was wearing a gray Woolrich jacket, sturdy boots, and striped hat. *Nature boy,* Laz liked to call him when he was in the wilderness. Even in the outskirts of New Jersey, he metamorphosed into a sort of well-heeled version of a scout leader, always prepared. Kane took out his Swiss army knife and sliced off a strip of bark.

"Is it fresh?" Grace asked.

"Grace, it's still growing. I just wanted to see if it was well hydrated." Kane motioned to a young guy leaning against a red pickup truck, apparently the universal signal that they'd chosen a tree and were ready to chop it down. Kane did the honors, as always, air cast notwithstanding, wielding the saw with the same unswerving focus that Grace's father used on the turkey with the carving knife.

After wrapping the tree in green plastic netting, Kane and the young guy managed to fit the tree crosswise in the Jeep, one end in the front seat and the trunk sticking out the rear window, leaving Grace to sit in the back. Kane gave her a plaid wool blanket to help her keep warm. Surrounded by branches and covered with the blanket, Grace felt as if she were in a fragrant nest. Kane pointed out sites along the way, offering bits of information in his tour-guide voice, like, "That's Twain's house—it's shaped like a hexagon," or, "Don't Pass Me By—the best banana cream pie in a hundred-mile radius."

They passed a lake on the left side. The surface was coated with frost, making it look frozen. With the unseasonably warm weather, though, it couldn't be more than just a superficial layer of ice.

It was almost dusk—that gray, undelineated time of day that Grace's father referred to as *accident time,* the time, he claimed, when overtired children had to be rushed to the emergency room for stitches, although Grace had never so much as skinned a knee. If Milton was driving at this time of day, he would pull into a roadside diner and wait for night to fall. It was usually only a twenty-minute stop, just long enough for a hot brisket sandwich with horseradish and a chocolate shake, which he consumed in religious silence.

Grace was about to suggest that she and Kane stop for a bite to eat—she was suddenly ravenous, when all day she hadn't had much of an appetite—but she wanted to leave enough time to get Laz's jacket from the bar. She thought about what she had to eat in the house—some leftover soy turkey loaf, pureed sweet potatoes, bagels, blinis, and enough frozen containers of Francine's meatballs to reach to Grace's fourth-floor window.

The fragrant smell of pine made Grace drowsy. She removed her boots and stretched her feet out over the divider in the front. Something about being driven home made her feel like a child. Kane was a good friend. She knew he always would be. Nothing had changed between them.

Grace felt herself drifting off, and in the last remaining minutes of twilight, she thought she felt Laz's hand on her foot. When she woke up, it was dark and her nose was tickling.

"Can we make a quick stop at Tap A Keg?" Grace asked, as Kane drove down Riverside Drive.

"Why? Are you up for a couple of rounds?"

"Hardly," she said. "I think I left Laz's jacket there last night. I can't find it anywhere." Kane looked at her in the rear-view mirror, his eyebrows raised.

"Well, you definitely didn't leave it at Tap A Keg. You had it on when we left."

"Are you sure?"

"I distinctly remember zipping you up outside," he said. "Right after your unfortunate fall."

Grace wrestled with this new piece of information. "Well, I'd like to check anyway," she said.

"Suit yourself."

Kane waited outside with the Christmas tree while Grace ran inside the bar. It was smoky, as usual, even though no one seemed to be smoking. The specials board listed Alaskan oysters and venison burgers, two dishes she would be suspicious of even in a four-star restaurant. Grace was relieved to see that the same bartender was behind the bar and that he recognized her.

"*I've never . . .*" he began, trying to contain his amusement, "had an affair with a bartender."

"Very funny," she said with a perfunctory smile.

"I guess that means no, huh?"

Grace scanned the room, pretending to ignore his last comment. "I think I left my husband's jacket here last night."

"Your husband's jacket?"

"Yes," she answered.

"I didn't find anything," Pete said, folding his arms across his chest. "But I'll ask the day guy when I see him tomorrow."

"I'd really appreciate that," Grace said, reaching into her bag for a pen. She wrote her telephone number on a cocktail napkin and asked him to call her if he found the jacket. Then she started for the door.

"Wait, I have something for you," he said, holding out a closed hand. Grace watched as he opened his hand to reveal two pink gumballs.

"How did you know?" she asked, taking the two gumballs from him.

"Just a hunch," he said. The gumballs had stained his hands pink, which he wiped on his white half-apron. Grace smiled and walked to the door.

"Don't be a stranger," he called after her. Grace was struck by the familiarity of the phrase. It was one her father used, and like most of his expressions, she was not used to hearing them in common parlance, at least not by anyone even remotely close to her age, and it engendered in her a feeling of kinship between herself and the bartender.

"I won't," she assured him.

KANE HAD TAKEN his time setting up the tree, puttering with the stand and turning the tree to get just the right angle. Now he was lying on the floor, adding a spoon of sugar to the water in the base, which he said was to help the tree stay hydrated, but which Grace took as a ploy to prolong his stay. She couldn't blame him —

he was probably hoping Laz would come home—but it was beginning to get on Grace's nerves.

"I'm meeting Laz in twenty minutes," she blurted out, finally. He stood up and wiped his hands on his jeans.

"I guess I better be shoving off. Unless you've changed your mind and you want to join us."

"Let's do it another time. Laz said he'd like to make it an early night. Say hi to Greg, though," she said, as she watched him get into the elevator.

Grace plopped down on the sectional couch in the living room and looked at the tree. Any other year she would have made mulled cider, and she and Laz would have been halfway finished with the decorations by now. Laz liked to throw the tinsel all over the room, creating an icicle wonderland. Even weeks after the tree had been taken down, the vacuum cleaner having inhaled more than its fair share of tinsel, Grace would find strands of it clinging to her clothing and hair.

She got up to change her clothes. As she walked out of the room, she became fixated with the indentation she'd made in the couch. Her body had left a noticeable depression in the down-filled cushion, which seemed somehow deeper than usual.

Grace looked at the calendar, turning it back to October. There was a pumpkin sticker on October 31. She tried to find the date of her last period, but no days were circled. None in September, either. Ever since fifth-grade sex education, she'd been religious about keeping track of her period. She remembered the way that the nurse had fastened a pink-stained sanitary napkin onto a stuffed Snoopy, emphasizing the need to keep strict records of their still-latent reproductive cycles. Grace took the message to heart, but the demonstration also had the effect of anthropomorphizing her stuffed animals in a way she had never imagined.

She flipped through the calendar once more. And then she remembered that she had started using Laz's date book in the fall to avoid scheduling conflicts. She went to his desk and turned the pages back. Opposite a picture of Monet's *Water Lilies,* there was a red circle on the fourteenth of October, making her period approximately two weeks late, but still well within her "usual" range. Coincidentally, that was the same date as the ticket stubs that had been in the pocket of Laz's jacket. Underneath the date, written in Laz's scrawl, Grace read: *Championship Game. Seven o'clock.*

The details came back to her with such precision that it was uncanny. Laz had wanted to cancel his plans that night because she hadn't been feeling well, but Grace had insisted he go. Before he left, he brought her a hot water bottle for the cramps and a cup of chamomile tea. He had been so solicitous, even calling her around ten to tell her the game had gone into overtime. When he came home that night, he set the trophy on the bedside table and covered her with the afghan.

"You missed a great game, Gracie," he'd said, stroking her hair. "I thought about you all night."

ANY FEELINGS OF doubt about that night flew out of her head. The memory was warm in her mind. Grace got the ticket stubs from the silver bowl. Laz had wanted to stay home, she reminded herself over and over again—as she tore the tickets into tiny pieces and watched as they fluttered into the garbage can.

# 12

# The Pink Tea Cup

The Pink Tea Cup was crowded when Grace arrived holding a tattered copy of *Oblomov*. Several sheets of yellow paper were tucked between the pages. Laz sometimes marked his spot in a book with a torn tissue or movie stub, never dog-earing the page, something Grace's father also abhorred. One Christmas, Grace had given Laz a silver bookmark adorned with a biblical scene that had yet to be identified, which he'd never used. It was still in the top drawer of his dresser, along with the gold pocket watch from his father and the key to his old apartment. Before she left the house, Grace had taken the key as casually as she might an old umbrella, just in case, and had put it in her purse—either a lucky charm or her last resort.

A loose approximation of a line had begun to form by the door, and the windows were fogged up, making it difficult to see in. She made her way to the front and down the steps. Once inside, she saw that all the tables were occupied. A tall young woman wearing black jeans and a camisole approached her.

"Can I help you?" she asked.

"I'm meeting my husband," Grace answered. The hostess nodded and walked away.

"That's a bit presumptuous, don't you think?" a voice said. She spun around to find a man with flyaway hair and a big toothy smile.

"Excuse me?" Grace said, moving slightly to the side. The man was uncomfortably close and smelled faintly of rubber cement. She had her answer. She knew full well that this man in front of her was one of the lunatics from A Perfect Match, but she made the choice to keep up the charade.

"I mean we've barely met," he said, chortling. He was dressed in a red turtleneck sweater and chinos, very unexceptional, except for his highly polished black wing tips. Underneath his cuffed pants, Grace saw a flash of white socks.

"I'm expecting someone," she lied, glancing toward the door.

"I know," he responded, giving Grace what he must have thought was a knowing look. She wasn't certain, but she thought she may have even detected a wink. She looked at her watch and tried to appear occupied, hoping he would move on. She was about to turn her back to him when he made a gesture with his hands like a magician and presented her with a single long-stemmed rose.

"Please," she said, trying her best to sound firm, but found herself feeling surprisingly touched. "I told you I'm meeting someone," she said again, this time more softly. Grace noticed he was holding a copy of *Oblomov*. The man hung his head and shuffled his feet.

"I understand. It happens all the time," he said as he backed away. "I just thought—since we had so much in common."

"I'm sorry," she started to say, looking down. But before she could continue, he was gone, leaving the book and the rose on a nearby table. She picked up his copy of *Oblomov* along with the rose and then left.

SHE STOOD OUTSIDE the door to Laz's old apartment quietly, as if waiting for an invitation, holding the key in her hand. The door had been sanded so many times that it looked like driftwood, the fine carved woodwork nearly washed away. Voices could be heard echoing down the wide hallway, and the sound of footsteps overhead was a distant aria. All sensation began to drain out of Grace, her breath sucked away. She mistook the rumble of the elevator for her racing heartbeat; the reactions of her body, for feelings. She was the trespasser here, all the while holding the key, but unable to enter what was once a home, but which was now a forbidden place.

Outside, gargoyles loomed above to protect the inhabitants from evil spirits. But what if those spirits had already slipped through, let in by the gatekeepers? She swayed a bit. She had come this far, but found she could go no farther. All she could do was stand at the threshold. She turned to go, dropping the long-stemmed rose and the key to the floor.

THE CHRISTMAS TREE looked ghostly in the dark living room without the adornment of lights or ornaments. It had only been two hours since Kane had left, but the apartment seemed completely abandoned.

She turned on the sconces above the mantelpiece as well as the table lamps, but it made little difference. Even the color of the walls seemed to drain the room of light.

The fiasco at the Pink Tea Cup had left her feeling dejected, though it hadn't been entirely her fault. Stuck between the pages of the man's copy of *Oblomov* she found a business card: Adrian

Dubrovsky—Private Investigator. On the same page, a passage was marked with a yellow highlighter: *Life is poetry, if people don't distort it.* In the margins, scrawled throughout the book, were notes written in ink in an unfamiliar language, which Grace took to be Russian.

Laz would have found the incongruity of this situation amusing, but for Grace, the evening's occurrences coupled with her feeling that she'd just been stood up by Laz left her with an emptiness she was unable to shake. Thankfully, Marisol would be in on Monday to string the lights and make the apartment hum again, but at the moment, it was as if Grace were in a black hole, deeper even than the utility closet.

She went into the kitchen, aware that all she had eaten since the morning were some stale sourdough pretzels that Kane had in his car and the two gumballs. She felt herself drawn to the utility closet, where she took out the picture from Halloween. Removing it from its frame, she studied it, trying to decipher Laz's body language. She couldn't tell if his arm was actually around Chloe, or just behind her.

Without thinking, Grace tore the photograph into small, centimeter-size pieces, which she regretted immediately. She sat down on the floor to try to fit the pieces back together, but no matter how she configured them, there was no repair.

Finally, she swept the torn pieces of the photograph into her hand, placing them in a plastic bag for safekeeping.

LAZ'S GLASSES LAY on the bedside table, as if he had just removed them to wash up for dinner. Grace lifted them from the nightstand and, holding them by the rims, inspected them in the light. She was careful not to disturb the traces of his smudged fingerprints, so as not to tamper with the "evidence."

She put them on. She didn't need glasses, and Laz's prescription was strong, but as her eyes strained to decipher the blurry images before her, Grace imagined what he might have seen if he'd been there. She looked in the mirror. Her features were undelineated. Laz might have walked right by her if he saw what she was seeing now. She tried to reach out to pick up a glass of water she had brought in, but with no depth perception found herself grasping at air. She closed her eyes, resting the tiny muscles and nerves that create sight. Suddenly, she remembered something that had occurred the day before with unnerving clarity. A headline she had seen in a newspaper at the corner newsstand flashed before her: BOSNIAN PRISON STORY UNCOVERED. She'd walked by quickly.

Her head was now swimming—the words appearing in her mind more like fragmented pixels than symbols. She opened her eyes and removed the glasses, her vision taking a while to readjust to normal. Then she placed the glasses back on the nightstand.

Grace spotted the Magic 8-Ball on the floor underneath the desk, back in its white box. She hadn't consulted it since the night of the anniversary party, having filed it away as a cute but useless item. Now, for some reason, she felt herself drawn to it. She picked it up as if holding something precious, gave it a good shake, and asked in a half whisper, "Am I pregnant?" The answer appeared: *Ask again later*. Very sound advice, she thought, although *later* was open to interpretation.

THE NEXT MORNING, Grace decided to tackle the bills. She had begun to avoid the dining room, which seemed uninviting without the Duro-Lites, and now the living room was haunted by the sight of the unadorned, seven-foot Scotch pine that resembled a Trappist monk. When Grace was alone at night, the only rooms in which she didn't feel like she was floundering were the bedroom and kitchen. She wondered if, after a while, the apartment, like her marriage, would begin to shrink from atrophy.

She went to the hall closet and looked for the Rolling Stones CD *Beggar's Banquet,* which Laz always played while he did the bills. Background music was a must for him no matter what was in front of him, and now Grace, too, thought that this was the only way bills were done. The CDs were neatly lined up and alphabetized on the shelf, but the one Grace was looking for was nowhere to be found. She even searched the piano bench, before deciding to choose a record from her old album collection.

After Grace met Laz, he had eventually replaced most of her records with CDs. Those albums that remained were stored in a carton on the floor of the closet. She opened the box and saw her soundtrack to *Fiddler on the Roof* and *My Fair Lady,* along with her Bangles and Carly Simon albums, none of which suited her mood. She settled for the Pretenders, *Learning to Crawl,* wiping the cover with her sleeve. It was an album that Chloe had given to her in college. She'd forgotten she still had it.

Chloe had written on the album cover: *To your New Wave. Don't go back to being a pretender.* Grace and Chloe had shared a dorm room during the fall of their junior year, while Chloe's roommate was on exchange in France. It was the one semester that Grace lived on campus, and it was now a distant memory for her. That semester, she and Chloe, wearing thrift-store clothes, studied until eleven each night and then went out to readings, parties, or to hear music in obscure basement clubs. Grace switched her major from Classics to Fine Arts and spent most of her time in the art studio sculpting.

When Grace returned to her parents' apartment at the end of the semester, her mother took one look at her hands, which were dry and cracked from working with clay, and said, "Get your coat!

We're going for a paraffin manicure." Grace's hands were dipped into a vat of hot wax and wrapped in Saran Wrap. After the wax hardened, it was peeled off, revealing Grace's smooth, exfoliated hands.

"Are you getting married?" someone next to her asked, as her nails were drying.

Grace hesitated. She didn't even have a boyfriend at the time. Her mother answered for her. "Yes, she is," she said. "We just don't know when."

THE LID TO THE record player was covered with dust, and Grace's fingers made long streaks across the smoky gray plastic. She had the distinct feeling of being watched, though she knew she was all alone. She put the record on the turntable, switched it on, closed the lid, and went into the kitchen.

The stack of bills seemed to have expanded like an accordion, the roll of stamps unfurling in front of Grace on the table. This may have been the first time she had ever done bills. When she lived alone, her father had set up a system so that all her bills were paid electronically. She'd never even balanced a checkbook. She was an accountant's nightmare. Not that she didn't keep records—she kept everything—she just didn't know where.

She shuffled the envelopes. Then she remembered about the bill underneath the *New York* magazine and ran to get it. She'd received letters with the words *Urgent* or *Past Due* on them before, but they were usually form letters from her congressman or credit card applications. Once, she accidentally tore up an envelope, thinking it was junk mail, only to discover that it had contained tickets to game six of the World Series. She was shocked to see that the letter under the magazine was an actual notice of eviction unless payment was received within two business days.

At first she assumed it was in reference to the mortgage payments on their co-op, but then when she read further, she saw that it was for back rent on Laz's old apartment. The letter was dated the day before Thanksgiving. She wrote out a check for it and decided it would be better to deliver it by hand as soon as possible. Grace could never fully understand why Laz needed to hold on to the apartment. She would have relinquished any part of her past if he'd asked her to.

She thought about the key frozen in the fishbowl. She tried to focus on the remaining bills, but the numbers swirled like confetti in her head. Finally, she got up from the table and walked over to the refrigerator.

As she opened the freezer door, her vision fogged from the burst of cold air. Behind the ever-increasing stacks of containers of meatballs and the box of frozen blinis from her father's sixtieth birthday Beluga Bash two years ago, she located the fishbowl. She removed it, holding it with both hands and gazing into its depths as if it were a crystal ball. She knew what Laz would say if he were to walk in on this scene: "Why spoil things?"

The ice had a bluish cast, completely unmarred by cracks. Grace thought about the lake at Kane's house. Each winter, the lake was covered by a dark layer of ice, forbidding and unfathomably deep; but in the summer, the water was so clear that the bottom looked magnified. She remembered how she and Laz had once sneaked out to skinny dip while Kane was making breakfast. As she held on to Laz's shoulders, gliding across the lake on his back, it was as if she were skimming air, not water. Grace always found it unimaginable during the winter that it was the same body of water that had seemed so inviting only months before.

The frozen key was just a faint glimmer within the sphere of ice. The bowl held approximately one gallon of water. She remembered the clerk in the pet store explaining the ratio of water to fish: for every inch of water, you could have one fish. He hadn't mentioned any such limit on keys or other unresolved marital issues.

Grace guessed that the ice could take several days to thaw. She considered putting the bowl in the microwave, but then remembered Francine's admonition about sparks from metal. And the glass might crack if she submerged it in a bath of warm water. She placed the bowl on the kitchen counter, moving it away from any heat that might be emanating from the counter's fluorescent light fixture, and wiped her hands on a dish towel. If she had a thermostat, she probably would have considered turning it down. She wasn't even certain if she was prepared to use the key this time. If the ice wasn't melted by Monday, she would have her answer. Time would tell, she decided, glad that the decision was out of her hands.

GRACE SPENT THE rest of the afternoon coordinating Laz's "comings and goings," so as to avoid any more conflicts like the one with Kane the previous day. She plotted Laz's life out in minute detail, using her pink pen to fill in his daily planner a month in advance, even down to such mundane activities as appointments with the dental hygienist and trips to the hardware store or to the Russian baths on Tenth Street.

She consulted her father's latest e-mail update for the extended weather forecasts and other family events. She'd have to check the date for Kane and Laz's annual ice fishing trip at the lake, but for now she penciled in an acute case of the stomach flu as well as a list of some ready-made excuses to have at her fingertips.

Most of the time, other people supplied her with the alibis: *Laz working as usual? Away, again? Off on some humanitarian mission?* She marked the days he would be "out of town" to coincide with family events, such as Grace's parents' annual Hanukkah potluck dinner or the Sugarmans' New Year's Day dim sum brunch. The pink pen she was using began to run out; she shook it and pushed on the tip, but it was dry. She switched to a blue pen and a legal pad, which was not nearly as pleasing, but considering the complexity and organizational demands of her mission, she felt she needed to adopt more serious tools.

Grace noticed that Laz had written *Contact, eight P.M.* on New Year's Eve in his calendar, and she figured he had ordered tickets for the play at Lincoln Center. He had obviously felt confident that he'd be back by then, sitting beside her to ring in the new millennium. When she got to her own birthday, she stopped. There was a red circle around the date. Underneath, Laz had written in almost illegible handwriting: *Grange, nine P.M.* Or did it say Grace? Grange Hall had never been one of her favorite restaurants, but she supposed it was the thought that counted.

Her birthday was only two weeks away. As a child, her parents used to take her to the Hawaii Kai for her birthday, which they pronounced as if it rhymed. She always felt like a princess as she drank out of a coconut and sat in a high-backed wicker chair, wearing several flower leis around her neck. Now she left the space as it was, wondering whether she'd be spending this birthday alone.

Once she finished organizing the next few weeks, she felt unusually celebratory, buoyed by a feeling of great accomplishment. She decided to treat herself to dinner, so she made a reservation at her and Laz's favorite restaurant. As she was getting dressed, the telephone rang.

"Just wanted to check and see what you were up to tonight," Kane said. Grace glanced at the date book to make sure she wasn't forgetting anything and then answered with confidence.

"Nothing much. Just a quiet dinner at des Artistes."

Kane was silent. He started to say something and stopped. "Sounds nice," he said, finally.

While cradling the phone under her chin, Grace attempted to fasten the clasp of her pink sapphire choker—a present from Laz last Valentine's Day. She had never been able to do it herself, sometimes even going downstairs and asking José for assistance. Laz had given it to her while she was in the shower. The three smaller jets had been on full force until the bathroom had steamed up and water dripped from the ceilings and walls, but even through the mist, the sapphires had glinted like stars as Laz had fastened it around her neck.

"About Monday," Kane said. "Greg wants to know if we can go to a place that has spelt pizza." Monday was Pizza Night. Every other Monday they went to Ralph's for deep-fried zucchini sticks and a large pie. Kane had cancelled the last two.

"Spelt pizza?" Grace asked. She put the necklace down, unable to clasp it. It wound around itself slowly like a jeweled serpent.

"Yeah, Greg has me off wheat. Something about the gluten."

"What else does Greg have you off?"

"Well, dairy, too," he admitted sheepishly.

"So we're having Spelt Night," she said. "Sounds appetizing."

"I'm not laughing," Kane said, not quite his snappy self. "If you guys can't make it, we'll understand." He seemed to be giving her a too-convenient out, which somehow took away the challenge for Grace. She had already penciled in a family emergency to get out of Pizza Night, but it was a last-minute excuse and she couldn't use it until Monday afternoon. Even though she'd never planned to go, she found herself irritated that Greg was trying to alter their plans.

"Count us in," she said adamantly, as if trying to protect her turf.

"You really won't be able to tell the difference. Except you have to drink a lot of water," he added.

CAFÉ DES ARTISTES was crowded when Grace arrived. The restaurant had a timeless quality. Everything, from the lacquered bar to the murals of nymphs on the walls, made Grace feel as if she'd stepped into another era. She indulged in the five-course tasting menu, including a cheese course, which featured unpasteurized delicacies smuggled in from France. No wine, just to be prudent. Her waiter was a handsome and ubiquitous young man, who stood nearby at the ready to refill her water glass, replenish the minibaguettes, or offer seconds on the beggar's purses.

As she was taking a bite of her pear sorbet, the waiter brought over two glasses of Muscato and set them down in front of her. Grace looked at him questioningly, as if to say he must have made a mistake.

"From a Mr. Kane," he said. Grace looked frantically around the dining room, trying to think how she would explain Laz's absence. Noticing her futile search, the waiter added, "He called and said to send his best." Grace tried to laugh it off, but even as she brought one of the glasses to her lips, she felt her heart pounding in her ears. Laz had once told her that *Muscato* meant "tiny flies" in Italian, and as she took one perfunctory sip, she imagined the carbonation like the flutter of wings.

Grace asked the waiter for the check, passing on the candied orange rinds and the madeleines. She waited for her coat by the entrance, protected from the wind by a glass storm door. Still slightly preoccupied by the near miss with the Muscato, she didn't notice a couple as they entered the restaurant. There was a sudden stir among the patrons as a celebrity entered the restaurant. The staff began flurrying about, and Grace felt herself pushed rather forcibly from behind as another couple passed by. Grace turned, and as if in slow motion, she took in fleeting details.

"A quiet table in the back, please," she heard the woman say, as the maître d' led the couple to a secluded booth.

The woman was striking, with wavy, shoulder-length auburn hair, probably only a few years older than Grace. She looked familiar, perhaps being an actress who played character roles. Grace glanced at the man accompanying the woman. From the side, he reminded her of Laz, and she dropped her coat as it was handed to her. She composed herself, blaming the sip of Muscato, and looked more carefully. There was a definite similarity, but he was much younger than Laz. In fact, he looked a lot like Laz had in his Dartmouth College yearbook.

As Grace turned to go, she caught another flash of the young man's face and couldn't shake the feeling that she had seen him somewhere before. Only later, on the walk home in the bitingly cold air, as she thought about the ice melting in the fishbowl, did it register: He was the young man at the bookstore.

THAT NIGHT, GRACE dreamt that she and Laz were lying in a hammock, their legs entwined. Laz murmured, "Baby, baby, baby," until the hammock began to sag and stretch from their weight, the diamond-shaped holes growing larger and larger, no longer able to sustain them. In the dream, Chloe was mending the hammock with variegated yarn spun from a giant spool. Grace awoke in a cold sweat, her T-shirt drenched, but the answer to her birthday dilemma was suddenly apparent—she would visit Chloe in Chicago.

# 13
# THE PAINTED LADY

It was tradition on the Sunday after Thanksgiving that the Sugarmans would host the weekly Scrabble game. What was not usual was the fact that Bert was doing the cooking, or that it was hibachi night. Bert had gone to great lengths to prepare the spectacular evening. He had even purchased a traditional Japanese charcoal grill. Earlier in the day, Francine called Grace expressly to tell her to dress in loose, comfortable clothing suitable for sitting on the floor. Grace was happy to oblige, as anything other than stretchy, oversize articles of clothing made her feel like lying down, especially after last night's five-course gustatory binge.

Grace showered, dried off, and surveyed her face in the bathroom mirror. She looked pale. She felt as if her mother's hand was guiding hers as she applied her makeup before heading over to the Sugarmans'.

. . .

GRACE ARRIVED AT Bert and Francine's penthouse apartment to a flurry of activity. Grace had brought a bouquet of white daisies and thistle, which she knew Francine liked. This, in turn, set off the obligatory commotion of a ten-minute appraisal of all the vases in the house and caused a lamentation about the Lalique that Bert had knocked off the mantelpiece ten years ago, which would have been simply perfect for Grace's bouquet. It was decided that the stems were too long and needed to be cut in order to look right in the Orefors vase.

Bert was dressed in a white bib apron and chef hat. He sharpened his knives on a carving stone in the kitchen as Francine hovered about silently, clucking her tongue. The hibachi grill was set up on a low, square coffee table in what Francine referred to as the Bali room. The room was a small token to appease Bert's lifelong yearning to live in Indonesia. A microcosmic replica straight from the pages of *Travel,* it was complete with low leather stools, embroidered throw pillows embedded with tiny mirrors, beaded curtains, and potted palms. Early on during Grace and Laz's courtship, Laz had given Bert a rare artifact he'd picked up on a trip to Borneo. It was now displayed on a pedestal by the window. That token, along with their shared affinity for etymology, served to ingrain Laz forever in Bert's heart. With floor-to-ceiling windows on all sides, in the summer months, the Bali room was like a hothouse. But on sunny winter days, it was usually quite pleasant. This afternoon, however, it seemed unmitigatingly gray.

Grace's father, seated on the floor and wearing a wool cardigan he had borrowed from Bert, was reading aloud the directions for the hibachi grill.

"It says here," he began, adjusting his reading glasses, which still had the drugstore price tag on the earpiece, "the grill should be ignited twenty minutes prior to cooking. And never used indoors."

"I have this all under control, Milt," Bert said, waving him off and proceeding to light the grill with a sparker. Grace saw a flash out of the corner of her eye and turned to see a huge flame shooting into the air. Bert quickly covered the grill, cautiously looking up to see if Francine had witnessed the pyrotechnics. Assured that she hadn't, he turned up the flame. "It heats up better this way," he explained. Then he turned his attention to the preparation of the mushrooms, slicing them an eighth of an inch thick with utmost precision. "Boy, Laz must really be tied up to miss this."

When everyone was seated, Bert bowed ceremoniously. Francine poured low-sodium soy sauce into small triangular dishes and passed out chopsticks and wasabi. Bert uncovered the grill and brushed the surface with oil. Shrimp, onions, and mushrooms sizzled as Bert tossed them high into the air with his spatula to a round of applause led by Milton. The smell of the shrimp was beginning to make Grace's stomach turn. Bert added the steak and, with a flourish, threw his spatula in the air. The white plastic spatula twirled like a drum majorette's baton. Everyone watched as it missed Bert's outstretched hand and landed instead on the grill, melting like wax onto the caramelized onions. Grace's mother gasped. Francine almost choked on a pickled carrot. Bert reacted quickly, dousing the grill with what he thought was soy sauce, but which turned out to be sherry. Flames soared and the guests ran from the scorching heat.

"My best spatula," Francine grumbled, as she got up from the floor, smoothed her skirt, and left the room.

Francine quickly returned calm and collected, carrying a fire extinguisher, and sprayed the grill with what looked like whipped cream. "No problem," Francine reassured everyone. "Chicken Kiev in three minutes and thirty seconds."

• • •

THE SCRABBLE BOARD was set up after dinner. They played several rounds while sipping steaming green tea and eating tender litchi nuts. Bert had planned to serve pineapple flambé, but everyone insisted it be eaten uncooked. Grace declined because of the brandy.

"First a vegetarian, now a teetotaler?" Bert asked.

"Whose turn is it?" Grace's mother interrupted.

"I think it's Paulette's," Francine answered.

"No, it's Grace's turn," Bert corrected her.

"It's my turn actually," Grace's father said in an unusually firm voice as he placed the letter *x* on the board to form *ox*.

"You opened up a triple-word score, Milton. Don't you have anything better? Laz would never have left that open."

"I'm planning ahead, dear," he said, picking up another tile. "Using a bit of strategy." Grace tried to focus on the board. The letters looked blurry, as if they were underwater. The thought that she might not be pregnant but have a brain tumor instead crossed her mind, and it almost seemed to make more sense. Laz would undoubtedly be there for her for cancer, but not necessarily for childbirth. Before they were married, he had been adamant about not having any children. They took up too much time and he said he didn't have the patience. His decision had seemed so overly intellectualized that Grace had thought he would eventually warm to the idea. It might even keep him home.

She rearranged her letters almost unconsciously and placed them on the board. She felt as if her very participation at these weekly gatherings was programmed into her.

"Flumm? What kind of word is that?" Bert asked. Francine shushed him. Grace moved the tiles across the board, attaching them to her father's *ox*.

"Flummox," Grace announced.

"Never heard of it," Bert said.

"Look it up in your *O.E.D.*," Grace's father suggested.

"Go ahead," Francine quipped.

"I'm sure it won't be in there," Bert said, getting up from the table and going over to the dictionary. He opened the volume and sighed. "I knew I should have gotten the abridged edition," Bert grumbled under his breath.

"Bravo, Grace," her mother said. Then, with a self-satisfied smile, she proceeded to add *ed* to *flummox*, her own score nearly tripling that of Grace's.

"Oh, by the way, how was your anniversary last night? We would have called, but we didn't want to bother you."

*Anniversary.* The word hit her like a burst of frigid air. She could not believe she'd forgotten. She tried to console herself with the idea that she had, indeed, celebrated at their favorite restaurant. The anniversary must have registered on some level, no matter how unconsciously so.

"We went to des Artistes," she answered, finally, growing queasier and queasier.

"You went to dinner?" her father asked, furrowing his brow.

"Lovely," her mother chimed.

Grace wobbled as she stood up from the table. Bert raised an eyebrow.

"Too much celebrating last night, it looks like," he said.

"Can I use your telephone?" she asked Francine.

"Certainly. You need to call Laz?"

Grace nodded. She feared if she tried to speak that she would not have been able to keep her food down.

"Use the one in the bedroom—it'll be more private," Francine offered.

• • •

Grace walked down the hall toward Francine and Bert's bedroom. Just as she was turning the corner, she saw her father standing in the shadows.

"Honey, I need to talk to you," he said softly, touching her arm.

"Sure, Dad," Grace said. As her eyes adjusted to the darkness she could see that his expression was grave. "Are you all right?" she asked.

"Oh, yes, I'm fine. Never felt better," he said, lightly patting his stomach. "Now that your mother has me doing laps around the reservoir." His expression changed quickly and he stammered to find the right words. "It's . . . about Laz," he said, finally.

"What about Laz?" Grace asked, trying to appear unfazed.

"Grace, I saw Laz on *Bookspan* last night talking to that guy who's been trying to discredit him. Something about an eyewitness in Kosovo who—" He paused. "I just thought you might need to talk, that's all." Grace's thoughts careened, trying to find the right response.

"He's been on that show several times," she explained. Grace's father looked at her with concern.

"It was live, Grace. From Washington. I turned it off before your mother came in the room. I didn't want to upset her. Are you and Laz having some kind of marital problems? Because when Bert and Francine went through their little rough patch a few years back . . ."

Grace remembered when Francine had gone to stay with Grace's parents for five days after a disagreement with Bert. She had slept in Grace's room and moped around the house in curlers, until Bert came over with a bouquet of roses and took her home. Grace felt herself beginning to lose her resolve as she took in the full measure of her father's concern, but the pretense was as much for him as for herself.

"Laz and I were out to dinner last night," she began. "That was just a rebroadcast of a show he did weeks ago. You know, because of the holiday. Don't worry, Dad, things couldn't be better between us." Grace tried to rein herself in. She knew she was beginning to sound manic. She took a deep breath. "Everything's fine. We had a wonderful anniversary."

"Oh, I'm so glad, sweetie. I knew there was a good explanation," he said, kissing her on the cheek. As he did, a small black comb fell out of his shirt pocket. He bent down, fumbling as he picked it up. "Now go call Laz and tell him he was missed. And let him know that I'll have the edition of Melville finished by next Friday, if I can swing it."

"I will," she assured him, watching as he disappeared down the hall.

GRACE SLIPPED THROUGH the half-open door to Francine and Bert's bedroom. Her feet sank into the soft-pile carpeting as she closed the door quietly behind her. The flowers she had brought were on Francine's ornately mirrored vanity by the window. She couldn't stop thinking about her encounter with her father in the hallway. The worst part for her was that rather than feeling regret for having lied to her father, she wished he'd taped the show so she could play it over and over again to look for some clue as to why Laz had left her.

For a second, Grace thought she saw something moving among the flowers. Unnerved, she went over to the bed and turned on a small lamp on the nightstand. She knew she was on Francine's side of the bed because the base of the lamp was a porcelain lady wearing a frilly petticoat. The mate was on Bert's side.

Small figurines were posed on every flat surface in the room like a display in a store window. She thought about Laz's wedding band behind the rusting can of shaving cream. It seemed so out of character for her to have forgotten her own anniversary when she'd kept track of everything else so well.

She looked out the window but all she saw in the glass was her own overly made-up reflection. Still feeling a bit queasy, she considered lying down but abstained, not one to take liberties in someone else's home. Instead, she sat on the edge of the bed, relieved to be alone. She felt an odd sense of calm among the frozen figurines. She picked up a small porcelain figurine next to the lamp. It was cold and smooth in her hand—a mother and child holding onto the brims of their watery-blue sun hats, perhaps walking on the beach.

She thought again about Laz and their first Valentine's Day together. The BE MY VALENTINE lift ticket was still on her ski jacket. The memory was clear in her mind. She could conjure every detail—the touch of Laz's lips on hers, the sting of the wind on her cheeks. She wondered if he remembered it, too.

And then another detail of that day, which she'd almost forgotten, began to surface. It had been late afternoon. Grace remembered the deep-blue color of the sky just before their last run. While they were on line for the lift, Grace noticed a young girl wearing a pale blue jacket who had fallen off the rope pull and was crying quietly. Grace knelt down to help her up. Laz stood blocking the sun behind her. *She's old enough to take care of herself. We're going to miss the last run,* he said, steering Grace toward the lift before it closed. Laz pulled the metal bar over Grace's legs, and she looked back once more as they left the ground and ascended into the clear blue sky.

GRACE WAS ABOUT to leave Francine and Bert's room when she became peripherally aware of a shadowy fluttering in the lamp shade. She immediately felt the familiar palpitating in her chest as she recognized the dull thump of a moth against the lightbulb. She rolled up Francine's *Redbook* magazine and prepared herself.

The moth fluttered against the shade, coming in and out of focus through the fabric, looming surreally larger as it pressed its wings against the shade. It reminded Grace of the giant Woodstock balloon that had almost crashed through her window. She struck the shade with the magazine, and the moth fell to the nightstand and lay motionless. She struck at it again, and then once more just to be sure, surprising herself with her spirit for retaliation.

The room suddenly grew bright, and Grace saw Francine and Bert in the doorway. Francine's mouth fell open as she digested the scene.

"Bert's Painted Lady!" she cried. "Grace, you just killed Bert's prized butterfly!"

GRACE'S GUILT OVER killing Bert's butterfly was offset by her elation at now having an excuse to leave the Sugarmans' early. The mood had changed after the incident, as if an ominous high-pressure system had descended upon them. Grace assured Bert that she would make reparations, although she had no idea where to find a replacement caterpillar. She'd seen cardboard butterfly kits sold at the Museum of Natural History, but she was doubtful they'd suffice.

Grace said her good-byes, and after a needless discussion about the best way to get back across town, she left, laden with two Food Emporium bags brimming with leftovers.

# 14

# THE DOPPELGANGER

When she arrived home, the first thing Grace did was to go into the kitchen and check on the fishbowl. The ice had melted substantially, and the key was now encapsulated within a smaller ball of ice, the size of a grapefruit. Like a fortune-teller, she held the fishbowl in her hands and gazed into the water. The ice would be melted soon, but the fishbowl did not contain the answers Grace was looking for.

Inspired, she went in search of other methods of prognostication. The Magic 8-Ball was still under the desk in the bedroom, and Grace decided there was no harm in giving it another try. Suitably skeptical, she gave the ball a gentle shake, not wanting to jostle it unnecessarily, and asked again if she was pregnant. She read the answer: *Yes, definitely*. At first she was incredulous, so she proceeded to ask again, watching with amazement as *Yes, definitely* appeared in the tiny window three more times in a row.

Grace hastily put on a pair of sweats and ran down to the corner drugstore to buy a pregnancy test. She asked the salesperson for a double bag in order to conceal her purchase, but from whom she wasn't certain. Once home, she immediately performed the test and waited, her hands shaking, until the three minutes were up. She scanned the results and sighed with relief as she saw that only one pink line had appeared in the test window, putting to rest any fears—along with any stray hopes and dreams—about having a baby.

Grace wrapped the pregnancy test in tissues, stashed it in the garbage can, and then went into the bedroom. She picked up the 8-Ball, embarrassed that she had given it so much credence, especially since the pregnancy test was ninety-nine percent accurate and there was no toll-free number on the back of the 8-Ball. She let the ball drop to the floor and gave it a good kick, watching as it rolled under the bed. It was just a silly plastic toy filled with colored water. And yet, as hard as she tried to ignore it, she couldn't help hoping it knew something that the pregnancy test did not. She lifted up the dust ruffle and rescued the 8-Ball from a field of dust bunnies. Leaning over the side of the bed, she turned the ball over to reveal the answer: *Yes, definitely.*

GRACE AWAKENED THE next morning filled with optimism. She had slept soundly. Marisol would arrive shortly and order would once again be restored. The lights would be strung on the tree, caramel custard would simmer on the stove, and the dust bunnies would be swept clean.

After bringing down José's coffee, Grace called Chloe and left a message that she and Laz would be in Chicago for her birthday. Then she began to straighten up, or, rather, to arrange the room so as to give the impression that the apartment had been inhabited by Laz. The amaryllis was almost in full bloom, with another flower about to burst open like a brilliant ruby flame.

She hummed as she displayed items around the house that she and Laz might have used over the holiday weekend—a pair of gloves, boots, two crystal flutes for their anniversary celebration, a half-eaten currant scone dripping with jam, *Oblomov* still marked with a folded scrap of yellow paper on the desk, a cashmere sweater on the coat rack. She even left drawers and cabinets half-open— one of Laz's habits, which used to drive her crazy but which now seemed endearing—as well as chairs pulled out from the table. It was the part of the day she derived the most pleasure from— setting the scene.

As she was leaving the evidence of Laz having eaten a peanut butter sandwich by scattering a few crumbs on the counter and leaving a knife in the dish drain, she glanced at the fishbowl and noticed that the ice had melted completely and that the key was lying at the bottom. She plunged her hand into the still-icy water and, feeling very much like a nursery rhyme character, pulled out the key. Even this she took in stride, secure in the knowledge that she was prepared to handle whatever she would confront in Laz's apartment.

The phone rang. It was Marisol's niece with the news that Marisol had eaten contaminated jambalaya and would not be in until Wednesday at the earliest. Grace spent the next few minutes walking aimlessly around the apartment, like a dandelion in search of a swift breeze.

Now that all her efforts that morning had been wasted, she needed something to occupy herself. Her grandmother's afghan, draped over the side of a chair, looking tattered and forlorn, provided her with the solution. She decided at once to take it to the yarn store on Broadway to see if they could repair it. It was as though she'd found her mission. With a few deft strokes, all would be right again, even if only with the afghan. And on the way home, she'd stop by the managing agent to pay the back rent on Laz's old apartment. After consulting the combination thermometer/barometer her father had installed outside the kitchen window, and with afghan, checkbook, and key in hand, Grace left the apartment.

On the front table in the vestibule, she noticed a white postcard from her gynecologist, reminding her of her appointment for her yearly exam. She took this, as opposed to all other signs, as proof that the planets were aligned and cooperating fully.

IT WAS A BEAUTIFUL, clear day and everything, including the sidewalks, sparkled. Grace felt enlivened, better than she had in weeks. She walked up the steep flight of carpeted stairs to the yarn store, which had been on Broadway for as long as she could remember, and pressed the buzzer. She heard the click and opened the door. She didn't see anyone at first as she walked inside. The walls were lined with skeins of yarn in every shade, balls of wool piled high in wicker baskets. Sweater samples hung on wooden dowels above the large windows, and in the middle of the room was a long wooden table with ornate legs and clawed feet. On it were half-finished pieces in an array of textures and patterns, unidentifiable swatches of knitting left in progress.

From behind the counter a woman appeared. She was lifting a large box from the floor, which she set down on the table. Her hair, the color of raspberries, was piled high on her head, and she wore an overly formfitting dress in a floral pattern, with a lavender shawl over her shoulders. Grace waited. Finally, the woman looked up and asked, "Can I help you with something?"

Grace opened her bag. "I was hoping someone could repair this."

"We don't do repairs," the woman answered curtly. "We instruct, make patterns, troubleshoot, sell the materials. But we won't do it for you."

"Oh," Grace said. "I don't know how to crochet."

"How bad is the damage?" the woman asked, softening a little. She put on a pair of tortoiseshell glasses and reached into the shopping bag, spreading the afghan out onto the counter, as if about to perform a complete medical exam. She ran her milky-white hands along the frayed edging, shaking her head as she assessed the situation.

"You're better off starting over," she said finally. "There's less here than is missing." Grace felt like snatching the afghan away from this woman, who bore a strong resemblance to a Little Kiddle doll.

"I couldn't do that."

"Start fresh. It's too *ungepatchket,* anyway," the woman said, without a trace of sentiment. Grace had heard her mother use that word to describe Francine Sugarman's taste in decorating. Actually, anything pre-1960s was *ungepatchket* in her mother's mind.

"I need to try at least," Grace said quietly. "I've had it for so long."

"Suit yourself."

"Do you sell this kind of rainbow yarn?" Grace asked.

"You mean ombré?"

"I guess so," Grace replied.

"We don't carry any acrylics. And Woolworths has been closed for years."

Grace's eyes inexplicably filled with tears as she folded up the afghan and put it carefully back into the bag. She turned to leave. Just as she was reaching for the doorknob, the woman approached her and put her hand on Grace's shoulder.

"I could teach you a few simple stitches. It might take your mind off of things."

Grace sat down on a small stool as the woman dug through a basket until she found a skein of ombré yarn in soft muted shades of purple, sage, and teal. The woman made a simple slipknot, looped it over the crochet hook, and within a matter of minutes was showing Grace how to make a granny square. Grace's hands moved slowly and awkwardly at first, until she began to get the hang of it. By the time she finished her square, she felt serene. She looked at the four-by-four-inch square in her hands and could not believe she'd made it.

"One by one," the woman assured her. "That's all it takes."

"I had no idea it was so simple," Grace said.

"What's your name?" the woman asked, snipping the end of the yarn with a pair of tiny gold scissors that were shaped like a stork.

"Grace," she answered.

"I'm Penelope. Grace, most things are simple—it's people who complicate things." She put five skeins of wool and a crochet hook in a plastic bag. Grace offered to pay, but Penelope refused. "I'll just put it on your tab," she said. "Come back when you've done a few, and I'll show you how to put them together. And leave the afghan. I'll see what I can do with it."

THE LOBBY OF LAZ's old building had been recently re-furbished, restored to an extroverted facsimile of its former Beaux Arts splendor, with a cobbled carriage entrance, gilt paneling, and crystal chandeliers. The limestone exterior of the building was being repointed, and the entire southern side was sheathed in black netting. It looked like a giant veil had been suspended from the cupolas. For all the improvements, though, the building still had the same stale smell that had always permeated the hallways and stairwell—a sort of olfactory melange of burnt toast, papaya, and mothballs.

The Barclay School of Dance that Grace had attended during all of her preteen years had occupied a grand studio on the mezzanine level in the same building, with floor-to-ceiling mirrors and double-height windows. Grace's mother used to sit on the faded chintz couches in the lobby, waiting for Grace to emerge, lollipop in white-gloved hands, usually a hole in the knee of her white tights from where she'd skidded in her Mary Janes across the polished floor. Laz thought the image was funny and had called Grace his little debutante, one night waltzing her down the marble hallway toward the elevator bank.

She and Laz had lived in his old apartment together for less than six months, until Grace could no longer tolerate the confined space and the noisy, whip-crazed neighbors, whom Laz had once threatened in the middle of the night by knocking on their door, wearing little more than his sheepskin slippers. The next night, the neighbors, Alexander and Julian, were invited over for brandied pear canapés and white wine sangria. Later, Laz laughed about the lively neighbors next door. He had a selective memory, as did she, but he only seemed to remember the good times in that apartment, most of which predated Grace entirely.

Grace recognized the concierge as she passed by on her way to the elevators. He waved as if he thought she still lived there. Grace took the elevator to the sixteenth floor, where the office of the managing agent was. She opened the door and approached the receptionist, who was tapping her long, turquoise nails against the desk.

"I'd like to pay this bill. It's two weeks late." She felt the words catch in her throat, feeling as if she had just told the receptionist that her period was late and not the rent. The receptionist took the bill from Grace's hands and studied it. Then she looked at the check Grace had written.

"You need to get this check certified," she said flatly. "And we need to schedule a date for the asbestos abatement."

"That shouldn't be a problem. I'll arrange it with my husband."

The woman gave Grace the once-over, her eyes eventually resting on the ring on Grace's left hand.

"That's some ring," she said, finally. Grace had grown accustomed to people staring at her engagement ring. It was quite a ring—a two-carat, emerald-cut diamond with sapphire trillions. When Laz gave the ring to her, Grace had at first been embarrassed by it. Laz had originally planned on giving her his grandmother's engagement ring, a more modest diamond in a basket setting, but a week before he was going to propose, his mother told him that the ring had been stolen. She had collected a huge sum of money from the insurance agent, enough not only for a replacement ring but also for her to remodel her kitchen. The ring was eventually discovered in her safety deposit box along with her stallion's certificate of genealogy, but by that point, Grace and Laz were already off to Belize.

"I should mention," said the receptionist, "there have been a few complaints about noise from your apartment." Grace tried not to appear startled by this information. After all, Laz had been known to sublet the apartment from time to time. He usually mentioned it to her, though.

"I'll take care of that," she assured the receptionist.

GRACE TOOK THE elevator down to the fourth floor and stood in front of the door to Laz's old apartment. The key and rose she'd dropped on her previous visit were gone. Even though she had the key from the goldfish bowl, she felt obliged to ring the bell. After waiting for an appropriate length of time, Grace put the key in the lock and opened the door. If anyone was living here, there were no visible signs of occupation—no food, recent newspapers, or disarray—nothing to suggest that the apartment was currently inhabited.

Laz's college desk and cinder-block bookshelves looked as if they hadn't been touched in years. Even the television that could access only the local stations, and then with plenty of interference, still had the tinfoil rabbit ears attached to the antenna. Grace noticed how dusty everything appeared, the surfaces covered not with ordinary soot and dust but with particles that had a shiny, almost opalescent sheen.

Grace continued to look around the room as if she were at an exhibit of pre-Columbian art. From the fluorescent light fixtures to the makeshift, faux–wood grain kitchenette, the apartment was no-frills. Laz had liked it that way, the antithesis to his mother's Bauhaus duplex on Park Avenue. The only remnants of this apartment's former glory were the sealed-off dumbwaiter, which had once brought up dinners to the hotel guests, and the gas fireplace. Laz's mother referred to the apartment as "the tenement." On Laz's thirty-second birthday, one of the few times his mother ever deigned to visit, Grace had prepared a dinner of rack of lamb and scalloped potatoes. The meal was eaten at a card table surrounded by metal folding chairs, and they spent a good part of the evening fanning the overly sensitive smoke alarm, which went off even when Laz blew out the candles on the Greenberg chocolate cake.

Grace was surprised to see the spinning pups on the coffee table, merrily skating across its dust-covered surface. And then she saw an extension cord, tangled with plugs, leading in all directions to various electronic appliances. It looked uncannily like the one she'd been missing. Where before she might have considered the mystery of the extension cord solved, now she had only more questions. She knew that these were not just simple coincidences; she began to wonder if she and Laz were engaged in an unwitting game of cat and mouse. Still married, but not together—it was as if they were playing chess, just not on the same board.

Grace sat down on the edge of the couch. It was an emerald green velvet pullout that Laz had slept on in college, with a concave Styrofoam mattress that was missing several springs. Laz used to replace them with twist ties, which Grace would later find underneath the couch when she dry-mopped. She recalled how much effort it used to take to fold the mattress and close the couch. Sometimes, she would have to physically jump on it. Grace ran her hand over the fabric. The velvet was worn to a pale green on the arms and seat cushions, which they used to flip regularly.

She remembered the morning not long after they'd moved in together, when she found a black-and-white photograph of a woman inside one of the zippered seat cushions. Laz had said that it had probably been forgotten by the previous owners of the couch. It was such a sensible explanation that she felt ashamed for even bringing it up. The next evening, he blindfolded her and led her down twisting corridors, up a spiral staircase, and outside. When he removed the bandana from her eyes, Grace was looking out over the skyline.

"I thought the roof was closed," she said.

"It is," he answered. "I paid off Jorge." Grace smiled, and then she noticed a hammock in the most northern corner, under a thatched covering, and a book on top of a stack of black roofing tiles.

"Look," Laz said, walking over to where the hammock was fastened, "someone's reading *Oblomov*." He and Grace had been reading it aloud nightly for weeks. He picked up the book and opened it, the spine cracking. They had bought their copy at the Strand bookstore, and it still had the price written in pencil on the inside cover and the ex libris bookplate from the previous owner.

Grace leaned against the metal railing, taking in the unobstructed view all the way up Broadway past Columbia University almost imagining that she could see the outline of the mansion where they'd first met. That night, as they lay in the hammock, Grace felt secure that these memories would always be there for her, grounding her and Laz, especially during the times when they were apart.

SHE COULDN'T REMEMBER now if they'd actually ever finished reading *Oblomov*. But it had never been about getting to the end. They had a way of stopping and picking up again without missing a beat. A wave of exhaustion came over her, so she put down the shopping bag and rested her head on a tasseled pillow. As she drifted off, she wondered how *Oblomov* ended.

The next thing she was aware of was a loud knocking on the door. It had grown dark outside. She heard the sound of rain on the air conditioner. As she tried to reorient herself, she recalled a fragment of a dream that hovered above her in her half-waking state. Laz was standing on the other side of a doorway, which was covered by a huge cobweb. As he walked through it toward her, not a trace of the web adhered to him.

She stood up from the couch to open the door and caught sight of a brown leather jacket that looked identical to Laz's hanging from a hook. Stunned, and afraid that she might still be dreaming, she reached out to touch it. She pulled the jacket off the hook, causing a windbreaker and a baseball cap to tumble to the floor. She pushed her arms through the sleeves and plunged her hands into the pockets. As soon as she did, her heart sank. The jacket she was wearing, although almost identical to Laz's, had no hole in the lining. As she took it off, she noticed two frayed army patches on the sleeves. It was not the missing jacket she was looking for, but it had clearly belonged at one time to the missing man.

• • •

As she was riding down in the elevator, Grace realized that she'd been so distracted by the leather jacket that she'd completely forgotten all about the person knocking at the door. Probably a maintenance man to schedule the abatement, she told herself.

When she descended to the lobby, another concierge was on duty. She glanced at a brass clock above the desk and saw that it was a quarter to six. She'd slept for over three hours! She hadn't yet canceled spelt night, and Kane and Greg would be expecting her and Laz at seven.

"You just missed Mr. Brookman," the concierge called to her, as she passed his desk. Grace stopped and turned around.

"Excuse me?"

"Mr. Brookman," he repeated. "You just missed him." The shopping bag with the crochet hook and wool fell out of her hands, and Grace watched as a ball of ombré yarn rolled away, leaving a rainbow trail in its wake.

"Laz was here?" she managed to say. The concierge shook his head and smiled.

"No," he corrected her. "The *young* Mr. Brookman. He just came by to drop something off."

# 15
## SPELT NIGHT

Back at her own apartment, Grace called Kane to cancel, but there was no answer. Then she reconsidered. She was so hungry that spelt pizza with tofu mozzarella was beginning to sound appealing. Just as she was about to leave, the telephone rang. It was her father.

"Been out?" he asked, not bothering with pleasantries.

"Yes, actually. I just got in. Why?"

"Mother's friend Mrs. Kreiger called and said she saw you in Laz's old building."

Grace was used to this level of surveillance. Still, it was shocking how quickly the information had been conveyed, as if it had been done by means of a global satellite scanner. There was a decided method to her father's interrogation, an occupation he relished, and no matter how mundane her crime, she knew she'd have to endure his inquisition. It was a nuisance at times, but she also knew how much he enjoyed it—a sort of holdover from his *Perry*

*Mason*–watching days, so she played along, answering his questions as if on the witness stand. While she was talking, she busied herself by unknotting the yarn that had spilled out of her bag. She heard a muffled cough on the extension, an indication that her father's very own sidekick was listening.

"Doing errands?" her father asked.

"I was just coming from the yarn store. The afghan Grandma Dolly made me needs some repair," she answered, yanking on a particularly tight knot. Grace's grandmother had once told her a story about how prospective brides in the shtetlach of Europe were given a knotted-up ball of yarn, and if they had enough patience to undo all the knots, they were deemed to be a worthy match. Over cups of tepid tea with lots of milk and sugar, Grandma Dolly had made Grace practice on shoelaces or delicate gold chains. Luckily for Grace, for whom a pair of sharp scissors seemed now the only solution to such knots, those customs had long been abandoned. She still had several unknotted skeins remaining, the shtetl's judgment of an old maid.

"But the yarn store is blocks from there."

"When it started raining, I ducked into the lobby to avoid getting wet," Grace answered. Laz's building had two entrances. She could actually walk a stretch of almost ten blocks virtually untouched by the elements by wending her way through various buildings, hotel lobbies, subway stations, garages, and covered courtyards, a route that her father had mapped out for her.

"Ah! Good thinking. Did you use the Hotel Mirabela's side entrance?" he asked.

"Of course," Grace answered, stretching the truth still further like a piece of warm taffy. "And the Apple Bank."

"I tried to show your mother once, but you know her—she could get lost in a phone booth." Grace heard the sound of "someone" clearing her throat. "Well, anyway, your mother got this silly idea that you were up to some sort of covert activity," he said, taking pride in his deductive skills.

"Well, you can reassure her I was not smuggling wool," she said. There was rustling on the extension and Grace could almost hear her mother bursting from the effort of trying to remain unobtrusive.

"I hope it's not real wool," her mother finally said. "Wool pills."

"Oh, and if you're going out," her father warned, "make sure you and Laz take mass transportation. It's going to be treacherous tonight once the temperature drops. Like a sheet of ice."

THE RAIN HAD ended, the temperature had dropped, and the streets were indeed treacherous. The taxi ride downtown to meet Kane was a more adventurous journey than Grace would have liked. She had no idea that cars could move sideways.

The restaurant was minimalist in style: long maple tables, chrome chairs, and a silent, rippleless waterfall cascading down a granite wall. Kane was sitting by himself at a table near the window. From his expression and the empty bottle of organic beer in front of him, Grace guessed that something was troubling him. She wondered if he and Greg had had an argument, and she felt relieved—though also a little guilty—that Laz's absence would now be eclipsed by Kane's greater need for comfort.

"Are we dining alone?" Grace asked. Kane got up from the table and kissed her on the cheek.

"Greg got caught up at the studio. You know how those things are."

"Yes, I do," Grace commiserated.

"Laz couldn't break away either?" he asked, taking a sip of his hops-free lager.

"Unfortunately not. And he was really looking forward to meeting Greg."

"Another time, I guess," he said.

"Definitely. We'll do it soon. The four of us." The conversation continued in this vein for another few minutes until Grace could no longer stand the forced civility and tried to concentrate on the menu. She reached for a spelt breadstick, which, she was loath to admit, was actually quite tasty.

The waiter, who, in Grace's mind, was paying an inordinate amount of attention to Kane, came over to take their order. Grace noticed the eye contact and the nuanced gestures of the waiter toward her old friend, and she felt suddenly proprietary toward Kane, who seemed completely oblivious to the waiter's overtures. They ordered a large spelt pizza with mushrooms, two organic fennel salads, and two soy milk shakes with wheat grass juice.

"That's my favorite," the waiter beamed, still hovering around their table.

"Hey, you know," Grace said, trying to ignore the waiter's unctuous glances, "I was looking at that picture of the four of us at Halloween. Remember—when Laz was the Invisible Man?"

"Yes, of course. I was there, remember? Me Tarzan, you Wilma."

"By any chance, do you happen to have another copy of that picture?"

"Why?"

"I thought I'd send one to Chloe," she answered, not mentioning that her copy was now torn to pieces.

"Are you sure Chloe would want a reminder of that night?" The question surprised her.

"What do you mean?"

"It was sort of weird, don't you think?" Kane looked down, smoothing out the tablecloth with his hands. "At least for me it was." Grace didn't know how to respond.

"Well, if you can find it," she said, finally.

"I'm sure I have it somewhere," he said. "Unless it pulled a vanishing act, like your husband. He's even more invisible than usual."

She had assumed that what Kane had been alluding to was Laz's very conspicuous absence over the last few weeks, but then it occurred to her that she must have been doing such a good job of simulating his presence that he was not even missed. Or maybe they didn't really miss him after all. And maybe neither did Grace.

"Oh," she said. "I see what you mean. Kind of like how my father covers every book in the house with plastic laminate." Kane broke into a smile.

"Exactly. Like the time he gave you a *Zagat* guide with a dust jacket?" he joked. Grace felt relief at their having finally begun to find their usual rhythm, the kind of easy conversation that she didn't have with anyone else, not even Laz.

"Yeah. He calls them prophylactic covers. Just in case anything spills on them. He even coats them with a special solvent to repel dust mites."

"Sort of like *safe texts?*" he asked. Grace gave Kane a disdainful look. The waiter returned with two salads and what appeared to be a soggy disk laden with mushrooms that was sprinkled with bits of unmelted shredded tofu.

"You always take things one step too far," she said. Grace took a bite of fennel salad, which tasted a little too close to Black Jack gum for her liking, a predilection she'd had for a while during her grammar school years. As she lifted the soggy slice of pizza to her lips, the mushrooms slid off onto her lap. "It's not too late to make a break for it," she conspired. "Ralph's is only two blocks from here. I promise I won't tell Greg."

"Speaking of Greg," Kane began, "We're thinking about moving in together." Grace almost spit out the water that Kane had advised her to drink in order to wash down the spelt, which had already begun to coagulate in her mouth.

"What? Isn't that a little premature?" she asked in a tone that sounded more accusatory than she'd intended.

"Premature? Do you think I would make this decision lightly?" he asked.

"No," Grace answered tentatively, trying to regain her composure. "I just mean you haven't known each other very long."

"Long enough to know we're compatible," he countered, spearing a cherry tomato with his fork.

"Haven't you considered that this might just be a passing fancy?"

"A passing fancy? Look, let's not talk about Greg right now."

"I just mean," she said, formulating her words slowly, realizing that she was in touchy territory, "that these things eventually tend to lose their appeal."

"Really?" Kane reached for his glass of water and leaned back in his chair as he took a long drink.

Grace knew she was walking a precarious line. She cringed at her words, but it was too late to take them back, and for some reason, she was unable to stop from adding more. "Once you get over the novelty of it, that is," she said.

"The *novelty*? I'm not quite following," Kane said, staring at her. "Maybe I'm just not ready to talk about Greg."

"Don't you want to at least see what Laz thinks about this?" she asked. Even before she said it, she knew she'd gone too far.

"Well, far be it from me to make any sort of informed decision without first clearing it with Laz. I thought you of all people would be happy for me." Just then, an attractive woman passed by their table. Grace was perplexed while watching Kane's head turn.

"You don't have to pretend with me," she blurted out. She wondered if the soy milk shake was spiked.

"Pretend? Grace, what are you talking about?" With that, he picked up his fork and focused on eating, looking up only once to motion for the check. Suddenly, Grace felt a hard lump forming in her throat. If she tried to utter a word—any word—she knew she would dissolve into tears.

Kane paid the bill, glancing repeatedly at his wristwatch, and they sat in silence as they waited for the change. The waiter had insisted on wrapping up what remained of the spelt pizza and fennel salad, which he handed to Kane.

"You take it home. For Laz," Kane said, passing it to Grace.

As Kane held the door of a taxi open for her, he barely met her eyes. Until just then, she had been so busy perfecting her performance, she hadn't realized she was lonely. As the taxi pulled away, Grace looked out the rear window, trying to catch a glimpse of Kane, but all she could see was the glare from passing cars. She had just offended one of the people closest to her. She searched in vain for an explanation for her erratic behavior. If it weren't simply a case of premenstrual hormones gone awry, and if she continued with this trend, then by the time Laz did finally come back, she might just have managed to alienate everyone within her proximity.

THAT NIGHT, SHE dreamt that Kane was driving her home in a car filled with sterling roses, but instead of stoplights, there were Magic 8-Balls at each corner. The 8-Balls glowed green like neon halos, but when she and Kane approached them, the 8-Balls turned red. At each corner, the same message was displayed: *You may deny it.*

# 16

## WATSON AND CRICK

There were seven messages on the answering machine when Grace got upstairs. It was only nine o'clock, but it felt like midnight. She wagered a guess before playing the messages that at least five of them were from her father, hopefully one from Kane. That would leave one remaining message. It was the last one that Grace held out for with white-knuckled tenacity, like a child clinging to a helium balloon.

The first one was from her father. *Hi, Gracie, it's Dad.* She skipped ahead to the next message, which was from Laz's mother, reminding her about an auction solicitations meeting on Wednesday. Then another one from her father. *Dad again. Just calling to see if you got home safely.* She assumed the next message would be her father again, but it was from Chloe.

*Hi. It's me. It's been a long time. I guess you haven't heard. My mother died in September. I was in briefly to sort through some things, but not really in the Thanksgiving mood. Call me. I'd love to talk to you.*

Grace replayed the message. She hadn't realized that she and Chloe had drifted so much that Chloe wouldn't have even called to tell her about her mother. She remembered when they used to talk every day.

She played the next message. *Grace, it's your father. Give a call when you get in.* She hit the delete button. The next message was garbled. She heard a woman's voice mumbling in Spanish. Grace recognized some of the words. *No está en casa.* Finally, after some confusion and shuffling sounds, she was able to discern Marisol's voice: *Señora Grace? My niece will be in tomorrow. The doctor says I cannot work until Thursday. Gracias.*

Grace played the final message. Just a long dial tone. She rewound it and played it again, turning up the volume in the hopes of hearing something that might indicate that the call had been from Laz, and not simply a wrong number. She was about to replay it for the third time when the telephone rang and she hit the delete button by accident. She picked up the phone and had already said, "Hi, Dad," when she heard an unfamiliar voice on the other end.

"Hello. Is Lazarus Brookman there, please?" a woman inquired. She had the kind of voice Grace recalled from poetry workshops she'd taken in college—self-assured and polished.

"Hello?" the woman said again.

Grace had a flash of recognition, like the sighting of a lightning bug, but each time she thought she'd caught hold of it she came up empty-handed. Grace was about to answer when the woman began speaking to someone in the background. "Let me handle it," the woman said, her voice slightly muffled.

"He just stepped out," Grace told her. "Can I take a message?"

"No, thank you. I'll call back," she said, hanging up before Grace could get her name.

Grace went to the closet to hang up her coat, and to her amazement, there on the same wooden hanger where it had always hung was Laz's leather jacket.

She touched the jacket and had a strange impulse to embrace it, instead zipping it up and adjusting it on the hanger, as if it were a disheveled child just home from school. In the morning, she'd take it to the tailor to get the pocket lining mended.

As soon as she closed the closet door, she was suddenly overcome with exhaustion, when only a moment ago she'd felt elated. The jacket had returned, but with it, only more questions. The Magic 8-Ball wasn't wired to deal with conflicted emotions, and neither was Grace. She proceeded to go into her default mode, blanking out all self-doubt and worry—even the sound of the woman's voice now escaped her—until the only thing she thought she needed was a good night's sleep.

WHEN SHE WOKE UP, she had no recollection of having fallen asleep, just the awareness that she'd had no dreams, a span of time with no thoughts—a feeling close to bliss, as if her memory, along with the dream about Kane, had been erased. It was still dark out. She thought it must be nearly dawn, but when she looked at the clock she saw that it was only four in the morning.

As a child, when she couldn't sleep, she'd think about her father's beige argyle sweater. Most of what he wore was either beige or some other neutral tone. Her father, a creature of habit, ate the same breakfast—cornflakes, half a toasted English muffin with currant jelly, and a cup of Postum with nondairy creamer—without fail each day. Grace found this predictability soothing, as regular and soporific as the pattern on his argyle sweater. She tried to close her eyes now, but she was strangely alert. She decided she might as well get up and string the Christmas lights.

The lights were in the utility closet inside two large plastic bags, next to some unopened cans of paint and tile grout that Laz had purchased during one of his home-repair phases, which had never come to fruition. The lights were a tangled mess of wires and bulbs, as Grace never had the patience to wind them back neatly. She preferred the stuff-them-in-a-bag-and-forget-about-them method of taking down the tree; she didn't mind the necessity then the following year of having to run out to the hardware store to buy new lights.

She set about trying to separate the strands that had twirled together like some genetic experiment gone haywire. There were equal numbers of white and colored strands, and many of each. Grace liked every inch of the tree to be lit up so that it blazed. Last year when they'd decorated the tree, Laz had said that if they strung the lights end to end, they would span the length of the George Washington Bridge.

As Grace untangled the lights, she thought of the meteor shower that she and Laz had seen on Block Island the first summer they were together. On a clear August night, they had been huddled by the dunes. Laz had pointed to the sky, which was streaked with sprays of light, and told her that for him it was what was in between the stars that intrigued him. Grace told him she preferred the stars themselves.

"Tell me what you can't do," he asked, pulling her closer. "I love you as much for what you aren't, as much as for what you are. Maybe more."

"I can't do a cartwheel," she said. "Or be alone." At the time, Grace had found the request strange, like trying to define something by its negative image, but now it made perfect sense. However, she still preferred the lights.

. . .

THE MOST DIFFICULT part of untangling the Christmas lights was having the restraint not to tug too hard, so as not to unwind the double wires that made up each individual strand. Grace found this particularly trying, as her initial inclination was to wrench them apart with brute force. Her second thought was to get a pair of scissors and cut them. She succumbed to neither strategy, forcing herself to remain in a state of calm and balance that was utterly unfamiliar to her. She had once read that the smell of lavender was supposed to have a relaxing effect on the mind, and she would have lit an aromatherapy candle now if she'd had one. Instead, she settled for trying to conjure a mental facsimile of the smell.

After several minutes, managing only a vague olfactory approximation of essence of apple, she gave up. Although unsuccessful, the distraction had served its purpose. In the meantime, she'd been able to disengage several strands from the chaotic jumble. She marveled at her work, then inspected each strand to make sure that no bulbs were missing or broken.

The tree had settled in over the last few days, spreading out like a houseguest with a lot of luggage. It looked significantly larger than when Kane had first set it up. Grace moved the furniture to give the branches more space and hoped that the tree would not continue to expand.

Once Grace began stringing them, the lights went up easily. She fastened the strands together, following the natural flow of the branches, and before she knew it, she was ready to plug the cord into the outlet. The tree lit up in a sparkle of white and jewel colors. Grace stood back to admire it. The lights soon began to blink in a perfectly timed sequence that, for Grace, mimicked and in some way even surpassed the randomness of stars.

She was tired when she finished, the first hint of morning a pale glow above the park. She prepared José's coffee, took it downstairs, and, exhausted, went back to bed.

GRACE HAD FORGOTTEN that Marisol's niece was coming that morning, so she was surprised when she was awakened by the sound of the vacuum. She looked at the clock. It was nearly eleven. Grace jumped out of bed, realizing that she'd neglected to leave any further evidence of Laz around the apartment. Laz's side of the bed appeared eerily unslept on, the pillows neatly stacked, the comforter uncreased. She pulled down the comforter, rumpled the sheet, and twisted it into a tornado-like formation. Laz was a fitful sleeper, often sprawling diagonally across the bed, the pillows ending up tossed on the floor. Grace, on the other hand, could sleep in one position all night. In the morning, all that was needed for her side was a light smoothing of the bedspread and fluffing of the pillows; otherwise, it was hard to tell that anyone had even slept there.

After a few final touches—Laz's razor blade and a tube of toothpaste in the garbage can; an unopened tin of Altoids on the dresser; his tattered black Dartmouth sweatshirt, now faded to a grayish green, slung over the back of the chair—the scene was set. It was more for Grace's own benefit, she acknowledged, than for Marisol's niece, on whom the fine attention to detail would be lost since she was not well acquainted with Laz's habits.

Grace bent down to retrieve Laz's sheepskin slippers out from under the bed and had the sudden impulse to try them on. They were far too large for her, of course. She could feel the indentations that his toes had made in the thick fleece. Instantly, her feet began to overheat in them. Laz wore them all the time, complaining that his feet were always cold, but still preferring the aesthetic of bare floors or area rugs to wall-to-wall carpeting. If pressed, though, it was the carpet's seeming permanence that scared him.

Except for the kitchen, every square inch of Grace's parents' apartment, including the closets and the bathrooms, was covered with a thick, wool Berber. To Grace, it felt homey. Her mother had put her foot down, however, when Grace's father had suggested using the scraps to line the kitchen cabinets. Her father had even invested in an industrial-strength rug shampooer, which he lugged out religiously every month.

Once, on a trip to Morocco, Grace and Laz had visited a local rug shop. An array of brilliant carpets hung from the rafters, others were piled high on the floor. Laz had remarked to the owner of the shop that he liked the fact that the carpets could be rolled up and taken with them if they ever moved.

Sipping a glass of mint tea, Laz pointed to a small flat-weave rug. The owner shook it out and let it fall gently to the floor. "This one I could slip into a backpack," Laz joked, making the merchant smile. When Laz saw the expression on Grace's face, he put his arm around her and pulled her close. "Don't worry, Grace, I'd slip you in there, too—if there was room," he said, laughing. "You never know, you might wind up leaving me. But you'd need a six-piece set of luggage, and that's not even counting the passage for your family. And you can't forget the Sugarmans. Travel light—that's my motto. If I teach you one thing, that should be it."

GRACE REMOVED THE slippers from her feet and arranged them to look as if Laz had just kicked them off. She bent down to smooth the dust ruffle. As she stood up, she felt a sharp twinge in her lower right side. She took three deep breaths until the pain subsided.

She looked around the room and admired her work, deciding she might have missed her calling as a stage manager, or at the very least, a competent window dresser. The room looked like a life-size diorama. As if the curator of a museum, she formulated the caption in her head: *Portrait of a Marriage, circa 1999.* She angled the door for the best possible view, stopping just short of cordoning off the room with a velvet rope.

Marisol's niece Dolores was polishing the silver when Grace walked into the kitchen. Grace was dressed in a black sweater and a pair of gray pants that had just come back from the dry cleaners and were a bit on the tight side. "*Buenos dias,* Señora Brookman," Dolores said, smiling.

"Good morning. Beautiful day, isn't it?" Grace said.

Dolores nodded. "*Sí,* but it's *mucho frío,*" she answered. Grace noticed that Dolores was still wearing her blue down jacket.

"Please call me Grace."

"Certainly, Señora Grace," she responded, as she carried the silver bowl into the dining room and placed it in the center of the table. Before Grace could warn her, Dolores flipped on the light switch. With a quick flash, the dining room fixture and the lights in the entire apartment blew.

When Grace called down for the handyman, the superintendent told her he'd send someone up right away—one of the many perks of being generous tippers at Christmastime.

The handyman arrived within minutes, once again removing his shoes, although Grace would have much preferred footprints to the sight of his canary yellow socks. It was only a matter of minutes before the apartment once again blazed with the light from the Duro-Lites and the Christmas tree sparkled in the living room.

"Remember to turn off the circuit breaker the next time if you need to replace the dimmer," the handyman advised her, as he bent down to put his shoes back on. She noticed that they were not his usual work boots, but a pair of shiny tap shoes, which, paired with his baggy blue carpenter's pants, gave him a Chaplinesque appearance. He stood up, lingering a bit until Grace pressed a twenty-dollar bill in his hand and bid him good-bye.

After he left, Grace went into the dining room to test the dimmer. She lifted it up and down and felt a sense of complete satisfaction as the Duro-Lites dimmed to a quiet, calming orange and then brightened. Out of the corner of her eye, she noticed a strange flickering from the living room, like the flashes from a silent summer lightning storm. To her dismay, she realized that the Christmas tree lights as well as the sconces above the mantelpiece and the Arts and Crafts lamps on the end tables were all dimming and brightening in unison with the Duro-Lites.

When Grace turned the light off, the lights in the living room went off as well. She flipped the switch back on quickly, hoping she could somehow fool the circuits. Once again, the Christmas tree and all the other lights went on. She jiggled the switch, thinking the wires were just stuck together and that she could somehow unstick them, but it didn't help. Her first inclination was to call the super again, but instead she decided to adjust the lights so that the Christmas tree and the Duro-Lites were all at a tolerable level of brightness.

Then she went to the closet to get Laz's jacket to take it to the tailor's, along with a pair of his pants that needed hemming. When she got back, she would call Chloe.

THE TAILOR AT Aphrodite Cleaners was busy sewing buttons onto a thick shearling coat when Grace walked in. He nodded for her to sit down on a folding chair, then he ended off, cutting the thread with his teeth, and walked over to her.

"These pants need hemming," she told the tailor, "and there's a tear in the pocket lining of the jacket." The tailor unfolded the pants and examined them.

"How long?" he asked. Grace hadn't remembered to measure the length of Laz's inseam, although she was certain she could come pretty close to the measurement if she tried the pants on.

"Is there someplace I can change into them?" she asked.

"Right in there," he said, indicating a small half-curtain to the left of his sewing table.

The tailor didn't question whether the pants were hers or not. She went behind the curtain into a space no larger than a telephone booth and put the pants on. They were not as large as she'd anticipated. Clearly, the sugar binge she'd been on over the last few weeks was beginning to take its toll. The waistband skimmed her pelvic bone. As she adjusted the pants low on her hips, she pictured how Laz's body fit into hers, the way his hands could practically circle her waist when he stood behind her.

"The hem should just graze the floor," she told the tailor when she emerged. She stepped up on a small stool and stood in front of the mirror as he knelt down and marked the pants with a white wax crayon. She was amazed by how much she resembled Laz, at least from the waist down, except for her shoes, which were high-heeled boots. She felt like a picture in one of those children's flipbooks that mixes and matches different heads and bodies—a strange hybrid creature. A Chimera. As Grace stood in front of the mirror, she wasn't sure where the line of demarcation was, where one began and the other one ended. And who was inhabiting whom now?

"Which one needs repair?" the tailor asked, picking up Laz's jacket and turning it inside out.

"Excuse me?" Grace asked.

"Which pocket has the hole?"

"Oh, the right one," she answered.

"Do me a favor and check to make sure there's nothing in the pockets. You wouldn't believe the things people leave."

She slid her hands into the pockets. These pockets that had once held Laz's keys and change, into which his hands had slid so many times to keep warm, were now empty. Not only was his PalmPilot gone, but so were the Life Savers. Grace felt as if she'd been fleeced by a phantom pickpocket. She wondered if the vanished items might lead her to her vanished husband, a trail she knew she wasn't yet prepared to follow. For now, it would remain another mystery.

DOLORES WAS STANDING in the doorway, waiting for Grace when she arrived home. She hung up her coat, ready to write the name of some cleaning product on a shopping list, assuming that Dolores had run out of Brillo Pads or Murphy's Oil Soap, which Marisol used liberally on all surfaces and that soaked through even the Sunday *Times,* leaving the pages nearly translucent.

"Excuse, me," Dolores began. "Marisol says Señor Brookman forgot to leave her pay." Grace was baffled. She'd been so diligent about writing checks to pay the bills, but then it dawned on her that Laz must have always paid Marisol in cash.

"How much do we owe her?" Grace asked.

"*Cinco* weeks," Dolores answered. Something about hearing the number, even in Spanish, made Grace's head spin. To her, it felt as if Laz had been gone no longer than a matter of days, despite all evidence to the contrary—such as the fact that the supply of deli cups, which had come in a pack of fifty, was more than half depleted. Grace had stopped counting the days sometime after Laz's birthday. November might as well have been frozen in one of Francine's containers.

"*Cinco?*" Grace repeated. She opened her wallet and gave Dolores all the cash she had on hand. "I'll go to the bank right away for the rest. Please tell Marisol I'm very sorry."

The telephone rang. She picked it up, half expecting it to be a bill collector.

"Grace? It's Chloe."

"Chloe," she said. "It's so good to hear your voice. I'm so sorry about your mother. I wish you had called to tell me."

"You know how it is." She paused, sniffling a bit. "It's been rough."
There was another pause. Then Chloe said, "So you're coming to
Chicago?"

"For my birthday," Grace answered, although she was already
having misgivings about the plan.

"Laz, too?" Chloe inquired.

"Yes, he'll be tied up with some conference, but I thought you
and I could spend some time together if you want."

"It's been a long time."

"I know. I'm really sorry I've been out of touch," Grace said.

"Me, too. Let's make sure to change that."

Grace hung up and dialed the toll-free number of the discount
travel agent whom her father had once told her about, and she
booked a flight to Chicago for the day before her birthday, using
frequent-flier miles accrued by Laz on his many transatlantic flights.
Out of force of habit, she asked for two bulkhead seats—Laz liked
a lot of legroom. By the time Grace had realized her mistake, the
agent had already put the order through, so Grace decided to keep
it. She told herself it was in order to avoid wasting more time, but
what she was really feeling was trepidation about traveling alone,
which was somehow alleviated by the thought of Laz's disembodied presence. He was like her new imaginary friend—if only he
didn't demand so much attention.

LATER THAT EVENING, Grace was straightening up after
Dolores. It seemed that Dolores had a similar propensity as Grace
did of shoving things in incongruous places wherever they fit, and
Grace noticed her bag of ombré yarn stuffed into the umbrella
stand.

She opened the bag and pulled out the crochet hook and a skein
of yarn. Removing the paper sleeve, she located the end and proceeded to begin a chain stitch. At first it was slow and laborious,

but soon the yarn began to slip easily through her fingers, the stitches forming as if automatically. When the chain was a good length, Grace began to crochet, pulling the yarn under and through and wrapping it around the hook until she came to the end of the first row. The edges curled up and it didn't look like anything, but after several more rows, Grace began to detect the beginnings of a pattern.

For an indeterminate span of time, no thoughts entered her mind. The yarn alternated in a pleasingly unpredictable way, varying in tone and thickness, with intermittent flashes of fuchsia. The rhythmic pattern was spellbinding. She wondered if crocheting could become addictive, as she considered the merits of a twenty-four-hour yarn store and tied the ends of one skein to the next.

After crocheting some more, she started to tire of repeating the same stitches and decided to make variations in the pattern by adding a stitch here or there, inserting the hook into the same stitch twice or dropping a loop, which created a clustered, starlike effect. She liked not having to follow a pattern; however, she did have to pull several rows when she tried to get too fancy.

Before she knew it, the bag of yarn was empty. Only after she'd ended off the last stitch did she realize that it was well after midnight and that she'd crocheted something—what, she wasn't sure, a sort of continuous flow of color and texture that spanned the entire length of her living room.

# 17
# A GRIMM TALE

Kane did not call the following day or the next. It wasn't noticeable at first. His calls were not all that regular—varying from once or twice a day to once a week, or even less frequently. It wasn't that he wasn't calling, it was the *way* in which he wasn't calling that Grace knew was somehow different.

She'd already left two messages for him. The first was to provide an excuse as to why Laz couldn't make hockey that night—a fundraiser his mother had roped him into—and the other was to try to make amends for the other night. Both calls went unanswered.

Another stack of mail had materialized on the front hall table. Grace likened the pile of mail that had begun to overrun her life to the suburban phenomenon of trying to maintain a manicured lawn, the bills like stubborn dandelions and the junk mail like fallen leaves. She wished taking care of the bills were as simple as upgrading to a more powerful leaf blower or a more potent weed killer.

Among the bills, she saw a letter from A Perfect Match. Ordinarily, she would have just ripped it in half, but after the meeting with the strange Mr. Dubrovsky, her curiosity was piqued. When she opened it, she saw that she'd been mistaken. The letter was from the lipstick company, informing her that they needed an additional five dollars and ninety-five cents per tube and another sample of the lipstick, if possible, which would have to be sent to the laboratory in Minnesota for further analysis.

Grace was disappointed. She was almost certain she didn't have anymore Velvet, but she went into the bathroom and dug into her vinyl makeup bag on the off chance that she had missed it. She stored the bag on the windowsill above the broken radiator because her mother once told her that the shelf life of makeup is shortened if it's exposed to heat or humidity, advising her to keep her extra lipsticks in the freezer. If Grace followed all of her parents' advice on proper storage, her freezer would be filled to capacity with film, batteries, stockings, and makeup, probably even Duro-Lites.

The bag overflowed with tester-sized tubes of moisturizers, eye shadows, perfume samples, lip and cheek stains, shimmery face powder, white lip gloss, metallic eyeliner, and an array of age-defying lotions that her mother had given her, none of which Grace ever used. Francine gave leftovers; her mother gave beauty products. Grace always felt a pang of guilt when she even entertained the idea of tossing the entire makeup bag in the garbage, just as she would have felt if the did the same with Francine's meatballs.

She was about to give up her search when she noticed an orange pump bottle containing a hydrating body mist called Happy. She read the directions on the back of the bottle: *Spray it. Be Happy.* Enticed by the promise it made, she opened the top and sprayed it over her neck and forearms. It couldn't hurt, her mother would say. The citrusy smell was pleasant enough, but Grace didn't notice any other effects. If only it could be that simple, she thought as she tossed it back into the transparent makeup bag and went to get dressed.

She chose what she considered to be one of her more pulled-together outfits—a cream-colored cashmere turtleneck and her new purple suede skirt—for her visit to her grandmother at the nursing home.

Grace was an unseasoned shopper and left most sartorial decisions to other people. Elliot, one of the salespeople at Barneys, called whenever something came in that they thought suited her, like a pair of must-have black pants, a puckered pink shell, or the beaded silk sarong that Grace had later found for a fraction of the price on a foray with her mother to the Woodbury Commons Outlet. Yesterday, Elliot had left a message telling Grace that he was holding a Katayone Adeli suede skirt for her, but when she went in to try it on, he made the gentle suggestion, not able to fully conceal his raised eyebrow, that they go up another size. Decorum stopped him from suggesting they go up still further. "It *will* stretch," he assured her.

Grace recalled numerous Saturday shopping expeditions with her mother over the years, the two of them often coming home with matching outfits, such as the satin blouses with bell sleeves and macramé vests, or the bright floral minidresses with white peace sign belts. Shopping was her mother's forte as well as her form of therapy—a cure-all for whatever ailed you. They'd spend hours scouring the racks and then, shopping bags in hand, find the nearest Burger Heaven for what her mother referred to as a little *lift*, which consisted of half a cantaloupe, a medium-rare burger on half a bun, and a large Coke. But at the end of the day, Grace would feel anything but uplifted. While clothes were her mother's means to attain her desired image of herself and that of her daughter, for Grace clothes would never be more than another ill-fitting costume.

WHEN GRACE WAS FIFTEEN, she broke up with her first boyfriend. Her mother wasted no time questioning her about the particulars of the breakup, bringing a box of Fiddle Faddle and some tissues to Grace's bedroom as though having prepared all her life for this mother-daughter bonding moment. Grace was too numb to cry.

"I hear you broke up with that sweet Jamie. What happened?" her mother asked. Grace pulled her feet underneath her and tried to find the right words.

"I didn't feel like me anymore," she said quietly. Her mother looked at her quizzically.

"You're still you. Jamie liked you just the way you are."

"It wasn't him. It was me. It was as if I had found the perfect outfit and wore it everyday and never wanted to change it—you know, like that polka-dotted dress I wore until it didn't fit anymore?"

"I know exactly what you mean," her mother said, nodding. "Variety is the spice of life. But that dress was adorable on you."

"Only the more I wore the dress, the less I liked myself in it. I didn't know who I was supposed to be or what I was supposed to wear. It was like I'd run out of outfits."

Her mother put her arm around her, and passed her the box of caramel corn and a handful of tissues.

"Honey, not to worry," she said. "Lord and Taylor is open until nine, and there's a sale in the junior department. We'll have you back to yourself in no time."

GRACE ZIPPED UP her skirt and pulled her hair back with a clip. There had never been any question in her mind that her mother was not capable of more. Grace had always tried to accept her mother's good intentions, even if they came in the form of frilly skirts and turquoise belts, but in Grace's mind she was still in some metaphorical dressing room, trying on clothes chosen by someone else.

Going into the kitchen for a quick cup of tea, Grace opened the cabinet, and there, next to a canister of peppermint tea, she saw the familiar silver tube of Velvet, shining like a beacon in the darkness. It did strike her as a rather odd place for the lipstick, but it was just like her to have absentmindedly put it in there. She felt the sense of elation she usually felt on Christmas morning.

Grace thought about the rhinestone lipstick holder that Laz's mother had coveted at last year's Historical Society auction. Even though the auction was for charity, and Laz's mother would have received a tax deduction for the purchase, she'd refused to go above the estimated value and had lost out to Francine Sugarman, who had instructed Bert to outbid anyone while she was at home with a case of the flu. Bert had waved his paddle as if he were a table tennis champion, once even bidding against himself as Laz's mother lowered her paddle to her lap.

Laz's mother still eyed the lipstick holder with a sneer every time she saw Francine pull it out of her purse—which Francine did often and with obvious pleasure—because she, Nancy Brookman, would never pay full price. Grace thought she might bid on it herself at this year's auction so that she would have a special place to hold her custom-blended lipstick, when it finally arrived. She regretted having not renamed the lipstick—"Velvet" seemed somewhat generic now.

She wrote a check for the required extra amount, placed the lipstick sample in an envelope, and sealed it. She felt as if she were participating in some cloning experiment and wondered if she sent them the smudged fingerprints from Laz's eyeglasses, would they be able to come up with a reasonable replica of him as well?

Taking the envelope, along with the bag containing her crocheting in case she had time to stop in for more yarn on her way to class, she went to visit her grandmother.

• • •

GRACE RODE THE bus up Riverside Drive just past Columbia Presbyterian Hospital to the nursing home. Grace's grandmother had lived in Washington Heights in a redbrick apartment house on the cliffs of the Hudson, overlooking the river for nearly forty years.

When Grace was a teenager, Dolly used to take her aside and tell her that when she died, the apartment would belong to Grace. "I know you'll take care of it—it's my museum. You understand." Grace had always thought she would move there, keeping it intact, as her grandmother had wished, but Laz wanted something "in the city." To him, Washington Heights was like another country, even though it was within the city limits. When Dolly had moved into the nursing home six years ago, the apartment had been given up, her possessions appraised and then sold.

After Dolly's first stroke, Grace had brought Laz to the hospital to meet her. Dolly had squinted her eyes and pointed at him. "I know you," she said, with seeming certainty.

Dolly had come to the United States from Lithuania with her older brother when she was nineteen. The rest of her family perished during the war a few years after that, at which point Dolly had begun collecting. While her children and husband were off at school and work, Dolly went scavenging in antique shops. "Junk shops," she called them. She would return with heavy pendulum clocks, porcelain teacups, carved wooden chairs, hiding her treasures in the closet until one day they'd suddenly appear, blending in among the other household items, as if always having been there.

The bus continued up Riverside Drive, past Grant's Tomb and the mansion where she and Laz had met. It was now abandoned, the property surrounded by a barbed-wire fence. The windows had been replaced with plywood, the doors boarded up. Grace looked back, hoping to glimpse some signs of restoration, until the bus turned and the mansion was no longer in sight.

GRACE GOT OFF the bus and walked up the stone steps of the nursing home, where she found Dolly propped up in bed, gazing out over the Hudson River.

"Grace," she said, slurring slightly. "When will this plane land?" Dolly's room was bare, except for an embroidered bedspread with silk tassels and an antique porcelain clock—one of dozens that she'd collected—that ticked loudly.

When Grace was in college, she had visited her grandmother weekly. Grace remembered the details of one particular visit as if it were yesterday. Dolly had come to the door wearing an ankle-length peasant skirt and a purple shawl around her shoulders. On her head she wore a flowered kerchief, her white hair braided and twisted into a tight bun, which was held in place with a tortoiseshell comb.

"Grace, you're here! I have spinach pie all ready for you. Come have a little something."

"Dolly, I told you I would bring lunch this time."

"What? You'd rather eat from a store?" she asked, putting her arm around Grace's waist.

"I have that cake you like."

"Well, with Zabar's, I can't compete. Come, let's sit."

Grace followed Dolly into her living room. The room was large but so crammed full of furniture that it was difficult to walk through without bumping into something. The door to the terrace was open and there was a breeze. Grace sat in the courtship chair. It had two worn mahogany seats, which faced in opposite directions. The carved center arms were linked together, as if in an embrace. Dolly took in the scene, smiling and nodding her head.

"You look perfect there. Just perfect."

Then Grace noticed a broken spinning wheel next to the fireplace. She'd never seen it before and went to touch it. "Is this new, Dolly?" she asked.

"Oh, no, Grace. It's been here all along."

GRACE NOW LOOKED at the outline of her grandmother's small frame under the bedspread, and at the bare, uncluttered room.

"Will this plane land soon?" Dolly asked again. Grace wondered which way her grandmother thought she was traveling—to America, or back to the girlhood home in Lithuania she'd spent her life trying to recapture.

"Soon, Dolly," Grace said. "I promise."

THE YARN STORE was crowded, and at first Grace didn't see Penelope. Then from out of a basement storeroom, Penelope emerged, huffing and puffing from the climb. She was carrying an armful of yarn, which she set down, and she nodded to Grace. One of the balls of yarn rolled off the counter and disappeared behind a basket like a frightened mouse. Grace bent to pick it up.

"Thanks," Penelope said. "It's Grace, right?"

"Yes," Grace answered. Another customer, a petite woman in a shearling coat and a black beret, was waiting to be rung up. Grace felt she was in good company. If only she'd discovered the meditative qualities of crocheting sooner.

"So, how's it going. Are you hooked yet?" Penelope asked, deadpan. She had clearly used the pun before and had no reason to punctuate it with a laugh. Grace smiled.

Grace placed her yarn bag on the counter and reached inside. "I'd like to buy more yarn."

"You're finished already?" Penelope asked, her eyes widening as Grace pulled out the seemingly never-ending stretch of crochet from the bag. Even Grace was surprised at its proportions, which seemed, like a yeast dough, to have more than doubled in size since the previous night.

"Once I started, it was hard to stop," Grace answered.

"I like the pattern. What book did you use?"

"I didn't," she admitted. "I sort of improvised as I went along."

By this time, a small group had gathered around the counter, hands outstretched to examine the length of Grace's crochet.

A tall woman wearing a long black coat that was covered with cat hair came over to the counter. "Interesting pattern," she said discerningly, as she inspected the edging. "But what are you making?"

"I'm not sure," Grace said. The idea that this would eventually have an end didn't appeal to her. Part of her believed she could just keep crocheting ad infinitum.

"It's a process," Penelope said with authority.

"Nice bobbles," another woman commented. Grace thanked her, even though she didn't have any idea what bobbles were, and in any other context she might have been duly insulted. A heavyset man, not more than thirty, with shiny brown hair approached the counter. Grace noticed that he was wearing a hand-knit sweater of a bright blue wool tucked into a pair of too-tight jeans.

"My grandmother taught me how to crochet when I was eight," he told Grace with a faraway look in his eyes. "Whenever anything was bothering me, we'd sit down to crochet, and it would all just go away. And that was before they knew about serotonin levels." Grace couldn't help but nod. "My name's Scott," he said, extending his hand. "I started a men's group called Crocheting Through. We meet in the basement of the Presbyterian Church every Thursday night. In homage to my grandmother." He sighed. Grace was afraid that he might start crying. "I really miss her a lot." She'd had no idea that people could bond over a few simple stitches.

"You've got the knack," Penelope said. "If I didn't know any better, I'd say you've been crocheting all your life. I started repairing that afghan you brought in, but I think you can handle it from here. Don't be afraid to rip. You have to be ruthless, otherwise you're wasting your time. If you don't do it right, it'll just fall apart in other places," she explained. Grace felt her cheeks grow warm. Somehow, after seeing Dolly in her bare room, the holes seemed preferable to the idea of undoing her grandmother's stitches.

"If you don't mind, I'd rather you did it," she said. Grace walked over to a basket and pulled out a ball of soft yarn.

"Those are nice if you're going to make a throw," Penelope told her. Grace liked the sound of that. It seemed less daunting than making a sweater or something else that required precise dimensions. A throw. Casual and homey.

"How many will I need?" she asked.

"It depends on how big you want it to be. One skein will work up to be about a ten-by-ten-inch square."

"Well, I guess I'll need about twenty, then," she decided.

"I should just give you some straw and see what you come up with," Penelope said with a laugh. Grace smiled but didn't get it. Noticing Grace's perplexed expression, she added, "You know, like Rumpelstiltskin."

"Oh, of course," Grace said.

Penelope put the yarn in a bag. "By the way, I've been looking for someone to work part-time. I don't know if you'd be interested."

"My days are pretty full," Grace answered. "Can I think about it?"

"Of course. Take your time." Grace was struck by the camaraderie and support among the patrons in the tiny, cramped shop. She pictured them all gathered around the long oak table, comparing stitches and giving advice on projects. If ever there were an actual Friends of the Friendless, this place was it.

CHIMERA BOOKS WAS moderately crowded for a Wednesday evening. Grace walked to the back of the bookstore, greeting the salespeople with a newfound openness. It was as though she were seeing the place for the first time, embracing every idiosyncratic detail of the store—from the worn wooden Escheresque steps to the warped bookshelves and the smell of cloves from the holiday wreaths. One of the clerks had brought in a bûche de Noël, and Grace decided she would not pass on a slice. She took out her supplies, placing the hand drills and metal burnishers on the long worktable alongside the three-inch-square sheets of gold leaf she'd bought at Lee's Art Shop.

The room didn't have adequate lighting—the antique brass billiard lamp that hung from the ceiling gave off barely enough light to read by. Yet the dimness didn't deter Grace's students in the least as they fashioned folios out of rag paper. Grace had brought in a few hurricane candles, which were useful not just for the added light they provided but also the added warmth, needed because of the draftiness from the large, warped windows. Some of her students actually preferred the dim lights, saying that it hearkened back to a simpler time. Grace agreed. In the low lighting, the gold leaf fluttered like butterfly wings. With a little ingenuity and a light dusting of gold, Grace thought she might even be able to fool Bert with a paper rendition of his beloved Painted Lady.

She heard laughter and the popping of corks from the front of the store, so she finished up her class preparations and decided to join the festivities. As she walked through the stacks, passing people as they browsed, she noticed an edition of Kafka's *Metamorphosis* and pulled it from the shelf to see if it was a first edition.

Her father had taught her how to identify rare books, and she was about to turn to the title page when she felt a hand on her shoulder. She turned around to see the young man from the other day, who was not only standing before her but wearing the leather jacket that she'd seen in Laz's apartment. The next thing she was aware of was a sharp pain in her lower abdomen and then the hard *thud* as she fell to the floor.

Grace had never fainted before, and even though she was lying down, she wasn't really sure what had happened. The concerned faces above her were a clear indication that something was wrong, so she immediately tried to get up. As she braced herself on a low shelf, she saw a book entitled *Your Natural Childbirth,* with a graphic photograph of a baby still attached to the placenta on the cover. Grace immediately felt herself growing woozy again. Maybe she should have put more faith in the 8-Ball and not the pregnancy test. She closed her eyes, then felt herself being lifted to her feet by a strong set of arms, which led her to the front of the store and eased her into a large leather club chair by a window. When she was seated, she looked up at the young man standing in front of her.

"Sorry I startled you. You were really out over there," he said, sounding a little impressed. "I'm Griffin."

"I just got a little dizzy, that's all," she told him. "I'll be fine, thanks. I have a class to teach."

Someone brought a glass of water, which Grace sipped slowly. Griffin pulled a chair beside her and sat down. Grace looked at his jacket. She knew there were things he could explain, but something held her back from asking. She pulled her hair into a ponytail and looked at him. He was sweet looking, and, close up at least, his resemblance to Laz was less noticeable. The jacket, however, was another story.

"Your jacket—" she started to say, and then stopped.

"Oh, yeah. It was my dad's."

"Your father gave it to you?" she asked. "When?" Once she started asking questions, she knew she'd be unable to stop.

"Well, he didn't exactly give it to me," he said. "I mean, I've never actually met him. My mom kept it for me. He wore it in college. It's not very warm, though, or maybe I'm just not used to the cold." It occurred to her that Griffin might be Laz's son. All the crocheting in the world would not make this go away.

"Why? Where are you from?" she asked.

"From Atlanta. But I go to college in Maryland. I'm a sophomore at Johns Hopkins. Premed."

As he spoke, all the strange occurrences of the last few weeks began to fit together like a puzzle—from the edition of Twain to the couple at the restaurant and the concierge's reference to the *young* Mr. Brookman. It had been Griffin all along.

"How did you know where to find me?" she asked.

"From an article my mother saw in a magazine. She wrote a letter to my father. Didn't you get it?" Grace shook her head, and then vaguely remembered the folded piece of paper stuck in the pages of *Oblomov.*

"So you came looking for him?" she asked. Griffin looked at his fingernails, which were chewed down to the cuticles, and then shoved his hands into his pockets. Laz bit his nails, too.

"I'm sorry I wasn't honest with you," he said, his voice melting into a more Southern tone. "I wasn't all that sure how I'd be received." His cheeks flushed all the way behind his ears. Grace could see he'd cut himself shaving.

"So," Grace started to say tentatively, "am I a stepmom?" It was a totally alien concept, especially considering that Laz couldn't have been more than Griffin's age when the boy was conceived. He smiled.

"I was hoping you could help me get in contact with my father, but I know this may be a bad time with the controversy and all."

Even if she did know where Laz was, she couldn't imagine that this would be a happy reunion. "He gave you the keys to his apartment, didn't he?" Grace asked, trying to change the subject.

"He left them for me with the concierge, but he never showed up. My mother says that's typical." He paused. "She didn't want me to get my hopes up, but I told her that I had nothing to lose." Grace nodded, but she knew he was wrong. Either way, he had something to lose. And more so if he ever met Laz.

"He's away now," Grace told him, trying not to meet his eyes. "At a conference."

"When will he be back?"

"He wasn't sure," she answered. "Sometime next week. I think." Grace felt perspiration trickling down her back. The store suddenly felt stiflingly hot, and Grace knew that she had to get outside.

"You're looking pale again," Griffin said. "Can I get you something?"

"Is it hot in here?" she asked. Not waiting for a response, she bolted for the door.

Once outside, Grace braced herself against a mailbox. It had begun to snow and big wet flakes stuck to her suede skirt. Griffin followed behind.

"Are you okay?" he asked, putting his jacket over her shoulders.

"I'm sorry. I just needed some air," she explained.

"I know the feeling," he said, reaching into his army-green knapsack. He rummaged through a zippered compartment and took out a box of Altoids, opened it, and held it out to her. Laz always had a box of Altoids in his pocket, too. Grace took one, marveling that a father and son who never knew each other could have the same small things in common. Maybe the gene for a predilection for peppermint was passed down like eye color or left-handedness. There was no need for genetic testing.

"My mother says peppermint lifts your spirits," he told her. It would have been preferable had Griffin appeared out of thin air. Having a mother implied a relationship with the father, and that was something Grace was not prepared to confront. "And ginger is good for motion sickness." He pulled out a bag of crystallized ginger. "You should try some for your stomach."

"My stomach?" Grace asked, perplexed.

"You're holding it. I thought it might be bothering you." Grace hadn't been conscious that she was clutching her stomach. She put her hands to her side, suddenly aware of a nagging pain. She wondered if it might be some kind of psychosomatic wishful thinking for a baby. Maybe Griffin's appearance triggered something, shining a light on possibilities she'd never allowed herself to dream of. Surprisingly, the mint did revive her.

"Thanks," she said. "I feel much better." She looked at Griffin and found herself trying to dissect his features, deciding which ones to embrace, which to disown—the squared-off angle of his chin, his long fingers, and even the way his hair fell over his forehead were all clearly from Laz. But his sad yet still trusting eyes, she knew, had to have come from someone else.

She looked at her watch. "I need to get back inside now." Griffin looked expectantly at her. She knew he was waiting for her to take some initiative, to invite him for dinner or suggest they meet sometime. "Will you be in town long?" she asked, finally.

"Until after the New Year," he said. "Then the next semester starts."

She hesitated. It wasn't enough that Laz had left her. His leaving now took on greater nonmarital dimensions—it was parental, as well. And, worst of all, he'd left her to clean up messes related to his leaving someone other than her.

He'd clearly been unable to confront his wife *and* his son. Laz's departure was perhaps beginning to make sense. After all, the deshrouding of his book and the return of his paternity-seeking son was a bit much for someone already predisposed as a marital flight risk.

She looked at Griffin standing in front of her with a look of hopefulness and expectancy. "You can call if you need anything," she said. She knew as she handed him a slip of paper with their phone number that what she was offering was inadequate, that anything less than making Laz materialize at this very instant would invariably fall short.

"Thanks," he said. Grace gave him back the jacket. She watched him zip it up, restraining that part of her that wanted to turn up his collar. He kissed her on the cheek, a gesture that took her completely by surprise, and turned to leave.

"Take care," she called after him as she watched him walk down the street, swinging his arms like Laz did. She felt a strong tug toward him as he turned the corner and disappeared from sight. Then she went back into the bookstore to teach her class.

# 18
# BRINGING UP BABY

O n Friday morning, the day of her gynecologist appointment, Grace noticed some light spotting. She chided herself for having even entertained the idea that she was pregnant, an idea that now evaporated from her consciousness. It figured—just like how her hair always looked its best on the day on which she was scheduled to have it cut, or how something missing turned up immediately after she'd either replaced it or forgotten about it altogether.

DR. SARAH GAYLIN's office was just off Fifth Avenue, on the ground floor of a town house. This was only the third appointment that she'd had with Dr. Gaylin. Her last gynecologist had had a lecherous manner, along with hair plugs that made him look like one of those pomanders stuck with cloves that Grace's mother made during the holiday season and that Grace dutifully hung in her closet until the orange shriveled and it was safe to dispose of.

Grace took the crosstown bus through the park. She spent a few minutes writing her to-do list in her Filofax—*pick up dry cleaning; order Fruit of the Month for Laz's editor; order champagne for his agent; send thank-you notes for anniversary presents*—feeling satisfied by how orderly she'd made her life.

The decor in the doctor's waiting room was Old World, with leather club chairs and heavy drapes, reminding Grace of the Oak Room at the Plaza Hotel, where Laz's mother had a standing Thursday night reservation. Grace half-expected to be offered a drink by a waiter in a dusty black jacket, except here the customers were an assortment of women in various stages of pregnancy, reading parenting magazines and eating dried fruit.

After twenty minutes, Grace was ushered into a small dressing room by a nurse in a pink uniform. She knew there was a reason she liked this place. Even the gowns were a soft rose color.

Soon after, Dr. Gaylin knocked on the door and walked in, greeting Grace with a warm smile. She was tall—probably close to six feet—and under her white coat, she was dressed in a tailored skirt, sheer stockings, leather pumps, and a long strand of pearls. Her head had a perpetual tilt to the side that gave her an approachable, friendly appearance, and her hair was an indeterminate hue that changed from gold to strawberry blond, depending on the light. She possessed a certain regal, angelic quality that Grace was drawn to.

"How have you been, Grace?" she asked, looking at the chart and then sitting down on a stool to begin the exam.

"Everything's fine. I've been a little tired, but who isn't? Oh, and my period was a little late this month."

"How late?" she inquired.

"About two weeks. Almost three, I think." Grace gazed at the pale, striped wallpaper.

"Was your period normal?"

"Well, today is the first day, and it's still very light. Probably just stress from the holidays," she said.

"Any pain? Cramping?"

"I did notice a sharp pain a few times," Grace said.

"On which side?"

"The right, I think," she answered. "Why? Is there something wrong?"

"Grace, I'm going to do some tests. It's really just a routine precaution that I like to take with my patients who have IUDs. When a period is late, I like to make sure that everything is normal by checking blood levels and doing a sonogram."

Grace swallowed hard.

"What are you checking for?"

"To rule out the possibility that you're pregnant."

"I couldn't be pregnant," she insisted. "I did a test."

"In very rare instances, those tests can yield false negatives. I'd just like to make sure."

"What kind of instances?" Grace asked. She was about to explain that her husband had not so much as touched her in the last five weeks, but stopped herself as she did some mental calculations and thought back to the night Laz left.

"Nothing to worry about. As I said, it's just a precaution," Dr. Gaylin reassured her, buzzing for the nurse.

"Let's check the beta hCG levels," the doctor told the nurse when she walked in. After drawing blood, the nurse prepared for the sonogram. Dr. Gaylin explained each step as she went along, but as the procedure progressed, all Grace was aware of was the halolike glow of Dr. Gaylin's golden hair and the faint humming of the machine.

GRACE LISTENED AS Dr. Gaylin explained about hCG levels and how in ectopic pregnancies that they don't double every forty-eight hours as they do in normal pregnancies. Although it was rare, the hormones had apparently been too low to register with a standard urine test. The information took time to sink in. Laz had never wanted children and Grace thought she'd accepted that. But as images of spinning musical mobiles, swaddling blankets, and her and Laz pushing a stroller along Riverside Drive flashed through her mind, she realized she had yearnings of her own. From one minute to the next, she bounced back and forth between feeling desolate and ebullient. And although she'd just been confronted with Laz's offspring, Griffin was not hers. Now she would have a child of her own.

"When will I be due?" she asked Dr. Gaylin.

"I don't think you understand. The embryo has embedded in the fallopian tubes. It's not a normal pregnancy."

"What chance is there that it will just get unstuck?" Grace asked. "And wind up in the right place?"

"I'm afraid that's not possible," Dr. Gaylin answered. "I'm going to have to administer a shot of methotrexate, which will in essence make the embryo disintegrate in the fallopian tube over the next several days." Grace found this information impossible to comprehend. How was it possible to lose something that five minutes ago she hadn't even known she'd had? The high beam from the halogen light turned Dr. Gaylin's hair a garishly unnatural cotton-candy pink.

Suddenly, Grace found the color repellent. "Will it be painful?" she asked.

"It shouldn't be. You can go about your daily activities, and then we'll check the hCG levels again in four days. We can call your husband to take you home, if that would make you feel more comfortable."

As Dr. Gaylin spoke, Grace felt a swelling in her chest. She was unable to breathe in deeply enough, as if it were a feeling she couldn't reach. Uncertain what she was about to do—cry or scream, or both —she waited until the urge subsided before she answered.

"He's out of town," she said softly.

THE WINDOWS OF the bus were covered with frost. Thoughts of Griffin surfaced again. She had an urge to crochet a scarf for him—a long, warm, tightly woven scarf, not as a consolation prize, or an affectionate gesture, or even to keep out the winter chill. Now she was deprived of both a husband and a child. She needed Laz home *now*. But not for her usual reasons—in order for Griffin to strangle his AWOL father with the scarf she would make him, Laz would have to be physically present.

She thought of the strange man she'd met at the Pink Tea Cup. Mr. Dubrovsky, she recalled, with the fluffy hair. She remembered the bold print on the card he had slipped in his copy of *Oblomov: Private Investigator.* He could help her track Laz down.

WHEN SHE GOT HOME, Grace turned on the dining room light and dimmed it (along with the Christmas tree and all the other fixtures in the living room). Everything seemed too bright. She noticed the amaryllis was still blooming.

As she searched for Mr. Dubrovsky's copy of *Oblomov,* she decided she'd treated him poorly at the restaurant and now regretted it. Hiring him to help her to find Laz might rectify the situation, but finding his *Oblomov* was an entirely different matter.

Marisol's niece had turned out to be a demon of a housekeeper, cleaning so well that Grace couldn't find anything. That morning, when she was looking for a washcloth in the linen closet, she discovered a stack of neatly folded shopping bags stuck between a stack of bath towels, and she found her moisturizer next to some Spanish olive oil in the pantry. The apartment was unquestionably spotless—the brass doorknobs buffed to a blinding sheen, the books dusted and replaced. However, now they were arranged by size, rather than alphabetical order. It was lucky that Laz wasn't there to witness the reorganization. It would have been too much for him. Plus, Dolores's caramel custard was tasteless and flat.

So it came as no large surprise to Grace to find both Mr. Dubrovsky's copy of *Oblomov* and her own in the kitchen, next to a cookbook of the exact size and color. She pulled the two books off the shelf, noticing the lemony smell of Murphy's Oil Soap emanating from their damp spines. As she held the books in her hands, Mr. Dubrovsky's business card fell onto the counter along with the two sheets of crinkled yellow paper from her copy. The yellow pages appeared to be a letter, and the writing was clearly a woman's handwriting. Grace wondered how long it would take for the ink to get bleached by the sun until not a trace would remain if she left the pages in direct sunlight.

She unfolded the letter and began to read:

> Brookman, It's been over nineteen years since we last saw each other. You can't keep denying that Griffin is your son. He's exactly like you, at least who you were then. He needs you now, and you must take responsibility. He's adamant about contacting you, even though you refuse to answer my calls. I can't stop him from going. Please have the decency to meet him. What happened between us is not the issue. Yours, Merrin.

Grace felt her head begin to pound and her eyes sting. Laz had never mentioned the name, not even in passing. Kane would probably know of her, although, maybe not the whole story. But even if they were speaking to each other, she still wouldn't have been able to ask. She folded the pages and placed them back in the book.

She left Mr. Dubrovsky's book on the front hall table, glancing at it one last time, as if she were checking to make sure an iron were unplugged so the counter wouldn't get scorched. Then she picked up Mr. Dubrovsky's card, and with a strong sense of purpose, walked down the hall to the bedroom.

The door was closed. She'd flung Laz's yellow Hermès tie over the doorknob and rumpled the bedcovers that morning. As she held the brass handle, letting the silk tie slip through her hand to the floor, she became aware of a slight humming sensation in the tips of her fingers, some incoherent impulses bumping around in her consciousness. She had almost been able to fool herself before. But now, as she stood in front of the bedroom door, she wished Laz really were in there. Not so she could greet him and welcome him home, but for the express purpose of doing him some sort of bodily harm. And then Grace had another incongruous thought, one in a series of non sequiturs: *And he can pick up his own damn dry cleaning, too!*

She went to the phone and dialed the number on Mr. Dubrovsky's card, but his voicemail picked up. After the beep, she began to explain: "Mr. Dubrovsky, this is Grace Brookman. You might not remember me. We met at the Pink Tea Cup. I apologize for the misunderstanding that night. I'm calling because I'm trying to locate someone. I can fill you in on the details when we speak. Also, I have your copy of *Oblomov*." She left her number and thanked him before she was disconnected.

Impulsively, she dialed the number of Flik's Video 2 Go store and asked them to deliver every Katharine Hepburn movie they had in stock as soon as possible, stressing her affinity for *The Philadelphia Story* and *Bringing Up Baby*. If that couldn't take her mind off the methotrexate coursing through her body and the letter she'd found in *Oblomov,* then nothing could.

Later that afternoon, the videos arrived, and suddenly life was refined, elegant, and romantic. Grace's mind wandered, conjuring scenarios. She imagined a reunion between Griffin and Laz: Laz would be overjoyed and beside himself with emotion, lifting Grace up and spinning her around, then embracing his son for the first time. Grace would prepare a light supper of penne with shiitake mushrooms and pan-seared tuna with a lentil salad. For dessert, a warm tarte Tatin with crème fraîche and espresso served out of the demitasse cups they'd bought in Portugal. They would eat in the kitchen because it was cozier. After dinner, Laz and Griffin would disappear down the hall to Laz's study to talk, and Grace would curl up with a cup of tea, admiring the snow falling outside and basking in their newfound familial bliss.

Grace wanted to jump up immediately and call Griffin with the good news, and then felt ridiculous when she realized that not only had she spent an inordinate amount of time planning an imaginary menu, but that there was, in fact, no news to tell.

Her thoughts turned to Kane. On their first quasi-official date, Kane had taken Grace to the Regency Theater for a Katharine Hepburn marathon film festival. He had brought along a wicker basket containing a loaf of raisin bread, Muenster cheese, Martinelli's apple juice, and Thin Mints, all of which they shared as they watched movie after movie until well after midnight. As Grace thought about how much she missed Kane, she wanted to scream out to Katharine Hepburn in *The Philadelphia Story,* "Don't lose him! He's your only true friend."

When her mother called, it was a welcome distraction. "Sweetie, you're home for once."

"Hi, Mom, how's everything?"

"Fine. Except for Francine. She's beside herself." Grace half-watched the film and half-listened, finding it was a perfect balance between reality and fantasy.

"Why, what's wrong?" Grace could hear her father saying something in the background.

"Milton, I'm talking to Grace. And it's my business what I tell my own daughter, thank you," she said. "Sorry, honey, your father says to send his love. Anyway, it's Bert, who else?"

"What about Bert, Mother?"

"Don't call me *Mother,* Grace. You know how that irritates me."

"Sorry, Mom. What's wrong with Bert?"

"He's been acting strangely lately. Francine doesn't know what's gotten into him."

"In what way?" Grace asked.

"You know—wearing turtlenecks, Kenneth Cole loafers, after-shave. And he's parting his hair on the other side. Poor Francine. She even found a copy of *GQ* in his briefcase."

For as long as Grace could remember, Bert had dressed in the exact same way: pressed polyester trousers, a collared shirt in a pale check or stripe, and white tennis shoes. Perhaps he was just compensating for his own insecurities about Francine leaving for two weeks. Grace didn't divulge this theory to her mother, afraid of the conclusions that her mother would invariably jump to, but did congratulate herself on her sleuthing abilities. Clearly, she could find Laz herself if she ever were to put her mind to it.

"I'm sure it's nothing," Grace said. "Remember when Dad brought home that Huk-A-Poo shirt from that business trip?" Her mother was silent. "Whatever happened to that? It's probably a collectible by now."

"I threw it out," her mother answered. "It was a woman's shirt."

"Oh." Grace realized that she'd taken the wrong path. She knew full well that if left to his own devices, her father would either violate every fashion dictum, or just stay in his pajamas for most of the day. Since the Huk-A-Poo incident, he was not permitted to pick out any of his own clothes. "Well, I'm sure it's nothing," she continued. "It's probably just a stage he's going through."

"Well, you can see for yourself tomorrow."

"Why tomorrow?"

"Grace, don't tell me you've forgotten about Francine's good-bye party? We're going gallery hopping and to Chanterelle for dinner. Honey, I left a message with that new Dolores of yours. Didn't she tell you?"

"I guess not." Grace tried to think of a way out. The thought of going anywhere while the methotrexate was taking effect, let alone an entire Saturday with the Sugarmans, was daunting to say the least.

"It'll be an adventure," her mother said. Grace had heard *that* expression one too many times. On one such "adventure," Grace's father had to be helicoptered out of Mesa Verde after he had become wedged in a crevice. "We'll pick you and Laz up at one. Francine and I are off to Loehmann's today to try and take her mind off things. I'll keep an eye out for something cute for you to wear for Mambo Night."

Before Grace could tell her mother that Laz wouldn't be able to make it — she couldn't remember if she had told them that he was in Yugoslavia or some other extinct locale — her mother had already hung up.

THAT NIGHT, GRACE dreamt she was in *Mary Poppins,* but instead of Julie Andrews and Dick Van Dyke, it was Grace and Kane floating above the tables in the Pink Tea Cup with Bert Sugarman and Griffin. They were all laughing and drinking tea out of oversize pink floral cups, and Grace kept spilling her tea. Every time she would try to right her cup, she would begin to descend slowly to the floor, and Kane would take her by the wrist and pull her back up. "We need to keep telling jokes," he said, but whenever Grace tried to tell one, she forgot the punch line.

Grace didn't like to dwell on her dreams, but the next morning, this one stuck with her in all its Technicolor details. As a child, she'd had a crush on Dick Van Dyke, his inclusion being the only element of the dream that made sense to her. Bert Sugarman's cameo in the dream would remain, for the time being, a walk-on without meaning.

# 19
# THE INSTALLATION

It was raining the following day, the kind of drenching rain that never lets up. Grace went into the kitchen to make tea, still holding out some hope that the outing with her parents and the Sugarmans would be postponed. Dr. Gaylin was right. There was no pain to speak of.

Just as the kettle was coming to a boil, Grace noticed that the amaryllis on the dining room table had begun to wilt. She propped up the stalks against the side of the bark trellis that encircled the crate, but the stalks just bent in the opposite direction like overcooked asparagus. She remembered the instructions to cut the plant down a few inches above the base of the bulb, but now, as she sipped her tea, she opted for neglect, deciding that it could wait until Monday.

FRANCINE, SWATHED IN a full-length silver trench coat, vinyl boots, and her signature plaid Burberry umbrella (large enough for a golf foursome), was not in the least deterred by the rain. Even Bert, whose new shoes were not waterproof, trudged on like a trooper. His appearance was indeed significantly altered. He sported a black fedora, and Grace could detect the beginnings of a goatee.

"Mother went on quite a spree," Grace's father said as they crossed Ninth Avenue. "Did she tell you?"

"Don't exaggerate, Milton. I just bought a few things, that's all."

"So, Francine," he continued, "you're off to Paris on Monday. It's going to be some trip, huh?"

"Of course, it will be. Even more, in retrospect," Francine answered. "Grace, tell Laz I'll whip him up some culinary delight when I get back from Le Cordon Bleu," she added, shooting Bert a punishing look as they walked down the street to begin their gallery-hopping adventure.

The galleries were on a side street, in renovated garages that bore no resemblance to their former incarnation, although Grace's mother kept insisting that she smelled gasoline. Bert held the door open for Grace and then sloshed his way through to the entrance of a photography exhibit. Grace felt as if she were sleepwalking as she followed her parents and the Sugarmans in and out of gallery after gallery. She was unable to absorb anything she saw, as though her mind was covered in some impervious, repellent material.

Their last stop on the tour was a huge installation by Damien Hirst. Grace could hear Bert's shoes squeaking across the floor as they all wandered about the gallery in their rain gear like a family of longshoremen. Grace walked in the opposite direction.

The exhibits were diverting enough—a blend of art, technological finesse, and arresting imagery—and Grace soon found herself mesmerized by the sight of a large white ball suspended by a current of air. In the next room, there was a huge glass tank filled with green water. Swimming around inside the tank were dozens of large black, orange, and silver fish. It was like the aquarium except for the life-size gynecologist's table complete with stirrups also inside the tank. The only thing missing was Dr. Gaylin in a wet suit.

The fish began to swim fervently about in what looked like a feeding frenzy, but there was no food, only large air bubbles coming out of a tube. Also in the tank, on a small table, was a rusting computer, a broken watch, and a white mug next to the computer keyboard. Grace walked around to the other side of the tank, and as she did, she saw that the mug had letters on it. She looked closer. They spelled out the name *Bert*. She read the title of the piece: *Love Lost*.

At first, she thought she must still be asleep, and that the whole day, including Bert in his hat and this strangely apt installation, was just a dream. But this was far too clever even for her, so she knew she was certainly awake. Her *Mary Poppins* dream now seemed patently obvious—Bert is the name of Dick Van Dyke's character in the movie. Grace was surprised that it had taken her so long to unravel the connection.

These images not only penetrated Grace's psyche, they had hooked her, and she felt as if she were about to be devoured by the fish. She walked over to a bench in the center of the room and sat down. She considered contacting Damien Hirst and asking him how on earth he'd managed to distill her life and encapsulate it into a seven-by-seven-foot tank.

Grace saw her father walking toward her. "Francine's getting antsy," he said. "Some exhibit, isn't it?" Grace took one of those deep breaths she'd learned in yoga but that she had never mastered, because holding her breath for any length of time, even for only seven seconds, terrified her. The breath, at least now, did serve to calm her somewhat.

"Yes, it's really something," she agreed, not sure what she was agreeing to. She heard someone approaching from behind. Bert sat down, holding his hat in his hand. A more dejected sight Grace had never seen, and she surmised that the new look had not served the purpose he'd hoped for.

"You have any Mylanta, Milt?" he asked.

"How many you need?"

"Two will do it, thanks," he said. Grace's father reached into his pants pocket and pulled out two tablets still in the plastic sleeve. Bert proceeded to pop them into his mouth and chew them, the white powder adhering to the corners of his mouth.

"Who's ready to eat?" Grace's father asked.

"Ready as I'll ever be," Bert said. Then he turned to Francine, who had joined them. "Time to shove off, honey." He reached for her arm, but she quickly pulled it away.

Grace stood up from the bench, but as she did, she felt the room grow dark.

"Grace, what's the matter?" her father asked. "You look peaked." He put his hand to her forehead. "And you're burning up."

There was a pounding in her ears and the room began to spin. As she fell back on the bench, an image of dozens of tiny, dazzling butterflies circled around her. When she opened her eyes, her parents and the Sugarmans were standing above her. She sat up slowly. Something flat and disklike was beneath her. She grabbed hold of it, and discovered Bert's now-flattened fedora, which she handed to him.

"For heaven's sake, Grace needs a doctor," Bert said in a panic. "Who has a cell phone? Someone should call Laz. Where the hell is he anyway? He should be here. Especially at a time like this. It would be easier to get Henry Kissinger on the phone!"

"Calm down, Bert, you're acting hysterical," Francine said.

"You're frightening Grace. She needs calm, rational people around her now. Why don't you take half a tranquilizer? It'll do you good. Grace doesn't need a doctor. Everything's fine. Look, the color's coming back into her face. Go make yourself useful and get some wet paper towels."

Bert scurried away and returned with a handful of soaking wet paper towels, a trail of water behind him. Grace pressed the towels to her forehead. She was beginning to feel better when she noticed bloodstains on her khaki pants.

"Honey, are you having pain?" her mother said quietly, sitting down on the bench beside her.

"Not really. It's just a very heavy period, that's all," she told her. "I got a little light-headed, don't worry."

Her mother, quickly assessing the situation, reached into her oversize tote bag and rummaged around. "Everything is under control. No need to get excited," she said and miraculously pulled out a pair of black satin cargo pants and a rhinestone belt with the Loehmann's tags still attached.

"Paulette to the rescue," Grace's father beamed.

"And here—you might need this," she said, stealthily handing Grace a blue-wrapped sanitary napkin as if it were a bag of hashish. "Why don't you go to the ladies' room and change? And here's a couple of Aleve. First thing Monday, we'll make you an appointment with this new doctor I found. Then we can have lunch at the Whitney. Doesn't that sound nice?" Grace hadn't really heard a single word. Her mother handed her the pants along with two white pills. Then, wrapping her raincoat around Grace's waist, she escorted her to the ladies' room and then waited for her outside.

Grace looked at herself in the mirror. Her complexion was the same pale yellow color as the letter from Griffin's mother. It would have been so much easier to go blank, but she couldn't. For once she agreed with Bert. Laz should have been here—just as he should have been at other times these past five weeks. She was afraid, and she wasn't supposed to be bleeding.

When she emerged from the ladies' room, still walking a bit unsteadily, she was met with nods of approval from Francine and her mother as if she were about to venture out for her prom night. Her father and Bert stood off to the side, Bert holding his misshapen hat in his hands.

"I knew they'd be perfect on her," her mother said. "See how they skim her hips and elongate her torso?"

"You do have an eye for these things," Francine agreed.

"They're one size fits most. No iron. Those pants, a crisp white shirt, a red cashmere sweater, a good pair of shoes, and you're ready for a week in Europe," she told Francine. "All set, everyone?"

Grace touched her mother on the shoulder. "I think I'm just going to head home," she said.

"Honey, are you sure? It might make you feel better to be with people."

"No, really," Grace said. "I'll talk to you later. Have fun." Grace kissed her parents good-bye and wished Francine a good trip. She watched as the four of them left the gallery. As soon as they were out of sight, Grace called Kane.

## 20
## LITTLE ODESSA

Kane picked Grace up right in front of the gallery. Miraculously, on the ride to Brooklyn, just as they were crossing the Manhattan Bridge, the rain ended, Grace's bleeding stopped, and the sky turned a deep, clear blue, with bright stars and light, puffy clouds.

They were on their way to Little Odessa, where a surprise birthday celebration for Greg was planned at a Georgian restaurant. Grace would have preferred the quiet of just Kane's company, but it was better than being alone while things were invisibly disintegrating inside her.

"I'm glad you called," Kane said, turning off his windshield wipers.

"I hated the way we left things the other night," Grace said.

"I know. Me, too."

"I didn't think you'd ever want to speak to me after all the awful things I said to you."

"You and Laz are two of my closest friends. I don't want there ever to be tension between us."

"I still don't know what came over me," Grace said.

"Too much wheat grass, I guess," Kane said.

"I don't know. Whatever it was, I'm sorry. We really are so happy for you."

Kane reached his hand out and touched Grace's arm. "It's all forgotten. I can't believe you're finally going to meet Greg."

Grace looked out the window at the passing neighborhoods—attached brick row houses delineated by only slight stylistic variations, and then stretches where there were only stores. Kane pulled off Kings Highway and drove through the center of Brighton Beach, although the idea that they were anywhere near the ocean seemed unbelievable to Grace. It looked like any outer borough of the city, except that the lettering on the storefronts—even the Duane Reade and the Barnes & Noble—was written in both English and Russian.

They parked and walked several blocks down the main thoroughfare, then turned left onto what looked like a deserted street. Kane's cell phone rang.

While Kane was on the phone, Grace saw his shoulders slump. "How long will you be?" she could hear him say. After a few minutes, he ended the conversation and put his phone away. "Looks like Greg won't be able to make it until dessert," he told her. "Some emergency at a photo shoot." Grace felt a sense of empathy toward Kane. Their relationships had more in common than he knew.

They walked in silence until, out of nowhere, a restaurant appeared, its lights blazing and its interior festooned with brightly colored streamers and red-and-green garlands. Even though it was only five-thirty, every seat, except for those at a long table reserved for Greg's party, was taken. A silver disco ball spun from the dropped ceiling, sending flashes of prismlike lights around the mirrored room.

In the back, on a raised platform, a man wearing a white jacket and tight spandex pants was playing a synthesizer, and Grace recognized the melody of "Surfin' U.S.A." Everyone at the restaurant was swaying and singing along, although the words were in Russian. She scanned the faces in the room as she followed Kane to their table, which, unfortunately, was right next to the speakers. Kane made apologies for Greg's absence, and just like at the anniversary party, things went on in spite of the missing man of the hour.

"Are you okay?" she shouted to Kane over the music as they sat down.

"Oh, yeah. Comes with the territory."

"I know what you mean. But at least we have each other," she said, linking her arm in his.

"Always will."

They didn't have to look at menus; Kane had ordered in advance. The food arrived on huge platters and bowls that were filled with Russian delicacies—grilled eggplant, spinach purée, smoked fish with pickled beets, spicy minced string beans, cheese-filled pie, and a basket of warm airy bread that the waitress placed on a high silver stand. Everyone took a spoonful of each dish and passed it along. Grace noticed that she'd worked up quite an appetite.

The man next to Grace turned to her and extended his hand. "I'm Carmine. Greg's old man."

"I'm Grace. A friend of Kane's."

"Gotta love that guy! Grace, you have any idea what this is?" Carmine asked, as he examined an unrecognizable dish.

"I think it's some kind of meat," Grace said.

"It's cabbage," the waitress said curtly, as she walked by.

"Tastes like my mama's meatballs, may she rest in peace," Carmine said. "Only without the meat, obviously."

Kane flagged down the waitress for another glass of wine. As Grace watched the spinning disco ball and listened to the warped sounds from the synthesizer, she found herself growing hypnotized. Even the Russian lyrics to the Beach Boys' song were beginning to sound comprehensible. She took a long swig of Kane's wine and looked at the people assembled for Greg's party. Friends and family. One of Greg's cousins got up to do the chicken dance, which Grace had once seen at a wedding. The setting and the cast of characters had changed, but not much else. With only a few minor differences, this was the Italian version of her parents and the Sugarmans. Even Grace's role was the same.

"Miss, this is the best wedding I've ever been to," Carmine said. The waitress gave a perfunctory smile.

"He thinks he's a comedian," his wife, Sophia, said, taking a bite of food and turning her back to him.

"What? I was just being friendly," Carmine said. "Grace, would you care to dance?" As Grace listened to the music, which now sounded a bit like a synthesized version of Elvis Costello's "Watching the Detectives," she thought about Adrian Dubrovsky—or was the elusive Russian detective watching her?

"Thanks, but I'm going to have to take a rain check," she said. Someone passed Grace a dish of something surrounded by a mass of clear jelly. Another mystery vegetable, perhaps. She looked at the pale, oval slices on the platter and decided to try one. She had just taken a small bite when she noticed the knuckles on the underside. They jiggled slightly. She set down her fork as she realized that she may have just ingested the toe of a pig. She felt nauseous and turned to Kane, unable to speak.

"Grace, what's wrong? You're breaking into a sweat."

"Nothing," she managed to say, feeling herself begin to gag. "I think I'm going to go."

"But Greg will be here any minute. Can't you stay just a little longer?"

"I really can't. I want to leave before I get up and start doing the chicken dance. Tell Greg I'm sorry."

"I wish I could drive you home," he said.

"It's Greg's birthday. You should be here."

"Why? Greg's not."

The DJ, who also happened to be the maître d', called a car for Grace. It arrived in less time than it took her to put on her coat.

Kane walked her outside and hugged her. "I'm really glad you came," he said. "I couldn't have gotten through this evening without you."

"If you only knew," she said, giving him a hug.

GRACE GOT INTO the back of the black sedan and gave her address to the driver, then dozed off despite the bumpy ride home. She awoke with a jolt to see someone other than José holding the car door open for her. As soon as she stepped out of the car onto the cobblestone driveway, she realized at once that she'd given the driver the wrong address. She was standing in front of Laz's old building. Perhaps some delusional side effect of the methotrexate had catapulted Grace five years back in time, so that when she turned the brass doorknob of the apartment, Laz would be inside waiting. She turned back to the car, but the driver had already sped off, without collecting his fare.

"Good evening," the doorman said. "Mrs. Brookman, right? I'm really enjoying the book Mr. Brookman gave me." She stared blankly at him.

"A travel book," he continued. "He left it for me yesterday." And then Grace understood. She knew what book without having to ask.

"*The Innocents Abroad*," he beamed. "A hand-bound, leather edition. I can't wait to read it."

"I'll tell him."

"He's such a nice young man," he said. She wondered why Griffin would have given away a book that had been a gift from Laz, but perhaps he felt that the books were poor substitutes and that he'd rather have nothing.

Grace walked into the building and down the marble corridor to the side entrance, where she could get a taxi heading in the right direction. The chandeliers gave off an eerie yellow light. Reflected in the Baroque mirrors that lined the hallway, Grace saw the fuzzy outlines of what looked like Mr. Dubrovsky sitting on a velvet chair. His legs were crossed, he wore black wing tip shoes, and on his lap he held a hat. She spun around to see if he was indeed really there, but the chair where she'd thought she'd seen him was now empty. No sign of Mr. Dubrovsky or his reflection.

Grace thought that she must have experienced some kind of Manhattan mirage, the consequence of too many blinis after having grown faint earlier. Then checking her own reflection in the mirror, she walked outside to find a taxi home.

"THERE'S A PACKAGE for you," José said, as she walked into the lobby. Grace was afraid that it was another dozen Duro-Lites. Her second thought was that her mother had dropped by with more spoils from her Loehmann's spree.

José went over to the concierge desk and lifted up a small, unmarked carton, which he brought over to Grace. "It was delivered by messenger," he told her. She cautiously took it from him. It was almost weightless. She turned it around to read the return address. There, in bold pink lettering, she read the words A Perfect Match.

Upstairs, Grace opened her front door to the sound of the telephone. It had been several hours since she'd left her parents at the gallery with the Sugarmans. They were likely to be checking up on her. Grace placed the box next to the stack of Katharine Hepburn movies on the hall table and picked up the phone.

"Grace—it's Griffin." His voice was muffled, as if he was talking to her from another planet.

"Griffin," she repeated. "I can barely hear you."

"I hope it's not a bad time."

"No, I just walked in. Is everything all right?" she asked, shrugging off her coat and walking into the living room. The satin pants her mother had given her at the gallery were slippery and made a distracting swishing sound as she walked. She sat down on the Victorian love seat that she'd just had reupholstered in a lilac chintz, and she had to hold on to the armrest to keep herself from sliding off.

"Well, I just thought you should know that they're going to start the abatement Monday morning."

"The abatement?" Grace asked.

"For the asbestos," Griffin answered. "They said it should take about a week or so. They've already covered everything in plastic."

"How can you sleep there?" Grace asked.

"I sort of made a slit in the plastic large enough for me to slide through. It'll be fine," he assured her. He paused. Grace could hear what sounded like hail falling on an air conditioner in the background. "Except for the falling plaster, that is."

"What plaster?" Grace asked, beginning to grow alarmed.

"They're working on a pipe upstairs."

"Griffin, it's not safe for you to stay there." She thought about the dismal black netting on the windows and imagined Griffin covered head to toe in white dust. She scolded herself for not having checked on him when she was there.

She was about to tell him that he should look for a room in one of the residence halls on Broadway when, without thinking, she told him he should come stay with her. There was plenty of room. It made perfect sense. There were two extra bedrooms, which were unoccupied. The more she thought about it, the more the idea of having somebody around began to appeal to her. It would only be for a week, and she was going to Chicago on Friday anyway.

"Are you sure that would be a good idea?" Griffin asked. Grace knew he was referring to Laz's lack of responsiveness. In a way, she thought his staying at their place would mollify the situation somewhat.

"Please consider it. I'd like to get to know you better."

Griffin hesitated. "You really don't need to do this," he said, finally.

"I know. I want to." Grace began to feel animated, more so than she had in weeks. She wanted to ask him all sorts of questions, like what kind of cereal he ate in the mornings, how he took his coffee, what section of the paper he read first. Toast or English muffins? Or she could make waffles. He was a bit on the thin side, after all, she could hear her mother saying.

She harbored a secret hope that he would eat Grape-Nuts cereal with two-percent milk, take his coffee black with two sugars, and read the Op-Eds followed by the sports section while holding a slice of lightly toasted raisin bread in his hand—just like Laz. Then with a start, she corrected herself. It wasn't Laz who liked raisin bread, it was Kane. How could she forget? Laz liked a currant scone covered with crème fraîche and a spoonful of raspberry jam, which inevitably dripped onto the newspaper.

It was agreed, after another few rounds of demurring and insisting, that he would come first thing in the morning. Grace sat in the darkness, holding the phone in her hand and enjoying the quiet with the knowledge that the end of solitude was in sight. She was also half-waiting for her father's postdinner, just-checking-up call, which, surprisingly, never came.

It was almost ten o'clock when she went into the kitchen to get a knife and proceeded to open the carton from A Perfect Match. Underneath several crumpled sheets of packing paper, she found a small, rectangular box sealed in bubble wrap. She undid the tape and let the wrapping fall away.

Inside were three pristine silver tubes. She cradled the lipsticks in her hand, reluctant to open them. How the lipsticks had arrived so speedily, she did not know, but she didn't question it.

She chose one, carefully pulled off the top, and twisted the bottom of the tube to reveal a perfectly angled tip, which she touched to the back of her hand. The consistency was smooth and cool, like the skin of an apple. She applied the lipstick without a mirror, following the contours of her mouth, and pressed her lips together. She could reorder to her heart's content and never run out. She walked over to the mirror.

Since Laz had left, except for hibachi night, she'd become accustomed to just a light coating of gloss. Velvet, the lipstick that she'd put on every morning for years, the color that had become second nature to her, now looked unfamiliar. She turned the dining room light on high and stared into the mirror. Her lips looked almost fake, not like hers at all. This was not the person she remembered. The Christmas tree began to blink as if objecting, too. Grace ran to the bathroom and wiped off the lipstick with a tissue and threw the tubes in the wastebasket. They landed with three hollow thumps on the bottom.

# 21

# DOWN THE HATCH

A little before eleven o'clock, the telephone rang. Grace let the machine pick up. She wanted nothing more than to rest and forget this strange day, and she was in no mood to hear the details of Francine's farewell dinner. She heard the sound of her mother's voice as she walked down the hall to the bedroom.

*Darling, it's Mom. We had a lovely evening with the Sugarmans. A shame you weren't feeling quite yourself. Dad wants to know if you'll tape his show for him. He felt a little twinge, so we took him to Lenox Hill for a thallium stress test. We're just waiting for the . . .* Grace ran to the kitchen and grabbed the phone so quickly that it almost flew out of her hand.

"Mom?" she said, out of breath.

"Grace. I was in the middle of leaving a message," she said, sounding slightly irritated that she'd been interrupted. "I didn't wake you, did I?" she added as an afterthought.

"No. I'm up. I heard the message. Why didn't you call me earlier? How's Dad?"

"We didn't want to worry you. It's probably nothing. They're just being very thorough."

"Do you want me to come over?" she asked, trying to hear through the static in her ears even though the line was clear.

"That's sweet of you, but Bert and Francine are here. Bert bumped into one of his old college friends in the waiting room. The man's wife has gallstones. Anyway, it shouldn't be too long. Don't worry. We'll call you first thing. You need to get some rest, dear. Give our love to Laz when you speak to him," she said and then hung up.

Feeling helpless, Grace went into the living room, sank down onto the couch, and stared at the blinking Christmas tree lights. Beside her was the bag of yarn still untouched from the other day, the perfect over-the-counter antidote to her racing mind. She took out some yarn and began a chain stitch, mindlessly crocheting as she allowed her thoughts to unravel. She could no more stop the obliterating effects of the drug in her system than influence the outcome of her father's tests, or telepathically summon Laz back to her side. However, she could create something out of, or in spite of, the chaos, something that had order, symmetry, and purpose—whatever that might be.

She continued crocheting well into the night and must have dozed off for a while when the telephone rang. The sky was pink—not a predawn pink, but the kind of pink that might signal snow. It could have been three in the morning or sometime past eight; it was impossible to tell. She'd tucked the phone underneath her legs, and she could feel the warmth emanating from the battery pack.

The results of her crocheting efforts covered her lap—a rectangle approximately two feet by four. It confounded Grace how the intervening hours had slipped by unnoticed, but the proof was in her hands. The dimensions were unremarkable. The stitches were plain, but pleasingly regular. It was too small for a throw and too large for a scarf for Griffin.

As she folded it back to retrieve the phone, tiny sparks of electricity sent a tingling sensation down her arms as she realized that what she had unwittingly crocheted was a baby blanket. She held the blanket in her arms, but it only accentuated the weight of an unfillable absence. She knew there was no way to mourn an unacknowledged loss, although her hands had so deftly tried to orchestrate a symbolic remedy. For the briefest of moments, she allowed herself access to the knowledge that she felt pain.

The phone continued to ring. As she pushed the button on the handset, she expected to hear her mother's voice telling her that everything was fine, but she was startled by an unfamiliar man's voice.

"Mrs. Brookman. Adrian Dubrovsky here." Grace bolted upright. "Mrs. Brookman?" he said again.

Grace could hear the quiet tapping of computer keys on the other end. Her father often fiddled with some gadget, too, while he spoke to her on the phone. She walked into the kitchen to check the time. The clock on the microwave read six-fifteen. "Do you realize what time it is?" she asked, slowly gathering her wits.

"I apologize for disturbing you so early, but my schedule is quite erratic and I felt that we must speak." His accent was difficult to place. "I got your message. When I met you at the Pink Tea Cup, it was not as it seemed," he said. "That is all I can say at this time."

"I'm not sure what you mean," Grace said.

"I was there under false pretenses," he continued. "My situation has changed, and although I cannot go into the details, I'm afraid that my working for you would be a conflict of interest. But I would like to arrange to pick up my book. I was concerned that it might have gotten into the wrong hands." Just then, another call came in and Grace asked Mr. Dubrovsky to hold on. She pressed the call-waiting button.

"Up and *Adam*," her father said in his chipper, early morning voice. He'd been saying the expression wrong for as long as Grace could remember, but she would never think of correcting him. He was usually up well before five in the morning, reading; and by six, he was ready to socialize.

"How are you feeling?" Grace asked.

"Fit as a fiddle. I got a clean bill of health. Just some acid reflux. The doctor said I just have to lay off the spicy food, that's all."

"I'm so relieved," Grace said. Then she remembered that Mr. Dubrovsky was on the other line. "Dad, I'm going to have to call you right back."

"We have to go to Wal-Mart for supplies. Call us around ten." Grace knew how much her father disliked shopping. He had devised a schedule that required them to shop only once every month, except for perishables, which they had delivered from the Food Emporium.

"Supplies? For what?" Grace asked.

"The blizzard. Could be two feet by tomorrow night. The worst in fifty years."

"Dad, I'm glad you're okay. You had me worried. Oh, and thank Mom for the pants," she said, looking down at the satin pants she was still wearing.

Just before she pressed the button to get back to Mr. Dubrovsky, she heard her mother call out from the extension, "Don't mention it."

There was a dial tone on the other end. Mr. Dubrovsky had hung up. An odd bird, she concluded, picturing him in his striped pajamas listening to *The Brothers Karamazov* on tape. Clearly, A Perfect Match needed to better screen their members—she, like Groucho Marx, not wanting to count herself among them.

Trying to put the whole conversation out of her mind, she walked into the kitchen to prepare José's coffee. On the way, she noticed Mr. Dubrovsky's copy of *Oblomov* next to the stack of Katharine Hepburn movies on the front hall table and picked it up.

The book had obviously been well read, some pages stained and rippled from water damage. She sat on the couch and flipped through the book, trying to find the place where she and Laz had last left off. A line, marked in pencil, caught her eye: *You had really parted before your separation and were faithful not to love but to the phantom of it, which you had yourself invented—that's the whole secret.*

The line was impossibly apt. It seemed almost as if Oblomov were addressing Grace directly and not his beloved, Olga. Could this be just a random coincidence, or was it a flicker of prophesy from the nineteenth century? Or did Mr. Dubrovsky know more than even Grace had supposed? She turned the page and read more. *The man before you is not the one you have been expecting and dreaming of. Wait, he will appear and then you will come to yourself.*

The passage took her breath away. They were the same lines that Laz had read to her, but never before had they reverberated as they did now. She found herself unable to concentrate on Goncharov's words and wanted to banish them, along with her feelings, to a place even less hospitable than a Siberian gulag. They were *too* close, as if resonating from inside her almost.

Just as she was about to close the book, she thought she recognized two words written in the margins in smudged blue ink. She held the book closer and examined the letters. The words were written in some language that resembled neither Anglo-Saxon nor Cyrillic, appearing more like a strange hieroglyphic code. She could have sworn she read the words as *Brookman Redux*. She looked again more closely, but the words swam on the page like a deep-sea Scrabble game with no rule book.

She gazed out the window at the pink sky. This was turning out to be an unsettling morning. She tried to focus on Griffin's arrival, but there were too many loose ends that nagged at her, and she thought it might help her clear her head to get some fresh air. If there was going to be a blizzard, it would be a good idea to do some shopping just in case they were snowed in as Milton had predicted. She would go to the Food Emporium, which was open twenty-four hours a day; on the way back, she'd return the videos.

Laz never returned anything on time. Every library book and video he had ever rented was kept well past its due date. Once, he was fined over two hundred dollars for losing *After Hours*. They'd never even gotten to the end of the movie. Grace had found it years later, stuffed in a box containing an old orange clock radio, some letters, and other miscellany that he'd no doubt neglected to return along the way. For Laz, like the movies he rented and the books he borrowed, this was a marriage in which he was willing to incur late fees, rather than to submit to a lifetime commitment. Grace was beginning to become aware that hers might be a marriage on loan, and not for keeps.

She poured José's coffee into the cup and pressed the lid on tightly. Then she grabbed her coat, along with the stack of videos, and went downstairs.

Grace placed the coffee cup on the mahogany concierge desk. As soon as she removed her hand, she imagined the gold letters that encircled the cardboard cup rearranging like air-popped popcorn until finally settling on another phrase, one more in keeping with her mood that morning: *We Are Happy to Preserve You.*

THE BLAZING LIGHTS at the Food Emporium gave it a surreal, timeless quality. The aisles were virtually empty, except for several stock boys who were sitting on boxes, reshelving items that seemed in plentiful supply. She thought of her parents at Wal-Mart, pushing their supersized carts down the wide aisles, buying gargantuan quantities of food. Her parents had shopping down to a science, each taking a list and a cart and heading in opposite directions, somehow always meeting in the frozen foods section simultaneously.

Grace began to fill her cart with food. The predictability of the store was reassuring as she went up and down each aisle, pulling items off the shelf that she thought Griffin might like—pretzels, blue corn chips, a six-pack of Coke, Mint Milanos. It had been a while since she'd been shopping. Filling the cart felt so satisfying. For herself, Grace stocked up on Boca Burgers, fresh vegetables and fruit, soy nuts, and bread. Gone were her cravings for pastries and sweets. She decided to prepare a spinach lasagna for dinner, so she went in search of part-skim ricotta cheese.

She went down the next aisle and stopped short. She found herself surrounded by neatly stocked rows of small jars of pureed vegetables, infant formula, tiny spoons, teething rings, sippy cups, shelves of diapers, and wipes. She had the urge to empty the shelves into her cart, as if by doing so, the rest would follow.

From a distance, she saw a woman wearing a familiar-looking silver trench coat reaching to pull down a box of Kleenex from a high shelf. The woman's back was turned, but as Grace drew nearer, she saw that it was Francine and walked over to help her.

"Francine, let me get that for you," she said, reaching up to get the box of tissues. Startled, Francine spun around, toppling over a tower of paper towels in the process.

"Grace," she said, with a tight smile. "So nice to run into you. Glad Dad's feeling better." Grace was about to respond when Francine thrust the box of Kleenex into her cart and said, "Sorry, but I've got to dash."

Francine's eyes were rimmed with streaks of black mascara,

which Grace had the urge to wipe away with a moistened Q-Tip, as her mother surely would have done. Francine was wearing the same outfit she had on the day before, but then Grace looked down and realized so was she.

"Is everything all right?" Grace inquired. Francine began to busily rearrange things in her cart and then, grabbing two double packages of napkins, placed them on top, as if in an effort to conceal what was inside.

"Oh, yes. Everything's fine. Good to see you," she said quickly, and then with a quick wave, and in a blur of silver, she was off. As Francine rounded the corner, her cart practically tilting on two wheels, Grace caught a glimpse of its contents. There were dozens of bottles of chili sauce and at least twice the number of jars of Welch's grape jelly, along with several bags of minimarshmallows —strange things to stock up on, stranger still since Bert was diabetic.

Grace finished shopping and made her way to the checkout line. She unloaded her cart and realized that she hadn't purchased so much as a package of Altoids for Laz, as though, if only in pretense, she was letting him fend for himself and go hungry, too. She presented the super-bonus-savings card that her father had given her to the cashier and glanced at the headlines of the nearby magazines. On the cover of one was a photograph of an emaciated man who was dressed in loose white clothing and standing next to a McDonald's restaurant in a bombed-out village. *Bosnian Prisoner Paid for Story.* Grace turned the magazine over and quickly scribbled her address on the delivery slips.

Outside, the sky was obscured by a dense layer of clouds, and there was the feeling of snow in the air. At the corner of Verdi Square, she could just make out the outline of the cupolas of Laz's old building through the black construction netting. From the exterior, the netting looked impervious and forbidding, as if no light could get through. Griffin was probably still asleep under his plastic-wrapped bed. Grace knew that "first thing in the morning" to a person his age might extend well past noon.

The storefront of Flik's Video 2 Go was covered with a corrugated metal gate. To the side was a graffiti arrow in red, white, and blue spray paint as well as a sign indicating a drop-off slot. Without the arrow, she could have easily missed it. Opening the slot while holding the stack of videos proved awkward, so she devised a system of dropping them in a few at a time while holding the door open with her hip—until several got jammed at once and she had to put them in one at a time. The videos hit the floor with a crash. She pictured them strewn across the linoleum in disarray. She placed the last one in the slot, and as it descended, she watched with utter dismay as Mr. Dubrovsky's copy of *Oblomov,* instead of a video, flew down the chute into the heap of Katharine Hepburn videos.

Grace tried to fish the book out, but the slot had obviously been engineered much like a mailbox, allowing things only to go in. Despite the queer looks that she received from a few people passing by with dogs, she tried to look inconspicuous as she shoved her arm into the chute all the way up to her shoulder blade, persevering for several minutes. Finally, forced to admit defeat, she headed home to wait for Griffin.

# 22

# The Abatement

Just as Grace was cleaning up the kitchen, the intercom rang. She closed the pantry door and pressed the button.

"Your guest is here," José announced.

"Thank you," Grace said. "Send him up, please."

The Christmas tree sparkled in the living room and the spinach lasagna was covered with tinfoil on the counter, ready to be popped into the oven. Grace smoothed her hair and, feeling very Florence Henderson–like, went to the door. She'd rehearsed her greeting several times in the mirror and had decided upon a welcoming but casual hello, as if she were in the middle of something and hadn't in fact been waiting for hours for his arrival. She flung the door open, surprised by the sight of Kane standing in the doorway with two white-and-orange bags from Citarella's.

"Kane?" she said, flustered.

"Glad to see me, I guess." He remained outside until Grace regained her composure and asked him in.

"It's just that I wasn't expecting you." Kane's cheeks were flushed from the cold.

"I can see. I ran into your mother buying whitefish this morning. She mentioned that you weren't feeling well. I brought you some barley soup. Why didn't you say anything last night?"

"You know how my mother is, always exaggerating," Grace said, taking the container of soup from Kane. "Thanks. But I'm fine. Was my father with her?"

"He was double-parked outside. I said hello to him on my way out."

"Did he seem all right?"

"Yes, except he kept mumbling something about battening down the hatches."

"Yeah. He's worried about the blizzard."

It was difficult to pretend with Kane. She fought the urge to tell him about the methotrexate, the Damien Hirst exhibit, the Duro-Lites, Griffin, and the strange Mr. Dubrovsky. And, of course, Laz. Kane was the only one who would understand.

"Is something wrong?" he asked.

"No, nothing's wrong," she answered, looking away. She felt like a bottle of soda that had been shaken but left unopened. Kane put his bags by the door and walked into the living room. Grace tried to look at her watch without him noticing. An accidental meeting between Kane and Griffin in her living room was more than Grace could safely negotiate.

Kane went over to the Christmas tree and touched a branch. The tinsel glistened.

"The tree looks nice."

"Thanks." He was about to sit on the couch when Grace steered him toward the window before he knew what was happening, and she took a quick peek to see if Griffin was walking toward the building.

"Greg and I are having a brunch this afternoon. We'd love it if you could make it. Just a few people." She avoided his stare.

"Thanks, but I have tons to do," she said, trying to think fast. "We're going to Chicago on Friday and I haven't done a thing."

"To see Chloe?" he asked.

"Yes. Her mother just died," she said.

"I'm sorry to hear that."

"And Laz has a conference," Grace added.

"Isn't your birthday on Saturday?" Kane always remembered.

"Yes." She began to grow excited at the prospect of a birthday celebration. Then, like all the other times she'd felt buoyed and optimistic during the past five weeks, Grace realized she had once again fallen into one of her own, well-fashioned traps. Kane reached into his jacket pocket and pulled out a canary yellow envelope and handed it to her.

"In case I don't see you."

"That's so sweet of you," she said, taking the card from him. She took his arm and escorted him into the dining room with the intention of getting him to the front door in what would seem like a natural and unchoreographed progression. As they walked through the kitchen, she hoped Kane wouldn't notice the tinfoil-covered lasagna.

"Having company?"

"Scrabble night," she said, her reflexes oiled like a finely tuned machine. In truth, she'd forgotten all about it, but that was the least of her worries. Getting out of Scrabble night was child's play.

"That's funny, I thought your mother said Scrabble was canceled because Francine needs to get ready for her trip."

"I wish someone had told me," she covered. "Well, you must have lots to do. Thanks for stopping by." She waited to see if he would take the cue and be on his way.

"Sorry you can't make it to brunch. Greg really wants to meet you."

"When we get back from Chicago. That is, if there really is a Greg. We'll make a date," Grace promised. Kane put his hands in his pockets.

"Grace?" he said.

"What?"

"Oh, nothing. Have a nice trip. Call me if you need anything."

"I will."

"And I mean anything," he said again, bending down and picking up his bags.

"Even to change a lightbulb?" she joked, but to her it wasn't really a joke, considering the unpredictability of the Duro-Lites.

"That happens to be one of my specialties," he told her.

"You know you'd be the first person I'd call if I needed anything," she said, although she knew she probably wouldn't call anyone.

As soon as she closed the door behind him, Grace went into the living room and collapsed onto the couch. Her heart was racing. She was still holding the yellow envelope, and unable to wait until Saturday, she tore it open. Out flew dozens of small strips of paper, newspaper clippings, and several fortunes from Chinese take-out.

She picked up a strip of paper to read: *Sagittarius. The planets are in line, making this the time to get what you have always wanted. Try it. Close your eyes. Make a wish. Open your eyes. Did it come true?* She turned it over. On the reverse side was the personal ad from *Time Out* magazine that Kane had cut out the day they went up to get the tree. She felt relieved and foolish to have jumped to the conclusion that Kane was out cruising. He'd always still be Kane— reliable and consistent. She read one of the fortunes: *The difficulties of life have been removed.* If Kane only knew how ironic that was, and would he agree that Laz was one of them?

After an hour, Grace decided she needed something to occupy herself, so she decided to confirm her flight. She dialed the number for the airline and waited for an operator to pick up. Chloe had recommended the airline, a small, Midwestern carrier that had good rates.

"Thank you for calling Highland Air. How may I help you this morning?" It never ceased to surprise Grace that people could be so pleasant and friendly. She was often told that she didn't seem like a New Yorker, but whenever she encountered someone outside of the tristate area, she felt as if she needed a crash course in manners. No matter how she tried, she couldn't match the effortless civility on the other end of the telephone.

"I'm calling to confirm my flight."

"If you give me your confirmation number, I'll be glad to help you." Grace gave the operator the information and waited on hold as Vivaldi's *Four Seasons* played.

"Sorry to keep you waiting. Yes, your flight has been confirmed. That's two first-class tickets to Chicago on Friday at ten A.M." It took a second for the mistake to register.

"I think that's two coach tickets," Grace said.

"You've been upgraded."

"I have?" Grace asked, confused.

"Ma'am, I'm showing two first-class tickets to O'Hare, with a return flight on Sunday at one P.M. You requested the vegetarian luncheon special with steamed edamame and miso soup, and you have a choice of grilled tempeh or a garden burger." Grace, who despised being called ma'am, once mistook a slice of tempeh for a scouring pad, but what concerned her was how this operator knew that she was a vegetarian.

"Garden burger, please," she answered.

"Will you be needing ground transportation once you arrive at

O'Hare? We offer complimentary limo service to your destination."
Grace began to feel lulled into a sort of sheeplike compliance.

"Yes, thanks." She was bewildered when she hung up the phone.
But after a few moments to reflect, the only explanation she could
come up with was that the upgrade must be an early birthday present from Chloe.

IT WAS NEARLY one o'clock and still no sign of Griffin.
Grace considered sitting down and crocheting the time away, but
then remembered that she'd neglected to cut down the amaryllis.
She'd once left an iris bulb in the soil too long, and the next year,
the plant yielded no flowers, just thin, grasslike leaves that eventually turned brown.

Grace got the shears out of the utility closet and went into the
dining room. The plant had definitely seen better days—its leaves
unfurled and wilted. She cut the stems two inches from the base
and placed the crate in a deep shopping bag, folding down the top,
which she secured with masking tape.

The coolest and darkest spot she knew of was in the butler's
pantry by the back door. The window faced an alley and received
no direct light. Sometimes, through the air shaft, she could hear
singing from a neighboring kitchen. Grace stored onions, potatoes,
and garlic in metal stacking baskets on the floor. The pantry radiator hadn't worked since they moved in, and there was a draft from
the lopsided, frosted window. She tucked the shopping bag under
the sill and, with a sense of having accomplished something, again
went to wait for Griffin, busying herself by tidying up and putting
the apartment back in order after Dolores's reorganization.

FINALLY, AROUND FOUR-THIRTY, the buzzer rang and
Grace ran to answer it. Unable to restrain herself, she waited by the

door until she heard the elevator arrive at her floor. The doorbell rang, and Grace took a breath before flinging the door wide open. Griffin stood in the vestibule wearing a gray-and-white wool hat, a black ski jacket, and jeans. He carried a small duffel bag over his shoulder.

"I was beginning to wonder about you," Grace said. All her preparations for a low-key welcome slipped away from her and she felt like a stereotypical overanxious parent.

"I guess I lost track of the time," he said, taking off his hat and running his hand through his hair. His tan canvas duffel bag was almost identical to one that Grace had had in high school. While hers had been covered with autographs, peace signs, and flowers drawn in magic marker, this one was covered with Pearl Jam and New Order stickers. Dangling from the frayed strap was a miniature snowboard key chain. Grace noticed an ironed-on patch of an airplane with an arrow pointing to a red heart. She wondered if it was a symbol of his trip to New York to find his father.

"Come in," she said to Griffin. "Let me show you where you can put your stuff."

Griffin slowly followed as Grace led the way down the hall to Laz's study. He seemed as if he wanted to take in every detail, stopping every so often to look closely at a photograph or print on the wall. When they reached Laz's study, Griffin put his bag down. Inside it, Grace could see a pair of brown hockey skates just like the ones the woman had been wearing at Sky Rink. As Griffin walked over to the walnut desk by the window, Grace realized that she had come face to face with his mother now on two occasions. Griffin sat down in Laz's leather swivel chair. The weight of his body compressed the air in the seat cushion, making a sound much like one of her father's long sighs, as if the chair, too, was relieved to have a body finally occupying it again.

The room faced north, overlooking the tops of neighboring brownstones. Grace was so used to the sight of Laz staring out the window while he was working that more than once she had mistaken the sight of the sheer curtains blowing in the wind for his silhouette. For however brief a time, those phantom images dulled the sting of his absence. Griffin seemed perfectly at home in the room. He folded his arms across his chest and leaned back, then smiled at her.

"Would you mind showing me some photographs? I only have this one picture of my parents," he said, taking a photograph out of his duffel bag. "It must be twenty years old, at least." Grace looked at the picture. If she didn't know better, she'd have thought she was looking at Griffin. "My mother doesn't have any recent pictures of my father."

The full meaning of the words took time to penetrate. Recent photographs. As if looking at them would mean that Laz was nearer to her somehow—but he was no more accessible in the photographs she had than in the one that Griffin was holding. The truth was, Laz was beginning to feel further and further away. Each day, even as she conjured him in her life with the finesse of a sorcerer, she was banishing him as well, sending him into an exile that was comparable to his own abandonment.

Grace pulled out a cloth-covered album with a tea-rose pattern from their honeymoon and sat down on the floor. Griffin sat next to her. She watched as he turned the pages—Laz waist-deep in the blue water; Laz on the porch in front of their thatched hut; Grace and Laz waving as they hiked up a dusty mountain trail before the monkeys chased them halfway down—images so burned in Grace's memory, she barely had to look at the photographs.

He closed the album and held it on his lap. "It looks like you two are really happy together," he said.

"We are," she said, unable to ignore the impact of her choice of tense. The truth fluttered around her like dust motes. *We are. We were. We will be, again.* But when? Griffin got up from the floor and placed the album back on the shelf. He picked up an ornate oval-shaped brass doorknob that had been painted silver, which was from Laz's old apartment. Laz had removed it from the front door and replaced it with a reproduction he had found at the flea market.

When Grace had been packing up to move in with Laz, he had come over to her place with a set of screwdrivers and had removed one of the original faceted crystal doorknobs. He'd done it as if it were an ordinary and usual custom, and with the same casual air that Grace's mother had when she dumped a basket of onion rolls or a plate of biscotti into her purse at a restaurant, or when she took a hotel ashtray as a souvenir. It had seemed odd at the time, but now, as Griffin touched the contours of the floral motif on the handle and measured the weight in his hand, Grace understood why Laz had taken it. There were several other doorknobs on the shelf that he'd collected from various apartments he'd lived in over the years, and she looked at them as if for the first time, wondering what other hands had turned them, what doors they had opened, and if perhaps one of them had come from an off-campus apartment Laz might have shared with Griffin's mother.

Griffin set the doorknob back on the shelf and grazed the spines of the books with his fingertips as if he were reading Braille. Grace had seen Laz do the same thing many times in secondhand bookstores, almost as if he thought he could glean something of the person who'd previously possessed the book. Griffin opened a book of poems and began reading the notes Laz had made in the margins. Then he put the book back on the shelf and went around the room, picking up objects—a silver-plated cigarette lighter embossed with an image from mythology, a small wooden puzzle box, an ashtray from a hotel in Prague, an ivory-handled letter opener.

Everything Griffin touched seemed suddenly brought to life and imbued with new meaning. The desire to discover was infectious, and Grace felt the urge to show him everything. She went to the closet and turned on the light. The closet smelled of cinnamon from a candle that had once been in there. Grace pushed some unpacked boxes out of the way until she located a metal container that was stuffed with letters. She held it to her chest as she carried it to the desk.

"He used to love to write letters," Grace told Griffin. In the top drawer of her dresser she had a stack of letters tied with silk ribbon that Laz had sent to her even though they were living together at the time. She read them often, especially when he began to feel remote to her. She sometimes even saved messages from him on the answering machine to play when he was away on a trip.

Inside the metal container were letters he'd sent home from camp and boarding school and college, as well as letters he'd written to his father over the years that had come back unopened. Laz's mother had once been on a cleaning binge and had come across the tin. When she had asked him what she should do with it, he'd told her to throw it out, but Grace had salvaged it from the discard pile and brought it home without telling him. Neither Grace nor Griffin spoke as they emptied the contents of the tin. Blue, green, and orange envelopes fluttered across the desk.

Griffin picked up one of the unopened letters and pressed the envelope between his palms. Each letter was thick, comprised of several folded pages. Laz's handwriting was visible through the envelope. Without having to say anything to each other, Griffin and Grace gathered the letters together and placed them back in the tin. There would be plenty of time to open them, if they ever felt the need.

Griffin shoved his hands in his pockets. Grace went to the closet, pushing aside a shopping bag, and placed the tin back on the shelf. Just as she was about to close the door, she saw a sealed plastic bag containing a block of clay. It had probably been in there for years. She knelt down and lifted it up, setting it on the floor. Amazingly, the clay still felt cold and moist.

"I had completely forgotten about it," she said. She could easily imagine the feeling of working the clay with her hands to get the air out, and the way that the dry, silky dust would remain on her fingertips for days afterward.

She glanced at the clock. It was nearly seven. She realized that she'd been so engrossed in their explorations that she hadn't even offered Griffin anything to eat or drink.

"Are you hungry?" she asked.

"Starving." She was about to mention the spinach lasagna with tofu filling that she had waiting in the kitchen when he said, "I've been really craving meat. It's been nothing but gerbil food since I got here." Feeling very Francinesque, she decided to freeze the lasagna for another time.

The only meat she had in the house were the two dozen or so containers of sweet-and-sour meatballs. She made a mental note to call the butcher, then went into the kitchen, thankfully able to stop herself before she uttered the words, "Dinner will be ready in ten minutes and thirty seconds."

FRANCINE WAS RIGHT—the meatballs seemed to be as fresh as the day they were prepared, whenever that was. Grace set the kitchen table with two woven place mats, cloth napkins, and the William Morris dishes that she and Laz had bought at the Victoria Albert Museum in London. The image of Francine at the Food Emporium was still vivid her mind. It had been a strange encounter, almost as uncomfortable as when she was a teenager and had bumped into her parents in the East Village, wearing their matching dungaree leisure suits. Her father still spoke about those leisure suits with great nostalgia, yearning for a bygone time. Francine had been quite ill at ease, as if she had been caught in a compromising position.

As Grace stirred the meatballs, she realized that she'd forgotten all about Mr. Dubrovsky's book, which was probably still on the floor of Flik's Video, when the telephone rang. The machine picked up and she heard Mr. Dubrovsky's voice. *Mrs. Brookman, it is vital that I speak to you . . .*

Just then, Griffin walked into the kitchen, and Grace rushed over to turn down the volume. Mr. Dubrovsky's voice trailed off. Grace wiped her hands on a paper towel and motioned for Griffin to sit down, placing the steaming bowl of meatballs on a trivet. He spooned almost half the contents of the bowl onto his plate. By the time Grace had taken a second bite of her grilled vegetable/soy burger, Griffin had all but cleaned his plate.

"These are amazing. What's in them?" he asked. Again, she couldn't tell him even if she'd wanted to. Francine never would have divulged her culinary secrets, however fond she was of Griffin's father.

"I'll try to get the recipe for you," she lied. "I actually didn't make them myself."

"Well, they're really good," he said again, reaching for the bowl. "Aren't you going to have any?" Grace shook her head, so he proceeded to spoon out the remaining meatballs.

"What would you like to do tomorrow?" Grace asked. "I could show you around the city a bit, if you like."

Griffin reached for a slice of peasant bread. "That sounds great, but I'm going up to Vermont for a couple of days to go skiing."

Grace watched as he spread a thick layer of butter over the bread, salted it, and took a huge bite.

"Alone?"

"No. Some girl I met invited me. She goes to the acting school in the building. A group of them are driving up in the morning, and they asked if I wanted to go with them." Grace had seen the acting students in Laz's building. They were always dressed in black and carried huge bags slung over their shoulders.

"When will you be back?" she asked, not wanting to sound intrusive but suddenly aware of a Stepford-like feeling of protection over him.

"Thursday late afternoon, I think."

"We're going to Chicago on Friday," she told him. Griffin put down his bread and looked up. Grace knew what he was thinking. She took a deep breath before she spoke. "But Laz is flying directly to O'Hare."

As soon as she'd uttered the words, she paused and tried to think of anyone over the course of the last six weeks to whom she had not lied, and realized that with the exception perhaps of Pete, the bartender at Tap A Keg, there was no one.

Grace brought a plate of cookies and a pot of chamomile tea into the living room. Griffin turned the Christmas tree on and off from the dining room light switch with glee, like a small child let loose at the planetarium.

"Cool light show," he said. Grace sat on the couch with her legs folded beneath her, sipping her tea.

"Glad you like it," she said.

EARLY THE NEXT MORNING, Grace went to prepare Griffin breakfast and found a note on the kitchen table. He hadn't wanted to wake her. The radiator hissed and clanked like someone knocking. Grace walked through the apartment and into the den, looking for remnants of Griffin's presence, some proof that he'd really been there. The least he could have done was to have left some traces—a half-empty glass of water on the nightstand, a paperback book, even a wet towel on the doorknob. Griffin, in this regard, was nothing like his father after all, who left evidence of himself whether he was in the apartment or not. Griffin had seemed to all but vanish. The bed was made, as if no one had inhabited it. Even the rug she and Laz had brought back from Morocco, which was constantly inching toward the window, was in its place, undisturbed.

She noticed that the light in the bathroom was on. She went to turn it off and saw Griffin's Dopp kit on the sink. It was wide open like a fish about to swallow a hook, and Grace looked at the contents: a tube of toothpaste, a double-edged razor, deodorant, dental floss, a nail clipper, and shampoo. Luckily, all the items inside were easily replaceable, although, with a blizzard about to hit, replacing them might prove difficult. She was about to zip the bag up when she noticed a familiar-looking white business card sticking out of the top. She reached for it, and as soon as she read Mr. Dubrovsky's name, she stuffed it back inside, turned off the light as if that would obliterate the knowledge, and fled the room.

Later that morning, she telephoned Flik's Video, but—as if they were Grace's willing accomplices—they claimed that they had found no evidence of *Oblomov* among the videos.

## 23
## FREQUENT FLYER

The snow arrived late Monday evening and continued through Wednesday morning. It was indeed a blizzard of immense proportions, some snowdrifts reaching as high as the parlor-floor windows of brownstones. With all the snow, which was considerably more than Milton had predicted, Grace imagined Laz couldn't have gotten home even if he'd wanted to.

The snow presented Grace with an early holiday gift of excuses to abstain from almost all daily activities, including teaching her class and attending any family functions during the week. She was thus exempt from the biweekly "ancient Chinese" facials on Mott Street that her mother swore by, which incorporated ground-up pearl powder and shark cartilage exfoliant, and which left Grace's skin sensitive and prone to breakouts, lunch at Ratner's, and the requisite quick peek in at S and W's discount clothing store in the garment district, as well as a charity meeting with Laz's mother. Nancy Brookman, not heeding the advice of her riding instructor, had gone out riding and fallen when the horse lost its footing on a patch of ice, spraining Nancy's ankle in the process.

The one appointment that Grace could not get out of was with Dr. Gaylin, and so she set out midafternoon on Wednesday, traversing the snow-covered park on foot. The sun shimmered off the unmarred white hills, a short reprieve as more snow was forecast. The park was silent, all but unpopulated, with no wind. Grace trudged through the surreal stillness.

As Grace neared the East Side, the park suddenly became animated—cross-country skiers threaded their way between benches and trees, then disappeared through covered overpasses; dogs trotted through huge drifts, in search of squirrels, occasionally chasing children whizzing by on Flexible Flyers and plastic saucers.

Almost without thinking, Grace walked along the twists and turns of the paths, as the synthesized activities continued around her. Fifth Avenue loomed ahead, the impressive limestone facades in deep shadow. Grace gazed back one last time at the idyllic snow-covered scene before crossing the street and heading toward Dr. Gaylin's office.

Once inside, Grace sat down on a leather club chair and opened a magazine. There were several women in the waiting area. One, who looked at least eight months pregnant, smiled at Grace, who smiled back politely.

"You don't recognize me, do you?" the woman said. She was wearing a black headband, and her auburn hair fell just to the nape of her neck. Her scarf, folded in a triangle and tied off to the side, was imprinted with horses and riding scenes. "I'm Patsy. Laura's daughter. Nancy and my mom ride together. I met you at last year's Historical Society auction."

"Oh, of course," Grace said. "I'm sorry. I was just a little preoccupied."

"Me, too," she said, patting her stomach. "How are you?"

"Fine, thanks. When are you due?" In the background, the radio was tuned to WQXR. A female journalist was discussing hoaxes in the media. *I've been a journalist for twenty-five years, and never before have I come across a case of such blatant fabrication as with the case of the Kosovo prison impersonation . . .*

"Hey, isn't that your husband's—"

"Shh," Grace said, raising her finger to her lips. The woman must have thought the gesture indicated Grace's desire to listen to the broadcast. Just then, the nurse came in to escort Grace into the examining room. The voice of the female journalist trailed off as Grace followed behind the nurse.

The results of the hCG test confirmed that the blood levels had returned to normal, as if nothing at all had ever inhabited Grace's uterus. After spending a few moments with Dr. Gaylin, Grace headed for home.

Her mood and the weather had changed dramatically. The sun was obscured by thick, gray clouds and the park was virtually deserted, as if all the activity of just an hour ago had been a figment of her imagination. She shivered in her red parka. It felt like dusk. As she approached the park exit nearest her street, Grace thought about her empty apartment and then continued north on the park drive toward the yarn store.

She rang the buzzer and waited. Just as she was about to leave, she heard the door click and went in. Penelope was not dressed in one of her usual floral outfits, but was wearing a formfitting, blue pinstriped pants suit with exaggerated shoulders and a peplum waist. Her pants were tucked into white, fur-lined boots.

"Grace!" she said, walking toward her, arms extended. "We haven't seen you around lately."

"I know. I got caught up with family stuff," she said. This was not a lie. She had lost a child, found a child, and her father had been hospitalized all in less than a week, not to mention her husband's ongoing unexplained absence.

The sight of the shelves newly stocked with yarn was reassuring. Grace touched the soft skeins. Each one contained the possibility of a new creation. Some were more suited to one type of form than another, and there was the variable of the person working the yarn, but still, the basic characteristics were innate, as if the light gossamer weave of a fine angora had only one option. Grace was drawn to a pale lilac yarn with flecks of white. She pulled a skein off the shelf.

"That's a very fine yarn," Penelope commented. Grace squeezed it. It felt almost like nothing in her hand.

"It's wonderful," Grace said. For the first time since she began crocheting, she felt the need to have a pattern. "What should I make out of it?" she asked.

Penelope's eyes widened. "You never had to know before. Why now? Take the risk, let go of the result," she answered. Just then, the young man with the crocheting workshop stopped by to pick up a package of labels to sew into his creations that read *Made expressly by Scott.* He was wearing a nubby yellow sweater he'd obviously knitted himself, tucked into a pair of tight, black ski pants. He looked like a bumblebee.

"Hello, hello," he said, greeting Grace like an old friend. She sat down at the long oak table and set to work. She hadn't discussed the offer for the part-time job that Penelope had made her, but it seemed as if no answer was required besides just showing up.

Grace assisted three customers with choosing yarn, and she demonstrated a scallop stitch to another. By the time she was ready to leave, it was dark out. As Grace put on her coat and packed up ten skeins of the lilac yarn, Penelope brought over a large plastic bag and set it in front of her on the table.

"It's your grandmother's afghan. I did a few repairs. Not like new, but it will hold up. I hope you like it." Grace had not forgotten about it. In fact, quite the opposite. It was like Laz's leather jacket, which was still at the tailor's—she simply had no use for it now. She reached into the bag and pulled out the afghan. There were no more gaping holes or frayed ends. The afghan was whole and intact, as perfect as the edition of Twain that her father had re-bound for Laz, and inasmuch, utterly unfamiliar to her. This was not the same afghan that had kept her warm the night Laz went to his hockey games. The holes were gone and with them the memories —the proof of being well loved and well used—the tenacity of fibers holding tight in spite of weaknesses.

"Penelope, thank you so much," she said, trying to hide her disappointment.

"My pleasure. But I told you you'd be better off starting over. It can never be the same. I'm closing up early today. I'm meeting someone," she said, batting her eyes. "A blind date." She lowered her voice. "Actually, I met him on the Internet. He's a linguist. We really hit it off. Who knows? He may be the one." Grace wished her well and closed the door behind her on the way out.

IT WAS SNOWING heavily when Grace walked out onto the street. At least another three inches of fresh snow now covered the parked cars. She pulled her hood over her head and steadied herself against the wind. The lights from the cars blended into one glaring stream as she crossed the street to find a taxi heading downtown. There were several people searching for taxis ahead of her, arms laden with packages.

Out of the corner of her eye, she saw a man in a black parka leaning against a mailbox, his head buried in a newspaper. It wouldn't have seemed out of the ordinary, except that people don't usually read newspapers or wear business shoes during blizzards. She knew those shoes. They were the same sort of wing tips that Mr. Dubrovsky wore. As she approached the man, she saw him turn his head away quickly, as if he didn't want to be identified. Instead of waiting for a taxi, she began walking, quickly. She looked behind to make certain he wasn't following her, but in the bracing wind and with the glaring headlights, she could no longer even make out the mailbox where he'd been standing.

Grace quickened her pace, rushing around the corner, then stopped briefly to catch her breath. All for a book. It seemed so ludicrous. Then she remembered the card in Griffin's bag, thinking that everything was somehow related, but she couldn't connect the dots at the moment. She ducked under the awning of the synagogue that her family went to on the high holy days, just off West End Avenue. Brushing the snow off her coat, she went in.

Her father had once led her through the synagogue on a rainy day. They had gone into the sanctuary and down a flight of stairs and through a neighboring church, miraculously emerging several blocks south, right in front of the crosstown bus stop—without getting wet. She wondered if she could reconstruct the route. She proceeded toward the sanctuary while trying to keep an eye out for Mr. Dubrovsky. Could he actually be following her?

An archway that was covered in small, brilliantly colored tiles led into the sanctuary, two large doors flanking it on either side. Each door was emblazoned with a seven-pronged gilt menorah and a colorful, fanning mosaic pattern, along with other symbols of Judaism with which Grace was not familiar. She pulled at the ornate brass handle of one of the doors, but it was locked. She tried the other. After a heavy tug, it opened. She glanced over her shoulder and thought she saw a hooded figure enter the synagogue just as she slipped through the door.

She descended a flight of unlit stairs until she reached a musty-smelling basement. An eerie orange glow emanated from the single bare lightbulb hanging from the ceiling. The bulb, covered with a thick layer of black soot, looked as if it hadn't been changed in forty years, clearly surpassing the Duro-Lite record for longevity.

Looking ahead and seeing only murky shadows before her, Grace had the urge to turn back. Harnessing her courage, she forged ahead down the maze of dark corridors. She traveled for what seemed to be several blocks, then she finally entered a brightly lit boiler room with an assemblage of pipes and gears, beyond which was a door with a lit red exit sign above it. She pushed the door open to find another flight of stairs. At the top of the landing, she came to a fire door, which she opened slowly, careful not to set off any alarms, and found herself standing in the church entryway.

The building smelled faintly of incense, and she saw the requisite bulletin board covered with church announcements. A notice for a lecture that evening caught her eye: *It's never too late to become who you could have been.* She recognized the quote from George Eliot. The lecture had probably been canceled because of the snow. She zipped up her jacket and was about to leave when she heard voices coming from inside the church. Wondering if the lecture was in progress, she opened the door a crack and peered inside. The pews were sparsely filled, and at the front of the sanctuary stood a man in his thirties wearing a jade-green fleece pullover, jeans, a backwards baseball cap, and hiking boots. His hair was long and shaggy, and he had a few days' growth on his face. He looked familiar. Laz occasionally didn't shave on the weekends, and by Monday morning, his face would be completely covered by a full beard. Once, when he had left the building after not having shaved, the doorman hadn't even recognized him.

Grace opened the door wider and tried to slip in unnoticed. The man at the front caught her eye and nodded. She sat down in the last row and listened.

"Try to think back to a time as a child when you were so occupied in something that you were completely unaware of the passing of time," the man said. "You were lost in your true selves. You haven't lost that, you've just forgotten."

At first the things he was saying were the kind of typical pop psychology that was promoted on daytime talk shows. It wasn't as if Grace even thought she needed to discover her authentic self. She was simply curious what these people thought they lacked.

"We all know," the man continued. "We either forget who we were, discount it, or never seek it because it didn't fit into the scheme of our family's, lovers', friends', employers', husbands', wives', or children's expectations. Remember: It's never too late. Who could you have been?"

He stopped, left the lectern, and walked down the aisle in Grace's direction. She glanced behind her, assuming he was headed toward the back of the church. But he wasn't. She felt like someone about to become an unwilling magician's subject. As he approached, Grace suddenly realized who he was and tried to reach for her bag in an attempt to escape before he recognized her. Too late. He stood in front of her.

"*I've never . . . ,*" he said, addressing Grace, with a wink. "You fill in the blank." He stared at her, waiting for a response. She stared back at him. Her heart began to pound. This meeting in the church was no drinking game. And whatever it was, Grace no longer wanted to play. Without the bar between them, she felt completely vulnerable.

"I'm sorry," she mustered. "But I really have to go." And she ran out of the sanctuary. On the street, she oriented herself and realized that she was directly across the street from Laz's old building. The snow was falling heavily and the streets were empty. The yarn and afghan in her bag were dusted with snow. She looked both ways. Thankfully, Mr. Dubrovsky was nowhere in sight. She decided to cut through the lobby of Laz's building. Her father had turned her into an urban groundhog, capable of giving a potentially danger-ous stalker—as well as an intrusive moonlighting bartender—the slip. She hurried through the revolving door into the lobby of Laz's building and then into the elevator and up to the fourth floor.

When she opened the door, she saw that the apartment was cov-ered entirely with sheets of plastic and a layer of fine white dust. By the window, under a single sheet of plastic, was an orchid. She went over to uncover the plant, which from a distance had looked too perfect to be real. There was no white dust on the leaves and, strangely, the soil was moist.

If Laz had been there, he had left no tracks. For now, the two of them, like the magnetic spinning pups, had reversed their polarity. It seemed that they could only push each other away. Snow swirled in the courtyard outside and Grace imagined a flurry of white busi-ness cards fluttering to the ground.

She was in no hurry to go home, now that Griffin was out of town. Here, in this unoccupied apartment, where no one else could possibly leave her, she felt safe. Still wearing her red parka, she laid down on the plastic-covered couch. Her eyes felt heavy. What was it about this apartment that always made her so sleepy? she won-dered, her last thought as she drifted off. She awoke to the sound of the asbestos workers entering the apartment the next morning. She left quickly, taking the orchid with her, her hair and clothing now covered in white dust.

GRIFFIN WAS DUE back that night. By nine o'clock, still not having heard from him, Grace decided to go to bed. She'd spent the evening packing—both her suitcase and a bag for Laz. With just a few well-chosen items, she was able to evoke the semblance of a whole life. At this point, Grace had it down to a science. The black satin pants that her mother had bought for her, when folded, took up no more room than one of Laz's pocket handkerchiefs. If she packed for Chicago according to her mother's principles, she would require a bag no larger than a manila envelope. She could mail her clothes to Chicago.

She pulled down a small duffel bag from the closet, filling it with Laz's clothes, shoes, an extra-warm sweater, as well as several talisman-like items, such as his eyeglasses and the gold pocket watch from his father. Ostensibly it was for Chloe's benefit—if she came to the hotel, there would have to be signs of Laz around the room, but it was really just as much for Grace's own peace of mind.

She opened the top drawer of Laz's dresser. Inside, there were belts from every trip Laz had ever taken—a white belt with blue embroidery from Morocco, a cowboy belt from Durango, a camel hair belt from Egypt. Grace could practically construct a map of the world by laying out the belts in longitudinal lines. Next to his passport, she placed the key to his old apartment. There was no need for her to ever go there again. Then she closed the drawer.

Her parents telephoned later that evening, wishing her a safe flight and a happy birthday in unison. *Call as soon as you land. What's the flight number again? You know it's going to be bitter cold in Chicago. Maybe you should go in the spring instead.*

When Grace finally heard the front door open around midnight, she remained in bed, as if physically weighted down. She couldn't face another leave-taking, not even one from this near stranger. She heard music coming from his room. Grace recognized the melody and the sound of Aimee Mann's voice—*One is the loneliest number that you'll ever do. Two can be as bad as one. It's the loneliest number since the number one.* Laz had played that song, too, sometimes over and over again.

She stared at the ceiling and thought about the fragment of the dream she'd had in Laz's apartment on her post-Thanksgiving visit. Laz had walked through the web with nothing sticking to him. She wondered why it hadn't occurred to her to try walking through the doorway herself.

The next morning, she left for the airport two hours early, long before Griffin would be up.

GRACE SETTLED HERSELF into the plush first-class seat. The seat next to hers was reclined, the buckle fastened as if a body were actually occupying it. Grace returned the seat to its upright position and opened her book.

She thought back to her first solo plane ride, when she was eleven. She had been going to Iowa for Christmas to visit Chloe, where Chloe's father lived. Grace's parents had driven her to the airport, but at the gate, Grace panicked and refused to get on the plane. Her father gave her half a Miltown tranquilizer that he had in his breast pocket. About fifteen minutes later, she was sitting limply strapped into the orange airplane seat on her way to Iowa City, even less present than Laz was now.

About forty minutes after the plane's takeoff, Grace found herself growing anxious. For the first time since Laz had left, she was traveling out of her comfort zone. Living in the city had lately become almost as provincial as a small town for Grace. Her life for the past six weeks had been mostly contained within the very circumscribed twenty-block area of the Upper West Side. But now she was taking "her act" on the road and suddenly, after this many weeks of performing, it was as if she couldn't remember her lines. Her mouth was dry. She asked for a glass of water.

Grace unwrapped a skein of the lavender angora yarn that she had bought the other day, her lifeline to familiar ground. As she began to crochet, the feeling of dread began to lessen, until gradually it was a mere wisp like the cirrus clouds that skimmed the blue sky. It wasn't like a pill that she had popped or like a muscle relaxer to soothe the mind during periods of turbulence. By creating something new out of whole cloth, her fingers were trying to show her she could lead the way.

A pattern began to emerge, and it was clear that this project was going to require more than the seven skeins she'd brought along with her. The yarn was so light that it took almost half a skein to crochet just five inches. She tried to ration herself, but as much as she willed herself to slow down, she couldn't. Before they had been airborne even an hour, the bag was nearly empty. Only one skein remained.

The flight attendant gushed over Grace's work as she passed by on her way to get the drink cart. Grace envisioned the finished crochet weightlessly skimming the top of the dining-room table.

She put down her crocheting and pressed her forehead against the window, peering out at the horizon. An image began to encroach like a storm cloud over her mind. She saw herself with Laz on the ski slope on their first Valentine's Day. From the vantage point of thirty thousand feet up in the air, she saw Laz's face as he had taken her hand and led her to the lift. *You're too sensitive,* he'd told her. *Who would ever want kids? They just tie you down.* He had proposed that afternoon on the last run of the day. The ski lift had taken off as the words left his lips. *Marry me.* She remembered how once they returned to the city, he didn't call for three days.

Despite all their premonitions and warnings about the weather, her parents never counseled their daughter on the fault lines and sinkholes of real life. They scoured the skies for forces of nature, but they didn't see that human beings and bad marriages have their own high-pressure systems. They misguidedly thought that Laz would elevate their daughter, but they confused his breeding and background with his worth. They hadn't been able to foretell that he would only elevate Grace to the status of a single wife.

Suddenly, she felt a tug on the yarn, as if she'd caught a fish. Before fully registering what was happening, Grace watched in horror as, row by row and down the aisle, her crocheting began to unravel, caught in the efficient wheels of the drink cart. The more she tried to save it, the faster it unwound. Grace's attempt to recover the unraveling yarn sent several opened cartons of milk and cups of coffee toppling over (and the flight attendant to lose her footing), until the entire length of the plane, from first class to coach, looked as if a soggy, purple spider's web had descended upon it.

# 24
## Soul Kitchen

The woman at the reception desk at the Four Seasons hotel very kindly informed Grace that they would require a different credit card.

"Has it expired?" Grace asked.

"No, actually," the woman answered with a sympathetic tilt of her head, "it's been frozen."

"That's impossible," Grace said. "I just used it." But as she uttered the words, she didn't remember exactly when the last time was that she'd used it. In fact, she couldn't recall having received her last monthly statement. Due to some recessive gene passed on through her mother, she was in the habit of paying with cash. What she hadn't inherited was her mother's penchant for haggling. Her mother would have asked the hotel concierge if she could do a little better on the rate.

"Let me call them," Grace said.

A lengthy conversation with the credit card company, a few

choked back tears, and a dose of reality later, Grace returned to the reception desk. The card had indeed been frozen, but by whom, Grace wasn't sure. She had just enough cash on her to pay for the deposit and a day's worth of expenses. She picked up her bags, noting how light Laz's duffel bag felt in her hand in comparison to hers and went upstairs.

THE ROOM SHE'D booked was spacious and tastefully decorated, if slightly generic. There was a vase of purple freesia and a fruit basket by the window, a floral down comforter and king-size pillows on the bed, cherry-wood dressers with matching nightstands. The room was orderly and utterly free of any residual history, which held a certain guilty allure for Grace. She felt as if she'd entered the Platonic ideal of a stage-set life.

Through the sheer curtains, from the forty-first floor window, Grace could see the shores of Lake Michigan. Noticing that the phone's red message light was blinking, Grace pressed the button and listened to Chloe's voice, welcoming her to Chicago. Grace called back, and they arranged to meet for an early dinner at a restaurant near Chloe's apartment in Wicker Park. Grace made the usual excuses for Laz, saying that he had a reception he had to attend.

Grace spent the day shivering as she wandered around downtown Chicago in her pink coat, visiting the tourist sights. Then she took a short walk along the shore. She returned to the room just after five o'clock and put on a thick pair of thermals and several sweaters over an ankle-length knit skirt. She removed the present she'd brought for Chloe from her suitcase—a blank book that she had made. On the cover, she'd mounted a packet of seeds for Chloe to plant in the spring on her porch. Underneath the packet, Grace had glued one of the fortunes that Kane had given her. The fortune had seemed more appropriate for Chloe, who was working on a novel: *You are a lover of fiction.* Grace had made the pages from shredded newsprint with flecks of wild flowers, spraying the pages with essence of bergamot, Chloe's favorite perfume. Grace thought that she might have overdone the perfume, as now the entire contents of her suitcase smelled like a very strong cup of Earl Grey tea.

Before she left the room, Grace gazed at Laz's unopened duffel bag on the wooden rack. Usually it made her feel less alone to display Laz's things, but in her present frame of mind, the last thing she wanted was his clutter to mar this wonderfully unblemished scene.

Soul Kitchen was nearly full, even though it was still early. The crowd was unusual, too—very young, tattooed, and imaginatively pierced. Chloe was seated at a round table in the center of the room. Her hair was no longer cropped short or dyed black, but fell past her shoulders in blond waves. She was wearing ripped jeans and a vintage cardigan covered with intricately beaded flowers over a pale blue T-shirt with the words *All About Me* embroidered across the front. Every once in a while, the light reflected off the beads on her sweater in a certain way, sending a sparkling shower of colors around the room.

"They're hipsters," Chloe said, referring to the other patrons. "It just comes naturally. We were never that cool."

Grace tried to take off one of her sweaters, but it got caught on her necklace and Chloe had to help her pull it off. The waiter, dressed in red jeans and a light-green shirt with depictions of major historical events on it, smirked as he filled her glass with ice water.

"Great shirt," Chloe told him. "Did you get it at Village Thrift?"

"No, at Una Mae's."

"I have to take you there, Grace," Chloe said. "You'll love it." The waiter and Chloe continued talking about their favorite vintage stores, and Grace thought at one point that he was going to join them at the table.

"Where are you from?" he asked, turning to Grace for the first time during the whole conversation.

"New York," she answered. Grace watched as the lines in his brow began to furrow.

"Like where? Upstate?"

"No, the city," she said.

He glanced at Chloe as if for verification. "Cool," he said, then went off—rather quickly in Grace's opinion—to get them menus.

Grace could barely finish half of the sweet potato ravioli and grilled spinach with dandelion greens. The waiter wrapped it up for them, and as they were getting their coats, he asked Chloe for her telephone number.

"I guess you like it here," Grace said, as they walked outside onto Milwaukee Avenue. They passed a small group of people who stood in line, waiting to get into a club next door. On the corner, Grace noticed a cluster of teenagers in hooded jackets, congregating in front of a small deli.

"A lot. I never felt like I could be myself in New York. I know you love it, but I just couldn't take looking out my window at a brick wall. Now that Mom's gone, there's not much left for me there."

"I can imagine."

"I'm still sort of waiting for her to come back." They walked around the corner toward the elevated train. Chloe stopped and turned to Grace. "If you have time, you should come over and see my apartment. Too bad it's not spring. We could sit on my porch."

"I'd really like to, but I think Laz will be finishing up with his conference soon, and I told him I'd meet him back at the hotel." She was thankful it was dark out.

"Grace——" Chloe began but then stopped. She put on a hat that looked like she'd sewn it together from some old sweaters scraps. "That's all right. Another time, then." She rummaged through her red vinyl purse for her keys. A cab pulled up in front of them. "Thanks again for the journal. Call me tomorrow and let me know what your plans are. I have a birthday present for you." As they hugged, Grace thought of the empty hotel room that awaited her. Chloe began to walk away.

"Chloe . . ." Grace called, waving the cab off. Chloe turned around.

"Did you forget something?"

"I think I have time to stop by your apartment. Let me call Laz and tell him I'm going to be late."

Chloe's apartment was a half mile from the restaurant in Bucktown. They took the long way home, walking along streets named after famous authors——Shakespeare and Dickens Avenues——that were lined with Victorian row houses and unadorned, low brick buildings with high fences surrounding them, which Chloe told her had been built before the area had become a designated landmark.

On the way, they made a stop at Myopic, a tiny independent bookstore with aisles barely wide enough for two people to stand without touching. The floor was covered with pencil shavings. Unvarnished raw wood shelves were crammed with titles that Grace had never heard of. Plaster statuettes peeked out from tiny nooks. A black cat nudged Grace's ankles and followed her around the store as she browsed. In the back, there was a garden with a round table and three chrome chairs. Chloe went upstairs to find a book about the subject of loss. Grace could hear the creaking of the floorboards above her, and she imagined the entire inventory of *A* through *F* crashing down on her.

She walked over to the register to wait and glanced at the

assortment of notices, mostly ads for sublets or part-time jobs, that had been stuck up with pushpins. Grace was about to go in search of Chloe when a yellow flyer caught her eye. It was a listing for an open pottery class. The bottom of the sheet was cut into a fringe on which there was a drawing of a tiny potter's wheel and a telephone number, written in calligraphy. It had been such a long time since she'd thrown a pot—the wheel spinning as she centered the clay, lifting the clay upward, and hollowing it until it seemed almost too thin to hold. The black cat played at her feet, scampering after a fallen pushpin, then Grace saw Chloe coming down the stairs. Before she knew it, Grace found herself tearing off one of the slips of paper and stuffing it into her pocket.

CHLOE UNLOCKED THE door to her second-floor apartment, turning the dead bolt and fastening the chain once they got inside.

"I never used to lock my door until after Mom died. I don't want anything else to be taken away."

"I know the feeling," Grace said as she walked into Chloe's kitchen. The floor was an old-fashioned, peach-colored linoleum tile with gold flecks that matched the countertops. The walls were painted a sunny yellow, and every available wall or surface was covered with artwork or knickknacks.

Grace thought of her grandmother as she looked around at the assortment of clocks, each with a different time. Antique dolls were displayed on top of the refrigerator, as were pieces of miniature furniture that could have fit in quite naturally with the Damien Hirst exhibit. Magnets and black-and-white photo strips covered the front of the refrigerator door. Grace saw a photo of her and Chloe from their senior trip to Rye Playland. The photograph was curled at the edges. In it, Grace was wearing a frayed jean jacket with a bandanna tied around her neck. Grace barely recognized herself. Even her smile seemed alien to her.

She thought of the drawer under her bed, where she suspected most of her high school paraphernalia still lay undisturbed. It would never have occurred to her to try to incorporate one part of her life into another. When one stage ended, she'd been taught to pack things away like old clothes into a camp trunk and move on to the next. Whatever didn't fit was left behind or sent to Goodwill.

When Grace first began dating Laz, her mother had taken her shopping and to get a new hairstyle. For the first time, they paid full price, trying on clothes with the solemnity usually reserved for a rite of passage. It was the culmination of all those years spent at places such as the Barclay School in preparation for this very moment. Like a shtetl bride who'd been shipped off with a goat and the family linens, Grace had a modern-day trousseau—hers from Bergdorf's, which secured her access into Laz's sphere. It wasn't what was included that had made the ultimate difference, it was what had been left out. With the aid of her mother's skilled hand, Grace had been delivered to the threshold of a marriage with one important thing missing. As she looked around Chloe's kitchen, she knew what it was. Here—in the clutter and the accumulation—was an uncensored life.

"Would you like a cup of chamomile tea?" Chloe asked. The question broke Grace's reverie and she found herself back in the false world that she'd been inhabiting all too easily over the past six weeks.

"Can I use your phone to call Laz?"

Chloe gave Grace the same look that she'd given her outside of Soul Kitchen, but this time she was shaking her head.

"Grace . . ."

"What?"

"Do you think I'm stupid?"

"Of course not. I just wanted to let Laz know I'll be late."

"Give me a break. I know what's going on. Maybe you think you can pull this off with everyone else. But Grace, please, with me? I've known you forever."

Suddenly, after a day of shivering, Grace was sweating. She wasn't sure what or how much to say.

"What do you mean?"

"Grace, Laz was in Chicago last week at a symposium on human rights, but he spent most of his time trying to defend his book, if you can even call it that. I think he even believes his story that he was in that concentration camp. It was in all the papers. He still claims he spent six weeks impersonating a prisoner. Paying one off is more like it. I even went to see him at the symposium."

"You saw him? Did he say anything about me?"

"Yes. But it was all a bunch of crap. And between the two of you, I don't know who's got the bigger problem. He had no idea that you were coming to Chicago. He wanted all the flight information. Like I'd ever give it to him. He hasn't changed one bit. I knew it from the first time I met him. I'm sorry, but I've never been a big fan of the guy." So Laz must have been the one responsible for the upgrade.

"I never meant to lie to you," Grace said, sinking into a chair.

"Why don't I make some tea and you can tell me what's been going on?" Chloe went to the cabinet and took out two unmatched mugs with floral patterns and set them down on the table, shoving aside a thick, marked-up manuscript and several back issues of *The New York Review of Books*.

Grace sighed. "I wouldn't even know where to begin."

"Wherever you want. We can edit later."

. . .

THAT NIGHT, LYING on the futon mattress in Chloe's second bedroom, Grace was unable to sleep. The talk with Chloe had been like a summer storm on a hot August evening that does nothing to unburden the night. The room was filled with sewing things. Chloe's mother had taught her how to sew and knit and embroider. A pair of gingham curtains hung from brass rods on the window and a hand-quilted blanket covered the bed. On a wooden table, an old Singer sewing machine that had belonged to Chloe's mother was set up with bobbin and thread, as if poised to begin whirring away. Next to it was a clear, plastic sorter stocked with buttons, hooks, thimbles, and metal spools.

Grace had a childhood memory of writing her name on the sides of her white saddle shoes while she was in grammar school. When her mother picked her up from school that day, she was beside herself. "Your brand-new shoes!" she'd cried. It hadn't been the first time Grace had written her name on things. She'd inscribe entire pages in her notebook with her name, etch it into her desk at school, scratch it on the upright piano in the living room. Her teacher had taken her mother aside and in a low voice suggested they set up a meeting. Grace caught the words *identity crisis,* and although she hadn't understood the meaning, from the way her mother reacted, she knew it was worse than the time she had to go to the speech therapist.

"She knows *exactly* who she is, and if she doesn't, I'll be the one to tell her, thank you," Grace's mother said in a high-pitched voice, zipping up Grace's coat and leading her down the limestone steps. When they got home, her mother handed Grace a brush dipped in peroxide and detergent. Grace's fingers turned white as she applied three thick coats of Kiwi shoe polish, setting the shoes to dry overnight on sheets of newspaper.

Tomorrow was her birthday. She would be celebrating without

Laz. Suddenly, like a homesick child at camp, she felt a longing—but not for her father's beige argyle sweater, climate-controlled rain showers, or her mother's elixirs, not even for Laz. It was a longing for something she could not yet name. When she returned to New York, she decided, she would tell her parents everything.

# 25

## GRACE'S INTERVENTION

Chloe was already up and working on her laptop at the kitchen table, wearing jeans and a purple sweater and slippers, when Grace walked in. There was a pot of coffee on the counter and the kettle was on.

"Hey. How did you sleep? Did the gunshots wake you?" Chloe asked.

"Gunshots?" Grace sat down at the table.

"It happens all the time. I'm so used to it now that I barely notice it; but the first time I heard them, I dropped to the floor and rolled like I was on *Miami Vice* or something."

"I guess I was out cold," Grace said, though she had no sense of having slept at all.

"Well, that's good." The kettle whistled. Chloe turned off the burner on the old gas stove and picked up a yellow watering can, then went over to water a flowering plant that was in a hanging basket by the window. She reached in to pick off what she thought was a dead leaf. "Damn it," she said, wiping her hands on a dish towel.

"What's wrong?" Grace asked.

"There are moths in my petunias!" Chloe unhooked the hanging basket and carefully held it out the door to the porch, giving it a vigorous shake, which caused at least a dozen gray moths to fly out and flutter away. "We've been having a real moth problem lately," Chloe said. "I'll spray later. I love my petunia, even though according to my grandmother, they're low-class flowers."

Chloe poured herself a cup of coffee. She brought over a tea strainer and some fresh mint and poured boiling water into Grace's cup.

"I want to take you to the Bongo Room for breakfast. For your birthday," she said, sitting down at the table. "They make the best eggs. A few of my friends will be there who I think you'll like. Then we could hit the vintage stores."

THE RESTAURANT WAS packed when they arrived. At first, Chloe didn't see any of her friends. The hostess, who wore a tight black turtleneck and low-waisted chinos, told them that the wait would be at least an hour.

"I don't mind waiting, if you don't mind," Grace said. But before Chloe could answer, three people at a big booth in the back waved them over.

"Oh, look. They're over here." Chloe pulled Grace by the wrist to the back of the restaurant and introduced her. "Guys, this is Grace, my friend from New York I'm always telling you about."

"Nice to meet you," Grace said, as she squeezed in between two girls named Kym and Sela, who were wearing matching llama-wool sweaters. Chloe sat down next to a guy with diamond studs in his ears and wearing a red velvet jacket over a worn blue T-shirt.

"Jeff, you wore your Kris Kringle jacket," Chloe said.

"Just trying to spread a little holiday cheer," he answered. Another friend of Chloe's arrived late, brought over a chair, and sat down at the head of the table.

"Hey, Ian," Chloe said. "This is Grace." Ian nodded to her. He kept on his navy blue pea coat and scarf, undoing only the top button. He drummed his fingers on the table, his hair filled with static electricity, almost as frenetic as his temperament. After they all ordered, Grace noticed that Ian was staring at her. She tried not to look back, but every so often she would check to see if he was still looking.

"So, have you been to Chicago before?" Jeff asked, picking a piece of lint off his crimson jacket.

"No, it's my first time," Grace answered.

"Chloe says you're a sculptor."

"No, I used to teach art, but I'm not a sculptor," she said, thinking about the notice for the pottery class and the block of clay in her closet. Besides modeling some Christmas ornaments out of plasticine, she hadn't sculpted anything in years.

"She is, too—she just doesn't remember," Chloe interjected.

"You know, I heard someone once say at a meeting," Jeff began, "'Leap and the net will appear.' It helped me get over my fear of auditioning." When he finished speaking, he had an expression on his face as if he'd just uttered a statement of profundity.

Grace had no idea what meeting he was referring to, or why he was addressing her as if she'd solicited his opinion. Anyway, the thought of leaping was unappealing enough, but the idea of doing so without the assurance of a sturdy net, harness, and a well-thought-out contingency plan was unfathomable to her. She began to feel slightly claustrophobic and took a deep breath to keep herself from scrambling over the two sweater girls to seek refuge in the ladies' room.

"Jeff, Grace doesn't know about Near West," Chloe said. Everyone at the table nodded gravely in a manner that made Grace feel slightly paranoid. "It's an AA meeting I've been going to since I moved here."

"Alcoholics Anonymous?" Grace asked. "You're not an alcoholic."

"I've been there, too," she heard someone say. Grace suddenly felt as if she'd stumbled into some lodge meeting and she didn't know the secret handshake.

"Grace, I've been sober for almost five years. And I think you knew." Grace couldn't recall the last time Chloe had gotten drunk. Of course, there'd been more than one occasion in college that she'd thought Chloe had overdone it with the melon ball shots.

"Why didn't you tell me?" Grace asked.

"I tried to on several occasions. You wouldn't hear it."

"Ain't just a river in Egypt," Jeff said.

"What does that mean?" Grace asked.

"*Denial.*"

"When did you start speaking in slogans?" Chloe asked Jeff, taking a sip of her orange juice.

"Trace it; face it; erase it," he continued.

"Replace it," Kym added.

"Enough," Chloe said, trying to stifle a laugh. "See what I have to put up with here? Maybe I'll just move back to New York and leave you loonies to fend for yourselves."

"*Grace* it," Jeff said.

"I actually like that one," Chloe said.

The omelets they'd ordered arrived on oval plates that were the size of Grace's mother's platters. Her omelet was so large, Grace guessed that it must have contained at least ten eggs, and with its side of hash browns and caramelized onions, she thought she'd never be able to finish it. Laz usually ate whatever was left on Grace's plate. She'd become so used to it that sometimes she wasn't sure if she was actually finished or just in the habit of leaving something for Laz.

Grace remembered a dinner she'd had with Laz at a bistro in Paris. Thick gold curtains had hung from the doorway to keep out the cold. She and Laz had been ravenous, having spent the day walking to Montmartre and the Jeu de Pommes. As always, Grace had left a bite of steak au poivre, a bit of pureed turnips, and a few *frites*, which Laz ate, dipping his bread in the peppered cream sauce on her plate. During dessert, she'd watched as he took the last spoonful of her crème caramel, now wondering whether he'd even considered that she might not have been finished yet.

"Your friend's a good eater," Jeff said to Chloe. Grace looked down at her plate and saw that she'd finished every last bite, while the rest of the group had barely started theirs.

"I didn't realize I was that hungry," she said.

"Take what you need and leave the rest," Jeff said. Chloe rolled her eyes. Again, Grace wasn't sure if he was talking about something other than eggs.

As Grace listened to the conversation, she began to feel a sense of belonging. Her shoulders relaxed and her breathing came easier. She found in this circle of Chloe's friends at the Bongo Room a place not to find answers—because, like Kane said, sometimes there aren't any—but to ask questions. They tumbled out fast, one after another, like somersaults. *If she gave up the illusion, who or what would be there to break her fall? And why did she need it in the first place?* Grace looked up to see Ian staring at her again. He unwrapped his scarf and finally took off his coat, throwing it over the back of his chair.

"Grace, I don't know you," he said, leaning across the table. "And if you were here longer, I'd probably ask you out. But slogans won't help you—you just need to take some steps." Even though his words seemed harsh, Grace was relieved that someone was speaking plainly.

She looked Ian directly in the eye for the first time. His eyes were pale blue, which from a certain angle looked almost silver. "You're right. I do. And that's just what I'm doing."

"Oh, thank God!" Chloe said, obviously pleased. "Everyone—meet my friend Grace."

AFTER BREAKFAST, GRACE and Chloe made the rounds at the vintage stores in the neighborhood. In one store, which was as large as one of the Price Clubs that Grace's parents frequented, Chloe pulled item after item from the tightly packed racks. She placed them in a metal shopping cart and proceeded down the narrow aisles toward the western wear department, which was next to the flannel section at the end of the aisle, just before the flowered muumuus.

Grace was struck by the vastness of the store, but what was even more amazing to her was that everything in the store had once belonged to someone else and that no two things were exactly alike. There was clearly more to this process than just finding something in the right size. She wondered what made one thing right for one person and not another. And did the clothes change the person, or the other way around?

When Grace and Chloe came to a rack of faux-leopard coats, Chloe stopped as if she'd just struck gold and looked at Grace.

"I don't think that's me," Grace said.

"Don't say that until you try it," Chloe responded, choosing one with a straight cut and checking to see if all the buttons were on. Then she grabbed a set of matching earmuffs and a pair of black motorcycle boots.

"It's lucky we got here early," Chloe said, examining the beadwork on a pearl-white cardigan. "You should see the line just to get in after twelve. And then all the good stuff's gone."

Chloe pushed the shopping cart to the dressing room and motioned for Grace to get in line. The woman ahead of her had so much in her cart that it looked like she was buying inventory to open her own vintage store. When it was Grace's turn, the attendant handing out the numbers didn't flinch at the abundance of clothes she was taking into what they called the dressing room— far too loose of a term for the sheer lack of space or privacy it offered. Basically, it was a circular area surrounded by a shower curtain. Grace hung her clothes on hooks that were originally hot-and-cold water faucets and looked down to make sure she wasn't stepping on a drain. Chloe stood outside, handing her clothes from the cart.

"Put this camisole on under the cardigan, and then try on the gray pinstripes. I want to see them on you, so come out," she instructed. "And don't forget the motorcycle boots."

When Grace emerged, she was not wearing a single item of clothing she had come in with, except her black gold-toe socks, which were Laz's, and her underwear. Chloe clapped her hands when she saw Grace, and immediately directed her to a full-length mirror that was leaning against the wall. She stood behind Grace and adjusted the collar on the leopard coat.

For the first time in years, Grace recognized herself. She liked what she saw—from the slouchy pants to the sturdy boots, and even the worn-in leopard coat. She felt awake, her eyes bright and her face glowing, without a stitch of makeup.

"You're back," Chloe said.

"I didn't know I'd been gone."

"Not gone—just in hiding," Chloe answered. "Come on, let's pay and then go get your stuff from the hotel."

"What about my clothes, the ones I came in with?" Grace asked, looking at her pink princess coat draped over a plastic chair.

Leave them. They belong to someone else anyway."

# 26
## MAMBO NIGHT

Grace listened as the pilot informed the passengers that because of dense fog and heavy traffic flying into La Guardia that they would be delayed for at least another hour. She was dressed head to toe in her new vestments, her leopard coat occupying the seat next to her like a wild animal escaped from captivity. The plane circled the airport in a nauseating figure eight. The irony was not lost on Grace, for whom another hour in a holding pattern would hardly make a difference.

When she finally arrived at home, she found a note from Griffin taped to the side of the orchid that she'd rescued from Laz's apartment. She read the letter, noting how similar Griffin's handwriting was to Laz's.

> I will always remember how you let me in and made me feel welcome. My father's lucky to have you. I've decided to go back to Maryland. I can't wait forever for something

that might never happen. It's time to get back to my life. Thank you for all your kindness. Griffin.

She stopped and took a deep breath, then folded the letter. She hadn't been honest with him and felt she deserved no thanks. She wasn't even sure if she had a life to get back to, and this kid knew that his was still waiting for him to return.

The only other sign that Griffin had been there was a stack of plastic containers that had been rinsed out and placed in the kitchen sink. Grace filled the sink with warm soapy water, knowing that Francine expected her containers to be returned in the exact condition that they'd been given, and she suspected the sauce might take some time to dissolve.

She opened the freezer to find that Griffin had defrosted and consumed more than a year's worth of sweet-and-sour meatballs and a dozen bagels in a mere two-day span. The freezer was now empty, except for the spinach lasagna, the birthday blinis, a box of Arm & Hammer baking soda, and two ice trays that Grace didn't even remember having bought.

There were two messages from her parents on the answering machine, confirming Scrabble night. *Best wishes to the birthday girl. And bring the blinis, if you still have them. We're doing a vodka tasting.* With Francine in Paris and Grace having missed celebrating her birthday with her parents, Grace felt obliged to go. She called to report the state of the blinis and to let her parents know that she had something she needed to discuss with them. She feared that if she didn't tell them immediately, she might lose her resolve.

She called the credit card company and was relieved to find that her charge card was no longer frozen, although the limit on her account had been readjusted. She left her suitcase to unpack later, stuffing Laz's filled duffel bag into the back of the hall closet. Then, still wearing her new outfit from Chicago, she grabbed her purse and the blinis and went downstairs to get a taxi.

When Grace arrived at her parents' building, she saw that it was draped with the same black construction netting that covered Laz's old building. Huge Dumpsters blocked the driveway, and she was directed to the service entrance by the doorman.

Milton and Bert were sitting at the kitchen table when Grace walked in. Bert had brought over an assortment of frozen delicacies —pierogi, caviar, as well as a bottle of Ketel One vodka. He'd already poured himself a glass. Grace opened the box of frozen blinis and put them on the kitchen table. Encrusted with a thick layer of ice, they looked more like sand-covered jellyfish than something edible. Grace's father rose and, standing on tiptoe, kissed her on the top of her head.

"Trip okay?" he asked.

"It was fine," she answered, unbuttoning her leopard coat.

"Laz working?" he asked, as if they'd rehearsed this exchange.

"Yes. He sends his best."

"You've got a good one, there. Don't let him go." She knew the next line by heart, but just couldn't manage to get the words out this time.

Her mother entered the kitchen and stood staring at Grace, dumbfounded. "What on earth are you wearing?" she said finally. Grace's father looked up.

"Just my usual," he answered.

"Not you, Milton. *Grace.*"

"She looks the same to me. Maybe a little taller," her father said, still under the misguided impression that he stood five feet ten and a half.

"It must be the boots, Dad," Grace said, feeling herself slouching slightly. She touched the beadwork on her cardigan sweater.

"Chloe picked out some new things for me while I was in Chicago." Her mother approached her, touching the leopard coat with trepidation.

"Secondhand," she determined. "And more than gently used. Well, it's lucky I didn't send that box of odds and ends to Goodwill yet. Oh, and I picked up a pashmina for you on sale at Filenes's to wear to Mambo Night."

"Thanks, Mom, but I already have something to wear," Grace said, shrugging off her coat as well as her mother's comments. "I noticed they're doing some work on the building," she said, hoping to change the subject.

"Keep your voice down," her mother said in a hushed tone. She pulled Grace aside and looked to make sure Milton was sufficiently occupied. "They're refacing the building," her mother whispered, "replacing the blue bricks. Daddy will be beside himself when he finds out—he thinks they're just sandblasting."

Grace knew not to push any further. It was an unspoken rule in her family that keeping people in the dark for as long as possible was a gesture of love and devotion, not deceit. Her mother would no doubt keep this from Milton until the last blue brick had been removed. But, short of giving him a pair of blue-tinted sunglasses, she could not keep him in this state of innocence forever. In a few months' time, he would begin to notice that, brick by brick, his beloved blue building was being transformed into something more subdued and in keeping with the upscale neighborhood in which they lived. If he couldn't take this, how could Grace expect him to take the news of Laz's disappearance? The urge to protect him was strong.

"What's all the whispering?" Bert asked, coming up behind them with a mouthful of caviar.

"Nothing," Grace covered. "Did Francine get off all right?"

"Oh, yes, fine, fine. Except she took enough luggage for an around-the-world tour—almost threw my hip out again. She said her meatballs made quite a hit. So, what were you two girls talking about?"

"I was just telling Grace that we're going to see *Miss Julie* on Friday night."

Bert looked blankly from Grace to her mother. Grace was impressed. Maybe it was from her mother that Grace had inherited her skills at deception.

"Miss who?" Bert asked.

"We have season tickets," Milton chimed in.

"Strindberg," her mother added.

"He's Swedish," Grace's father said, in explanation. Her father always did research before attending a cultural event, reading the scores before attending operas or looking up artists on the Internet before seeing an exhibit. "A disciple of Schopenhauer and a notorious misogynist."

"A misogynist, really?" Bert piped up, as if elated that he was finally able to make a contribution to the conversation. "What kind? Deep tissue or craniosacral?"

Paulette gave Bert a quizzical look. Bert let out a deep sigh when his comment was dismissed and took a sip of his drink. Grace felt a genuine tenderness toward Bert, on whom Francine's absence was clearly taking its toll.

"What was it you wanted to talk to us about, dear?" her mother asked, popping the blinis into the microwave. Grace looked at her father, who was occupied so contentedly at the table with a new gadget that she felt her newfound resolve swiftly fading. Maybe in a day or two, when he'd come to terms with the fate of his beloved blue building. Surely it could wait.

"I was just thinking," Grace said, noticing a few scuff marks that her motorcycle boots had left on her mother's vinyl flooring, "it's been a long time since you've been over. Why don't you and Dad come for dinner Tuesday? I can make a pot of chili."

"You mean the vegetarian one from *The Moosewood Cookbook*?" her mother asked.

"Yes. The one I made for Laz's birthday last year."

"That sounds lovely. I'll bring the entrée."

"That is the entrée," Grace said.

"But you know how much Laz loves my veal roast with the wild rice stuffing."

"Laz won't be there. He has to give a talk in Pittsburgh."

"He can eat it when he gets home. He'll need some protein." Grace noticed that she was beginning to resent her mother's unending doting on Laz. The last thing she wanted was to start filling up the freezer again with things she couldn't eat, now that it had been emptied.

"Tuesday's out," Bert said. "Remember? It's Mambo Night. Must have just slipped your mind, I guess."

"We could make it a late supper," Grace suggested, hoping to allay his fears, but in truth, she'd blocked it out altogether. "After Mambo Night." Nothing short of an act of God could get her out of the Hadassah dance at this point.

"Well, how about we pop over for a quick cannoli from Café La Fortuna?" Grace's father suggested.

"Milton, you know the doctor told you to cut down on saturated fats."

"I can have a taste," he said. "Just a bite. I'll eat the part with the air."

"How's ten?" Grace asked, looking at Bert for approval. She didn't want him to feel slighted. He nodded, closing his eyes and shaking his head resignedly, as if having just given in to a tough all-night negotiation.

"We wouldn't miss it," her mother said.

GRACE THOUGHT OF nothing else over the next two days but how to break the news about Laz to her parents. She didn't know which would be harder — telling them or watching their reaction. If only she didn't have to actually be there. It could go two possible ways.

In the first scenario, after they recovered from the initial shock, her parents would assume total responsibility. In some convoluted way, they would recast the events until the entire thing was their fault. Her father, unable to take another bite of his cannoli, would then walk toward the window, thrust his hands deep into his pockets as if they might contain the solution and not just a crumpled shopping list and a few quarters, and gaze out over the park, at a loss for words. Grace's mother, growing flushed and increasingly frenetic, would spend several minutes deliberating over whether to wrap up the leftovers or do the dishes first. Her father would then notice the state of the Duro-Lites and proceed to disengage the dimmer switch and rewire the circuit that connected to the Christmas tree, after a great fuss about the possibility of being electrocuted. Then, they would all collapse into the sectional couch and put on *The Charlie Rose Show*.

The other, more likely scenario involved her parents coming over for cannolis, and Grace not saying a single word.

PERHAPS IT WAS the salty beluga caviar that her parents had picked up at Costco and Grace had indulgently eaten that caused her hands to retain water. Even two days later, Grace's fingers were swollen and her engagement ring and wedding band were uncomfortably tight. Edema, her father always called it, pumping his fingers and waving his hands in the air after he'd been to a Chinese restaurant, even though he had specified no MSG. Grace removed her rings and dropped them into a small jar, which she filled with sudsing ammonia and water. She gave the jar a shake and watched the glint of diamonds, sapphires, and bubbles swirling around. She turned it upside down. The rings made a hollow tinny sound as they hit the lid.

She found Laz's wedding band right where he'd left it, behind the can of shaving cream in the medicine cabinet. Strangely, the can felt almost empty, even though no one had used it recently, as if in the intervening weeks its contents had just dematerialized. Grace slipped his ring on her finger, imagining the configuration of Laz's knuckles, the indentations and bends in his fingers. She took it off and held it up to the light. The ring all but disappeared as she squinted through it, just a thin circle that from a certain angle was barely detectable.

The more she looked at it, the more she began to see the ring as nothing more than a piece of soldered metal badly in need of cleaning. She tried to rekindle her faith in its powers, but instead, the longer she held it, the more diminished it became. She dropped it into the jar of ammonia with her ring and gave the jar another quick shake, hoping to renew some of its former luster. A marital snow globe. The rings settled in the jar with distance between them, like two caged animals.

It was getting late. Grace rummaged through her closet, looking for something to wear to the Hadassah dance. She found a low-cut red dress and a pair of strappy sandals she'd bought before she met Laz. The one time she wore the outfit, Laz told her she looked like a contestant in the Miss America pageant. She hadn't known how to take the comment at the time, so she had relegated the dress to the back of the closet in case she needed it for a costume party. This seemed an appropriate occasion.

In a last-ditch effort to distract herself from the inevitable pain of telling her parents the truth, she prepared and fussed over a plate of brandied figs on rice crackers. It was amazing how long it took to get the figs to look just right—a task that could have expanded indefinitely, if only she'd actually had the luxury of time. She knew Bert would not appreciate her being late. She covered the plate with plastic wrap, even though the platter was still sorely lacking in aesthetic value. She was about to head out the door when the phone rang.

"Grace? Bert, here." He didn't sound quite like himself.

"Is everything all right?" Grace asked.

"I'm sorry to have to disappoint you, but I threw my hip out, and I'm just in no shape for Mambo Night. You should have seen the cortisone shot they gave me. Francine could skewer a horse with the needle they used." Grace tried to conceal her delight at this turn of events.

"Well, there's always next year," she assured him.

"I know how much you were looking forward to it."

"Don't give it another thought. I'll find something to do. Just take care of that hip."

Grace hung up the phone and was on her way into the bedroom to change when she caught sight of her reflection in the full-length mirror. She walked toward the mirror, lifting the scalloped hem of the skirt a bit, revealing her black fishnet stockings. She had a vague memory of learning to samba at the Barclay School, where she had snapped a pair of castanets in her hands and stamped her feet on the polished floor.

She hadn't danced in ages, but now, all dressed up with nowhere to go, she suddenly felt the urge. She found a Latin music compilation CD that she and Laz had won as a door prize at some charity event, and put it on.

The music was loud and the beat was infectious. Before Grace knew it, she was not only mamboing around the room, she was twirling and shimmying like a Brazilian showgirl. She didn't know what had come over her. All along, she'd been dreading the evening, and here she was having a private Mambo Night by herself. She kicked her leg high in the air, nearly knocking over a standing lamp and almost losing her balance, but it didn't stop her. She felt flushed and unencumbered—she could have danced for hours—until reality once again descended upon her. Her parents were due in less than an hour.

She sat down on the window seat, clutching her knees to her chest, and pictured her parents at home getting ready—her mother telling her father to wear his ecru pullover with the burgundy tie, her father calling down for the car to pick up the cannolis he wasn't even permitted to eat. Grace felt herself faltering. She closed her eyes and thought about the horoscope that Kane had given her for her birthday: *Make a wish. Open your eyes. Did it come true?*

As she tried to formulate her wish, she found her mind wandering off as if in an enchanted forest. The more she tried to bring herself back, the more her mind went around another bend. She found herself wishing for things that made no sense—the taste of pure dark chocolate, a wisp of lilac, untrodden snow, a lump of soft clay, a stretch of silence without fear—all things with no definite beginning or end. Strange wishes. There were none about Laz coming home and their life picking up where it had left off.

She made one last attempt to pinpoint and crystallize her wish. She concentrated. *Did it come true?* She opened her eyes. Kane was standing before her. She got up and turned off the music.

"What are you doing here?" she asked.

"I let myself in," he said. "The doorman buzzed, but no one was picking up. Grace —"

She looked at him and realized from his expression that something was terribly wrong.

"What is it?" she asked.

"Your mother called me from the hospital," Kane said. "She tried calling here, but there was no answer. It's your father. He's had a heart attack."

The room began to spin. Kane put his arms around her, and then they went downstairs to get a taxi to Lenox Hill Hospital.

# 27
# VISITING HOURS

Grace was in the backseat of the cab with Kane, her faux-leopard coat over her shoulders. Even with the heat on, she was shivering.

At the hospital, they rode up in the elevator to the seventh floor, where they found Grace's mother in the waiting room sitting on a nubby, purple armchair. Everything in the room was a different shade of either purple or green, even the huge abstract painting on one wall.

As Grace and Kane approached, Grace was struck by her mother's complete lack of makeup and her unkempt hair. She was dressed in a flannel shirt that belonged to Grace's father, and underneath she had on only sheer stockings and a pair of black snow boots. To Grace, her mother's appearance was a clear indication that the situation was far more serious than she feared. Her mother rushed over as soon as she saw them, dissolving into Kane's arms like a small child.

"He's still in the emergency room," she sobbed.

"Can we see him?" Grace asked.

Her mother shook her head. "Not yet."

"Will he need surgery?"

"They're not sure. They need to see the results from the angiogram first," she said. Kane gave Grace's mother a squeeze. Her eyes began to fill with tears. "My Milton."

"Can I get you anything?" Kane asked.

"Maybe a cup of hot tea, that's all," she answered. "Earl Grey, if they have it. If not, a bottle of seltzer."

Grace walked with Kane down the tiled hallway to the elevator. "I wish Laz were here," she said, half to herself. "If only he were back from his trip."

Kane didn't respond. They stepped into the elevator, which stopped on each floor, although no one got on or off. They walked to the cafeteria in silence. Grace watched as orderlies pushed patients on gurneys down the corridor. The cafeteria was empty, except for one table at which a man and woman were bent over a turkey sandwich that was still wrapped in plastic.

Kane filled a Styrofoam cup with boiling water and picked up a foil-wrapped Earl Grey tea bag. He paid for the tea and handed the cup to Grace.

"I should go. Your family needs you," he said.

"Kane—" she began, then fell silent.

"Don't worry, everything will be all right. I'll call you later," he said, hugging her. Grace watched as he walked down the hall and into an awaiting elevator.

"Thanks for everything," she called after him. He didn't respond, and she wasn't certain whether he'd heard her or not. She stood watching until the elevator door closed, and then she went back upstairs to the waiting room.

GRACE'S MOTHER WAS by the window. Two women in full-length fur coats sat holding hands on a small green couch. Bert had arrived and was in the process of trying to unwrap a bar of Toblerone without making any noise, when he saw Grace approaching and pretended he was just reading the ingredients.

"White chocolate has much more saturated fat than dark chocolate, did you know that?" he asked, placing the bar back on the table.

"How's your hip?" Grace asked, although she didn't see even the slightest evidence of a limp.

"Much better, thanks. Cortisone is a miracle drug," Bert said, giving his hip a pat. He paused and took a deep breath. "Actually, my hip's fine," he said, fumbling with the top button of his overcoat. "It's just that I couldn't bear to go without Francine." Grace put her hand on his shoulder.

"You don't need to explain," she said. Grace could tell he seemed relieved not to have to say more.

"Kane brought you to the hospital?" he said, after a while.

"Yes."

"He's a decent guy," Bert said. Grace nodded in agreement. Then they both sat down to await news about Grace's father.

IT WAS JUST after two o'clock in the morning when the doctor finally came to give them a report, leading them down to the recovery room. "We'd like to keep an eye on him for a few days, just to make sure." As Grace and her mother walked down the hall, the emergency room nurses looked at Grace strangely.

"Only members of the immediate family are allowed in the recovery room," one of the nurses told her.

"I'm his daughter," she said. Grace's mother whispered something to one of the nurses, who nodded and let them go in.

"What did you tell them?" Grace asked.

"I said you had just come from a costume party. What else?"

"It wasn't a costume party," she said, sounding embarrassingly like a nine-year-old after an all-night sleepover party. She couldn't help thinking that if the music hadn't been so loud, she would have heard her mother's call.

"Anyway, that coat is frightening. Now, which room did they say he was in?" Grace's mother stuck her head behind several curtains before locating her husband, who was lying on his back, eyes closed, sucking on a green lollipop.

"He's still a little groggy," a stocky nurse said as she made some notations on a chart with a chewed pencil. Grace sat on the edge of the bed, her mother on the only chair in the room. Her father began to stir. He opened his eyes and smiled weakly.

"Gracie," he said faintly, still sucking on the lollipop. He tried to raise his arms to embrace her, but with the tubes, he could only make a feeble attempt. "Would you like anything to eat or drink? There's ice water and some tea biscuits," he said, pointing to the nightstand. "They said later I can have some chicken broth."

Grace was almost brought to tears by her father's display of hospitality, as if he were hosting a party. Grace's mother got up to examine the ingredients on the package of tea biscuits. She took out her reading glasses from her purse and went over to the light.

"These are fine," she determined, opening the plastic wrapper and offering one to Grace, who shook her head.

"You look good, Dad," she said, although his body looked small and frail in the thin cotton hospital gown.

"Sorry we couldn't make it tonight," he said. "You wanted to tell us something?"

"Another time," she said, rubbing her hands together, even though she wasn't cold anymore. "When you're feeling better. You should rest now." He closed his eyes again. He was wearing a pair of blue paper slippers on his feet. A plastic balloonlike instrument was wrapped around his calves, automatically filling with air every few seconds and then deflating, to prevent blood clots. Grace's mother motioned for her to come near.

"You really should go home and get some rest, Grace. No need for all of us to stay. Bert's here if I need him. Come back in the morning when your father's feeling more himself. Visiting hours start at nine."

"If you're sure you'll be okay. I can go by the apartment if you need anything."

"Well, only if it's not out of the way. Maybe a pair of slippers and a robe, for your father. And my makeup kit."

THE FIRST THING that struck Grace when she walked into her parents' apartment just before four in the morning was how dark and empty it was. The television was tuned to the Weather Channel, but the sound was muted. She'd become so used to conjuring Laz's presence; but now, as she walked through the empty apartment closing doors and turning on lights, she realized that her actions weren't done in order to conjure a life, they were to ease the pain.

Her parents had clearly left in a hurry. All the signs of panic were there: an overturned container of buttermilk on the countertop, pulled-out chairs, the refrigerator door left open.

She pictured her mother running to her father's aid in the bedroom, where drawers were flung open and an empty bottle of medicine was on the nightstand. In the adjoining bathroom, she found cotton balls tumbling out of the medicine cabinet, a wet washcloth on the floor, and her father's black comb with a few white hairs on it. Grace began to clean up. She stuffed the cotton balls back into the now-bulging box, threw the washcloth in the hamper, and went back to the kitchen. But even when everything was put back in order, Grace could do nothing to obliterate the emptiness that remained.

She found a small, black WQXR tote bag still wrapped in plastic underneath the coat tree, like a forgotten present on Christmas morning. Her father's maroon bathrobe was hanging in his closet next to his beige and pale gray button-down shirts. With its pointed shoulders and slouched back, the robe looked only slightly less inhabited than her father had in his hospital gown. She folded it neatly and placed it into the tote bag along with his corduroy slippers. Her mother's supersize, clear-plastic makeup bag was too large to fit, so she put it with a pleated skirt, a pair of shoes, and sweater set into a plastic grocery bag.

Walking aimlessly around the apartment, Grace found herself pausing in front of her old bedroom. She went in and knelt down on the soft green carpeting. In the fifth grade, Grace had brought home two gerbils, which in a matter of weeks had multiplied to twenty-eight. The plastic cage, filled with cedar shavings, had toppled over one afternoon, sending the gerbils scampering across the kitchen floor, running behind the refrigerator and stove, never to be seen again. As Grace opened the drawers underneath her bed, she half-expected to find a scene straight out of *Miss Bianca*—her long-lost gerbils sitting on silver swings and having a tea party in a white pagoda.

Inside the deep double drawers were her possessions, although none of them were even vaguely familiar to her as she inspected them. She waited for the memories to kick in, as if somewhere encoded in the fibers of the clothes or the books there was preserved a strand of her former self.

As she rummaged through the drawers, Grace felt as if she were invading someone's privacy. The things she was looking for were no longer there and never had been. They were the things she'd lost along the way—the twenty-eight gerbils, the calculator pen, the holes in her grandmother's afghan, Laz, and herself. The things unrecoverable. The unopened drawers had once held out the possibility of recovery, and now that was lost, too. She thought about her father offering her tea biscuits from his hospital bed. She couldn't bear to lose him also. She closed the drawers and laid down on the carpet. Then finally, the tears came, silent and streaming down her face.

THE CLOCK ON the blue nightstand read six-fifteen when she awoke. Still nearly three hours until she could go back to the hospital. She went into the guest bathroom and splashed cold water on her face. On the marble pedestal sink, there were candles and beauty products arranged in neat white baskets. There were even products *pour hommes,* in case a male guest needed a bit of freshening up.

She applied some alpha-hydroxy moisturizer with aloe to her face and dabbed chamomile gel on her noticeably puffy eyelids, convincing herself that she could see changes occurring right before her eyes. The urge to improve herself was hard to resist. Suddenly, her mother's makeup kit held out a kind of promise. She got the bag and unzipped it, looking at the array of products with confusion. What looked like mascara turned out to be a mauve eye stick, the tube of what she thought was lipstick was actually cream blusher.

After she was finished, she looked like a character in a black-and-white movie that had been improperly colorized. She washed the makeup off her face and zipped up her mother's makeup kit. It would always be a bag of tricks that required a proper magician.

The clock on the nightstand in her bedroom still read six-fifteen. She went into the kitchen and stared at the clock on the wall in disbelief. It was nearly ten-thirty. She pulled on an old pair of Levi's she'd found in her closet, a light blue turtleneck sweater (slightly moth-eaten) from the top drawer of her dresser, and headed back to the hospital.

WHEN GRACE ENTERED her father's hospital room, it was as if her mother had aged ten years from the night before. Her hair was pulled back in a short ponytail and she had raccoon eyes from lack of sleep combined with crying. Her father appeared to be asleep, but as soon as Grace walked in, he began speaking.

"Is that you, Grace?"

"Yes," she answered, bending down to give him a kiss.

"So good of you to come." His voice sounded weak.

"How are you feeling?" she asked.

"Just fine. I should be home by tomorrow. Friday by the latest."

"I brought you your slippers and a robe." He reached his hand out to touch her on the arm. His eyelids began to flutter.

"I don't know what I would do without you and Laz. And mother," he added. "It was so nice of Laz to come this morning."

"This morning?" Grace turned to her mother for verification. Her mother was leafing through the current issue of *The New York Review of Books*. She looked back at her father and saw that he'd drifted off again. Grace had expected that he would be groggy, but delusional was another thing altogether.

"Did you say something, honey?" her mother asked.

"Dad says Laz was here."

"Oh, yes. I guess I just missed him. I went down to the cafeteria for a cup of tea. I tried to make a manicure appointment at Pinky's, but they weren't open yet."

"What time?" Grace asked.

"Around six-fifteen," her mother answered. "They really should have all-night manicurists." Grace's heart froze in concert with all the clocks.

"I thought visiting hours didn't start until nine," she said. For all she knew, Laz might have been there—but just as easily not. Grace understood that this was a time when her father would have needed Laz. At his most fragile, he needed to summon his family to his bedside. Her father could tolerate Laz's absence at Scrabble games, just not when it came to heart attacks.

"The nurses must have let him sneak in," her mother said matter-of-factly. "You know how he charms people." Her father began to stir.

"He read me a chapter of that *Oblomov* book you two like so much," he said, not missing a beat. He was able to drift seamlessly in and out of conversations—even consciousness—while listening to a particularly soporific Debussy piece at Avery Fisher Hall, during one of Grace's mother's lengthy and detailed accounts of her shopping expeditions, or at a lecture at the Ninety-second Street Y, and yet still remain completely engaged. It was a talent that now seemed that much more precious to Grace as he lay recuperating in a hospital bed. "He says I'll be back on my feet way before that Oblomov guy gets out of his robe."

Grace looked around. There was no book in sight, only a tattered issue of *Reader's Digest* on the nightstand. She guessed that the drugs must still be in his system, but whether Laz had been there or not was not important. He was there now just as much as he had ever been.

Bert walked in the room carrying a huge basket of what Laz liked to call *bon voyages* fruit—apples, pears, and mangoes fit for Gulliver. On his head, Bert sported a dapper fedora, around his neck a silk scarf. He looked well rested and in good spirits, better than Grace had seen him since Francine's departure. He placed the basket of fruit on a table by the window and waited for some sort of acknowledgment, which when received, he quickly brushed off.

"It's the least I could do," he said, reaching into his breast pocket and taking out a travel-size Scrabble board. Grace was convinced that in some other pocket he had a miniature twin edition of the *Oxford English Dictionary.* "Anyone up for a friendly game?" he asked, assuming it was a rhetorical question and proceeding to set up the board.

Grace walked over to the window and stared out over the tops of low buildings that were all the same generic tan or white brick. Soon her parents' building would blend in among the rest of them, distinguishable only by slight design variations and the street address marked on the awning.

"Can we entice you to join us?" Grace's mother asked. The game was already in progress. Her father had a tile rack and was shuffling his letters, but Grace could detect the faraway look in his eyes. She recognized the tendency in herself, too, her mind evaporating into utter blankness. She, however, had not perfected the ability to remain engaged while also being elsewhere.

"I'm sorry, what did you ask me?" Grace said.

"Do you want to join us?" her mother asked again.

"I think I need to get some air," Grace said.

GRACE WALKED AROUND the corner to Le Pain Quotidien, a restaurant with long, rough-hewn tables and French country decor. Almost all the patrons in the restaurant wore large hats, their faces hidden behind newspapers. She pulled up her sleeves and leaned on the table. When her pot of Earl Grey tea arrived, the bergamot smell reminded her of Chloe. She poured a cup. Some loose tea leaves swirled to the bottom. She looked for some sign in the pattern, but none appeared.

In Chicago, everything had seemed so simple. She recalled the sight of herself in the mirror at the thrift shop. For some reason, she pictured herself unpacking a car filled with her belongings in front of a Victorian row house on a snowy street in Wicker Park. It all seemed so real—everything from the lime-green Volkswagon bug to the fuzzy purple hat on her head, until she remembered her father in the dreary hospital bed. She felt she'd never have the courage to leave.

Owning up to the truth, which in Chicago had come to her surprisingly easily, now seemed impossible. But the idea that her own father had succumbed to the power of self-deception was a far more unsettling prospect. It was like leaving her father snared in a web while she held a pair of scissors in her hand. She understood the impulse to believe in the status quo. They all wanted Laz to be there. Even in his absence, he still existed for them, as if it were as simple as slipping into one of his dove-gray T-shirts and waiting for sleep. Her father would be expecting Laz to visit again. More than anything, she didn't want him to be disappointed. Even if Laz had been there, it didn't mean he would come again. She couldn't protect her father forever. The best she could do was cushion the blow.

Just as she had poured her second cup of tea and was about to reach for a packet of raw sugar, she sensed she was being watched. She glanced up quickly. Across the wide table she saw a man, the brim of his hat pulled down over his brow. He was leafing through the peach-colored pages of *The Observer*. She noticed the headline: PULITZER PRIZE RESCINDED FOR KOSOVO CAMP ACCOUNT. The man nodded to her. A complete stranger. She gave a sigh of relief that it hadn't been Mr. Dubrovsky, but part of her was disappointed. For all the uneasiness the idea that she was being followed caused her, in some way it gave her a small amount of comfort. Someone, for whatever reason, would have been watching over her. She nodded back to the gentleman as the sugar crystals dissolved into her steaming cup of tea.

GRACE STOPPED IN the hospital gift shop for a pack of gum before going up to her father's room. As she was on line to pay, she noticed a stack of Hadassah cookbooks. Grace leafed through one, turning the pages and looking absently at the familiar, tried-and-true recipes. She was nearing the end of the book, having just passed a kugel recipe made with pineapple and maraschino cherries, when she saw a recipe for Trudie's Famous Sweet-and-Sour Meatballs. She read through the list of ingredients: two parts chili sauce to one part Welch's grape jelly. A bag of minimarshmallows were needed to sprinkle on top for a glaze.

Grace was about to close the book when she recalled the incident with Francine in the Food Emporium, Francine's cart precariously loaded with enough jelly and chili sauce to drown several cows, and it all began to make perfect sense: everything from Francine's adamant refusal to give away her secret recipe to her quick exit at the supermarket, and finally her excess baggage. She had obviously smuggled the ingredients in her suitcase for a recipe even the French would not be able to duplicate. All these years of subterfuge, and here was the recipe in bold type for the bargain price of ten dollars.

Although the vehemence with which Francine had guarded this secret was out of proportion to the reason, the idea that a secret— even one so seemingly insignificant—had grown to such consuming magnitude was as familiar to Grace as her favorite pillow. She had an overwhelming feeling of compassion for Francine. She understood the impulse to maintain the illusion. Indeed, there was safety in it, but at the same time it invariably kept everyone at arm's length. Grace and Francine were in the same self-made predicament. The deception wasn't just for them. The result of going this far and with such success was that everyone around them became invested in it. Francine may have known this, protecting her illusions like a mother lion her cubs. Taking it away seemed wrong, although Grace knew she must. The dilemma now was about finding the right time for it to be undone.

Grace's father was asleep when she entered the room. She recalled a phrase she had heard her mother once use when his mother died. *It took the starch right out of him.* She imagined her father hanging limply on a clothesline, as if all that was required to resurrect him now was the simple addition of the right solvent to the rinse cycle.

Bert and her mother were nowhere in sight, the Scrabble match abandoned midgame. Grace read the words on the board: *frigid, agog, genus, kin, null.* The usual assortment of esoteric words. She wondered how many words Bert had challenged. She glanced at her father's letters. In front of his tile holder, next to the plastic pitcher of water on the wood-grained Formica swinging table, he had spelled out the word *grace.*

Even Grace, a novice in the world of etymology, could see that there was no place on the board where it could possibly fit.

Grace sat at her father's bedside and waited. She hoped the words would come when she needed them. She looked at her left hand, and saw that she had forgotten to put her rings back on. Strangely, there was still a deep indentation in her skin where the rings had been. Her father began to stir. Then he opened his eyes.

"Grace," he said. "How long was I sleeping?"

"Not long."

"You should have woken me."

"Dad?" she said, quietly. "I need to talk to you about something. Is this an okay time?"

"It's always a fine time to talk to my daughter." The room began to grow dark. Grace looked out the window. She could see menacing storm clouds gathering in the distance. She thought about the rain showers her father used to give her.

"Do you still have that Mary Poppins umbrella?" she asked. He smiled, closed his eyes again.

"I think it's in the front hall closet. Why?"

"Just asking."

"What's it like out today?"

"It looks like it's about to storm."

"Did you wear boots?"

"Yes," she said. Grace touched her father's hand.

"What is it, Grace? Something wrong?"

"It's just that I miss you."

"I'm right here, sweetie."

"This is hard," she said. "It's about Laz."

"Laz?" he repeated, slowly.

"He's not coming tomorrow."

"Hmm," he said.

"He's not coming tomorrow or the next day. He didn't come today. He doesn't even know you're in the hospital. He's been gone. Since Halloween. I know this won't make any sense to you right now, but I did all this to protect you and Mom. I thought he was coming back. I'm sorry I didn't tell you. If I could change things, I would. Please forgive me." Grace stopped. The words seemed disembodied, even though she knew they had come out of her mouth. Tears ran down her cheeks. She looked at her father's face. His expression was calm and placid. He touched her arm.

"What's that, honey?"

"Laz is gone," she said, reaching for a tissue and blowing her nose.

"That's nice, dear. Send him our best." Grace wiped her eyes and watched the rain pelting the windowpane.

"I will," she answered. "As soon as I see him."

# 28

## THE UNINVITED GUEST

The next morning, when Grace arrived at the hospital, a resident was talking to her mother in that disturbing hushed tone that doctors use when something's wrong.

"His enzymes are high. We think there may still be a blockage in one of the arteries."

Grace walked closer. Her heart began to palpitate, and she considered asking for her own thallium stress test. Her first thought was that the conversation she'd had with her father the day before had registered on some corrosively subliminal level, and that it was now wreaking havoc on his system. She wished there were a version of the M.R.I. to determine whether her words had penetrated his consciousness. She feared that the truth might have done more damage to him than withholding it. Maybe the truth was vastly overrated. Maybe lies were the glue that bound people together like connective tissue, maintaining the fibers of interpersonal relationships, allowing for freedom of movement without pain. Maybe some truths are not meant to be known. Grace couldn't forgive herself. She should have let him be.

She stood next to her mother and listened to the prognosis. Then, as they wheeled her father down the hall for his second procedure in two days, Grace ran downstairs and onto the street, heading to Kane's. She would tell him everything.

SHE RODE THE elevator to the ninth floor and rang the bell. She rang again. She was about to leave when she heard sounds from within. The door opened. Before her stood a woman with long, tousled dark hair, wearing only a large blue hockey jersey. Grace checked to make sure she had rung the right bell.

"Can I help you?" the woman asked.

"Is Kane here?" She hesitated, then said, "It's Grace." The woman smiled and motioned for her to come in.

"Hold on, I'll get him." She turned to walk into the other room, and as she did, Grace saw white lettering on the back of the shirt. It spelled out the name *Gregg*. Grace's mind tried to assimilate the barrage of information that was whizzing by her. Slowly, it began to make sense. This person in front of her was Kane's Greg, only *this* Gregg was a long-legged, half-naked woman who spelled her name with two *g*s. Grace heard Kane from the bedroom. She wanted to bolt for the elevator, but he appeared before she could make her getaway.

"Grace," he said when he came out, wearing only a pair of boxers. Between the two of them, they had one complete outfit. "Is something wrong?"

"I just wanted to let you know that my father's going into surgery again. There's another blockage." Grace thought about her father undergoing surgery, entering that state of twilight sleep where there is no pain.

"Come on in. Let's talk."

"No, I really should get back," she said, glancing at her watch. She couldn't stay. Not now, with Gregg here. She knew she had no right to feel jealous, but still, with all her might, she wished this long-legged interloper would disappear. Kane was supposed to be hers—gay, straight, or otherwise.

"Stay for a little while. Are you hungry? Gregg's making blueberry pancakes." Grace imagined the wheat-free, gluten-free, egg-free, dairy-free, fat-free concoction and shook her head, knowing that she was being offered a breakfast without ingredients.

"I'd really like to, but I need to get back to the hospital," she said again. What she really needed at that time was, as her father would say, a mystery to her.

"We'll be thinking about you," Kane said, giving her a hug. "Let me know how it goes."

"Nice to finally meet you, Grace," Gregg said, slipping her arm around Kane's waist. "Kane never stops talking about you."

"You, too," Grace said, and then quickly walked to the elevator.

THE SURGERY WENT WELL—Grace's father was back in the recovery room sucking on another lollipop, Bert was in the hallway in yet another hat, and Grace's mother was giving makeup tips to a woman about to undergo radiation treatment. Although Grace had no proof that her confession had actually penetrated deeper than the surface of her father's tympanic membrane, it was a beginning, and her faith in the curative power of truth was once again restored.

"Makeup is for life," she heard her mother say. "It makes all the difference. For you and everyone around you. That, and a great outfit, of course." Grace had visions of an infomercial hosted by her mother, and she avoided looking at her for fear of being doused with some hypoallergenic beauty product or accosted with an implement supposed to endow her with perfection. Grace stayed until visiting hours were over, kissed her still groggy father on the cheek, and told him she'd see him in the morning. Then she rode back to her apartment through the park.

José held the door open for her when she stepped out of the taxi. He looked her up and down as her mother had done numerous times since her return from Chicago, and Grace prepared herself for whatever comment awaited her.

"Nice coat," he said, after appraising it. "I like your new look."

She smiled. As she passed him and walked toward the elevator, she said, "It's not new, actually. Just something I'd forgotten I had."

When the elevator doors opened and Grace stepped out into the hall vestibule, she saw dry cleaning hanging from her front door. Through the plastic, she could see Laz's leather jacket and pants, returned like homing pigeons. On the small table next to the door there was a package tied with kite string. It was about the size of one of her father's old cigar boxes, and written on the front in black marker was Grace's name and apartment number. There was no return address. She wasn't in the mood for any more surprises.

She brought the dry cleaning and the mysterious package inside, hanging Laz's jacket back in the closet. She looked down at her polyester-blend, faux-leopard coat and grazed the soft pile with her hand. She wondered if it, too, wasn't just another kind of wrapping.

But then she realized the difference — she had chosen it not to fit in or to transform herself in some way, but because for once it fit her, instead of the other way around. Maybe another day she would feel like wearing pink polka dots, or white tulle with sequins, or nothing special at all. The only thing that mattered was that it would be *her* choice.

She went into the bedroom to unwrap the package, and just as she was cutting the string, the telephone rang.

"Grace," her mother said, cheerfully. "Thank you for the raisin biscotti. Daddy loved them." While her mother was talking, Grace went into the bathroom, cradling the phone under her chin, and reached under the sink for the jar of ammonia. She fished her wedding and engagement rings out with a pencil, dried them, and slipped them on her finger—but they wouldn't go farther than her second knuckle. Her mother had always told her never to take off her wedding ring. Now she understood why.

"Cholesterol-free, and no one would ever know it," her mother continued. "If you dip them in coffee, they're just perfect." Grace was about to say that she had no idea what her mother was talking about when she realized what was in the package that was lying on her bed. She lifted it up and weighed it in her hands.

She could visualize the words, the lines, even the spaces between the words—the silent, blank patterns that emerged like breaths separating the lines. Her mouth moved as she recited a phrase from memory: *Life is poetry, if people don't distort it.* Her life was more like Silly Putty, stretched and contorted, rendered silly beyond recognition. Her life, far from poetic, was collecting dust.

She slid her finger underneath the butcher paper and let the book fall into her hands. It was Mr. Dubrovsky's beaten up, scrawled-upon copy of *Oblomov.* She had no idea how it had gotten there and even less how to return it to him. The definitive edition of *Oblomov Uninvited.* She tossed it on the comforter. Oblomov was back in bed once more.

Unless, like the raisin biscotti, it had delivered itself. Grace preferred not knowing who had sent it.

"I'm glad he liked them," she said to her mother.

# 29
## SPRING CLEANING

A week after her father's first surgery, and three days before Christmas Eve, Grace decided it was time to tell her parents the truth.

"To what do we owe this pleasure?" her father asked, when he answered the door. He was wearing a button-down shirt and pajama bottoms.

"Why didn't you call first?" her mother asked, rushing down the hall and untying her apron. "We might have been out."

"We're not out, Paulette. You haven't let me out in a week, except to go to the doctor's."

"How are you feeling, Dad?"

"Fine. The doctor says I'll be back to my old self in no time. Better than new."

"Can we sit?" Grace asked. "There's something I have to tell you."

"Sure, honey," her mother said. "I'm making some turkey broth for your father. You'll stay for lunch."

Grace and her parents walked into the living room and sat down on the couch. The shades were drawn to block out the afternoon sun. She began to tell them the story of the past three months, this time unabridged. While he listened, Milton sighed deeply and grasped for his wife's hand, which she pulled away, running it through her hair.

"There's no point in saying I'm sorry." Grace paused, then ended by saying, "It won't make this easier or take away the pain. But I am. And I love you both very much." After she was finished, the three of them sat in silence.

Finally, her mother spoke. "He'll be back—he wouldn't leave us. And we'll just act like nothing happened."

"I can't do that anymore," Grace said quietly. Her father began to sob, covering his face with his hands.

"What, Dad?" Grace asked, moving closer to him and putting her arm around his shoulder.

"I can't help you," he said, through his tears.

"That's okay. I don't need help now." Grace held out the box of tissues. He took one.

"How are we going to tell Bert and Francine?" he asked, blowing his nose.

"Why involve them yet? Nothing's definite," her mother said. Grace looked at her parents. She knew that they weren't ready to see the finality of the situation, and that this was all they could do. For now. But she also knew she had to do more.

THE ONLY DIFFERENCE preconfession and postconfession was that where before every conversation had been peppered with references to Laz, now his name simply never came up. With Grace's parents or the Sugarmans, his name was not only avoided, it was verboten, but not for the reasons that might be commonly expected. It wasn't to spare Grace's feelings or to protect her from what they feared might turn out to be a harsh reality; it was as if the mere utterance of Laz's name might in some way actually awaken the dead. It was a *shonda*—a word that almost defies translation. So, instead, they went through the motions and kept things hushed, in the hopes of not jinxing what they secretly wished would turn out to be a happy reunion.

For Grace, though, it was significantly worse than before. Now she was truly alone. While in some ways her parents' denial looked like a rather comfy choice, it was an option no longer available to her. Denial was not a gift certificate in a self-addressed, stamped envelope, redeemable at any time. It had run its course in Grace's case. She'd invented this story of a stable, stationary husband in order to keep things in place, a bracket around the relationship, a scaffolding to hold things up while she contemplated an entirely new marital strategy. But there was nothing left to hold up. The bricks were coming down.

ON CHRISTMAS EVE, Laz's mother hosted an annual evening of caroling at her building on Park Avenue and Ninety-second Street. Grace arrived early to tell her about Laz. Nancy Brookman was the only one who wasn't at all fazed by her son's departure. In fact, she had anticipated it all along. "Like father, like son," she said. It wasn't a matter of *if* he would leave, but *when.*

Nancy had hired a choir of Juilliard students to lead the carols throughout the building, with the party eventually winding up upstairs at her penthouse duplex for crepes and Irish coffee by a roaring fire. The carolers stopped in each of the four stairwells, singing several traditional arrangements as the sound echoed up the marble vestibules. The stairs were lit with votive candles, the air perfumed with frankincense. The caroling culminated with *Silent Night* around the brilliantly lit twenty-foot Douglas fir in the center of the courtyard.

Grace sang out as if she'd gone to parochial school instead of a progressive independent school on the Upper West Side. After the final refrain of *Silent Night,* her mother-in-law approached her.

"I hope you're not going to waste your time pining away for that husband of yours. You can't expect a Brookman to make good, you know. Hopeless dilettantes, all of them. At least his father had the sense to leave before he scandalized the rest of the family," she said, stopping to adjust the velvet collar on her jet black suit. "Thank God, I had the prescience of mind to readjust Lazarus's credit card before it was too late." She followed the carolers up the stairs from the courtyard into the building, teetering on her slender heels. "He may be my son, but it's my family's money he's been squandering. And I hope you don't expect me to support you, either."

Grace felt emotions swelling inside her as they had that day in Dr. Gaylin's office, but this time the right words came. "I can't believe you would think that about me," she said. "But if that had been my intention, I would have been entitled to the money."

"That's what Merrin said, too, and look where it got her."

"Merrin?"

"She can write all the letters she wants, but Griffin is not my grandson, no matter what she says." Laz's mother stood in the doorway as if blocking Grace's entrance. Grace thought about the child she might have had with Laz, and that this selfish woman would have been its grandmother.

"Excuse me," she said, gathering her courage, "Nancy." The name stuck in her throat as she uttered it for the first and last time. "I've met him. He definitely is Laz's son. And you don't deserve him."

"You've never spoken to me like this before," Nancy replied, raising her eyebrows.

"I'm just sorry it wasn't sooner," Grace said as she turned to leave.

AFTER HEARING THE news of Laz's departure, Marisol, in what could almost be described as post-traumatic stress syndrome, became obsessed with cleaning out Laz's closet. It was not in an effort to purge the apartment of his presence, rather it was with the express purpose of preparing for what she believed would be his inevitable return.

"Señor Lazarus will be with us soon. I know he will. *Mi lindo, lindo,*" Marisol would mumble periodically to herself throughout the day.

Grace allowed the proceedings to continue, partly out of sympathy for Marisol and partly because the closet had become so overrun with dust, plastic wrapping, and wire hangers from the dry cleaners that it had become impossible to find anything inside. Not that she really needed anything from it. Other than stationery supplies and tax returns, there was little of use at all to Grace and apparently to Laz, as well.

Everything in the closet was covered with opalescent white dust, as if the asbestos that had been removed from Laz's old apartment had migrated through the pipes and underneath the floorboards. Laz's shoes looked like they'd just returned from a walk in the snow. Marisol carefully took each pair out of the closet as if she were holding Cinderella's precious glass slippers, and lined them up on newspapers in the pantry, where she waxed and buffed them to a high-glossed sheen.

Marisol hand-washed each of Laz's Brooks Brothers shirts, painstakingly pressing them, replacing cracked buttons, and blowing into the sleeves to prevent creases, which made them eerily appear to be inhabited by an invisible body. Then she hung them on wooden hangers that had been covered with tissue paper. The shirts looked like new. Although Grace kept the thought from Marisol, the thrift store wouldn't know what had hit them when they eventually received the donation. Grace gathered up the pile she had made of plastic wrap, compressed it, and brought it to the back door, where she stuffed it into the garbage can. It took up less room than a bag of daily trash—all air and no substance.

The reorganizing and cleaning took several days to complete. Nothing was left undone, unturned, or unpolished. Once the closet was all finished, Grace had trouble closing the door. As hard as she tried to get the door to stay shut, it kept springing back open. The hinges had just given out. Laz's possessions were now on twenty-four-hour display. Each time Grace passed the closet, she was brought to tears. To her, it was akin to looking at an open casket. It bothered her so much that she put a large stack of books in front of the door, but after a while, the books were pushed out and the door would once again open. After several days, as with most unpleasant things, she learned to live with it.

Marisol and Grace continued for days as if possessed, until the entire apartment was not only organized, it was also alphabetized. Even the piano bench and utility closet were now showcases of organization, and Grace had found the missing extension cord inside an empty thermal bag, where it had been all along. Nothing was out of place or missing—except for Laz. And although his presence had shrunk considerably (now measurable in cubic feet), Grace still wasn't ready to fill the space with anything else.

One thing that Grace made sure that she salvaged was the block of clay she had found with Griffin, which Marisol had put out by the back elevator along with the trash. Marisol, having recently seen an episode of *Martha Stewart Living* concerning the proper way to fold towels, was busy attacking the linen closet, as Grace smuggled the clay back inside.

LATE THAT NIGHT, Grace sat at the dining room table with the block of clay in front of her. She unwrapped it, touching the cool surface. Its blankness beckoned to her. She looked at her hands, her only tool, and began to work the clay.

Her fingers felt clumsy at first, and she wasn't sure what she wanted to make. She pounded the clay with the heel of her hand. The more she tried to force it into a shape, though, the more resistant the clay became. She added some water with a sponge. After a while, she simply allowed the clay to move in her hands, rolling and pressing it, following its contours. As she did, she found it became more malleable, until she began to see an emerging form. In a flash, she could envision what it would be.

The sheer texture and possibility of the clay became intoxicating. Like her first crochet stitches, this piece began to take on a life of its own. She looked at the form before her. It was rough, but its dimensions, curves, and lines were clear. It was a woman sitting in a chair, her back straight, her chin lifted. But the more Grace looked at it, the more ambiguous it appeared. She couldn't tell if the woman was in the process of sitting down or getting up, as if the figure were caught midway between the two. Grace rested her hands on the table, then wrapped the sculpture in wet towels. There was plenty of time to decide.

TWO DAYS BEFORE New Year's Eve, Kane called to see if Grace wanted to take a quick ride up to his lake house. The pipes had frozen and burst, and he needed to oversee the plumber. Gregg was off on a photo shoot in Europe.

"It will be good for you to get away," he told her. "You can't stay in that apartment forever."

"Why not?" she asked, only half-joking. Truthfully, Grace had had enough of watching Marisol organize the closets. "But only if you promise not to talk about anything of substance."

"No problem. I won't say a word. We won't even look at each other if that makes you feel better."

"It does."

"Great. I'll bring the sandwiches. You bring your skates." Kane had already hung up before Grace could protest.

During the two-hour drive up to the cabin, Kane, true to his word, did not initiate any conversation other than innocuous subjects, such as rising gas prices or random icicle sightings. They arrived at the house around two. Kane carried Grace's skates as he walked up the slate steps and held the door open for her. The house smelled of pine and wet wool, just as she had remembered. She couldn't recall whether the last time she had been there it had been winter or summer, if they'd skinny-dipped or if Laz had ventured out onto the ice. It was as if a crucial file had been erased.

Kane dropped off the bag of sandwiches in the kitchen and headed out the back door, beckoning for Grace to follow him. They walked down the narrow wooden dock to the lake and Kane sat on a makeshift bench at the end of it. He put on his hockey skates and laced them up. Looking out at the lake, which was covered with a thick layer of ice, he handed Grace her skate bag and waited. She stood motionless, pondering how to get out of doing this. She gazed out over the tundralike vista, then sat down on the bench next to Kane and unzipped her bag. Once on, her skates were tight. Her ankles wobbled as she walked back down the dock and stepped carefully onto the edge of the frozen lake.

"I think I'll just watch for a while," she said. "You go on."

"Suit yourself," he said, pushing off onto the ice and skating away as if chasing a puck in a championship game. He looked so untethered. Grace tried to talk herself through her fear. What was there to fear, after all, besides falling into the depths of an icy black abyss?

She scuttled to the side and was about to get off the ice when she remembered what Chloe's friend Jeff had said over those huge omelets: *Leap and the net will appear.* She certainly hadn't been doing any leaping as of late. That would require actually leaving the apartment.

She admired the expanse of white before her, pure and unadulterated like the untouched clay. She imagined her feet making interlocking loops, a pattern she could not only follow, but could direct. She closed her eyes, pushed off, and found herself gliding out across the ice. She did a figure eight and an arabesque. When she opened her eyes, she saw Kane skating toward her.

"Can I talk now?" Kane asked.

"Will it do any good if I say no?"

"Probably not," he said, skating backward. "That was great. I just wanted to tell you that I knew you could do it. And your skating's improved, too."

"Thanks. I didn't." She felt herself inhaling deeply as if for the first time.

"Kane?"

"Yes, Grace?"

"How long did you know about Laz?"

"The day we went to get the Christmas tree," he answered. Grace remembered how he'd lingered at the apartment when he was setting up the tree. "I didn't know whether I should shake you or the tree. Maybe I should have tried harder, but I was feeling the loss, too. Laz is my best friend, and you and I have this weird relationship. Before Gregg, it was like we were this threesome. Now I have no idea where any of this is going."

"Come on," Grace said. Then she took his hand, and together they skated off to the far side of the lake.

# 30
# LIGHTS OUT

The Scrabble-game-cum-Mexican Fiesta Night at the Sugarmans on New Year's Eve was less than festive. Even though the
Bali room had been transformed into a millennium Mayan temple,
complete with ceremonial statues and traditional painted bark decorations hanging from the windows, the evening was noticeably
muted. While the whole city was divided between gearing up for an
all-holds-barred last night of the century or stocking up on bottled
water, videos, and Y2K restoration kits, Grace's parents and the
Sugarmans were just laying low, hoping not to cause any more unnecessary rifts.

The Mayan temple theme, Grace thought, was quite apt—a
bulwark against encroaching enemies and evil spirits. She just wondered who would be offered up as the sacrifice.

It was cold in the Bali room, so Grace's father and Bert had
hooked up a space heater, which glowed orange like the mouth of a
volcano. The combination of the heater and Bunsen burner for the

blue corn quesadillas made the glassed-in room fog up. With the mirrors covered by swaths of fabric, it was as if, in a way, they were all sitting shiva for the dead in a Mayan temple.

Francine was dressed in a long, white authentic Mexican wedding dress, which she'd bought for twelve dollars on a cruise that she and Bert had taken to Acapulco last March. She was still very much on a high from her culinary excursion, the evidence of which was laid out in Aztec crockery and woven baskets, a veritable feast of authentic delicacies. Grace's father looked tired, but he didn't complain, participating with his usual gracious enthusiasm.

"Francine, you've outdone yourself," Bert said, taking a bite of grilled octopus with mole sauce. "You always cease to amaze me."

Francine rolled her eyes. "I think you have that backward," she said.

"You mean *I* always cease to amaze *you*?" he asked. "Why, thank you."

"Something like that," Francine answered, kissing him on the cheek.

"Looks like the honeymoon isn't over yet after all," Bert said, winking at Francine.

"Don't press your luck," she said, before walking briskly into the kitchen to attend to the black-bean soufflé.

AFTER DINNER, THE Scrabble board was set up. Between bites of warm sopaipillas dripping with honey, the game proceeded as usual, except with an eerie lack of spirit. Bert, uncharacteristically, did not challenge a single word. He brought out his *O.E.D.*, but only for inspection by Grace's father's trained eye.

"Could definitely use a new binding," Milton pronounced. "I guess you dropped it one too many times. I'll take it home with me and have it back to you good as new in a jiffy."

"Much appreciated," Bert said. "I owe you one."

"I can cover it with an antimold laminate cover, if you like."

"Only if it's not too much trouble."

"Not at all," Milton replied, more animated than Grace had seen him in weeks. "Glad to do it."

Words slipped by like minnows through a net—slang, proper names, egregious misspellings. At one point, even Grace found herself moved to challenge, but as she watched her father add up her mother's triple-letter score on the word *twizzler*, she could not bring herself to go through with it.

"Well done, my dear," her father said, bursting with pride. "This is quite a contentious match. Hats off to you all."

A little before eleven, Grace began to prepare her parents and the Sugarmans for her ensuing departure, which she knew might be a lengthy affair. Because of the fear of some millennium bug striking at midnight, the elevators in her building were going to be shut off for an hour. She thought it was a good excuse to leave early.

"You can't ring in the New Year alone. It's unheard of," Francine objected.

"Have a quick glass of eggnog with us. I made it with Egg Beaters for your father," her mother said.

"And I have my usual to-die-for chocolate mousse," Francine added.

"You don't know what you're missing," Bert said. "And I'm not even allowed to eat it."

"Bert will drive you home right after," Francine offered, as if that would entice her to stay.

"Thanks, but I really can't," Grace answered. "I have some things to do in the morning."

"You'll be here for dim sum tomorrow, won't you?" Francine inquired.

"I wouldn't miss it," she answered.

ON HER WAY to get her coat, Grace saw Bert's plastic butterfly garden on a small drop-leaf table in the front hall. Hanging from the top circular window were three grayish chrysalises, each one engaged in its own process. Their outer wrappings were beginning to take on the formation of wings. It would not be long before they molted. Grace buttoned her coat and felt a chill run up her spine as thoughts went unregistered. Her coat seemed tighter under the arms than it had before.

She walked home through the park. If she walked quickly, she would make it home before eleven-forty-five. It was a windless, cloudless night—a night when weather prediction would have been superfluous. The park was populated with midnight runners, couples carrying bottles of champagne arm-in-arm on their way to the Great Lawn to watch the fireworks, many likely to become engaged in a few minutes. A man wearing a glittery top hat ran by. Someone dressed as Baby New Year rode by on a bicycle. It was beginning to feel a little too much like Halloween.

As Grace continued along Park Drive, she felt as if she were wearing someone else's shoes that were both too large and too heavy for her. The motorcycle boots felt like a burden and her ankles ached. Each step was overly labored, and she walked with a self-consciousness she was unused to, as if she had to think about where to place each foot. She felt like a newly hatched duckling.

In the distance, she saw a crowd of runners beginning to congregate near Tavern on the Green. Just as she was about to head out of the park, she was startled by a hand on her shoulder. In the glare of the streetlight behind her, Grace had trouble making out anything more than silhouettes and obscured features.

A couple stood before her. The woman was sausaged into a shiny pink warm-up suit, matching rabbit-fur headband, and running shoes. She had reflector stripes on her jacket. The man wore a nondescript, black running outfit and ski hat. The only thing that registered about the man was his blindingly white socks. Grace couldn't process anything familiar about them until she heard the woman's voice and realized that it was, of all people, Penelope.

"Grace, what a wonderful coincidence," Penelope said, wrapping her fuchsia arms around her. "We were just talking about you."

"You were?" Grace supposed that this was the man that Penelope had met online. The man, still in the glare of the streetlight, seemed about to step forward.

"We're on our way to do the Midnight Run and then to celebrate our engagement. Adrian has just popped the question. It's a real *shiddach*." Penelope took the man's arm and brought him out of the glaring light. "You must join us."

The man's features came into view, and Grace saw the same flyaway hair underneath the black hat that she'd first glimpsed at the Pink Tea Cup, and she knew without a doubt that the person arm-in-arm with Penelope was none other than Mr. Dubrovsky, Private Investigator. Grace wasn't sure whether it was wiser to act nonchalant, wish them a Happy New Year, and make a quick exit, or to warn her friend that this guy was a nutcase. She was mulling over her options when Mr. Dubrovsky reached out his hand. Grace flinched reflexively.

"Ms. Brookman," he said, bowing slightly from the hip. "I will be forever indebted to you." As he spoke, Grace detected a hint of Maurice Chevalier in his voice, a whiff of aftershave in the bracing air. Penelope all but swooned. Grace felt herself immediately disarmed and became even more defensive. She took Penelope aside.

"Do you know who this is?" Grace whispered.

"Of course, I do. He told me the whole story."

"Penelope, allow me," Mr. Dubrovsky said, patting her lightly on the arm. "May I call you Grace?" he asked. Grace didn't respond. The whole situation was ludicrous, even by the reality-lax standards of her life, but she remained, in the hopes that it might somehow begin to make sense. He continued. "I must apologize for having deceived you. When Griffin's mother, Merrin, called and asked me to locate Mr. Brookman, I had no idea how entangled this situation would become. If I have caused you any injury, I am sorry and I would like to try to make amends. But my involvement with you has indeed changed my life. If not for you, I would never have found my Penelope."

"Oh, Adrian," Penelope said, nuzzling his neck. Grace felt herself about to sneeze, that nose-tickling sensation when things seemed right. Grace pictured the three of them strolling around the reservoir, admiring the cherry blossoms the following spring. Even Griffin and Kane along with Chloe and Pete popped into view like a Japanese paper fan opening to its full peacocklike splendor.

"I have your book," she told him.

"I have no need for it now," he answered, linking Grace's arm in his, as they continued down the path.

When Grace entered her building, she knew something was amiss. José was directing people to the stairwells, and the fire doors were propped open. Instead of the usual overhead lights, there were lanterns placed along the corridor.

"Happy New Year, Mrs. Brookman," José said as she walked into the lobby.

"Thank you, José. Happy New Year to you, too. Why is it so dark in here?"

"When they shut down the elevators, the whole building blacked out. The generator is on a timer. Should come on about twelve-thirty, one o'clock. What a night! And the people in 10J were having a karaoke party."

Grace walked up the stairs to her apartment. A lantern had been placed at the top of each landing, and she noticed her shadow growing longer and longer with each step.

She opened her door, then walked into the kitchen. On the table, in front of Laz's place, was a folded napkin and knife, a half-filled glass of water was on the counter. She must have placed it there absently. Old habits, she realized, were hard to break. She could have kept up the pretense in her sleep. Opening the utility closet, she took out a flashlight, a perfunctory gesture since due to Marisol's reorganization, there was really no need for light. She could find anything, even with her eyes closed.

In the distance, she heard fireworks. She went to the window and watched the muffled pyrotechnics display. Everyone was ringing in the New Year—Penelope and Adrian were no doubt toasting at the finish line; her parents and the Sugarmans would be squabbling about how much they would pay for Francine's chocolate mousse, all over a cup of low-cholesterol eggnog; and somewhere, Laz, too, was celebrating, even if by proxy. Tonight she and Laz were supposed to have been at Lincoln Center. Laz had written *Contact* in his date book. Grace had always wanted to see that play.

Although it was not late, she was exhausted. She threw off her coat and left her clothes on the bedroom floor. Then she collapsed into bed.

She was awakened by a dream so vivid that she felt every muscle in her body vibrating. It was as if Laz were inside her mind and body. He spoke to her through synapses that she thought had been sealed off: *I'll never leave you again.* She heard the words like a distant melody. They were the very words she'd imagined in her head day after day, the words she would have had him say if she could have orchestrated his homecoming as precisely as she had perfected his presence.

*I'm here, Gracie. I'm home for good. I'm never going to leave you again.* The words reverberated in her head.

So hard had she wished to hear those words, and for so long, yet something about them rang false. She was sweating. She felt a weight on her chest. Suddenly, the bedside light went on as if José, himself, had switched it on from some central circuit breaker. She opened her eyes and realized she was neither dreaming nor hallucinating—Laz was lying next to her. It was not a phantom of him, airbrushed and absent of anything as unseemly as a stray hair follicle, body odor, rough hands, a too-studied look, or a masking smile, but Laz in the flesh. He was almost unrecognizable. A stranger was in her bed.

Laz lifted her hair off the nape of her neck and kissed her the way he had on the ski lift. She shut her eyes, and it was as if no time had passed and her feet were once again off the ground. She opened her eyes and saw herself reflected in his pupils.

"Happy New Year, sweetness. I love you," he said, rolling onto his back. His voice was low and slightly hoarse. "I'm so sorry. I put you through hell. But you know how I am—it was just too much for me. I couldn't take it. But none of that matters anymore. Not even the Pulitzer. What matters is that we're back together. And we always will be. This is only the beginning. I promise. I need you now more than ever." He closed his eyes. Grace pictured his side of the bed in the morning—a rumpled, twisted frenzy—unsure that he could produce evidence of himself as finely wrought as she had. "I missed you so much. I promise things will be different. You're the only one I've ever loved."

He kissed her again and wrapped his arms around her. She was about to tell him it was as if he'd never left, when he fell asleep.

The flash from the lights going on had distorted Grace's vision, making everything she looked at glow green, like a modern-day, urban Emerald City. But she hadn't been torn away from home in the wake of Laz's tornado. She was already home, no more or less now than ever.

She put her head on the pillow, staring at the ceiling. The man before her was not the one she had been expecting. She had finally come to herself. The dream was what she had thought she had wanted all along, and now that it had arrived, she was free to let it go.

AT DAWN, GRACE slipped out of bed to make a cup of tea and to get José's coffee. It had become her ritual, but today she prepared it in an earthenware mug that Marisol had found in the music cabinet. The mug had been filled with pencil stubs and rubber bands. Grace knew she was supposed to feel unencumbered by her uncluttered apartment—no more secrets hiding in crevices, no mysteries, no surprises under the bed, nothing lost along the way, no treasures undiscovered. Everything in its place. She should have experienced something of a catharsis, but instead, she felt an absence. It had been her clutter, her circuitous route, detours and all. She just hadn't realized it until now.

The living room was ablaze as the Christmas tree and the Duro-Lites blinked in unison. She left them on and went into the bedroom to put on her motorcycle boots, taking care not to wake Laz. He was a sound sleeper. The room smelled different to her, as if she'd forgotten their particular alchemy of pheromones. She opened the window a crack and then went to stand by the door. He was home. His legs dangled off the side of the bed, the sheet twisted underneath him. His watch was on the nightstand, his shoes and pants in a corner by the ottoman. Generic details, totally lacking imagination and flourish. If she hadn't heard the sound of his breathing, she would barely have known he was there.

She ripped a page out of one of her blank books. *Glad you're back, but I'm sorry, I can't stay. I don't live here anymore. Grace.*

She placed the note, her engagement ring, and wedding band next to the orchid on the dining room table, and left her clay sculpture of the woman rising from the chair alongside, directly in the spotlight of the Duro-Lites. Then she took her grandmother's afghan, along with Mr. Dubrovsky's copy of *Oblomov*—which she would finish this time—and went downstairs to bring José his coffee before venturing out into a driving rain, as prepared as she ever needed to be.

*Lanterns on the Levee*

Library of Southern Civilization
*Lewis P. Simpson, Editor*

# Lanterns on the Levee

## RECOLLECTIONS OF A PLANTER'S SON

William Alexander Percy

*With an Introduction by WALKER PERCY*

**Louisiana State University Press**
Baton Rouge

ISBN 0-8071-0072-2 (paper)
Library of Congress Catalog Card Number 73-90687
Copyright 1941 by Alfred A. Knopf, Inc.
Copyright © renewed 1968 by LeRoy Pratt Percy
Introduction copyright © 1973 by Walker Percy
Manufactured in the United States of America
Published by special arrangement with Alfred A. Knopf, Inc.
Second printing

*FOR*

*WALKER, ROY, & PHIN*

*FOR*

*ADAH, CHARLOTTE, & TOM*

# Introduction

WALKER PERCY

I remember the first time I saw him. I was thirteen and he had come to visit my mother and me and my brothers in Athens, Georgia, where we were living with my grandmother after my father's death.

We had heard of him, of course. He was the fabled relative, the one you liked to speculate about. His father was a United States senator and he had been a decorated infantry officer in World War I. Besides that, he was a poet. The fact that he was also a lawyer and a planter didn't cut much ice — after all, the South was full of lawyer-planters. But how many people did you know who were war heroes and wrote books of poetry? One had heard of Rupert Brooke and Joyce Kilmer, but they were dead.

The curious fact is that my recollection of him even now, after meeting him, after living in his house for twelve years, and now thirty years after his death, is no less fabled than my earliest imaginings. The image of him that takes form in my mind still owes more to Rupert Brooke and those photographs of young English officers killed in Flanders than to a flesh-and-blood cousin from Greenville, Mississippi.

## INTRODUCTION

I can only suppose that he must have been, for me at least, a personage, a presence, radiating that mysterious quality we call charm, for lack of a better word, in such high degree that what comes to mind is not that usual assemblage of features and habits which make up our memories of people but rather a quality, a temper, a set of mouth, a look through the eyes.

For his eyes were most memorable, a piercing gray-blue and strangely light in my memory, as changeable as shadows over water, capable of passing in an instant, we were soon to learn, from merriment—he told the funniest stories we'd ever heard—to a level gray gaze cold with reproof. They were beautiful and terrible eyes, eyes to be careful around. Yet now, when I try to remember them, I cannot see them otherwise than as shadowed by sadness.

What we saw at any rate that sunny morning in Georgia in 1930, and what I still vividly remember, was a strikingly handsome man, slight of build and quick as a youth. He was forty-five then, an advanced age, one would suppose, to a thirteen-year-old, and gray-haired besides, yet the abiding impression was of a youthfulness—and an exoticness. He had in fact just returned from the South Seas—this was before the jet age and I'd never heard of anybody going there but Gauguin and Captain Bligh—where he had lived on the beach at Bora Bora.

He had come to invite us to live with him in Mississippi. We did, and upon my mother's death not long after, he adopted me and my two brothers. At the time what he did did not seem remarkable. What with youth's way of taking life as it comes—how else can you take it when you have no other life to compare it with?—and what with youth's incapacity for astonishment or gratitude, it did not seem in the least extraordinary to find oneself orphaned at fifteen and adopted by a bachelor-poet-lawyer-planter and living in an all-male household visited regularly by other poets, politicians, psychiatrists, sociologists, black preachers, folk singers, itinerant harmonica players. One friend came to seek advice on a book he wanted to write and stayed a year to write it. It was, his house, a standard stopover for all manner of people who were trying to "understand the South," that perennial American avocation, and whether or not they succeeded, it was as valuable to me to try to understand them as to be understood. The observers in this case were at least as curious a phenomenon as the observed.

Now belatedly I can better assess what he did for us and I even have an inkling what he gave up to do it. For him, to whom the world was open and who felt more at home in Taormina than in Jackson—for though he loved his home country, he had to leave it often to keep loving it—and who in fact could have stayed on at Bora Bora and chucked it all like Gauguin (he told me once he was tempted), for him to have taken on three boys, age fourteen, thirteen, and nine, and raised them, amounted to giving up the freedom of bachelorhood and taking on the burden of parenthood without the consolations of marriage. Gauguin chucked it all, quit, cut out and went to the islands for the sake of art and became a great painter if not a great human being. Will Percy not only did not chuck anything; he shouldered somebody else's burden. Fortunately for us, he did not subscribe to Faulkner's precept that a good poem is worth any number of old ladies—for if grandmothers are dispensable, why not second cousins? I don't say we did him in (he would laugh at that), but he didn't write much poetry afterwards and he died young. At any rate, whatever he lost or gained in the transaction, I know what I gained: a vocation and in a real sense a second self, that is, the work and the self which, for better or worse, would not otherwise have been open to me.

For to have lived in Will Percy's house, with "Uncle Will" as we called him, as a raw youth from age fourteen to twenty-six, a youth whose only talent was a knack for looking and listening, for tuning in and soaking up, was nothing less than to be informed in the deepest sense of the word. What was to be listened to, dwelled on, pondered over for the next thirty years was of course the man himself, the unique human being, and when I say unique I mean it in its most literal sense: he was one of a kind: I never met anyone remotely like him. It was to encounter a complete, articulated view of the world as tragic as it was noble. It was to be introduced to Shakespeare, to Keats, to Brahms, to Beethoven—and unsuccessfully, it turned out, to Wagner whom I never liked, though I was dragged every year to hear Flagstadt sing Isolde—as one seldom if ever meets them in school.

"Now listen to this part," he would say as Gluck's *Orfeo* played—the old 78s not merely dropped from a stack by the monstrous Capehart, as big as a sideboard, but then picked up and turned over by an astounding hoop-like arm—and you'd make the altogether unexpected discovery that music, of all things, can convey the deepest and most unnameable human feelings and give great pleasure in doing so.

Or: "Read this," and I'd read or, better still, he'd read aloud, say, Viola's speech to Olivia in *Twelfth Night*:

> Make me a willow cabin at your gate,
> And call upon my soul within the house;
>
> .    .    .    .    .    .    .    .    .    .    .    .
>
> And make the babbling gossip of the air
> Cry out "Olivia!"

You see? he'd as good as say, and what I'd begin to see, catch on to, was the great happy reach and play of the poet at the top of his form.

For most of us, the communication of beauty takes two, the teacher and the hearer, the pointer and the looker. The rare soul, the Wolfe or Faulkner, can assault the entire body of literature single-handedly. I couldn't or wouldn't. I had a great teacher. The teacher points and says *Look;* the response is *Yes, I see.*

But he was more than a teacher. What he was to me was a fixed point in a confusing world. This is not to say I always took him for my true north and set my course accordingly. I did not. Indeed my final assessment of *Lanterns on the Levee* must register reservations as well as admiration. The views on race relations, for example, diverge from my own and have not been helpful, having, in my experience, played into the hands of those whose own interest in these matters is deeply suspect. But even when I did not follow him, it was usually in *relation* to him, whether with him or against him, that I defined myself and my own direction. Perhaps he would not have had it differently. Surely it is the highest tribute to the best people we know to use them as best we can, to become, not their disciples, but ourselves.

It is the good fortune of those who did not know him that his singular charm, the unique flavor of the man, transmits with high fidelity in *Lanterns on the Levee.* His gift for communicating, communicating himself, an enthusiasm, a sense of beauty, moral outrage, carries over faithfully to the cold printed page, although for those who did not know him the words cannot evoke— or can they?—the mannerisms, the quirk of mouth, the shadowed look, the quick Gallic shrug, the inspired flight of eyebrows at an absurdity, the cold Anglo-Saxon gaze.

(For he was this protean: one time I was reading *Ivanhoe,* the part about the fight between Richard and Saladin, and knowing Richard was one of Uncle Will's heroes, I identified one with the other. But wait: wasn't he actually more like Saladin, not the sir-knight defender of the Christian West but rather the subtle easterner, noble in his own right? I didn't ask him, but if I had, he'd have probably shrugged: both, neither . . .)

There is not much doubt about the literary quality of *Lanterns on the Levee,* which delivers to the reader not only a noble and tragic view of life but the man himself. But other, nonliterary questions might be raised here. How, for example, do the diagnostic and prophetic dimensions of the book hold up after thirty years? Here, I think, hindsight must be used with the utmost circumspection. On the one hand, it is surely justifiable to test the prophetic moments of a book against history itself; on the other hand, it is hardly proper to judge a man's views of the issues of his day by the ideological fashions of another age. Perhaps in this connection it would not be presumptuous to venture a modest hope. It is that *Lanterns on the Levee* will survive both its friends and its enemies, that is, certain more clamorous varieties of each.

One is all too familiar with both.

The first, the passionate advocate: the lady, not necessarily Southern, who comes bearing down at full charge, waving *Lanterns on the Levee* like a battle flag. "He is right! The Old South was right!" What she means all too often, it turns out, is not that she prefers agrarian values to technological but that she is enraged at having to pay her cook more than ten dollars a week; that she prefers, not merely segregation to integration, but slavery to either.

The second, the liberal enemy: the ideologue, white or

black, who polishes off *Lanterns on the Levee* with the standard epithets: racist, white supremacist, reactionary, paternalist, Bourbon, etc., etc. (they always remind me of the old Stalinist imprecations: fascist, cosmopolitan, imperialist running dog).

*Lanterns on the Levee* deserves better and of course has better readers. Its author can be defended against the more extreme reader, but I wonder if it is worth the effort. Abraham Lincoln was a segregationist. What of it? Will Percy was regarded in the Mississippi of his day as a flaming liberal and nigger-lover and reviled by the sheriff's office for his charges of police brutality. What of that? Nothing much is proved except that current categories and names, liberal and conservative, are weary past all thinking of it. Ideological words have a way of wearing thin and then, having lost their meanings, being used like switchblades against the enemy of the moment. Take the words *paternalism, noblesse oblige,* dirty words these days. But is it a bad thing for a man to believe that his position in society entails a certain responsibility toward others? Or is it a bad thing for a man to care like a father for his servants, spend himself on the poor, the sick, the miserable, the mad who come his way? It is surely better than watching a neighbor get murdered and closing the blinds to keep from "getting involved." It might even beat welfare.

Rather than measure *Lanterns on the Levee* against one or another ideological yardstick, it might be more useful to test the major themes of the book against the spectacular events of the thirty years since its publication. Certainly the overall pessimism of *Lanterns on the Levee*, its gloomy assessment of the spiritual health of Western civilization, is hard to fault these days. It seems especially prescient when one considers that the book was mostly written in the between-wars age of optimism when Americans still believed that the right kind of war would set things right once and for all. If its author were alive today, would he consider his forebodings borne out? Or has the decline accelerated even past his imaginings? Would he see glimmerings of hope? Something of all three, no doubt, but mainly, I think, he'd look grim, unsurprised, and glad enough to have made his exit.

Certainly nothing would surprise him about the collapse of the old moralities, for example, the so-called sexual revolution which he would more likely define in less polite language as alley-cat morality. I can hear him now: "Fornicating like white trash is one thing, but leave it to this age to call it the new morality." Nor would he be shocked by the cynicism and corruption, the stealing, lying, rascality ascendant in business and politics—though even he might be dismayed by the complacency with which they are received: "There have always been crooks, but we've not generally made a practice of re-electing them, let alone inviting them to dinner." All this to say nothing of the collapse of civil order and the new jungle law which rules the American city.

Nothing new here then for him: if the horrors of the Nazi holocaust would have dismayed him and the moral bankruptcy of the postwar world saddened him, they would have done so only by sheer dimension. He had already adumbrated the Götterdämmerung of Western values.

But can the matter be disposed of so simply: decline and fall predicted, decline and fall taking place? While granting the prescience of much of *Lantern on the Levee's* pessimism, we must, I think, guard against a certain seductiveness which always attends the heralding of apocalypse, and we must not overlook some far less dramatic but perhaps equally significant counterforces. Yes, Will Percy's indictment of modern life has seemed to be confirmed by the holocaust of the 1940s and by American political and social morality in the 1970s. But what would he make of some very homely, yet surely unprecedented social gains which have come to pass during these same terrible times? To give the plainest examples: that for the first time in history a poor boy, black or white, has a chance to get an education, become what he wants to become, doctor, lawyer, even read *Lanterns on the Levee* and write poetry of his own, and that not a few young men, black and white, have done just that? Also: that for the first time in history a working man earns a living wage and can support his family in dignity. How do these solid social gains square with pronouncements of decline and fall? I ask the question and, not knowing the answer, can only wonder how Will Percy would see it now. As collapse? Or as contest? For it appears that what is upon us is not a twilight of the gods but a very real race between the powers of light and darkness, that time is short and the issue very much in doubt. So I'd love to ask him, as I used to ask him after the seven o'clock news (Ed Murrow: *This*—is London): "Well? What do you think?"

The one change that would astonish him, I think, is the spectacular emergence of the South from its traditional role of loser and scapegoat. If anyone had told him in 1940 that in thirty years the "North" (i.e., New York, Detroit, California) would be in the deepest kind of trouble with race, violence, and social decay while the South had become, by contrast, relatively hopeful and even prosperous, he would not have believed it. This is not to say that he would find himself at home in the new Dallas or Atlanta. But much of *Lanterns on the Levee*—for example, the chapter on sharecropping—was written from the ancient posture of Southern apologetics. If his defense of sharecropping against the old enemy, the "Northern liberal," seems quaint now, it is not because there was not something to be said for sharecropping — there was a good deal to be said — and it is not because he wasn't naive about the tender regard of the plantation manager for the helpless sharecropper — he was naive, even about his own managers. It is rather because the entire issue and its disputants have simply been bypassed by history. The massive social and technological upheavals in the interval have left the old quarrel academic and changed the odds in the new one. It is hard, for example, to imagine a serious Southern writer nowadays firing off his heaviest ammunition at "Northern liberals." Not the least irony of recent history is that the "Northern liberal" has been beleaguered and the "Southern planter" rescued by the same forces. The latter has been dispensed by technology from the ancient problem, sharecroppers replaced by Farmall and Allis-Chalmers, while the former has fallen out with his old wards, the blacks. The displaced sharecroppers moved to the Northern cities and the liberals moved out. The South in a peculiar sense, a sense Will Percy would not necessarily have approved (though he could hardly have repressed a certain satisfaction), may have won after all.

So Will Percy's strong feelings about the shift of power from the virtuous few would hardly be diminished today, but he might recast his villains and redress the battle lines. Old-style demagogue, for example, might give way to new-style image manipulator and smooth amoral churchgoing huckster. When he spoke of the "bottom rail on top," he had in mind roughly the same folks as Faulkner's Snopeses, a lower-class, itchy-palmed breed who had dispossessed the gentry who had in turn been the true friends of the old-style "good" Negro. The upshot: an unholy hegemony of peckerwood politicians, a white hoi polloi keeping them in office, and a new breed of unmannerly Negroes misbehaving in the streets. But if he — or Faulkner for that matter — were alive today, he would find the battleground confused. He would find most members of his own "class" not exactly embattled in a heroic Götterdämmerung, not exactly fighting the good fight as he called it, but having simply left, taken off for the exurbs where, barricaded in patrolled subdivisions and country clubs and private academies, they worry about their kids and drugs. Who can blame them, but is this the "good life" Will Percy spoke of? And when some of these good folk keep *Lanterns on the Levee* on the bed table, its author, were he alive today, might be a little uneasy. For meanwhile, doing the dirty work of the Republic in the towns and cities of the South, in the schools, the school boards, the city councils, the factories, the restaurants, the stores, are to be found, of all people, the sons and daughters of the poor whites of the 1930s and some of those same uppity Negroes who went to school and ran for office, and who together are not doing so badly and in some cases very well indeed.

So it is not unreasonable to suppose that Will Percy might well revise his view of the South and the personae of his drama, particularly in favor of the lower-class whites for whom he had so little use. In this connection I cannot help but think of another book about the South, W. J. Cash's *The Mind of the South,* published oddly enough the same year by the same publisher as *Lanterns on the Levee.* Cash's book links Southern aristocrat and poor white much closer than the former ordinarily would have it. Both books are classics in their own right, yet they couldn't be more different; their separate validities surely testify to the diversity and complexity of this mysterious region. Yet in this case, I would suppose that Will Percy would today find himself closer to Cash in sorting out his heroes and villains, that far from setting aristocrat against poor white and both against the new Negro, he might well choose his present-day heroes — and villains — from the ranks of all three. He'd surely have as little use for black lawlessness as for white copping out. I may be wrong but I can't see him happy as the patron saint of Hilton Head or Paradise Estates-around-the-Country Club.

For it should be noted, finally, that despite conventional assessments of *Lanterns on the Levee* as an expression of the "aristocratic" point of view of the Old South, Will Percy had no more use than Cash for genealogical games, the old Southern itch for coats of arms and tracing back connections to the English squirearchy. Indeed if I know anything at all about Will Percy, I judge that in so far as there might be a connection between him and the Northumberland Percys, they, not he, would have to claim kin. He made fun of his ancestor Don Carlos, and if he claimed Harry Hotspur, it was a kinship of spirit. His own aristocracy was a meritocracy of character, talent, performance, courage, and quality of life.

It is just that, a person and a life, which comes across in *Lanterns on the Levee.* And about him I will say no more than that he was the most extraordinary man I have ever known and that I owe him a debt which cannot be paid.

# *Foreword*

The desire to reminisce arises not so much I think from the number of years you may happen to have accumulated as from the number of those who meant most to you in life who have gone on the long journey. They were the bulwarks, the bright spires, the strong places. When they have gone, you are a little tired, you rest on your oars, you say to yourself: "There are no witnesses to my fine little fury, my minute heroic efforts. It is better to remember, to be sure of the good that was, rather than of the evil that is, to watch the spread and pattern of the game that is past rather than engage feebly in the present play. It was a stout world thus far, peopled with all manner of gracious and kindly and noble personages—these seem rather a pygmy tribe." After a while, particularly if you have cut no very splendid figure in the show, indulgence in this sort of communing becomes a very vice.

*With some addicts it takes the form of dreaming; silently —the best way, I fear—and these are mostly women; with others, of conversation, and these are mostly old men— very tiresome unless you are one too; but the most abandoned of the whole lot insist they must write it all down, and of them am I. So while the world I know is crashing to bits, and what with the noise and the cryings-out no man could hear a trumpet blast, much less an idle evening reverie, I will indulge a heart beginning to be fretful by repeating to it the stories it knows and loves of my own country and my own people. A pilgrim's script—one man's field-notes of a land not far but quite unknown— valueless except as that man loved the country he passed through and its folk, and except as he willed to tell the truth. How other, alas, than telling it!*

# CONTENTS

# CONTENTS

*Lanterns on the Levee*

# CHAPTER I

# The Delta

My country is the Mississippi Delta, the river country. It lies flat, like a badly drawn half oval, with Memphis at its northern and Vicksburg at its southern tip. Its western boundary is the Mississippi River, which coils and returns on itself in great loops and crescents, though from the map you would think it ran in a straight line north and south. Every few years it rises like a monster from its bed and pushes over its banks to vex and sweeten the land it has made. For our soil, very dark brown, creamy and sweet-smelling, without substrata of rock or shale, was built up slowly, century after century, by the sediment gathered by the river in its solemn task of cleansing the continent and deposited in annual layers of silt on what must once have been the vast depression between itself and the hills. This ancient depression, now filled in and level, is what we call the Delta. Some say it was the floor of the sea itself. Now it seems still to be a floor, being smooth from one end to the other, without rise or dip or hill, unless the mysterious scattered monuments of the mound-builders may be called hills. The land does not drain into the river as most riparian lands do, but tilts back from it towards the hills of the south and east. Across this wide flat alluvial stretch—north and south it measures one hundred and ninety-six miles, east and west at the widest point fifty miles—run slowly and circuitously other rivers and creeks, also high-banked, with names pleasant to remember—Rattlesnake Bayou, Quiver River, the Bogue Phalia, the Tallahatchie, the Sunflower—pouring their tawny waters finally into the Yazoo, which in turn loses itself just above Vicksburg in the river. With us when you speak of "the river," though there are many, you mean always the same one, the great river, the shifting unappeasable god of the country, feared and loved, the Mississippi.

In the old days this was a land of unbroken forests. All trees grew there except the pine and its kindred, and, strangely enough, the magnolia. The water-oak, the pecan, the cypress, and the sweet-gum were perhaps the most beautiful and home-loving, but there were ash and elm, walnut and maple, and many others besides. They grew to enormous heights, with vast trunks and limbs, and between them spread a chaos of vines and cane and brush, so that the deer and bear took it for their own and only by the Indians was it penetrable, and by them only on wraiths of trails. Wild flowers were few, the soil being too rich and warm and deep, and those, like the yellow-top of early spring, apt to be rank and weed-like. A still country it must have been then, ankle-deep in water, mostly in shadow, with mere flickers of sunshine, and they motey and yellow and thick like syrup. The wild swans loved it; tides of green parakeets from the south and of gray pigeons from the north melted into its tree-tops and gave them sound; ducks—mallard, canvas-back, teal, and wood-duck—and Canadian geese, their wedges high in the soft air of autumn like winter's first arrows, have still not deserted it.

Such was my country hardly more than a hundred years ago. It was about then that slavery became unprofitable in the older Southern states and slave-holders began to look for cheap fertile lands farther west that could feed the many black mouths dependent on them. So younger sons from Virginia, South Carolina, and Kentucky with their gear, live-stock, and chattels, human and otherwise, started a leisurely migration into the Delta. Forests were cleared, roads constructed (such dusty or muddy roads!), soil shaped into fields, homes built. They settled first on the banks and bends of the river, later on the banks and bends of the smaller streams, for those were high ground over which the then yearly inundations of the river, as yet un-curbed by levees, never quite reached. There is still a great curve of the shoreline called Kentucky Bend, and another, mostly sandbar now, called Carolina.

The roads they built were local affairs, connecting plan-tation with plantation or with hamlets which grew slowly and without booms into our present small towns. In wet weather, of which we have much, they were bottomless, and old-timers believed they could never be anything else.

The real highway was the river. All life, social and eco-nomic, centered there. The river steamers furnished trans-portation, relaxation, and information to the whole river people. In our town the *Pargo* landed regularly on Sun-day, usually between eleven o'clock and noon. Everybody would be at church, but when she blew, the male members of the congregation to a man would rise and, in spite of indignant glares from their wives and giggles from the choir, make their exits, with a severe air of business just remembered. With the *Pargo* came the week's mail and gossip of the river-front from St. Louis to New Orleans and rumors from the very distant outside world. If the occasion was propitious a little round of poker might be started and a few toddies drunk. They were a fine fleet, those old sidewheelers which plied between St. Louis and New Orleans and stopped on signal at the various plantations and river settlements—the *White*, the *Pargo*, the *Natchez*, the *Robert E. Lee*. The last and least of them was the *Belle of the Bends*, which as a small boy I could never see steaming majestically through the sunset to the landing without a fine choky feeling. They had pleasant outside cabins opening on an enormous white dining-saloon, decorated in the most abandoned gingerbread style, which after supper became a ballroom. Almost as comfortable as our ocean liners of today, they were far easier and more sociable; anybody who was anybody knew everybody else, and each trip was rather like a grand house-party, with dancing and gambling and an abundance of Kentucky whisky and French champagne. The ladies (who never partook of these beverages—maybe a sip of champagne) were always going to New Orleans for Mardi Gras or to shop or to hear the opera (well established there before it was begun in New York) or to visit cousins and aunts in the Louisiana and Natchez territory; and as those were days of enormous families, cousins and aunts were plentiful. There never was a Southern family that was a Southern Family some member of which, incredibly beautiful and sparkling, had not opened the ball with Lafayette. For years apparently his sole occupation was opening balls in New Orleans, Charleston, Natchez, and St. Louis. After looking at a hundred or more badly painted portraits of these belles I am a firm believer in this tradition.

If the ladies loved going to New Orleans, the men-folks were never at a loss for reasons to take the same trip. Memphis was hardly more than a country town. The commission merchants (forerunners of the modern bank, co-operative association, Federal Land Bank, insurance company with funds to invest) had their offices in New Orleans and it was they who supplied the planters with the cash for their extensive and costly operations. Here was an ever ready reason to board the boat going south, and one that made unnecessary any reference to the lottery, the races, the masked balls, the fantastic poker games, the hundred and one amiable vices of that most European and sloe-eyed of American cities.

Our Delta culture stemmed from an older one and returned to it for sustenance and renewal, but it lacked much that made the older culture charming and stable. We had few of those roomy old residences, full of fine woodwork and furniture and drapery, which excellent French or English architects built in the Natchez and Charleston neighborhoods and in the Louisiana sugar-cane territory. The few we had have caved into the river or burned. But a library was as portable as a slave, and excellent ones abounded—leather-bound sets of the *Spectator,* the *Edinburgh Review,* the works of Mr. Goldsmith and Mr. Pope, *Tom Jones* and *A Sentimental Journey,* translations of Plutarch and Homer, amazing poems about plants and flowers by the grandfather of Darwin, *The Faerie Queene* and Bobbie Burns. (I never came across a copy of Shelley or Keats or Wordsworth in these old collections.) On the bottom shelf would be a fat Bible, the front pages inscribed with long lists of deaths and births in a beautiful flourishing hand. On the top shelf, presumably beyond the reach of the young and impressionable, would be the novels of George Sand and, later, of Ouida. *Paul and Virginia* too was a favorite, but who can now recall that title, though no book ever had more warm and innocuous tears shed over it?

I recall one survivor of that generation, or rather of the one immediately following it. Aunt Fannie, my great-aunt by marriage, was in looks all that the Surry of Eagle's Nest and Marse Chan school of writers would have you believe elderly Southern gentlewomen invariably were. She had exquisite slender white hands, usually folded in idleness on her lap; upon her neat curly white hair, parted in the middle, reposed a tiny white thing of frills and lace which may have been a cap but which looked more like a doily; her face was small and white, with truly a faded-flower look; her dress was black and fitted well and with a sort of chic her still slender figure; she smelled faintly of orris-root, a bit of which she usually chewed with no observable cud-motion. (I don't know why old ladies abandoned orris-root—it's the right smell for them. But, after all, there are no old ladies now.) It was not these things, however, but certain little personal eccentricities of Aunt Fannie's that endeared her to me as a child. She would suddenly drop into a little nap, sitting bolt upright in her chair and with the animated company around her pretending not to notice it. Or, equally inexplicably and with equal disregard of surroundings, she would sob gently and delicately and wipe quite real tears from her eyes with her diminutive orris-scented handkerchief. I attributed this phenomenon to some old and overwhelming sorrow which she carried in her heart and was too proud and ladylike to reveal. Only years and years later I learned that these engaging little habits of hers arose from another little habit: Aunt Fannie took her grain of morphine every day. Being the only wicked thing she ever did, it must have been doubly consoling.

Nevertheless it was this same Aunt Fannie who, a newly arrived bride from Nashville, by raising a moral issue threw the countryside into violent commotion, almost caused a duel, and established a social distinction in our county which has survived more or less to this good day. She gave a house-warming, a large affair, with dancing and champagne and a nougat from New Orleans. In selecting her guests she flatly refused to invite a prominent planter because he openly and notoriously lived with a Negro woman. For some reason the logical duel did not take place; the planter found it easier to move from the community than to live down the stigma or to acquire a paler bolster-companion. Aunt Fannie's husband died, she saw the war and poverty and reconstruction, she raised a daughter and saw her die, she lived on into a new order unsure of itself and without graciousness—if a bit of morphine would blur the present and brighten the past for her, who could have had the heart to deprive her of it?

But, after all, I suppose my paternal grandmother, Mur, was more typical than Aunt Fannie, more illustrative of the class to which she belonged. Left on the plantation during the war, alone with her three babies, while my grandfather, an opponent of secession and a lukewarm slave-owner, was away fighting to destroy the Union and preserve the institution of slavery, she not only raised her little bro⸫ ¹ single-handed and under the handicap of increasing poverty, but managed the thousand-acre home place. When the effect of the Emancipation Proclamation was realized by the slaves, they became restless, unruly, even dangerous. Her position was one of great difficulty, if not of peril. One evening in the spring of 1864 she learned that the remaining slaves (for many had run away) had met and decided not to plant or work the crop. She immediately called them together and ordered them to meet her in the field the next morning at sun-up. They were there and so was she, sitting in a rocking-chair at the end of the turn-row. (Rocking-chairs have disappeared, a great and symbolic loss.) They met in this manner every morning till July, when the crop was laid by. When the war ended and my grandfather returned penniless, his family managed to live for a year or more on the proceeds from the sale of that cotton crop. At that time my grandmother was twenty-nine, very pretty, with a keen sense of the absurd, and how she could play Strauss waltzes!

Indeed, indeed, the lily-of-the-field life of the Southern gentlewoman existed only in the imagination of Northern critics and Southern sentimentalists, one about as untrustworthy as the other. They had too many duties even in slavery days to be idle. It is true, charm was considered the first and most necessary course in female education, as it is among French women today, and this seems to me sound, because it was a gregarious, sociable, and high-spirited world into which they were born, much addicted to dances and parties of all sorts and visitings and love affairs, and whether that world was delightful or vulgar depended on whether or not the women were ladies. To manage a single household competently is a sizable job. These women on country estates so isolated as to be of necessity self-sustaining and self-governing had the direction of the feeding, clothing, education, health, and morals, not only of their own families, but of the dark feudal community they owned and were responsible for. When there were no bakeries or corner grocery stores or Kress's and Woolworth's, they had to know how to make cloth, bake bread, smoke meat, design quilts, pickle and preserve, nurse and concoct medicines, and supervise the cooking of all and sundry. They held Sunday school for their own and the darkies' children and generally taught white and black alike reading, writing, arithmetic, and the Bible. From them we inherit those golden recipes which give the lie to foreign critics when they say Americans know nothing of gustatory joys, eat to live, and are unaware that good cooking is one of the few things that make life bearable. What of Virginia hams, Maryland terrapin, Charleston roe and hominy, New Orleans gumbo-filé, griades, fourchettes, sea-food—oysters, crabs, shrimp, pompano, red snapper, crawfish, sheepshead—and the hundred exquisite ways of preparing them known to the Creoles, not to the Parisian? What of coffee, dish-water in the North, chicory abroad, but strong and hot and clear and delectable on any Southern table? And the hundred varieties of hot breads? Oh, the poor little boys who never put a lump of butter into steaming batter-bread (spoon-bread is the same thing) or lolled their tongues over pain-perdu! There should be a monument to Southern womanhood, creator of the only American cuisine that makes the world a better place to live in.

Instead, you will find in any Southern town a statue in memory of the Confederate dead, erected by the Daughters of something or other, and made, the townsfolk will respectfully tell you, in Italy. It is always the same: a sort of shaft or truncated obelisk, after the manner of the Washington Monument, on top of which stands a little man with a big hat holding a gun. If you are a Southerner you will not feel inclined to laugh at these efforts, so lacking in either beauty or character, to preserve the memory of their gallant and ill-advised forebears. I think the dash, endurance, and devotion of the Confederate soldier have not been greatly exaggerated in song and story: they do not deserve these chromos in stone. Sentiment driveling into sentimentality, poverty, and, I fear, lack of taste are responsible for them, but they are the only monuments which are dreadful from the point of view of æsthetics, craftsmanship, and conception that escape being ridiculous. They are too pathetic for that. Perhaps a thousand years from now the spade of some archæologist will find only these as relics of and clues to the vanished civilization we call ours. How tragically and comically erroneous his deductions will be!

My memorial to Southern cookery would be more informative. Or one to Southern hospitality, concerning which so many kindly things have been said. And that tradition too must have begun in those earlier times. In such a purely agrarian and thinly populated country there were no hotels or lodging-houses of any kind. The traveler could buy neither bed nor food, but had to hope some resident would give them to him as an act not so much of hospitality as of sheer humanity. A stranger in the Navajo country of Arizona or in Arabia experiences the same difficulty today and has it solved for him in the same way—the natives receive him as their guest. Frequently this must have been trying to the ladies of the household. I have always heard, though I will not vouch for the story, that a stranger dropped in for the night on one of my Louisiana kinsmen and remained a year. The stranger was Audubon, the ornithologist. My French grandmother, whom I called Mère, was not quite so cordial. Neither her plantation home nor her English vocabulary was large. When my grandfather, whom I called Père, unexpectedly appeared one nightfall with a number of friends who had been bear-hunting with him, she first said to him: "Mais, Ernest"—and he quailed, for it was one of her favorite phrases and it could mean all manner of things, but it always *meant*—then she observed to the guests: "Welcome, messieurs, I can eat you but I cannot sleep you." She was a remarkable woman, and very firm.

Well, she has joined the lovely ladies who opened the ball with Lafayette, and the forest country, only half conquered in her day, has become an open expanse of cotton plantations, though woods, unkempt remnants, still cling to their edges and rim the creeks and bayous. Railroads have come, and almost gone, thanks to the shoving and obese trucks and busses. The roads are now of concrete or gravel and there are thousands of miles of ugly wires crossing the landscape bearing messages or light. The river town has a White Way, picture shows, many radios, a Chamber of Commerce, and numerous service clubs. We have gone forward, our progress is ever so evident.

And the river? It is changed and eternally the same. The early settlers soon began to rebuff its yearly caress, that impregnated and vitalized the soil, by building small dikes around their own individual plantations. This was a poor makeshift and in time, not without ruction and bitter debate, was abandoned in favor of levee districts which undertook to levee the river itself at the cost of the benefited landowners within the districts. After reconstruction no more vital problem perplexed Delta statesmen than how to convince the Federal government of the propriety of contributing to the cost of building levees. At first they failed, but later niggardly aid was doled out —a bit some years, others none. Only within the last fifteen years has the government accepted the view urged for half a century by our people that the river's waters are the nation's waters and fighting them is the nation's fight. The United States Engineers under the War Department are now in full charge of levee and revetment work from one end of the river to the other.

But this work has not changed the savage nature and austere beauty of the river itself. Man draws near to it, fights it, uses it, curses it, loves it, but it remains remote, unaffected. Between the fairy willows of the banks or the green slopes of the levees it moves unhurried and unpausing; building islands one year to eat them the next; gnawing the bank on one shore till the levee caves in and another must be built farther back, then veering wantonly and attacking with equal savagery the opposite bank; in spring, high and loud against the tops of the quaking levees; in summer, deep and silent in its own tawny bed; bearing eternally the waste and sewage of the continent to the cleansing wide-glittering Gulf. A gaunt and terrible stream, but more beautiful and dear to its children than Thames or Tiber, than mountain brook or limpid estuary. The gods on their thrones are shaken and changed, but it abides, aloof and unappeasable, with no heart except for its own task, under the unbroken and immense arch of the lighted sky where the sun, too, goes a lonely journey.

As a thing used by men it has changed: the change is not in itself, but in them. No longer the great white boats and their gallant companies ply to and fro on its waters. A certain glamour is gone forever. But the freighters and barge lines of today keep one reminder of the vanished elder packets—their deep-throated, long-drawn-out, giant voices. And still there is no sound in the world so filled with mystery and longing and unease as the sound at night of a river-boat blowing for the landing—one long, two shorts, one long, two shorts. Over the somber levels of the water pours that great voice, so long prolonged it is joined by echoes from the willowed shore, a chorus of ghosts, and, roused from sleep, wide-eyed and still, you are oppressed by vanished glories, the last trump, the calling of the ends of the earth, the current, ceaselessly moving out into the dark, of the eternal dying. Trains rushing at night under the widening pallor of their own smoke, bearing in wild haste their single freightage of wild light, over a receding curve of thunder, have their own glory. But they are gone too quickly, like a meteor, to become part of your deep own self. The sound of the river-boats hangs inside your heart like a star.

# CHAPTER II

# Delta Folks

I may seem to have implied that all Delta citizens were aristocrats travelling luxuriously up and down the river or sitting on the front gallery, a mint julep in one hand and a palm-leaf fan in the other, protected from mosquitoes by the smudge burning in the front yard. If so, I have misinterpreted my country. The aristocrats were always numerically in the minority; with the years they have not increased. It may be helpful to mention the other and very different children of God who took up their abode beside the waters of the great river.

The Indians left not a trace except the names of rivers, plantations, and towns, the meaning of which we have forgotten along with the pronunciation.

Another element leaving almost as little impress, though still extant, is the "river-rat." He is white, Anglo-Saxon, with twists of speech and grammatical forms current in Queen Anne's day or earlier, and a harsh "r" strange to all Southerners except mountaineers. Where he comes from no one knows or cares. Some find in him the descendant of those pirates who used to infest the river as far up as

Memphis. It seems more likely his forefathers were out-of-door, ne'er-do-well nomads of the pioneer days. His shanty boats, like Huck Finn's father's, may be seen moored in the willows or against the sandbars as far up and down the river as I have ever traveled. He squats on bars and bits of mainland subject to overflow, raises a garden and a patch of corn, steals timber, rafts it, and sells it to the mills, and relies the year round on fishing for a living. He seems to regard the White River as the Navajos regard the Canyon de Chelly—as a sort of sanctuary and homeland, and it supplies the clam shells from which he makes buttons. Illiterate, suspicious, intensely clannish. blond, and usually ugly, river-rats make ideal bootleggers. The brand of corn or white mule they make has received nation-wide acclaim. They lead a life apart, uncouth, unclean, lawless, vaguely alluring. Their contact with the land world around them consists largely in being haled into court, generally for murder. No Negro is ever a river-rat.

Every American community has its leaven of Jews. Ours arrived shortly after the Civil War with packs on their backs, peddlers from Russia, Poland, Germany, a few from Alsace. They sold trinkets to the Negroes and saved. Today they are plantation-owners, bankers, lawyers, doctors, merchants; their children attend the great American universities, win prizes, become connoisseurs in the arts and radicals in politics. I was talking to one, an old-timer, not too successful, in front of his small store a short time ago. He suddenly asked in his thick Russian accent: "Do you know Pushkin? Ah, beautiful, better than Shelley or Byron!" Why shouldn't such a people inherit the earth, not, surely, because of their meekness, but because of a steadier fire, a tension and tenacity that make all other whites seem stodgy and unintellectual.

Other foreigners arrived with their gifts, more or less battered, of other cultures. When the levees were being built with hand-labor and wheelbarrows, the Irish came, many remaining to run excellent saloons or to fill minor political offices. They quickly merged into the life of the community, though their warm-heartedness, love of brawling and excitement, and high-spirited humor were fortunately not lost in the process. From southern Italy and Sicily came fruit-venders who made unobtrusive good citizens, wise in turning a penny and keeping it, taking small part in community life and rarely appearing in the courts. I have noticed that these Latins brought from the Mediterranean thrift and industry, unhurried energy, a sober and simple culture, earthy and warm; but their American offspring seem to regard it as their patriotic duty to unlearn these virtues. Second-generation Italians rival the Anglo-Saxon tough in vulgarity and loudness, their sole saving grace being charm and impulsiveness. Even Asia has contributed to and drawn from the Delta. Small Chinese store-keepers are almost as ubiquitous as in the South Seas. Barred from social intercourse with the whites, they smuggle through wives from China or, more frequently, breed lawfully or otherwise with the Negro. They are not numerous enough to present a problem—except to the small white store-keeper—but in so far as I can judge, they serve no useful purpose in community life: what wisdom they may inherit from Lao-tse and Confucius they fail to impart. Not infrequently they are indicted for crimes of violence occurring among themselves. Representatives of the implicated tongs rush down from Chicago, the Chinese consul rushes up from New Orleans, there are parleys, threats, general excitement. The jury convicts or not. But no one ever supposes the true facts have been developed in court, though all suspect complete knowledge of them reposes in numerous celestial bosoms.

All of these—Jews, Italians, Irish, Chinese, Syrians—contribute to the Delta way of life points of view, rudiments of cultures, traits, more or less assimilable though not yet assimilated. Almost any American community, I suppose, has similar bright strands being woven into its texture. But the basic fiber, the cloth of the Delta population—as of the whole South—is built of three dissimilar threads and only three. First were the old slave-holders, the landed gentry, the governing class; though they have gone, they were not sterile; they have their descendants, whose evaluation of life approximates theirs. Second were the poor whites, who owned no slaves, whose manual labor lost its dignity from being in competition with slave labor, who worked their small unproductive holdings ignored by the gentry, despised by the slaves. Third were the Negroes.

The poor whites of the South: a nice study in heredity and environment. Who can trace their origin, estimate their qualities, do them justice? Not I. Some say their forefathers served terms in English prisons for debt and were released on condition that they migrate from the mother country to the colonies. The story continues that they congregated in Georgia. The story may or may not be true; it is unpopular, needless to say. This much, however, it is safe to assert: they were not blest with worldly goods or mental attainments. The richer coast and tidewater country was not for them; their efforts at tilling the soil had to be among the unfertile hills. Farther and farther west they were pushed by an unequal competition until they lodged in the mountains of North Carolina, Tennessee, and Kentucky and in the clay hills of Alabama and Mississippi. Pure English stock. If it was ever good, the virus of poverty, malnutrition, and inter-breeding has done its degenerative work: the present breed is probably the most unprepossessing on the broad face of the ill-populated earth. I know they are respon-sible for the only American ballads, for camp meetings, for a whole new and excellent school of Southern litera-ture. I can forgive them as the Lord God forgives, but admire them, trust them, love them—never. Intellectually and spiritually they are inferior to the Negro, whom they hate. Suspecting secretly they are inferior to him, they must do something to him to prove to themselves their superiority. At their door must be laid the disgraceful riots and lynchings gloated over and exaggerated by Negrophiles the world over.

The Delta was not settled by these people; its pioneers were slave-owners and slaves. One exception may be noted. Forming a small intermediate white class were the managers and slave-drivers and bosses, men of some abil-ity and force, mostly illiterate. These in time became plantation-owners, often buying up and operating suc-cessfully the places lost by their former employers. Here is an ironic and American and encouraging phenomenon. Their children are being what is known as well educated. They will be the aristocrats of tomorrow; they make ex-cellent professional Southerners now.

But the poor whites—"hill-billies," "red-necks," "pecker-woods," they are often derisively called—did not remain outside the Delta. Twenty-five or thirty years ago they began to seep in from the hills of Alabama and Missis-sippi, probably the more energetic and ambitious of them. The Delta soil seemed good to them; they came as ten-ants and remained as small farmers. In certain counties they so throve and increased that they now outnumber the Negroes, control the local government, and fix the culture—God save the mark!—of those counties. That fate is probably in store for my own county. I am glad I shall not be present to witness its fulfillment. The river folk do not like white tenants or "red-neck" neighbors. When these shall have supplanted the Negro, ours will be a sadder country, and not a wiser one.

Just now we are happy that the brother in black is still the tiller of our soil, the hewer of our wood, our servants, troubadours, and criminals. His manners offset his inefficiency, his vices have the charm of amiable weaknesses, he is a pain and a grief to live with, a solace and a delight. There are seven or eight of him to every one of us and he is the better breeder. Ours is surely the black belt. It is all very well for Cheyenne or Schenectady or Stockholm or Moscow, where a black-faced visitor is a day's wonder, to exclaim: "There is no race problem! Southerners are barbarians and brutes." There never is a race problem until the two races living in close contact approach numerical equality. The belle of Kamchatka could marry the Crown Prince of Nigeria and the union could be blest past telling, but a hundred years afterwards the Kamchatkans would be unaffected and undarkened by the incident. In our country if such an incident became a custom, the end of the century would behold a Delta population neither white nor black, but hybrid. Many philanthropists, the usual run of sentimentalists, and some scientists are confident this would be well and is in fact inevitable. Assimilation they are sure is the solution, and a desirable one, so long as they do not have to co-operate personally in the experiment. The trouble is that the white Southerner is stubbornly averse to playing the necessary role of party of the second part in the experiment. Whatever his practice may be, he agrees in theory with Anglo-Saxons living among darker races the world over that the hybrid is not a desirable product, that amalgamation is not the answer so far as he can prevent it.

I often conclude that the only Southerners worth talking about are the darkies. But what can a white man, north or south, say of them that will even approximate the truth? The one thing we are certain of is that they are one people, of one blood, with identical background, tradition, environment, alike as peas in a pod—and this is untrue. When the New England and English slave-dealers captured their human booty, they combed a vast section of Africa, populated by tribes unalike in physique, physiognomy, and customs; some were of small stature, stupid; others were superb physical specimens with a certain tribal history and pride; some were blue-black, others brown or reddish brown; some had flat noses and great loose lips, others had features almost as regular and fine as Arabs; some were princes and rulers, others slaves. Now and then the slave-dealers brought along for good measure the Arab tribesmen who had captured and collected the natives for them. All these strains, these differences, may be detected in the Negro population of the South today. These facts are unknown to the Negro and to the generality of whites, both of whom attribute any deviation from the black, spread-nosed, thick-lipped type familiar in caricature to some intermixture of white blood. No race probably ever had less knowledge of its own past, traditions, and antecedents. What African inheritance they still retain lies in the deep wells of their being, subconscious. They know not whence they came nor what manner of life they led there. Their folklore, rich and fascinating, is American, not African. Only in their practices in voodoo, their charms, potions, and incantations, can we catch glimpses of customs practiced by them in their mysterious homeland. This failure on their part to hold and pass on their own history is due, I think, not so much to their failure to master any form of written communication as to their obliterating genius for living in the present. The American Negro is interested neither in the past nor in the future, this side of heaven. He neither remembers nor plans. The white man does little else: to him the present is the one great unreality.

In slavery days the darkies lived in "quarters," a group of cabins not far from the "big house" of the owner. To-day each family on a large plantation lives in a two- or three-room house on the fifteen- or twenty-acre tract it is renting and working. Many of them own their own farms, generally forty acres, rarely more than one hundred and sixty. And many, of course, have abandoned farming and moved to town, where they hire out as servants or do manual labor for the railroads, the lumber companies, the government forces on the levee, or grace in idleness the poolrooms and gambling-halls of the colored end of town. None of them feels that work *per se* is good; it is only a means to idleness ("leisure" is the word in white circles). The theory of the white man, no matter what his prac-tice, is the reverse: he feels that work is good, and idle-ness, being agreeable, must be evil. I leave it to the wise to say which is the more fruitful philosophy, but I know which best develops the capacity to wear idleness like a perfume and an allurement. A white poolroom or soda-water stand is a depressing place where leisure does not seem excellent or ribaldry amusing. But Negro con-vocations, legal or otherwise, are always enjoyable affairs right down to the first pistol-shot.

So the Delta problem is how all these folks—aristocrats gone to seed, poor whites on the make, Negroes convinced mere living is good, aliens of all sorts that blend or curdle —can dwell together in peace if not in brotherhood and live where, first and last, the soil is the only means of livelihood. Most of our American towns, all of our cities, have their unsolved problem of assimilation. But the South's is infinitely more difficult of solution. The attempt to work out any sort of one, much less a just one, as a daily living problem, diverts the energies and abilities of our best citizenship from more productive fields. A certain patience might well be extended to the South, if not in justice, in courtesy. . . .

But in this respect we of the Delta have been fortunate in our misfortunes. Time out of mind we have been gifted with common disasters, all-inclusive tragedies that have united us or at least made us lean together. The old yellow-fever epidemics were especially helpful. And there's no better cement for a people than moderate poverty. No class or individual with us has ever known riches. Some years the crop and price are good and we take a trip or sport an automobile or buy another plantation; most years the crop fails or the bottom drops out of the market and we put on a new mortgage or increase the old one. Even then no one goes hungry or cold or feels very sorry for himself. If we become too prosperous and entertain the impression we are independent and frightfully efficient (farmers feel that way any good year), the levee breaks and the wise river terrifies his silly children back into humility and that cozy one-family feeling of the inmates of the Ark. Behind us a culture lies dying, before us the forces of the unknown industrial world gather for catastrophe. We have fields to plow and the earth smells good; maybe in time someone will pay us more for our cotton than we spend making it. In the meantime the darkies make up new songs about the boll-weevil and the river, and the sun pours over us his great tide of warmth which is also light.

# CHAPTER III

# *Mur and Nain*

I
n this kind of country and among this sort of people I was born, in 1885. That the month should have been May seems a debatable blessing, for in that season of bloom and untarnished green you are always brimming with delight or despair, groundless in either case, and, worse still, it is then that spirit and body are one and indistinguishable and your thoughts are feelings and the word is made flesh every hour. Besides, it happened to be the morning of Ascension Day, a fact I used to consider significant or symbolic, but of what I could never decide. Yet a pagan month and a Christian day for a start still seem to me a stimulating handicap, with possibilities. Unfortunately my coming impressed no one sufficiently for him to remember the hour, much less the minute, so my friends who ponder horoscopes have never been able to chart me properly between Taurus and Gemini, Venus and Mercury; they only insist the stars were badly tangled at my arrival and no great good can be expected of me, a prophecy I sometimes find comforting in view of the outcome. Anyway, I was born and in May and on Ascen-

sion Day, and I have picked up the information that the incident overjoyed no one, because Father and Mother were young and good-looking, poor and well-born, in love with each other and with life, and they would have considered the blessed event more blessed had it been postponed a year or two. No matter how unfavorably I impressed them at the time, they impressed me not at all, and for a much longer period afterwards. I have no single memory of them dating from the first four years of my life. The only persons whose activities were important enough to dent the fairly undentable tablets of my memory were Nain, my colored nurse, and Mur, my grandmother.

Southerners like to make clear, especially to Northerners, that every respectable white baby had a black mammy, who, one is to infer, was fat and elderly and bandannaed. I was a respectable and a white baby, but Nain was sixteen, divinely café-au-lait, and she would have gone into cascades of giggles at the suggestion of a bandanna on her head. I loved her devotedly and never had any other nurse. Everything about her was sweet-smelling, of the right temperature, and dozy. Psychiatrists would agree, I imagine, that I loved her because in her I found the comfort of the womb, from which I had so recently and unexpectedly been ejected and for which I was still homesick. The womb may be comfortable, but I have my doubts, and, without a little first-hand information, I shall continue to believe I loved her for her merry goodness, her child's heart that understood mine, and her laughter that was like a celesta playing triplets. Chiefly I remember her bosom: it was soft and warm, an ideal place to cuddle one's head against. My earliest clear recollection is of a song she would sing me so cuddled—rather, not of the song itself, but of its effect on me. The words and tune have gone, but not what they did to me.

A poor egoistic sort of memory I know, that records nothing of the outer world, but only how certain bits of it pleased or distressed me, yet mine, and no better now than it was then, and no different. Nain would hold me in her arms and sing this song, rocking herself a little. I would try not to cry, but it made me feel so lost and lonely that tears would seep between my lids and at last I would sob until I shook against her breast. "Whut's de madder, Peeps?" she would say. "Whut you cryin' fur?" But I was learning not so much how lonely I could be as how lonely everybody could be, and I could not explain. If she innocently endowed me with a sense of the tears of things, she gave me something hard to live with, but impossible to live, as I would live, without. If her music opened vistas and induced contemplations, unbearably poignant and full of pity, I should perhaps thank her for the Good Friday Spell and the Dance of the Blessed Spirits, for certain Bach chorales and Negro spirituals that, awakening kindred compassions in the core of my being, have guided me more sure-footedly and authoritatively through life than all ten of the Commandments. *Lachrymæ rerum* in a baby's vacant heart? A silly question, but one of the many I do not know the answer to.

Nain possibly comes back to me more as an emanation or aura than as a person. But, no mistake, Mur was a person. She was my first chum. I slept in her room, calcimined a lugubrious blue, whether in a bed of my own or hers I can't recall, and was often awake when she prepared herself for the night. It was a splendid ritual. First she removed her switch, a rather scrawny, gray affair, like a diminutive horse's tail, which, when on duty, enlarged the knot of hair at the nape of her neck. Then she combed it briskly until it fluffed out into a fascinating silver cone before she rested it for the night on the bureau.

Next, and this was awe-inspiring, she removed from her mouth one single tooth attached to an amazing red thing like a live and oddly shaped eave and dropped it into a glass of water. Last she poured something from a brown bottle into another glass of water and drank it. I wondered and wondered why that was necessary, but to my questions she always replied it was Crab Orchard Water. The answer cleared up nothing then or now. Through these mystic rites she was fully clad, only she started out in her black dress and ended up in her white nightgown. I never understood how this transformation was accomplished, though it proceeded under my very eyes, without her being at some stage of it undressed; this was more than modesty, it was legerdemain. When these vivid preliminaries were over, it was time for prayers.

Mur, being an Armstrong by birth, was of Scotch descent and Presbyterian to the marrow. She never outlived the drastic piety of that angular creed, but after she married my grandfather, whom others called the Gray Eagle of the Delta but I called Fafar, she became an Episcopalian, out of deference to his Church of England traditions and leanings. She was as broad-minded as a Presbyterian could be and by temperament neither austere nor intolerant, but I could tell she feared my pretty Papist mother would neglect my spiritual needs. Therefore she taught me the Lord's Prayer to replace Now-I-Lay-Me and every so often read me her two favorite passages from the Bible. I think the Lord's Prayer took all right, but from the start I was immune to the Bible. I did not like those passages of hers and, though one is not supposed to have moral convictions at so tender an age, I did not consider them good morally. One concerned Dives and Lazarus, the other the Prodigal Son. Lazarus had too many sores to be attractive. Abraham must have been horrid with that peculiar roomy bosom of his like a hair-lined cupboard, and it was downright ugly of him not to let Lazarus give a little drop of water to poor old Dives. I could feel Dives' torment and the prickle of Abraham's beard and I was sure Lazarus would have received something nourishing if he'd asked for it instead of for such silly canary-fare as crumbs. I developed a strong distaste for paradise. Nor was the Prodigal Son any better. He could have found a more sanitary place to stay in than the hog-wallow, he just didn't try, and when he came on home he deserved a good whipping instead of a party. The nice boy, who had never run away and got hog-smelly, had a right to be upset.

These thoughts I kept to myself, sitting quietly by Mur, who read the lovely words softly and drew comfort from them and hoped they might teach me goodness. How little our wisest teachers guess what effects their best-intentioned efforts are producing in the minds and imaginations of the bland-eyed neophytes at their knees! Many people these days have Abraham's antipathy for purple raiment and his obsession that a case history of sores is the only admission card to paradise. I cling to my childish preference for hell. With Achilles and Dives and Frederick II for company one could gaze afar off and see Abraham and Mahomet and the Blessed Damozel and be right well content.

Although allergic to Mur's spiritual provender, I found her pantry and general back-gallery doings altogether delectable. Meals in those days managed to be pretty fabulous affairs anyway—always soup, two or three meats, vegetables innumerable, never less than two hot breads— but besides all these Mur habitually had *two* desserts. Imagine ice-cream *and* pudding, ambrosia *and* pie! I don't know whether this glorious termination of dinner was a

custom of the times or a personal eccentricity, but I approved of it from the depths of my being. As Christmas
time approached, the actual celebration of which left no
impression on me whatever, she made elaborate fruit
cakes, some blond and some brunet. For that undertaking,
which required much thought and measuring, she would
spread newspapers before the fire in her room and pile
them with pyramids of assorted currants and raisins and
nuts. I would lie in bed and watch them in the firelight,
quaking deliciously inside and my nose twitching like a
rabbit's, though I never actually liked fruit cake.

Dinner parties were rare at our house and I disapproved of them because they meant my enforced withdrawal from the dining-room. But nearly always there
were extra and often unexpected guests for meals. Once
the ice-cream gave out just before my turn came. This
was my first experience of the injustice of things. One is
not born a Stoic. I took the event lying down, under the
table, loud with woe, and was hustled out, conspicuous in
misery. Generally, however, meal time was a nice time
and everybody talked a lot. The best thing about it was
watching Willis, Mur's very black waiter. When the dining-room was frigid Willis piled the coals high in the fireplace. When he piled them too high it was too hot on
Mur's back and she made him stand between her and the
fireplace, almost in the fire, an elegant human fire-screen.
It was agreeable to watch him break out into a profuse
sweat without any loss of dignity—indeed, with increased
immobility and self-importance. He must have got dreadfully hot behind. His was a lofty character.

He and I, while not intimate, were on friendly terms
and he always let me witness the first stages of turtle soup.
To the grown-ups turtle soup was simply the predestined
last act of a soft-shell turtle's career and one worth waiting

years for. But Willis and I knew the terrific drama preceding it. Someone would bring one of the great monsters
to our back steps and leave it there as a gracious and esteemed gift. To Willis fell the hard lot of converting it
from an unlikely reptile into a delicacy for Dives and his
kind. The turtle gave no co-operation. It resented the
situation and withdrew from it by tucking head and flip-
pers into its shell and refusing to emerge. Willis would
then give him a jab in the armpit and out the obscene
head would dart, the slit eyes pale with hatred, and the
horny beaked mouth snapping dangerously at all of us.
Nain would scream and snatch me up and scuttle to safety on top of the cistern, while the cook would emit Fo'-
Gods, interspersed with strictures on the cannibalism of
white folks. Finally that dreadful head would come out
long enough for Willis to whack it off with the ax, at
which the rest of the turtle would walk off hurriedly, as if
the incident were closed. Even this was not the climax of
the gory horror—Willis still had to break off the top shell.
When this was accomplished, before your startled eyes
lay the turtle's insides, unharmed, neatly in place, and still
ticking! They did not seem to miss the head, but acted
like the works of a watch when you open the back. It was
the nakedest thing I ever laid eyes on, and usually while
you were watching, fascinated, the whole thing walked
off, just that way, and the cook would almost faint. Turtle
soup indeed! I don't miss it and I hope not to meet up
with it unexpectedly in elegant surroundings.

Mur always dressed in black because my grandfather
had not been long dead. It is a pity some of the painted
and bedizened old ladies, who have grandchildren but
are not grandmothers, cannot know how beautiful and
useful and real she was. She taught me to see flowers, and
of course anyone who sees them loves them. It would

have gone hard with me in certain later hours without that training. She showed me dog-tooth violets outside of Birmingham and so many flowers around Asheville that we invented a game to see which one could spot a new variety first. There must have been many kinfolks and mountains and various happenings around these towns during our visits, but my only memories of them are of wild flowers and Mur. On the other hand, her appreciation of good china, glass, furniture, and draperies was singularly deficient: she aimed only at comfort and had no special genius for that. I remember her horsehair sofas. Her only pictures, besides the oil paintings of prissy-looking great-aunts and such, were an engraving of the Sistine Madonna and another large and quite terrifying one of the death of Queen Elizabeth. After growing up with the latter I understand why one of those fool early Percys was beheaded for attempting to rescue Mary Queen of Scots. In the fine arts Mur's sole flair was for music. Young people loved to dance to her piano-playing and she loved to play for them. Her touch was firm and her sense of rhythm contagious. As I was either moved to tears or bored by anything slower than an allegretto, I recall only her waltzes, marches, and polkas.

Mur's figure was ample and she moved splendidly and serenely like an ocean liner. Back of her silver white pompadour she wore a small widow's bonnet, from which hung a widow's veil to her waist, and there was white ruching at her throat and wrists. Every afternoon she took a nap (which should be compulsory in the interest of sanity), and after her nap she took a walk. I was permitted to be her companion except on those days when her door would be closed and she would walk the floor of her room and Mother would explain: "Mur is thinking about Fafar." On our promenades I sometimes carried her fan as Peter did the nurse's, and we had endless invigorating and informative conversations. There may have been something quaint in our sedate pilgrimages, but no young Mercutio of the countryside ever dared to address her with Mercutio's levity. She suffered fools, but brooked no impertinence; she feared nothing except sin and no one except God. On nights when Father and Mother were out at some party or other and she and I were left alone in the house, which suddenly seemed very big, Mur would stoke up the coal fire and thrust a heavy iron poker deep into its embers where they were turning lavender. The poker point would become red-hot. With that reliable and effective weapon at hand we would settle down to a safe and cheerful evening. Father often teased her by asking what she would do with the poker if a burglar did actually come in. But I knew, and I think he did, that she would have attacked and routed him; he would have been sizzled and spitted like a chicken liver on a brochette. I always hoped just a little bit to witness such a dramatic victory. Instead the poker grew whiter and the flames quieter and bluer and I would move my chair close to hers and she would read aloud to me. What superb things she chose when she was not Bible-minded! Grimm and Hans Andersen, *Huckleberry Finn* and *Uncle Remus, The Rose and the Ring,* and *A Christmas Carol, Pilgrim's Progress* and *Alice in Wonderland.* Mur's reading was not condescending; she loved it as much as I did. She cried at the same places I did, and when she laughed she shook till her glasses fell off. Of course, when we cried—say at the story of the Frog Prince or the Little Boy with Ice in His Heart—we said nothing about it to each other, though Mur sometimes had to stop and blow her nose. Perhaps a diluted course in Lenin and Marx with passages from *Mein Kampf* or a handbook on electricity and aviation would have better prepared a youngster for life as it is. But not, I think, for life as it should be. Old orders change I know, and Mur knew, having herself lived through the death throes of one with all its wreckage of aspirations and possibilities, with bitterness to master and new hope to create. But new orders change too. Only one thing never changes—the human heart. Revolutions and ideologies may lacerate it, even break it, but they cannot change its essence. After Fascism and Communism and Capitalism and Socialism are over and forgotten as completely as slavery and the old South, that same headstrong human heart will be clamoring for the old things it wept for in Eden—love and a chance to be noble, laughter and a chance to adore something, someone, somewhere. Mur and her books did not inform me, they formed me. She should have lived forever to read to one generation after another of little boys, but one night as she was sleeping she died, without premonition or pain, her face no paler than it always was, and a charming smile on her lips. I was a little boy then, but I have never been so close to any living creature since.

# CHAPTER IV

# Mère and Père

Although Mère and Père, Mother's parents, were born in New Orleans, they were just as French as if they had landed day before yesterday from Lyon or Tours. Mère was plump, squat, and blue-eyed, with a soft face that never learned wrinkles or unlearned its miraculous pink and white. She wore pretty things, light in color, and little bonnets with forget-me-nots and pink rose-buds, and she always managed to look cool, in crises or midsummer. Père would not have had any particular look at all except for his beard, which was so long and silky it could be plaited into one, two, or three plaits and when hooked under and over his ears produced an amazing effect of benign ferocity. The year of fifty-cent cotton Père bought a Delta plantation on Deer Creek and bid adieu to crêpes suzette, absinthe, the old French Opera House, and all his kin except Uncle Alfred, whom no one spoke to or of because he had sold out to Ben Butler. He loaded Mère's nice French furniture, her Pleyel piano, and four little girls, of whom the blondest and prettiest was my mother, on the boat bound for Greenville, and launched forth to make his fortune in the un-French, uncivilized, undeveloped Delta country.

Père was merely bon bourgeois. But through Mère's veins coursed the blood of the Générelly de Rinaldis. Having somehow failed to stumble on this truly magnificent name in song, story, or archive, I recall the tentative inquiry I once made of Mère concerning her forebears. I was told positively, though a bit vaguely, it seemed to me, that the original old Rinaldi from his castle in thirteenth-century Italy had descended on a lovely lady in a neighboring castle and made her, in disregard of her wishes, his consort, and that this exploit satisfied the family's yen for romance and heroism for five or six centuries—in fact, until Mère's grandfather, a dashing and aristocratic youth, was hustled out of revolutionary France by a faithful servant after untold hardships and escapes, and turned up in New Orleans with a few charming water-colors of tulips and roses and a deep sense of wrong. A trifle tenuous, perhaps, as proof of glorious lineage, but Mère was calmly adamant in the conviction that her blood was blue, which gave her the upper hand over Père right from the outset. This was rather sad, because he was a sweet and infinitely polite soul and had been a Captain under Beauregard. Nor did he improve his status with Mère by acquiring this outlandish Delta property. Though she could pioneer, she had neither admiration nor liking for the role—no French woman ever has—and I suspect he rather misrepresented its charm and elegance, being as he was on the poetic and sentimental side. Even naming the place Camelia after her did not pacify her or compensate for its living-quarters, which, far from being a mansion with white columns, were, I must confess, a log cabin, though a commodious one and fairly comfortable for those days. No, Mère never forgave him; you could tell it when she said "Mais, Ernest"; and even when with an "Ach" she tapped me on the head with her thimbled first finger, I suspected the correction was meant for him as much as for myself. Père was not lazy or even fundamentally incompetent, but his competency never got itself focused. He lost the plantation, moved his family to town, started one business venture after another, and failed in all of them. When Father married his daughter she was a very poor girl who made her own clothes—pretty ones I am told—and had never seen more of the outer world than New Orleans and the Sacré Cœur Convent, where Père somehow managed to have her educated. Père was miscast; besides having little girls, his only accomplishment was raising roses. His Maman Cochets and Malmaisons and Maréchal Niels were famous, or should have been in any civilized community. He should have been provided with dominoes, a desiccated crony or two, a siphon, a bottle of Amer Picon, and a corner in a dingy café where some broad-bosomed madame queened it behind an elevated guichet—and of course he should have had seats for the opera twice a week, including Sunday night.

Instead, his life petered out in a drab little country town, very Protestant and very Anglo-Saxon. In such a setting the French family must have seemed an oddity, but it never tried to be less odd or less French. The little girls continued to play croquet on Sunday, to the scandal of everyone, and to enliven shamelessly that dour and boring day by dance tunes on their little French piano, while their betters attended divine services. Their trouble, and their strength, was that they recognized no betters. Not that they minded Anglo-Saxons or took their own religion hard, but they regarded their poverty as an incident and their position as an immutability. Mère would never have sought the advice of a priest, or anyone else, but she could not have imagined herself anything but a Catholic—it was a habit, a good one, she was sure, but not interesting and distinctly not a subject for conversation. Nor would she have called on members of the congregation whom she considered excellent in everything except social standing, or on anyone in this semi-civilized community, first. As the little French girls grew up they were attractive and popular, which made things easier for everybody, yet Mère permitted courting only within the strict French convention. She was a pain to suitors, chaperoning her daughters everywhere and sitting in her corner of the parlor, playing solitaire, when they came courting. She maintained this observation post—half dragon and half Brangäne—even after Mother was engaged to Father, and his only revenge was occasionally to swipe a card from her deck so she couldn't make it. Father was the catch of the town, but Mère had no enthusiasm for the match: she knew he was what Aunt Nana would call "something of a gay blade," and it never crossed her mind that the Percys were any better than the Bourges.

Were they? In the South a question of that kind is apt to fling family skeletons from their closets into the middle of the parlor floor and to set extant sibs and collaterals shrieking like mandrakes. Even today from Virginia to Texas, from Charleston to Natchez, ten thousand crepuscular old maids and widows in ghostly coveys and clusters are solving such unsolvable issues. They are our Southern Norns, keepers of family Bibles, pruners of family trees, whose role is to remember and foretell—to remember glory and to foretell disaster—while in the gaudy day outside the banker's daughter, Brunhilde, elopes with the soda-water jerker. Père had he been less polite, Mère had she been less assured, might have introduced such devastating evidence into the Bourges-Percy controversy as would have titillated Norn circles for months. They must have known the bleak facts of my paternal ancestry, which confidentially were these:

The first Percy in our part of the South, my great-great-grandfather, was Charles. He blew in from the gray or blue sea-ways with a ship of his own, a cargo of slaves, and a Spanish grant to lands in the Buffalo country south of Natchez. Court records show that he was made an Alcalde and called Don Carlos by the Spaniards, and his house was known as Northumberland Place. This was shortly after the Revolution. Where did he come from? How came he by a Spanish grant? What were his antecedents and station? To such questions climbers in the family tree have found no answers: Don Carlos came from nowhere, he issued suddenly from the sea like the Flying Dutchman or Aphrodite—though Mrs. Dana once darkly confided to me that on his westerly flight he had landed at one of the Caribbean Isles and left a record behind him there nothing short of "lamentable, lamentable." Was he a pirate? Or the lost heir of the earls of Northumberland? Or a hero of the Spanish wars? Silence. Mystery.

Don Carlos settled down on his plantation and married him an intelligent French lady from the other side of the river. The Lord blessed them with progeny, and things seemed to be going well and quite respectably when a lady suddenly appeared from England and said to Don Carlos: "I am the long lost wife of your bosom." As if that was not enough, she added: "Behold, your son and heir!" Whereupon she tendered him, not a wee bairn, but a full-grown Captain in the English Navy, also yclept Charles. Certainly a discouraging business all round. It is not recorded that Don Carlos slapped the lady, but of course he was thoroughly provoked and everybody immediately began suing everybody else. Somewhere during the commotion Don Carlos walked down to the creek with a sugar kettle, tied it round his neck, and hopped in. The creek is still there and is called Percy's Creek to this good day. His will left his holdings, not to his English, but to his American family, whether from pique, outrage, or affection I can only surmise. The wives continued their litigation for a while, wrote eloquent letters to the Governor, and acted as outraged gentlewomen usually act. Then everything was hushed up or patched up without a court decision; both families calmly settled down in the same neighborhood and lived happily ever afterwards. Need I say the English lady was not my ancestress? I have a tender feeling for Don Carlos and wish I could ask him confidentially a few leading questions. He was not exactly a credit to anybody, but, as ancestors go, he had his points.

I once drove to Woodville, a little town which has grown up near the old Percy place, to see if I could discover the grave of Don Carlos. I thought his dates might be clarifying, and once in a while an inscription on a headstone is penetrating to the point of cruelty, if you know half the story. Of the usual engaging youth at the filling station I inquired: "Can you tell me where Charles Percy is buried?" "No," he replied, "didn't know he was dead." I elucidated vaguely. He laughed. "Maybe he'll know, he's a Percy," he said, pointing to a pleasant-looking, countryfied man sitting on the ditch bank, spitting tobacco juice. "No," drawled my half cousin, "we never could find where the old bird was buried. I reckon it was on the creek bank, and the creek's changed its course."

Playing Tarzan in the family tree is hazardous business; there are too many rotten branches. Mère and Père would have put such irrelevancies in the class with religion, as distinctly not a subject for conversation. The Percys were nice people; the Bourges were nice people—voilà tout! But I cannot help wondering what were the qualifications that admitted to the post-Civil-War aristocracy. Apparently not pedigree, certainly not wealth. A way of life for several generations? A tradition of living? A style and pattern of thinking and feeling not acquired but inherited? No matter how it came about, the Bourges and Percys were nice people—that is what I breathed in as a child, the certainty I was as good as anyone else, which, because of the depth of the conviction, was unconscious, never talked of, never thought of. Besides Southerners, the only people I have ever met graced with the same informal assurance were Russian aristocrats.

I suspect, however, that no pair ever looked less aristocratic than Père and I, he in his neat but well-worn and out-of-style sack suit, I barefooted and hatless, as we rushed up the levee to see the *Floating Palace* come round the bend. The blast of the calliope way up the river had electrified the countryside. All the Negroes, all the children, and half the adults were swarming to the levee. From the thick of the laughter and shoving and pointing, he and I would watch the magnificent apparition sweep down the center of the stream, black smoke pouring from its funnel and white plumes of steam from the calliope, whose stentorian cacophonies were like the laughter of the gods at some pranks of Hebe's, only off key. Waiting for dark and the show to begin was unbearable. At last the calliope would hit a high note and hold it, until you almost burst, then dash into "Dixie," and we would rush down the levee, squeeze on to the gangplank, buy our tickets, and at last, at last, enter—Elysium. Such a grand, exciting smell of sweating people, everybody eating pink popcorn and drinking pop, such a dazzle of lights, such getting stepped on and knocked over and picked up, and at last the show, the beautiful, incredible show! A little Japanese with jerky angular gyrations climbed a ladder of sharp swords on feet as bare as mine; an adorable lady in pink tights floated through the air with ravishing grace while an elegant gentleman in full evening dress explained she came from the Garden of Eden; a baker's daughter hid seven suitors from her father in his oven and when he returned he built up the fire and they were baked to a crisp; in fact, the baker took them out of the oven for you to see and they were flat and brown, exactly like gingerbread men. This last was surpassingly horrible and gave me nightmares for a solid week, to the confusion of the family, who finally in desperation administered castor oil followed by raspberry jam. But all the rest was divinely beautiful. Show-boat! I never heard of such a name in my time. Everybody knew it was the *Floating Palace* and worthy, a thousand times, of its title.

Mère and Père were at their best, I think, at Roxbury, Aunt Nana's place in Virginia, or possibly I saw them there less interruptedly and less flurried by such incidents as beset those who can't quite make both ends meet. It was an old run-down place, far out in the country, and Mère's corner room was full of sunlight and breeze. On afternoons when it was too hot for me to go on expeditions with the little darkies, the three of us would convene there and Mère would bring out her quilting materials, needle and thread, and that thimble of hers. Aunt Nana might rustle in with glasses of blackberry vinegar, which apparently went out when cocktails came in. It had a kingly color and when chilled with ice, which Uncle George had harvested last winter from the pond and stored in sawdust against such occasions, it tasted like those snow and honey concoctions of the Greeks, just sweet enough and just sour enough and altogether Olympian. Mère's quilts were marvels of skill and took months and months to make. They were born from the tails of neckties and scraps of velvet and silk from petticoats, bustles, and linings. She first sewed the scraps into squares, then she sewed the squares on each side of a panel of watered silk into a quilt shape; next she bordered the whole with a hand's width of velvet, and last she embroidered all of it with wonderful flowers and birds and vines and bows and even little baskets. The result was as personal as that web of Penelope's and as French as the illegitimate daughters of Louis XIV. In the making the vexatious æsthetic problem was to match the colors of the scraps. She tried them out this way and that, sometimes even consulting Père and me on the effect, though this I fancy was mere affability. Pink, of course, matched with blue or lavender or even light green, but never with red. It was unthinkable to set green and blue side by side, or blue and lavender. Red was always difficult, but yellow could be sprinkled nearly haphazard. I would watch with deep interest and so received my first lesson in color-consciousness. Perhaps I should thank her for later hours of delight with Rembrandt and Titian, and blame her perhaps for my being still a little scared and shocked by El Greco.

Meanwhile Père would start humming, and that would be my cue to ask him what opera the tune was from, was it grand or comic, heavy or light, what was the plot, was it as good as *Les Huguenots*? *Les Huguenots* was his classic example of a heavy opera, into which category fell *Aïda*, *Faust*, and an opera new to New Orleans called *Lohengrin*, which he had been told was *very* heavy. *Les Huguenots* was also grand opera. Grand opera always ended with a death or a suicide, usually two or three of each. Then why was not *Carmen* a grand opera? Well, it was heavy but not grand, because they gave it on Sunday nights in New Orleans, and at the Comique, not the Opéra, in Paris. What! *Carmen* on Sunday nights, like *La Belle Hélène* and *La Fille de Madame Angot* and *Giroflé-Girofla?* Why did they do that? As these distinctions became more tenuous and Pére more hard-pressed, Aunt Nana, who loved peace though she never abandoned an argument, would cough and observe that everybody said the New Orleans Opera House really was more beautiful than the Paris Opéra. Mère would observe: "Évidemment," since the Paris Opéra had no loges découvertes. Père out of the exuberance of his memories would start singing "O mon fils" from *La Juive* and go on louder and louder until he came to shocking grief on the high C of the climax. Mère would look over her glasses and exclaim: "Mais, Ernest," but not in her usual Fricka-to-Wotan manner, indeed so sympathetically that in a distrait moment she would sew crimson next to shrimp pink.

The French do actually love music, but in a maddening way. When a favorite passage is well sung the thing to do is to cheer and cry "Bravo! Bis!"; you do not swoon. Mère would have had no patience with swooning for any cause, or with ecstasy as a result of music any more than as a result of religion. Music was a charming décor, a delightful adjunct to living, in the same category as chic clothes and a considered cuisine. The great French artists felt the same way about it: Clouet, Poussin, Chardin, Renoir never attempted ecstasy. If you wish to express sentiment, that is permissible, in the manner of Greuze and Massenet, but ecstasy, no, ecstasy is too much. Verlaine and Debussy tried it, but they were more neurotic than French, and their success lay not in content but in style, which in its perfection was absolutely French. It is a rare Frenchman who really prefers *Pelléas* to *Héro-*

*diade,* or Verlaine to de Musset. Mère and Père wouldn't have done so; that I do only proves, I suppose, that moony strain of Don Carlos.

Music would be continued on a less exalted plane by Aunt Nana and me after supper. We would open the parlor, always shuttered and musty and cool by day, light the candles on each side of the black upright piano, and sing duets. "Just a Song at Twilight" and "Love's Old Sweet Song" were our favorites, and we liked a new piece, "After the Ball," which was very sad, almost as sad as the tune Mother used to sing to herself while sewing, "Tit Willow, Tit Willow, Tit Willow." I cannot explain why I so completely misinterpreted Gilbert and Sullivan's intention. I have made such mistakes all my life, and it's too late now to change. It was too late from the beginning. The color of our temperament, our chief concern, is nothing of our making. If we are pink, we can only hope that fate will not set us cheek by jowl with red. If we see the world through mauve glasses, there's no sort of sense in wishing they were white. We may only console ourselves by noting that a certain opalescence, like sun through the misty mornings of London, is not without a loveliness denied the truer and cruder white noons of the desert.

# CHAPTER V

# Playmates

ny little boy who was not raised with little Negro children might just as well not have been raised at all. My first boon-companion was Skillet, the small dark son of Mère's cook. He was the best crawfisher in the world and I was next. Instead of closed sewers our town had open ditches, which after an overflow swarmed with crawfish, small clear ones, quite shrimp-like, whose unexpected backward agility saved them from any except the most skilful hands, and large red ones, surly and whiskered, with a startling resemblance to the red-nosed old reprobates you saw around the saloons when you were looking for tobacco tags in the sawdust. When these rared back and held their claws wide apart, Skillet said they were saying: "Swear to God, white folks, I ain't got no tail." Theoretically it was for their tails that we hunted them, because when boiled and seasoned and prayed over they made that thick miraculous pink soup you never experience unless you have French blood in the family or unless you dine at Prunier's. Of course anyone could catch crawfish with a string and a lump of bacon, and anyone knows their family life is passed in holes, like snake-holes, from which they must be lured; but who except Skillet had ever observed that a hollow bone lying on the bottom of a ditch is bound to be occupied by one? Maybe he sat there as in a summerhouse thinking or catching a nap or saying to himself: "These boys will never think of this." If you waded up noiselessly and clapped both hands suddenly and simultaneously over both ends of the bone, he was yours and went into the bucket outraged and blowing bubbles, nothing appeased that his high destiny was to contribute his bit to a bisque d'écrevisses.

Skillet's sister Martha was a virago. Like Goneril she never reformed and so kept the plot boiling. She constantly threatened to do away with our crawfish in some low diabolical manner. This led to a painful incident. After an especially successful day we decided to hide from Martha our water-bucket brim-full of the simmering live catch and chose for that purpose an obscure corner behind the bookcase in Mère's parlor. Black fate decreed that on that very night Mère should give what was called a soirée. Now, the parlor was the hallowed place to receive guests, gay and beribboned and with splendid bustles. Fruit punch seemed to make them as lively as cocktails do now (I think Père spiked it). Mrs. Holland sang the Jewel Song from *Faust* and as an encore "Three Little Pigs Went to Market." Everyone said she should have joined the New Orleans Opera instead of marrying Mr. Holland, as obviously she would have had a succès fou in *Mignon* or *L'Africaine,* but Mother insisted she was a natural comédienne and would have been irresistible in *Orphée aux Enfers* or *Les Cloches de Corneville.* Then someone began playing dance music, which, if I recollect accurately, was as enticing and stimulating as the radio, but in a nice way, and without interpolations concerning liver pills and tooth paste. After the dancing, Mother and Mr. Harry Ball were to have sung a duet—they had "parlor voices, but sweet"—and it may have been sung, but I was not destined to hear it. At that moment a ladylike scream stopped the music and threw the gathering into consternation. Mrs. Holland had stepped on a large red crawfish in the attitude of "Swear to God, white folks." It made a crunchy sound. Another was discovered and another; they were all over the place. Mère was indignant, but Mother, though she retired me hastily, and in bad odor, really wanted to laugh. Skillet and I were in disgrace; Martha—need I say?—escaped unscathed.

Crawfishing was not Skillet's only excellence. As a conversationalist he outdistanced any white child in inventiveness, absurdity, and geniality. In Mère's back yard we would sit in a row-boat, a relic of the last overflow, and for hours ply imaginary oars toward an imaginary land that we described and embellished as we approached. These voyages afforded endless opportunity for discussions. One in particular drifts back to me across long years. It was one of those still, hot days when earth things lie tranced at the bottom of a deep sea of summer sun. We were resting on our oars at the moment. Far, far up buzzards circled dreamily, their black wings motionless, tilting, banking, coasting in wide arcs, somnambulistic symbols of the drowse and delight of deep summer. Watching them, Skillet observed in a singsong: "If they was to ever light, the world would burn up." As the birds seemed fixed at their vast altitude, this was a safe prophecy. But I was skeptical, as could have been expected of any horrid little white realist. Skillet, though, was so eloquent in citing reasons and authorities that my disbelief weakened and by degrees I was convinced, for the old excellent reason that I wanted to be. As we watched, the buzzards, careening and narrowing their circles, began to descend. It was exciting to see them drop lower and lower and to think what might happen. At last we could discern their horrible necks and heads. Skillet rose in a kind of ecstasy, thrusting out his arms, flexing his knees, and chanting: "Don't let 'em light, God, don't let 'em light." The flames of a consuming world were practically around us. Only the fire music as it came to Mime about the time Siegfried rushed in with the bear could have expressed our abject and delicious terror. They were hovering over our own back yard and, last touch of horror, there lay one of Mère's chickens dead—indeed, more than dead—their target, stark and untidy on the crust of the earth so unconcerned and so doomed. One of the ghastly creatures suddenly rocked, flapped its wings, and settled down awkwardly on the fence between us and the Fergusons'. "Look, I told you so, the world didn't burn up," I almost sobbed, torn between relief and disappointment. "He lit on a fence. He ain't never teched the ground," whispered Skillet. The buzzard gave an ungainly bound and landed on the too, too solid earth. "Look," I wailed. "He lit on a chip," Skillet observed affably. I was outraged.

Calling to mind with gratitude those to whom we are indebted on our journey is not only a sort of piety, but one of the few pleasures that endure without loss of luster to the end. I like to imagine that Skillet is not in jail or dead, but that he lords it in a Pullman car or pulpit, or perhaps has a farm of his own and many little crawfishers—in fine, that the swooping dark wings continue for him to light on a chip. He is all my memory records of what must have been long months of my childhood; all others it seems were lay figures.

Equally treasurable were Amelia's children on Aunt Nana's farm in Virginia, where I was deposited so many summers. I don't remember the house well except that it was square, airy, and very old, with a corridor behind leading to the kitchen, storerooms, and Amelia's sleeping-quarters; the old furniture and woodwork made no impression whatever. All around were cornfields and dabs of woods, and a few hundred yards in front the small cool river. I must have seen it rain there often, but like a sundial I remember only sunlight, acres and acres of it: sometimes merely pale and fresh and still on the pasture; or heavy like a great depth of blue sea-water on the undulating rows of corn, which, tired of the weight, sagged limply; or in splotches and scarves and sudden widths of glitter on the river; or, best, early in the morning, when it slanted in long gray panels through the orchard and barely silvered the small yellow pears with a sweat of cold dew on them and dew on the grass where they lay. Quantities of little wiggly paths, cow-paths likely, meandered everywhere and nowhere, bordered by straggling colonies of tawny lilies and bushes of pokeberry, indispensable for war-paint on our Indian days. They too were sunny, but managed to make every patch of shade a port of call, and two of them met in the little wood where an old fox-grape vine with the kindliness and humor of old age crooked one arm into a perfect swing. The swing itself would be in shadow, of the breezy arrowy kind, all shreds and patches on you as you swung through it, but you looked out from under the branches across all that shining clearness that lay on the fields and the aspen woodland to the old house far off to the left, and you knew you needed nothing else. When your peace is without grayness, it comes seldom and does not stay long; some are still hunting for it and some are trying to find it again, but know they won't.

At Aunt Nana's there were so many fascinating spots you couldn't make the round of them in a week, and all of them smelled good. The dairy, round, with thick walls and no windows, where the crocks of milk and clabber and cream stood in live spring-water, smelled cold and slightly sour. The corn-bin had a warm yellow smell like a loaf of bread at the moment Amelia opened the oven and pawed it out with the edge of her apron. The barn, from the pile of manure in front (which Père said Uncle George was too lazy to scatter over the fields, and it was beautiful manure) to the stalls, soggy with corn-shucks and urine, had an exciting smell, like autumn, but the smell was definitely good. Of course the kitchen was so full of things to whiff and sniff and inhale with eyes closed that you could stay there all day, only you were always being shooed out, on lucky occasions with the batter-bowl to lick. The best smell, however, was undoubtedly at the mill. That mill was none of your modern contraptions, spotless and intricate and unintelligible. You saw how it worked when it worked, which was occasionally. There was the dam, and the mill-pond above and behind it; there was the huge water-wheel which sloshed and turned when the sluice was opened; there were the great mill-stones, likely the very ones the gods used to use, between which the corn filtered to its golden doom; and there was the miller, a bit sweaty and covered with a lovely creamy dust of meal, especially his eyebrows and mustache. Sometimes I was allowed to ride behind Reuben when he took a sack of corn to be ground. We would wait till the resulting sack of meal was ready to be put over the pommel and jogged home to Amelia, by her to be manipulated into corn-pones of unspeakable crunchiness and savor. The meal would be still damp and warm when turned over to

[51]

us, and it was hard not to eat it raw, like chickens, so rich and sweet and really fundamental it smelled.

Reuben was too old to be interesting, perhaps eighteen, but Amelia's children—Ligey, Martha, Cora, Friday, and a few more I've forgotten—were exactly the right ages. They seem to have arrived precisely a year apart and all were dark, but some were darker, and no two of them looked alike. I often wondered who and where their father was, and once put the question to Aunt Nana, but she developed one of those little attacks of hurry and said, as well as I could gather, he was a traveling man. However, it must have been a fine father or set of fathers, because they were fine children and as playmates perfection. Small satyrs and fauns could not have been more instructive or resourceful or absurd.

We harried the hillsides for arrow-heads and found many splendid ones—training I found invaluable years later when between showers I hunted sea-shells in Bora-Bora. Sometimes we spent days on end in full flight from a murderous band of gypsies. Cora's cries on one occasion when she was almost captured were so blood-curdling we rushed off down the road and abandoned her to her fate, quite forgetting the plot she furthered with such histrionic fervor. Friday had a genius for discovering hornet-nests. Silvery and rather Burmese in design, one would be hanging on a tree conveniently low, its irascible inmates in a stew and a lather, storming in and out. Led by Friday, we would approach as near as we dared and let fly our barrage against the patiently built castle of the poor earnest insects. But they, unadvised of the other-cheek doctrine we have so long been beseeching one another to follow, would sally forth in the best modern echelon formation, armed to the tip, and we, sounding precipitate and individual retreat, would scatter yowling.

If someone was not badly stung, to be borne lamenting loudly to Amelia's soda and scarifying invective, it was a disappointing adventure.

In our milder moods the river was a favorite haunt. It was the right sort of river. With the dam closed, it could be waded and was all pools and trickles and slimy shelving rocks. Although not scorning such lesser quarry as eels, leeches, water-snakes, and frogs, our constant ambition was to discover a giant sturgeon. This ambition was unlikely but not impossible of fulfillment, because one had found its way into our river as a result of the Johnstown flood and we had seen it with our own eyes hanging from the ceiling of the tool-house, its tail sweeping the floor, glittering in the lamplight, magnificent even in death. We noticed when it was split open that with just a little more room Jonah could have sat inside. We discussed this and kindred issues for days afterwards.

During one of these theological sessions I swallowed a persimmon seed. Doctors had recently discovered appendicitis, attributed it to the swallowing of a seed, and considered it fatal. Solemn with this medical erudition, I explained the grisly situation and announced my approaching demise. All accepted the news with delight and prepared for the end. I lay on the ground and my faithful retainers knelt around me, in the manner of sundry versions of the Assumption of the Virgin. I closed my eyes, and fervent prayers rose loudly. Nothing happened. Nothing ever did happen. Reviving was undignified and bitterly disappointing to all concerned. As a corpse I was a fiasco, but as mourners my colored entourage displayed genius. Racially they are the best diers in the world anyway: they put more force and enthusiasm into the scene, being seriously aware it is the climax of the show, their curtain. If Friday had swallowed my persimmon seed, he

would beyond question have died outright and to perfection, although it's a role one can't rehearse.

So many things to do and each summer so short. To
chase rats in the barn, a dangerous and slightly sickening
enterprise; to teach the kitten to play circus (our cats
were Manx, with stubs for tails and bouncing rabbit motions); to climb the roof of the corridor and watch the
ducks file out to the pond, cracking dry mirthless jokes to
one another and sometimes laying an egg, shamelessly
and without stopping, on the bare ground with no thought
of a nest; to be allowed to help with the cider press where
all the apples with a rotten spot, those claimed and contended for by the yellow-jackets, disappeared into the
hopper and gushed out the sides in a seethe of bubbly
brown liquor, fit for Ceres; to hunt in the mold of the
wood-pile for the turquoise bits that were fox-fire and find
instead a land-terrapin closed up safe from the mad world
in his neat hinged box, and to devise means to make him
come out—so many things to do, and summer so short.

Supervised play and summer camps came after my
time. I missed learning the principles of team work and
many games which must be helpful if you can think of
nothing to do. Instead, Friday's accent, Cora's intonation,
and Ligey's grammatical uses contaminated beyond hope
of purification the wells of what should have been my
pure English undefiled. That was their only evil influence.
Of nastiness and bad manners they taught me nothing;
older boys of my own color and caste were later to be my
instructors in those subjects. From Amelia's children I
learned not only gaiety and casualness and inventiveness,
but the possibility that mere living may be delightful and
that natural things which we ignore unless we call them
scenery are pleasant to move among and gracious to recall. Without them it would probably never have oc-

curred to me that to climb an aspen sapling in a gale is one of those ultimate experiences, like experiencing God or love, that you need never try to remember because you can never forget. Aspens grow together in little woods of their own, straight, slender, and white. Even in still weather they twinkle and murmur, but in a high wind you must run out and plunge among them, spattered with sunlight, to the very center. Then select your tree and climb it high enough for it to begin to wobble with your weight. Rest your foot-weight lightly on the frail branches and do most of your clinging with your arms. Now let it lunge, and gulp the wind. It will be all over you, slapping your hair in your eyes, stinging your face with bits of bark and stick, tugging to break your hold, roaring in your open mouth like a monster sea-shell. The trees around you will thrash and seethe, their white undersides lashed about like surf, and sea-music racing through them. You will be beaten and bent and buffeted about and the din will be so terrific your throat will invent a song to add to the welter, pretty barbaric, full of yells and long calls. You will feel what it is to be the Lord God and ride a hurricane; you will know what it is to have leaves sprout from your toes and finger-tips, with satyrs and tigers and hounds in pursuit; you will never need again to drown under the crash of a maned wave in spume and splendor and thunder, with the white stallions of the sea around you, neighing and pawing. That must have been the very wood old Housman had in mind when he sang "We'll to the woods no more." But when he found his way to it he was alone, and it was autumn.

# CHAPTER VI

# A Side-Show Götterdämmerung

The most moving book ever written, more moving than *Jean-Christophe* or *Death Comes for the Archbishop* or *Anna Karenina*, is *In Silken Chains*. No one ever read it except Aunt Nana and me, and we never finished it. The heroine's beauty—raven hair, magnolia skin, purple eyes—made you feel like the string section of an orchestra, and she was in deep trouble, I don't remember what about, but it was not her fault. Aunt Nana had been reading this gem to me for weeks and we had just reached an unspeakably poignant climax when Father appeared in our midst. "Nana, what in the world do you mean by reading such trash to that child?" Aunt Nana was crushed, I was desolated, he was adamant. We asked weakly what please could we substitute, and unhesitatingly he answered: "*Ivanhoe.*" He did not often lay down the law, but then and there he ruled as authoritatively as Moses that there would be no other novel-reading to poison my mind until I had finished Scott, Bulwer-Lytton, Dickens, and a little Thackeray. This injunction remained in full force until I left for college with a volume of Stanley J. Weyman under one arm and Rider Haggard under the other. In the meantime Aunt Nana and I dutifully settled down to *Ivanhoe*. It produced unpredictable results: Aunt Nana wept herself into an illness over Rebecca, and I, far from being inspired to knightly heroism, grew infatuated with the monastic life, if it could be pursued in a cave opening on a desert.

Father rarely gave advice and never unless he'd taken it himself. He read *Ivanhoe* once a year all his life long, and *The Talisman* almost as frequently. Because of or in spite of Don Carlos he was kin to Hotspur and blood-brother to Richard Cœur de Lion, and he looked the part. No one ever made the mistake of thinking he wasn't dangerous, and to the day of his death he was beautiful, a cross between Phœbus Apollo and the Archangel Michael. It was hard having such a dazzling father; no wonder I longed to be a hermit. He could do everything well except drive a nail or a car: he was the best pistol-shot and the best bird-shot, he made the best speeches, he was the fairest thinker and the wisest, he could laugh like the Elizabethans, he could brood and pity till sweat covered his brow and you could feel him bleed inside. He loved life, and never forgot it was unbearably tragic. His appearances during Virginia summers were brief and legendary—he had to be home, making a living for us.

Uncle George was not deeply concerned with making a living, for in a mild way it made itself from those hundreds of acres in corn and orchard. His real worry was whether or not the fish were biting. After Father's electric advents, Uncle George was restful: he didn't say much or do much or think much, but unquestionably he was a good fisherman. Often when you asked him a question, he grunted for answer and you could take it either way. This usually occurred when we were in the boat on the pond, and the fish weren't biting. He wore a wide limber straw hat, like Matahi's Sunday best in Bora-Bora, and he clenched a stubby pipe between his teeth. He didn't mind just sitting, but after two hours without a nibble, he would take his pipe out, tap it on the side of the boat, and observe: "When the wind's in the east, the fish bite least." To which I would counter: "When the wind's in the west, the fish bite best." Though I knew the answer, I could never resist asking: "When the wind's in the south, what do they do?" "Bite in the mouth," replied Uncle George. "But what does that mean?" "What it says," snapped Uncle George, and though that sounded like sense, it wasn't, and I'd do useful ruminating over how many things sounded like sense and passed for sense which were nowhere near sense. Of course there was no use asking about the north wind: to that I'd never got anything better than a grunt.

If fish could bat their eyes or wall them like El Greco's saints, their death throes would be unbearable to watch and no one would ever have the heart to fish. Even as awkward and impersonal as they are, floundering about on the bottom of a boat, I soon came to the conclusion that fishing was not my sport and hunting was even more lacerating to the spirit. Yet fishermen and hunters are the most pitying, the most gentle and understanding people in the world, and I suspect anyone who isn't one or the other. They are curative to a degree; Uncle George was. You walked along carrying the empty fish-basket and felt easy and liked his grumpiness. Of course he wasn't comparable to Father on the nights he came in from bird-hunting. That never failed to have a home-from-the-wars, home-from-the-seas, ballad brilliance about it. In the first place he looked so heroic and gay, smelling warmish of feathers and corduroy and dogs, and togged out in boots and sweaters and jackets full of pockets, all brown as a cocklebur; and then he never failed to bring in a big bag. He'd tell how each bird was killed and what the dogs did, as he sat before the fire, feeling simply great and drinking slowly a very long toddy, while Mother bustled about the kitchen, making him an oyster soup. To be reared among wise earth-people that way gives you a lifelong distaste for the fidgety folk of cities who palaver and intellectualize and use their features but not their hands and feet.

Long after these things, when Uncle George was broke and had moved down from Virginia to our town, Father managed to find him a poorly paid job as road-inspector. I look at Uncle George's section of that road every now and then; it pulls me together. The concrete north and south of his section is warped and cracked, but his after twenty years stands solid and level. The contractors couldn't buy Uncle George, though he knew ahead of him lay an old age of penury and dependence.

The only thing I held against Uncle George was the stories he'd tell me just about my bedtime when we'd all be sitting in the dark on the front porch. I tried the patience of them all, begging for stories. Père was the most accommodating and the most inept. He would start off in the tempo of the prodded dormouse: "There was once a beautiful little princess and she lived in a wood; she had long gold hair and blue eyes, and wore the most exquisite little dress, all white, with pink and blue ribbons," and then he would give up. I never learned what happened to the little princess: Père was long on feminine pulchritude and short on invention. An unfinished fairy story, like the old South. Uncle George's stories, on the other hand, featured bears or hyenas coming down the chimney, a chimney exactly like ours, and they were blood-curdling. When my last excuse for staying up had been overruled, I'd be sent up the stairs alone to the dark upper story where there wasn't a living thing except probably a bear or a hyena, and I'd be clammy with terror. But no one knew, no one ever did know, not to this good minute. Psychiatrists to the contrary notwithstanding, it was splendid training, most useful in later years.

So I don't bother about Don Carlos's missing link or the Bourges being in trade or about that Italo-French mésalliance of Mère's ancestor or the border cattle-stealing blood of the Armstrongs, who to the scorn of the Whig Percys were Democrats and close friends of Andrew Jackson's, or all the other vague and mixed ghosts back to Adam which went into the creating of my body and temperament. In time we are all good democrats; in the manger we look the same and in the grave. But at this particular time and place, viewed not from a peak in eternity but from the ephemeral now, I rejoice to be of a caste which, though shaken and scattered, refuses to call itself Demos.

In Virginia the big event of the summer was the trip to Fredericksburg. May and Maud, the slickest mules in the county, would be hitched to the carriage that on such occasions replaced the buckboard in which Uncle George and I drove twice a week to Guiney's for the mail. The carriage, of course, dated from before the war and fortunately refused to fall to pieces. It was elegant but shabby, with a sort of prenatal bulge reminiscent of the stage coaches in the Musée Cluny, and there was mold in its color and smell. The winding dirt pike we took passed through a country almost as haunted as Greece: to the right stretched the Wilderness; just over the ridge Stonewall Jackson was shot and was caught dying in the arms of Captain Randolph, whose daughter now earns her living by selling shrubs from her little nursery on the edge of our home town; beyond was Guiney's, where he breathed his last; Spottsylvania Court House was up the right-hand road and we would be going there next week for a barbecue of squirrel—more popular with spiders and ticks than with me; ahead, in their gardens, stood the quiet homes of General Washington's mother and friends. Aunt Nana described it all as we drove along and, although few of the facts lodged with me, I knew it was holy ground and in every field and thicket men had given up the breath they loved for something noble they loved more. It was a countryside of proud ghosts.

Fredericksburg reached, Uncle George would disappear while Aunt Nana and I paid calls. I do not remember the old houses and gardens or the people, but the return trips made a great impression. Uncle George while away from us always picked up a headache. He was not given to headaches and Aunt Nana always inquired, with what seemed to me undue asperity, how he came by this one. Uncle George attributed his condition to peanuts. Aunt Nana replied it seemed strange to her how he always ate peanuts in Fredericksburg when he knew they always gave him a headache. I had never eaten peanuts except at a circus and I would wonder if Uncle George had sneaked off to one without taking me. My inquiries about this were ignored, and even the silence was tart. Finally Uncle George would ask fretfully if a man couldn't eat peanuts *once a year* without being persecuted. I enjoyed the drive home, but no one else did. They seemed dreadfully fuzzed-up over peanuts.

Aunt Nana, descending from her mule-drawn, ancient vehicle in a home-made print dress did not seem shabby or peculiar or anything less than aristocratic to Fredericksburg folk, high or low. Today she couldn't come to town in a T-model Ford, dressed in home-made clothes and un-adorned by beauty-shop ministrations and a permanent, without snickers and comments from the ladies of the Saturday Night Bridge Club as well as from the barber's wife. Maybe this is as it should be, but I don't think so. I'm unhappily convinced that our exteriors have increased in importance while our interiors have deteriorated: it is a good paint job, but the lighting and sanitation are execrable. A good world, I acknowledge, an excellent world, but poor in spirit and common as hell. Vulgarity, a contagious disease like the itch, unlike it is not a disease of the surface, but eats to the marrow.

As a class I suppose the Southern aristocrat is extinct, but what that class despised as vulgar and treasured as excellent is still despised and treasured by individuals scattered thickly from one end of the South to the other. Those individuals born into a world of tradesfolk are still aristocrats, with an uncanny ability to recognize their kind. Their distinguishing characteristic probably is that their hearts are set, not on the virtues which make surviving possible, but on those which make it worth while. They could drive tomorrow to the guillotine in Aunt Nana's shabby ante-bellum carriage with so bland and insolent an air that passing Fords would take to the alleys and a Rolls-Royce would stop dead in its tracks, realizing itself parvenu. Having neglected the virtues that have survival value, these charming people are on their way to extinction, while the vulgar are increasing and multiplying and prospering and will continue to do so until their children or their children's children, having attained security, will begin all over again to admire and cherish the forgotten virtues we were not strong enough to maintain. Perhaps in every age an aristocracy is dying and one is being born. In any event aristocratic virtues and standards themselves never die completely and never change at all. General Lee and Senator Lamar would have been at ease, even simpatico, with Pericles and Brutus and Sir Philip Sidney, as Washington was with Lafayette.

This is chilly comfort, however, to the living members of an aristocracy in the act of dying. Under the southern Valhalla the torch has been thrust, already the bastions have fallen. Watching the flames mount, we, scattered remnant of the old dispensation, smile scornfully, but grieve in our hearts. A side-show Götterdämmerung perhaps, yet who shall inherit our earth, the earth we loved? The meek? The Hagens? In either event, we accept, but we do not approve.

My generation, inured to doom, wears extinction with a certain wry bravado, but it is just as well the older ones we loved are gone. They had lived, for the most part, through tragedy into poverty, which can be and usually is accomplished with dignity and a certain fine disdain. But when the last act is vulgarity, it is as hateful and confused a show as *Troilus and Cressida.*

During their last years Mère and Père lived with us most of the time. Père was ill a long while, but no one was very much interested. He had to sit in a dark room days on end, and there were no radios then or phonographs, and no one read to him. He rarely complained and seemed to know that those he loved were vital and busy with their living. I hope he remembered pleasant things most as he sat in the dark and awaited the end.

Nor was Mère spared. I suppose her strength was a temptation to death. No wonder we hate him so unforgivingly: his ways are humiliating and his approaches brutal. His indignities we fear, not him. Mère's heart gave way, she could not breathe, but she could not die. For months she fought. Being propped with pillows eased her a little. Mother was her nurse, for there were no hospitals or trained nurses in our county then, and Mother, because her heart was compassionate and her hands tender and knowing, was an excellent nurse. At last we had to set Mère bolt upright in a straight chair and tie her to its back so she would not topple over when the merciful moments of sleep came. One night she woke suffocating. Mother said: "It will be all right, it will pass. It's a little spell." But Mère gasped: "C'est la mort." Mother leaned to her and whispered: "Tu n'as pas peur?" Mère steadied herself on the arms of her chair and said distinctly and firmly: "Non." So death took her.

# CHAPTER VII

# *A Small Boy's Heroes*

F ather and General Catchings and Captain McNeilly and Captain Wat Stone and Mr. Everman would forgather every so often on our front gallery. These meetings must habitually have taken place in summer, because I remember Mother would be in white, looking very pretty, and would immediately set about making a mint julep for the gentlemen—no hors d'œuvres, no sandwiches, no cocktails, just a mint julep. After the first long swallow— really a slow and noiseless suck, because the thick crushed ice comes against your teeth and the ice must be kept out and the liquor let in—Cap Mac would say: "Very fine, Camille, you make the best julep in the world." She probably did. Certainly her juleps had nothing in common with those hybrid concoctions one buys in bars the world over under that name. It would have been sacrilege to add lemon, or a slice of orange or of pineapple, or one of those wretched maraschino cherries. First you needed excellent bourbon whisky; rye or Scotch would not do at all. Then you put half an inch of sugar in the bottom of the glass and merely dampened it with water. Next, very quickly—and here was the trick in the procedure—you crushed your ice, actually powdered it, preferably in a towel with a wooden mallet, so quickly that it remained dry, and, slipping two sprigs of fresh mint against the inside of the glass, you crammed the ice in right to the brim, packing it with your hand. Last you filled the glass, which apparently had no room left for anything else, with bourbon, the older the better, and grated a bit of nutmeg on the top. The glass immediately frosted and you settled back in your chair for half an hour of sedate cumulative bliss. Although you stirred the sugar at the bottom, it never all melted, therefore at the end of the half hour there was left a delicious mess of ice and mint and whisky which a small boy was allowed to consume with calm rapture. Probably the anticipation of this phase of a julep was what held me on the outskirts of these meetings rather than the excitement of the discussion, which often I did not understand.

General Catchings was our congressman. He was short, with a fat stomach, a wide face, and heavy fat jowls. Yet he did not resemble Humpty Dumpty or Henry VIII. If I had not seen him I could not have believed that fat men could make tragic figures or that Burbage could have played Hamlet. He had a cold analytical mind of the first water, plus an arrogant integrity. His political weakness was that he could not kiss babies and considered it indecent to rhapsodize over the purity of Southern womanhood. So he was always about not to be re-elected. His English was all sinew and no color, his rare adjectives were like bullets, and he had some strange expressions of his own. He would say to Father: "It is bitter as gar-broth, LeRoy," and I would lose the rest of the discussion wondering what gar-broth might be. I never found out, but in my mind it was associated with those rueful liquors in which the sponge was dipped that they lifted to the lips of Jesus. I realized vaguely that he was always about to be crucified by the people for serving them so devoutly.

Cap Mac, for so we called Captain McNeilly, the editor of the local paper, was bitter too and old and tired and even poorer than the others, who were poor. He read Gibbon and Carlyle and Thucydides and Voltaire till all hours of the night, and his pen was dipped in gall. But he read also the New Testament and the *Sentimental Journey*, and when his heart was moved he could break yours. His paper was his own, hated by many and feared throughout the state, because he had a wrath like the Lord God's and words for the unrighteous in high places that withered and blasted. He loathed corruption and hated public iniquity. The intelligent few worshipped him, the unintelligent many scuttled for cover at the first hiss of his lash. We loved him for his weaknesses as much as for his strength, for his inability to manage his own affairs or his family, for his poor marksmanship when he was constantly being threatened with duels and assassinations, for his failure to appreciate beauty except in women, nature, food, and drink. Father was elated when, showing him a sizable copy of Canova's *Cupid and Psyche*, his sour and single comment was "Kind of raw." The very best brand of Puritan, simple and afraid, and unremittingly a fighter. He is completely forgotten now except by a few hold-overs from his world, soon to join him, and except by those who, delving into the archives of the Mississippi Historical Society, come wiith amazement across his articles on the reconstruction period, so trenchant, so accurate, so cold with fury.

Captain Wat and Mr. Everman were strophe and antistrophe to the tragic matters under way. Captain Wat had been a professor of Greek in Missouri before the war; he was sententious, moralizing, and a trifle eloquent. His bent was philosophizing on a situation instead of solving it. Mother, who was always dropping into and out of the discussions, would invariably grow impatient and exclaim: "Oh, Captain Wat, you never want to take sides. For heaven's sake, stop talking and decide"—which amused him. Mr. Everman agreed with her to the core of his being, because he was red-headed. I loved to watch him. He was incontestably the ugliest man in the world—tall, shambling, with tiny pale eyes, extravagant sandy eyebrows gone to seed, and a masterpiece of a nose that Ghirlandajo would have given his life to paint. He always suggested things vehemently, was always overruled, always accepted the adverse decision, and always concluded with: "Well, LeRoy, what do you say? I'm an old fool." They knew him to be sound of heart and character and it took only a little time to calm him down and start him off right, quivering with ardor and invective, sputtering the fire and smoke of righteousness from corner to corner of the little town, like a disjointed pinwheel.

In these parleys I recall the protagonists far better than the plot. Yet scraps of it come back to me: their hatred of Bryan and free silver; their adoration of Cleveland; their contempt for the nepotism of the then Governor; their determination to elect Captain Hunt sheriff because he was a gentleman and of course honest, courageous, and bankrupt; first, last, and always, their search for means to protect the country from overflow, which involved re-electing General Catchings to Congress and inducing the Governor to appoint able men on the local levee board. These were the men who, before I was a listener, bore the brunt of the Delta's fight against scalawaggery and Negro domination during reconstruction, who stole the ballot-boxes which, honestly counted, would have made every

county official a Negro, who had helped shape the Constitution of 1890, which in effect and legally disfranchised
the Negro, who still earlier had sent my grandfather to
the legislature to help rid the state of "old Ames," the car-
petbag Governor.

It is not what they discussed so much as how they discussed it that still makes those meetings so memorable to
me—indeed, so epic. They were leaders of the people, not
elected or self-elected, but destined, under the compul-
sion of leadership because of their superior intellect, training, character, and opportunity. And the people were
willing to be led by them because of their desperate need
of leadership in those tragic times, because they recognized their fitness to lead, tested and proved in the series
of revealing crises that only began with the war, and because they came from the class which traditionally had
led in the South. Applause or aggrandizement played no
part in their calculations. They knew leadership was a
burden, they knew there was no such thing in the long
run as public gratitude for public service, they also knew
that unless the intelligent disinterested few fought for
good government, government would be bad.

Even at that time, however, the leadership of the wise
and the good never went unchallenged. Rascals and
grafters, ambitious men on the make and personal enemies
fought them and what they stood for tirelessly and unceasingly. Then too the first trickle of poor whites from
the hills into the Delta had already begun. It was often
necessary to get in touch with Charlie Scott in Rosedale,
Sam Neill in Indianola, the Farishes in Mayersville, and
those amazing Kentuckians, Colonel Mat Johnson, Johnson Erwin, and Mr. Merritt Williams, down on the lake.
If the matter were of national concern, Father would be
delegated to go over to Yazoo for counsel with John Sharp

Williams, who loved him. Though they were decreasing-
ly on the winning side, they were always live forces and
rallying-points for righteousness, respected and greatly
feared. When they lost, it was a public loss.

One particular local tragedy did much to undermine
their prestige and influence. I was too young to understand it all, but I grew up knowing it was a terrible thing.

General Ferguson was one of their intimate friends and
advisers and, further, he was the friend of General Wade
Hampton, whose friendship was an accolade and a passport. He had been the beau ideal of a soldier, handsome,
young, daring, adored by his men, with a record of brilliant military achievement which won him the rank of
general at an age when others were lucky to be captains.
His home was the center of frivolity and hospitality, famous
in the countryside for high spirits and wit. I cannot
recollect seeing the General himself when I was a little
boy, but I climbed his kitchen roof, taunted to evil by his
small daughter, who was a tartar, and I marveled at her
older sister, Miss Natalie, galloping by in her long black
velvet riding habit, by general consent the most dashing
horsewoman in the Delta. In those poverty-stricken years
the General was elected by his friends treasurer of the
levee board, though he had neither aptitude for nor experience in business or accounting, besides being high-
handed and utterly unmethodical. After some years Mr.
Everman, secretary of the board and his close friend,
checked the books and found him twenty thousand dollars
short. It was unthinkable. He had always been a man of
unimpeachable rectitude, of untarnished honor. And he
had nothing to show for it: he did not gamble, he had no
extravagant habits, his possessions were his home and a
run-down plantation, both heavily mortgaged. He could
give no explanation. Then, while the enemies of the old

regime were in full hue and cry, and our people distracted, humiliated, and incredulous, he did the inexplicable, the unpardonable thing—he fled to South America.

It was recent history when I was scraping the bottom of mint-julep glasses, and it still rankled. He lived for years in exile with his family; then, the bitterness having diminished, his property having been seized and sold to pay his deficit, the rank and file having as usual forgotten, he drifted back to his own country and settled down in poverty and obscurity on the coast.

I went to college and law school, the world began to acquire that momentum commonly mistaken for progress, incidents like the disappearance of trust funds occurred daily and caused no special stir, and I don't suppose a dozen people in the town could have told you the Robertshaw house was once the Ferguson house. One cold night during the holidays we were giving a dinner party for some of my Eastern schoolmates—pretty girls and young men, pleased as cockerels. It was still the custom then to entertain at home. We were dressed in our giddiest as a dance was to follow. Mother and Father, at the ends of the table, were as usual in fine form and more fun than any of us. Unexpectedly a knock sounded at the front door. The colored waiter, who was also butler, answered it. We could feel the cold air from the open door and hear the scraps of a conversation that seemed to go on and on. I went out to see what the trouble was. In the light of the doorway against the blustery dark stood a little shabby old man in a gray suit and a bright red tie, his white hair untidy, his white beard untrimmed, with something childlike in his wide, vague, very blue eyes. He said: "Is LeRoy home?" I answered impatiently: "Yes, but—" "Tell LeRoy I must see him now." Father, joining us as he said these words, exclaimed softly: "Why, General Ferguson! Come in. Won't you have some dinner with us?" "Of course, LeRoy," murmured the little old man, and he came into the light still wide-eyed like a ghost, a ghost that is not afraid, but only uncertain, a ghost that can't remember. He sat down with those youngsters in their party clothes just as Banquo's ghost did, but mercifully they knew nothing and rattled on, though I could see Mother wanted to cry. He hardly touched his food and sat quietly, looking but not seeing, trying to remember something. Once he leaned to Father and said softly: "I have come back to go through those records. It was all a mistake. They will show everything was in order." Father said: "Of course, General."

For a month or more he haunted the courthouse and the levee board, pulling out the heavy record books, carrying them unsteadily to a desk, turning their pages backward and forward, and making notes. His presence in the town created little flurry. It had all been too long ago. At last he drifted away. He was mad.

People steal public funds now, but the public is cynical, no one is horrified, and the accused, guilty or innocent, seldom goes mad. Going mad for honor's sake presupposes honor. In our brave new world a man of honor is rather like the Negro—there's no place for him to go.

No one took l'affaire Ferguson more to heart than Mr. Merritt Williams, for he had loved the General and to the end of his days believed in his integrity. When the scandal was at its height, Mr. Merritt, small of stature, but of fabulous strength, was called to New Orleans and boarded the boat at Greenville. At supper he sat across the table from two strangers who began to disparage General Ferguson. Mr. Merritt said: "Gentlemen, I will ask you not to discuss the General." His manner was quiet, almost diffident, and his appearance belied his stoutness. The strangers looked him over and continued the tenor of their conversation. Mr. Merritt said, still more quietly: "Gentlemen, General Ferguson is my friend." The strangers ignored his warning. Mr. Merritt picked up his coffee-cup, a thick old-fashioned weapon weighing about a pound, and hurled it across the table. It hit one of the men squarely between the eyes and laid him low. Before the other could recover from his astonishment, Mr. Merritt was over and across the table and had fallen on him with murderous fists, one on the jaw finally putting him where he belonged. Then Mr. Merritt finished up with the first, who was recovering from the coffee-cup. When it was over, he flicked a crumb from his lapel, strolled forward, sweetly at peace, and watched the moonlight from the bow. The strangers were borne off at the next landing, on stretchers.

I asked Mr. Merritt about it years after when he was well over ninety. He was still diffident and said it was just a little personal matter.

Good men nowadays question what form of government is best and search like Plato for a formula, following which this benighted race of ours may automatically perfect itself. The Delta sages of my youth knew there was no such formula. Being convinced no system of government was good without good men to operate it, they considered it their bounden duty, their prime obligation as members of society, to find such men and elect them to office. Concerning democracy they had no illusions, their fears for it were prophetic; they esteemed it a poor makeshift, but the best devised by man for keeping the peace and at the same time permitting personal liberty. Their point of view, their sense of duty, their relentless striving, while certainly not appreciated or understood by me in my childhood, seeped into me, colored my outlook, prescribed for me loyalties and responsibilities that I may not disclaim—no, not though the sirens call and the flutes sound over the hill. Nor in this respect was my training unusual in the South of my generation. Anybody who was anybody must feel *noblesse oblige,* must concern himself with good government, must fight, however feebly or ineffectually or hopelessly, for the public weal. One of the first things I did after returning home from law school was to stump off to a mass meeting with Mr. Everman at which we read aloud bitter denunciations of a crime of violence. He thought that was the thing a man had to do, even if we were shot for it, as he believed we would be. And so did I. (When I started publishing verse Mr. Everman simply ignored it.)

During my day I have witnessed a disintegration of that moral cohesion of the South which had given it its strength and its sons their singleness of purpose and simplicity. Today there is fretting and fuming on the part of young people over what they should do, how they should act, what is worth while. Standards are in flux: there is no commonly accepted good way of life—and the hospitals can't hold the neurotics, the mental cripples, the moral anemics, the blasted who strove to build a pattern because none existed.

Epstein with his heads neurotic, restless, ugly, is the appropriate portraitist of this generation, but Cap Mac and Father and General Catchings would have been at home on the west portal of Chartres with those strong ancients, severe and formidable and full of grace, who guard the holy entrance.

What was the pattern that gave them strength and direction, that kept them oriented, that permitted them to be at once Puritans and Cavaliers? To recapture the recipe might give sustenance to the undernourished of these times, but I suspect, lacking pepper and tabasco, it would be unpalatable to my contemporaries.

Sipping the dregs of a julep among the patriarchs of Chartres with the Queen of Sheba in her summer dress shedding immortal grace—in what better way could a little boy learn that the austerities of living are not incompatible with the courtesy and sweetness of life? I never heard them over their juleps express a philosophy of life, and if I had it would have been incomprehensible to me, but a philosophy was implicit in all their thoughts and actions. It probably made the Southern pattern. Perhaps it is all contained in a remark of Father's when he was thinking aloud one night and I sat at his feet eavesdropping eagerly:

"I guess a man's job is to make the world a better place to live in, so far as he is able—always remembering the results will be infinitesimal—and to attend to his own soul."

I've found in those words directions enough for any life. Maybe they contain the steady simple wisdom of the South.

# CHAPTER VIII

# Learning from Teachers

The time came when Mother and Father had to decide on what might be termed my formal education. So far the only efforts of that sort had been Aunt Nana's piano lessons and Mère's instruction in French pronunciation. Neither was too successful. I developed a nice touch, a moderate ability to read notes, and a hatred for Aunt Nana because she would not permit me to step on the loud pedal during scales. But I was a lazy and ungifted musician. My French accent got me to Belgium and France during the war, and delighted no one after I arrived. Heaven help parents worrying over what to do with children a little out of the ordinary! It's a dark problem even with the recent assistance of Doctors Freud and Jung; when Mother and Father faced it they had to decide by ear. I was a sickly youngster who never had illnesses, who hated sports partly because they didn't seem important and mostly because I was poor at them, who knew better what I didn't want than what I did, who was sensitive but hard-headed, docile but given to the balks, day-dreamy but uncommunicative, friendly but not intimate—a frail problem-child, a pain in the neck. To make matters harder, the choice of what to do with me was restricted. I was too young to be sent to boarding school even if Father could have afforded it, there were no local private schools, and Mother had a wise intuition that, though I needed the rough and tumble of a public school, I didn't need as much as I'd get. In desperation they chose the local Roman Catholic convent for little boys and girls run by the Sisters of Mercy and started me off one September morning with a basket of lunch and no advice.

The first thing I learned there was the existence of evil. All the boys were herded together in the same classroom, presided over by Sister Evangelist, a midget of a nun with the valor and will-power of an Amazon, who taught every class, held prayers, occasionally larruped the wayward with the thin cane pointer she always carried, bullied, cajoled, and beguiled us unflaggingly and devotedly. But there was one boy she was afraid of, though I have seen her whirl into him dauntlessly and whip him until he whined. The oldest and biggest boy in the school, he was a monster of evil—cruel, nasty, bullying—with face and body so like Mansfield's Richard III that they published his qualities. All of us knew what he was and feared him. I once saw a rattlesnake in a bare spot of the woods coiled and rattling. That dry incessant hypnotic sound hushed the little sounds of the forest—bird-song, beetle-drone, wing-whir—the little things stood still and held their breath; you could hear the terrified silence. It was that way when this boy standing behind Sister faced us with some obscene pantomime: we were hypnotized with horror and helpless. A sickening lesson but a necessary one for those of us with third-rate bodies who insist on living uncowed in a world of evil. How cope with concrete active evil when your body is weak and the fear in your throat is like cold bile? How breathe the same air with the vicious who are strong? How fashion weapons against such a one and what shall the weapons be? If the gods are good, try charm; if not, try guile; both failing, try flight. Survival virtues, you know. Once there was another defense in vogue—every youth was taught the use of sword or firearms. In the South it was the pistol, as deadly in the hands of the little fellow as of the giant— and the little fellow made the poorer target. Many contend that if you fight with your fists well and honorably and are whipped, your self-respect is saved. Not mine. You meet a brute and a bully—what consolation is there in trying to knock his lights out and having your own dimmed in the effort? But with a pistol, ah! There are too many villains abroad, the well-disposed need breathing-space anyhow. Well, none of us little boys had pistols and our tormentor still lives, a wake of wickedness behind, a long life ahead. Left on his own, death has a poor sense of selection. Anyway, that boy started me thinking about defense weapons and I've thought a lot about them ever since.

Determination ranked high among Sister's virtues, and among other things she determined that mine was a likely soul and she was going to save it. I gave up; there was no use resisting; into her hands I committed my spirit. She would have succeeded in her determination had not I incautiously remarked one day to Mother, who was bending over an ailing Cape jessamine at the moment, that I had decided to become a priest. I had anticipated dismay but not indignation. Mother rose from the flowerbed to her full height, the height, say, of Lady Macbeth or Clytemnestra; too late under the solemn fillet I saw the scorn. But her only observation was that there was no excuse for talking like a fool at my age. I must have been an unbearable little prig. I do hope I've outgrown it. If not, it wasn't Mother's fault. I shouldn't blame Sister Evangelist for my unbridled mystic fervor at this time; evidently my ground was plowed and harrowed waiting for her sowing. I became intolerably religious, going to early mass at the slightest provocation, racking my brain to find something to confess once a month, praying inordinately, and fasting on the sly. It was infinitely trying to the family and so unexpected, so unlike anything in the case-history of any recorded member of the clan, French, English, or Scotch. I just couldn't help it, it was a violent attack, perhaps I've never fully recovered. Indeed, painful as it all was to the family, it was anguish and ecstasy, but mostly anguish, to me. I wanted so intensely to believe, to believe in God and miracles and the sacraments and the Church and everything. Also, I wanted to be completely and utterly a saint; heaven and hell didn't matter, but perfection did. Yet never, never for a moment, was my belief without doubt: the Satan of my disbelief was at my elbow scoffing, insinuating, arguing, day and night. I'm certain Shelley never sank upon the thorns of life and bled nearly so often as I did between ten and sixteen. To be at once intellectually honest and religious is a rack on which many have perished and on which I writhed dumbly, for I knew even then there were certain things which, like overwhelming physical pain, you must fight out alone, at the bottom of your own dark well, beyond ministration of assuagement or word of advice, incommunicado and leper-lonely. If you die it is natural; if you live you have learned pity and the strength of silence.

I didn't die, and, curiously enough, neither did Sister Evangelist. Only last year I saw her, and she must be approximately a hundred. Sister Scholastica, my old music teacher and the only teacher I ever feared because she was absolutely impervious to my charm, telephoned me and announced that I was a godless, ungrateful, heartless monster (she always telephoned that way, never giving her name and knowing I would recognize her voice and style), that Sister Evangelist was on her deathbed in Vicksburg, that she loved me more than any of her thousand pupils, that in my baseness I ignored her and would not even take the trouble to visit her, dying, in fact barely this side of rigor mortis. As usual I took Sister Scholastica's hint and dashed to Vicksburg. At the convent door a scared rabbit of a little nun asked my name and mission, suspiciously admitted me to the cool bare sitting-room, and left me there. There was a long pause during which I assumed they were propping up Sister Evangelist so that she could reach out feebly and blindly to give me her last blessing. It was pretty staggering, therefore, when Sister Evangelist came tripping in, unbent by her hundred years and vivacious as a cricket. She immediately loosed a diatribe of piety and invective, contrasting the promise of my past with the worm-eaten fruit of my present, and all with no more pause, punctuation, or capitalization than the last forty-six pages of *Ulysses*. At the first drop of a comma I got a word in edgewise: "Heavens, Sister! You talk as if God didn't have any sense of humor." She burst into gales of laughter, exclaiming: "Everybody forgets it; even I do sometimes," and the next two hours were chuckling gossip, singularly naïve and gay. The incident helps me to understand better why St. Francis would drop over to visit Santa Clara when he was tired, and to appreciate Fra Angelico's versions of walking all over God's heaven. Those two old ladies with Machiavellian heroism and saintly mendacity had made one last try at saving my soul.

Bless them, I wish they had succeeded!

So probably Mother was right when after two or three years she concluded the convent had done me all possible good but held possibilities of harm. After grievous cogitation she and Father chose as my next teacher Judge Griffin, who lived across the street and had never taught school. To church-goers he was the town atheist, which is only one more proof that the churches wouldn't recognize religion if they met it in the middle of the big road, for he was a saint. His house, where I went for lessons, was a turmoil of grandchildren, dogs, models of inventions, bundles of cotton lint, sacks of cottonseed (he was a great hybridizer), silkworms eating mulberry leaves and spinning cocoons, books on tables, on chairs, in stacks on the floor, and old furniture too big for its quarters, knee to knee everywhere—plus a raccoon. Judge Griffin's father had been the largest cottonland-owner in the world, before the war and the river destroyed his holdings, and he himself had studied at universities east and abroad and had gained knowledge of every world but this one, and much wisdom. Others had become rich from the gadgets he had invented for cotton gins and roller-skates while he became poorer and retired farther from community life into his own family and his own thoughts. With his silver hair and beautiful benign face I had long recognized him as a friend and was enchanted at the prospect of hobnobbing with him as a teacher. I anticipated golden hours and was not disappointed. We browsed and ranged and broke every law of pedagogy. He read me *Paradise Lost* and Cary's translation of the *Divine Comedy* and I perceived grandeur and nobility and heroic struggle, even when I didn't understand. We pondered and discussed the Doré illustrations, which I am told are pretty bad, but which we considered magnificent. He even told me a lit-

tle about the epic he was writing, *Ruin Robed,* in which
Napoleon replaced Lucifer; but I could never induce him
to read it to me. And Shakespeare—but there a distressing
memory intrudes. We were reading *Othello*—I must have
been about ten—and it came over me horribly and deliciously during the first act that Iago's conversation was
unadulterated smut. I certainly didn't understand it, but
I sensed it, I knew in my soul it was pornography and I
enjoyed it exquisitely. ("Je tremble délicieusement," sang
Louise.) It was shortlived bliss; torture followed. Conscience pointed out unanswerably not only that my spasm
of enjoyment was in itself sinful but that to continue reading such immorality would be willful and therefore mortal
sin; furthermore that the excuse I offered of being only a
pupil with no control over my teacher's assignment was
false, insincere, and cowardly. Torn between what I knew
to be my duty and a terrified shyness at mentioning such
a thing, especially to my old mentor and friend, I presented myself to the Judge next morning resolute, dry-
tongued, and sick through every inch of me. When he
picked up his beloved volume of Shakespeare I said thickly but audibly: "I don't think we ought to read any more
*Othello.* It's—it's immoral." My venerable master was
speechless. He gazed uncertainly and a little mournfully
at his chela. At length he said: "Iago does do some ugly
talking. Maybe we'd better try *The Merchant of Venice.*"
It was one of the two occasions in my life when I showed
courage, and in such a poor cause. As usual the reward
was incommensurate: *The Merchant of Venice* seemed
tame, and still does.

Of Judge's pedagogy I recall little and that not to his
credit. Struggling with my handwriting, he suggested that
the best-looking hands were those in which the tall letters
and the short letters approximated each other in height.

I should like to think that advice was the corrupting influence which, exfoliating in my subconscious, has rendered my script unintelligible to anyone, including myself,
but I doubt it. As with all great teachers, his curriculum
was an insignificant part of what he communicated. From
him you didn't learn a subject, but life. I suspect anyway
that the important things we learn we never remember
because they become part of us, we absorb them. We
don't absorb the multiplication tables (at least not the
seventh and eleventh), but those things that are vitamins
and calories to the spirit, the spirit seizes on and trans-
mutes into its own strength, wholly and forgetfully. Tolerance and justice, fearlessness and pride, reverence and
pity, are learned in a course on long division if the teacher
has those qualities, as Judge Griffin had.

What with learning the eternal verities from my old
friend and talking poetry instead of doing sums, Mother
judged I was growing a trifle remote from ordinary doings. French, practical, opposed to excess even of virtue,
she concluded a further change was needed in my scho-
lastic career. So I was transferred to Father Koestenbrock,
the parish priest, for mornings of French and Latin, and
to Mr. Bass, superintendent of city schools, for afternoons
of whatever else immature minds require.

Mr. Bass was red-haired except that he was bald, and
he had the sort of pale eyes and vague pinkish features
red-heads grow when they decide not to be beautiful. Almost everybody recognizes the temperament common to
red-heads—irascibility, generosity, nervous energy, mental
quickness, with just a touch of flightiness: Mr. Bass didn't
miss a one. I wonder why when the obvious connection
between the innards and out'ards of red-heads is generally
conceded, it is doubted in people of slant eyes and yellow
skins and flatly denied in people of kinky hair and black

skins. Someone's always drawing the color line; now they won't let the Negro's interior be as individual as his exterior. I am told there is no relation between what you see of him and what there is of him: the only difference is a sort of hallucination in the eye of the beholder, he's a white man inside. Very like, very like. Mr. Bass, though, was different: his insides matched up perfectly with his outsides. He'd come storming into the classroom with a cocoon when I'd prepared with boundless boredom the lesson on Burke's *Speech on Conciliation,* and the hour would trip by gaily while he explained that the cocoon's poor inmate never got to be a person but was always a transition. Always a becoming, never a being—a sort of Bergson bug. One day he brought in a lunar moth, a fabulous thing of silver-white wings, lyre-shaped, with a breath of apple green over them and frugal markings of rose. Milton for all his headachy classical allusions was abandoned, though the ghost-creature was obviously just blown from the bosom of Demeter's lost daughter. Milton studied and Milton read were quite different, I found. Judge Griffin's was the only method. Poetry should never be taught.

Although a school-teacher from his youth, Mr. Bass, I believe, hated teaching and learning by textbook. He would sit on the edge of his chair as though about to leap up, and flop his knees together very fast as if a grasshopper's sound-box ought to be between them, and you knew he wanted to dart off somewhere and you knew going with him would be much more interesting than staying anywhere. Further, you had a definite hunch where he longed to be going—to his garden. It was the worst-looking garden I ever saw, with no design, no order, really no sense, a hodge-podge of flowers and vegetables. But everything grew there and throve and bloomed as it did nowhere else. He had no preferences: a carrot was as dear as a peony, a black-eyed Susan as a rose; it only mattered that they were living things mysteriously standing in the earth and reaching for the sun. The mystery was everything to him. I never knew a heart so capable of wonder, though of an earthy unmaudlin sort. When soaked with sweat and dabbed with dirt from digging, his ugliness rather resembled Pan's—not the maligned Pan of the nymphs, but that gaunt mysterious god of flocks and herds, of crops and weathers that rustics worshipped. The rustic Pan in him made his garden for use, not looks. Any morning, if you were an early riser, you could catch a glimpse of him hatless, dirty, untidy, a basket bulging with green things under his arm, and on the run. He dropped into people's front yards unbeknownst and planted unpredictable things—iris and tulips of course, but just as likely salvia against a brick wall. Even more secretive were his vegetable errands. Before anyone was out or up, he'd leave heaps of them—tomatoes, corn, okra, and the like—on the back steps of his friends or preferably of the unknown and sensitive poor. Many a family he half supported whose name he never knew.

All of this by some unaccountable transmutation got itself into his teaching. The way he scuttled in and out of the classroom caused a draught, and if you'd seen grass growing from his ears you wouldn't have noticed. Yet he had principles and ideas galore and never hesitated to express them, no matter how hostile the audience. His vehemence was infectious and you knew he was right when you knew he was wrong.

One summer he took me out West—my first real trip. He was an ideal traveling companion. He had the gift of being informal without being intimate, and his eyes and ears were born anew every half hour. We drove in a stagecoach behind ten span of horses from Flagstaff to the Grand Canyon and I almost died happy at the sight of it. It is God's most personal creation; you feel He's just walked off and is expected back any minute. But of course Mr. Bass in his heart of hearts preferred the flower fields and enormous forests of California.

He wasn't Mississippi-born. To be accurate, he was earth-born but he hailed from a farm in Missouri—a farm, not a plantation. His people farmed not to make money but to live well, and they succeeded, not only in that respect but in developing character, individuality, and easy-going self-respect. Many such are scattered over all the states of the South and they constitute its greatest hope. They were here before the Civil War, they will be here when wars have ceased. They, the aristocrats, and the Negroes are the only three classes in the South of which God must be proud. Mr. Bass was plain through and through and rich and unadulterated. Wherever he is sleeping he is thinking how good the earth is and wondering what flowers are just overhead.

Father Koestenbrock and I were rather cronies anyway, he having heard every confession I'd ever made, having given me my first communion and prepared me for confirmation, and, not least, having talked to me about his plans for the new church. He was not a saint and nothing shocked him. I used to peep at him through the confessional grille and he seemed half asleep, only he couldn't have been because he was too big and fat for his side of the confessional and it must have been uncomfortable. He never was interested in my sins and I believe if I had whispered: "I killed Aunt Nana with the butcher knife because she wouldn't let me hold down the loud pedal!" he would have replied: "Say ten decades of your beads, go in peace, and sin no more." Maybe it all came from his being Dutch, a Dutch nobleman. When he said in a special tone "my native city of Haarlem," you smelled great quantities of rich food and the bouquet of four different wines and saw fat strong women in layers of petticoats prodding among piles of red cheeses.

Naturally, he smoked a huge meerschaum pipe which it had taken him twenty years to color a dull Rembrandt gold and which rested on the first pleat of his stomach when he settled back in his chair and said unromantically: "Give the present tense of *amo.*" If you didn't, believe me, the very furniture rocked until it looked to be drawn by Van Gogh, and like a car of Juggernaut he lumbered over you and you stayed flattened out until he relented. The thing to do during such a cataclysm was to figure ways of diverting the conversation to Haydn—not always easy. That quieted him and presently he'd be laughing like a Frans Hals, exclaiming: "Ach! Haydn! He knew more than all the rest. Chopin—sick! Beethoven—too religious! Mozart—too elegant! But Haydn—that is music, happy and sober, sane as sunshine!"

With any kind of tact and luck he could then be led to analyze Rubens's *Descent from the Cross* and Raphael's *Christ and Saint Veronica,* engravings of which "from the old country" hung on the walls of his study, or to discourse on Dutch Gothic, the style of architecture he'd chosen for the church he was determined to build. I don't understand how his love of Haydn taught him to sing high mass, but something did, and more understandingly and movingly and musically than ever I heard it sung. The magical melodic line of his Pater Noster with its earnestness and pleading could keep you holy for a week.

But ordinarily in religious matters he was earth-treading like Mère: he was not one to receive the stigmata. Once I thought he failed to see a delicate spiritual point with almost willful obtuseness. I had gone to confession in the afternoon preparatory to Holy Communion at early mass next morning. That night I felt so sanctified that at some mundane intrusion I lost my temper and answered back with more than asperity. It was a bad night I passed, thinking over my sin and debating how I could take communion with it unshriven. Mass had started when I entered the church, so there was no chance for a word with Father beforehand. He knew every member of his little flock and had clearly in mind those who were to take communion that morning. The moment arrived, he stood with the host facing the congregation, and the communicants, in-drawn and bowed, walked up the aisle to the communion rail. I stayed where I was, miserably. Then the unforeseen, the impossible happened. When he had given the host to the last communicant, he looked over the church as if searching for someone, saw me, and, standing before the high altar, in full view of the congregation, motioned me to come to the rail. I went up the aisle alone and conspicuous, knelt at the rail alone and conspicuous, and when he bent over me with the host, whispered: "I can't take communion," turned and walked back to my seat. It took every ounce of courage in my whole being. After mass Father called me to the sacristy and demanded an explanation. I explained. He looked as if he wanted to box my ears and blurted out: "Ach! Don't act like a fool. Kneel. Say an act of contrition," and placed the wafer between my lips. His manner worried me, but it never crossed my mind I wasn't right. It never does.

Père said Father Koestenbrock's French accent was painfully Dutch, which infuriated me as it smacked of disloyalty, though doubtless his French was no better than his English, and I knew it. By temperament I'm afraid I'm partisan and attain impartiality, if ever, only by an effort of will. However Dutch Father's French *r*'s and *n*'s, his enthusiasm for certain phases of French literature would have done credit to a French curé. He adored Bossuet and Fénelon, and when he started reading aloud the *Oraisons funèbres* or *Télémaque* with spacious eloquence, there was no telling when he'd desist. I would be bowed with boredom, for they seemed to me in spite of the rolling periods about as unctuous and self-satisfied as *Sandford and Merton* (one of Mur's less inspired selections).

Every six months or so I would come for lessons and find him sitting in his bedroom instead of the study, without pipe or glasses, and in his undershirt. He would look at me dully and from a distance and say thickly: "Go away." At home Mother would explain Father was sick again, but she would be visibly upset and a little angry. He would be sick for several weeks. At first I didn't understand, but after a while it came to me one way or another that my teacher was on a drunk. Drunkenness was bad and Father wasn't bad—my first lesson in reconciling the irreconcilable. The immature must be ruthless and intolerant while their own uncertain inner principles and ideals are hardening into the patterns within which they must enact their own future dramas. We must demand of them much, but not tolerance. Father did nothing improper or public, he just stayed drunk in his room, alone, for weeks and weeks. I would have hated another priest for doing the same thing, it would have been immoral and disgraceful. But Father was not immoral, he was good. Suddenly I experienced the beginning of wisdom. Father was lonely, he never would be or could be anything else. Realizing that hurt me a lot. But I thought Father was single and unique in his loneliness: it was only the beginning of wisdom.

As he grew older and tired, he became impatient about

his new church. He ordered the plans, and for a year or more studied and changed and caressed them. His congregation being poor and he a most shy collector of pew-rent, the building fund remained stationary. He talked of visiting his native city of Haarlem, but always found some excuse for not going. At last to everyone's astonishment he announced that the contract for the building of the church had been let. How could it be paid for? The congregation was in a flurry. But he was gay as Papa Haydn and busy, busy from morning to night. The contractor he selected was an elderly German, a proud fine craftsman, with a fiendish temper and an unquenchable thirst. Then began two years of heroic battle: the two old gentlemen fought all over the place, about every item and detail, they throve and battened on the conflict, you could hear them high up in the scaffolding in outbursts of bilingual denunciation that would have done credit to Michelangelo and the Pope. At last the building was completed, the yellow brick walls, the Gothic windows and arches, the rather stumpy steeple of gray slate—a little Dutch Gothic church, well built, homey, in good taste. And the congregation began to inquire about the mortgage. There would be no mortgage. Father had paid for it all himself. His patrimony, hoarded by a prudent Dutch father to protect the old age of his son, had gone into his church, every nickel of it, and he was happy and old and penniless.

The loneliness came back on him, stronger than ever, and there was nothing much to live for. He was an old man and very tired. So he gave up his parish and retired to a home for superannuated priests on the coast, leaving his little church and us. He'd done his best with both. He returned once years afterwards during our Ku Klux fight, and he was glad to be home. He and I talked about things for hours. At last I said:

"This is the only time within a year that two people have talked in this county for as long as we have without mentioning the Ku Klux Klan. What do you think of the Klan, Father?"

"I do not think of it," he replied. "The Church has been here a long time; it will be here a much longer time, after all these klans and foolish things are forgotten. And it is good for the Church. You remember Luther. The Church was rotten in his day, it needed to be attacked. Old Luther made the Church cleanse herself. So now. The Knights of Columbus, worthy souls, became filled with their own importance during the war and did a great deal of foolish bragging. The Klan will bring them to their senses. It is a very good thing for the Church." He rose to go. We knew we should never see each other again. He looked at me, but his voice was matter-of-fact:

"You always had a spiritual nature. As a little boy you were almost a saint. I—I never had a spiritual nature. I only tried my best." I was never so shamed.

Judge Griffin, Mr. Bass, Father Koestenbrock—their names are being forgotten in our little town, the town where they lived. They have gone the way we all take and they left no mark on the world. But before I join them, I bear testimony they left shining marks on one little boy's heart that shine still.

# CHAPTER IX

## Sewanee

I had been exposed to enough personalities mellow and magnificent to educate a Hottentot and in the process I had somehow received enough formal instruction to condition me for college. Fafar and his brothers had gone to Princeton, Father and his brothers to Sewanee (The University of the South, an Episcopal institution) and to Virginia Law School. Where I should go no one knew, least of all myself, so because it was fairly near and healthy and genteel and inexpensive, Father and Mother drew a long sigh, set me on the train bound for Sewanee, and betook themselves to Europe with Mr. Cook, on their first foreign tour. I was fifteen plus one month, in short trousers, small, weakly, self-reliant, and ignorant as an egg. I had the dimmest notion of how children were born though I knew it required a little co-operation; I had never heard of fraternities, I had never read a football score, I had never known a confidant or been in love. My instructions had been to enter the preparatory school, which was military, but I watched the grammar-school boys in their dusty ill-kept uniforms and I suspected they

smelled bad. I developed an antipathy to the military life
—which I've never overcome—and so, to the astonishment
of the college authorities, I presented myself to them for
entrance exams, and passed.

By no means brilliant, I studied hard, often getting up
at six, to the scandal of other students, to struggle with
Latin and math, and I made excellent grades. I don't
know why I studied hard, but I had no shadow of a doubt
it was the thing to do. English was my favorite course,
whether because of the huge undigested gobs of the best
I'd already read or because of Dr. Henneman, it would be
hard to guess. He was passionate, black-bearded, bespectacled, with an adoration for *Beowulf*, Chaucer, Shakespeare, a grimace for Dr. Donne and the metaphysical
school (oh, woeful unshakable influence), and, much more
important, a capacity for furious moral tantrums in which,
his beard on end clear out to his ears, he would beat the
desk with his fist and roar:

"My God, gentlemen, *do* something!" We earnestly intended to, after such a scene.

And the other great course of those days was Dr. Du-
Bose's Ethics. He was a tiny silver saint who lived elsewhere, being more conversant with the tongues of angels
than of men. Sometimes sitting on the edge of his desk in
his black gown, talking haltingly of Aristotle, he would
suspend, rapt, in some mid air beyond our ken, murmuring: "The starry heavens—" followed by indefinite silence.
We, with a glimpse of things, would tiptoe out of the
classroom, feeling luminous, and never knowing when he
returned to time and space.

It was a small college, in wooded mountains, its students
drawn from the impoverished Episcopal gentry of the
South, its boarding-houses and dormitories presided over
by widows of bishops and Confederate generals. Great

Southern names were thick—Kirby-Smith, Elliott, Quintard, Polk, Gorgas, Shoup, Gailor. The only things it wasn't rich in were worldly goods, sociology, and science. A place to be hopelessly sentimental about and to unfit one for anything except the good life.

Until I came to Sewanee I had been utterly without intimates of my own age. I had liked children whose pleasures were my pleasures, but they had not been persons to me and had left no mark. Here I suddenly found myself a social being, among young creatures of charm and humor, more experienced than I, but friendly and fascinating. I was never generally popular, but I had more than my share of friends. I am never surprised at people liking me, I'm always surprised if they don't. I like them and, if they don't like me, I feel they've made a mistake, they've misunderstood something. There's so much backing and filling about getting acquainted—indirection confuses and sometimes deceives me.

Probably because of my size and age and length of trouser I was plentifully adopted. It is a long time now: some of them have gone the journey, others have fallen by the road and can't go on and are just waiting, and a few have won through to autumn. But then the springtime was on them and they taught and tended me in the greenwoods as the Centaurs did Achilles—I don't know how I ever recovered to draw my own bow. Percy Huger, noble and beautiful like a sleepy St. Bernard; Elliott Cage, full of dance-steps and song-snatches, tender and protective, and sad beneath; Paul Ellerbe, who first read me *Dover Beach,* thereby disclosing the rosy mountain-ranges of the Victorians; Harold Abrams, dark and romantic with his violin, quoting the *Rubáiyát* and discoursing Shaw; Parson Masterson, jostling with religion, unexpected and quaint; Sinkler Manning, a knight who met a knight's death at Montfaucon; Arthur Gray, full of iridescence, discovering new paths and views in the woods and the world; Huger Jervey, brilliant and bumptious then, brilliant and wise now, and so human; and more, many more, all with gifts they shared with me, all wastrel creditors who never collected. Peace to them, and endless gratitude.

I suppose crises occurred, problems pressed, decisions had to be made, those four shining years, but for me only one altered the sunlight. Once a month I would ride ten miles down the wretched mountain road to Winchester, go to confession, hear mass, and take communion. I had been thinking, I had never stopped thinking, I was determined to be honest if it killed me. So I knelt in the little Winchester church examining my conscience and preparing for confession. How it came about did not seem sudden or dramatic or anything but sad. As I started to the confessional I knew there was no use going, no priest could absolve me, no church could direct my life or my judgment, what most believed I could not believe. What belief remained there was no way of gauging yet. I only knew there was an end, I could no longer pretend to myself or cry: "Mea culpa. Help Thou mine unbelief." It was over, and forever. I rode back to the leafy mountain mournful and unregretful, knowing thenceforth I should breathe a starker and a colder air, with no place to go when I was tired. I would be getting home to the mountain, but for some things there was no haven, the friendly Centaurs couldn't help: from now on I would be living with my own self.

There's no way to tell of youth or of Sewanee, which is youth, directly; it must be done obliquely and by parable. I come back to the mountain often and see with a pang, however different it may be to me, it is no different, though Huger and Sinkler and I are forgotten. Then with humility I try to blend and merge the past and the present, to reach the unchanging essence. To my heart the essence, the unbroken melodic theme, sounds something like this:

The college has about three hundred young men or inmates, or students as they are sometimes called, and besides, quite a number of old ladies, who always were old and ladies, and who never die. It's a long way away, even from Chattanooga, in the middle of woods, on top of a bastion of mountains crenelated with blue coves. It is so beautiful that people who have once been there always, one way or another, come back. For such as can detect apple green in an evening sky, it is Arcadia—not the one that never used to be, but the one that many people always live in; only this one can be shared.

In winter there is a powder of snow; the pines sag like ladies in ermine, and the other trees are glassy and given to creaking. Later, arbutus is under the dead leaves where they have drifted, but unless you look for it betimes, you'll find instead puffs of ghost caught under the higher trees, and that's dogwood, and puffs of the saddest color in the world that's tender too, and that's redbud, which some say is pink and some purple and some give up but simply must write a poem about. The rest of the flowers you wouldn't believe in if I told you, so I'll tell you: anemones and hepaticas and blood-root that troop under the cliffs, always together, too ethereal to mix with reds and yellows or even pinks; and violets everywhere, in armies. The gray and purple and blue sort you'll credit, but not the tiny yellow ones with the bronze throats, nor the jackrabbit ones with royal purple ears and faces of pale lavender that stare without a bit of violet modesty. If you've seen azalea—and miscalled it wild honeysuckle, probably —you still don't know what it is unless you've seen it here, with its incredible range of color from white through shell pink to deep coral (and now and then a tuft of orange that doesn't match anything else in the whole woods), and its perfume actually dangerous, so pagan it is. After it you'd better hunt for a calacanthus with brown petals (what else likes its petal brown?) and a little melancholy in its scent, to sober you. We call our bluets "innocence," for that's what they are. They troop near the iris, which when coarsened by gardens some call fleur-de-lis, and others, who care nothing about names, flags. Our orchids we try to make respectable by christening them "lady-slippers," but they still look as if they had been. designed by D. H. Lawrence—only they're rose- and canary-colored.

After Orion has set—in other words, when the most fragile and delicate and wistful things have abandoned loveliness for fructifying—the laurel, rank and magnificent for all its tender pink, starts hanging bouquets as big as hydrangeas on its innumerable bushes. But on moonlight nights there's no use trying to say it isn't a glory and a madness! And so the summer starts—summer, when we're not seraph-eyed enough to see flowers even if there were any. In the fall, when our souls return, a little worse off, a little snivelly, there are foggy wisps of asters whose quality only a spider would hint at aloud, and in the streams where the iris forgathered there are parnassia, the snowdrop's only kin. Mountain-folk alone have seen their virginal processions, ankle-deep in water, among scarlet leaves, each holding a round green shield and carrying at the end of a spear, no thicker than a broomstraw, a single pale green star. Last, chilly and inaccessible and sorrowful, in the damp of the deep woods, come the gentians, sea-blue and hushed.

Now all these delights the Arcadians not infrequently neglect. You might stroll across the campus and quadran-

gles of a sunny afternoon and guess from the emptiness
and warm quiet there that they had gone out among the
trees, lying perhaps in shadow, idly, like fauns, and whistling at the sky. Some may be so unoccupied, though not
faun-like to themselves. But more I fear will be amiably
and discreetly behind closed doors on the third floor, playing not flutes or lyres or even saxophones, but poker. Still
others will be bowed over a table, vexed to the soul with
the return of Xenophon or the fall, too long delayed, of a
certain empire. A few will be off in the valley bargaining
for a beverage called mountain-dew with a splendid virile
old vixen who in that way has always earned a pleasant
livelihood. Later they will have consumed their purchase
to the last sprightly drop and will be bawling out deplorable ballads and pounding tables and putting crockery to
uncouth noisy uses in the neighborhood of one or another
of the old ladies, who will appear scandalized as expected,
but who in the privacy of her own chamber will laugh
soundlessly till her glasses fall off on her bosom and have
to be wiped with a handkerchief smelling of orris-root.

Yet I would not have you think that the Arcadians are
all or always ribald. Even those with a bacchic turn are
full of grace and on occasion given to marvels. I myself
have witnessed one of them in the ghastly dawn, slip-
pered and unpantalooned, his chaplet a wet towel, sitting
in the corner of his room, his feet against the wall, quite
alone, reading in a loud boomy voice more beautiful than
chimes *Kubla Khan* and the *Ode to a Nightingale*.
One afternoon of thick yellow sunshine I was audience to
another who stood on an abandoned windlass with tulip
trees and a blue vista for backdrop reciting pentameters,
which though you may never have heard, we thought too
rich and cadenced for the race of men ever to forget. I
can remember them even now for you:

I dreamed last night of a dome of beaten gold
To be a counter-glory to the Sun.
There shall the eagle blindly dash himself,
There the first beam shall strike, and there the Moon
Shall aim all night her argent archery;
And it shall be the tryst of sundered stars,
The haunt of dead and dreaming Solomon;
Shall send a light upon the lost in hell,
And flashings upon faces without hope—
And I will think in gold and dream in silver,
Imagine in marble and in bronze conceive,
Till it shall dazzle pilgrim nations
And stammering tribes from undiscovered lands,
Allure the living God out of the bliss,
And all the streaming seraphim from heaven.

Perhaps a poet whose dear words have died should be content if once, no matter how briefly, they have made two lads in a greenwood more shimmery and plumed.

Nights, spring nights in special, temper and tune the Arcadian soul to very gracious tintinnabulations. Three Arcadians on one occasion, I recall, sat through the setting of one constellation after another on a cliff in the tender moonlight with a breathing sea of gray and silver tree-tops beneath them and discussed the possibility and probability of God. One, upholding the affirmative, announced that he needed no proof of divinity beyond the amethyst smudge on the horns of the moon. This was countered by the fact that this purple lay not in the moon itself but in the observer's eyes. The deist, troubled, at last concluded anyway he'd rather be a god looking out than look out at a god. Only this was all said with humor and a glistening eagerness—a sort of speech I could once fall into, but long ago.

Myself one of these mountain dwellers for four years, I

have observed them, off and on, for thirty more. It is to be marveled at that they never change. They may not be quite the same faces or the precise bodies you met a few years back, but the alterations are irrelevant—a brown eye instead of a blue one, a nose set a little more to the left. The lining is the same. Neither from experience nor observation can I quite say what they learn in their Arcadia, though they gad about freely with books and pads. Indeed, many of them attempt to assume a studious air by wearing black Oxford gowns. In this they are not wholly successful, for, no matter how new, the gowns always manage to be torn and insist on hanging from the supple shoulders with something of a dionysiac abandon. Further, even the most bookish are given to pursuing their studies out under the trees. To lie under a tree on your back, overhead a blue and green and gold pattern meddled with by the idlest of breezes, is not—despite the admirable example of Mr. Newton—conducive to the acquisition of knowledge. Flat on your stomach and propped on both elbows, you will inevitably keel and end by doting on the tint of the far shadows, or, worse, by slipping into those delightful oscillations of consciousness known as cat-naps. I cannot therefore commend them for erudition. So it is all the more surprising that in after years the world esteems many of them learned or powerful or godly, and that not infrequently they have been the chosen servitors of the destinies. Yet what they do or know is always less than what they are. Once one of them appeared on the first page of the newspapers because he had climbed with amazing pluck and calculated foolhardiness a hitherto unconquered mountain peak, an Indian boy his only companion. But what we who loved him like best to recall about that exploit is an inch cube of a book he carried along with him and read through—for the hundredth time,

likely—before the climb was completed. It was *Hamlet*.
Another is immortal for cleansing the world of yellow fever, but the ignorant half-breeds among whom he worked
remember him now only for his gentleness, his directness
without bluntness, his courtesy which robbed obedience
of all humiliation. Still others I understand have amassed
fortunes and—to use a word much reverenced by my
temporal co-tenants—succeeded. That success I suspect
was in spite of their sojourn in our greenwoods. The Arcadians learn here—and that is why I am having such difficulty telling you these things—the imponderables. Ears
slightly more pointed and tawny-furred, a bit of leafiness
somewhere in the eyes, a manner vaguely Apriline—such
attributes though unmistakable are not to be described.
When the Arcadians are fools, as they sometimes are, you
do not deplore their stupidity, and when they are brilliant
you do not resent their intellectuality. The reason is, their
manners—the kind not learned or instilled but happening,
the core being sweet—are far realer than their other qualities. Socrates and Jesus and St. Francis and Sir Philip
Sidney and Lovelace and Stevenson had charm; the Arcadians are of that lineage.

What Pan and Dionysos and the old ladies dower them
with is supplemented by an influence which must appear
to the uninitiated incompatible. By the aid of a large bell
jangled over their sleeping heads from the hands of a per-
ambulating Negro, the Arcadians at seven each morning
are driven, not without maledictions, to divine service. A
minute before the chapel bell stops ringing, if you happen
to be passing, you may imagine the building to be on fire,
for young men are dashing to it from every corner of the
campus, many struggling with a collar or tie or tightening
a belt in their urgent flight. But at the opening of the
first hymn you'll find them inside, seated in rows, as quiet

as love-birds on a perch. More quiet, in fact: as the service progresses you might well mistake their vacuity for devotion unless you happen to notice the more nocturnal souls here and there who, sagging decorously, have let the warm sleep in.

Nevertheless, the Arcadians add to their list of benefactors those elderly gentlemen about King James who mistranslated certain Hebrew chronicles and poems into the most magnificent music the human tongue has ever syllabled. In their litanies should be named no less those others (or were they the same?) who wrote the Book of Common Prayer. Each morning these young men hear floating across their semi-consciousness the sea-surge of their own language at its most exalted—clean and thunderous and salty. Some of the wash of that stormy splendor lodges in their gay shallows, inevitably and eternally. Who could hear each morning that phrase "the beauty of holiness" without being beguiled into starrier austerities? If someone daily wished that the peace of God and the fellowship of the Holy Ghost might be with you always, could it help sobering and comforting you, even if God to you were only a gray-bearded old gentleman and the Holy Ghost a dove? Suppose you had never rambled from the divine path farther than the wild-rose hedge along its border, still would not the tide of pity for the illness of things rise in your heart at hearing: "We have wandered and strayed from Thy ways like lost sheep"? Lusty Juventus hereabouts may reflect and forget that there was a modern spiciness in the domestic difficulties of David, but it treasures unforgettably: "The heavens declare the glory of God, and the firmament sheweth His handiwork," and "He maketh me to lie down in green pastures, He leadeth me beside the still waters." Such glistening litter is responsible, perhaps, for the tremulous awe and rever-

ence you find in the recesses of the Arcadian soul—at least
you can find them if you are wary and part very gently
the sun-spotted greenery of Pan.

Girders and foundations are fine things; and necessary,
no doubt. It is stated on authority that the creaking old
world would fly into bits without them. But after all what
I like best is a tower window. This hankering is an endless source of trouble to me and I like to think to myself,
in defense, that it comes from having lived too long
among mountain-folk. For they seem always to be leaning from the top of their tower, busy with idle things;
watching the leaves shake in the sunlight, the clouds tumble their soundless bales of purple down the long slopes,
the seasons eternally up to tricks of beauty, laughing at
things that only distance and height reveal humor in, and
talking, talking, talking—the enchanting unstained silver
of their voices spilling over the bright branches down into
the still and happy coves. Sometimes you of the valley
may not recognize them, though without introduction
they are known of each other. But if some evening a personable youth happens in on your hospitality, greets you
with the not irreverent informality reserved for uncles,
puts the dowager Empress of Mozambique, your houseguest, at her ease, flirts with your daughter, says grace before the evening meal with unsmiling piety, consumes
every variety of food and drink set before him (specializing on hot biscuits) with unabashed gusto, leaves a
wake of laughter whenever he dips into the conversation,
pays special and apparently delighted attention to the
grandmother on his left, enchants the serving maid with
two bits and a smile, offers everyone a cigarette, affable
under the general disapproval, sings without art a song
without merit, sits at last on the doorstep in the moonlight, utterly content, with the dreamy air of the young

Hermes (which only means the sense of impending adventure is about his hair like green leaves), and then if that night you dream of a branch of crab-apple blossoms dashed with rain—pursue that youth and entreat him kindly. He hails from Arcady.

# CHAPTER X

# A Year Abroad

Arcadia no more. But what next? Father thought I'd overstudied and I was undoubtedly puny, so a year's respite from schooling seemed advisable. But how employ it? Had there been dude ranches in those days I don't doubt I should have landed on the back of a broncho and swung a lariat with the worst of them, but thank God they were still in the womb of time along with movies. From first childhood I had saved every penny of birthday and Christmas money for a trip abroad. It was my obsession, my one mundane objective—and I had amassed five hundred dollars. Here was my great opportunity; so, Mother and Father dubiously consenting, I seized it.

They traveled to Paris with me and uneasily sought respectable quarters I could afford. Our choice wasn't a triumph. It was a third-floor room in what was coyly termed a hotel, on the rue de Vaugirard, opposite the Senate. French rooms can smell damper and look dowdier in a pretentious way than any in the world. (In comparison the cabins on my plantation seem air-conditioned, riant, and functional.) Mine contained a thick bed curtained in morose red with coarse linen sheets eternally damp; the sparse furniture, though stuffed and overstuffed, was neither sittable nor lyable, and a quiet moist dinginess exuded, from the walls like mold or gangrene. It was fit habitat for a rubber plant, and its tutelary deity was Marie, the homeliest femme de chambre in Paris and scatter-brained to boot. I added hopefully a small upright piano and bought boulets for the tiny fireplace, but that room never attained cosiness or even comfort. Its sole recommendation was the rental, which came to exactly eight dollars a month, not including Marie's tip.

So far as I could detect, I had only two co-lodgers: a desperately poor medical student, a Pole, and a blowzy girl whom I sometimes passed on the dark stinking stairway as she started on her professional rounds. The Pole and I finally spoke, but as I didn't recognize his "Varsovie" as among my geographical familiars nor he my "Paderewski" as an entity of Polish affiliation, we didn't progress far. Nevertheless once a month we found our way together to the Concerts Rouges, each paying his own admission and fifty centimes for a vile concoction with a cherry in it. Looking back I know he was a courageous noble creature and we could have meant much to each other. He and Marie taught me a great and needed lesson in compassion. I had the American contempt for whores, but they never referred to the blowzy young girl as anything except "la pauvre" and were sorry for her when business was bad. My only real intimate was the charming old lady who collected fifty centimes at the cabinet d'aisance opposite the Luxembourg. We met every lucky morning and exchanged pleasantries, she dignified and very sage, because, I suppose, of her unimpeded opportunities for observation.

Even at this age I had great affection for the world and did not want to miss any of its beauties. This obligated me to appreciate whatever men of taste and heart found lovely, which in turn drove me to study, to school my eyes and ears, to train the sensitive and unruly bondsman in my body. I attended free lectures at the Sorbonne along with Russians and Poles who could find no other place to keep warm in this piercing French winter, and I hoarded every cent for theaters, concerts, and operas. To please Father, I joined—and this still doesn't sound true— a fencing school. The results were meager. I developed my single visible muscle on the inside of my right leg, for which I have never since found any use, and one of my fellow students opened my eyes to the possibility of conjugal infelicity by referring to his wife as "un sac." I practiced hours on my tinkly piano, the only hard practicing I ever did, and it seems sad my assiduity was expended on Mendelssohn's *Songs without Words*. Every Sunday afternoon found me at the Concerts Colonne or Lamoureux sitting on the floor of the top balcony amid bespectacled music students out of the Ark with scores in their laps. At the Comique the fabulous Mary Garden was singing Mélisande and Louise, and at the Opéra Bréval was looking exactly like Brunhilde. Bernhardt was still doing Tosca and Phèdre, the Odéon as usual was putting on *L'Arlésienne*, and Bartet and Sorel were declaiming shapely lifeless hexameters at the Comédie. Réjane's homeliness and style were exquisite though her plays on the eternal French theme were a trifle disturbing to my American Puritanism. I adored all French actresses and considered all French actors conceited and artificial.

My best hours, though, were the many I spent in the Luxembourg Gardens. Having paid two sous to the wretched perambulatory old shrew for a comfortless iron chair, I would drag it against one of the big boxes holding a pomegranate bush, tilt back, and read aloud, for the good it would do my accent, *La Cousine Bette* and *Salammbô*. You may have read Proust and Villon, Racine and Rabelais, you may have lived a year in Tours, you may have drunk Vouvray and eaten escargots and *tripes à la mode de Caen*, you may have scrutinized Mont Saint-Michel, the Eiffel Tower, and the Musée Cluny, you may have visited the tomb of Napoleon, you may have slept with ten cocottes and got lost in the Métro, but you still haven't halfway understood France and the French unless you have loitered hours and hours in the Luxembourg Gardens in autumn.

I was talking to a Japanese gentleman once after I'd come from weeks of prayerful solitude at Nikko, steeped still in the dream of its vast cryptomerias, its gold and scarlet temples, its terraces rising higher and higher to unexpected *torii* and tombs, its fantastic bell-towers and stone lanterns, its pools and rivulets, its guardian beasts and writhing gods, its limpid gloom and exalted airiness, and I questioned him concerning the miracle of its creation. He answered:

"What is most abhorrent to the Japanese soul is obvious plan. The expected is uninteresting. Plan, of course, there must be, so subtle it is concealed, so imaginative it appears unplanned. Axes and balances, geometrical design, formal arrangement—anyone can learn these; they must be avoided if your creation is to appear not man's but the excellent whimsy of the gods. Nothing is so tedious, so obvious, so boring to the Japanese soul as the garden of Versailles. It is a problem in mathematics. Nikko is as inconceivable as a sunset or a moth's wing."

The Luxembourg is mathematical, it is not a whimsy of

the gods; gods I suppose wouldn't walk in it, but men—
men with the pathos of autumn in their souls, disillusioned
of high endeavor, patient and thankful for the late sunshine and quiet little things, men can walk there in peace,
a peace full of sadness and without regret. It was made
by men, for men, on man's scale: it is full of comfort and
tenderness. Its chestnuts have a somber gold and their
leaves fall slowly, in zigzags, filling the fountain of the
Medici and glancing from the shoulders of the children
as they whip their tops and roll their hoops. The old men
in their corner behind the Palace play croquet passionately, but the leaves drift through their fiery outbursts and
clutter the course to the next wicket. They sprinkle with
cicada rustlings the amazing tennis courts between their
rows, where the players never play but always are hunting the ball, there being no backstops. They lay a tar-
nished curtain between Polichinelle and Pierrot bickering
stridently in the little marionette theater and their won-
der-eyed birdlike audience in twittering rows. They even
blow into the central fountain flanked by its prim beds
of asters and dahlias and mingle their sunset barques
with the small boys' sail-boats that eternally head for the
drip of the upper basin and turn over, necessitating rescue
squads from the ranks of passing elders. But it is all a
dream, a tender gracious unreality, like Watteau's *L'Em-
barquement pour Cythère*: the children's cries and laughter are muted; the slow-passing lovers cling wordlessly
together; and each bench has its single occupant looking
out over the autumn, over the gold trees in their sculp-
tured masses and the pale bubble of the Panthéon, over
the curving balustrades and the queens of France in their
still white rows, and seeing maybe nothing, or maybe the
enchanted world that does not last and time that does not
pause. They ask little, for they know it is little they will

receive for all their asking, but that little is so dear, as it always is to the autumn-hearted who know life is pitiful and infinitely sweet.

No one ever missed so much during his first year abroad as I. I was desperately shy: my French was halting and ungrammatical; buying tickets, engaging rooms, asking directions, ordering meals were delicate tortures; and to make it worse I was constantly going places and doing things because I was afraid to. Except for the merciful and occasional appearances of Huger Jervey, Arthur Gray, and Huger Elliott, I saw and spoke to no one, I was completely unconscious of human beings. I lived with John Addington Symonds, Ruskin, Cellini, and Shelley. Yet despite all this, or because of it, I betook myself, trembling and hopeful, to almost every nook and corner of France and Italy, even landing before the winter was over in Egypt.

I haunted art galleries and churches like a New England spinster and must have passed months in the Louvre, the longest, tallest, widest, worst-hung, most exhausting, irritating, and magnificent gallery in the world. There wasn't a room of it I wasn't familiar with, and by the aid of a compass I even found the Houdons (west by north) and the Michelangelos (north by northeast). I specialized in madonnas, holy families, and allegorical pieces, and was cold to portraits unless they were by the early Florentine sculptors and to everything Dutch except Rembrandt. Murillo was the only Spanish painter and Ingres the only French. Manet was shocking and Monet impossible.

Because I was less sensitive to sculpture than to painting, I tried harder to appreciate it and spent hours with the Greeks. My admiration was for the conventional masterpieces—the *Venus de Milo,* the *Niobe,* the Naples *Psyche,* the *Victory* of Samothrace, the Pompeian bronzes —and I missed completely the *Birth of Venus,* the *Sleeping Fury* and the *Charioteer* of Delphi. I was always happening on a Hermaphrodite, in some discreet alcove, and I would examine the sleazy mock-modest little monster with horror and fascination. I could never imagine how it could have been created by the Greeks, usually so healthy and frank. I stumbled on the answer years later. When the Greeks practiced bisexuality honestly and simply without thought or condemnation they did not create these slick symbols of love divided in its objectives. It was a later, more sophisticated, more prurient age, the age of the nasty *Crouching Venus* of Syracuse, that, titillating and ahing, symbolized what they understood and were ashamed of by these sentimental decadent man-woman creatures, false art and false biology.

It's a grievous and a long way you travel to reach serenity and the acceptance of facts without hurt or shock. By that time you are too old to practice your wisdom and to young ears your advice might as well be uttered in Icelandic. Ripeness is all, said the wise one, and I suppose that's all there is to it. But one isn't ripe at nineteen. I was gourd-green, fearful, treading ledges without a Virgil.

While I was missing so much, I collected some imperishable memories: Luxor in moonlight; Notre-Dame in any light; the hill-towns of Italy, particularly Perugia; my first nightingale at Nîmes; my first Greek temple at Pæstum; the brumal gold interior of St. Mark's before it was cleaned; Shelley's grave with camellias blooming against the wall of the Protestant Cemetery and violets in purple shallows over the graves; the tall Egyptian women at dusk bearing on their heads to the Nile their water-jugs, the night air stirring the veils half from their faces and flattening their single garments in ripples against their straight proud bodies.

But it was lonesome going. I missed Mother and Father and the Centaurs, yet I wasn't suffering regular homesickness or ordinary loneliness. At sight or sound of something unbearably beautiful I wanted desperately to share it, I wanted with me everyone I'd ever cared for—and someone else besides. I was sick for a home I had never seen and lonely for a hand I had never touched. So for a year I ate and walked and lived and slept with loneliness, until she was so familiar I came not to hate her but to know whatever happened in however many after years she alone would be faithful to me and, departing a little way for some brief beatific interlude, would always return. And that perhaps is the only important thing I learned that year. What must be learned at last had as well be learned early.

# CHAPTER XI

# At the Harvard Law School

This year of travel after college was supposed to have afforded me a breathing-spell during which I could judiciously select my future means of livelihood. I agreed uneagerly with Father that a man should earn his keep, and Father was willing to give me an education in any profession I might choose or to set me up in business. No young man could have asked more; it was a magnificent opportunity. I found myself not only bewildered but uninterested. In my day people didn't flatfootedly choose to be teachers or scholars, scientists or preachers, much less hermits or saints. I had no penchant for any business, no talent for any art. Weighing my abilities, I had to confess they were of no commercial value and, to be honest, were, so far as I could judge, non-existent. The necessity of earning a living plus a desire to live plus the failure to discover in myself any quality convertible into cash—here was a combination sufficient to fling one tailspinning into the deepest inferiority complex. All along of course I had a sneaking persistent desire to write, but I realized I had nothing to write about, being ignorant of man and of his home, this dark sphere, and even of that palpitating speck, myself.

So I did not choose the law, it chose me. Father was a successful lawyer, as were his brothers, as had been his father. With his growing reputation and practice and because he loved me he would be glad to take me into his office. I was not more unfit for the law than for anything else I could think of. Ignobly and without decision I asked Father to send me to the Harvard Law School. After all these years I look back on that request as craven and unimaginative. But I don't regret it and if I had it to go through with over again I should be equally nonplussed and not more courageous. On leaving college if we had some inkling of our own aptitudes we could plan our lives more usefully and more happily. For the unfortunate without aptitudes of course there's no hope of direction except from wind and tide. Conceding myself to have been an extreme case of jelly-fish, yet I notice today that college graduates continue to be distressfully disoriented and, remembering, I grieve for their waste and pain. Yet down wrong turnings too there's plentiful adventure.

Harvard's law school was my own choice, not Father's, for he leaned to Virginia, where he and his brothers had sat worshipfully at the feet of old Minor. The reason for my selection had little enough to do with law. I wanted to be near Boston with its music and theaters, which I would miss the rest of my life in my future Southern home, and I wanted to meet the damyankees.

Carl Sandburg observed casually in the preface to his life of Lincoln that one of my grandfathers fought in the Union Army. I rejoice in his error because except for it my name would never have found its way into the pages of his magnificent study. I probably told my poet friend that Fafar made speeches against secession, that he was a Whig and something less than an admirer of Jefferson Davis and that his two older brothers had felt so bitterly the unwisdom of secession that they refused to enlist in the Confederate Army. Fafar, though, enlisted; in fact, he raised a company which he captained and at the time of the surrender he was a Colonel on Bowen's staff. But he never spoke of the war, it hurt too much, and besides, silence was General Lee's example. So they never talked of the war at home and I never heard Yankees referred to as damyankees. My feeling toward them was one of curiosity, not hostility. Yet when I lit in their midst I did feel a drop in the temperature. It wasn't Sewanee or the Delta.

I have enjoyed spells of more intense happiness but never three years of as uninterrupted happiness as I did at the Harvard Law School. I was aware it was my last fling at life unweighted by responsibility and that awareness tautened my every sense to miss no vibration. By good chance I roomed at Winthrop Hall, which stands in a green space back of the Longfellow House and which was then the popular dormitory for law students from Yale. With my usual desire to like and be liked, I was a little dazed at first by the atmosphere of reserve, by the angular restrained manners. Grace wasn't abounding, but I came to find that character and intelligence were. I sensed that I was under inspection and on probation until I proved myself "the right sort," which it seemed to me anyone should have known me to be from the start, and besides I couldn't imagine what harm anyone would have come by had I turned out to be the wrong sort. Southerners are far easier to meet and never so intimate after meeting.

I found myself in a strange land but a pleasant one. It's

easy to remember why it was pleasant, but not easy to explain or analyze why it was strange. It lacked something of giddiness and absurdity. The ability to be a trifle daft, which I had considered native to young people, was unhappily absent. A certain rigidity hinted of pomposity or dullness ahead, as well as of strength. Even now, if I think of the Brattle Hall dances, I feel the way a banana plant looks after a frost. New England's self-consciousness was without artlessness and its show of superiority betrayed unsureness. People tried to impress one another, and real folks make no such effort.

On my first vacation South Mrs. Lovell, whom I loved most of all the old Sewanee ladies after Mrs. Preston, asked me a startling question: "Will, up North there did you meet anyone who was"—she paused—"a gentleman?" My emphatic and amused "Yes" didn't convince her. "I mean among the Northerners." No amount of affirmatives could have convinced her. She counseled quietly: "I'm certain you will find you are mistaken." Being a daughter of General Quitman, famous in the Mexican War, and having been born and bred in one of the great homes of Natchez perhaps accounted for her provincialism, but she was a good hater anyhow and she had seen reconstruction. I am not a good hater. I detect likenesses more readily than differences and the former strike me as the more important and the more interesting. That one of my fellow creatures happens to be a German or a Hottentot or even a Northerner seems less exciting to me than that he is a human being, engagingly and pitifully like me. Mrs. Lovell was wrong, no doubt of that whatsoever, but, all the same, Harvard was un-Southern in feel, though I can't recall instances of difference to prove it. Yet these inconsequentials stick in my mind as if they meant something.

For the first month or two a chap named Freddie sat next to me in class and we usually exchanged casual remarks. He seemed nice and I knew nothing about him except that he was a real Hahvard, by which we outlanders meant a graduate of Harvard College with a broad *a*. I learned later that Freddie had been something of a person in college and came from an old and rich Boston family. One day as I was walking to the Square Freddie came toward me from it. It was our first meeting outside of classroom. He glanced up and recognized me. As I started to speak he looked me through and cut me dead. It was the first time I had ever been cut. I have never been more surprised or more angry. Inquiring later the reason for this gratuitous rudeness, I was told a Harvard man's prominence was gauged by the number of men he could afford to cut. Things may have changed there since my day. I hope so. With us a cut is used as a moral weapon, except by social climbers. It was our third year before Freddie and I met again as members of one of those silly exclusive clubs which young people, at best hopeless snobs, persist in forming, and on that occasion, I must confess, he was more affable than I. I think he really was a nice and intelligent young American. He just hadn't been brought up right. Gus Westfeldt, my roommate from New Orleans, had a similar experience, but his reaction was more instantaneous and effective than mine. He delivered the *Mayflower* princeling a sock on the jaw and a bit of advice which I recall but can't repeat. I guess they thought Southerners were queer too.

My next lesson in differences was more amusing. Harley Stowell and I had been invited to dine with a middle-aged professor and his wife at their home. Except for the usual bolt-upright atmosphere it was a tasteful house and everything except me ran smoothly and decorously. An immense bird-cage full of canaries filled the end of the dining-room to my right behind our host. On each plate sat a snowy napkin innocently folded and refolded into a sort of battleship. I must have been feeling unpardonably vivacious, for in undoing my napkin I gave it an airy little flirt to the right, and to my horror out of it soared a small brown roll shaped like a torpedo which described a slow parabola and lit with a wiry bang on top of the bird-cage. No one could pretend it hadn't happened. A bandersnatch or a whooping crane flying across the room could not have had higher visibility. The impact with the bird-cage sounded like a Stravinsky chord on an untuned harp, and all the canaries burst into a pæan of dismay or applause. I couldn't decide whether I wanted to die or giggle. But my hosts never batted an eye. They were wonderful; their nerves must have been shattered, but, without allusion to projectiles, we proceeded with the soup course. To ignore completely such a calamity takes praiseworthy poise, but I'd have felt more reorganized if they all had gone Japanese and bombarded the bird-cage with their rolls or, better still, if everyone had burst out laughing and cheered: "Good shot" or "It's a birdie" or "The last time Senator Omygosh did that he hit two canaries and killed the auk." Someone would surely have been that silly and that merciful a thousand miles south of the Charles.

My last example of difference isn't worth recording except for its mention of some wholly charming New Englanders. Bobbie Schurman had a genius for discovering beautiful girls whom Aunt Nana would have described as "comme il faut." One fine fall day he lured the Crocker girls down from Fitchburg for an afternoon concert of the Boston Symphony. They had as much chic and loveliness and animation as any Southern belle, but that afternoon they felt positively dashing because they were going unchaperoned to the symphony with two young men. I fancied their flurry on this score was one of those mysterious aberrations of feminine coquetry, but realized the error of my diagnosis when I suggested after the concert that we go for tea to the most proper of Boston hotels (and I imagine that meant the most proper hotel in the world). They were scandalized by the suggestion. It wasn't proper, it wasn't ladylike, it just wasn't done. We argued and pleaded so chivalrously and dolefully that finally, unable to resist the sheer bravado of the proposal, they actually drank tea and nibbled toast with us in a huge oak-paneled dining-room heavily populated with dowagers. It was far less intimate than the Boston Common, and the girls felt like soubrettes. Fascinated, I mused that no Southern girl would have given our proposal a thought, unless it had not been made.

After tea we accompanied the girls up to Fitchburg, where Bobbie and I were to be their guests over the weekend. We quaked a little about our reception after such devilish gallantries and with cause, for all of us were sternly scolded. Not between Tierra del Fuego and the Arctic Circle could a more gracious and delightful household have been found than that of the Crockers in Fitchburg in those days. It was everything a home full of young people should be. Yet even there I experienced a contretemps which I hope was typical of nothing. One of President Theodore Roosevelt's sons was also a houseguest. Although I suspected he might be fairly dour and lofty, after dinner I rambled over to him and began talking of an incident which had occurred to his father and mine on a bear-hunt they had recently taken together. As I began to talk, his expression took on the glassy hauteur of the Ritz head waiter when he wordlessly reminds a couple from Hushpuckna where they came from and where they should go. Snubbed. I left the story unfinished. But this time I wasn't surprised or angered. Surely he belied his breeding. I was in the midst of proof that bad manners were not inculcated in these parts or indigenous. Before the Civil War a good many of the Southern leaders were guilty of this same sort of stupidity. Not satisfied with knowing they were as good as anyone else, they came to believe they were better than anyone else. Always a fatal delusion. They should have remembered hubris from their Greek. Except for them the Civil War could possibly have been avoided, as could, except for their like, many a modern conflict between capital and labor and between nation and nation. Manners are essential and are essentially morals.

Beyond peradventure there were differences, but so oblique and unessential that after a few months I was not conscious of them. My intimates, except Gus, were all Northerners and, curiously enough, all from New York State. Mentally they were more disciplined and morally more innocent than the Southern boys. Everyone studied seriously and dissipation of any sort was almost unknown. A Saturday night Boston binge was an event, and drinking in the dormitory was restricted to our annual beer night. Our chief dissipation was conversation. Every night at eleven, after study was over, a coffee percolator would be started in someone's room and weary students would drop in. It was a superior brand of talk we indulged in, covering a wide range of subjects, with a minimum of inhibition and a maximum of gusto. Occasionally sparrows on the roof or that wretched woodpecker on the tin gutter would halt our sessions with news of the sunrise. I wonder if this most civilized form of entertainment is fated for extinction by man's most effective mental opiate, the radio? Instead of hot orchestras, impromptu interludes often interrupted our symposiums. It would cross someone's mind that I had been less than appreciative of Bobbie Schurman's Christmas gift, a copy of *Uncle Tom's Cabin.* The rebel would be pinned to the floor and sat on by rowdy well-wishers while others would read aloud Mrs. Stowe's more sadistic and blood-boiling passages, with Simon Legree gestures. Or Stanleigh Friedman, fresh-laureled as composer of "March, March on Down the Field," would start playing the score of *Tristan und Isolde* and in his mounting passion would burst into astonishing song as he reached the "Liebestod." They were splendid evenings.

By day of course sterner doings were afoot. We were attempting to learn the law and we took it hard. The first year our confusion mounted to despair. One night Jakie Smith rushed into my room with the sudden illumination: "I know what it is! The law is common sense plus clear English!" I've never heard a better definition of what the law should be and isn't. In comparison "Pop" Gray's dictum: "The aim of the law is settlement, not justice," seems weary and defeatist. The virtue of the Socratic method of the Harvard Law School is not that from it you learn what the law is, but that by it you learn how to think. Whatever ability I may have to reason in a straight line from premise to conclusion derives from the discipline of those three years and especially from Professor Williston and his horse Dobbin. I lost hours of sleep, pounds of flesh, buckets of cold sweat over Dobbin, the hero of every supposititious contract, the villain of every supposititious sale. From Professor Williston I also learned that one can be proved a fool so quietly and inexorably that the fool will harbor neither anger nor resentment. But this technique I have never been able to master. Cold logic I admire, but have no talent for. My sort works only above boiling-point.

Whatever I learned in class was absorbed and left no conscious memories. I recall less of that phase of my life in Cambridge than of any other. The grace of New England elms, whiffs of New England lilacs, spring which came in May and for its tardiness came with intolerable rapture, the long winters with crystal storms and interminable widths of snow never the same color, the sound of the puckered thaw like crabs feeding, walks around frozen ponds on snow-shoes or through sparsely green woods, in either case well-companioned, often by Elsie Singmaster or Bob Black, the red winter sunsets which turned the bare branches to amethyst and crimson—such items I recall far more vividly than torts or the statute of uses. And then the Boston Symphony on Saturday nights and the week in spring when the Metropolitan came! To have the great masterpieces of music, matchlessly performed, poured into your fresh ears with Harold Bruff or George Roberts or Harley Stowell in the seat next to you —well, one could ask nothing more of life—that was ecstasy. We cherished Gadski, though she looked like a horse, and when she lay down by Tristan's body she couldn't rise by her own power. We beamed on Schumann-Heink as she stood on the deck of Tristan's boat gazing seaward and trying to look tragic but failing because of her funny nose and her arms too short to meet across the bolster of her bosom. But when her voice poured from the tower across the moonlight we shuddered, knowing that never in life would we again hear any slow river of sound as beautiful. We adored Farrar with that ineffable springtime voice of hers, and for us there could never be another real Mimi or Nedda or Butterfly or Elizabeth. When Papa Hertz's black beard stood on end and he began bouncing at a climax we were blissfully happy. And, besides, there were Caruso and Sembrich, Louise Homer and Scotti, and, most glorious of all, the divine Fremstad with her head high, her shoulders back, her goddess figure, as though she had just stepped from the porch of the Erechtheum. We were critical and ignorant, but our reactions were ardent and genuine and we held no truck with those clichés which lend a spurious air of knowledge and appreciation to musical conversation. When Karl Muck, whom we considered Wagner's son and the most electric and impeccable of conductors, played Mahler or Bruckner or Sibelius we felt personally affronted, and, unbelievable as it seems now, we were apt to be heavy-lidded through Bach and Brahms. There was so much that we had not yet experienced and that lay ahead, particularly fiery furnaces and anvils of pain. But every concert was an adventure and usually we'd be plumed and dripping fire as we made for the Brattle Street trolley through the winter murk.

Boston meant nothing to me. Cambridge meant nothing to me. The ghosts of Emerson and Thoreau did not haunt my ways nor the tall shadows of William James and Santayana cross my paths. The strong tart flavor of New England was not savored by my palate. I missed much, as usual, but much more I did not miss. I had daydreamed too long, and though dreamers are needed by this world of ours, day-dreamers are not, nor sleep-walkers. The law was a dash of cold water, a first film of nacre for a very shell-less oyster. However uncertainly and shyly, I could proceed into the frightening concourse of men at least awake and not wholly unarmed. I had gathered a kitful of new memories, Elysian sounds and sights, for the rigorous journey, and in the enemy country

I had taken hostages against the long cold, new friends to whom I could shout when the going was rough and on whom I could brood when, silence answering, I knew for them the going had been too rough. Harold Bruff and George Roberts were worth three years of any man's life.

# CHAPTER XII

# The Return of the Native

Probably there is no nostalgia so long-lived and hopeless as that of the college graduate returning to his native town. He is a stranger though he is home. He is sick for a communal life that was and can never be again, a life merry with youth and unshadowed by responsibilities. He is hungry for the easy intimacies which competitive anxious living does not provide. He is unproved when proof is demanded on every side. In this alien environment, the only one he may now call his own, he is unknown, even to himself.

My case was no different from most, I suppose, and I hated it: eight years of training for life, and here I was in the midst of it—and my very soul whimpered. I had been pushed into the arena and didn't even know the animals' names. Besides, I labored under individual disabilities: I had been to Europe; I had been to Harvard; my accent, though not Northern, was—well, tainted; I had had it easy; I probably considered myself *it*. For crowning handicap, I was blessed with no endearing vices: drunkenness made me sick, gambling bored me, rutting per se, unadorned, I considered overrated and degrading. In charitable mood one might call me an idealist, but, more normally, a sissy.

It must have been difficult for Father too. Enjoying good liquor, loving to gamble, his hardy vices merely under control, he sympathized quizzically and said nothing. But his heart must often have called piteously for the little brother I had lost, all boy, all sturdy, obstreperous charm. Fortunately I wasn't meek and I wasn't afraid. When put upon, I discovered that a truculent tongue did more to save than a battalion of virtues. But it wasn't fun. I had attacks of nausea, but not of tears.

Yet these handicaps on my debut were a minor worry. My real concern was what the show was all about and what role I should or could play in it, queries which, since the curtain was up and I on the stage, seemed fairly belated.

For eight years—in fact, for twenty-three—a great number of people had been pouring out money, skill, time, devotion, prayers to create something out of me that wouldn't look as if the Lord had slapped it together absent-mindedly. Not Alexander the Great nor Catherine II had been tended by a more noble corps of teachers. It humbles me to call their roster, but calling it is no penance: Nain and Mur, Mère and Père, Sister Evangelist and Judge Griffin, Father Koestenbrock and Mr. Bass, Dr. Henneman and Professor Williston, the Roman Catholic Church and Browning, the sea and the sun, Beethoven and Wagner, Michelangelo and Andrea del Sarto, loneliness and friendship, Sinkler and Harold, Mother and Father. They made a longer procession than the Magi and the shepherds combined, and the gifts they brought were more precious. Obviously I was cast to justify the ways of man to God, as it were. But how? What does one do with a life, or at any rate intend to do? It was time to inventory my ambitions and, having selected one as paramount, to pursue it whole-heartedly. For months (maybe for years, maybe until now) I hunted about for a good ambition. Money? No, positively—not because my financial future was assured or my financial present anything more than adequate to supply my simple needs, but it wasn't interesting and it wasn't worthy. Nothing to debate here. Fame as a lawyer? I had been a B man at the law school, which is eminently respectable but not brilliant as Harold and George had been. I suspected that if I should give everything I had to the law I might realize such an ambition, but I had no notion of doing any such thing. I wanted to do whatever piece of work fell to my care as well as I could, but beyond that I wasn't concerned over what opinion my brethren of the bar held of me. Power? I knew nothing about it and it certainly wasn't my métier. Civic usefulness? Perhaps; that was getting warmer, but I had no desire to hold office and I knew no way of dedicating one's unendowed life to usefulness. Other things, I did not know what, except that they were things inside, seemed realities, while money, fame, power, civic virtue seemed things which required an audience to become real. So with my ruminations I reached nowhere, a lonesome sort of spot. Now that the show is nearly over, I'm only just beginning to see what one may truthfully call the good life, but of the plot I still know so little that I can't swear whether it's been tragedy or comedy, though I have an inkling. Perhaps, after all, stumbling through life by ear, though slower, makes more exciting traveling, and if you have a good ear you're just as apt to arrive as if you'd dipped about in the wake of one of those twitchy compasses.

I didn't exactly plunge into life, rather I tipped in, trepidly. In spite of doubts and misgivings, there was living to be done and I set about it. Our town wasn't a thing of beauty in those days. The residences looked like illegitimate children of a French wedding cake. Besides all the icing they usually sported a turret or cupola to which Sister Ann couldn't have climbed if she *knew* somebody was coming, for it never had stairs. The brick stores, most of them still in situ, as we lawyers say, managed to look stark without looking simple. Curbs, gutters, and open ditches, while satisfactory to such stalwart conservatives as crawfish and mosquitoes, still abided hopefully the coming of the W.P.A. Sidewalks were often the two-board sort that grow splinters for barefoot boys, and the roads, summer or winter, were hazards. There were lovely trees and crape myrtles but where they grew was their business. There were flowers, but no gardens. Just a usual Southern town of that period, and its name was Greenville. There must be something in that name attractive to towns because every state in the Union has one. It's a name without charm for me. I prefer Alligator or Rolling Fork or Nitta Yuma or Rosedale, our neighbors— at least they have individuality, of one sort or another. But, aside from all that, in 1909 I retook Greenville for my home (and kept it) and could boast that I was a full-fledged practicing attorney-at-law.

While not what you might call indispensable in the office, I looked up authorities for Father with great interest and once or twice stumbled on an original legal theory, the discovery of which pleased him even more than myself. I was terrified at the thought of arguing a case, particularly before a jury, but somehow I steeled myself to do it and with some passion, though never brilliantly and never to this day without a spasm of nerves before and after. But the law was the least of my troubles. Making

a rut, for comfort, was a grimmer endeavor, one that required years of effort—probably it is one of those lifetime
jobs, and just when you are beginning to feel snug you
are routed out permanently.

In those days the center of social life for the young
people was the Elysian Club. The oldsters played poker
at the Mississippi Club and the middling mature indulged
their usual bacchanalian bent, unassisted by pards and
mænads, at the Elks'. No doubt about it, our town was
plumb social. Although it cherished a "reading-room" and
a poolroom, our club's raison d'être was its dance floor. It
was a fine floor, but it was housed in a room replete with
unsynchronized angles and curves which it must have
taken the local builder months to conceive and no time
to execute. Beyond question it was the ugliest room in
the world, but thoroughly entrancing when Handy appeared and the dancing started. Delta girls are born
dancing and never stop, which is as it should be, for surely it is the finest form of human amusement except tennis
and talking. The club's dances were famous from Hushpuckna to Yazoo City, and they were the right sort of
affairs, with rows of broad-bosomed lares and penates
against the wall and so many good-looking animated girls
drawling darkest Southernese and doing intricate steps by
instinct or inspiration that no one could think of going
home before daylight. Drinking was not permitted in the
clubhouse and there were no parked cars for intermissions. An intoxicated youth was a crying scandal and an
intoxicated female would certainly have caused hara-
kiri or apoplexy among the penates. There are dances
now in the Delta, a never ending round, but I am told
they are more stimulated and less stimulating.

Now and then Father and Mother appeared at our
functions and remained an hour or two because they loved

young people. Father himself would occasionally indulge in a whirl on the dance floor, but, being practically tone-deaf, he was an awful dancer and knew it, though fairly unabashed and invariably amused. Mother never understood or forgave in me a certain lack of enthusiasm for things social. People, whole throngs of them, delighted her, and her delight was infectious. Everyone became a little more charming than he was meant by God to be when she was around. I liked people, too, but individually and separately, not in throngs. I soon learned, when surrounded, not to go bounding off like a flushed fawn, but crowds were not then and are not now my natural habitat, and even individuals, no matter how fascinating, I find more exhausting than hard work or boredom. Mother regarded my antisocial tendencies as pure mulishness, but Father, although disappointed no doubt, never showed it except by a far-away expression and a little smile.

I often took to the levee in sheer lonesomeness and confusion of soul. Our woods are not made for walking because the vines and bushes are too rampant and the rattlesnakes too much at home. But the high levee is perfect for a stroll, which you can extend, if so minded, a hundred miles in either direction. Across the river you see Arkansas, a state almost as unfamiliar to us as Montana, but we know it has one great virtue—it grows willows and cottonwoods right down to the water line. In spring they are done by Puvis de Chavannes in pastel green, in summer they are banked in impenetrable tiers of lushness, in fall they have a week of pale flying gold, and in winter they are at their best with their wands rose- and copper-colored and their aisles full of blue smoke. There wasn't a time of year I didn't walk there and watch them across the vari-colored river, which, though it seems home, seems too the most remote and secret stretch of all God's universe. It is most itself and to my liking when with the first crystal rush of winter the ducks and geese and water-turkeys, in wedges, follow its pale protecting sandbars south. At first I walked there alone, but later I discovered three familiar spirits who also enjoyed walking and talking. Will Francis and Lyne Starling and George Roth certainly tided me over a bad passage and are with me still.

It was on these levee walks that I began to think of poetry and to jot down lines. At Sewanee I had tried my hand at lyrics and unfortunately, as I was editor of the college magazine, some of them found their way, anonymously, into print. I reread them a few years ago and I cannot imagine an experience more embarrassing. In Paris I had written a feeble sonnet on Chatterton and at Harvard I improved slightly with two winter songs, one of which, to my amazement and delight, *McClure's* published, still anonymously. All these were secret indulgences and only Miss Carrie knew of them.

This is not an account of my poetry nor of me as a poet. But since much of my life has gone into the making of verse which I hope is poetry, I may as well state now and as briefly as I can how and why I wrote.

What I wrote seemed to me more essentially myself than anything I did or said. It often gushed up almost involuntarily like automatic writing, and the difficulty lay in keeping the hot gush continuous and unselfconscious while at the same time directing it with cold intellect into form. I could never write in cold blood. The results were intensely personal, whatever their other defects. But by some quirk I was always aware in the act of putting words to paper that what I was feeling and thinking had been felt and thought by thousands in every generation. Only that conviction would have permitted me to publish without feeling guilty of indecent exposure.

I judge there's nothing at all unusual about such mental processes, or about these:

When you feel something intensely, you want to write it down—if anguish, to stanch the bleeding; if delight, to prolong the moment. When after years of pondering you feel you have discovered a new truth or an old one which suddenly for you has the excitement of a new one, you write a longish poem. To keep it free from irrelevant photographic details you set it in some long-ago time, one, of course, you love and perhaps once lived in.

That is how I wrote and why I wrote. As to technique I tried to make it sound as beautiful and as fitting as I could. Old patterns helped, but if rhyme seemed out of place, the choruses of *Samson Agonistes*, some of Matthew Arnold's unrhymed cadences, and Shakespeare's later run-on pentameters suggested freer and less accepted modes of communication. As far as I can make out, the towering bulk of English poetry influenced me tremendously, but not any one poet, though I hope I learned as much as I think I owe to Browning's monologues and to Gilbert Murray's translations of Euripides.

Thinking of these lonely trial years would be impossible for me without thinking of Caroline Stern. Everybody in town called her Miss Carrie. The first time I saw her I was far gladder than she realized. One of the convent boys, a fattish one who loomed huge to my apprehensive vision, had announced to me as we dawdled on the corner that I would have to fight him then and there. As in so many conflicts, the casus belli was obscure and immediately forgotten. I accepted the challenge with the least possible enthusiasm and began taking off my coat very deliberately, to give the Lord time to take a hand.

At this moment Miss Carrie appeared, surveyed the scene, and paused. The conflict petered out before a blow was struck. Evidently my guardian angel had taken the form of Miss Carrie. It was an unusual guise. She was as tiny as Sister Evangelist, but birdlike. She must have weighed eighty pounds. She had a sensitive face, pale, with a large Jewish nose and enormous brown eyes, lustrous and kind. Her hair, which curled pleasantly, was just darker than wasp red. But I found later there was nothing else waspish about her, though she was a gallant fighter. She never thought anything was worth fighting for except moral issues, and it sickened her when an individual or a nation refused to fight for them. On this occasion she stopped and viewed our bellicose stance, meaning no doubt to whirl in if developments required. Then as always she looked tidy but a tiny bit disheveled, as if a not very rough breeze had just deposited her unexpectedly. She had the air of a volunteer as we gardeners use the term, and that air always kept Mother from appreciating her, because Mother by instinct and training was chic.

Miss Carrie—she must have been in her twenties then, though of course she seemed to me far gone in overblown maturity—had mistaken my unwilling preparations for battle for simon-pure heroism and, since she admired nothing more than knightly prowess, I found myself a few days later a visitor in her little house. It was a bare little place with an improvised look and hardly enough furniture for convenience. Her dwarf of a father, an Alsatian Jew, lived with her, a querulous old fellow who had failed as a country merchant and, now idle, lived by her scanty earnings as a teacher. She tended and scolded him as if he were a child. Her passionate adoration had been for her mother, whose death a few years before had left her the bread-winner and spiritually in solitary confinement. It would have been mortally lonely for her had she not known Judge Griffin, who gave her the nourishment she needed, his deep patriarchal love.

Miss Carrie's passion for painting was beyond bounds, consuming. While still in her teens, by impossible denials and scrapings, she had managed to save enough money to study in New York for a year. I think she must have lived in a state of ecstasy that whole year—she needed to, for I am sure she went hungry half the time. She would tell me about the classes, about copying the head of Bastien-Lepage's *Joan of Arc,* about her friend Annie Goldthwaite, who became famous, about all the young doings of the League. She loved to remember it and longed to go back. But hardly had she returned home to her school work than she developed lead poisoning. Her doctor forbade her to paint again. Against orders she was trying it when I met her. While sketching me, she would say with shy pride: "At the League they said I had a real sense of color. Someone once mistook one of my oils for a Henner," and she laughed softly at the delightful recollection. But in a year or two the blood-poison returned and she had to give up painting again, this time forever. It was her whole life and that meant she had lost her life and must find another. If this had been different and that had not happened, she might have become a great painter. Instead she became a great soul.

She was a teacher born. Mr. Bass recognized her gift and soon had her teaching anything, everything—painting, history, English, whatever classes happened to be without a teacher at the moment. She was always exhausted, generally undernourished, and always eager. The children adored her. She read me my first poetry (Milton and Shakespeare didn't count, they were just Milton and Shakespeare) and I resisted it mightily. This resistant attitude of mine lasted for years—in fact, until I read *Dover Beach* at Sewanee. Perhaps it was due to Father's having read me when I was a little fellow Tennyson's *I'm to be Queen of the May, Mother,* which I had found so unbearably pathetic I had burst into tears. Or perhaps I did actually detest poetry's inversions and circumlocutions as much as I thought I did. But poetry fascinated me, like a fearful sin, and Miss Carrie kept on reading it to me. Mother disapproved of these goings-on and observed, accurately enough, that there was no telling what kind of impractical notions Carrie was putting into my head, and my visits to her must stop. Father wondered if they did any harm anyway. But I announced I was going to see her when I wanted to. Mother closed the discussion, not weakly but impotently, by remarking that for an obedient child I was the most hard-headed she had ever encountered.

I kept on seeing Miss Carrie until I could see her no more. Many of the young people, mostly her former students, felt similarly drawn to her, and those who had moved from town were eager to visit her on their return trips. We came to her as to a clean upland spot smelling of pine. There was a childish gaiety about her, and her great wisdom was completely innocent. Apparently she made no effort to be right, she just was right. She gave you the fine feeling you were shielding her when in fact you were drawing from her your strength.

While I was at college she joined the Episcopal Church. That must have been a cruel decision for her to feel she must make, for it meant, and she knew it meant, breaking with her own people and with the faith of her fathers. The Jews at home never forgave her for it. After a few years she stopped attending church, and that too must have meant a grievous struggle. So she went her way alone and built her own lonely altar. She must have been a very Jacob for wrestling with God, but when I knew her best, after her youth, she didn't wrestle any more, she merely walked with Him and leaned on Him when she was tired. It's a good thing He was there because she was often tired and she had no one else to lean on.

Beginning with my return home from Harvard, every scrap I ever wrote I showed Miss Carrie or mailed to her, coming by her house Sundays for her criticism. Though a partial critic in my case, she was a sensitive and a fearless one. We fought over words and cadences and sometimes I was worsted. She knew far better than I when I was growing didactic, and vehemently opposed the tendency. One week I sent her three or four short pieces and when I arrived I was pleased and astonished to hear her say ardently: "At last you have written a perfect poem!" I didn't know to which one she was referring, but it was *Overtones,* the one poem of mine which critics and anthologists, almost without dissent, have liked. At the very time she was giving me so much, she was making a selection of her own poems and saving every nickel to have them published. For years she had been writing poetry and a good many of her lyrics had appeared in the more distinguished magazines. At last she named her collection and found a publisher, one of those who advertise little and charge much. Denied an outlet in painting, she had turned to poetry, and now her very own book—*At the Edge of the World,* by Caroline Stern—in a pretty yellow binding was to appear in the kindly world. She was so excited and hopeful, she often wore a cherry-red ribbon at her throat, but though it was not her color, none of us would tell her so because that ribbon made her feel reckless and mischievous. Although there was plenty of Joan of Arc and St. Theresa in her, she was fundamentally a little girl. Her book appeared, and that was all. The critics ignored it, there were no sales, after a year the publisher wrote no copies were available. It did not deserve such treatment. Though she had more fancy than imagination, more feeling than art, and though she was not endowed with the sense of the magic word, they were good poems, charming, and so like her. She was hurt inside, but she did not complain and she never grew accusatory or bitter. When she read favorable reviews of my volume, a little later, she thrilled, and when the reviews were unfriendly she was furious. All the while she continued to teach with undiminished enthusiasm hundreds of children and to give cheer or comfort to her numerous young friends in their happiness or troubles.

After her father's death she had built herself a small home with two extra rooms which she rented as an apartment. Between paying by the month for it and paying for the publication of her poems she had little enough left to fill her birdlike needs. When I think of the stark little living-room where I found so much peace and encouragement and of the scanty meals she referred to vaguely and when I remember I never gave her a present worth having or thought of helping out in any one of a hundred possible ways, I am appalled at the self-centered egotism of youth and its incapacity for real understanding or pity.

Once in a while you would find she had visited the doctor or was not feeling so well, but none of us was disturbed or really interested—people were always getting sick and Miss Carrie was naturally frail. She was alone most of the time and bought a Ouija board for company. It did astounding things for her—wrote hours on end faster than anyone except her could read, leaped into the air, went into frenzies, or moodily refused to budge. It amused us enormously. But I found after a while it wasn't so amusing to her. Her mother would speak to her, and God, and Matthew Arnold would send me long messages. She was puzzled and incredulous, but Ouija became almost alive, almost a person to her. She had no one else to live with except God, and He isn't enough by Himself. One night when Ouija had announced God was speaking and she was listening intently to the strange poetic moralizing, the wretched three-legged thing suddenly bounded into the air and spelled out violently: "Carrie, you are a damn fool. This isn't God. Good night," and could not be coaxed into further comment. The incident distressed her more than she would confess.

Once as I was leaving she told me quietly she was going to the hospital next day—an operation, she didn't know what for; she'd be out in two weeks. She was out in a few days, although they had operated. Then she began to waste away before our eyes. Soon she was taken to the hospital again, and this time for good. Although she didn't complain she asked everyone what was the matter with her. At last they took Ouija away from her. One afternoon when I came in she smiled and said: "I know the truth now. I asked the nurse and as she was leaving without answering I picked up a pencil and said: 'Ouija, tell me,' and it wrote: 'Cancer.'" The last time I saw her she had drawn a heavy white veil across her face and her body weighed no more than a bird's.

Miss Carrie was not "my favorite Jew." I have had dozens of favorites. To no people am I under deeper spiritual obligation. But I am not unaware of the qualities in them (absent in her) which have recurrently irritated or enraged other people since the Babylonian captivity. Touch a hair of a Jewish head and I am ready to fight, but I have experienced moments of exasperation when I could willingly have led a pogrom. No, Miss Carrie was not my favorite Jew. She was my favorite friend. She never failed me, but looking back I am not certain I did not fail her despicably—I suspect I was patronizing. She was so different, so unworldly, so fundamentally inno- cent, and her friendship was so unwithheld and shameless. I don't often trouble to be ashamed, but if I was patroniz- ing, Miss Carrie and her God would have to forgive me. I never could.

Miss Carrie had failed in everything—in painting, in poetry, in making money, in winning love, in dying easy. Yet she was one of the few successes I ever knew. I think I learned more from her of what the good life is and of how it may be lived than from almost anyone else.

# CHAPTER XIII

# The Bottom Rail on Top

Hardly had I fallen into my stride—not a very springy one—when I was called to Sewanee because of Dr. Henneman's death and asked by the desperate Vice-Chancellor to help my Alma Mater through the ensuing crisis. Arriving on the mountain I was presented with the English department, all five classes, everything from *Beowulf* to American literature (which meant the New England school with Lanier and James Lane Allen thrown in for lagniappe), and no assistants. I couldn't spell or punctuate or paragraph or construct a sentence that didn't wobble like a caterpillar. But I got by—partly by not pretending to possess these necessary qualifications and mostly by being gifted with a handwriting nobody could read even when exposed on a blackboard. The students liked me, and I found I had some of that peculiar gift, a talent for teaching, which consists, I suspect, largely in communicable ardor and which in any event does not derive from erudition. Nevertheless, my ignorance of English literature was a real handicap, because, after all, that was what I was supposed to be teaching. When we came to Marlowe I talked about Giorgione and the Venetians, and when we came to prose I gave up and talked about morals and Southern deficiencies. At that, some of those boys, hardly younger than myself, grew to love Browning and Shakespeare. I worked all hours to keep one hop ahead of the classes and, whatever they may not have learned, I learned a lot, particularly about human nature. I also discovered I couldn't teach and write poetry at the same time—they tapped the same reservoir. So after my six months were up, refusing an offer of the chair of English, I returned home, and Mother and Father were glad to have me back.

As a youngster I had not loved Father deeply, though I had admired him boundlessly. He was stern, though he never corrected me, and shy, and high-spirited at all the points where I was flat. During my religious period I resented his unchurchliness. I must have been a hard child to get close to. But now that I had learned a little sense, though not much, he was my chief delight. Of all my experiences our daily walks together to and from the office are those I would least want to forget, and they continued through the years, until I had to do my walking alone. He emitted sunshine and strength. We talked of everything—of the condition of the crops (it was always too wet or too dry), of the market, which, to my disapproval, he loved to play, of the Mississippi judiciary and its decline, of the parlous state of American politics, of friends and enemies, of everything. Once—this was in the early days—I asked him if he'd heard that one of our young married friends had brought on a miscarriage. He looked vague. I launched into a moral diatribe and averred that such conduct merited social ostracism. He still looked vague. It dawned on me that he knew all about it and was not aghast. I sensed we were diverging in judgment on a matter I considered important: I was confused and distressed. He knew I would learn in time and he knew that a narrow idealism at the start is bracing and formative. But he said nothing—advice was for those not strong enough to make their own decisions or to apply the decisions others make for them, advice was waste of time.

As summer approached we would always concoct delirious plans for trips to strange ports. Travel and the thought of travel fascinated him as much as they did me and he thoroughly approved my reckless determination to spend every cent I earned on going places. We barred Australia, Siberia, South Africa, and Iceland, but every other nook of the globe allured us, especially those full of the ghosts of countless generations, holy with their dust and tears.

When he would stop suddenly with his hands in his pockets and exclaim: "Consound Cam's kittycats!" I would know what had happened: Mother had filched more than her quota from his trousers pockets as he slept. It was a custom, one indulged in by her with skill and elaborate secrecy and consented to by him with considerable amusement. She could and did check unreservedly on his account, but the booty from these forays was her very own and she never reported the uses to which it was put. She would decide some poor girl needed a new evening gown, or the washerwoman needed a ton of coal and a gold tooth, or Mrs. X's roof was leaking, or Mrs. A should go to Memphis for the opera, and she supplied their needs by this violent brigandage. He never upbraided her, but only tried to resolve after some especially outrageous depredation to carry less cash on his person. He could never remember his resolution, and Mother never repented or reformed.

After a while I discovered to my amazement that Father

did not like to work. He was a tireless worker and had a large demanding practice, but he worked only because he had a family to support and wanted the pleasant things of life for himself and them. He would have preferred to play golf with that extravagant high-betting foursome of his, or to hunt lions in Africa or tigers in India or moose in Alaska, or merely to lie on the deck of a sunny steamer with a hundred detective novels, *Ivanhoe,* and *The Light of Asia.*

He was hunting birds in Arkansas when Senator Mc-Laurin of Mississippi died. It was a death that did not stir my pulse or suggest to me consequences that might have any personal bearing on me or mine. It was a turning-point in my life.

The most prominent politician in Mississippi at that time was James K. Vardaman, a kindly, vain demagogue unable to think, and given to emotions he considered noble. He was a handsome, flamboyant figure of a man, immaculately overdressed, wearing his black hair long to the shoulders, and crowned with a wide cowboy's hat. He looked like a top-notch medicine man. He had made a good governor of Mississippi and he craved public office because the spot-light was his passion and because, eternally in need of money, he abhorred work. At the slightest opportunity he would quote Bobby Burns fervently and with appreciation, but his oratory was bastard emotionalism and raven-tressed rant. For political platform he advertised his love of the common people and advocated the repeal of the Fifteenth and the modification of the Fourteenth Amendments to the Federal Constitution. He did love the common man after a fashion, as well he might, but although he hated the "nigger," as he called the Negro, he had never studied the effects of the abolition of the Fifteenth Amendment and he had never considered by what verbiage the Fourteenth Amendment could be modified. He stood for the poor white against the "nigger"—those were his qualifications as a statesman. He was very popular in Mississippi; they called him the Great White Chief.

Father rather liked Vardaman—he was such a splendid ham actor, his inability to reason was so contagious, it was so impossible to determine where his idealism ended and his demagoguery began. Besides he had charm and a gift for the vivid reckless phrase. A likable man, as a pool-room wit is likable, but surely not one to set in the councils of the nation. Father considered his Negro-baiting mischievous and his proposed changes in the Constitution impractical and undesirable. He was not a moral idiot of genius like Huey Long; he was merely an exhibitionist playing with fire. So Vardaman announced his candidacy for the United States Senate while Father was hunting quail in Arkansas.

Father wanted to be a force for good government, but he did not want to hold office. He did not want to be senator from Mississippi, but he wanted to keep Vardaman from being. Vardaman stood for all he considered vulgar and dangerous. Most people we knew felt the same way about him. The vacancy created by Senator McLaurin's death was to be filled, not by popular vote, but by the Mississippi legislature. Everyone conceded that on the first ballot of that body Vardaman would receive a plurality, but it was hoped that if several anti-Vardaman candidates ran, between them they could muster a majority and hold it until they could agree on the strongest of their number as the anti-Vardaman candidate for the final ballot. With this strategy in mind and confident that no Delta man and no gentleman could possibly be elected, Father consented to be one of five prominent citizens to enter the race against Vardaman. The strategy decided on succeeded, but only after an increasingly bitter battle in the legislature which lasted for fifty-seven interminable nerve-racking days. When the last ballot was cast, only five votes prevented Vardaman from representing Mississippi in the Senate. The anti-Vardaman forces won and the state was torn to shreds.

I don't suppose a state legislature is ever an impressive body of men. Mississippi's at that session was not: its members were not venal, but most of them were timid and third-rate. I moved to Jackson, the state capital, for the eight weeks of the fight in order to be with Father and to help as best I could, and Father's two brothers, Uncle Walker from Birmingham and Uncle Willie from Memphis, both brilliant and both popular, joined us. Father couldn't get chummy with people and, though his friends worshipped him and would have died for him, they did not call him LeRoy. As the struggle in the legislature progressed he became beyond question the dominant figure of the anti-Vardaman forces, although on the first ballot he had received only thirteen votes. His trouble was that he was a natural leader of men. Unwillingly the other four candidates conceded his pre-eminence and fitness and on the fifty-seventh ballot withdrew in his favor. So, at the last, it was Father against Vardaman. On the night of Washington's birthday 1910, a night of frenzied excitement, by a vote of eighty-seven to eighty-two, Father was elected United States Senator from Mississippi.

Nothing is so sad as defeat, except victory. There was the wildest enthusiasm among our people. Arriving home by train the next night, we were greeted by crying crowds, bands, and a torchlight procession. They had even found a little cannon for the levee, about like the one Fabre and his grandchildren used to test the hearing of cicadas. Our townsfolk were as deaf with joy as his cicadas. But Father was worn out and oppressed by the responsibilities ahead. Mother and I, though happy in a way, were dazed. And I was haunted by that desperate figure of Vardaman rushing up and down the rostrum after the last ballot screaming: "Black as the night that covers me."

The years Father served in the Senate were not dramatic or crucial years in the history of our country, but they were the end of a period in which great men represented our people. Father admired Mr. Root and Joe Bailey, disliked Lodge, loved John Sharp Williams, and was drawn to that Western group, so able and so feared by the Republicans, Dolliver, LaFollette, Borah, Cummings, and Norris. He fought the Civil War pensions racket, opposed our breach of faith with Great Britain in the Panama tolls case, helped with levee legislation, concerning which he knew more than any other man in Congress, and contributed materially to an excellent survey of our immigration laws. President Taft trusted and liked him in spite of Father's friendship with the ex-President; and Secretary of War Dickinson was his old and good friend. Had he been returned to the Senate he would have served our people helpfully and with distinction during the great period of the war.

But he was not returned by the people of Mississippi. Hardly had he taken his seat in Washington when he became engrossed in his race before the people for re-election, probably the most vicious and sordid campaign experienced by Mississippi since reconstruction days. While the overt issue in Father's race with Vardaman before the legislature had been Vardaman's stand on the Negro question, the undeclared issue had been the unanswerable charge against Father that he was a prosperous plantation-owner, a corporation lawyer, and unmistakably a gentleman. In his race before the people the Negro issue was to disappear with the emergence from under cover of the increasingly popular social issue and with the unexpected appearance of a new issue.

About two months after Father's election one of Vardaman's supporters in the legislature appeared before a grand jury and announced that one of Father's supporters had bribed him to vote for Father, that he had accepted the bribe money in bills, that he had taken them home and kept them in his safe, that he was now returning them intact to the grand jury. He added that he had broken his promise to vote for Father and instead had voted for Vardaman. We were stunned. Although we knew the shady reputation of the accuser we were not sure his story was false because the alleged bribe-giver was no intimate of ours but only an enemy of Vardaman. We were sick to the soul. But it occurred to the district attorney to examine the bills left with the grand jury. It was found to our own astonishment and relief that many of them had been issued after the date on which the self-accused bribe-taker said he had received them; indeed, after the date of the election. His story was a palpable and proved lie. But it was a lie with a thousand lives. The liar became the hero of the hour and his lie Vardaman's campaign ammunition. Vardaman's stand on the Negro question, Father's stand on current legislation in the Senate, simply held no interest for the sovereign voters of Mississippi. They were eager to learn if Father was a member of any church, if he hunted on Sunday, if his house was painted, if he had Negro servants, if Mother was a Catholic. They printed such questions and presented them to him when he spoke. He answered them truthfully, and unsatisfactorily. All over the state roved the self-accused bribe-taker vomiting his own infamy and cheered to the echo. The Hearst papers took up the hue and cry; George Creel published a foul attack in the *Cosmopolitan;* the professional lovers of carrion snickered and pointed. A man of honor was hounded by men without honor—not unusual perhaps, but the man was my Father.

The man responsible for tearing Father's reputation to tatters and saddening three lives was a pert little monster, glib and shameless, with that sort of cunning common to criminals which passes for intelligence. The people loved him. They loved him not because they were deceived in him, but because they understood him thoroughly; they said of him proudly, "He's a slick little bastard." He was one of them and he had risen from obscurity to the fame of glittering infamy—it was as if they themselves had crashed the headlines. Vardaman's glamour waned and this man rode to power.

Such was the noisome situation in which Father found himself mired and out of which he must fight his way with only integrity, courage, and intelligence for his weapons. A different assortment was needed—those count only in a world of honor. But the world in which he used them was not a world of honor; it was a new-born, golden age of demagoguery, the age of rabble-rousers and fire-eaters, of Jeff Davis and Tillman and Bleese and Heflin, of proletarian representatives of the proletariat. Vardaman was not the first nor Huey Long the last. I accompanied Father and his dear friend and campaign manager, Will Crump, from one end of the state to the other, at the first to try my hand at being agreeable to the voters and at the last to guarantee that Father received sherry and raw eggs and a little rest every day, for he was fagged and weak and, though not a big man, he had lost thirty pounds.

I recall a speaking at Black Hawk in a clearing of the woods with a few hundred persons present in spite of the drizzle. I had learned that the crowd planned to rotten-egg Father. I had found the hampers of eggs and stood by them with a pistol in my pocket which I intended to use. I looked over the ill-dressed, surly audience, unintelligent and slinking, and heard him appeal to them for fair treatment of the Negro and explain to them the tariff and the Panama tolls situation. I studied them as they milled about. They were the sort of people that lynch Negroes, that mistake hoodlumism for wit, and cunning for intelligence, that attend revivals and fight and fornicate in the bushes afterwards. They were undiluted Anglo-Saxons. They were the sovereign voter. It was so horrible it seemed unreal. But they didn't throw any eggs. They didn't refrain from fear of me, but Father was not the sort of person you threw eggs at—his eyes held a fearful warning. I have seen him cow better men than that gang of poor degenerates.

The worst day of all, as I remember it, was at Lauderdale Springs. A few of us had gone over from home to hear the speech, armed and sick at heart. Uncle Walker came to my room after midnight to say that one of our group would have to kill the bribe-taker in the morning as he was to attend our meeting and was scheduled to denounce Father. At six we met in the cold dreary dining-room for breakfast, Uncle Walker, his seventeen-year-old son, LeRoy, and I sitting at a table to ourselves. I had target-practiced most of the night in front of the mirror, so as not to forget to release the safety. A few yards from us at a table alone sat our intended victim.

Uncle Walker had a voice like Polyphemus', but he couldn't hit a balloon. Suddenly he leaned across the table, pointed to the man, and boomed out the epithet which makes an American fight if he's a man. The object of his outburst did not fall for the ruse, he made no motion to his hip or elsewhere, he kept on eating oatmeal.

At last we arrived at Lauderdale Springs, where a thousand or more people were seething about in front of a vacant hotel from the porch of which Father was to speak. Father's few local supporters drew him aside and told him the situation was grave. They insisted that on no account should he mention Vardaman or his henchmen in his speech, but that he must confine his remarks to non-controversial topics like the tariff. Otherwise there would be bloodshed. With that admonition they took the morning train back to Meridian. Father and Uncle Walker sat together an hour, painfully weighing this advice. They concluded it was too late in life to start being intimidated and this was not the occasion to talk tariff.

When Father rose to speak he was greeted with a roar of boos, catcalls, hisses, and cries of "Vardaman! Vardaman!" It was impossible to hear a word he might say. The din was insane and intolerable, and it showed no sign of diminishing. Obviously the crowd was determined to make it impossible for him to speak at all. The self-accused bribe-taker sat smiling on the porch at his immediate left. Father faced that obscene pandemonium, paused for the courtesy of silence, and, when he did not receive it, his eyes narrowed. Then burning-cold insults poured from his lips, he jeered them as cowards afraid to listen, and dared them to keep on. He cowed them by sheer will-power and lashed them into silence by leaping invective. At last the whole crowd was shamed into silence except one heavy man who sat in the middle toward the front and kept on howling insanely: "Vardaman! Vardaman!" I was glad to observe Billy Hardie immediately behind him with his pistol across his lap. Suddenly out of the crowd leapt a wiry stranger who jumped to the porch and, holding to a post, leaned out over the audience. He pointed into the face of the big man screaming "Vardaman" and called: "I know who you are and you know who I am. Shut up—or I'll come down after you." His eyes blazed like gray fire. The man shut up. He was wise. We found afterwards our unknown ally was Hunter Sharp, the best pistol-shot in Mississippi, noted for his daring and the number of his victims. Quiet restored, Father launched into the most scathing denunciation I have ever heard from human lips. It was the only speech of the kind he made during the campaign. He exposed Vardaman in all his weakness and the methods used by his henchmen with his consent. At the climax he turned to the man sitting next to him and, white with avenging anger, blasted him with his own infamy. The bear-baiting cowardly crowd, wild with excitement, cheered and cheered and cheered.

A few weeks before election day, coming back together from a hard week, Father asked me: "What do you think of it?" and I had to answer: "Not a chance." He smiled a little and said: "Right." The night the polls were closed and all Mississippi was counting ballots, Father, Mother, and I felt so relieved to be at last from under the long humiliating strain that we went to bed early and slept soundly. Father was not only defeated, but overwhelmingly. Thus at twenty-seven I became inured to defeat: I have never since expected victory.

Father did not like to lose at poker or golf or politics; in fact, he couldn't be called a good loser, if by that is meant one who loses without visible irascibility. But in this, the great defeat of his life, he was tranquil and found smiles and little spurts of merriment for his broken-hearted supporters. The only effect on him I could detect was an inner sadness, beyond reach, the kind of look I suppose Lazarus never outgrew after he had once died. A letter from him written about this time to one of his supporters is typical:

Greenville, Miss.,
November 19th, 1912.

Mr. W. W. Cain,
West, Miss.
My dear Mr. Cain:

Your letter is like "the voice of one crying in the wilderness." I have always thought that it is worth while to have made the fight and lost for the sake of the friends I have made, and your letter convinces me of the correctness of that view. I do not expect to shirk any duty that comes my way, but I am not seeking or desiring any political preferment. There is no office of honor that does not carry with it corresponding duties, responsibilities and work. I have no hunger for the honors and less for the work.

If I can keep this small corner of the United States in which I reside, comparatively clean and decent in politics and fit for a man to live in, and in such condition that he may not be ashamed to pass it on to his children, I will have accomplished all that I hope to do.

A good deal has been written about "shooting at the stars." I have never thought much of that kind of marksmanship. It may be characterized by imagination, it is lacking in common sense. I rather think it is best to draw a bead on something that you have a chance to hit. To keep any part of Mississippi clean and decent in these days, is a job that no man may deem too small. I certain-

ly appreciate your kind expressions. With best wishes,
I am,

Cordially yours,

*LeRoy Percy*

An old man wet with tobacco juice and furtive-eyed
summed up the result: "Wal, the bottom rail's on top and
it's gwiner stay thar." He wasn't much as a human
being, but as a diagnostician and prophet he was first-
rate. It was my first sight of the rise of the masses, but
not my last. Now we have Russia and Germany, we have
the insolence of organized labor and the insolence of
capital, examples both of the insolence of the parvenu;
we have the rise of the masses from Mississippi east, and
back again west to Mississippi. The herd is on the march,
and when it stampedes, there's blood galore and beauty
is china under its hoofs. As for Mississippi, I don't mean
to imply she has reached the nadir toward which she is
heading. We still have Will Whittington in the lower and
Pat Harrison in the upper house of Congress and that's
creditable for any state. When Father was defeated good
men all over the South were heart-broken, but today Mississippi is like the rest of the South, and the South is like
the rest of the nation: the election of demagogues horri-
fies nobody. The intelligent are cynically amused, the
hoi-polloi are so accustomed to victory they no longer
swagger. The voters choose their representatives in public life, not for their wisdom or courage, but for the
promises they make. Vardaman was a great forerunner
of a breed of politicians not more able but less colorful
than himself.

Perhaps it is a strengthening experience to see evil triumphant, valor and goodness in the dust. But whatever

the value of the experience, it is one that comes sooner or later to anyone who dares face facts. Mine came sooner because of Father's defeat. Since then I haven't expected that what should be would be and I haven't believed that virtue guaranteed any reward except itself. The good die when they should live, the evil live when they should die; heroes perish and cowards escape; noble efforts do not succeed because they are noble, and wickedness is not consumed in its own nature. Looking at truth is not at first a heartening experience—it becomes so, if at all, only with time, with infinite patience, and with the luck of a little personal happiness. When I first saw defeat as the result of a man's best efforts, I didn't like the sight, and it struck me that someone had bungled and perhaps it wasn't man.

After the election not only Father but Mother needed desperately some interlude of peace. I hardly know what Father would have done in Washington without Mother. She laughed at his shyness, made him meet people and go to parties. More important, he thought aloud to her every problem he pondered, and her unfailing sanity clarified his thinking and freshened his spirits. During the long anguish of the campaign, she set her heart not on winning but on sustaining him and on keeping home pleasant and full of life. So we all needed a trip and chose the one Father and I had most wanted to take for years. We sailed for Greece.

Our approach was roundabout and leisurely. From Italy we dawdled down the beautiful Dalmatian coast, along Montenegro and Albania (ravaged that summer by cholera), turned the Leucadian promontory, passed Ithaca, and finally, with considerable peace of soul, pulled into the harbor of Patras and touched the soil, the hot, sandy, unkempt, sacred soil of Greece. We reached Athens after dark. In bed that night I figured I couldn't possibly wait until after breakfast to see the Acropolis, and besides it would be great fun to put one over on Father and tell him all about Athena's Hill over coffee and rolls. At six o'clock, with Baedeker under my arm, I rushed, as fast as my feet and my ignorance of the way allowed, to the Acropolis. No one was ascending the broad flight of steps to the Propylæa, but as I stood in its shade trying to catch my breath after the climb, I heard a great hubbub within the enclosure. I stepped in, facing the Parthenon. Voluble workmen in a group at the foot of a ladder were gesticulating and protesting. Father had beaten me to it. He was sitting on the pediment of the Parthenon where the Parcæ had sat and looking across Mars Hill to the blue sea and the mountains beyond. The curative morning was flooding over him, and he laughed when he saw me.

# CHAPTER XIV

# 1914-1916

Ishmael lived one hundred and thirty-seven years. During that time he must have laughed and joked and loved; he must have looked at the sky and sat beneath the cool palm trees; he must have been glad—but he was a wanderer and a stranger all his days.

The North destroyed my South; Germany destroyed my world. In the dog-days of 1914 the mad dog of the world broke loose. After 1918 the world forgot that hydrophobia is curable only by death and it is paying for the oversight now. Again the mad dog is loose. His victims clutter the roadside, but still my own people, with the mentality of priests and tradesmen, prefer to pass by on the other side. In 1914 I didn't like the other side and I didn't want to pass by. All of me that said this is right and that is wrong said France and England must not be destroyed; Germany must not dominate: my mind did not judge, my being affirmed. Nevertheless I did pass on the other side. I was a tourist in a tourist's world, with no premonitions. An entrancing world it was, where prices were low and passports unheard of, where scenes fit for postcards were round every corner and treasures of art at every turn.

I was spending the midsummer of 1914 in Sicily and because of the heat I had the whole island to myself. As I had always been tormented by acrophobia I decided it would show a deplorable lack of nerve if I failed to climb Mount Ætna for the sunrise (double-starred by Baedeker). It was a long, tiresome ascent, beginning in a carriage, continuing by donkey, and ending afoot with a scramble through the ashes of the cone. By dark the donkey-boys (aged sixty) had become howling drunk and were bawling out bawdry while they hung for support to the tails of the donkeys. There was bright moonlight and a bitter wind. My guide, who stank unforgettably of civet and garlic, was chattering with cold and I had shrunk to half my size. At the observatory, where we were to have three hours' sleep before the ascent to the crater, if we could ignore fleas and bed-bugs, I asked him disagreeably, as I was trying to make myself comfortable in the hay in the corner, if Ætna donkey-boys always got drunk. He said no, but they were scared this time because ours was the first ascent anybody had made since the last eruption. He added that the last person he had guided to the top was an Austrian Grand Duke. I was not interested in Austrian grand dukes and wished he would shut up. He continued that in yesterday's paper he noticed the Grand Duke had just been assassinated at Sarajevo; one duke more or less—what time did we start up the crater for the sunrise? After the sunrise would be Taormina and Assisi and Paris. What a fascinating world!

Even in Paris I felt not the least tremor of doom. I paid my respects to Notre-Dame, looked in on the Salon Carré for old times' sake, paused in the gold gloom of Saint-Germain-des-Prés before the Mater Afflictorum with her

cluster of candles and her small coterie of petitioners.
That night I joined Frank Hoyt Gailor for sole cardinal,
a bottle of Graves, and raspberries with sour cream. It
was so pleasant a world we decided to watch it drift by
from one of its most agreeable spots—a chair behind a
table on the Grands Boulevards. We taxied to our favorite corner. The chairs were gone! There were no chairs
or tables on any Paris sidewalk! We knew the world had
come to an end. Within three days we had been involved
in street-rioting, Mme Caillaux had been acquitted of murder, Jaurès had been assassinated, and war was declared.
My world fell to pieces before I felt it tremble. I was to
be a bit of an Ishmael the rest of my days, but I didn't
know it then.

Safely back home, I wondered why I had left France.
I was miserable. Men were fighting for what I believed
in and I was not fighting with them; men were suffering
horribly for my ideals and I was safe at home applauding
and sympathizing. I tried the usual opiate—travel—and
my private opiate—writing poetry. But I was shot through
with discontent and probably with self-disappointment. I
could have enlisted in Canada—why didn't I? There were
excuses enough, I suppose, and I adopted them as reasons. Physically I was not made for a soldier, nor spiritually, for that matter. I was an only son; men around me
were not enlisting; et cetera, et cetera aplenty. But from
this vantage point of age and safety I think, granting
everything, that for me, feeling as I did, not to have enlisted was inconsistent and shabby.

My cousin, Janet Dana, who had led as sheltered a life
in New York as I had in Greenville and who alone of all
my intimates felt as passionately about the war as I, entered training as a nurse and in due course reached a
hospital in France. This was the last straw. Yet I tem-

porized and equivocated. By accident I came across an advertisement in the *Outlook* asking for volunteers to join the Commission for Relief in Belgium under Mr. Herbert Hoover. I boarded a train for New York, applied to join the Commission for service in Belgium, and was accepted. My qualifications were that I spoke French quickly and inaccurately and that during the Mississippi floods of 1912 and 1913 I had headed the relief work in my section of the Delta. I hardly surmised what the work of the Commission covered or what service I could be to it. Americans under Hoover were feeding the starving Belgians— this much I was certain of and it seemed enough. Of course I hoped it would be a trifle heroic.

I remember nothing whatever of the partings at home or of how I got from Greenville to London. But I remember well the opal mornings of London and the cold velvet-black nights with the single corner lights blue and hooded, and I remember what seemed to me the youth of all the world in uniform, walking the streets, crowding the tea-rooms and pubs, on leave from France, from Gallipoli, from Palestine, gay and aureoled with daring. I was more eager than ever to get going, to be working at something related to the war, even though it were safe and minor. After waiting three weeks for a permit and a boat to cross the North Sea, at that time a perilous crossing, I finally received my orders, caught the deserted mail-boat at Harwich, a boat from *Outward Bound,* and by morning was safely ashore at Rotterdam. Then a week's dreary delay in slush and rain while spies ransacked my hotel room, and at last I was hustled across the border into the forlorn and snowy flatness of Belgium.

During the first days of the war Mr. Hoover, a rich mining engineer unknown to the American public, had had the imagination and energy to gather together what

young Americans were within reach and to form them
into a committee to feed the civilian population of Belgium and of the enemy-occupied area of northern France.
At no time were there with him within the German lines
more than forty-two Americans. They were novices, volunteers, and they did a surpassingly fine and ingenious
job, by ear. Mr. Hoover collected money where he could
find it, procured the necessary permissions and promises
of co-operation from the Germans, and was himself the
buying agent for wheat, corn, and meat the world over,
from the Argentine and Australia to Canada. Germans,
Belgians, French, English, and Americans trusted him,
not only for his integrity but for his organizing genius and
for his passionate non-partisanship. When his work was
finally established in Belgium, he left Brussels for London
and single-handed, against bitter opposition, persuaded
Lloyd George and Lord Eustis Percy to finance his operations and to continue them under his direction for the
duration of the war.

When I arrived in Brussels, the romantic pioneer period
of the Commission's work had ended and Mr. Hoover's
young Americans occupied positions of prestige and authority, while an enormous Belgian committee administered the details and performed the wearisome chores.
The Belgians could have done the work equally well without us, but we were needed to maintain civilian morale,
to act as liaison with the Germans, and to guarantee that
the food distributed went into Allied and not into German mouths. There was nothing dangerous or onerous or
exciting about our tasks, though in the sectors where we
were required to live with and be directed by German
officers, whom we called our "nurses," they sometimes
tested our tact and temper. The simple truth is we were

the spoiled darlings of Belgian society, entertained, furnished with servants, and provided with handsome residences richly furnished in the worst Victorian. For us, if it was war, it was war de luxe. It should have been a delightful experience—everyone, except an occasional German officer, was more than kind, my fellow Americans were fine intelligent chaps (particularly that red-headed, husky-laughtered running-mate of mine, Pink Simpson), and there was no lack of excellent food, excellent wine, and red-cheeked healthy Belgian girls who liked to laugh and to show you their albums of family photographs after dinner. It should have been great fun—but as far as I was concerned it wasn't.

No, in spite of the pleasant luxury, I didn't enjoy my life as member of the Commission. There was plenty of surface gaiety, but there were too many glimpses beneath. Across the golf-links and the moated parks of our friends' estates where we strolled week-ends, during lulls in the winter's bluster, drifted, like rumblings of far-off summer thunder, the sound of artillery fire from the front, and the ease and the laughter would seem inane, and I would wonder how many were mangled by that burst.

I don't suppose the dull ache which made the pedal-point of my waking hours was solely my unfulfilled desire to be a soldier in the trenches. Probably I had never been at peace. Probably I had always wanted to escape a life that had seemed to me filled with nothing and less noble than a human life need be. Probably, although I had no liking for hardships, a soldier's hardships and his likely end seemed to me a better poem than I could ever hope to write. And yet it is true that in a quiet, drugged fashion I was tormented by the thought that others were suffering for what was right and I was not suffering.

Furthermore, in Belgium we could never quite forget we were prisoners, well treated, indeed pampered trusties, yet prisoners.

I remember one winter twilight walking down a broad Brussels boulevard. The lights were just on, ice glinted from the trees, snow was deep and dry on the ground, pedestrians were hurrying home for supper through the crunchy silence. Plodding along, I became conscious of someone whistling a tune and suddenly the name of the tune came back to me—the *Marseillaise!* That martial air was forbidden by the Germans; to sing, play, or whistle it meant imprisonment. I looked around for the dare-devil whistler and saw instead the other passers-by becoming aware of what was happening. Everyone stopped or looked over his shoulder or into the eyes of those near him; everyone straightened up, quickened his step, and smiled. One after another we located the brash offender and were filled with warmth and excitement. It was a hulking young driver of a van pulled by two magnificent Percherons. Slouched over the reins, devil-may-care, in his workman's corduroys and broad red sash, without lifting his eyes or looking to right or left, he whistled piercingly and accurately from end to end the forbidden thrilling music.

But there was no such recompense when I watched the Germans herd together the unemployed civilians (called "chômeurs" at the time) and send them as slaves into Germany to work in the munition factories. German "atrocities" in Belgium were widely advertised and for the most part non-existent, but the wholesale enslavement of the able-bodied males of a helpless little country received slight publicity and only passing condemnation. Yet it was an example of wicked stupidity that Germans alone could have been capable of. The Belgians—of whom I was not an unqualified admirer—reacted to the indignity with a heroism beyond all praise. Most of them refused doggedly to work in the munition plants, and the Germans with their usual ruthless logic attempted to force them to do so by starvation. The Belgians were starved, actually and literally, but they were not starved into making munitions. When they had become physical wrecks, the Germans, finding them useless, returned them to Belgium. I saw trainloads of them arriving in the Antwerp station. They were creatures imagined by El Greco—skeletons, with blue flesh clinging to their bones, too weak to stand alone, too ill to be hungry any longer. This was only a miniature venture into slavery, a preliminary to the epic conquest and enslavement of whole peoples in 1940, but it seemed hideous and unprecedented to us in 1917.

When, therefore, in the early spring news reached us that our country was about to enter the war and had broken off relations with Germany, there was only shouting in my heart. Indeed, all of us walked on air and found it difficult to hide from our Belgian friends, terrified at the prospect of our withdrawal, our pride and enthusiasm. I at once applied for permission to return home. The Commission did not relish my request and pointed out the indispensable humane service we were rendering. I listened but did not hear. I insisted on the safe conduct out which had been promised me when I came in. Six other kindred spirits joined in my revolt: we were intractable and eloquent rebels. So the anxious Commission requested of the Germans a safe conduct for us through Germany into Switzerland. It was intimated that we would be required to take an immunity bath of several months in some German concentration camp so that any knowledge we might have of troop movements would by the time of our release be too stale to help the Allies. But we were undismayed. The whole Commission became interested in us as a test case. Finally the permits were granted and all arrangements completed for us to board a train to the Swiss border under the protection of a German officer, our last "nurse." With mingled emotions of sorrow and gladness we spent the last day telling our pitiful Belgian friends good-by; then the seven of us met for our last Belgian dinner at the Palace Hotel, across the street from the railroad station.

We took a table in the brilliant crowded dining-room, feeling, after our feverish day, flat and full of foreboding. We were leaving these wretched civilians to the mercy of the German army; they were afraid and we were afraid for them. We realized that each of us had reached his individual crossroads where the sign-posts showing the mileage and the destination had been blown down; and we were troubled by the possibility, now to be tested, of internment in Germany. We took a cocktail, ordered our meal and a bottle of wine. We were very sad. As it was not customary for us Americans to frequent the Palace, it being the favorite resort of German officers, our presence was noticed and commented on by the other diners, and we soon realized we were creating something of a sensation. A stray attaché joined us and asked us to drink with him one last solemn toast in champagne. We accepted. A Portuguese gentleman rushed over and greeted us as long-lost allies; another bottle was opened. Two young German officers who had been "nurses" of ours in northern France drew their seats up to our table and began fraternal lamentations. "Alas," said the little one we all liked though he was a confirmed embusqué, "to think that in a few months we shall be at the front line together, you on one side, we on the other, trying to kill each other!

Waiter, a bottle of champagne." We all wept and our spirits rose. Others joined us, vague individuals. It became a celebration. Everybody felt better and better. We all loved one another and said so and pledged our devotion in glass after glass of magnificent champagne.

At last someone thought to look squarely and honestly into the face of a watch and discovered we had ten minutes in which to collect ourselves, pay the check, get across the street to the station and into the train. There was a stampede. In the mêlée Arthur Maurice lost his hat and overcoat. But we made it across the icy street more or less upright, and debouched into the waiting-room of the station in superb spirits, giddy with love and optimism, teeming with becks and calls and wreathèd smiles. It was something of a set-back therefore to find the whole staff of the C.R.B. and half the Brussels population jamming the waiting-room, in tears, anxiously and solemnly waiting to bid us adieu. They had brought hampers of food, cases of wine, and bouquets of flowers, and only our tardiness had kept the weeping burgomaster from delivering an oraison funèbre of incomparable poignancy. Our German nurse had been frantically looking for us for an hour. He collected our remnants, and as the train pulled out we were boosted into it through the windows amid the sobs and cheers of our sorrowing friends. We landed in different compartments and it took hours to collect us. Our poor nurse was a nervous wreck. United at last, we settled down to headaches.

The next few days would have been dismal enough even had we been feeling first-rate. Rain, rain, rain—heavy, unceasing, cold—in Cologne, up the Rhine, into Switzerland. The landscape was a blur, the faces along the way gray and mirthless. Of course there were no sleeping-accommodations on our train and we dozed as we could, our nurse being unfailingly thoughtful and courteous. About the second night, while the others were sleeping, we stopped at some city, soaked and dimly lighted. It was about two in the morning, a miserable hour at best. I heard German voices outside our coach and the phrase by which they called us: "die amerikanische Hilfskommission." My heart sank, for I felt certain we were at last to be hauled from the train and headed for a concentration camp. I wakened our nurse. Outside, in the torrent, stood an old gentleman in a superb uniform of scarlet and gold with a few attendants. He was the burgomaster of the city and said he had come to the train to meet us in order to present the respects of himself and his city to the gallant and ardent young Americans who under untold difficulties had fed the population of unfortunate Belgium. The gallant and ardent were rumpled, unshaven, and half-asleep, but touched to the quick, and they truly regretted their inability to respond in words equally courteous and kindly. I should like to know the name of that old gentleman's city—I am sure it was not Prussian.

I cannot describe the feeling of breathing the free Swiss air, of touching the soil of a republic, without seeming exaggerated and sentimental. For months we had not dared speak of subjects nearest our hearts, we knew we were being watched and ears were everywhere. We were not anxious to say things, but we were choked by the things we were forbidden to say. Americans at home cannot possibly know what that feeling is, and so they cannot possibly appreciate the freedom so abundantly theirs. The right to call the President of the United States a dog-faced son of a sea-cook or something fancier, though you believe him the Messiah, is a right worth dying for. Liberty unthreatened is always liberty about to be lost. In

Switzerland we avidly read the newspapers so long denied us and talked at large and wondered about our own
country, what it would do, for none of us doubted what
it should do. At last our band of seven, papers in order,
permits granted, boarded the night train for France—for
Paris! Our elation was almost unbearable.

About five in the morning we piled out at a way station
to hunt for hot chocolate. As we were drinking, news-
boys came rushing up, crying at the top of their lungs:
"la guerre," "les Etats-Unis," "la victoire," "le Président
Veelson." Hurriedly we bought the morning paper.
America had declared war on Germany! We could hardly
see to read the President's incredibly moving and just
words. We were spectators no longer, we were part of
the tragedy.

Paris was brilliant with sunshine, our flag, so poignantly
beautiful in foreign lands, was flying from every window,
bunting and streamers festooned the streets, bands were
playing. It was the glory of war and we were glorious,
then if never again. We couldn't take time to wash or
shave or stay indoors, and all Paris knew we were Americans. We trailed from bar to bar, the toast of strangers,
passers-by, Frenchmen, Englishmen, soldiers, civilians. It
was all vague and beautiful, it was fun turned ecstasy,
drunkenness after Bacchus' own heart.

When we finally made it back to our hotel in the afternoon, a magnificent gentleman in a Prince Albert with the
red button of the Legion of Honor on his lapel was awaiting us. We were bidden to attend as guests of the French
Senate the speech of Premier Ribot welcoming our
country into the war. We were dashed by the grandeur
of the situation and by the unworthiness of our general
appearance and condition. But stranger things had happened (though not to us), so we climbed into the sleek

waiting automobiles and were borne in state to the Palais du Sénat. We looked like hobos, and our liquor was wearing off. We sat in our box and surveyed the French Senate with as much aplomb as we could muster. My recollection of Monsieur Ribot's address is singularly dim, but at its close a startling incident occurred. The senators from occupied northern France, whose guests we really were, in their overflowing enthusiasm for us, for America, for the Allies, for everything, turned to our box from their places on the floor of the Chamber and burst into cheers of "Vive l'Amérique!" "Vivent les Alliés!" finally producing a huge American flag and waving it violently at us. The rest of the senators, assuming of course that if we were not President Wilson in person, we were at least the American Ambassador and his suite, rose and joined in the uproar. We limply got to our feet and acknowledged the overwhelming though mistaken ovation. Across from us, neglected and unobserved, stood at the front of his box the real American Ambassador, hunting an opportunity to bow. When those Frenchmen discovered their mistake—O mon Dieu! it was moving in the extreme. And we teetered out, wrecked with laughter, and heading for a hot bath via the American bar.

# CHAPTER XV

# The Peewee Squad

Although I made the trip from Paris to Greenville in record time, the fever of war had beaten me home. The Delta was in the first throes of heroics. Women were knitting and beginning to take one lump of sugar instead of two, men within the draft age were discussing which branch of the service they had best enter, men above the draft age were heading innumerable patriotic committees and making speeches. People found themselves all of a sudden with an objective in common, with a big aim they could share, and they liked it immensely. You could sense the pleasurable stir of nobility and the bustle of idealism. Life that had seemed a habit and not a particularly good one had become overnight purposeful adventure, brisk with fine things to do and finer though more tragic things to anticipate. The Delta had reached the stage of exaltation. I loved it unreservedly. But Mother and Father looked as if they had just taken communion: there was a stillness in them which covered, I suspected, a great sadness.

I wanted to join the army, the infantry, at once. But,

being a year over draft age, my only chance was to enter an officers' training camp, and the first one had already started. A second, however, would open in two months. All the young men I knew had entered or been rejected by the first camp, or were trying for the second.

The most miserable people in the home town were the boys who had been rejected. Among them were two of my best friends, Tommy Shields and Widdie Griffin. Tommy's disqualification arose from a badly infected sinus which he must cure before he could be accepted in any branch of the service. It took him six months of operations and torture to effect that cure, but he stuck it out and he served. More than six months, maybe more than a lifetime, would be needed for Widdie to recover from his experience at camp. He had always been one of my favorite people, he was one of Judge Griffin's grandchildren, and we had played Buffalo Bill and Indians together. He was a woods creature, all eyes and ears, with a leprechaun shyness and whimsicality. When a baby, he had been dropped by his nurse and in consequence his shoulders were stooped, but he had no scar or break, he could accomplish miracles with a gun or a fishing rod, he excelled at track and baseball, and he had won the state championship for trap-shooting. He didn't like war or politics, but he was a gentleman, he was in love with danger, and he had infinite grit. So among the first to present themselves at Fort Logan H. Root for admission to the first officers' training camp was Widdie. One of the preliminary requirements was a physical examination, during the course of which Widdie found himself, along with some hundred other youngsters, all stark naked, filing before the desk of an examining officer, a Major in the medical corps. The Major had a voice of brass. When Widdie approached him he rasped out: "What to hell are you doing here? Fall out of that line, you're nothing but a damn hunchback." When Widdie returned home he told nobody what had happened. He went about as quiet as a ghost and his eyes looked as if he had been crucified.

With a stay in Belgium to my credit during which I had doubtless seen real German soldiers and heaps of German atrocities, I was inevitably expected to be a rabble-rouser at all patriotic convocations within the radius of two hundred miles. My first month home was a crowded itinerary of speeches. With emotions all over America waiting to be fired, the smallest spark in any speaker fell on audiences all tinder. I tried my best because I believed in what I was saying and audiences were distressingly responsive, but I have reason to suspect my speeches were pretty bad. I don't remember a single word of any one of them. Yet I must qualify that statement: one speech I remember very clearly. I received an unexpected invitation to address the officers' training camp at Fort Logan H. Root. For once I accepted with eagerness an invitation to speak. The meeting was held out of doors. The whole camp—about twenty-five hundred men —was present, the student officers sitting on a fan-shaped slope of grass, and between them and me a huddle of officers. About ten feet in front of me sat the Major who had examined Widdie. I started off with the usual items— the Belgian civilians and their troubles, the German army and its occasional insolence, the deportation of the chômeurs and their tragic saga. This live young bunch was so hungry for authentic news from abroad they followed me with real interest. Then I began to discuss German and French officers I had met and the difference between them, due to the different theories of discipline in which they had been schooled. I described the German officer's attitude toward his subordinates as arrogant and harsh, his will imposed by fear, if necessary by cruelty, and I contrasted that with the attitude of the French officer, who was a father to his men, guiding and protecting and controlling them as if they were his children. Surely the German system was inimical to all we cherished. Surely with Americans the French system could be made to work. But in which school were American officers, these very student officers before me, being trained? I had learned of recent happenings which had made me wonder and doubt and fear. I began citing concrete instances, and the crowd stiffened with excitement. I have no orator's eloquence, but sometimes when I am shaken with feeling, that feeling in spite of the words communicates itself to my listeners. On this occasion I was shaken with indignation and the desire to avenge Widdie. I began slowly to tell the story of Widdie's examination by the Major sitting in front of me, omitting nothing except his name and Widdie's. By the sudden stir and whispering of the crowd I saw they were familiar with the incident and knew my target. Then I told what I thought of the Major whose manners and brutality had been typical of the worst tradition of the German army and I closed by appealing to them not to follow his example.

When I had finished, no officers lingered to congratulate me, but the students were beside themselves with excitement and, if I remember accurately, the Oklahoma contingent had me on their shoulders and were yelling like coyotes.

My speech-making came to a sudden end when I discovered thirty days before the opening of the second camp that I was twenty pounds underweight. No amount of ardor and patriotism would be accepted as a substitute for those missing pounds. I immediately took to bed. Daily I managed to get into me and keep down four tablespoonfuls of tanlac, six raw eggs, a quart of cream, and the three usual hefty meals. On the fateful day I was to be weighed I supplemented the ration with four bananas and a quart of water. I tipped the scales at 135, a net gain of 23 pounds in thirty days. I was as proud as if I had captured a machine-gun nest. When I brought the good news to Mother, she looked incredulous; then she looked like Mère when she would tap me with her thimble, and suddenly she left the room. I was at last about to begin to be a soldier.

The second officers' training camp for our part of the South was held at Leon Springs, Texas. It bulged with five thousand anxious, husky young Southerners who believed that if they failed to become officers the war would be lost and they might just as well have been born out of wedlock in New England. A vast army was being created out of nothing in no time, it would be sent overseas, and men of the training camps were to be its officers. I don't suppose any of us ever felt, before or since, so necessary to God and man. To save the world we were called on to learn in three months what it takes West Point four years to inculcate. If any of us failed, he would have usurped the place of some other chap who could have made the grade, he would have wasted his government's time and money, he would have disgraced his family, and he would have failed in the supreme test of his whole life.

Of the dozen home-town boys in camp, five of us landed in the peewee squad of Company D. Every company has two ends, a big end composed of six-footers, flashy and incompetent, who lead when the company is marching and are the joy and pets of the instructors, and a little end composed of pale runts whom the big end calls peewees and the instructors ignore. In the little end reside the brains of the company. We watched with growing contempt the ineptitude and bland blockheadedness of the big end and tightened our belts. When anyone fainted as we were lined up to pass a doctor with a hypodermic needle, he was always one drawn by Michelangelo. When after paratyphoid shots on Saturday afternoon someone collapsed in the barber shop or the hotel lobby, crashing loudly like a tree, you didn't need to look around, it was one of those superb military figures, all brawn and no guts. Who got themselves lost on night maneuvers and fell over parapets in the trenches? Big 'uns. Who, when asked an intelligent question in class, looked like God's afterthought? The question answers itself.

The five peewees from home were Allen Crittenden, Emmet Harty, Sam Weil, Ferman Millette, and myself. We just soldiered. In uniforms too big for us, we had no air martial or otherwise; indeed, to the naked eye we were undeniably insignificant. The physical work in camp was too much for us and we had the Pauline propensity for dying daily. Someone—a whole crowd of unfortunate someones—was going to be sent home ("broken" was the term used) and we knew it would be us. We banded together in an offensive and defensive alliance, and the woes of one were the woes of all. Although no one noticed us, we found some consolation in analyzing our superiority to the big stiffs. They had always been able to rely on their bodies, hence they had never been forced to develop their self-control and their will-power. When their bodies failed them, they had nothing else to fall back on and they merely passed out. The peewees of the world, never having been able to rely on their bodies, had always had to develop their strength in their souls. From the beginning most situations had been impossible for them, so they had been forced to spin from their intestines grit and endurance. Peewees stuck till they broke.

There was a dash of truth in our cheering theory. Most of the men I saw screaming and gibbering in battle or weeping at the whine of a shell or sniveling in the dark were big blonds who didn't know they had a nerve in their bodies.

Our bunch bunked side by side at one end of the barracks, we coached each other in book work, we whispered correct commands to whichever one of us had the misfortune to be corporal, we hazarded disgrace by helping one another reassemble in order the contents of our packs, when, spread on the ground at inspection, they seemed maliciously bent on disintegration—in brief, we stood by in every emergency, and there was one an hour. No soldier can soldier alone. The tasks assigned are too numerous and too intricate for one man, peewee or big stiff. A buddy is as necessary as a rifle. Of our quintet I was the greatest recipient of aid and solicitude because I was more incompetent and they more kind. Any afternoon by the time of the four-o'clock rest period I was strewn on my bunk, three-fourths corpse and too far gone to pray for resurrection or dissolution. I would hear Emmet's deep serious voice above me: "Percy, can you make it?" As I never knew the answer I never gave it. "I'll step over to the canteen and get you a cup of cold milk"— and he half dead himself!

Weeks passed and none of us had been sent home. We began to be hopeful. We even began to like our instructors. But I continued to hate Captain Harris. Having been until recently a top sergeant of the regular army he was uneducated and brusque. Every morning he inspected our barracks to see that we had made up our bunks and had policed around and under them. I labored piously at this chambermaid's job. One morning as he passed slowly between the double row of bunks with that quiet X-ray gaze of his, he stopped in front of mine and inquired: "What's that under your bed?" I unbent from attention to a humiliating angle and spied with despair one single tiny white feather which undoubtedly had just blown there from beneath Emmet's bunk. It was poised like a fairy caravel, but to me it looked as big as a battleship. "A feather," I murmured weakly. "Looks to me like dirt and I don't want to find it there tomorrow." He moved down the line. I was apoplectic and longed for the eye of a basilisk. Besides, I heard suppressed snickers from the other peewees, who were supposed to be at attention.

A week or two later as we lay on our bellies in the broiling Texas sun after a long day of hell, I again and unfortunately attracted Captain Harris's attention. We were doing an exercise invented, I take it, by the Inquisition and known as "push and pull." You thrust the rifle from your shoulder to your full arm's length, then snap it back, and thrust it out again and back again, and on and on and on. After about the tenth thrust I found there wasn't another thrust left in me: I couldn't push and I couldn't pull. I lay on my stomach—and I giggled. At any rate it was better than crying and I didn't care if Emmet did kick me. At that moment Captain Harris's voice, registering zero, poured over me: "Mr. Percy, this ain't no kindergarten." It certainly wasn't. Oh, how I hated that man!

After such a reverse it was a genuine pleasure to hear Sam Weil denounce the stupidity of the army, the inefficiency of the instructors, the general injustice of life. He was highly articulate, had no illusions, and not only looked facts in the face but smote them between the eyes. After taps, when the rest of us were bordering on collapse, he would rouse to loud and colorful conversation.

indiscreet, corrosive, and passionately just. The next day he would answer questions as accurately as a Red Seal record and he always made a hundred on quizzes. Scholastically the acknowledged superior of any other man in the company, the peewees were proud of him. But he had the defect of his qualities. The commanding officer picked the hottest day of the year to order us for the first time to put on full packs. Each weighed seventy pounds. By late afternoon, when we had marched countless miles, done push and pull, attacked dummies with bayonets, crawled and charged, we knew they weighed a hundred. We were limp, our tempers frayed, our morale gone, with it our strength, and it was time to start to camp if we could make it back without being carried. This was the moment our bumptious tactical officer selected to call us to attention and make a speech. He announced that we would double-time into camp! It would be hard, he conceded, but it would separate the men from the boys, and anyone who couldn't take it would return to his civilian habitat tomorrow morning. Choking with thirst, reeking with sweat, furious and exhausted, we started double-timing, those packs like stone mummies between our shoulders. The little end of the company happened to be in front. After a few minutes I got the blind staggers, which is as hard on the man each side of you as on yourself. We were in a column of fours and Sam was of the first four. Suddenly he fell, lay flat on his face like a sprawled-out starfish, and split the double-timing cursing column from end to end. He had fainted. But we peewees were outraged. We knew he hadn't fainted, he had only decided it was one stupidity too much.

Sam's departure was our first casualty. It was almost like a real death. Our fear of suffering his fate grew into an obsession.

Millette had been no favorite of ours at home nor we of his. But army life is peculiarly revealing because it affords no privacy. You can't eat and sleep, march and undergo hardships and humiliations with a man twenty-four hours on end, day after day, without becoming his dear friend or his bitter enemy. You have seen him all over, nakedly, the way God and Velásquez see men, and he must be little better than a jelly-fish if he inspires any less neutral emotion than loving or loathing. It wasn't long before we were finding Millette a very fine peewee. He was better company than any of us, he had wit and an exuberant sense of fun, and he could do more extraordinarily and unexpectedly kind things than you had any right to expect from a lifelong friend. Such things he did only because someone needed them done. He had given up an excellent job to enter camp and we felt confident he would pull through; in fact, we were more certain of him than of any of the rest of us.

Our prognostications would have been justified had it not been for that battalion drill. Our inexperience made of it a terrifying ordeal. The officers themselves were excited over it (I suspect some higher-ups were lurking about the outskirts). By some misfortune Crit, Emmet, and I were separated from Millette and placed in the second squad from the rear, while he drew a corporal's position in the rear squad. We assembled on an unfamiliar wide parade ground under a summer sky. The stir and commotion were hard on the nerves even of peewees. Watching so many soldiers drilling at once with new commands being bawled at us and new officers in charge got us weak-kneed, lathery, and a trifle addled. We wheeled and marched, circled and sidewised, we became giddier and giddier. At last a strange voice bellowed the command by which companies fall into a battalion front, each squad in staggered formation marching up separately and coming to a halt on the company front at the corporal's command: "Squad—halt!" Our squad had made it to its place without mishap, had halted, and was standing at attention. Behind us we could hear Millette's squad marching up to take its place on our left. It's a beautiful formation and we were doing it well. Everybody was watching with pride and enthusiasm. Millette's squad was the last to move into place. Except for it the whole battalion was standing at attention. Suddenly we heard his voice, clarion-clear, like a major's or maybe a general's, with a triumphant ring in it. But, unseated I suppose by the splendor of it all, his ringing command was "Battalion—halt!" instead of "Squad—halt!" His three bunkies standing at attention and listening breathlessly almost dropped in their tracks. But his squad, instructed to disregard mistaken commands, kept marching. The parade ground was stricken with horror. Every eye was on that squad. It kept on marching. Again Millette's gallant voice rang out: "Company—halt!" The squad kept marching; it marched now like Beatrice Lillie, *vi et armis*, clear through an unyielding detachment planted in front of it. Corporal Millette gave no further command. His vocabulary had excommunicated the word "Squad" and without it that wretched unit of his gadded on like Dukas's broomstick. The last we saw of them they were disappearing into the woods. Homeric laughter shook the parade ground. It would have been funnier if it hadn't been so sad.

So that left Crit and Emmet and me. We didn't feel like three musketeers. In spite of all our intelligence we felt so, so like peewees. It must have been about this time that the epidemic of Liberty Loan drives swept the country. Our camp planned a huge "pep" meeting designed to sell bonds to us student officers. I was invited (a polite army term for "commanded") to make a speech as representative of the students. Mother visited us a few days before the event and, on seeing me, burst into tears, explaining that I looked like a "picked chicken." But the speech went off well—better, if I may judge by the applause, than any other I have ever made. I was vastly assisted by the preceding speakers, old army officers who were not only platitudinous, but neither earnest nor sincere. Bonds were bought in quantity and consequently my fellow students were convinced I deserved and would receive a captaincy at least and—well, there was just no telling. I knew that by no stretch of the imagination was I qualified for any rank higher than that of lieutenant, but I wanted to be that with all my heart. And I suspected that because of the speech and because it had become known that I was an ex-Senator's son I would realize my ambition. But this being a mere suspicion, I relaxed my efforts no whit.

Crit and Emmet, however, had made no speech and had no ex-Senator for father. Their sole qualification was excellence, and, they being peewees, that had gone unobserved. The three of us had known each other and been friends always. Now the bonds between us were so close they hurt. The night study-hour was the period of our chief terror, because toward its close an orderly would enter the cold windy mess-hall where we hunched over our books and announce: "The following student officers will report to the Captain's room." He would then read the list of the condemned. Either those named would disappear next morning, sneaking home with the conviction they were failures, or they would be subjected to some public test that always broke them. Only a certain number of us could be given commissions and therefore hundreds of us would have to be broken. The officers increasingly looked for signs of weakness or ineptitude. Theirs had to be a superficial hit-or-miss judgment, and peewees were their natural prey.

One morning Emmet was called out to lead a platoon in setting-up exercises. He did it hesitantly and without style. Crit and I thought he was gone. But he was Irish and red-headed and mean-looking. You could tell at a glance that his was the face that launched a thousand revolutions, not to mention uprisings, brawls and free-for-alls. I think the officers lost their nerve. They probably figured that if they ordered him home he would then and there draw a shillelagh and lay the camp waste.

Emmet and I worried continually about Crit. He was the best soldier in the company, but he just soldiered. We would rage and condemn, but Crit never complained or criticized and day by day he seemed to get smaller and paler and more little-boy-looking. The three of us were intact the beginning of the last week of camp. We thought we had won through. But that night Crit's name was called out.

Emmet and I went to our bunks. Taps sounded. We undressed and lay down and waited for Crit. Lights were out so fortunately we couldn't see each other. About midnight Crit came in and sat on the edge of my bunk. He said simply:

"Well, Bill, I've got to go."

"When?" we asked.

"First thing in the morning."

"It's impossible," I stormed. "You're the best soldier of the whole bunch. Something's got to be done. It's an outrage, a disgrace to the camp."

"Whatever is done has to be done now, tonight," said Crit.

I got up and put on my uniform, rebellious, impotent, and crying.

"Do your best, Percy," came from Emmet's bunk.

I left the barracks and stood in the dark before the Captain's door. At last he came out and I asked permission to speak to him. I am certain that I made the most eloquent plea I ever made or ever will make. I would have lied willingly, but all I needed to do was to tell the truth, all of it. Finally the Captain said, more in sympathy than in encouragement: "Well, I'll give him a chance—tomorrow morning."

The three of us lay in our bunks with the news, with the hope. We didn't do any talking. I guess we prayed most of the night.

Next morning we went through the usual routine. Neither Emmet nor I could look at Crit or speak to him. One formation after another was lived through and nothing happened. At last, just before mess time, the Captain called out: "Mr. Crittenden, take the company." He stepped out of the ranks and stood before the company, so small, so quiet, so beyond anyone's help. It was unbearable. Then the officers fell on him with intricate directions which he must translate into commands and must see that the company execute. He had never drilled the company before. First one officer and then another took up the goading. No one else in our company had been subjected to such a grueling. But Crit never wavered or slipped. His voice with the correct commands rang out clear and self-possessed and stern, but pitifully young. He was magnificent. It was a triumph of nerve. Emmet and I in our squad stumbled along blindly, as proud as if we'd been presented with a helmet full of D.S.C.'s.

So the three of us received our commissions and we'd rather have had those single bars on our shoulders than celestial wings.

The first person to congratulate me was Captain Harris, who observed sourly but with a twinkle: "Well, Lieutenant, you made it, didn't you?" Even I had come to love him. What he knew he knew thoroughly; what he didn't know he made no pretense of knowing. He never bluffed and he never played favorites. Those of us who received commissions gave him a banquet and I made the speech telling what we thought of him. We were all pretty broken up and moist, and he had to leave the room, because of course top sergeants don't cry.

It wasn't easy for us three buddies to part, but the first chapter was ended, and honorably. I started for France, Crit for Oklahoma, and Emmet began his adventurous trek toward the First Division. We never met again till the war was over. And now a bit wizened, like picked chickens, I suppose, peewees still, our exploits forgotten except by us, our world slipping away, we hear the younger generation demanding peace and isolation and we feel sorry for them, knowing they missed a lot of fun and a lot of grief that was better than fun.

# CHAPTER XVI

# Getting to the Front

On the camouflaged but unconvoyed vessel that bore me to England, I met Gerstle Mack, sat with a life-preserver in my lap anticipating doom, and read *She* (forbidden by Father) to keep from being seasick. Ours was a shipload of casual officers, unassigned, ignorant, cheerful, and complete strangers to one another. We landed in Liverpool the day a transport was torpedoed in the Irish Sea and without delay were whisked across England, lovely even at that drab wintry season. To survive the rest-camp in which we were deposited required real stamina. We lasted out an all-night dash across the Channel, herded standing in the hold of a mouse of a boat that jumped and shied and all but turned over. Curled up in a baggage rack on the wall I watched between paroxysms of nausea the pale flower of the American army wilt with seasickness. Another rest-camp, half completed, leaking the ample French rain, slathered with mud, awaited us in Le Havre. There our individual assignments to posts of duty reached us and we dribbled out apprehensively to our various locations. I drew Tours via Blois.

Tours had not yet become the Sargasso Sea of sunk military careers, but the basin of the watery graves was in the building, though they hadn't started hauling in the seaweed. I reached there about the second day of creation and was immediately made a billeting officer. The job required a little tact, a little French, and considerable energy. It could have been done as well by a civilian.

All morning I would inspect and grade rooms offered by the townsfolk to the American army for its officers and non-coms. The rooms were usually tousled and always smelly, for the French are pretty bitter against fresh air and consider night air fatal. All afternoon I would assign the rooms I had inspected to officers applying for billets. A general rated a bathtub, a lieutenant anything that was left. I did well by myself, but only after tricking my conscience.

A middle-aged woman, pretty and chic, came into the office to offer the Americans a room in her home. She was obviously a lady and scared to death. You could tell her decision to permit a stranger under her roof had been an ordeal, and it must have taken sleepless nights to find the courage to invade this office full of uniformed men who couldn't speak her language and might not realize she was a gentlewoman. On seeing her I decided hers was the house in which I wished to be quartered. Three hours later, without inspecting her room (so that I could assure my conscience I didn't know whether it was good or bad), I drove up to 18 rue de Clocheville, deposited my baggage on the steps, dismissed the driver, and rang the bell. Mme Thierry opened the door, surprised at seeing me so soon and flustered at recognizing me. I said I wanted to move into the room she had offered. She objected that I hadn't seen it. I countered I had seen her. She was horrified at my impertinence and admitted me dubiously. Of course it was a delightful room, fit for a major general.

Mme Thierry's husband was the best doctor in Tours and one of the kindest men in the world. Her nineteen-year-old son, Jean, was at the front. It was the only time I ever lived in a French family—French families being notoriously partial to leaving the stranger at the gate. After two months of it I not only tolerated but applauded the French lack of interest in other peoples and their exclusive and passionate love of the French. Although realists and rationalists, they treasure sentiment as décor, and irony as wit and not as bitterness. I could never understand how a people could be so disillusioned and yet retain so bright a zest for living. They seem to consider life a raw deal and within limits very agreeable.

It was the winter of our discontent, that winter of 1918, full of foreboding, almost of despair. We thought Amiens would fall before the Americans could arrive in numbers, and after Amiens, Paris—in which event our army would have to scuttle over the Pyrenees to safety and disgrace. The Thierrys were heavy-hearted for their boy and saddened daily by news of some friend's death at the front.

To cheer them up two old friends of theirs came down from Paris for a visit, Rodin's rival, the great sculptor Sicard, and his beautiful Russian wife. They were often joined by an army chaplain, his uniform plastered with medals and a black patch over one eye. The five of them would while away the depressing winter evenings by reading aloud eighteenth-century memoirs, those just a little naughty. The chaplain was a wag as well as a hero, and his remaining eye burned with life and malice. Sicard, broad-shouldered and dour-looking, could be roused to memorable gaiety. Charming people, and so civilized. Their breed is not increasing.

I was often invited to family dinner, which would have been more than acceptable even without that miraculous Vouvray from the doctor's own vineyard. I should probably have been invited oftener had my French been house-broken. It took a sudden turn for the worse at the biggest party of the winter.

For the occasion the usual number of aunts and a grand-mère or two had been hauled from the attic, brushed off, and freshened up with ruching at the wrists of their black basques. They made me homesick: they looked like Aunt Fanny, their appetites were gargantuan like Aunt Nana's, and though entirely worldly-wise, their manners were delicately jeune-fille and conventual like those of old maids in Charleston. By the end of the soup course (served with Barsac) the interchange of chirpings had reached such a tempo I gave up trying to follow the sense and was sitting peacefully and contentedly thinking how nice they all were, and how alike nice people were the world over, when an Aunt Fanny, remembering it wasn't well-bred to omit the stranger from the conversation, asked across the table: "And now, Lieutenant Pairsee, won't you tell us something of the fauna and flora of your dear Southland?"

All French ladies are impervious to the facts of geography. You can do nothing about their impression that the Mississippi is a branch of the Amazon, and the Delta borders Tierra del Fuego on the north. I ransacked my brain for a topical theme. Or should it be tropical? Panic enfolded me. What can you say about the Delta? I became distraught in my search for a Southern theme. Rattlesnakes! Oh, how I hated them! But they were pretty Southern and not in the least French. I tried to dismiss them. They became an idée fixe. At the same time my French vocabulary suddenly wasted away. Slowly and pausefully I began on rattlesnakes. This is the information I imparted: "In my country there lives a serpent." Mild ah's. "He is three or four kilometers long." The ah's pick up. "He always carries little chimes." Great flurry of ah's and extraordinaire's. I ceased, but Aunt Fanny, unhappily roused to enthusiasm for natural history, insisted on knowing where this amazing reptile carried his chimes. On his head? What in heaven's name was the word for tail? I lunged and missed by a bare inch. Out of my naïve mouth leaped that most shocking of French words, a word which sounded to an American ear like the one I sought. A snowfall of silence covered the company. Aunts and grandmères tilted their eyes to the ceiling, saint-wise. Then the aumonier choked, threw his napkin over his head, and burst into a bellow of laughter. The rest followed suit. They rocked and wept and choked and stopped and started again. I, still guiltless as a clam, sat unnerved to the point of catalepsy. Clochettes dans le —— oh Lord!

No sooner had I become proficient at billeting than I was yanked out of it and assigned as flunky and handy man to the post commandant, Colonel B. We didn't take to each other. I recognized in him the regular-army outline without its content. He knew but two verbs: pass-the-buck and get-by-with-it. Having nothing for me to do, he made up things. The only definite assignment I received was to fix a smoking stove in the office. Two moronic doughboys were donated as my assistants. I knew if I booed at them they'd run into the woods and start whinnying. After two days of tussle with that stove-pipe we succeeded in blackening the office so completely it seemed paneled in ebony and looked rather handsome. The Colonel asked what progress we were making. I explained it was the nature of that stove to smoke out generals, and personally I couldn't do anything about it. He wanted to bawl me out, but decided it wasn't any use—and it wasn't.

Those would have been wretched days under Colonel B. had it not been for occasional glimpses of Gerstle and Frank Hoyt and an unexpected visit from Father.

Despairing of active service, Father had joined the Y.M.C.A. as one of an advisory committee of three and was making speeches at the canteens throughout the American sector. In his Y uniform he looked so strikingly like General Pershing he was always being embarrassed by salutes from green doughboys and embarrassing them in turn by his dreadful return salute, as sketchy as a general's. Some divine innocence in him made him believe nothing was too intelligent or too idealistic for our soldiers and they responded by loving his speeches. That same quality led him to regard me as a hero, though I had never seen a trench.

The Thierrys and the Sicards were great friends of Anatole France, who was living that winter in Tours. They must have mentioned me to him because he sent me an English translation of *Thaïs* with a charming inscription and a sheaf of American periodicals, the most unlikely imaginable, such as the *Ladies' Home Journal.* Twice he invited me to his Sunday levée and I longed to attend, but when I asked permission of Colonel B. he was so irritated at never having heard of Anatole France that he refused. So he was glad when a hurry-up order came from Paris for a lieutenant who could speak French. Protesting, I told him I wanted to go to the front and not to Paris. He observed that as far as he was concerned I could go to hell, but for the present I might try the next train to Paris and report to the purchasing agent of the American army, Colonel Charles Dawes. I tried the next train to Paris.

Colonel Dawes's small office contained two straight chairs, the Colonel, and a desk, on which reposed the Colonel's feet. I came snappily (I hope) to attention, saluted, and said: "Sir, Lieutenant Percy begs to report." He gazed at me anxiously but without interest. "Oh, for God's sake, Lieutenant, don't stand at attention! It worries me." I relaxed, almost crumpled. "All this saluting and carrying on gives me the fidgets. Now, Lieutenant, what do you want?"

"Nothing, sir. I thought you wanted me."

"What to hell do I want with you?"

"I can't imagine, sir. You sent for me in a hurry from Tours. I speak French."

"Good God," he burst out, "and now I've forgotten what I wanted you for. Sit down, sit down, Lieutenant, and help me remember."

I sat down and was about to suggest that anywhere he might send me, just so it was farther, might satisfy us both, when he exclaimed: "Old Jones, that's it, old Jones (Major Jones, I should say) needed you. Do you know Jones? Nice chap. You'll like him. Know where he is? Well, I'll take you down to him. Hell, what a mind I've got, what a mind! This goddamn army!" He led me down three flights of dark stairs and turned me over to old Jones. I batted my eyes to collect myself and stood at attention.

Major Jones was oldish and amiable and had the sort of face you couldn't possibly remember. I would scrutinize him, wishing he had one eye or three ears or a long scar so I could recognize him tomorrow. But it wasn't necessary. He was so pleased with the girls and the

liquor and the safety of Paris he had little time to inter-
fere with my work, much less to supervise it.

It was curious work for an infantry officer. My duty
was to supply civilian labor for the American army, usually for Gerstle, who apparently was running engineer
headquarters round the corner. The only civilian labor
left in Paris was apaches, pickpockets, gutter-snipes, and
syphilitics. I operated through the French Bureau of
Labor in this manner: Gerstle would order ten carpen-
ters, fifteen masons, twelve plasterers, six painters, and
one cabinet-maker (never more; I wonder why); the
Bureau would summon the scum of Paris into my presence; I would sift it for the craftsmen requisitioned and
direct them to meet me at the railroad station next morning. They would be booked to build a hospital at Saint-
Etienne or barracks at Bordeaux. I would secure their
reservations, meet them in front of the station, call the
roll, get their tickets, and put them into their compartments. In this way I became thick and friendly with the
underworld of Paris. No one ever came to tell them good-
by except me (perhaps because no train in any direction
could be induced to leave later than six a.m.) and they
were always in high spirits. Their baggage consisted of
a long loaf of bread, a large bottle of pinard, a cigarette
behind one ear and a flower behind the other (by preference a carnation). For traveling costume they wore big
baggy corduroys, tight at the ankles, a shirt without a
collar, a black skimpy muffler, and a wide red sash yards
long. Their hair was always dripping wet and carefully
parted, with an elaborate spit-curl on the forehead. They
would greet me loudly with "Hé là, mon lieutenant, ça
va?" and when I put them on the train I would shake
hands with them all, down to the last ax-slayer.

After they had been on their jobs a week, the Bureau

of Labor would receive from them an indignant telegram saying that they were rioting, that American food was impossible, fit for swine but not for civilized Parisians, that they demanded return fare to Paris immediately. About the same time Major Jones would hand me a telegram from the commanding officer of the camp to which they had gone to this effect: "Labor rioting. Fantastic complaints concerning American food. Riot quelled. Can't understand your selection. Labor shortage continues. Situation acute. Do you call this co-operation? For God's sake rush labor less epicurean and revolutionary who will work." The Bureau would treat the incident as if the Bastille was about to fall again and would confidentially implore me to reform the American army's cuisine. In a few days the rioters would all be back, delighted with the trip, glad to see me, ready to go elsewhere. I would again hire and ship them, they would again riot and return. The French never did come to think it was funny, or place the blame on those charming cut-throats of mine. We became so chummy I would take them cigarettes as a good-by present. I wished for a bitter enemy so they could do him in for me, ferociously and with gusto, just for sentiment's sake.

Although these goings-on occupied my waking hours amusingly enough, that spring in Paris was not a happy one. The marronniers bloomed sullenly under sunless skies, there was no heat in any hotel, Big Bertha boomed by day and planes dropped their loads by night, news from the front was increasingly terrifying—fear clung to Paris like mold. But these were not the true causes of my restlessness and unhappiness. Poilus from the trenches walked the boulevards, thick and stocky, dowdy in their horizon-blue uniforms, and sad-eyed. Spruce Australian, English, and New Zealand officers, on leave from the front, filled the bars and cafés. I began to believe these true soldiers knew I worked in an office, in a safe place, like a damn civilian. To men from the line an assignment in Paris was a badge of disgrace. No use to argue that it wasn't your fault, you were obeying orders, orders you hadn't asked for—I became convinced that without suffering there was no real soldiering and that the eye of every real soldier accused me of being an embusqué. An embusqué, everyone knew, was an officer who had got himself a soft safe berth by pull.

To let things take their own course meant to remain in the Labor Bureau for the duration. I brooded miserably on the situation and finally spied a faint ray of hope. The only "pull" I could possibly have would be through Huger Jervey, who at the time was in Saint-Aignan acting as chief of staff of the replacement division. I wrote and begged him to get me out of the S.O.S. and toward the front. He knew me and he knew how any soldier would feel under the circumstances, but, thinking of Father and Mother, he hated to help me out of safety and toward possible danger. Being a Southerner, a Sewanee man, and one of my oldest and dearest friends, however, he couldn't refuse. Major Jones received a request for my transfer to Saint-Aignan. The Major summoned me to his office and said affably: "Lieutenant, I have received a request for your transfer to the replacement division. You are indispensable to my department. I have recommended you for promotion. I have refused the request for transfer." My only chance to be a real soldier gone, gone because of this lazy old embusqué! Merciful anger saved me from tears. In Homer's phrase, I summoned my stout heart and spoke wingèd words:

"Major Jones, you've been good to me. May I speak to you man to man? I have watched you here in Paris doing your duty efficiently and on the surface cheerfully. But you haven't fooled me: I know you have been eating your heart out. The one thing in the world you want is to get to the front. You are soldiering, but it's killing you. Major, if you feel that way, think how I must feel, so many years younger than you. This is my only chance. My whole future is in your hands. You can keep me here for the rest of the war or you can let me do what you want to do, what every real American wants, what I want. Don't deprive me of my one chance. Major, let me go."

I almost believed my own eloquence and my voice was trembling. The Major's eyes became moist and he murmured emotionally: "Go, my boy, go. I understand. I can't hold you here. God bless you."

Although I knew they were crocodile tears, I felt like busking that old man on his bald spot. I had always considered Machiavellian tactics abominable, and guile and flattery the most contemptible of the survival virtues, but I had not one regret, no remorse, no repentance. I was spilling over with happiness. I wanted to share it with Gerstle and Charlotte and Frank Hoyt, but I couldn't locate any of them. So I walked on air down the Champs-Elysées repeating: "My heart is like a singing bird whose nest is in a watered shoot" and wondering what a watered shoot might be. I floated up the grands boulevards like a very luminous jack-o'-lantern, found by instinct the Café de la Paix, pulled out an iron chair that felt like down, took a seat, and ordered a whisky and soda.

It was at this point that I beheld an apparition of joy which almost floored me: Lieutenant McCloud of Leon Springs came sauntering down the boulevard. He had been the orneriest, wildest backwoodsman in camp and he hailed from Sullivan's Hollow, than which there is no more blood-spilling, moonshine-drinking, tobacco-spitting nest of outlaws in all the South, no, not excepting Louisiana's Tangapahoa or Kentucky's Harlan. When I had known him he couldn't speak English, much less French. But here he was strolling in front of the Café de la Paix in the snappiest of uniforms, with the sauciest of overseas caps over one eye, and on his arm the most flamboyant little cutie in Paris. He approached with a dazzling grin, as if we'd just finished squads-right together: "Hey, Percy, what's the French word for bolts?" "Bolts and shackles?" I ventured. "No, just bolts. My job is buying bolts for this man's army." He strode off in male grandeur, his little sweetie nestling warmly, but kicking up one heel behind her à la Moulin Rouge and giving me a wink as they faded out. Shades of Sullivan's Hollow!

Saint-Aignan was the liaison between the front and rear of our army, and Huger, apparently, was its presiding deity. Very splendid and dignified, he asked me where I wanted to go from there. I had had three months within which to learn the duties of an infantry officer and six months within which to forget them. Obviously I still wasn't fit to handle a platoon, so we decided the place for me was the officers' school of the line at Gondrecourt, completing which, one would be sent to the trenches as a replacement.

Gondrecourt was much like Leon Springs, but less taxing physically and unendearing. The officers taking the course were from line outfits to which they would be returned. I was an outsider and beneath notice. So I studied hard while they went through the motions, and for my virtue was rewarded as virtue is so often rewarded —instead of being sent to a division in the line as platoon leader I was made an instructor. I protested passionately and was told to shut up and report immediately to General Hay of the Ninety-second Division.

I had never heard of General Hay or the Ninety-second and I scoured France looking for them with the least possible enthusiasm. When I finally entered the division area, looking out of the train window, I decided that in a fit of homesickness I had lost my mind—the landscape was speckled with Negro soldiers! The Ninety-second was the much publicized Negro division, in which all officers except supply officers and those above the grade of captain were Negroes. Not knowing whether to laugh or cry and wishing I could see somebody from Trail Lake, I located the inhospitable division headquarters and asked for General Hay. They pointed him out, entering his car, a bleak, austere man with a hurt, forbidding look and a cold voice drained of color by the long giving of commands.

Standing on the sidewalk at attention, I introduced myself by the usual formula.

"What are you reporting for?" he demanded harshly.

"As instructor, sent from Gondrecourt."

"I didn't ask for an instructor and I don't want one," said the General. (I've sometimes thought the army's manual of manners must be *Alice in Wonderland* instead of Emily Post.) I was fed up with bad manners and bawlings out.

"Sir, I didn't ask to be sent here and I don't want to be here."

"Why?" he snapped.

"Sir," I proceeded as if he liked me, "can you imagine anyone *choosing* to be an instructor, particularly to an outfit that doesn't want him?"

He sized me up grimly and I didn't feel big.

"What have you learned over here that may help my men?"

"Map- and compass-reading, message-sending, and the

new French open-order formations." (I refrained from saying reeling, writhing, and fainting in coils.)

"Can you teach these subjects?"

"Yes, sir."

"Do you know anything else?"

"No, sir, I'm one of these new officers out of civilian life. I know nothing at all, sir, except a little human nature and good manners when I see them." I smiled cheerfully.

He meditated: "Hard on both of us."

"Not so very," I answered sincerely.

"Well, get in the car. We'll try it," said the General.

General Hay's headquarters were in a hovel of a village where the remaining civilians were shockingly poor and dirty-looking. Next morning I felt at home when upon asking a Negro orderly for some warm water he averred there warn't none and you couldn't git none. I suggested borrowing from the house across the street. He sighed and commented: "Lawd, that woman ain't seen no warm water since the last time she cried."

For a few days I drove with the General over his brigade on inspection trips. He was grim and aloof, but I noticed he inspected closely and asked me many questions, none personal. One night he knocked at my door and said: "Lieutenant, I'd like you to come to my room."

I went, puzzled and curious. He sat down stiffly but wearily and motioned me to a chair. "Lieutenant, I notice you are not afraid of me."

"No, sir, not a bit."

"I have an unfortunate manner. I appear cold and stern. My officers are afraid of me, all of them. For that reason they will not talk to me candidly. I am responsible for seventy-five hundred men, a whole brigade, and in all my army life, ever since I graduated from the Point, I have never commanded more than a hundred. For many years I have been a desk officer. I need to learn everything anyone can teach me. We are all like that, we ranking officers of the old army. Your first duty, Lieutenant, is to instruct me and to protect me from mistakes so I may protect my men. Will you promise to criticize me and give me any information you have and I haven't, as if we were of equal rank?"

I promised.

"I am making you brigade instructor. Half of your time will be spent in one regiment, half in the other. Any officer you recommend for demotion I shall demote. I will trust the honesty of your judgments."

I felt like putting my hands between his and swearing fealty. Without the oath, I was his man. He carried out his promise to the letter and I never tried harder not to fail a man. He was promoted before the war ended and I rejoiced, knowing he merited it. Only divine devotion to duty could have induced so self-contained and proud a man to open his heart and call for help to a shrimp of a lieutenant.

My classes were held for Negro officers, the majority of whom outranked me. I knew they would be looking out for slights and condescensions, especially after they recognized me as a Southerner. I wanted to give them their every due, to pay them their every military respect, but at the same time I was not going to permit them to be familiar. So I was punctilious about saluting them first, and for the rest I knew that nothing keeps one at arm's length so effectively as meticulous politeness. To satisfy their curiosity they tried me out once by inviting me to mess with them, but when that failed, our relations became cordial and natural. We treated one another with deserved deference which satisfied us both.

I don't like to say anything disparaging about the Ninety-second Division, because an outside instructor is helpless unless the outfit's regular officers co-operate with him, and the officers of General Hay's brigade co-operated with me to the limit. But believing that the Negro's first need is not sympathy or patronizing or even help, but the truth, I must set down here what I believe to be true of the division's Negro officers. Those who came from the regular army, where they had been sergeants, made splendid officers; those who came from civilian life by way of training camps were lazy, undevoted, and without pride. Both dressed well, but the latter were peacocks in splendor and strut. I couldn't judge the enlisted personnel—I liked them of course, they reminded me of home, but I feared for them under test.

After I'd been teaching four or five weeks, two of the Negro captains took me aside and did me the honor to unburden themselves to me. Earnest men of innate dignity, they were able, devoted officers. They asked if anything could be done to keep the division out of the line. They insisted it was unfit for line service. Without bitterness but with profound sorrow they confessed that under battle conditions it would disgrace our country. I was distressed for them and inquired the reason for their fears.

"Lieutenant," said the more articulate of the two, "you know. Don't make us say. These men are not going to follow us into battle because we are Negroes. You say we are able officers. That makes no difference. A Negro won't follow a Negro. We have enough pride in ourselves and in our race not to want to see that happen. Try to do something about it, Lieutenant."

I did try. I wrote Colonel Quekemeyer, General Pershing's aide and an old Delta boy, and told him what I had observed and learned, what these officers had told me, and what I feared. I suppose sending such a letter broke all rules and regulations. Of course I received no answer. I expected none. But, after the Armistice, Quackmeyer told me that General Pershing appreciated the facts, shared my fears, but because of political pressure could do nothing about it. He was forced to give them their chance in the line.

The Ninety-second Division returned to New York in splendor, marched down Fifth Avenue and was applauded and publicized as heroes. Its only major engagement had been in the Argonne. Of its exploits there General Pershing wrote: "The 92nd Division attacked but did not hold all its gains." His words win my admiration as a masterly example of the glacial tact of understatement, the polar pity of reticence.

I have another reason for disliking to criticize the Ninety-second: it was with them I got my break. The Colonel of the regiment in which I was instructing was promoted. He was a kind and intelligent gentleman, with a drooping mustache and an air like the White Knight's. A general's first need is an aide. White lieutenants being practically non-existent in these parts, General Jackson called me to his room and said in his pleasant, informal way: "Percy, how'd you like to be my aide-de-camp?"

Thanking him, I said I understood an aide was the lowest form of military life and all I aspired to be was a platoon leader at the front.

He laughed. "I have just seen the order for your re-appointment as instructor, Percy. You will be teaching in the training area till peace is signed and you'll be so deep in the woods you won't know it. My brigade is at the front now and I'm joining it Wednesday."

I gulped and sat down. "General, I'll join you Wednesday."

# CHAPTER XVII

# At the Front

25 Sept. 1918—9 p.m.
With the Armies

*Mother dear:*

Just a hurried line. Unless the order is changed we're going into a gorgeous big battle in a few hours, of which you'll know the full results long before this reaches you. I've no premonitions and few apprehensions, though battles of course aren't safe things. And for good luck, letters came from you and Father today. I'm glad he liked my little "Squire's Song." It was written at Tours with Frank Gailor in mind as he was going off to the Messines show, but it holds true for any soldier fighting in the great cause. One must be a soldier these days—there is no other part a man may play and be a man. Should anything ever happen to me over here, you and Father must, and I know you will, feel that it was a great privilege for us to be allowed to go forth with the heroes. I've had too much and too keen happiness out of this life to want to leave it or to leave it without regret, but this cause is too great to count the cost or speculate on the outcome to the individual. All that's good in me comes direct from you and Father, and my only ambition in this business is not to be unworthy of you. And whatever happens we'll be together in the end.

. . . I'll write you in a few days. Now for a little much-needed sleep.

All my love to you both.

Your devoted son,

*O.K.–W. A. Percy,*
*1st Lt. Inf.*

*W. A. Percy*

[*After the Argonne*]
*October 4, 1918*

*Dear Father:*

I have been through hell and returned without a scar. Already it seems a lifetime distant. I cannot recall the sensations clearly, the sheer relief of getting away from it is so great that it will be impossible to give any vivid account of the experience. Here I've a room to myself, a bed, we've just finished a hot supper served on plates with knives and forks and spoons, and we are so happy to be alive that the nightmare we've just left seems unreal, a thing that could not actually have been experienced.

We were rushed up the night before the attack and at midnight the barrage commenced. Although it was a fearful din I was somehow disappointed in it; in fact, slept from sheer exhaustion through most of it on the concrete floor of our dugout. At dawn we attacked. I went to an O.P. (observation post) in the woods to watch, but the mist was so thick I could see nothing and my only sensation as the sun came up was listening to the wild canaries which were suddenly and strangely moved to music that could be heard above the thunder of the guns. The General and I started forward in side-cars, but the roads were so choked with traffic that we abandoned them and followed the assaulting lines on foot. Our first experience of battle was in a shattered hull of a town on the edge of our side of No Man's Land. Troops, wagons, guns, ambulances were surging through in inextricable confusion when suddenly a shell fell on the crossroads, 50 yards ahead of us. An ambulance went up in a puff of cotton, horses and men fell; then another shell. One of our batteries on a slope at the crossroads was replying, and as a third shell fell who should rush down from it, to grab my hand, sing out hello, and rush back, but Gus? I haven't seen him since.

We finally got out of town and into the torn and scarred region between the lines, where already the engineers were attempting to build back the roads. Our troops had swept at once into the woods and were going forward under the barrage with little opposition. We followed them and their wake was clear from the rubble and refuse of battle—abandoned packs and guns, rarely a dead German, ammunition, helmets, then trenches and shelters that had been "cleaned out," as the saying is, for throwing grenades into them. The enemy, holding the first few kilometers lightly, had evidently been surprised by the onslaught. We lunched in a German kitchen off of German food—tea, coffee, potatoes, cabbages, purple and white, and, most surprisingly, good bread and fifty pounds of lump sugar. The day was clear and cool —picnic weather—and that first day was like a picnic. At leisure we examined the marvelous German system of defense, dugouts fifty and sixty feet deep, many of them concrete, often comfortable, sometimes even elegant, for one had a shower-bath and another was papered with burlap. The fine German equipment was scattered broadcast for the troops coming on in reserve to choose souvenirs from, knapsacks, warm socks, helmets (all camouflaged), big blankets, grenades and ammunition galore, shoes, underwear, personal property of all kinds, letters, pictures, books (I found a copy of Scott's *Waverly*), bottles of mineral water, canteens, and pistols. All the resistance that first day was made by machine-guns, which were cleaned up without much difficulty. It was rather a rollicking army that went forward those first six or seven kilometers. But that night it rained.

Next night as I rode forward in the darkness the roads over which all our food and supplies had to come were already becoming muddy and the mud from that time on was one of the things we had to fight. Perhaps you'd like to know what I wore and carried into the affray. A helmet, a gas mask, your field glasses, a heavy cane, a case, a pistol, belt and canteen, a trench coat, a musette bag containing one loaf of bread, a can of corned beef, a pair of socks, a toothbrush (never used), a few letters, a compass, the *Oxford Book of Verse*, and a shaving set. It's easy to tell these simple things, but I can't catalogue the sensations or the events of the next two or three days.

I once wrote Mother not to pity the soldier. Well, now I think the infantryman is the most to be pitied person in the world. The sheer misery he endures is not approached by men in any other branch of the service. He not only fights, but he marches unending miles, carries all he has to eat or keep himself warm with on his back. The artilleryman rides with his guns and sees little of the actual horror, the airman is just a mad adventurer, but these doughboys! I don't see how they do it. If there were no such thing as bullets and shells and bayonets, what they suffer in hunger and cold and exhaustion would earn them eternal reverence.

The second day was cold and rainy. I was detailed at a crossroads behind the assault echelons to direct the wounded and send back the stragglers. It developed into a big undertaking. The wounded themselves were tractable enough—many bad cases and some hit by shrapnel and machine-gun bullets—but every litter had extra volunteers as carriers whom I had to send back and all the unheroic of the battle came my way—the cowards and deserters and malingerers. The drawn faces of these were more awful than those of the wounded. Once a whole line broke and came tumbling back, led by an officer gone mad with shell-shock. I ordered and pleaded and threatened and just as things were at their worst there was the sound of horsemen galloping to us up the road from the rear and it was our artillery coming up to support us, headed by Colonel Luke Lea.

That day was bad enough, but the next was worse. The generals rode up to the front lines to investigate and encourage the men. I followed on foot, and on reaching the forward dugout was told my General had gone forward, so without orders I started out to find him. As I wandered along wondering vaguely where he was, the enemy's barrage suddenly opened up and I was caught in it. I had no duties of any kind, so I hopped into a shell-hole for a minute and waited; then, thinking that was poor business, went on. To be shelled when you are in the open is one of the most terrible of human experiences. You hear this rushing, tearing sound as the thing comes toward you, and then the huge explosion as it strikes, and, infinitely worse, you see its hideous work as men stagger, fall, struggle, or lie quiet and unrecognizable. I was on a wide reverse slope, where there was no timber or shelter, and where the shells were falling ceaselessly in groups of three. Suddenly over the crest a company broke and I saw their Colonel single-handed trying to rally and direct them. So I joined him and took over the company. A fine young chap by the name of McSweeney (General Farnsworth's aide) joined me. It was a vivid, wild experience and I think I went through it calmly by refusing to recognize it was real. You couldn't bear to see men smashed and killed around you and know each moment might annihilate you, except by walking in a sort of sleep, as you might read Dante's *Inferno*. The exhilaration of battle—there's no such thing, except perhaps in a charge. It's simply a matter of will-power. As for being without fear, I met no such person under this barrage, though most played their parts as if they were without it. When we had rallied the men and put them in shell-holes, I went up to the crest and as our advance had ceased sat down in a fox-hole which a soldier had dug the night before, next to that of a French lieutenant. With slight intermissions the barrage continued for four hours. We sat there laughing and talking and wondering if the next one would get us. He had a wife and child and had seen four years of this hell; once he remarked: "Oh, we will never leave here," but he was coolness and politeness itself. Hits within twenty yards almost deafened us, but we both escaped without a scratch.

That night the two of us and some twenty more passed in a dugout listening to the shells and awaiting the counter-attack, which did not develop. That dugout I shall never forget. It was about ten feet wide and forty feet long. The two sides were of mud, dripping and shiny, likewise the floor. The roof was a few logs and a layer of elephant iron which, far from furnishing protection from shell bursts, did not even keep out the rain which all night long trickled through onto our faces and hands and down our backs. We sat shoulder to shoulder on the floor in two rows, our backs against the mud of the walls, our feet against the feet of the man opposite. One candle made visible our weariness and discomfort. I've never seen such tired men. We'd all been a bit gassed and during the night four mustard shells fell at the door and forced us to climb into our masks (all but me, who was in charge and answering the telephone all night). The features of the men had sagged and run together with fatigue; it was cold and they had no blankets; our only food for two days had been bread and corned beef. The horror of the impending destruction tortured them while it could not hold them from sleep. They slept prone in the mud or propped up against each other; clothes, helmets, hands, faces, and hair all one color—mud. There was no complaining, little talking, and no thinking. Fatigue, cold, and hunger quickly made of us mere animals. It was a long night and outside the soldiers were lying under the rain and bitter wind, unfed, but holding.

The next morning the General and I went back to the elegant dugout of the artillery and Luke Lea served us a meal which was so good it almost brought tears to my eyes; no other meal will ever be as good. Coffee, broiled bacon, hot cakes, and syrup. I may sometimes forget Luke's cordiality, but his breakfast never.

Well, we're out of it all now. Most of the mud is scraped off. I've washed my face again and brushed my teeth and slept in a bed. The hardships and miseries are almost forgotten and we're looking forward to several weeks of training and instruction in this pretty country, almost within sight of the cathedral and moated town you visited.

Nuff said. I'm living and awfully glad to be alive. I've gone through unforgettable experiences and I have nothing to regret. Will write again shortly. Best love to you and Mother.

> Your devoted son,
> *W. A. Percy*
> *1st Lt. inf.*

*On the Lys*
*4 November 1918*

*Mother dear:*

The shells have stopped. It's just this side of midnight, everyone except the telephone man and myself has rolled into blankets on the floor or into bunks left by the Boche; there's still three inches of candle left. It's Sunday night —so I'll drop you a line about our recent doings. Our second battle is over and we've done well, advancing some seventeen kilometers, crossing the river and rather leading the divisions on either side of us. Things have run more smoothly than in our first attempt, and for us back at headquarters there have been less fatigue, less excitement, and fewer personal adventures.

Our start was really a rather beautiful thing—and that is noteworthy as there's so little beauty—at least, physical beauty—in a battle. For a P.O. we'd taken a small farmhouse with a red roof and drying tobacco hanging like a frieze under the eaves. Just at dawn our barrage started under a faintly pink sky. You could see endlessly in every direction, for the country is flat as ours and without woods, just miles of turnip, beet, and cabbage fields, little orchards, and quiet homey farmhouses. When the big guns started we seemed to be in the midst of an amphitheater, and all around us clear to the horizon we could see them flame and hear them roar. And they'd hardly started when, suddenly, against the forward skyline where the enemy lay, rockets began to leap of all colors and kinds, the enemy's signals of distress and vain calls for assistance.

We went forward almost at once across the river with the lovely lily name to follow the advancing infantry, and selected as our new P.O. what had been a charming home, sitting back in a small park with trees and flower-beds and a small artificial lake. Its owners had fled only a few days before, leaving their personal effects scattered wildly about (Delft china plates still on the walls, an old cashmere shawl hung over one chair, a woman's hat on another), but shells had dashed out the windows, torn the roof, smashed the piano, and littered the place with debris. It wasn't a nice neighborhood. The civilians remaining, after their days of hiding from bombardment in the cellars, were too dazed to rejoice at their deliverance. When we moved into the town, the Boche proceeded to shell it, and the bleak streets were only too often horrible with the evidence of his accuracy.

But the second day was rather a triumphal procession. After a bitter rear-guard resistance, the enemy retired, and we pursued him through a town where, in one of those fine bursts of patriotism small towns are sometimes capable of, all the civilians had refused to leave, and when our troops entered, they rushed out from their cellars and hiding-places wild with joy. We were the first friends they'd seen in four years, and our presence was the first news they'd had of the coming of Americans. Flags, so long forbidden, were hung in all the windows, and, lining the streets, they waved and cheered us as we passed. . . . We need to remember that day of glory now, for today and yesterday have been pretty bitter. We reached our objective, a river-bank, and were later under a hail of lead and gas while we attempted a crossing. I've suffered personally none of the agony that the men and line officers have been called on to endure; and they only a small part of what these French and British have been enduring for four years. Certainly, no one can ever hate war as a soldier does: it is the wickedest, most hateful thing man was ever guilty of.

I don't remember these last days as a connected story:

most of the time I wasn't doing anything except thinking
and observing, the former not apt to make one buoyant,
the latter not fruitful. But I've a few vivid impressions
of unimportant incidents. You never realize how many
different kinds of soldiers are called on for heroic, unre-
warded tasks, just as a matter of course. A truck-driver
wouldn't occur to you as a subject for song or story,
yet there's something almost epic in seeing a train of provisions or ammunition moving up to supply the front
line at night. The road is spotted by enemy artillery,
and all night the shells fall on it or near it, and, when the
shells stop, there's a dreadful whir overhead, and you
know a plane with bombs is searching for the best place
to drop them. Yet these men drive on in the pitchy darkness, in terror doubtless, but without halting. A shell
catches them: men and horses are killed; but the rest
of the train moves on, for without them the infantry
could not carry on. . . .

The first night we reached the river, I went down to
get a report from the Major and to see what was doing.
It's a mystery how our army ever gets to its destination.
All movements are at night, over an absolutely strange
country, only the officers can read maps, and most of
them have a fearful time with French maps; when you
come to a crossroads and stop to locate yourself, you
either find your searchlight refuses to work, or an enemy
bombing-plane is in the neighborhood and you don't
dare use it; and if by good luck you find a native and ask
him the way, you almost blow up to discover he doesn't
speak French. Well, as I started to say, I roved down
toward the river—I'm always remembering a magic line
of Verhaeren's: "Toujours l'énorme Escaut roule dans mes
pensées"—and on the way stopped by the P.O. of a battalion. It was in the kitchen of a farmhouse just off

the road. In the wide low-ceiled room one candle was burning, in the shadows about the big Flemish fireplace clustered two peasant women and four children, all quiet and watching, still with wonder, the Americans. The Major and another officer were studying a map and sending occasional messages to units scattered somewhere out in the night—where the guides would meet them, which one should move up, where the kitchens had been left, whether the ammunition train had arrived, etc., etc. These days the work of an officer, when his troops are not actually engaged, is getting them fed, clothed, supplied, moved without too great exhaustion and without being detected. There's no drill or instruction and little discipline. While we were discussing the orders for next day, one of the women set down on our table three cups and a pitcher of steaming milk. She couldn't speak a word of French or English, but she had a cheery, brave, bustling way about her, and in sign of friendship she was giving us all she had. In the old days, when Beowulf fought dragons and fly-by-nights, it was always the wife of the king who poured the mead cup for the heroes before battle, but her gesture could never have been as simple and fine as that peasant woman's. And the milk was delisch—the first I'd had in four months.

The hamlet on the river-bank was the peacefulest place you ever saw, the curé and a few civilians still remained, and under a velvet sky, all stars, our soldiers drifted about almost carelessly. Twenty-four hours later the hamlet was not on the map; it had vanished and in its place lay a rubble heap.

On my way back they began shelling the roads, which makes the going fairly interesting. They say English officers never duck shells, and it's probably true. I don't know of any rule in our army, but there's the universal custom for all ranks and grades, when you hear the scream coming your way, to dive into the nearest ditch, or, if none's handy, flat on your stomach. Well, I was flat a considerable portion of that night, and twice it seemed as if that would surely be my permanent position. But I guess you and Adah and Janet and Miss Carrie have worried the good Lord into taking care of me personally. . . .

Well, I'll stop. Lots of love to you and Father.

Your devoted son,

*W. A. Percy*

*Monday, November* 11, 1918

*Mother dear:*

Today is the impossible great day for which the world has been waiting four years and which it seemed we'd never see arrive. The armistice is signed and peace now is a matter of putting terms on paper. For us it came just in time. We'd started an advance of very great difficulty, with the enemy holding the heights on the other side of a bridgeless river and scourging our men, as they tried to cross, with high explosives, shrapnel, and machine-guns. Last night I was wrapped up in Father's Alaskan robe and trying to sleep in a corner between bursts from a long-range big-caliber battery stationed in our garden. Sleep wasn't easy as a window crashed in at every burst, and the air displacement almost blew us off the floor. The telephone was constantly ringing— Where were the engineers with the pontoon material? Could we give a carrying party for the infantry? Last attempt to cross had failed; machine-gun fire unceasing; the French on our left held up: gas shells falling in the town. And there was the weary confusion of mid-battle as seen from brigade headquarters, when suddenly at

2.10 in the morning I heard Moore—the other aide—gasp: "What's that?" And it was the Armistice! Signed, sealed, and delivered! Stop the artillery, no further advance necessary; wake up the General; the hubbub outside is only the French returning from the line singing and calling to our men: "La guerre est finie!" It's morning now, and we are loitering around waiting for our next orders. We don't know the terms, we don't know where we are going, we can't realize the immensity of this news. We can step out the door without fear of a shell, we can walk down the road without a gas mask, I can sit in comfort by a fire or a desk and not be haunted by the thought of men lying out under the wintry sky, hungry and riddled by shell and bullets. This physical relief is so great that I can't begin to appreciate the enormous spiritual results, this wave of gladness sweeping over the world, the home-turning of those who have fought, "the tears of recognition never dry."

I haven't got a captaincy, for which the General recommended me. So I'll bring home no honors. But I didn't go into it with the hope of getting any, and rewards given by other men have never impressed me. I've seen unforgettable sights. I've done my part to the best of my ability in a great cause, my life has been spared—certainly it would be churlish to ask more or to do other than to thank the merciful God for what He has granted. . . .

Well, it's all very wonderful: the times are so much greater than I am. I can't realize that I am playing in the last act of the world's greatest tragedy. Love to you and Father. Letters should go to and fro without trouble now. Watch for the fro.

Devotedly your son,
W. A. *Percy*

[213]

This is what my letters home said. But soldiers' letters from the front, if I may judge from my own, are gauche outpourings, too hot and too cold, too eloquent in a distressing amateurish fashion and too reticent, at once accurate and misleading. Their deficiency springs not so much from the haste of their composition as from the soldier's effort to express enough of the truth to give a glimpse of what he is going through, yet not enough to distress the devoted reader to whom he is writing. Rereading mine, after these twenty-two sobering years, I find they record all I have forgotten and omit all that I remember, all that made my stay at the front a test and a turning, the most memorable and maturing experience of my life. What soldiers write home about must be supplemented by what soldiers do not write home about, if one is to gain an inkling of why a soldier is more and less than a man.

When we were pulled out of the quiet Baccarat sector, where I had joined General Jackson and the Thirty-seventh Division, we knew we were in for trouble. You could feel it in the air, electric with hurry and secrecy. The first great battle of the massed American army was imminent, the battle of the Argonne. We were to be a part of it. Green as we were, General Pershing had assigned to us a sector near the center of the line to the west of Montfaucon, which, washed in yellow sunlight on its rise above the tree-tops, glowed like a Maxfield Parrish dream of a fortress.

On the second night before the Argonne I lodged in the small first-floor room of a two-story house that opened on the road. It was a poor little house that was home to poor people. I lay in my narrow bed by the open window and couldn't sleep. It was deep quiet night and the village was still as death. I listened to the ominous dull thunder from the front. I was tired. Then I heard upstairs above me a couple in bed making loud love. It should have seemed ribald and amusing; it seemed only obscene and pitiful. That poor poilu home on two days' leave and his shapeless, hard-working wife! This was love, this animal-sounding thing. I remembered that love had once seemed tender and beautiful. It wasn't any more. The sounds died down. I hoped they had enjoyed themselves and wondered if they were crying now, clinging to each other whimpering. I closed my eyes and the sleepless hours began.

After midnight I heard on the road the tramping of feet. It was soldiers marching with the snap gone out of their rhythm and that sound of shifting and bumping of gear a jaded outfit makes. As they paused outside my window a young voice, frayed and listless, called: "Platoon—halt. Left face. At ease." They shifted their feet and sighed, cleared their throats to spit, and cursed a little. The platoon leader's voice said drearily:

"Check up on 'em, sergeant. Where's Smithy?"

"Dropped out, sir," answered a steadier voice.

"And Weems?"

"Taken sick, sir."

"And Odell?"

"Guess he couldn't make it."

"Well, we got to go on, sergeant. Right face. Forward march."

Where were they going this time of night? Did they know themselves? Were they lost? A battle was ahead. They had to get there. But where or why? They were too tired, they couldn't remember. I lay still and listened to them tramping into the wide night. They were so much younger than French soldiers.

The next night my billet had no bed and the roof had

been torn away, but there were walls and a floor. I lit
a candle, hunted for a clean corner, and spread my
blanket. Then my eye fell on a small print pinned loosely
to the wall, the only object in a naked room. It was an
Italian Madonna. As I looked at it dully, knowing it was
familiar and trying to remember the artist's name, a wave
of anger and nausea swept over me. Art? What was
art, painting, music, poetry, all that stuff? Child's play,
the pastime of weaklings, pointless, useless, unmanly,
weak, weak, weak—I had loved it once and men had
wasted their lives on it. I blew out the candle, lay down
in my blanket, and shook in the darkness. It took me a
year to remember it was a Luini.

When the first picnic day of the Argonne had closed
in rain, four or five of us started to our new headquarters
on horseback. The darkness had substance; it touched
you. We could not discern the country through which
we were passing, we could only sense the deeper darkness of trees on each side of the road and the silence,
as if no one was there or had ever been there or ever
would be there. A weeping rain fell, cold, eternal, incon-
solable. It had been a long, exciting, exhausting day, our
first day of battle, and it followed three nights of half-
sleep. We let the horses guide themselves and in our
saddles fought sleep. Each man wondered wildly within
himself how long he could last. This was always the
inner terror—would the sleeplessness and exhaustion be
too much for the frail machine that was a man? Would
the machine break? We rode in silence through a nightmare of silence. It was broken wildly by a long-drawn
animal scream. But we knew the animal was a man. It
was repeated and repeated, full of torture and fear. We
realized it was trying to talk, to talk to us, from out there
in the woods alone. We rode on and said nothing; we

didn't dare. We learned next day it was a German soldier with his jaw shot away.

About two o'clock we found our overnight headquarters, a hole in the earth, but it had chicken-wire bunks. I fell into one and was immediately asleep. In fifteen minutes the General shook me awake: "Sorry, Percy. You must walk back a mile and a half to the crossroads and wait for the second battalion. Show them to their positions. You're the only person handy who knows them." I grabbed the short staff with a leather thong which I had found in a shell-hole and stumbled out. Somehow I reached the crossroads, meeting no one, hearing nothing, the only living creature on that vast battlefield. I was sure if I sat close to the road I couldn't miss them and if I sat up straight I couldn't fall asleep. I sat down on the muddy bank of the road with my knees drawn up, stuck the staff in the ground between my feet, and leaned my chin on it. The rain dribbled down my neck. When I awoke I was sitting in the same position and it was light. Asleep at the post of duty! The road was empty. Stiff with cold and desperate, I stood in the rainy half-light and prayed that the battalion had not passed. In a few minutes I saw it marching up the road toward me, beautiful as marching seraphim. For such a dereliction ordinary soldiers, yokels who didn't know or care why they were fighting, had been shot at dawn. I led the battalion to its position.

Next night our headquarters was that deep dugout which I shall never forget, as familiar to me still as my own bedroom. It was a German dugout and for our purposes faced the wrong way: it gaped to receive a shell. Sixty precipitous steps led down to its interior, dripping and dark like a cave. Two tiers of chicken-wire bunks flanked its long narrow corridor, and mine was a top one, so close to the ceiling you had to slide in sideways. Its last occupant, troubled by a dribble of water from above that leaked on his throat, had ingeniously attached a tin can to the ceiling and it required some skill and no thickness to sidle in and out without striking it and dousing yourself with the icy contents. Whenever I fell asleep, the telephone would ring or my name would be called, and, starting up, nervously, I'd hit that can and be splashed into cold bright consciousness. In spite of its convenience, I never grew to like it, but I grew more and more fond of that unknown predecessor of mine. He became a mystical bunkie, and I hoped we hadn't killed him.

Water stood on the floor of the dugout and there was no room to move about. The steps, steep as a ladder, were slick with slime, and some soldier, awkward in his heavy gear and sloppy with mud, would always be slipping and crashing down them heavily to our feet. He would lie there moaning a little or cursing softly and none of us would help him up or notice him. We were all holding more than we could contain, like a glass of water too full and held from spilling by tension. The slightest jar, even a sigh, would break it into overflowing. We didn't know what form the overflow might take—tears, hysteria, madness—but we knew laughter could be the jar and pity the sigh, and we couldn't risk either. For our protection we substituted dull anger.

From where we were, the forest stretched darkly behind us to the rear, and before us flowed undulations of open country as far as Ivoiry, our immediate objective. Everything happened under a morose dripping sky. In my recollection I seem always to have been standing in front of that dugout of ours. I watched little groups at the edge of the woods burying their comrades, just to get them out of sight. Around a shell-hole, half full of brown water, another group knelt with safety razors, making a woebegone effort to clean up and feel less lousy and less forgotten of God. Once a squadron of American planes in V formation roared over us toward the front, but from above, from nowhere, dropped an enemy squadron. The sky was littered with dog-fights. One American plane after another burst into flames and corkscrewed down, screaming like a siren in anguish, while the victors re-formed and darted proudly homeward. You could almost see them wag their tails.

But it was all unreal, like a slow-motion nightmare, and unreal incidents kept happening. You would see a regiment in extended formation, wide space between each two men, and from the look of them you couldn't tell what outfit they were, the 147th or the 148th or some unknown brown army from another planet. They marched stiffly down the slope in front of us and up the bare wide hillside to the lighter east. As they reached the crest each man against the sky became a giant twenty feet tall. They would seem to linger without stopping in the silver light of the top, still giants, and suddenly disappear down the farther slope. In the top of your brain you knew it wasn't true, they were only our men going into action against the brighter skyline, but in your darker deeper brain you noted the miracle and cringed.

That was the hill-crest where the best-known man in the division lay (for the roads crossed there), only he wasn't a man. I saw the thing as I passed with the General and, not recognizing it, went back and poked with my stick. It was a torso, a big one, without arms or legs or head, its lower part obscenely naked, the rest dressed in a German officer's uniform. Under a sack lay the mess of his spare parts. It couldn't be real. If it was real, you'd scream or burst into tears or shoot somebody.

The Italian boy with the long ugly face and the enormous dark eyes, speechless from the shell-splinter in his back—he wasn't real as I leaned over him, and his eyes drew all the strength from his dying body into one stare's terrified question: "Am I going to die?"

It couldn't be real. Under the barrage that creature wrapped in white cerements from his waist up his body and over his face and head, who would rise from the shell-hole suddenly and wave his stiff arms—he was Lazarus. The sharp thin sound stabbing the roar of the shells— that wasn't the crack of a rifle, and the boy screaming: "What am I going to tell my papa? What am I going to tell my papa? I shot myself in the hand!"—that didn't happen, the red hole in his palm wasn't a bullet-hole, it was something else, perhaps the stigmata.

And I walking quietly under the rain of shells from one shell-hole to another saying: "Get your heads down. Keep under cover. Relief's coming up in a minute. Hold on," knowing I bore a charmed life and couldn't be hit, knowing everyone else would be killed, but not I, smiling to know I would sit down again in the sun-parlor at home with the summery wind blowing the fresh curtains and Mother serving me breakfast as she laughed and talked and the water clean and cold in the sweating glass—I wasn't real. When Colonel Galbreath cited me because I strolled up to him through the leaping geysers and called: "Pretty warm day, Colonel, but you can't stay here. Get back where you belong. You've no right to be here," he thought I was gaily self-possessed and efficient —but I wasn't even there, I was lying in the bottom of a dark well shaking with horror.

The other battles in which our division engaged varied in detail from the Argonne, but varied not at all in those essentials that concerned the pitiful creatures who did the killing and were killed. For them every battle was merely strain and keeping on in spite of strain, merely fear and fear overcome, horror and horror made casual. For them after the battle there was no exhilaration but only animal exhaustion. Each man had had his own little adventures, desperate and precious to him—I had mine—but they were less desperate and less precious to him than the adventures of his squad or his company or his division. To each man battle was horrible and innocent, despicable and divine, torture but so austere and exalted that it invested the lowliest rumpled, unshaven participant with a fierce dignity, an arrogant worth. Although you felt like a son-of-a-bitch, you knew you were a son of God. A battle is something you dread intolerably and for which you have always been homesick.

After the Argonne our division fought honorably on the Belgian fronts out from Ypres between the Scheldt and the Lys. I remember it all. But over and above more important events I remember one inconsequential morning because somehow it seemed a symbol or an allegory. I had gone through the town of Olsene afoot and alone, carrying a message to the 148th, which was attacking. I found the Colonel in the ticket office of an abandoned railway station. A gloomy room and gloomy soldiers gathered there, for things were going badly and the shells fell like slow large snowflakes. My message delivered, as I started on my return trip and stepped from the doorway, one of them crashed a few yards from me and ripped the belly from a friend of mine. They tended him, and I went on across the turnip fields alone. A young soldier with a smashed ankle hobbled up and asked for a drink of water. That cold feeling was in my stomach's pit. I reached the village of Olsene again, desolate and gray as an hour before. Its single street was straight, narrow, and cobblestoned; its small stone houses, touching one another, stood flush with the road, dripping wet, blank-faced. Now, though, the village was not unoccupied as I had left it. But it was as silent. The bodies of forty-two Americans, my comrades, lay on the cobblestones in two short parallel rows, one behind the other. Their guns were in their hands. Their packs were on their backs. They had not fired a shot. They were not yet cold. They lay in uncouth attitudes, though I saw no blood. They did not seem asleep, but frozen in some profound discomfort, their faces yellow-green and strangely old. I walked between their short and sprawling rows and I was afraid. I wanted to run, to hide in a house, to escape this unending nightmare. Then the shelling began. It watered the road I was walking. The shells fell thickest ahead, near the crossroads I had to pass. The cold was now in my throat. I must not run, even to get by the crossroads. There was no one anywhere, but the shells kept falling ahead, they were finding the range of the crossroads. At last I reached them. I would soon be past and safe. I wanted to break into a run and not be left battered and nasty on the naked cobblestones. I was halfway across. And I stopped. There in the very middle, sitting on the ground with a broken telephone wire across his lap, a kit of tools by his side, busy with his task, was a single doughboy. No officer was near, no buddy was helping him. But about him the shells were falling and they gouged the shaking earth. I paused by him and said: "Hey, buddy, you've got pretty good nerve." He looked up, dirty, hard-boiled, absorbed: "Hell, somebody had to do it." And I went on, ashamed, knowing we were gods.

The matter which with the least decency you could have written home about would have been how we really felt that day when war stopped. In the tender aimless sunshine, in the incredible silence, we roamed the little town singly, like drifting shades. The physical relief, the absence of apprehension, brimmed us with ease and thanksgiving, but for each of us our bliss and serenity were only the superstructure over a hidden tide of desolation and despair. Each of us was repeating to himself in his own dim words something I heard crying out in me:

"It's over, the only great thing you were ever part of. It's over, the only heroic thing we all did together. What can you do now? Nothing, nothing. You can't go back to the old petty things without purpose, direction, or unity—defending the railroad for killing a cow, drawing deeds of trust, suing someone for money, coping again, all over, with that bright rascal who rehearses his witnesses. You can't go on with that kind of thing till you die."

That short period of my life spent in the line is the only one I remember step by step—as if it moved *sub specie æternitatis*. Not that I enjoyed it; I hated it. Not that I was fitted for it by temperament or ability, I was desperately unfitted; but it, somehow, had meaning, and daily life hasn't: it was part of a common endeavor, and daily life is isolated and lonely.

On my way home I landed in New York and found Mother and Father at the dock waiting for me. I had on a rakish overseas cap, a snappy uniform with Sam Browne belt, gold service stripes on the cuffs, a captain's silver bars on the shoulders, and on the breast a Croix de Guerre with a gold and a silver star. They were so happy, so filled with pride and thanksgiving, it was embarrassing. I tried, too, to be glad and proud and thankful, but I have never before or since felt so incapable of emotion, so dead inside. A chapter was ended which had been written in capital letters of red and purple with Gothic curlicues of gold, but ahead lay other chapters, and I knew they were written in fine black print, too small to read without glasses, preferably rose-colored ones. It was as if in the midst of a reading from Homer you turned the page and your eye met the society column of the *Daily Democrat.*

# CHAPTER XVIII

# *The Ku Klux Klan Comes and Goes*

Gervys Lusk left home a wastrel and returned a hero; he departed with a black eye and came back with a D.S.C. During that spiritual interregnum when both of us were fumbling to become good citizens (an undertaking in which he was entirely successful) Gervys confided to me that the home town had felt distinctly let down when I returned from the wars intact. It reasoned that not having been outstandingly useful—"indispensable" would have been Major Jones's adjective—I could have afforded to be ornamental by making "the supreme sacrifice." I was cast for the role—a poet (so they had heard), young (at least youngish), slender (thin, in moments of non-exaltation). It seemed churlish of me not to have seized the opportunity. I felt rather the same way about it, now that the opportunity was safely out of hand.

My destiny apparently is to pick up the pieces and start over. A lame start it was in 1919. I spent the first few months tinkering with the manuscript of *In April Once* and almost ruined it—April was over; I made numerous speeches over the state for something like the Second Liberty Loan;

for six months I again taught at Sewanee, and would probably be teaching there now had not one or two of the digni-
taries questioned my papist affiliations. Briefly I did a deal
of floundering before I could settle down all over again to
living, mere living.

During that period I evidently did some thinking about
our Southern race problem because I recently came across
this letter addressed to the *New Republic* (though of
course never published nor acknowledged):

*Sewanee, Tennessee*
*September 6, 1919*

*The New Republic*
*New York City*
*Sirs:*

Your intellectual fearlessness and sincerity prompt me to
write you regarding the recent outbreak of lawlessness in
Knoxville, Tennessee, which the newspapers have delighted
to call a "race riot." I am an average educated Southerner
and I want to give you the point of view of my class. The
Northern press will doubtless see in this occurrence merely
another instance of what it imagines to be the South's hostility and cruelty to the Negro, its inability to deal justly
with him without Northern interference. But the moral is
not so stereotyped. Viewed in its true relations, the Knoxville outrage is indicative of a situation more complex, and
full of pathos, and difficult of adjustment, than any our well-
meaning Northern friends conceive. This was no race riot.
It was a burst of hoodlumism which protected itself under
the local excitement and indignation at a ghastly and terrifying crime committed by a Negro.

It is clear from the newspaper reports that the mob at
first made no attack on the Negroes, but turned against the
jail from which they knew the Negro they wanted had been
taken. The jail was wrecked, the criminals within released,

jail records and property destroyed or stolen, and finally the house of the sheriff, who at that time was on his way to Chattanooga with the prisoner, ransacked and rifled. Hardware stores were next broken into for ammunition and arms. Thereafter conflicts between these hoodlums and terrified blacks were inevitable. A good Southerner considers this incident, as does any other good American, a national disgrace.

You in the North always assume there are two attitudes toward the race question—one pre-empted by the enlightened benign citizen of Northern birth, the other peculiar to the narrow heartless citizen of Southern birth. There is no such difference. I live in the Mississippi Delta, where a full half of the white population, outnumbered ten to one by the Negro population, is Northern by birth and rearing. Yet the attitude of that one half differs in no wise from the attitude of the other half born and bred in the South. Under similar conditions, and it matters not where those conditions arise, it may be Chicago, South Africa, Washington, or Knoxville, white men of Anglo-Saxon descent, whether Northern or Southern born, act in precisely the same way toward the Negro. Inhabitants of Maine, and France and Finland, can afford to toy mentally with the race problem and the theories they arrive at may be widely divergent. But among white men for whom the problem is a bitter and pressing fact, who live with it, there is no difference of opinion as to the problem's solution, based on difference of place of birth or of education. There is only a difference on this as on all questions between those Southerners who through poverty, lack of inheritance, and ignorance misunderstand and dislike the Negro, and those who by training and opportunity feel themselves his friend and protector.

Here are the two questions, or rather the two phases of

one question, with which we live: first, how best to protect and educate and deal fairly with a race which at its present stage of development is inferior in character and intellect to our own (this is the phase of the question in which the North is perennially interested); second, how best to develop so upright a character in our own people that they will resist the ever present temptation to prey and batten on this inferior race (this is the phase of the question in which the North is never interested, of which indeed it is hardly cognizant). To solve these questions in wisdom, justice, and kindness is difficult under any circumstances, but there are thousands of unadvertised leaders of thought in the South capable of working out such a solution if left to themselves —not quickly nor easily, but through the years. And they are the only people who can: it is their problem, their burden, their heavy heritage.

And the Knoxville crime illustrates the strongest force against which these leaders have to fight; to wit, the lawlessness and hoodlumism of our uneducated whites. The same force at work in politics produces vicious unworthy Southern governors and congressmen. Our fight to protect the Negro is merely part of our fight for decency in politics, for law-enforcement. The fight is often lost, but it never ceases; indeed, it gains in strength and in the end it is certain of victory.

You will wonder perhaps why I am telling you our troubles. My reason is quite simple: I want you to know why it is that we whose hearts are essentially as yours in this matter fear unjust criticism, unwise advice from the North. It makes a good Southerner's task only the harder. We could afford to be indifferent to your misunderstanding were it not that the inflammable, uneducated whites whom the best part of our lives is spent in controlling and teaching seize on the indiscreet utterances and unmerited strictures of the

Northern press as excuses for their own excesses and injustices. Nor is the effect on the Negro himself less deplorable. Doing no good in themselves, these utterances and strictures greatly lessen our force for good.

To you our tragic situation, calling for courage and wisdom and unselfishness and patience, is a theory, a subject for criticism, suggested panaceas, scorn. We know the solution, the only one; for there is no short cut. It is in the first place education for the whites and in the second education, simple and practical, for the Negro. For the rest common kindness must be the guide in this as in all human affairs. My plea to you is that you trust us who are fighting the fight in the South, and that you accept my assurance we are not a corporal's guard.

Respectfully yours,
W. A. Percy

I drag in this communication because after twenty years it still seems to me to point out the South's two major deficiencies—character and education—which, after all, are world deficiencies, and to indicate the lines along which the "solution" of our race problem must proceed. Of course the letter expresses the Southern point of view of a so-called conservative, which is deplored to the point of tears by the so-called liberals. There's an enduring quality to truth exceedingly irritating to fidgety minds. In the South our anxiety is not to find new ideas, but to bring to realization old ones which have been tested and proved by years of anguish—a far more difficult undertaking. We Southerners aren't as bright as we are right. But when we do hit on a new idea, it's not only wrong, it's inconceivable.

The years following the war were a time of confusion not only to ex-soldiers but to all Americans. The tension of high endeavor and unselfish effort snapped, and Americans went "ornery." In the South the most vital matter became the price of cotton, in the North the price of commodities. Idealism was followed by the grossest materialism, which continues to be the order of the day.

Our town of about ten thousand population was no better or worse, I imagine, than other little Southern towns. My townsfolk had got along pretty well together—we knew each other so well and had suffered so much together. But we hadn't suffered a common disaster, one that was local and our very own, like a flood or a yellow-fever epidemic, since the flood of 1913, and that had failed as a binder because it didn't flood the town. Unbeknownst, strangers had drifted in since the war—from the hills, from the North, from all sorts of odd places where they hadn't succeeded or hadn't been wanted. We had changed our country attractively for them. Malaria had been about stamped out; electric fans and ice had lessened the terror of our intolerable summer heat; we had good roads and drainage and schools, and our lands were the most fertile in the world. We had made the Delta a good place in which to live by our determination and our ability to endure hardships, and now other folks were attracted by the result of our efforts. The town was changing, but so insidiously that the old-timers could feel but could not analyze the change. The newcomers weren't foreigners or Jews, they were an alien breed of Anglo-Saxon.

Although I was always traveling to strange places, I loved Greenville and never wanted any other place for home. Returning to it was the most exciting part of a trip. You could find friendly idlers round the post-office steps pretending they were waiting for the mail. You could take a coke any time of day with someone full of important news. There'd be amiable people running in and out of the house, without knocking, for tennis or golf or bridge or poker or to join you at a meal or just to talk. It was a lovable town

I suppose the trait that distinguished it from neighboring towns was a certain laxity in church matters. We didn't regard drunkenness and lechery, Sabbath-breaking and gambling as more than poor judgment or poor taste. What we were slow to forgive was hardness of heart and all unkindness. Perhaps we were overstocked with sinners and pariahs and publicans, but they kept the churches in their places and preserved the tradition of sprightliness. Of course we had church folk, plenty of them—Episcopalians, not numerous but up-stage, whose forebears came from Virginia, Kentucky, or South Carolina; Catholics from Italy or Ireland or New Orleans; Methodists, indigenous and prolific; Baptists, who loved Methodists less but Catholics least, swarms of them; Presbyterians, not directly from Geneva or Edinburgh, but aged in the wood, fairly mellow considering they were predestined; and Jews too much like natives even to be overly prosperous. There were bickerings and fights during election time, but day in and day out we were pretty cozy and neighborly, and nobody cared what to hell was the other fellow's route to heaven. There was no embattled aristocracy, for the descendants of the old-timers were already a rather seedy remnant, and there was no wealth. White folks and colored folks—that's what we were—and some of us were nice and some weren't.

I never thought of Masons. Most of my friends wore aprons at funerals and fezzes (over vine leaves) at knightly convocations. Even Père had been a Mason, to the scandal of the Church and the curtailment of his last rites, but he took it easy. I thought Masonry a good thing for those who liked that sort of thing.

We had read in the newspapers that over in Atlanta some fraud was claiming to have revived the old Ku Klux Klan which during reconstruction days had played so desperate but on the whole so helpful a part in keeping the peace and preventing mob violence. This Atlanta monstrosity was not even a bastard of the old organization which General Forrest had headed and disbanded. This thing obviously was a money-making scheme without ideals or ideas. We were amused and uninterested. Even in Forrest's day the Klan had never been permitted to enter our county. It couldn't happen here. But reports of the Atlanta organization's misdeeds—masked night parades to terrorize the Negro, threatening letters, forcible closing of dance-halls and dives, whippings, kidnappings, violent brutalities—crowded the headlines. As citizens of the South we were ashamed; as citizens of Greenville we were not apprehensive.

Then in the spring of 1922 a "Colonel" Camp was advertised to speak in our courthouse for the purpose of forming a branch of the Klan in Greenville. Thoroughly aroused, we debated whether to permit the speech in the courthouse or to answer it there. We couldn't learn who had invited him to speak or who had given him permission to use the courthouse, but evidently some of our own people were already Klansmen—fifth-column tactic before there was a Hitler. Our best citizens, those who thought for the common good, met in Father's office and agreed almost unanimously that the Colonel should be answered and by Father.

The Klan organizer made an artful speech to a tense crowd that packed every cranny of the room; and every man was armed. Who killed Garfield? A Catholic. Who assassinated President McKinley? A Catholic. Who had recently bought a huge tract of land opposite West Point and another overlooking Washington? The Pope. Convents were brothels, the confessional a place of seduction, the basement of every Catholic church an arsenal. The Pope was about to seize the government. To the rescue, Klansmen! These were statements which any trained mind recognized as lies, but which no man without weeks of ridiculous research could disprove. It was an example of Nazi propaganda before there were Nazis. The very enormity and insolence of the lie carried conviction to the simple and the credulous. The Colonel was listened to with courtesy.

To his surprise, Father answered him: he had never been answered before. I have never heard a speech that was so exciting and so much fun. The crowd rocked and cheered. Father's ridicule was amusing but bitter; and as he continued, it became more bitter, until it wasn't funny, it was terrifying. And the Colonel was terrified: he expected to be torn limb from limb by the mob. I don't blame him. At the close of Father's speech the crowd went quite mad, surging about, shouting and cheering, and thoroughly dangerous. A resolution was passed condemning the Klan. Colonel Camp scuttled out of a side door, appealing to a passing deputy for protection. The deputy, an Irish Catholic and the kindliest of men (out of *Henry IV*), escorted him ceremoniously to his hotel.

It was a triumphant meeting, but for the next two years our town was disintegrated by a bloodless, cruel warfare, more bitter and unforgiving than anything I encountered at the front. In the trenches soldiers felt sorry for one another, whether friend or enemy. In Father's senatorial fight, we were surrounded by ferocious stupidity rather than by hatred. But in the Klan fight the very spirit of hatred materialized before our eyes. It was the ugliest thing I have ever beheld. You didn't linger on the post-office steps or drink cokes with random companions: too many faces were hard and set, too many eyes were baleful and venomous. You couldn't go a block without learning by a glance that someone hated you.

The Klan did not stand for, but against. It stood against

Catholics, Jews, Negroes, foreigners, and sin. In our town it chose Catholics as the object of its chief persecution. Catholic employees were fired, Catholic businessmen were boycotted, Catholic office-holders opposed. At first this seemed strange to me, because our Catholics were a small and obscure minority, but I came to learn with astonishment that of all the things hated in the South, more hated than the Jew or the Negro or sin itself, is Rome. The evangelical sects and Rome—as different and uncomprehending of each other as youth and old age! One seems never to have glimpsed the sorrowful pageant of the race and the other, profoundly disillusioned, profoundly compassionate, sees only the pageant. One has the enthusiasm and ignorance of the pioneer, the other the despair of the sage. One's a cheer-leader, the other an old sad-eyed family doctor from Samaria. We discovered that the Klan had its genesis, as far as our community was involved, in the Masonic Temple. The state head of that fraternal organization, a well-meaning old simpleton, had been preaching anti-Catholicism for years when conferring Masonic degrees. He joined the Klan early and induced other Masonic leaders to follow his example. These composed the Klan leadership in our county, though they were aided by a few politicians who knew better but who craved the Klan vote. It was a pretty leadership—fanatics and scalawag politicians. But not all Masons or all the godly were so misguided. The opposition to the Klan at home was led by a Protestant committee (and every denomination was represented in its ranks), who fought fearlessly, intelligently, and unceasingly this evil which they considered as unchristian as it was un-American. Father was not only head of the Protestant anti-Klan committee but of the anti-Klan forces in the South. He spoke as far north as Chicago and published probably the first article on the Klan in any distinguished magazine. It was reprinted from the *Atlantic Monthly* and distributed over the whole country. He felt the Klan was the sort of public evil good citizens could not ignore. Not to fight it was ineffectual and craven.

It's hard to conceive of the mumbo-jumbo ritual of the Klan and its half-wit principles—only less absurd than the Nazi principles of Aryan superiority and lebensraum—as worthy of an adult mind's attention. But when your living, your self-respect, and your life are threatened, you don't laugh at that which threatens. If you have either sense or courage you fight it. We fought, and it was high time someone did.

The Klan's increasing atrocities culminated in the brutal murders at Mer Rouge, where Skipwith was Cyclops. Mer Rouge is across the river from us, on the Louisiana side. It is very near and the murders were very ghastly. The Klan loathed and feared Father more than any other man in the South. For months I never let him out of my sight and of course we both went armed. Never before nor since have our doors been shut and locked at night.

One Sunday night of torrential rain when Father, Aunt Lady, and I sat in the library and Mother was ill upstairs I answered a knock at the door. It was early and I opened the door without apprehension. A dark, heavy-set man with two days' growth of beard and a soft-brimmed black hat stood there, drenched to the skin. He asked for Father and I, to his obvious surprise, invited him in. He wouldn't put down his hat, but held it in front of him. I didn't like his looks, so while Father talked to him I played the piano softly in the adjoining room and listened. The man's story was that he came from near our plantation, his car had run out of gas a few miles from town, he'd left his sister in the car and walked to town, he couldn't find a service station open, and would Father help him? Father, all sympathy, started phoning. The stranger seemed neither interested nor appreciative. I watched him with mounting suspicion. Father's effort to find a service station open having failed, he said: "My car is here. We might run out and get your sister—I suppose you can drive my car?" The stranger brightened and observed he could drive any make of car. The two of them were still near the phone when Father's three bridge cronies came stamping in, laughing and shaking out the rain. As they came toward Father, the stranger brushed past them and had reached the door when I overtook him. "Say, what's the matter with you?" I asked. "Wait a minute and some of us will get you fixed up." He mumbled: "Got to take a leak," walked into the rain, and disappeared.

We waited for him, but we did not see him again for two years. Then he was in jail charged with a string of robberies. When he saw I recognized him, he grinned sourly and remarked: "Old Skip nearly put that one over." He refused to enlarge on this statement, which presumably referred to Skipwith, Cyclops of Mer Rouge. We found from the neighbors that the night of his visit to us he had arrived in a car with another man and parked across the street from our house.

It looked too much like an attempt at kidnapping and murder for me to feel easy. I went to the office of the local Cyclops. He was an inoffensive little man, a great Mason, and partial to anti-Catholic tirades. I said: "I want to let you know one thing: if anything happens to my Father or to any of our friends you will be killed. We won't hunt for the guilty party. So far as we are concerned the guilty party will be you."

There were no atrocities, no whippings, no threatening letters, no masked parades in our town. The local Klan bent all of its efforts toward electing one of its members sheriff.

If they could have the law-enforcement machinery under their control, they could then flout the law and perpetrate such outrages as appealed to them. Our fight became a political fight to prevent the election of the Klan's choice for sheriff. The whole town was involved and the excitement was at fever heat. What appalled and terrified us most was the mendacity of Klan members. You never knew if the man you were talking to was a Klansman and a spy. Like German parachute jumpers, they appeared disguised as friends. For the Klan advised its members to lie about their affiliation with the order, about anything that concerned another Klansman's welfare, and about anything pertaining to the Klan—and its members took the advice. The most poisonous thing the Klan did to our town was to rob its citizens of their faith and trust in one another. Everyone was under suspicion: from Klansmen you could expect neither frankness nor truth nor honor, and you couldn't tell who was a Klansman. If they were elected judges and law-enforcement officers, we would be cornered into servility or assassination.

Our candidate for sheriff was George B. Alexander, a powerful, square-bearded, Kentucky aristocrat drawn by Holbein. He was one of those people who are always right by no discernible mental process. His fearlessness, warm-heartedness, and sheer character made him a person you liked to be with and for. He was Father's favorite hunting companion and friend.

On election night the town was beside itself with excitement. Crowds filled the streets outside the voting booths to hear the counting of the ballots as it progressed. Everyone realized the race was close and whoever won would win by the narrowest of margins. The whole population was in the street, milling, apprehensive, silent. When the count began, Father went home and started a bridge game. I waited at the polls. About nine o'clock a sweating individual with his collar unbuttoned and his wide red face smeared with tears rushed out on the steps and bellowed: "We've won, we've won! Alexander's elected! God damn the Klan!" Pandemonium broke loose. Men yelled and screamed and hugged one another. Our town was saved, we had whipped the Klan and were safe. I ran home with the news and Father's bridge game broke up in a stillness of thanksgiving that was almost religious.

Mother was away. Being a Frenchwoman, she had been neither hysterical nor sentimental during the months and months of tension and danger. But none of us knew what she went through silently and it was then her health began to fail.

While we were talking about the victory, a tremendous uproar came to us from the street. We rushed out on the gallery. From curb to curb the street was filled with a mad marching crowd carrying torches and singing. They swarmed down the street and into our yard. It was a victory celebration. Father made a speech, everybody made a speech, nobody listened and everybody cheered. Klansmen had taken to cover, but the rest of the town was there, seething over the yard and onto the gallery. They cut Mr. Alexander's necktie to bits for souvenirs. And still they cheered and swarmed.

Father, nonplussed, turned to Adah and me and laughed: "They don't seem to have any idea of going home and I haven't a drop of whisky in the house—at least, I'm not going to waste my *good* liquor on them." Adah and Charlie dashed off in their car and returned with four kegs. Father called to the crowd: "Come on in, boys," and into the house they poured. That was a party never to be forgotten. While Adah was gone, Lucille and her band appeared, unsummoned save by instinct. Lucille, weighing twenty stone, airily pulled the grand piano into her lap, struck one tremendous chord—my Steinway's been swayback ever since—and the dancing began. Adah never touches a drop, but she mixes a mighty punch. Things got under way. There were few inhibitions and no social distinctions. Dancers bumped into knots of heroes who told one another at the same time their harrowing exploits and unforgettable adventures. A banker's wife hobnobbed with the hot-tamale man, a lawyer's careened with a bootlegger. People who hadn't spoken for years swore deathless loyalty on one another's shoulders. The little town had come through, righteousness had prevailed, we had fought the good fight and for once had won. Everybody was affectionate with everybody else, all men were equal, and all were brothers-in-arms.

Hazlewood, the gentlest and most courageous of men, kept on making speeches from the front gallery long after his audience had adjourned to the dining-room and were gyrating like flies around Adah. He was so mortified at this treatment (when it came to his attention) that he joined them and was consoled and liberally refreshed. When at a late hour he started to leave, he couldn't find his hat and became whimpery. After discovering it under the radiator, he couldn't pick it up. When he was hatted at last and started on his way, Fletcher met him on the steps, gasped: "Oh, Hazlewood!" and kissed him. Hazlewood exclaimed: "Fletch, Fletch, you shouldn't have done that," burst into tears, and walked home down the middle of the street, sobbing bitterly.

From down Lake Washington way the swarthy tribe of Steins journeyed in, all seven of them, one behind another, the old man, broad-shouldered, arrogant, and goateed, leading the advance through the side door. You felt certain they'd left a tent and a string of camels under the porte-cochere. Solemnly they shook hands with everyone down the line, curved into the dining-room around the punch bowl, shook hands again, told everyone good-night, and left through the front door. We had barely recovered from this princely visitation when they again hove into view through the side door, went through the same exchange of courtesies, pausing a bit longer at the punch bowl, and disappeared out the front door. All during the evening, just about time you were getting settled in your mind, this apparition of a Tartar tribe would materialize, unhinge you, and withdraw, always with decorum but with mounting elation. The last time I expected them to produce cymbals and go to it, but instead Mrs. Stein staged a thrilling fandango with Mr. George B.

Old man Finch, bolt upright in a throne-like chair, fell sound asleep in the very center of the revelry. Well-wishers bore him to a car, drove him home, and deposited him with the greatest tact in the swing on his own front gallery. Later he fell off and cut his forehead. Wakened by the bump, his daughters swarmed out, found him unconscious and bathed in blood, summoned half the doctors in town, and went to keening. Next morning Louise telephoned asking if I'd found Papa's teeth. I'm afraid another guest wore them off.

Long after midnight I looked into the pantry and beheld my favorite barber, a plumber acquaintance, an ex-sergeant, and the hot-tamale man seated at the pantry table eating supper. They'd raided the ice-box and found besides a bottle of liquor. They graciously invited me to join them. Instead I routed out my husky soldier friend, Howard Shields, and admonished him to get those people out of the house, one way or another. Howard bowed stiffly and answered: "Certainly, leave it to me." A bit later I again looked into the pantry; Howard was standing with a glass full of straight whisky in his hand making an undisciplined speech about the virtues of his squad. His four listeners beamed foolishly. One of them managed to observe: "Didn't know Howard waised squabs," and went off into giggles, then into hiccups, then into tears. I addressed Howard sternly: "Go to bed," and he disappeared upstairs. On the way to my room I looked in on him: he was sound asleep. Actually, he hadn't taken off a stitch, he was lying under the sheet fully clothed and anticipating my inspection. The coast being clear, he slipped out, found his buddy, George Crittenden, knocked him cold, and lit out in his car for Clarksdale.

It was a memorable evening. On the way home people fell off bicycles and into gutters, ran over street signs and up trees—and all happy (except Hazlewood). The police radiantly gathered them up and located their destinations.

We decided it was just as well, after all, that Mother had been out of town. It wasn't her sort of party. She'd have started clearing the house at the first drunk, victory or no victory.

Our Ku Klux neighbors stood on their porch watching—justified and prophesying Judgment Day.

It had been a great fight. It was also a ruthless searchlight on character, of one kind or another. My generation still remembers it, though it all happened eighteen or nineteen years ago, and that's a century of any other time. An old Klansman, one who, being educated, had no excuse for being one, asked me the other day why I'd never forgiven him. I had to answer: "Forgiveness is easy. I really like you. The trouble is I've got your number and people's numbers don't change."

# CHAPTER XIX

# *Hell and High Water*

Forty-seven years ago—to be accurate, on May 13, 1893—the Greenville *Democrat* carried this appeal:

ON GUARD—This week guard duty has been continued, and the need of it, we may briefly tell thus: As long as there is a foot of water against our levees there is danger.

The Levee Board has done well, and at the approach of high water of this year they could say with a confidence, never possessed before, "We turn over to you earth works sufficient to withstand the strain of any previous flood and ask you as citizens to guard them from unforeseen foes."

To refuse or neglect to do your individual duty proclaims you wanting in those characteristics which would prove your patriotism in a time when your country is threatened. . . .

Capt. LeRoy Percy relieved Capt. Alexander at Camp Cousens and now has charge with J. H. Wynn, Alf H. Stone, Van B. Boddie, H. T. Ireys, Jr., A. Lewenthall, David Stone, Harvey Miller and Edgar Baker.

The levee at Camp Cousens, which Father's guard protected in 1893, was about four feet high, had been built

by Irishmen with wheelbarrows and paid for by local taxa-
tion; it always broke. The levee of today is forty feet high,
has been built by caterpillars and drag lines and paid for
by the United States government; it sometimes breaks.
The old guards were volunteers; guards nowadays are
hired by the Levee Board.

The new levee is stronger, but the old guards—well, perhaps I exaggerate their excellences, but to me their names
are innocent and idolized and more familiar than those of
my fellow Rotarians I lunch with every Thursday. All of
them except two are dead. When they were doing their
turn at guard duty they were undistinguished citizens of
the countryside, but the roster of the dead includes a captain in the Spanish-American War, a circuit judge, a leader
in the state legislature, two sheriffs, a distinguished Cin-
cinnati attorney, and a United States Senator. Of the living, one is a Major General in the United States Army, and
Mr. Alf, of course, is not only an author and an ex-president of the National Tax Association, but the most trusted
and beloved public citizen in the state. Guard duty or
something in the Delta way of life must have made men
strong in those days or else they came of strong stock.

I asked Mr. Alf the other day if he remembered old
Camp Cousens and, as I expected, he remembered it all, in
detail. While off duty the guards played freeze-out poker
for licks administered by the winner with Mr. Cousens's
broad, water-soaked razor strop to the squinched posterior
of the loser as he bent miserably over a log. No winner
ever stayed his arm because of friendship or compassion.
The game was gay and brutal. Hotspur and the heroes
beneath Troy would have joined it and have been com-
panionable in that company. It attracted participants from
the whole neighborhood. One planter, affable and tipsy,
rode up on his fine five-hundred-dollar mare as the players

were recovering from the last game in a swim. Without dismounting he whipped his snorting mount into the thick of the swimmers, roaring out the while: "Gotta head like a fish and a tail like a man. I'm a mare-maid." Evidently the Delta gentry of fifty years ago were not effete or decadent. I like to hear about them—theirs was such a magnificent male combination of gentleman and pioneer—but I doubt if I should have been at ease living among them. They were a bit too lusty and robustious; that good rough streak of Rabelais in them was unfortunately omitted from my make-up.

The low levees of 1893, ineffectual as they were to keep the Mississippi off the cotton fields, themselves had certain real advantages. When they broke, the water trickled in gradually, stood quietly over the land two or three weeks, deposited a fine nutritious layer of sediment, and withdrew without having drowned anybody or wrecked any buildings or prevented a late planting of the crop. You called that an overflow. Our great dikes of to-day, when once breached, hurl a roaring wall of water over the country, so swift, so deep, so long-lasting, it scours the top soil from the fields, destroys everything in its path, prevents crop-planting that year, and scatters death among the humble, always unprepared and unwary.

My first overflow I recall as a very jolly affair. In town the water was only two or three feet deep and by picket fences and floating board-walks you could climb and slither from the north end of Walnut Street, where the levee now stands, to Washington Avenue, where Rattlesnake Bayou once ran. Crawfishing was super-excellent, and if you fell in, it was adventure enough for a lifetime.

It must have been during this overflow that Father permitted me to go with him in a skiff from Greenville to the old Percy plantation ten miles to the east, where stands now the town of Leland. Overflow water is depressingly brown, the glare was terrible, and from trees and bushes hung snakes, which I loathed and which loved to fall into boats. I was utterly bored and despondent. Sitting in the bow I sought refuge from the dreary present in the thrilling pages of *The Last of the Mohicans.* Father was disgusted with me: here I was mid-stage in drama and romance and I preferred reading about them! I sensed distinctly he wanted to box my ears, but I kept on reading. He was diverted by sight of the old Hood house, forlorn in the watery desolation. When we toured the county together, he could never resist talking about the old times and he repopulated it with the rash amazing folk by whom it had been settled. His were often rip-snorting yarns of killings and poker games and duels, more thrilling than any Western and not unlike them. But this time he was merely laughing at his recollection of Major Hood.

A testy old gentleman who lived a few miles from the Major had named his plantation Ararat because, situated on the high banks of Deer Creek, it had never been overflowed. They were great friends though rarely on speaking terms. During an unprecedentedly high water in which even Ararat had gone under, Major Hood rowed over to the house, where his old crony was sitting in a rocking-chair on his veranda, comforting himself with a long toddy as he scanned venomously the surrounding waste of water. Without getting out of his skiff the Major drew alongside and snickered maliciously: "Ararat?" (only he pronounced it "Arry-rat"). "Should have called it 'Nary-rat.'" Without another word he rowed home, leaving his old friend apoplectic. For months they never spoke; then the master of Ararat dropped over to call on the Major and they went off together on a famous jamboree.

Now a battlement of levees extends for a thousand miles

on each side of the river from Memphis to New Orleans, without break in the battlement except where the hills crowd down to the bank for a glimpse of the old yellow snake or where tributaries like the Arkansas, the White, the Yazoo, and the Red join it with their own mighty contents. It towers forty feet above the country it protects and its sloping thickness is a hundred feet wide at the base.

All of us who grew up in the Delta have had experience aplenty in guard duty, or "walking the levee," as we call it. The earliest reason given for this custom was the fear that folks from the other side of the river would sneak over in a dugout and dynamite our levees in order to relieve the pressure on theirs. I doubt if anyone on either side ever attempted such a crime, but, the tradition having been established, armed citizens must guard the levee all night, listen for marauders in the willows, and shoot to kill. A soberer reason for the custom was to discover weak spots in the levee, particularly "boils."

A boil is a small geyser at the base or on the berm of the levee, on the land side, of course. It is caused by the river's pressure fingering out some soft stratum in the soil of the levee or by a crawfish hole. If the geyser runs clear, it is being filtered and is comparatively harmless; but if it runs muddy, it is in direct contact with the river and you'd better shoot your pistol, yowl to the next guard, and do something quick. What you do, if you have the gumption of a catfish, is build with sacks of earth a little "run-around"— that is, a small levee around the geyser to the height of its jet. That stabilizes the pressure, and the boil is safe, but should be flagged and watched. The levee generally breaks from boils enlarging themselves and not from the river running over the top.

So during every high-water scare Delta citizens walk the levee all night with pistol and lantern, nowadays with flash-light. If you won't volunteer for that duty, you should return to the hills from which obviously you came. If a guard gets lonesome he may gig a frog, whose croaking makes everything lonesomer, or take a little drink. During these times the river is a savage clawing thing, right at the top of the levee and sounding at night like the swish of a sword or the snarl of a beast. It puts ice in your heart when you're trudging the darkness on the slippery berm and hoping not to step on a snake. Each guard walks alone, and the tiny halo of his lantern makes our fearful hearts stouter.

I'd done so much guard duty during the years that I gave myself a holiday in April 1927. The American Legion boys had taken over the job and were handling it conscientiously and efficiently. Besides, during the three rainy nights preceding the break, I was in a writer's tantrum, the remaining proofs of which are *Three April Nocturnes*. But all good men and true except me were at Scott, fifteen miles above town. There five thousand Negroes, innumerable army and Levee Board engineers, plantation-owners, managers, old-time high-water fighters were battling with sandbags and willow mats to save a weak section of the levee. It was cold and a steady rain fell, freezing the workers and softening the levee. The greatest flood in the history of the Mississippi was roaring south between levees that trembled when you walked on them. The workers knew the fight was well-nigh hopeless, but there was nothing else to do but fight. They knew that if they lost, terror and desolation and death would spread over the hundred miles of thickly populated country from Cleveland to Vicksburg, over the fifty miles from Greenville to Greenwood. In the glare of improvised flares and flood-lights they swarmed over the weak spot like ants over an invaded ant-hill. But about daylight, while the distraught engineers and labor bosses hurried and consulted and bawled commands, while the five thousand Negroes with croker sacks over their heads and hundred-pound sandbags on their shoulders trotted in long converging lines to the threatened point, the river pushed, and the great dike dissolved under their feet. The terrible wall of water like an imbecile blind Titan strode triumphantly into our country. The greatest flood in American history was upon us. We did not see our lands again for four months.

If the Lord was trying to cement us with disaster, He used a heavy trowel that night.

# CHAPTER XX

# The Flood of 1927

The 1927 flood was a torrent ten feet deep the size of Rhode Island; it was thirty-six hours coming and four months going; it was deep enough to drown a man, swift enough to upset a boat, and lasting enough to cancel a crop year. The only islands in it were eight or ten tiny Indian mounds and the narrow spoil-banks of a few drainage canals. Between the torrent and the river ran the levee, dry on the land side and on the top. The south Delta became seventy-five hundred square miles of mill-race in which one hundred and twenty thousand human beings and one hundred thousand animals squirmed and bobbed.

In the thirty-six hours which the river required after its victory at Scott to submerge the country, panicky people poured out of Greenville by the last trains and by automobiles over roads axle-deep in water. These were mostly frantic mothers with their children, non-residents from the hills who regarded the river hysterically and not devotedly, and the usual run of rabbit folk who absent themselves in every emergency. During the same hours of grace panicky people poured into Greenville. These were mostly Negroes in dilapidated Fords, on the running-boards of trucks, or afoot carrying babies, leading children, and pulling cows, who are always at their worst in crises. Outside of town stock was being rushed cross-country to the levee, and Negroes were being piled into lofts, gins, and compresses by plantation managers. For thirty-six hours the Delta was in turmoil, in movement, in terror. Then the waters covered everything, the turmoil ceased, and a great quiet settled down; the stock which had not reached the levee had been drowned; the owners of second-story houses with their pantries and kitchens had moved upstairs; those in one-story houses had taken to the roofs and the trees. Over everything was silence, deadlier because of the strange cold sound of the currents gnawing at foundations, hissing against walls, creaming and clawing over obstructions.

When at midnight the siren of the fire department by a long maniac scream announced to the sleepless town that the water had crowded over the town's own small protection levee, we knew the last haven of refuge had been lost. In each home the haggard family did its hysterical best to save itself and to provide for the morrow. Outside on the sidewalks you heard people running, not crying out or calling to one another, but running madly and silently to get to safety or to their loved ones. It was a sound that made you want to cry.

At home Mother, Father, and I had been waiting for that signal, like zero made audible. When it came we telephoned a few friends and then half-heartedly began dragging upstairs such furniture as we could manage and Father filled the bathtubs with water. No one knew how high the flood would rise. By breakfast time it had still not entered our neighborhood. We stood on the gallery and watched and waited. Then up the gutter of Percy Street we saw it gliding, like a wavering brown snake. It was swift and it made toward the river. It spread over a low place in the yard and covered Mother's blue larkspur. We said nothing, but suddenly Mother called the terrified little Negro chauffeur and jumped into the car. She had forgotten to buy an oil stove. Our protests were useless. She was in one of those intrepid moods when Frenchwomen had best not be crossed. Up the street a truck-driver was abandoning his truck and splashing wildly home through the water. It was three months before we saw it again. When Mother and the car reappeared, it was between two flanges of spray and hub-deep. Father looked somberly over the drowning town. I think he was realizing it was the last fight he would make for his people. He was sixty-seven and though unravaged by age he was tired. But he only said: "Guess you'd better go while you can. I'll be along." I waded to relief headquarters.

Our kindly old Mayor had appointed me chairman of the Flood Relief Committee and the local Red Cross. I found myself charged with the rescuing, housing, and feeding of sixty thousand human beings and thirty thousand head of stock. To assist me in the task I had a fine committee and Father's blessing, but no money, no boats, no tents, no food. That first morning when the water reached Greenville we of the committee traipsed through the mounting flood to the poker-rooms of the Knights of Columbus, hung out a sign labeled "Relief Headquarters," installed a telephone, and called on the Lord. That calling on the Lord was a good idea, for our first job was to get people out of trees and off of roofs, which, in addition to good will and heroism, of which we had plenty, required motor boats, of which we had none. We were desperate, but the Lord, overlooking our lack of faith, performed one of His witty, whimsical miracles: out of the White River poured a daring fleet of motor boats—the bootleggers! They shot the rapids of the break and scattered into the interior. No one had sent for them, no one was paying them, no one had a good word for them—but they came. Competent, devil-may-care pariahs, they scoured the back areas, the forgotten places, across fences, over railroad embankments, through woods and brush, and never rested until there was no one left clinging to a roof or a raft or the crotch of a tree.

The next problem up for immediate solution was how to stop the looting and burglarizing which had already begun. Without boats the small force of local law-enforcement officers was cooped up impotently in the courthouse and the police station. We telephoned the Governor and asked him to send us National Guards. They arrived, a gay, busy bunch, ably officered and inveterate saluters. With their breeches rolled up to their thighs and their cheeks and legs pink with cold, they splashed about through the icy water trying to look military and succeeding in looking like an army of Kewpies. But their mere presence restored and maintained order.

Our first acts, though in defiance of all law, were effective: we seized and manned all privately owned motor boats, skiffs, pleasure craft, wagons, and trucks (with these we had the nucleus of a transportation system); we confiscated all stocks of food and feed stuff in the local stores (with these, even beleaguered as we were, we shouldn't starve to death for the immediate present). However, for the indefinite future our need of money, tents, and motor boats was desperate. We sent out a nation-wide appeal. The response was immediate and on a grand scale. Friends from the North wired me ten thousand dollars, local citizens raised an equal amount, and through the Red Cross campaign, headed by Mr. Hoover, the people of America gave millions. Whenever you are just about to decide that Americans are selfish, unpatriotic, and unintelligent, they always prove themselves the most liberal and lovable people in the world. You simply can't stay disgusted with them. What a pity they are not disciplined enough to survive!

With Red Cross funds came the Red Cross personnel from Washington, trained, patient, and easy to work with.

Perhaps these early accomplishments of ours sound routine and inevitable, but in fact they taxed our ingenuity, our strength, and our judgment. At headquarters we slept three or four hours a night and, when not sleeping, lived in bedlam. It fell to my lot as chairman to make hundreds of decisions each day and the impossibility of investigation or second thought made every decision a snap judgment. Of necessity I became a dictator, and because the Red Cross controlled the food supplies and transportation I could enforce my orders. The responsibility didn't daunt me, but the consciousness that my judgments were often wrong was a continuing nightmare. If I had to be a despot I was very anxious to be a beneficent one.

At headquarters we couldn't have functioned except for the telephone. Our lives seemed to be one long conversation with Washington or Memphis or Vicksburg, while people seethed in and out of the office with every imaginable request, well-wishers from Biloxi to Memphis insisted on tendering their heroism personally and in detail, and the local phone gabbled like a half-wit:

From Miss Lou: "A man just turned over in front of my house; he nearly drowned and he is now on my front gallery. Send a motor boat for him right away." All boats are more fruitfully occupied. "Miss Lou, have you a man in the house?" "Will, you know I haven't." "Well, you need one, keep him."

From the hospital: "Get some anti-typhoid serum at once, by plane."

From the sheriff's office: "The five hundred darkies in this courthouse can't be fed and the place smells like a slaughter-pen. Get them out of here and up to the levee." How deep is the water between the courthouse and the levee? We have only two motor boats available. "Chippy" (my junior law partner, proper peewee size), "get them to the levee somehow." It was an inspiring sight to see him leading his black army in single file through the water, he spectacled like an owl, bald and chin-deep in the current, they trailing behind him, moaning and shuddering—a small heroic Moses for whom somebody had forgotten to part the waters.

From an unknown hysterical lady: "There's a dead hog on my back porch; come and get him quick."

From an exasperated committeeman: "Those rations for the Mound turned over in twenty feet of water. Must we let them have another load?"

From a bootlegger: "Ain't you got any mash for chickens? My chickens goin' ter starve."

From doctors' headquarters on the levee: "Another Negro baby has just been born. Mother says it's got to be named after you, but it's a girl. How about Wilhelmina instead?"

From Tommy: "Our wagon full of milk for those babies started floating and turned over. The horses were drowned, the milk-cans were lost, and the babies still need milk."

From an Avon committeeman: "The truck goin' down the levee with rations fell off in the river." "Did the driver drown?" "I forgot to ask." Something always happening at Avon—rations get stolen, committeemen fight and resign, and now their truck in the river!

Voice from the Alfalfa Mill, where four hundred Negroes are conglomerated: "A woman done died out here." (What a selfish time to die!) "All right, I'll send a boat out." Hours later the same voice: "That woman out here's still dead." "All right!" (Dying, with all we've got to do!) Next day the same voice tearfully: "If that woman stays here, us kaint." "Chippy, that wretched woman is still dead. Please do something about her." After three hours of battling currents Chippy returns, bustling and competent: "Everything's fixed. All we need's a shroud." Good God! I might just as well be asked for a Poiret model. I spied the sheet which covered a poker table. "Chippy, look! a perfect shroud." "Never had a better one," agreed Chippy sardonically, and disappeared with it. He supervised the rites in the river, but the Negroes maintained that such watery graves were what kept the river up.

Whatever we had accomplished, recklessly and chaotically, those first few days of the flood, one problem, the vital problem of our whole situation, had not been solved: how could we feed the whites and the blacks scattered broadcast through the town in second stories, in attics, in office buildings, mills, and hallways, in inconceivable nooks and crannies? We did not know who or where they were; they could not get to us and we could not get to them. Our problem was essentially a choice between mass feeding and evacuation. For the whites we chose evacuation. I issued an appeal very much in the nature of a command, I am afraid, for the old, the women, and the children to leave town and proceed by boat to Vicksburg. We begged the necessary boats and barges from the Standard Oil Company. They landed at the foot of Washington Avenue and blew a long blast to their prospective passengers as solemn and mandatory as Gabriel's trump. Everything that could float was mustered into service, and from the interior of the town to the levee the flotilla wobbled and ricocheted its way with its freightage of the old and ailing, women and children.

When they had reached the wharf there was a scene of desperate confusion: invalids on cots, old people, querulous and uncomfortable, whining children, addle-pated mothers, squalling babies, having been got to the levee with the utmost difficulty and with great reluctance on their part, tried suddenly to board the boats at the same time. Everybody was short of money, short of temper, short of reasonableness. They milled and stampeded. The space available on the boats was limited and reserved, but in the confusion there were able-bodied men who tried to slip on, pleading sickness or urgent business or what not. We turned them back. It was horrible to see them plead and to hear the crowd from the boats hiss and jeer them. Cowards are not numerous, but they generally manage to be wretchedly conspicuous.

Mother was not among those present. After issuing the evacuation order, I asked her if she was not going to co-operate with the chairman, who happened to be her son. She looked at me as if she had seen me for the first time and was not gladdened by the sight. A Gallic "Psct" of contempt made itself unmistakably audible and she announced: "Adah and I have no idea of leaving. I should like to know how you and LeRoy and Charlie could manage without us!" As the chairman had not envisaged such a calamity he withdrew with some hauteur but without dignity. Many of the older women, those who had seen floods come and go, were similarly disdainful and insubordinate.

What should we do with the Negroes: evacuate them in the same manner or feed them from centralized kitchens as the Belgians had been fed? There were seventy-five hundred of them. It was raining and unseasonably cold. They were clammy and hungry, finding shelter anywhere, sleeping on any floor, piled pell-mell in oil mills or squatting miserably on the windy levee. The levee itself was the only dry spot where they could be assembled or where tents by way of shelter could be set up for them. In spite of our repeated and frantic efforts we had been unable to procure a single tent. We feared disease and epidemics. Obviously for them, too, evacuation was the only solution. Therefore the Red Cross prepared them a camp in Vicksburg and procured two large steamers with barges. At last the innumerable details for their exodus were arranged and the steamers, belching black smoke, waited for them restlessly at the concrete wharf.

It was at this juncture that the Negroes announced they did not wish to leave and a group of planters, angry and mouthing, said they should not and could not leave. I was bursting with fury when Father overtook me on the levee. I explained the situation and he agreed I should not, of course, be intimidated by what the planters said, but he suggested that if we depopulated the Delta of its labor, we should be doing it a grave disservice. I insisted that I would not be bullied by a few blockhead planters into doing something I knew to be wrong—they were thinking of their pocketbooks; I of the Negroes' welfare. Father intimated it was a heavy decision, one I should not make alone. He suggested that I call into consultation the heads of all of my committees. I said they had been consulted and were of one mind: as we couldn't provide an adequate camp for the Negroes, we must evacuate them. Father urged that in fairness to everyone I should recanvass the situation and abide by the decision of my committee. Although nothing new had happened to cause them to change their minds, I promised Father I would call them for a last consultation that evening. The boats in the meantime were tied up and their captains were glowering at the delay. At the meeting of the committeemen I was astounded and horrified when each and every one of them gave it as his considered judgment that the Negroes should remain and that we could provide for their needs where they were. I argued for two hours but could not budge them. At the end of the conference, weak, voiceless, and on the verge of collapse, I told the outraged captains that their steamers must return empty.

The next day the Lord again assisted, this time with two miracles—the sun came out warm and the tents arrived. Seven miles of encampment were set up on the levee, kitchens were established, the doctors devised a sanitary system that worked—the Negroes stayed home and everyone was satisfied. After Father's death I discovered that between the time of our conversation and the committee meeting he had seen each committeeman separately and had persuaded him that it was best not to send the Negroes to Vicksburg. He knew that the dispersal of our labor was a longer evil to the Delta than a flood. He was a natural gambler: he bet on warm weather and tents. Knowing that I could not be dissuaded by threats or even by his own opposition, he had accomplished his end in the one way possible and had sworn the committee to secrecy. Of course, none of us was influenced by what the Negroes themselves wanted: they had no capacity to plan for their own welfare; planning for them was another of our burdens.

Those first weeks the citizens of my little town were magnificent: they relearned friendliness; they re-established unity; they cleansed themselves of some of the venom and nastiness left by the Ku Klux Klan; they worked without pay for the general good, and no work was too hard and no hours too long. Those I had not placed on committees lent a hand independently and made jobs for themselves wherever they saw there was a need. Even Klansmen cooperated, even doctors worked together. Lawyers, ministers, insurance men, dentists, merchants, salesmen, cotton factors, hotel men, slaved at unaccustomed tasks—cooking for the Negro kitchens, convoying women and children from their homes to outbound boats, guarding warehouses, issuing clothes and rations, erecting wooden walkways above the flooded sidewalks, building camps and latrines, assembling data for Mr. Hoover, supervising and checking the loading and unloading of supplies from the steamers, caring for ten thousand head of stock on the levee, sending fleets of motor boats to the beleaguered inland towns. Once more I was proud of my people. My old army buddy, Emmet Harty, was my personal assistant, and Father, though he was not a member of the committee, was the brains and the faith back of everything, the strong rock on which we leaned and in whose shade we renewed our strength. He was our liaison with the outside world and most of his time was spent in arduous trips through the flood waters to meetings and consultations held from New Orleans to Washington. For eight weeks we were as heroic a people as you would wish to find. Then came the June rise.

In June the river was supposed to fall; that was its unbroken custom and surely its clear duty. Indeed, it started to fall. It fell possibly a foot. Home-folk outside the flooded area immediately went into tantrums of homesickness and made life for us at headquarters miserable by their pleas for return transportation. Negroes dropped apparently from the sky and insisted on going to their cabins (standing nine feet deep instead of ten) to see about their "thangs." Then the river rose again and fell no more until the last week of August.

Undoubtedly the flood should have ended in June. If it had, we could have remembered ourselves as paragons of unselfishness and devotion. But it didn't and, descending precipitously from our heights, we lapsed into true, everyday sons of Adam. We were tired out; we wanted to think of our own troubles; we longed to get back to our own concerns. We had risen to an emergency, but we couldn't stay risen. Perhaps the June rise had nothing to do with our lamentable reversion to type. Perhaps the cause was less picturesque and more depressing. I have noticed that if you afford people a chance to give, they are little less than angels; but if you afford them a chance to receive, they almost convince you somebody is right about the need of a hell. The shabby truth is that in June the Red Cross began its campaign of rehabilitation, and people began to receive —food and clothing of course, but in addition household goods, farm supplies, and money. Not only did the Red Cross do a magnificent job of giving, but I don't think there was a church, a fraternal organization, or an organized charity in America that did not donate almost prodigally. Particularly I recall the generosity of the Masons and the Christian Scientists. Our heroic people became mere people: they not only received, they grabbed. Everybody wanted what was coming to him and a little more. The deterioration of the populace affected even our workers: committeemen sulked or fought among themselves or resigned; everybody criticized everybody else; from whites and blacks alike came improper demands, and here and there we discovered simple undiluted dishonesty. It was a wretched period.

One evening I motored home through the rasping currents particularly depressed. It had been one of those days that turn Spartan souls into fidgety, irascible old men. Besides, my boat had torn into my favorite crape myrtle and almost turned turtle. Mother gave me a helping hand as I stepped unsteadily from the bow to the gallery. But I noticed her air was remote and determined and boded no good. Father and Charlie Williams were taking a drink in the library, both looking haggard. I joined them, but in spite of Father's Four Roses we all remained exhausted and depressed. As we sat down to dinner Mother looked us over and announced:

"We've got a crawfish bisque tonight, a good one. . . . You men have got on my nerves. I know you come home every night tired out, worried sick, and all in. But do you think Adah and I are enjoying ourselves? Adah works hard all day on the concrete wharf and I don't have a pleasant time keeping this house going with water all around, the servants scared to death and worthless, Will not letting me have anything that even smells of Red Cross, and all of you hauling in people to meals without a minute's warning. Now I want you to stop looking like sick kittens. Nobody has a right to act down just because he is down. Buck up!"

And we bucked up, believe me. It was a princely bisque.

A few days later she was almost in tears when she confided to me that Minerva, the cook, had struck and refused any longer to serve breakfast for Charlie and me at six o'clock. I asked her to leave Minerva to me and stomped off to the kitchen. I faced that saddle-colored mountain of laziness, that iniquitous amorist, that awful genius of the domestic hinterland, and addressed her spleenfully:

"Just one more word from you about not getting breakfast at six o'clock and I'll haul you out of those comfortable rooms of yours over the garage and deposit you on the levee. I'll give you a tent that leaks and put you on half rations. Also I'll bring back that worthless husband of yours so he can beat the hell out of you every night."

The insurrection collapsed.

I suppose the June rise was responsible also for one of the most memorable and least important incidents of that unhappy time. Early in the flood an ancient brownie appeared at headquarters and without explanation asked to be made the official feeder of all stock marooned on dredge banks. As I had overlooked the appointment of such a dignitary, I cheerfully inducted him into office by presenting him with a bale of hay. I was not certain he wouldn't use it as a personal nest, for he was four feet tall, bewhiskered, toothless, and incredibly dirty. Nobody had ever seen him before the flood and nobody ever saw him after the water subsided. Apparently a kind-hearted water-gnome. Weekly he entered the office without knocking, sat on an imaginary chair (he accomplished this unusual feat by crossing one leg over the other and balancing himself against the wall on his diminutive rump), grinned, and announced: "Here I is." I never questioned him, but always gave him a ration of four bales of hay and a sack of oats.

One of his ports of call was "Dredge Ditch No. 9" or "No. 9," as the Negroes called the drainage canal a few miles east of town through whose spoil-banks we had dynamited a passage for boats to and from Leland. The cross-currents at that point were terrifying. To navigate the opening was an aquatic feat, a sort of shooting the rapids which we Delta land-lubbers found disconcerting in the extreme. If a motor went balky it meant certain disaster, and even under the best conditions there were frequent upsets, rescues, and hair-breadth escapes. That passage was our Scylla and Charybdis. On the embankment overlooking it lived one solitary mule. His interest in seeing whether a boat maneuvered the rapids or turned over was extreme and personal. He would come down from his perch to the water's edge and watch quizzically, ears forward. He was not hysterical or even sympathetic, but distinctly he was interested. Everybody in the county knew that mule.

In June a wild-eyed Negro rushed into the office wailing that his mule had been stolen. Impossible! You couldn't take a mule anywhere if you stole it. The Negro insisted he had seen the marks of a barge on the mud of the embankment. I shuddered with premonition. What embankment? Yes, it was No. 9, and *his* mule was *the* mule. Here was not only wickedness but impiety. Boat-loads of the mule's outraged friends and well-wishers scoured the county for three days in search of him or his abductor. In vain. At the gnome's next visit I advised him of the monstrous occurrence. He sat on the wall, frowned, and cogitated darkly, his finger against his fore-head. Then I heard a chuckle and a series of "Umph! Umph! Umph!s" Still chuckling mysteriously he left with-out his hay and oats and disappeared in his rickety bateau up Poplar Street. Guided doubtless by some terrene telep-athy, he discovered that sprightly quadruped standing shoulder-deep in water in his own back yard. In a sudden attack of nostalgia he had swum the three miles to the cabin where he lived. Evidently he was not expecting the June rise. I am told he leered at the gnome when they met and followed him jocosely back to No. 9, snorting like a hippo.

It was also about this time that the Negro press of the North, led by the *Chicago Defender*, started an eight weeks' campaign of vilification directed at me. I had been rather amused at Mr. Hoover's pain when his devout efforts and the Red Cross's extraordinary accomplishments had elicited no word of praise or appreciation from that press. So I had to take lightly their accusations that I had dumped the town's sewage into the Negro residential section while the white folks were playing golf at the Country Club, and they were easy to take lightly because the golf-links at the moment were still four feet under water and the town sewerage system never ceased to function. I was even rather thrilled when the *Chicago Defender* climaxed an eloquent editorial by observing that until the South rid itself of its William Alexander Percys it would be no fit place for a Negro to live. But I ought to have been as pained as Mr. Hoover by these libels, because the Negroes at home read their Northern newspapers trustingly and believed them far more piously than the evidence before their own eyes.

The Negroes had behaved admirably during the first weeks of the flood. The camp life on the levee suited their temperaments. There was nothing for them to do except unload their rations when the boats docked. The weather was hot and pleasant. Conditions favored conversation. They worked a little, talked a great deal, ate heartily of food which somebody else had paid for, and sang at night. During the recent clamor for greater leisure for the children of men, I have often wondered what men are worthy of leisure. As far as I have been able to observe, only saints, a few aristocrats, and Negroes. These adorn what to the generality is deteriorating. But perhaps to be an ideal adept in idleness one should be illiterate. At any rate it was unfortunate that the Delta Negroes could read Negro newspapers during the flood.

I sensed this dimly when, as houses began to emerge from the water, we felt the need of a committee to list, by a personal house-to-house inspection, the individual losses in household goods. At the suggestion of a charming and idealistic Red Cross worker from Washington we decided to appoint for this purpose a committee of Negroes, thinking such a show of confidence would appeal to the Negro's pride and to his possible aspiration to do his part. I selected for the committee a doctor's widow, a dentist, a mail-carrier, and two other intelligent and trustworthy residents. They accepted their assignment of duties enthusiastically and we felt sure our experiment would be a success. But we could get no report from the committee. After waiting ten days we called them in for an explanation. We all felt desperately sorry for them: in tears they explained that the Negroes would not permit them to enter their homes, but slammed the doors in their faces, accusing them of having "sold out" to the whites. Regretfully we had to replace them with white committeewomen, who after weeks of hard work assembled the necessary information, on the basis of which we issued to the Negroes household goods to replace those they had lost.

I feel sure that the most painful incident of the flood would not have occurred had it not been for the embittering influence of the *Chicago Defender*. It was a general rule of the Red Cross that recipients of its bounty should unload it gratis. This meant in our instance that meal, flour, meat, sugar, and tobacco, ninety-five per cent of which went to the Negroes, must be unloaded by them without pay. When the water began to fall, the Negroes in the levee camp, where they were housed and fed under sanitary conditions, began to steal back to their soggy, muck-filled homes in the town. They always chose the hour of a boat's arrival for their sentimental journey rather than meal time. It became increasingly difficult to collect an unloading crew. If there was no such crew waiting, the steamer would immediately proceed with its sacred cargo to some more interested port. For that reason we had already lost one boat-load of provisions and our stocks were running low. Mr. Davis, in charge of the wharf, grew daily more frantic. At last he asked my permission to get the police to round up a gang of laborers to unload the next boat. I refused, because that meant forcing labor to work and the Northern press would surely accuse the Red Cross of peonage. Mr. Davis insisted that in no other way could a crew be assembled—he had tried every other method permitted by the Red Cross and had failed. I still refused, and he angrily and properly resigned. I gave up. The police were sent into the Negro section to comb from the idlers the required number of workers. Within two hours the worst had happened: a Negro refused to come with the officer, the officer killed him. The details were obscure and irrelevant. The Negro was a good man, the policeman young and inexperienced. It was no consolation to remember that we were not the first who with the best meaning had incurred the worst.

The next day my trusted Negro informant told me the Negroes had worked themselves into a state of wild excitement and resentment. He feared an uprising. They far outnumbered the whites, and when aroused they are not cowardly. Keeping the peace under these circumstances was my responsibility. I told my informant I would call a meeting of the Negroes for that night and speak to them in one of their churches. He vehemently opposed this course, saying the Negroes were all armed and all of them blamed me for the killing. Nevertheless I called the meeting and requested that no white person except myself be present.

At the designated hour the church was lighted but completely empty except for Mr. Davis and his wife, who to my surprise were seated in the front row. One by one, glum and silent, the Negroes trickled in, all men. As they entered, there was none of the confabulating and handshaking customary on such occasions. I waited in the ominous silence for the church to fill. It was the surliest, most hostile group I ever faced. A massive black preacher rose and announced starkly: "I will read from the Scripture." Without comment, he read the chapter from Genesis on the flood. It was as impressive as ice-water. Then he said: "Join me in a hymn." It was a hymn I had never heard, a droning, monotonous thing that swelled, as they repeated verse after verse, from an almost inaudible mutter to a pounding barbaric chant of menace. I could feel their excitement and hate mount to frenzy. In the quivering silence that followed the last defiant roar from those dusky throats and deep chests, the preacher turned toward me, and I wondered if he would dare introduce me to this audience with the usual fulsome phrases. Instead his words were gaunt: "I present Mr. Percy, chairman of the Red Cross." I knew there was no chance here to appeal to reason. Retreat was out of the question. Attack was imperative. Unapplauded I mounted the pulpit and spoke slowly and bitterly:

A good Negro has been killed by a white policeman. Every white man in town regrets this from his heart and is ashamed. The policeman is in jail and will be tried. I look into your faces and see anger and hatred. You think I am the murderer. The murderer should be punished. I will tell you who he is. . . . For months we Delta people have been suffering together, black and white alike. God did not distinguish between us. He struck us all to our knees. He spared no one. He sent His terrible waters over us and He found no one of us worthy to be His friend as Noah was. He found no one of us worthy to be helped by Him, so we had to help ourselves. For four months I have struggled and worried and done without sleep in order to help you Negroes. Every white man in this town has done the same thing. We served you with our money and our brains and our strength and, for all that we did, no one of us received one penny. We white people could have left you to shift for yourselves. Instead we stayed with you and worked for you, day and night. During all this time you Negroes did nothing, nothing for yourselves or for us. You were asked to do only one thing, a little thing. The Red Cross asked you to unload the food it was giving you, the food without which you would have starved. And you refused. Because of your sinful, shameful laziness, because you refused to work in your own behalf unless you were paid, one of your race has been killed. You sit before me sour and full of hatred as if you had a right to blame anybody or to judge anybody. You think you want avenging justice, but you don't; that is the last thing in the world you want. I am not the murderer. Mr. Davis is not the murderer. That foolish young policeman is not the murderer. The murderer is you! Your hands are dripping with blood. Look into each other's faces and see the shame and the fear God has set on them. Down on your knees, murderers, and beg your God not to punish you as you deserve.

They went on their knees and we prayed. The danger was averted, but when I called for volunteers to unload the next boat only four stood up—a friend of mine, a one-armed man, and two preachers who had been slaves on the Percy Place and were too old to lift a bucket.

During the last week of August the river crawled back to its bed through the trail of its slime and desolation. The Red Cross settled down to intelligent, constructive routine, performed largely by its own personnel. I was exhausted and I felt I had the right to resign as chairman. Having persuaded my friend Hazlewood Farish—later my law partner and the grandfather of my namesake—to take my place, I sailed for Japan. I had never imagined I was naturally given to attacks of hubris, but the painful truth is that when I left the work to which I had devoted myself exclusively for four months, I was convinced it would suffer because of my absence. I suspect I even hoped it would. Human beings are engagingly absurd, we oscillate between being insignificant and imagining ourselves God. It is a small man indeed who is not made big by a big job, but never as big as he imagines. I returned from Japan to find that the relief work had proceeded distressingly well without me. Actually the two really great contributions made to the Delta by the Red Cross had been made without me and without my connivance: we learned to conquer pellagra and to raise alfalfa. The Red Cross had substituted in the plantation ration salmon for salt meat because salmon was cheaper, and so we stumbled on the fact that you can't have pellagra if you eat enough fish. Since the flood did not permit us to plant our usual spring and summer crops, Mr. Hoover hit on alfalfa as a fall crop and distributed free alfalfa seed. Now alfalfa is our standard hay and our best soil-builder.

If out of the 1927 flood our people learned mutual helpfulness instead of the tenets of the Klan, our farmers learned the cultivation of alfalfa, our Negroes learned how to avoid pellagra, and our government learned the necessity for flood control, we Delta folks will have to pronounce that flood an unqualified success. If I learned from it due humility as to my own indispensability and due wonder at that amazing alloy of the hellish and the divine which we call Man, I, too, should recall it only with gratitude, though I hope even the liveliest appreciation would not require me to want to go through it again.

# CHAPTER XXI

## *Planters, Share-Croppers, and Such*

Father was the only great person I ever knew and he would not have been great without Mother. They died two years after the flood, mercifully within a few weeks of each other. Without them my life seemed superfluous.

Holt, a hunting partner of Father's and an ex-slave, came up to the office to express his grief. I met him in the hall, but he motioned me to Father's desk, saying: "Set there where he sot. That's where you b'long." He took the chair across the desk from me, filling it and resting his strong hands on the heavy cane he always carried and needed. He was a magnificent old man with massive shoulders and a noble head. For some minutes he struggled silently, sitting there in what had been Father's office, then he let the tears gush unhindered from his eyes and the words from his heart: "The roof is gone from over my head and the floor from under my feet. I am out in the dark and the cold alone. I want to go where he is." He rose and hobbled out. Many of us felt that way.

From Father I inherited Trail Lake, a three-thousand-acre cotton plantation, one of the best in the county and unencumbered. I was considered well-to-do for our part of the state. Father loved the land and had put into it the savings of a lifetime. Perhaps he loved it because he and his brothers and sisters had been born on it and had passed their childhood among country things. His grandfather had obtained title to the Percy Place about 1850. It was a patch of woods then and many slaves had to labor many months before it could properly be termed a cotton plantation. This grandfather, whom the family affectionately, but rather disrespectfully, referred to as Thomas G., had been the favorite son of old Don Carlos and had married a famous beauty from Huntsville named Maria Pope. If you had lived as long as I have with that oil painting of him in the library over the fireplace, you could easily deduce why Maria and Don Carlos loved him. It reticently and through a fume of chiaroscuro reveals a personable young chap in a black stock and a black waistcoat adorned with four stylish brass buttons. At first perhaps you won't notice his smile, but it's there, all right, at the corner of his mouth, very shadowy and knowing, a little hurt but not at all bitter. It's by that smile I really know him, and not by his descendants, who mostly are the kind you like to descend with, or by the tender trusting references to him in Don Carlos's will. Though I've always lived with the remnant of his brown English library (each leather volume numbered and marked with the book-plate bearing his name sans crest or escutcheon) and always loved his enormous mahogany dining-room table with its carved legs and brass claws, around which all of us have eaten meals together going on six generations now, it's not they but his smile that makes him a familiar and a confidant of mine—that and the fact he cut no very great figure in the world. He isn't a demanding ancestor.

He seems to have felt that if he raised his sons to be gentlemen he would have done his full Christian duty by them and indeed by life. Training in a profession, though ornamental, was unnecessary for a gentleman, but of course you couldn't be one at all unless you owned land. Therefore, Thomas G. casually made doctors of his two older boys, Walker and LeRoy, and a lawyer of Fafar, after whom I was named, but having done that, without, of course, expecting them to practice medicine or law, he settled down gravely to the really serious business of getting them a plantation. He decided on a place in the Delta, paid for it, manned it with enough slaves to clear and cultivate it, and shipped his sons, all three of them, down to live on it.

When I was a youngster, I quite often spent the week-end on this plantation of theirs, which is still called the Percy Place. Already the slave quarters looked ramshackly, the woods had disappeared, the loamy creek land seemed thin, and the residence, from which the ells had fallen away, was ugly and plain, more full of room than anything else and split amidships by an enormous drafty hall, a very cave for coolness and emptiness.

I am sure in these days and times no wise father would dare bundle off three sons, two of them married, and expect them to live forever after under the same roof without kicking it off. Uncle Walker was married to Aunt Fannie, Fafar to Mur, and Uncle LeRoy (whom everybody loved and the youngsters called Uncle Lee) was the bachelor—scholar and gallivanter of the trio and so destined to endure gracefully occasional admonitions and rakings over the coals from his young sisters-in-law. Yet all reports agree that the Percy household was not only amiable but full of fun. Apparently they were a cheery lot who liked life.

Then the war came, and everything changed. By the

time of the surrender Uncle Walker had died, Uncle Lee had been stricken with paralysis, and when Fafar, the youngest and the soldier of the three, returned, it was to a diminished and penniless household of which he found himself the head and the bread-winner. The women and children and sick were still clinging to the place, but there wasn't a servant or a field-hand on it. All the slaves had left. I suppose he and Mur must have done some pretty tragic planning together the night he got home. Mur brought out from hiding the last of the plantation's horses, Fafar mounted this priceless, unlovely steed—his name was Bill Jack—and jogged off to Greenville, which then was a mere river-landing at the end of ten miles of impassable road. Fafar was over thirty years old and a Colonel of a defeated army. He hung out a shingle announcing to the bankrupt countryside that W. A. Percy had opened offices for the practice of law. In time he became one of Mississippi's famous lawyers, but Father said that right from the start he always managed to collect more clients than fees.

Fafar was fifty-five years old when he died. Long before his death people had been calling him "Old Colonel Percy" and "The Gray Eagle." His life had been crowded with usefulness and honor, but it ended when he was fifty-five. That is my age now. When I consider all he did and all I haven't done, I feel the need of taking a good long look at Thomas G., debonair and wistful, expecting nothing.

Of course the stage that Fafar trod after the war was no ordinary stage, and the play no ordinary play. Those days you had to be a hero or a villain or a weakling—you couldn't be just middling ordinary. The white people in the whole Delta comprised a mere handful, but there were hordes of Negroes. Poor wretches! For a thousand years and more they had been trained in tribal barbarism, for a hundred and more in slavery. So equipped, they were presented overnight with freedom and the ballot and told to run the river country. They did. They elected Negroes to every office. We had a Negro sheriff, Negro justices of the peace, Negro clerks of court. There were no white officials, not even carpetbaggers. It was one glorious orgy of graft, lawlessness, and terrorism. The desperate whites though negligible in number banded together to overthrow this regime and chose Fafar as their leader. His life work became the re-establishment of white supremacy. That work required courage, tact, intelligence, patience; it also required vote-buying, the stuffing of ballot-boxes, chicanery, intimidation. Heart-breaking business and degrading, but in the end successful. At terrific cost white supremacy was re-established. Some of us still remember what we were told of those times, and what we were told inclines us to guard the ballot as something precious, something to be withheld unless the fitness of the recipient be patent. We are the ones I suppose who doubt despairingly the fitness of Negroes and (under our breath be it said) of women.

Father considered Fafar superior to any human being he had ever known: he insisted he had a finer mind, a greater gusto, a warmer love of people, and a more rigid standard of justice than any of his sons. But for Fafar's efforts at running the plantation Father had only amused and tolerant scorn.

It appears that Fafar practiced law in order to be able to practice husbandry. He retained title to the Percy Place by paying its taxes with fees. But never, never, during all the years he managed it, did it yield one penny of profit. Father contended the reason for this deplorable result was Fafar's inability to say no to any Negro in wheedling mood. I suspect, however, the main reason was the low price of cotton and the South's economic collapse following Gettysburg.

After the first fine frenzy of emancipation, although Negro politicians and carpetbaggers were riding high and making prosperity look like sin, the rank and file of ex-slaves, the simple country Negroes, found themselves faring exceedingly ill. They had freedom, but nothing else. It's a precious possession, but worthless commercially. The former slave-holders had land, but nothing else. It's as precious, nearly, as freedom, but without plow and plowmen equally worthless. On ex-slave and ex-master it dawned gradually that they were in great need of one another—and not only economically, but, curiously enough, emotionally. Holt killed a Yankee officer for insulting Colonel Howell Hines, his old master. Fafar had Negro friends without whose information and advice he and the other political rebels of the time would have suffered under this reign of scalawaggery even more grievously than they did. To each plantation drifted back puzzled, unhappy freedmen who had once worked it as slaves and who were discovering that though slaves couldn't go hungry, freedmen could and did. Ex-slaves returned to the Percy Place and asked for a chance to make a crop on it. Fafar had little to offer them except good land and leadership. He puzzled over what was just to do and what he could do. He concluded by offering his ex-slaves a partnership with him. The terms of it were simple.

In simple words, about like these, he explained it to them:

I have land which you need, and you have muscle which I need; let's put what we've got in the same pot and call it ours. I'll give you all the land you can work, a house to live in, a garden plot and room to raise chickens, hogs, and cows if you can come by them, and all the wood you want to cut for fuel. I'll direct and oversee you. I'll get you a doctor when you are sick. Until the crop comes in I'll try to keep you from going hungry or naked in so far as I am able. I'll pay the taxes and I'll furnish the mules and plows and gear and whatever else is necessary to make a crop. This is what I promise to do. You will plant and cultivate and gather this crop as I direct. This is what you will promise to do. When the crop is picked, half of it will be mine and half of it yours. If I have supplied you with money or food or clothing or anything else during this year, I will charge it against your half of the crop. I shall handle the selling of the cotton and the cottonseed because I know more than you do about their value. But the corn you may sell or eat or use for feed as you like. If the price of cotton is good, we shall both make something. If it is bad, neither of us will make anything, but I shall probably lose the place and you will lose nothing because you have nothing to lose. It's a hard contract these hard times for both of us, but it's just and self-respecting and if we both do our part and have a little luck we can both prosper under it.

This was the contract under which Fafar operated the Percy Place during his lifetime, under which Mur operated it after his death, under which Father operated it from the time of her death to the time it was sold. It changed in no essential during all those years except that with better times the promise to keep the Negroes from going hungry and cold became a fixed obligation to lend them a stated amount of money each month from the first of March, when planting started, to the first of September, when cottonseed money began coming in. After the place had been worked for years under this arrangement—years during which nobody grew rich and nobody suffered for necessities—Father decided that it was getting run down, it was too old, it was worn out. Miserable, but feeling foresighted and awfully business-like, he sold the Percy Place.

I rode through it last week and the crop was twice as big as either Fafar or Father had ever raised on it. Modern methods of farming, government-inspired diversification of crops, and the use of fertilizer have made it more productive than when Thomas G.'s sons planted their first cotton crop in its virgin soil with slave labor.

Let no one imagine that because Father sold the Percy Place he was landless. Far from it. Instead, he'd been watching longingly the new part of the county, the Bogue district, and little by little, bit by bit, over a period of ten years, he'd been buying a plantation there. It was his very own, his creation, and he loved it. He started with a batch of virgin timber and cleared that. Next he won in the cotton market and put the winnings into that section of Doctor Atterbury's, good land and mostly in cultivation. Then he added the desolate-looking deadening along Deep Slough. At last he bought the Cheek Place and the Ross Place. In all he finally acquired title to a single block of land of over three thousand acres—some cleared, some half-cleared, some in cultivation, part of it paid for, part mortgaged, most of it magnificent ridge-land, a few hundred acres swampy and sour. He named it Trail Lake after a singularly dilapidated-looking slough which meandered half-heartedly into the center of the place before petering out from sheer inertia. When I was going to Sewanee the whole property looked ragged and unkempt, full of fallen logs and charred stumps, standing and prone. It was at the end of the world, in a turkey and panther country. You could reach it only by a rocking impromptu trainlet called the Black Dog. The trip from Greenville and back required twenty-four hours.

Trail Lake was so far from anywhere, so inaccessible to "the law" and to the infrequent neighbors, that the Negroes ran off one manager after another and terrified the whole countryside. Father almost lost the place because the Negroes wouldn't let any white man stay on it. At last, in desperation, he sent down a young manager from Arkansas, Billy Hardie, who shot a tenant the day of his arrival and single-handed dispersed a crap game his first Saturday night. Quiet ensued. It's a pleasant country, but even now not safe. If you haven't got a few pioneer virtues thrown in with the run-of-the-mill sort you'd better move on to a more cultured environment.

I have no love of the land and few, if any, pioneer virtues, but when Trail Lake became mine after Father's death, I must confess I was proud of it. I could reach it in three quarters of an hour. It was a model place: well drained, crossed by concrete roads, with good screened houses, a modern gin, artesian-well water, a high state of cultivation, a Negro school, a foolish number of churches, abundant crops, gardens and peach trees, quantities of hogs, chickens, and cows, and all the mules and tractors and equipment any place that size needed.

Father had operated it under the same contract that Fafar used on the Percy Place. The Negroes seemed to like it and I certainly did. I happen to believe that profit-sharing is the most moral system under which human beings can work together and I am convinced that if it were accepted in principle by capital and labor, our industrial troubles would largely cease. So on Trail Lake I continue to be partners with the sons of ex-slaves and to share fifty-fifty with them as my grandfather and Father had done.

In 1936 a young man with a passion for facts roved in from the University of North Carolina and asked to be allowed to inspect Trail Lake for the summer. He was Mr. Raymond McClinton, one of Doctor Odum's boys, and the result of his sojourn was a thesis entitled "A Social-Economic Analysis of a Mississippi Delta Plantation." That's coming pretty stout if you spend much of your time trying to forget facts and are stone-deaf to statistics. But some of his findings were of interest even to me, largely I suspect because they illustrated how Fafar's partnership-contract works in the modern world. In 1936, the year Mr. McClinton chose for his study, the crop was fair, the price average (about twelve cents), and the taxes higher than usual. Now for some of his facts:

Trail Lake has a net acreage of 3,343.12 acres of which 1,833.66 are planted in cotton, 50.59 are given to pasture, 52.44 to gardens, and the rest to corn and hay. The place is worked by 149 families of Negroes (589 individuals) and in 1936 yielded 1,542 bales of cotton. One hundred and twenty-four of the families work under Fafar's old contract, and twenty-five, who own their stock and equipment, under a similar contract which differs from the other only in giving three-fourths instead of one-half of the yield to the tenant. The plantation paid in taxes of all kinds $20,459.99, a bit better than $6.00 per acre; in payrolls for plantation work $12,584.66—nearly $4.00 an acre. These payrolls went to the Negroes on the place. The 124 families without stock of their own made a gross average income of $491.90 and a net average income of $437.64. I have lost Mr. McClinton's calculation of how many days of work a plantation worker puts in per year, but my own calculation is a maximum of 150 days. There is nothing to do from ginning time, about October the first, to planting time, about March the fifteenth, and nothing to do on rainy days, of which we have many.

These figures, as I read them, show that during an average year the 124 families working on Trail Lake for 150 days make each $437.64 clear, besides having free water and fuel, free garden plot and pasturage, a monthly credit for six months to cover food and clothing, a credit for doctor's bills and medicine, and a house to live in. The Negroes who receive this cash and these benefits are simple unskilled laborers. I wonder what other unskilled labor for so little receives so much. Plantations do not close down during the year and there's no firing, because partners can't fire one another. Our plantation system seems to me to offer as humane, just, self-respecting, and cheerful a method of earning a living as human beings are likely to devise. I watch the limber-jointed, oily-black, well-fed, decently clothed peasants on Trail Lake and feel sorry for the telephone girls, the clerks in chain stores, the office help, the unskilled laborers everywhere—not only for their poor and fixed wage but for their slave routine, their joyless habits of work, and their insecurity.

Even with a place like Trail Lake, it's hard to make money farming. Although I kept myself helpfully obscure during the first years of my plantation-ownership, retaining the same excellent employees and following Father's practices, I began losing money almost at once, and in two years (they were depression years for everybody, I must confess) I had lost over a hundred thousand dollars and Trail Lake was mortgaged to the hilt. For the next four or five years I was in such a stew and lather getting that mortgage reduced and taxes paid, I lost track of goings-on in the outside world and missed the first tide of talk about sharecroppers. Those hundred and twenty-four families of mine with $437.64 in their jeans worked "on the shares" and called themselves "croppers," but I wasn't familiar with the term "share-croppers." As used by the press, it suggested to me no Delta group and I assumed vaguely that sharecroppers must be of some perverse bucolic genus that probably originated in Georgia and throve in Oklahoma. But one day I read that the President of the United States had excoriated bitterly and sorrowfully "the infamous share-cropper system." I asked a Washington friend of mine in what locality that system of farming prevailed. He knocked the breath out of me by answering: "On Trail Lake." I woke to the discovery that in pseudo-intellectual circles from Moscow to Santa Monica the Improvers-of-the-world had found something new in the South to shudder over. Twenty years ago it had been peonage. In the dark days when the collapse of the slave-trade had almost bankrupted good old New England, it had been slavery. Now it was the poor share-croppers—share-croppers over the whole South, but especially in the Delta. That very partnership of Fafar's which had seemed to me so just and practical now was being denounced as avaricious and slick—it was Mr. Roosevelt's "infamous system." We who had operated our plantations under it since carpetbag days were taunted now with being little better than slave-drivers by the carpetbaggers' progeny and kin. Obviously we are given to depravity down here: the South just won't do. In spite of prayers and advice from the "holier-than-thou's" it's always hell-bent for some deviltry or other. At this moment there's another of those great moral daybreaks on, and its east is Washington. In the glow I realize that Fafar and Mur, Father and I suffered from moral astigmatism—for all I know, from complete moral blindness: we were infamous and didn't even suspect it. Well, well, well. That makes a Southerner feel pretty bad, I reckon.

Notwithstanding an adage to the contrary, truth, as I've observed it, is one of the least resilient of herbs. Crushed to earth, it stays crushed; once down, it keeps down, flatter than anything except an oat field after a wind-storm. The truth about share-croppers has been told and retold, but, being neither melodramatic nor evidential of Southern turpitude, it isn't believed. I am not a well-informed person, but I know the truth about share-cropping and in this chapter I have told enough for earnest seekers to infer what it is; I have not done this, however, in the naïve hope that my words will do the slightest good or change the views of a single reader; my reason is other and quite unworthy: there's a low malicious pleasure in telling the truth where you know it won't be believed. Though rightly considered a bore and a pest in the best Trojan circles, Cassandra, no doubt, had her fun, but, at that, not nearly so much as the Knights of the Bleeding Heart who in politics and literature years from now will still be finding it fetching and inexpensive to do some of their most poignant public heart-bleeding over the poor downtrodden share-croppers of the deep South.

Share-cropping is one of the best systems ever devised to give security and a chance for profit to the simple and the unskilled. It has but one drawback—it must be administered by human beings to whom it offers an unusual opportunity to rob without detection or punishment. The failure is not in the system itself, but in not living up to the contractual obligations of the system—the failure is in human nature. The Negro is no more on an equality with the white man in plantation matters than in any other dealings between the two. The white planter may charge an exorbitant rate of interest, he may allow the share-cropper less than the market price received for his cotton, he may cheat him in a thousand different ways, and the Negro's redress is merely theoretical. If the white planter happens to be a crook, the share-cropper system on that plantation is bad for Negroes, as any other system would be. They are prey for the dishonest and temptation for the honest. If the Delta planters were mostly cheats, the results of the share-cropper system would be as grievous as reported. But, strange as it may seem to the sainted East, we have quite a sprinkling of decent folk down our way.

Property is a form of power. Some people regard it as an opportunity for profit, some as a trust; in the former it breeds hubris, in the latter, noblesse oblige. The landed gentry of Fafar's time were of an ancient lineage and in a sober God-fearing tradition. Today many have thought to acquire membership in that older caste by acquiring land, naked land, without those ancestral hereditaments of virtue which change dirt into a way of life. On the plantation where there is stealing from the Negro you will generally find the owner to be a little fellow operating, as the saying goes, "on a shoe-string," or a nouveau riche, or a landlord on the make, tempted to take more than his share because of the mortgage that makes his title and his morals insecure. These, in their pathetic ambition to imitate what they do not understand, acquire power and use it for profit; for them the share-cropper system affords a golden opportunity rarely passed up.

Two courses of action would be effective against unworthy landlords: the Negroes could and should boycott such landlords, quietly and absolutely; the government could and should deny government benefits to the landlord who will not put the terms of his contract in writing, who will not carry out those terms and who will not permit the government to prove by its own inspection that they have been carried out. In place of these suggested remedies, I can only recommend changing human nature. All we need anywhere in any age is character: from that everything follows. Leveling down's the fashion now, but I remember the bright spires—they caught the light first and held it longest.

So much that was fine and strong went into the making of this Delta of ours! So much was conquered for us by men and women whose names we have forgotten! So much had to be overcome before ever this poor beautiful unfinished present was turned over to us by the anonymous dead—malaria and yellow fever, swamp-water and rain-water and river-water, war and defeat, tropic heat and intemperate cold, poverty and ignorance, economic cruelty and sectional hatred, the pathos of a stronger race carrying on its shoulders a weaker race and from the burden losing its own strength! They must have been always in the front line fighting for us, those builders of the Delta; they could never have stopped long enough to learn of leisure and safety the graces of peace. But there are those who live in fear as in a native element, and they are beautiful with a fresh miraculous beauty. It is watching for unseen death that gives a bird's eyes their glancing brilliance. It is dodging eternal danger that makes his motions deft and exquisite. His half-wit testament to the delight of living, terror has taught him that, shaking the melody from his dubious innocent throat. Perhaps security is a good thing to seek and a bad thing to find. Perhaps it is never found, and all our best is in the search.

# CHAPTER XXII

# *Fode*

People are divided into Leaners and Leanees: into oaks more or less sturdy and vines quite, quite clinging. I was never a Leaner, yet, although seldom mistaken for one, I find people are constantly feeling impelled to protect me. Invariably they are right and I accept their proffered ministrations gratefully. I cannot drive a car or fix a puncture or sharpen a pencil or swim or skate or give a punch in the jaw to the numerous parties who need punching. My incompetency is almost all-inclusive, but it must have a glow, for it attracts Samaritans from miles around. I have been offered a very fine, quick-working poison for use on my enemies or myself; I have had my rifle carried by a soldier who disliked me, just because I was all in; a bootlegger once asked me to go partners with him because I looked seedy; a top sergeant, icy with contempt, put together my machine-gun when its disjecta membra unassembled would have returned me in disgrace to America; a red-headed friend of mine had to be restrained from flinging a red-headed enemy of mine into the river for some passing insolence; an appreciable percentage of the hard-boiled bastards of the world have patched tires, blown life into sparkplugs, pushed, hauled, lifted, hammered, towed, and sweated for me because they knew that without their aid I should have moldered indefinitely on some wretched, can-strewn landscape. If you mix incompetency with a pinch of the wistful and a heap of good manners, it works pretty well. Men of goodwill are all over the place, millions of them. It is a very nice world—that is, if you remember that while good morals are all-important between the Lord and His creatures, what counts between one creature and another is good manners. A good manner may spring from vanity or a sense of style; it is a sort of pleasant fiction. But good manners spring from well-wishing; they are fundamental as truth and much more useful. No nation or stratum of society has a monopoly on them and, contrary to the accepted estimate, Americans have more than their share.

The righteous are usually in a dither over the deplorable state of race relations in the South. I, on the other hand, am usually in a condition of amazed exultation over the excellent state of race relations in the South. It is incredible that two races, centuries apart in emotional and mental discipline, alien in physical characteristics, doomed by war and the Constitution to a single, not a dual, way of life, and to an impractical and unpracticed theory of equality which deludes and embitters, heckled and misguided by pious fools from the North and impious fools from the South—it is incredible, I insist, that two such dissimilar races should live side by side with so little friction, in such comparative peace and amity. This result is due solely to good manners. The Southern Negro has the most beautiful manners in the world, and the Southern white, learning from him, I suspect, is a close second.

Which reminds me of Ford. (He pronounces his name

"Fode" with enormous tenderness, for he is very fond of himself.)

In the South every white man worth calling white or a man is owned by some Negro, whom he thinks he owns, his weakness and solace and incubus. Ford is mine. There is no excuse for talking about him except that I like to. He started off as my caddy, young, stocky, strong, with a surly expression, and a smile like the best brand of sunshine. For no good reason he rose to be my chauffeur; then house-boy; then general factotum; and now, without any con-tractual relation whatever, my retainer, which means to say I am retained for life by him against all disasters, great or small, for which he pays by being Ford. It was not because of breaking up the first automobile, coming from a dance drunk, or because of breaking up the second automobile, coming from a dance drunk, that our contractual relation was annulled, but for a subtler infamy. I was in the shower, not a position of dignity at best, and Ford strolled in, leaned against the door of the bathroom, in the relaxed pose of the Marble Faun, and observed dreamily: "You ain't nothing but a little old fat man."

A bit of soap was in my eye and under the circumstances it was no use attempting to be haughty anyway, so I only blurted: "You damn fool."

Ford beamed: "Jest look at your stummick."

When one had fancied the slenderness of one's youth had been fairly well retained! Well, taking advantage of the next dereliction, and one occurred every week, we parted; that is to say, I told Ford I was spoiling him and it would be far better for him to battle for himself in this hos-tile world, and Ford agreed, but asked what he was going to do "seeing as how nobody could find a job nohow." As neither of us could think of the answer, I sent him off to a mechanics' school in Chicago. He returned with a diploma and a thrilling tale of how nearly he had been married against his vehement protest to a young lady for reasons insufficient surely in any enlightened community with an appreciation of romance. With Ford's return the demand for mechanics fell to zero—he always had an uncanny effect on the labor market—so he took to house-painting. His first week he fell off the roof of the tallest barn in the county and instead of breaking his neck, as Giorgione or Raphael would have done, he broke only his ankle and had to be supplied with crutches, medical care, and a living for six weeks. It was then that I left for Samoa.

But I should not complain. Ford has never learned anything from me, but I am indebted to him for an education in more subjects and stranger ones than I took at college, subjects, however, slightly like those the mock-turtle took from the Conger eel. The first lesson might be called "How Not to Faint in Coils." Ford observed:

"You don't understand folks good as I does." I was appalled. "You sees what's good in folks, but you don't see what's bad. Most of the time I'se a good boy, then I goes nigger, just plain nigger. Everybody do that, and when they does, it hurts you." I was pulverized. It may not have taken a wicked person to think that, but it certainly took a wicked one to say it.

That I have any dignity and self-respect is not because of but in spite of Ford. We were returning from a directors' meeting in a neighboring town and he was deeply overcast. At last he became communicative:

"Mr. Oscar Johnston's boy says Mr. Oscar won't ride in no car more'n six months old and he sho ain't goin' to ride in nothin' lessen a Packard."

I received this calmly, it was only one more intimation that my Ford was older than need be and congenitally unworthy. Ford continued:

"He says Mr. Oscar says you ain't got near as much sense as your pa." I agreed, heartily. "He says you ain't never goin' to make no money." I agreed, less heartily. "En if you don't be keerful you goin' to lose your plantation." I agreed silently, but I was nettled, and observed:

"And you sat there like a bump on a log, saying nothing, while I was being run down?"

"Well, I told him you had traveled a lot, a lot more'n Mr. Oscar; you done gone near 'bout everywhere, en he kinder giggled and says: 'Yes, they tells me he's been to Africa,' en I says: 'He is,' en he says: 'You know why he went to Africa?' en I says: ''Cause he wanted to go there,' en he says: 'That's what he tells you, but he went to Africa to 'range to have the niggers sent back into slavery.'"

I exploded: "And you were idiot enough to believe that?"

"I'se heard it lots of times," Ford observed mildly, "but it didn't make no difference to me, you been good to me en I didn't care."

Having fancied I had spent a good portion of my life defending and attempting to help the Negro, this information stunned me and, as Ford prophesied, it hurt. But hiding my wounded vanity as usual in anger, I turned on Ford with:

"You never in your life heard any Negro except that fool boy of Oscar Johnston's say I was trying to put the Negroes back in slavery."

"Lot of 'em," reiterated Ford.

"I don't believe you," I said. "You can't name a single one."

We finished the drive in silence; spiritually we were not en rapport.

The next morning when Ford woke me he was wreathed in smiles, suspiciously pleased with himself. He waited until one eye was open and then announced triumphantly:

"Louisa!" (pronounced with a long *i*).

"What about Louisa?" I queried sleepily.

"She says you'se goin' to send the niggers back into slavery!"

Louisa was our cook, the mainstay and intimate of the household for fifteen years.

"God damn!" I exploded, and Ford fairly tripped out, charmed with himself.

I dressed thoughtfully and repaired to the kitchen. My intention was to be gentle but desolating. Louisa weighs over three hundred, and despite a physical allure I can only surmise from the stream of nocturnal callers in our back yard, she distinctly suggests in her general contour a hippopotamus. When I entered the kitchen I found her pacing ponderously back and forth through the door that opens on the back gallery. It seemed a strange procedure—Louisa was not given to exercise, at least not of that kind. The following colloquy ensued:

"Louisa, what are you doing?"

"I stuck a nail in my foot."

"Why don't you go to the doctor?"

"I'se gettin' the soreness out."

"You can't walk it out."

"Naw, suh, the nail is *drawing* it out."

"What nail?"

"The nail I stepped on."

"Where is it?"

Louisa pointed to the lintel of the door. A nail hung from it by a piece of string; under it Louisa was pacing. I left her pacing. I didn't mention slavery then or later.

My bitter tutelage didn't conclude here. In late autumn we drove to the plantation on settlement day. Cotton had been picked and ginned, what cash had been earned from the crop was to be distributed. The managers and bookkeeper had been hard at work preparing a statement of each tenant's account for the whole year. As the tenant's name was called he entered the office and was paid off. The Negroes filled the store and overflowed onto the porch, milling and confabulating. As we drove up, one of them asked: "Whose car is dat?" Another answered: "Dat's *us* car." I thought it curious they didn't recognize my car, but dismissed the suspicion and dwelt on the thought of how sweet it was to have the relation between landlord and tenant so close and affectionate that to them my car was their car. Warm inside I passed through the crowd, glowing and bowing, the lord of the manor among his faithful retainers. My mission concluded, I returned to the car, still glowing. As we drove off I said:

"Did you hear what that man said?"

Ford assented, but grumpily.

"It was funny," I continued.

"Funnier than you think," observed Ford sardonically.

I didn't understand and said so.

Ford elucidated: "He meant that's the car *you* has bought with *us* money. They all knew what he meant, but you didn't and they knew you didn't. They wuz laughing to theyselves."

A few days later the managers confirmed this version of the meaning of the phrase and laughed. I laughed too, but not inside.

Yet laughter singularly soft and unmalicious made me Ford's debtor more even than his admonitions and revelations. I still think with gratitude of an afternoon which his peculiarly Negro tact and good manners and laughter made charming. I was in what Ford would call "low cotton." After a hellish day of details and beggars, my nerves raw, I phoned for Ford and the car. On climbing in I asked dejectedly:

"Where shall we drive?"

Ford replied: "Your ruthers is my ruthers" (what you would rather is what I would rather). Certainly the most amiable and appeasing phrase in any language, the language used being not English but deep Southern.

"Let's try the levee," I suggested.

Although nothing further was said and Ford asked no questions, he understood my depression and felt the duty on him to cheer me up. He drove to my favorite spot on the levee and parked where I could watch across the width of waters a great sunset crumbling over Arkansas. As I sat moody and worried, Ford, for the first and only time in his life, began to tell me Negro stories. I wish I could imitate his exact phrases and intonations and pauses, without which they are poor enough stories; but, in spite of the defects of my relaying, anyone can detect their Negro quality, care-free and foolish and innocent—anyone, that is, who has lived among Negroes in the South.

Here are the three I remember in something approximating Ford's diction:

"There wuz a cullud man en he died en went to hevven en the Lawd gevvum all wings, en he flew en he flew" (here Ford hunched his shoulders and gave a superb imitation of a buzzard's flight). "After he flew round there fur 'bout a week he looked down en saw a reel *good*-lookin' lady, a-settin' on a cloud. She wuz *reel* good-lookin'. En he dun the loop-the-loop.

"The Lawd cum en sez: 'Don't you know how to act? There ain't nuthin' but nice people here, en you beehavin' like that. Git out.' But he told the Lawd he jest didn't know en he wuzzent never gonner do nuthin' like that no mo', en please let him stay. So the Lawd got kinder pacified en let him stay. En he flew en he flew. En after he had been flying round fur 'bout a week, he ups en sees that same good-lookin' lady a-settin' on a cloud en he jest couldn't hep it—he dun the loop-the-loop.

"So the Lawd stepped up en he sez: 'You jest don't know how to act, you ain't fitten fur to be with decent folks, you'se a scanlus misbeehavor. Git out.' En he got.

"He felt mighty bad en hung round the gate three or four days tryin' to ease up on St. Peter, but St. Peter 'lowed there wuzn't no way, he jest couldn't let him in en the onliest way he might git in wuz to have a *conference* with the Lawd. Then the man asked if he couldn't 'range fur a conference en they had a lot of back-and-forth. En finally St. Peter eased him in fur a conference." (Ford loved that word, it made him giggle.) "But the Lawd wuz mad, He wuz mad sho-nuff, he wuz hoppin' mad en told him flat-footed to git out en stay out. Then the cullud man sez:

" 'Well, jest remember this, Lawd: while I wuz up here in yo' place I wuz the flyin'est fool you had.' "

Since the thirteenth century no one except Ford and his kind has been at ease in heaven, much less confident enough of it to imagine an aeroplane stunt there. And I do hope that good-looking lady saw the loop-the-loop.

The second story is just as inconsequential:

"A fellow cum to a cullud man en promised him a whole wagen-load of watermelons if he would go en set by hisself in a hanted house all night long. Well, the man he liked watermelons en he promised, though he sho didn't like no hanted house, en he sho didn't wanter see no hants. He went in en drug up a cheer en set down en nuthin' happened. After so long a time, in walked a black cat en set down in front of him en jest looked at him. He warn't so skeered because it warn't much more'n a kitten, en they both uvvem jest set there en looked at each uther. Then

ernurther cat cum in, a big black 'un, en he set by the little
'un en they jest set there lookin' at him, en ain't sed nothin'.
Then ernurther one cum en he wuz big as a dawg en all
three uvvem jest set there en looked at him en sed nuthin'.
Ernurther one cum, still bigger, en ernurther, en ernurther,
en the last one wuz big as a hoss. They all jest set there in
a row en sed nuthin' en looked at him. That cullud man he
wuz plum skeered en he had ter say sumpin so he 'lowed all
nice en p'lite:

"'Whut us gwiner do?'

"En the big 'un sed: 'Us ain't gwiner do nuthin', till
Martin comes.'

"The cullud man says reel nice en p'lite: 'Jest tell Martin
I couldn't wait,' en he busted out the winder en tore down
the big road fast as he could en faster, en he ain't never
taken no more interest in watermelons since."

"But, Ford," I asked, "who was Martin?"

"I dunno," said Ford and chuckled, "but I reckon he wuz
big as er elly-fant."

I reckon so too, and twice as real, so far as I am concerned.


And now the last:

"A cullud man cum to the white folks' house in the country en sed to the man:

"'Boss, I'se hongry; gimme sumpin t'eat.'

"The man sed: 'All right, go round to the back do' en tell
the cook to feed you.'

"The cullud man sed: 'Boss, I'se neer 'bout starved, I ain't
et fur a whole week.'

"The man sed: 'All right, all right, go round to the kitchen.'

"The cullud man sed: 'Boss, if you gimme sumpin t'eat

I'll split up all that stove wood you got in yo' back yard.'

"The man sed: 'All right, all right, go en git that grub like I tole yer.'

"So he went. After 'bout three hours the man went to his back yard en saw the cullud man, who wuz jest settin'. So he sed:

" 'Has you et?'

"En he sed: 'Yassir.'

"En he sed: 'Has you chopped up that wood-pile?'

"En he sed: 'Boss man, if you jest let me res' round till dinner time, after dinner I'll go en chop out that patch of cotton fur you.'

"So the man sed: 'All right, but don't you fool me no more.'

"After the cullud man had et him a big dinner he started out to the cotton patch en he met him a cooter [a mud-turtle] en the cooter sed to him:

" 'Nigger, you talks too much.'

"The nigger goes tearin' back to the big house en when he gits there the man cums out en sez:

" 'Nigger, has you chopped out that cotton?'

"En the nigger sez:

" 'Lawd, boss, I wuz on my way, fo' God I wuz, en I met a cooter en he started talkin' to me en I lit out from there en here I is.'

"The boss man was plenty riled and he sez:

" 'Nigger, take me to that cooter en if he don't start talkin', I'se goin' to cut your thoat frum year to year."

"So they bof uvvem started fur the cotton patch en there in the middle of the big road set that cooter. En he never opened his mouth, he ain't sed nuthin'. So the man hopped on the nigger en whupped him sumpin' scand'lous en left fur the big house mighty sore at niggers en cooters. Well, the cullud man wuz neer 'bout through breshing hisself off en jest fo' moseying on off when the cooter poked his head out en looks at him en sez:

" 'Nigger, I tole you you talks too much.' "

Can it be wondered at, now that Ford is sojourning in the North beyond the infamous housing conditions of the South, comfortable and healthy in his own little room with four young Negro roommates, a single window to keep out the cold and a gas burner for cooking and heat—can it be wondered, if now when the phone rings and the operator's voice says: "Detroit, calling collect," that I accept the charge, although I know who it is and why he is calling? It is Ford and he is drunk and he is incoherently solicitous for me and mine and for his mother and wants to come home and needs five dollars. I reply I am glad to hear his voice, which is true, and hope he is well, and advise him to be a good boy and stick to his job, and a letter will follow or shall I wire? Of course, he has no job, except with the W.P.A., to which he has attached himself by fictions and frauds with which all good Southern darkies with itching feet are familiar. I hope the government supports him as long and as loyally as I did, because if it doesn't, I must. I must because Ford is my fate, my Old Man of the Sea, who tells me of Martin and admonishing cooters and angels that do the loop-the-loop, my only tie with Pan and the Satyrs and all earth creatures who smile sunshine and ask no questions and understand.

I wish my parting with him could have been happier or that I could forget it. He had abandoned his truck in a traffic jam and forfeited his job, one that I had procured for him with much difficulty and some misrepresentation. Then he had got looping drunk and last, against all precedent and propriety, he had come to see me; it was late at night when he arrived, stumbling and weeping. He threw himself across the couch and sobbed without speaking. I could not get him up or out, and he wouldn't explain his grief. At last he quieted down and, his face smeared with tears, managed to gasp:

"You cain't do no good, Mr. Will. It don't make no difference how hard I tries or how good I bees, I ain't never gonner be nuthin' but jest Fode."

I wish I had never heard him say that. There are some truths that facing does not help. Something had brought home to Ford the tragedy of himself and of his race in an alien world. Had he been in South Africa or Morocco or Harlem or Detroit, his pitiful cry would have been equally true, equally hopeless and unanswerable. What can we do, any of us, how can we help? Let the man who has the answer cry it from the house-tops in a hundred languages. But there will be no crier in the night, and it is night for all the Fords of the world and for us who love them.

CHAPTER XXIII

# A Note on Racial Relations

A superabundance of sympathy has always been
expended on the Negro, neither undeservedly nor helpfully,
but no sympathy whatever, so far as I am aware, has ever
been expended on the white man living among Negroes.
Yet he, too, is worthy not only of sympathy but of pity, and
for many reasons. To live habitually as a superior among
inferiors, be the superiority intellectual or economic, is a
temptation to dishonesty and hubris, inevitably deteriorating. To live among a people whom, because of their needs,
one must in common decency protect and defend is a sore
burden in a world where one's own troubles are about all
any life can shoulder. To live in the pretense that whites
and blacks share a single, identical culture and way of life
is not only hypocritical but illusory and obfuscating. And,
last, to live among a people deceptively but deeply alien
and unknowable guarantees heart-aches, unjust expectations, undeserved condemnations. Yet such living is the
fate of the white man in the South. He deserves all the
sympathy and patience he doesn't get. Poor as his results
have been, they are better than any wise realist could have
anticipated.

[298]

It is true in the South that whites and blacks live side by side, exchange affection liberally, and believe they have an innate and miraculous understanding of one another. But the sober fact is we understand one another not at all. Just about the time our proximity appears most harmonious something happens—a crime of violence, perhaps a case of voodooism—and to our astonishment we sense a barrier between. To make it more bewildering the barrier is of glass; you can't see it, you only strike it.

The incomprehension is wider than the usual distance between practitioners of the security and of the survival virtues. Apparently there is something peculiarly Negroid in the Negro's attitude toward, and aptitude for, crimes of violence. He seems to have resisted, except on the surface, our ethics and to have rejected our standards. Murder, thieving, lying, violence—I sometimes suspect the Negro doesn't regard these as crimes or sins, or even as regrettable occurrences. He commits them casually, with no apparent feeling of guilt. White men similarly delinquent become soiled or embittered or brutalized. Negroes are as charming after as before a crime. Committing criminal acts, they seem never to be criminals.

The gentle, devoted creature who is your baby's nurse can carve her boy-friend from ear to ear at midnight and by seven a.m. will be changing the baby's diaper while she sings "Hear the Lambs a-calling," or indulges in a brand of baby-talk obviously regarded as highly communicative and extremely amusing. All white families expend a large amount of time, money, and emotion in preventing the criminals they employ from receiving their legal deserts. They feel that the murderers and thieves in their service are not evil and have not been made more unfit for society by their delinquencies.

Prosecuting attorneys, judges, and police officers are

eternally at their wits' end trying to deal justly with crimes committed by simple and affectionate people whose criminal acts do not seem to convert them into criminal characters. To punish them as you would a white man appears not only unjust but immoral. Consequently, for a stabbing or a shooting a white man will be charged with assault with intent to kill (a felony), but a Negro with simple assault (a misdemeanor). Those convicted and sentenced to a few weeks in the city jail are often turned loose at night, so they may enjoy the pleasures of domesticity. The injunction to return next morning in time for breakfast is always obeyed.

I asked a learned gentleman from Yale, who was psychoanalyzing the whole Negro population of a neighboring town in three months, for some explanation of the Negro's propensity to crimes of violence. The oracle spoke: "I should say, tentatively you understand, that the frustrated hatred of the Negro for the white man, because of the frustration, is transferred to his own kind for fulfillment." It sounded like Uncle George's "They bite in the mouth."

I submitted the problem to Ford: "Ford, why do colored folks fight, shoot, stab, and kill one another so much?"

Ford giggled: "Well, s'pose a woman comes home and finds her man in bed with another woman—she's sho goin' to slap him in the face with the lamp, ain't she?"

This seemed to me only an argument for rural electrification, so I urged Ford to proceed.

"Well, s'pose some nigger crooks you in a crap game— you sho ain't goin' to let him get away with that and with your thin dime too, is you?"

I demurred and Ford went further:

"To tell the truth, most scrappin' and cuttin' and sech comes from checkin'."

"What in the world is checking?"

"Well, a bunch of boys starts off jest talkin', then they starts kiddin', jest for fun, you know, and then they starts checkin'. That's kiddin' what's rough. Everybody gets kinder riled and biggety. Then some fool nigger puts you in the dozen."

Ford stopped as if the problem had been completely elucidated.

"What's putting you in the dozen?"

"That's sho nuff bad talk."

"Like what?"

"Well," said Ford, modest and hesitant, "that's talkin' about your mommer."

"What do they say?"

Ford was scandalized by the request.

"I couldn't tell you that, Mr. Will, it wouldn't be nice."

Explaining that my inquiry was solely in the interest of science, Ford divulged sheepishly:

"Somebody says: 'Well, your mommer hists her tail like a alley cat.' Then the shootin' begins."

It would require a fat volume to record all the crimes which were committed on my plantation during the nine years I managed it—the thieving of corn and gasoline, of gear and supplies, of hay and merchandise, the making and selling of whisky, the drunkenness and gambling, the adultery and bigamy, the cuttings, lambastings, and shootings. That volume I shall never write, but I can't help believing that some short mention of a few of the casual incidents which within that same period have befallen the transitory dark members of my own ménage might help the earnest outlander to understand, if not to alter, the moral climate in which the well-meaning, puzzled, exasperated Southern white man, day in and day out, pursues his foggy way in his dealings with the Southern Negro.

The last time I saw Mims I asked him how he and his

wife were getting along. He poked out his mouth: "Pretty good, pretty good, I reckon. Cose, I always goes up the front steps whistlin'."

I praised his cheerfulness.

"That ain't it, Mr. Will. I want to give anybody what's in the house and don't belong there time to git out the back way. You know I never did like no rookus."

And then there was Nick's contretemps which came near being serious. He gravely told me about it. Nick had dignity, besides a certain astuteness.

"I knew that woman was married and her husband was servin' time up in Leavenworth. I told her when he got out he could have her back. So we was runnin' the café, doin' very good, and I was treatin' her right. We slept there too, in a little room, and kept the café open all night. It was hard work, but we'd kept at it four years and was doin' good. Well, here last week, in walks that husband of hers from Leavenworth. Cose, it was all right 'cause I had told her it would be all right. They went on to bed and I kept on workin'. I was tired and she couldn't help me none that night. 'Bout four o'clock out they come from the bedroom. I didn't fire but two shots, Mr. Will, but I got 'em both."

Nick paused reflectively and gave me a quick intimate glance. "I forgot to say, cose he made a motion-like in his bosom before I shot."

Nick had destroyed the evidence and in court bore down hard on that "motion-like." When the charge against him had been dismissed he thanked me for a message I'd sent him, but said he hadn't needed no lawyer. He hadn't. That astuteness of his coupled with the excellence of his aim made one unnecessary.

Ernest was a truly devoted creature and loved Mother, but when after ten years in our service I discovered his thefts, he merely observed: "Well, to tell you the truth, Mr. Will, I just love money too much."

Of course drunkenness and running off with automobiles and smashing them up cannot be assigned to the category of crimes. When, however, Lige (the gardener) at high noon on Sunday, against my vigorous instructions, in a Dionysiac frenzy, drove my new car to the top of the levee and turned somersaults down the other side, I was unduly fretted. I lay in bed next morning preparing a speech designed to annihilate him, but while I was putting on the last scarifying touches, Lige glided in with a folded trunk strap, came to the bedside, and presented it to me. "Whup me," was his sole remark, and mine was about as brief: "Get out! Get out!" We have never referred to automobiles since.

Jim was different. He was the most efficient and intelligent servant I ever had in the house; besides he had book-learning and read the Bible assiduously. When I first saw him he was being borne into my office with a cracked skull and trembling as if with palsy. He wanted me to sue the sheriff. He had been in jail on a charge which he convinced me had been trumped up and, while there, had been struck over the head, accidentally or maliciously, with a billet of wood by the jailer. Thoroughly indignant, I procured a doctor and filed suit against the sheriff. The sheriff was furious, stormed, threatened, and became my bitter enemy. I recovered a few hundred dollars for Jim and, considering it inadequate, gave it to him without deducting a fee. But the whole sheriff's office was so venomously hostile to me and to the Negro that I feared he might be attacked and hid him for three weeks on the plantation. Then, to keep him near me for safety, I gave him a job as house-boy and a room on the yard.

Within a few months Jim had stolen all the personal

trinkets on the premises, everything from German field glasses to rings and studs. The colored population was familiar with the whole story. Jim is now a dapper and popular preacher in good standing.

Thinking over these incidents, so close to me and so usual, I wonder and fear. Is the inner life of the Negro utterly different from ours? Has he never accepted our standard of ethics? I remember too those fragments of another world on which I have stumbled, hints of a traditional lore alien to us and unfathomable by us.

I remember the sick Negro in the clinic at Leland, which I visited on an inspection trip during the flood. The doctors explained to me their dilemma: the Negro said he had been hoodooed by a witch-doctor and was going to die on the following Friday. Physically he was perfectly sound, they had made every kind of examination and test—but he was fading away before their eyes. I suggested getting the witch-doctor and forcing him to remove the spell. He had disappeared into the flood. I looked at the Negro. He was quiet, lying on his cot and gazing at the ceiling. I spoke to him. He heard and understood, but was not interested. His eyes were smoldering with terror. On Friday he died.

I asked Jim if he believed in hoodoo. He said, of course not, but he knew of a curious thing that had happened a little while before just three blocks down Percy Street. The sister of a friend of his was low sick; she got thinner and thinner, till you could see her bones. The white doctor couldn't do nothing, so her brother got up the money and sent to New Orleans for the big hoodoo doctor. He came to her bedside, leaned over her, said some strange words, and announced she had swallowed a frog. The frog jumped out of her mouth. The hoodoo doctor went away and the girl began to recover. She gained flesh and strength, then once more she went into a decline and became nothing but skin and bones and eyes. The hoodoo doctor returned. He leaned over her and said: "You've swallowed a cooter. I can't do nothing 'bout cooters." In a few days she was dead.

The county prosecuting attorney (incidentally he had been the Cyclops of the Klan) asked me what to do in a pending criminal case. A woman had cut her husband to shreds with a long knife the Negroes call a crab-apple switch. He was recovering. She acknowledged the occurrence, but pleaded in defense that he had placed a spell on her by means of a cunjer-bag. The bag, still in his possession, contained a piece of her red flannel drawers and a hank of her hair. Its effect was to rob her of connubial allure—in her words, "it stole her nature." She pleaded justification and I thought clearly she was justified. After many consultations with the distracted justice of the peace, on our recommendation the charge against her was dismissed. In the crowded court-room we expected an emotional scene of gratitude. Instead, the woman burst into tears. She lamented that it didn't make no difference to her if she was out of jail, seeing as how she didn't have her nature back. This seemed reasonable and we asked what we could do about it. We were advised that if we could git that cunjer-bag, she could sew the piece of red flannel "back where it come from" and all would be well. We told the husband he'd be immediately chucked into jail if he didn't fetch that bag instanter. He disappeared, while we waited in the court-room. In an incredibly short time he was back with it. The judge solemnly presented the bag to the woman. Everybody was happy. The couple left arm in arm, showing signs of resurgent nature.

How is it possible for the white man to communicate with people of this sort, people whom imagination kills and fantasy makes impotent, who thieve like children and murder ungrudgingly as small boys fight?

Appreciating as I do the Negro's excellences—his charm, his humor, his patience, his exquisite sensibilities, his kindness to his own poor, his devotion and sweetness to all children, black and white, his poetry of feeling and expression, his unique tactual medieval faith, his songs more filled with humility and heart-break than Schubert's or Brahms's—I want with all my heart to help him. But helping him is well-nigh impossible because of one tragic characteristic. No Negro trusts unreservedly any white man— that is understandable enough, though exceedingly unfortunate—but, still more unfortunate, no Negro trusts unreservedly any Negro. That too is understandable, because his leaders betray him, either from their childish ambition to appear "big shots" or from their willingness to exploit his simplicity. So the Negro has cut himself off from any leadership, and leadership is desperately needed by him. He turns not to the rare but magnificent leaders of his own race, but to his country preachers, uneducated, immoral, and avaricious. Trusting no one, without moral stamina, without discipline, without standards, the Negro gropes blindly through an alien white man's world, intricate in the extreme, and gleaming with attractive shoddiness.

The whole atmosphere of America is such as to mislead and endanger the Negro. The sickening adulation paid to Negro athletes and artists, not because of their great abilities but because they are Negroes; rumors of what the Negro does in Paris, in Moscow, in the Northern cities; the promises and bribes of demagogic politicians interested not in his welfare but in his vote; the Negro press's hatred of the white man, its demand for social equality, its bitterness, its untrustworthiness—all these combine to create about the young Southern Negro an atmosphere as dangerous as it is febrile and unwholesome. The work of white sentimentalists is equally perilous. When personal relations with the Negro are too familiar, they are misinterpreted by him. He reasons, plausibly, that if you are willing to dine with him, you are willing and probably anxious to sleep with him. With the genius of the poor for misinterpreting the motives of the rich, added to the Negro's own special genius for suspicion and mistrust, it should require little except common sense to deduce what the efforts of white sentimentalists may lead to. The noblest of them, such as Mrs. Roosevelt, accomplish their insidious evil quite unsuspectingly and with the highest motives. It will never occur to them that the results, however pitiful or savage, will have been of their making.

It is said that race relations in the South are improving because lynching has declined to the vanishing-point and outbursts of violence against the Negro are almost unknown. It should be noted, however, that the improvement, if improvement there is, is due solely to the white man. It should be further noted that the Negro is losing his most valuable weapon of defense—his good manners. When a Negro now speaks of a "man" he means a Negro; when he speaks of a "fellow" he means a white man; when he speaks of a "lady" he means a Negress; when he speaks of a "woman" he means a white woman. Such manners are not only bad, they are not safe, and the frame of mind that breeds them is not safe. Covert insolence is not safe for anybody, anywhere, at any time.

The Negro, not having assimilated the white man's ethics, giving only lip service to the white man's morality, must for his own peace and security accept whole-heartedly the white man's mores and taboos. In the South the one sacred taboo, assumed to be Southern, but actually and universally Anglo-Saxon, is the untouchability of white women by Negro men. It is academic to argue the wisdom or justice of this taboo. Wise or unwise, just or unjust, it is the cornerstone of friendly relations, of interracial peace. In the past it has been not the eleventh but the first commandment. Even to question it means the shattering of race relations into hideous and bloody ruin. But I fear it is coming to be questioned.

It is not difficult to reason why the young Negro is beginning to question this taboo their forefathers accepted so whole-heartedly and unthinkingly. Every black buck in the South today has gone or will go to Chicago, where it is not only possible but inexpensive to sleep with a white whore. Likewise, there are Negro bell-boys in Southern hotels frequented by white whores. But there is a further and more humiliating reason. In former generations, when the taboo was unquestioned, Southern women felt a corresponding obligation so to conduct themselves that any breach of the taboo was unthinkable. Those were the times when Southern white women were either ladies or loose. Today white women drink in public places, become drunk in public places, and public places are filled with scandalized and grossly human Negro waiters. Cars at night park on the sides of roads, and Negroes, like everyone else, deduce what the couple inside is doing. Whenever there's a moral failure on the part of the Southern white, there's a corresponding moral failure on the part of the Southern Negro.

Influenced by bitter half-castes, the young Negro argues that there is no justice in the white man's woman being untouchable to the Negro man, while the Negro woman is not untouchable to the white man. On the surface this seems an unanswerable argument, but it is not even sincere. The whites make outcasts of their white women who have violated the taboo, sometimes punishing them as grossly as they punish the offending Negro. Never are they accepted into even the lowest stratum of white society. But when a Negro girl sleeps with a white man, not only is she not ostracized by the Negroes, she becomes an object of increased allure to Negro youths. Unconsciously and pitifully they pay tribute to the white man by finding desirable his cast-off baggage. The Negro's resentment toward the practice springs from jealousy and from his imitation of the white man's fury when his own women are touched. Though they are sincerely bitter, theirs is only a pseudo-indignation. The Negroes themselves could stop the practice, if they truly resented it, by treating their offending girls as the white man treats his. The Negro's incapacity for moral indignation is one of his most terrifying characteristics. His moral flabbiness is his charm and his undoing.

It is not pleasant to make these bald and bitter statements. I make them because they are true and because I am afraid for the Negro. Only the truth can help him, and that can help him little unless he helps himself.

I have received visits from so many people whose sole reason for wishing to see me was their interest in the Negro problem that I am forced to conclude I am regarded in some quarters as an authority on the problem or as a typical Southerner who happens to be articulate. I am certainly no authority, and I doubt that I am entirely typical. I claim only to be one of that vast number of men of good will who try, with indifferent success, to see wisely and to act justly. As such, I would say to the Negro: before demanding to be a white man socially and politically, learn to be a white man morally and intellectually—and to the white man: the black man is our brother, a younger brother, not adult, not disciplined, but tragic, pitiful, and lovable; act as his brother and be patient.

# CHAPTER XXIV

## For the Younger Generation

My favorite cousin, LeRoy Percy, died two months before Mother's death, and his brave and beautiful wife, Mattie Sue Phinizy, two years after Father's. Their three boys, Walker, LeRoy, and Phinizy, came to live with me and I adopted them as my sons. Walker was fourteen, LeRoy thirteen, and little Phin nine. Suddenly my household was filled with youth, and suddenly I found myself, unprepared, with the responsibility of directing young lives in a world that was changing and that seemed to me on the threshold of chaos.

Even physically what had seemed adequate and fitting for me seemed primitive, even barbarous, to this generation. I had learned to read—indeed, had done my most absorbed reading—by oil lamps whose wicks forever got lop-sided and smoked. My drinking-water had come from the cistern in the back gallery and sometimes it suffered attacks of wiggle-tails. During mosquito time there were no screens, but we got along under a smudge of insect powder and slapped. If we were hot, we stayed hot and never missed electric fans or air-conditioning. If we were chilly, we ran out and got another scuttle of coal and pulled up closer to the fire. When the unloved, once-a-week ritual rolled round, I didn't turn on the hot and cold water, but quaked on the edge of a tin bathtub six inches deep which brought goose-bumps to the side away from the fireplace. At nature's beck I rushed out in the back yard and sat amid the unpleasant fumes of lime on a splintery seat that could be dismally cold and drafty.

Such early experiences make one apathetic to modern philanthropy which avows that the poor are being brutally treated unless somebody provides for them at somebody's expense electric lights, screens, running water, and modern plumbing. How out of step I find myself when I can't help regarding these things as delightful luxuries one must earn and not as basic necessities of the good life one may demand!

I was equally at sea when I considered how and where the boys should be educated. In my day education had been a disagreeable discipline by which one acquired, if susceptible, strength of soul and delight of mind. Now education is regarded as an easy but expensive aid to crashing society or procuring a better job.

Mother, ably backed by Aunt Nana, used to correct my manners, issue ukases on conduct, render innumerable decisions without written or oral opinions, and it would have been safer to jump in the river than question them openly. Now, I am admonished, a child's personality is as fragile as precious and if you try anything stronger on him than sweet reasonableness you will warp his psyche, foster complexes, and probably end up with a paranoiac or a Jack the Ripper on your hands.

I don't know how I'd have managed if the boys had not saved me the trouble by deciding to be good and infinitely considerate.

The house swarmed with young people. For me it was

delightful, but I knew a reciprocal duty rested on me to direct them toward the good life in so far as I had discovered it. But what good life that I had ever glimpsed was suitable and effective for this world where these children must earn a living and fashion their own happiness? The old Southern way of life in which I had been reared existed no more and its values were ignored or derided. Negroes used to be servants, now they were problems; manners used to be a branch of morals, now they were merely bad; poverty used to be worn with style and dignity, now it was a stigma of failure; politics used to be the study of men proud and jealous of America's honor, now it was a game played by self-seekers which no man need bother his head about; where there had been an accepted pattern of living, there was no pattern whatsoever.

I had no desire to send these youngsters of mine into life as defenseless as if they wore knights' armor and had memorized the code of chivalry. But what could I teach them other than what I myself had learned? True, it was not the South alone that had been killed, but its ideals and its kind of people the world over. The bottom rail was on top, not only in Mississippi, but from Los Angeles to New York, from London to Moscow. In different quarters the effects were dissimilar, but the cause was always the same. In Russia, Germany, and Italy Demos, having slain its aristocrats and intellectuals and realizing its own incompetence to guide or protect itself, had submitted to tyrants who laughed at the security virtues and practiced the most vile of the survival virtues with gangster cynicism. In the democracies Demos had been so busy providing itself with leisure and luxury it had forgotten that hardihood and discipline are not ornaments but weapons. Everywhere the security virtues appeared as weaknesses and the survival virtues as strength and foresight.

Should I therefore teach deceit, dishonor, ruthlessness, bestial force to the children in order that they survive? Better that they perish. It is sophistry to speak of two sets of virtues, there is but one: virtue is an end in itself; the survival virtues are means, not ends. Honor and honesty, compassion and truth are good even if they kill you, for they alone give life its dignity and worth. Yet probably England and France and all the good and the noble and the true of all the world will die and obscenity will triumph. Probably those that practiced virtue will be destroyed, but it is better for men to die than to call evil good, and virtue itself will never die.

We of my generation have lost one line of fortifications after another, the old South, the old ideals, the old strengths. We are now watching the followers of Jesus and Buddha and Socrates being driven from the face of the earth. But there's time ahead, thousands of years: there is but one good life and men yearn for it and will again practice it, though of my contemporaries only the stars will see. Love and compassion, beauty and innocence will return. It is better to have breathed them an instant than to have supported iniquity a millennium. Perhaps only flames can rouse man from his apathy to his destiny.

There is left to each of us, no matter how far defeat pierces, the unassailable wintry kingdom of Marcus Aurelius, which some more gently call the Kingdom of Heaven. However it be called, it is not outside, but within, and when all is lost, it stands fast. To this remaining fastness I knew I should help the children find their way. Yet, knowing how purblind a guide I was, I sent them to the churches. It seemed to matter little what sect they sought for guidance: they and their young friends returned confused, resentful, and distressed. Desperately and as a last resort they came to me with the old ultimate problem which time out of mind has vexed the children of men. None of us, I suppose, has found truth, but we can attain honesty, and that at least the young may demand of us.

One night as Father and I sat talking in the library I remarked flippantly that I couldn't understand the common fear of ghosts, adding I'd like to talk to one. Father was silent and then said in a low, curiously vibrant voice: "I'd crawl across the Sahara on my knees to meet a ghost." He wasn't given to exaggeration. Much later, as he lay dying, he roused after a night of coma and startled me by observing thoughtfully: "I nearly crossed over. You know what I've been thinking? All the while I've been pitying the thousands who have been sent across, terrified by the lies of priests in all the ages. There's nothing to fear."

Those quiet passionate words of his come back to me when I talk to the youth of today and observe their bewilderment, their craving, in a world without faith, among a people without gods. There's plenty of lip service to gods today and fear, but no easy unshakable faith. I think of what is being offered to our young people in their need by the churches, and my heart is filled with anger and sorrow. I asked a clergyman recently why it was that so many prominent church-goers were crooks in business and hypocrites in private life. He replied: "They have been born again." This clarified nothing for me and I told him as much. He explained sadly: "When they are born again, they are certain of salvation, and when you are certain of salvation you may do what you like." But I urged, horrified: "People don't really believe that!" "Hundreds of thousands of them," he rejoined, obviously as grieved as I. "The ethics of Jesus do not interest them when their rebirth guarantees them salvation."

Thus the Negroes believe! Religion to them is an emotional experience, orgiastic or mystic according to temperament, but not related to morals; so their ministers may steal and commit adultery without fear and without inconsistency. As I think of what that implies and of how much it explains, my memory fills with the ghosts of dead phrases —salvation, washed in the blood of the Lamb, He descended into hell, the resurrection of the body, born of the Virgin Mary. They are not the sort of ghosts I care to meet.

Where lies the virtue in attempting to persuade honest young minds to entertain such outworn rubbish? And what have such tenets to do with religion? How nearly impossible the churches have made it for such minds, earnestly seeking the truth, to join a church or even to remain religious! Not science but the Christian sects are causing the death of religion. The pitiful part of it is that it is as true now as it ever was that without faith the people perish, and they are perishing before our eyes. As object of faith Hitler has offered Race, Stalin the State, America Success, which is Mammon. These youths of ours know none of them is worthy, they know too they are sick, but when they turn for cure to the churches, the prescription handed them is written in the language of Hippocrates. These youngsters crave community of aspiration and purpose, they fear to be alone and outcast. A church forgetting its devitalized patter and meaningless incantations could tell them simply there is no unity except the unity of brotherhood, no brotherhood without a common father. Philosophical conceptions—the Trinity, the atonement, the fall, the redemption—cannot save this generation, for they speak a beautiful dead language, when what we need is live words, tender with meaning and assurance. Without them the young drift through the world, aimless, unemployed, with no certainties in their heart to give them anchorage or peace.

However young our old age is to us, to youth it is very

old, a thing depersonalized, spent of passion, by mere duration barnacled with knowledge if not with wisdom; so the
young speak aloud to us their troubled queries as they spoke
them centuries ago to the riddled rock of the embarrassed
Sphinx. In some such fashion I've heard my share of the
searching and seeking of young folk today, a brave breed,
more honest though no more wise than the youth of my
day. It is a sober thing when they come to you so lost
and ask the way. I am always afraid for them and afraid of
myself. But out of my own darkness, having first placed
in their hands the Gospels and the *Meditations* of Marcus
Aurelius, I try to point out to them the pale streak I see
which may be a trail:

The Gospels were written by simple men who earnestly
and with a miraculous eloquence tried to report events
which they themselves had never witnessed but of which
they had been told. Even what these writers of hearsay
set down we have never seen in the words they used, but
only in later Greek translations. Consequently the narra-
tives of the four Evangelists as we read them are full of
misunderstandings and contradictions and inaccuracies—
as every lawyer knows any human testimony aiming at
truth is sure to be—yet they throw more light than darkness on the heart-shaking story they tell. They are pitifully
human and misleading, but drenched in a supernal light
and their contagion changed the dreaming world.

The self-communings of the Emperor, though often cold
to clamminess, convince a man he never need be less than
tight-lipped, courteous, and proud, though all is pain. It is
saving to rest our eyes on nobility, severe and unalloyed,
such as a god might pattern after, and in these books, the
Gospels and the *Meditations,* we find such nobility like
strength turned beauty, a nobility the mere certitude of
which makes rational the frantic hope there never was a

woman great with child but she had listened to ecstatic Gabriel.

We often forget how pitifully unendowed we are. All we can know is through the tidings brought us by our five inaccurate senses. Others, perhaps, here or elsewhere, may be more suitably equipped with six or a hundred, but we have only five and they rusty and defective. We cannot hear the rushing spheres of our own universe though they must make a sound like trains loaded with thunder. We cannot hear the chirps and squeaks of the insect world which fragile insect ears hear plainly. We cannot see color at night as the owl can, or the rays that dart through space on mysterious errands, or even the germ that kills us. We cannot smell what a dog or Helen Keller or an eagle smells. Our diminished sense of taste has become a mere organ of luxury. Though we can feel the touch of another's hand, we cannot feel the dust on our own lips. Only the faintest wavering glimmer of the shouting light of creation penetrates our dark diminutive cell. Yet our whole knowing must be got through this crude outmoded equipment. No wonder our modes of thought are only three-dimensional!

Mathematicians and philosophers assure us that there's a fourth dimension which, if our faculties could master it, would unfurl to us widths of new knowledge. And if there is a fourth, surely there must be a fifth, and why could there not be a tenth, a hundredth?

But, circumscribed and blunted as we are, we men have always sought a god, a mind at work, a Master Schemer. Through all the centuries we have cried out: "These blue and starred heavens with all their intricate beauty and with man riding the darkness like a god, how come they here? If no god coaxed them out of nothingness, how then were they born, how did they grow and shape themselves, why are they here? And why, why, why are we here?" And finding no quick answer to this, the eldest and most pitiful of all our queries, time out of mind we have complained of the sorry scheme of things, confident it is sorry, dubious it is scheme. But is not our complaint a child's cry of pain rather than an adult's effort of mind? Must not the qualities of the Master Schemer's mind be either subhuman or human or superhuman? Good men in all the ages, materialists and atheists, have averred, bitterly or sadly, it was subhuman, it was no-mind, it was merely matter moiling, and the curve of their argument has always run thus:

In the beginning was the Atom. No one knew how it got there or what it was made of. Perhaps the void flinched. Later some changed its nature a little by calling it an electron, and others irritably dubbed it a particle of electricity. Whatever its name and nature, one day the Atom met up with another atom (antecedents unknown). So, like people, they got together in all that nothingness, and other atoms were the result. Atoms are blessed with a gaudy fecundity, so in no time they were all over the place. They like to agglomerate in outposts and sizable hunks. Heat developed somehow, though they didn't have a Prometheus, and that helped. They passed laws and stuck to them, and became enormously ingenious, forming colonies and sending out pioneers and settlements. At last they formed nations and called them by fancy names—liquids, gases, solids, metals, elements, and the like. They kept on building and gathering and bumping into one another because there was nothing else to do and they had so much room. They even formed into stars and suns and strange rays and marched to an ordered music, though none knew why. But all the time there were just atoms, nothing but atoms, clustering together like hornets or bees. It seems odd, but once, far down in an obscure corner, one tiny cluster, riding a larger cluster, spoke, and it said: "In la sua

voluntade e' nostra pace," and another cried out ecstatic-
ally: "Heilige Licht," and another said very softly: "Father,
forgive them, for they know not what they do." So that is
the way the world began and kept on. It would take less
than a one-dimensional mind to believe that was the way.

Because that cannot have been the way, because the
Master Mind cannot be subhuman, must it be like our own,
so defective, so unlighted, so unsteady and afraid? We
know that thinking like ours could not have created even
this paltry world of ours, yet we know equally that the injustice and horror of the world would not be tolerated by any
good three-dimensional mind. We complain of the sorry
scheme of things because against all reason and all evidence we assume the Schemer's mind to be dimensioned
like our own. We forget that the Master Schemer, worthy
of our loyalty and able to conceive and make what our poor
faculties perceive, must be possessed of faculties so far
beyond our own that the pattern of their functioning, if explained, could not make sense to us. The only god we
would be willing to adore must have a god's mind, not a
man's, and the hundredth-dimensional mind of a god we
could no more comprehend than a beetle could comprehend our own. To the mind that could dream and shape
our beaconed universe, what is injustice to us may be unfathomable tenderness, and our horror only loveliness misunderstood. If we but knew, all we ask is that what we see
and live in be not chance-built and accident-directed. Our
fear is to be participants in unplanned chaos. The rest
doesn't matter. We need not assail the sorry scheme—the
chaos we see is a hundredth-dimensional plan glimpsed by
three-dimensional perceptions.

If the theory of naked matter re-creating itself witlessly
be unbelievable and the God-Mind that plans and directs
be to us unknowable and incomprehensible, where then

may the young neophyte turn for certitude and easing of his loneliness? Where all other young neophytes have turned in the long processional of man's aspiring. Some day we may find we possess new senses with which to perceive, some day we may develop further dimensions in our thinking process: there are intimations of undiscovered powers and aptitudes in our ephemeral bodies—visions and levitations, prophecies and cures, telepathy and communications. But through the equipment we now possess, these five poor senses of ours, we can see daily what no atom built and no dust bred: it is given man to behold beauty and to worship nobility. He is shaken when he sees these two, but not because he feels them alien. Only when he is in their presence does the air taste native and the place seem home. These only are reality to his profoundest self; he needs no proof of them and no explanation. They are, he is, and over him there passes the shudder of a recognition. These recognitions are brief moments, but moments we may live by for our brief years. Who gave us these perceptions gave too, no doubt, the heavens' laws and conjured up creation. I think if one would sit in the Greek theater above Taormina with the wine-dark sea below and Ætna against the sunset, and if there he would meditate on Jesus and the Emperor, he would be assured a god had made earth and man. And this is all we need to know.

But we trouble our hearts with foolish doubts and unwise questionings—the fear of death, the hope of survival, forgiveness, heaven, hell. Rewards and punishments hereafter? What bribes we ask for our perfunctory righteousness! The oak spreads its arms in the sun, puts out leaves and tassels, and, if the season wills, scatters down acorns. But it does not querulously demand to know where fall its seeds or whether they will root and grow to saplings. There should be no question of reward: to function is the task assigned. To seek outlet for our emotions, our intellect, our spiritual cravings, to blossom and fruit with our whole nature, to keep its unity and proportion, of such is our occupation.

As to our pathetic plea for personal survival with all the quirks and foibles that alone make personality identifiable—there is nothing to fret about here. We survive or we are annihilated, and all our anguish cannot undo our fate one way or the other. But we may assuage our vanity by listening to the Buddha's thought. Our dread and torment in this life we lead are its apartness, its eternal isolation. We try to rid us of ourselves by love, by prayers, by vice, by the Lethe of activity, and we never wholly succeed. Above all things we desire to be united and absorbed. Must we insist that our besetting anguish go with us past the grave? To become part of the creating essence and of all things created by it, in this alone might be found fulfillment, peace, ecstasy. At the intensest peak of our emotions—lying on the bosom we love, or lost in a sunset, or bereft by music—being then most ourselves, we dissolve and become part of the strength and radiance and pathos of creation. When most ourselves, we are most not ourselves and lose our tragic isolation in the whole. To be a drop of water, trembling alone forever, lacks something of the peace and grandeur of being one lost drop in the immortal undivided ocean.

Death, Heaven or Hell, Rewards or Punishments, Extinction or Survival, these are epic troubles for the epic Mind. Our cares are fitted to our powers. Our concern is here, and with the day so overcast and short, there's quite enough to do.

So I counsel the poor children. But I long for the seer or saint who sees what I surmise—and he will come, even if he must walk through ruins.

# CHAPTER XXV

# A Bit of Diary

Geoge and Janet sometimes ask me what I do with my time down in the deep South, now that I've stopped practicing law and LeRoy is managing the plantation. I can never remember. To satisfy my own curiosity I've jotted down the doings of my last week-end. I never heard of anything more inconsequential and daft.

### THURSDAY

9.30 a.m. — Ancient sharp-eyed Negress appears in back yard, announces belligerently she has been waiting three hours for me, adds she used to farm on Trail Lake, made ten crops, raised six head of chillun and nursed all white babies from Arcola to Darlove. I ask her to get to the point. She says the point is fifty cents. I see the point.

10 a.m. — Meeting of executive committee of Delta Council. Shall the council endorse a bill now pending before Congress to levee the Yazoo River? Oscar Bledsoe argues it is economically unsound. I suspect it is unsound engineering. Billy Wynn says under all the circumstances our

endorsement is expedient. Long digression on what's intellectually honest and what's expedient. But Will Whittington wants it, so it must be right. All agree, with misgivings. Committee joins Levee Board. Everybody makes a speech. We endorse bill, gingerly, comforting ourselves it won't pass anyhow.

Noon — Rotary Club luncheon. Shall Rotary Club join other service clubs in urging city council to build a hundred-thousand-dollar swimming-pool with W.P.A. funds? Everybody thinks pool fine for underprivileged; nobody wants to increase taxes. Will Francis observes Wage and Hour Law bestows leisure on those unaccustomed to it— would they swim or continue to shoot craps? I mention bread and circuses. Everybody uncomfortable. Action deferred.

1.15 p.m. — An hour of dictation to Mitchell: letters to Lindley about his arthritis, to a gentleman from Tulsa who inquires if I have published "a volume of verse," to the twentieth lady asking permission to set *Overtones* to music, to the Children's Home saying they are mistaken, I am not on their directorate, to a nursery asking about spring planting of camellias and the habits of *Ilex rotundifolia*, to the university saying I will not make a speech on poetry or interracial relations, or the rise of the moron, or anything whatsoever, but I will be present to hiss Dave Cohn's oration.

2:30 p.m. — Pop-eyed youth, hitherto unknown to me, calls to say he must drop out of high school unless I give him financial assistance. It develops under cross-examination he has two grown brothers and lives with his widowed mother. I ask if he dropped out what would be his fate.

Answer: he would have to go to work. I inquire why not. Purposes of education explored with considerable incoherence. I decide he's the kind that would never get educated if he divided the rest of his life between Oxford and the Sorbonne. We part, youth observing he wants to be something better than a ditch-digger, I asking what's better. No conclusion reached.

3 p.m. — Try to nap. Boo [my Persian cat] jumps on my stomach. Wake in vile humor.

3.30 p.m. — A lady I can't identify enters to report that she has just discovered her husband is a drunkard and an alley cat. I brace myself to the melancholy disclosure and ask what I can do about it. Discussion follows on sobriety, fidelity, men, women, fate. No conclusions reached. She says she feels better, thanks me, and withdraws.

4.15 p.m. — I start hunting Lige. Decide he must be in his room asleep. As I approach his door to haul him out, hear unmistakably feminine titters. So outraged, forget why I started hunting him. Try to calm myself by considering it is an old custom—Malvolio on a day-bed with Olivia.

4.45 p.m. — Talk over troubles of Federal Art Center with Leon Koury. Is art compatible with continence and sobriety? Apparently not. But if you were a lady along in years and on W.P.A. wouldn't you fall for something too, almost anything? Leon has no right to have so much sense with so few years and no experience: he's just a genius.

5.30 p.m. — Toddy with Tom and Roy just in from plantation. Discuss price of alfalfa meal.

# A BIT OF DIARY

6.30 p.m. — Bob and Sammy arrive, unannounced, from New Orleans.

6.30 to 9.30 p.m. — Conversation. Subjects: fate of Finland, freight rates in the South, what cures gapes in baby chicks, the diet and discipline of babies, that scene in *Gone with the Wind* where Scarlett's in bed and smiling, politics (national, international, state, and municipal).

10 p.m. — I read *Time*. Turn on radio, turn off radio. Start to glance through Housman's *Collected Poems*, but in interval have lost reading glasses.

10.30 p.m. — Knock at door. Negro friend in tears. Displays lacerated arm which he says wife has bitten from shoulder to elbow in a fit of unwarranted exasperation. Question submitted: shall he kill her or call the law? I give him a dollar and advise him to spend night away from home.

11 p.m. — Go to bed. Phone. Negro friend after receiving dollar and advice went home, gave wife terrific beating, threw neighborhood into uproar, and is now in jail. Will I go his bond? I will.

Midnight — Phone. Same Negro on being released again went home and visited even more memorable chastisement on his consort. Again in jail. Will I bail him out? I will not.

2 a.m. — Long-distance. Detroit calling collect. Ford, of course. I refuse call. Hear Ford observing to operator being as how I near 'bout raised him it sho looks like I'd be willing to talk to him.

[325]

2 to 6 a.m. — Can't sleep. Take dose of somnos. Wonder if Ford is in jail and for what.

### FRIDAY

Sick in bed. Electric pad on back of neck.

### SATURDAY

8 a.m. — David wakes me with best breakfast in world— grapefruit, coffee, grits, and bacon—and the newspaper. Absorbing Popeye, Mickey Mouse, the Gumps, a sex murder, M. Daladier's fall, and Walter Lippmann, when Lige pops his head in door and announces them skrubs has came.

9.30 a.m. — Moping around the stricken long-leafed evergreens. Wizened gentleman appears without warning, announces he's read in *Good Housekeeping* I'm a gardener, and as he is a gardener on his way home to Ohio from warmer climes, thought he'd drop in and chat with me. He chatted: don't I disbud my peonies? Nice tulips, but haven't I any Clara Butts? His father taught Clara Butts to sing. How old do I think he is? No, no, no! He's sixty-five. It's gardening has kept him young: his wife can hardly believe it herself. What is my specialty? He specializes in Madonna lilies. He'll send me a photo of himself with his prize specimen. He leaves me, clammy with apprehension. Good God! At sixty-five shall I be specializing in Madonna lilies and thinking I look young?

10.30 a.m. — Edmund Taylor calls for me to go on our rounds collecting for the Boy Scouts ( or is it the Y or the Red Cross, this time?). What a creature! A Methodist and a successful businessman compounded of pure goodness! Pity he isn't a Catholic, so he could be martyred, canonized, and leave behind a legend of quaint miracles.

Noon — Gentleman from Oklahoma wants to buy oil rights on Trail Lake. I don't want an oil well. He guarantees well on plantation at his expense. I refuse permit unless he guarantees not to strike oil. He leaves hastily, figuring I'm insane.

1.30 p.m. — Will Francis rehearses speech on Great Ironists he is to deliver at Ladies' Night of Moorehead Rotary Club. Splendid speech and they'll love it, though they won't understand a word.

2.30 p.m. — Young lady simpers into library, whinnies at ancestors on wall and Epstein's Dave Cohn on mantel. Interview. Excuse: she's "doing" my poetry for her thesis. Archly imperturbable, asks impertinent questions. I inquire if she has read my poems. She has not, but expects to. I burst out, look her over, see there's no use.

3.30 p.m. — Young man calls to see me about his wife's insides. Appears she is practically hollow. Doctors did thorough job snipping off anything in the way. She's recovered from operation but is losing her mind. Injections of some sort, one a week for three months, alone can restore her. The shots cost $13.00 each; he makes $12.00 a week.

4.30 p.m. — As I hover over Bermuda grass praying for energy, old lady peers through garden gate appraisingly and venomously, a real gardener's look. Obviously poor and hard-working. I ask her in. She walks slowly and observantly, insulting me every step. She sniffs: "Horse! Should have been cow." None of my flowers floriferous as hers. I conclude she hasn't a house, much less a garden. On leaving, after standing me down my prize Mrs. Krelages are paper-whites, she proves her case by musing wearily:

"I don't know what I'd do without a garden. I just couldn't stand it."

5.30 p.m. — Whipped down. Julep with Tom and Roy. Helps.

7.30 p.m. — One of Levee Board engineers wants to come out and discuss Morganza spillway. Can't take it. Too tired. To bed.

### SUNDAY

8.30 a.m. — Over breakfast study *Delta Democrat Times* and approve Donald's editorial handling of situation we had discussed. Ask David to send in Lige. Lige can't be found.

9 a.m. — Gervys turns up with his colored movie camera to take garden pictures.

9.30 a.m. — Tommy reports new hardening room in his and Crit's ice-cream plant is completed.

10 a.m. — Police telephone Lige is in jail after a night of wassail.

10.30 a.m. — Rufus drops by from mass to say his and Marion's sinuses were miraculously cured by Florida's sunshine.

11 a.m. — Roy and Tom stop painting their fishing-boat in back yard and perch on foot of my bed for Coca-Cola and conversation.

11.30 a.m. — Adah joins us and reports on all and sundry. I remember I've forgotten to ask Aunts to dinner. Send David with conciliatory messages.

Noon — School of fish-faced strangers ask if they may walk through garden. Are joined by another similar school who don't ask. They streak through, looking as if they were inspecting a morgue, and vanish without audible gratitude.

12.30 a.m. — Head of state Federal Art Projects rushes in to wonder which of us would be more unpopular before the city council when the needs of the project must be presented.

1 p.m. — Dinner. Aunts present, 83 and 74, respectively. Their appetites and zest appalling. We marvel.

2 p.m. — I turn on radio for Philharmonic. Curse static. Roy and Sarah flee to golf-links. Aunts ignore static and indulge in a little free-for-all on some topic not related to music.

4 p.m. — Tom, Marie, and children take me for a drive in country. Discuss whooping-cough and public-school system.

5 p.m. — Negro I never laid eyes on says he's Baptist preacher and asks donation for church. Ingratiatingly observes cullud couldn't do nothing without the help of their white friends. I ask how many Baptist churches there are in town already. He doesn't know. I do—fifty-three Baptist, eighteen Methodist, one Episcopal, one Catholic, and a scattering of Sanctified, Holy Rollers, and Latter Day

Saints. I ask why another church is needed. Replies vaguely, concerning sisters who weren't satisfied and wanted to secede from Mount Horeb. Diatribe from me on the Negro's needs—hospitals, playgrounds, clinics, etc.—for which the Negro never raises one penny, while disreputable Negro preachers incessantly milk their congregations for funds to build an unneeded church and keep most of the money in their own pockets. He listens politely, murmurs assent, and beats hasty retreat. All true, but I feel like a miser.

7 p.m. — Memphis chap on verge of nervous collapse drives up, recounts latest symptoms, and asks advice. Give same advice I gave Sunday before last. He feels better and agrees to follow advice, as he agreed Sunday before last. He will be back Sunday after next for same interchange.

8 p.m. — Listen to Marian Anderson on Ford Sunday Evening Hour.

9 p.m. — One of police force drops in to discuss best method of handling dangerous breach of mores which is not breach of law. We agree on a course illegal but wise as it will keep the peace.

10 p.m. — Telephone. I refuse to answer.

10.15 p.m. — Regret I did not answer. It might not have been Ford.

10.30 p.m. — Hear someone outside whistling Tschaikovsky's Andante from the Fifth Symphony. Step out on gallery and see colored delivery-boy on bicycle, feet on handlebars. His rendition loud, inaccurate, and soulful.

10.32 p.m. — Put Boo out.  See Orion.

11 p.m. — Crawl into bed, thankful for a beauty-rest.

❧

There is no logical ending to an autobiography, once you've had the effrontery to start the thing, this side of the last gasp.  Facts keep on happening and the more of them you set down, the less progress you seem to make toward a likeness.  This bit of diary, if continued indefinitely, would not help my guardian angel to recognize me if he met me coming down the middle of the big road.  Evidently what doesn't happen is all-important, rather than what does.  To catch the likeness of this queer creature with whom I have lived always and for whom I have developed a sort of grumpy affection, I suspect I'll have to ease up on him unbeknownst—say when he is sitting in the garden idly, bemused, not even noticing the wasps on the fat peony buds.  It's getting too late for facts anyway and they have a way these days of looking like the Gorgon's head seen without the mirror Perseus used.  The garden's the place.

# CHAPTER XXVI

# *Jackdaw in the Garden*

Adah and Charlotte and Tom are real gardeners, dirt gardeners, of Mr. Bass's breed. They love the feel of the earth on their naked hands. They attain an intolerable serenity and conceit when because of their ministrations (plus the processes of heaven and luck, which they ignore) a tendril or a tiny green sail or a clenched rosy fist thrusts up where before there was unadorned ground. Tom in April always has the air of the Lord God after He did it in seven days. Adah plants seeds on the sly, not telling you what or where and in burning summer when you haven't so much as a lank strand in any bed you are infuriated to discover her yard strutting with color (though part of it *is* salvia). Charlotte can grow Oriental poppies and gentians, which sets her apart and makes her insufferable. I know my garden's prettier than theirs and gets itself photographed by the *National Geographic* and written about by Julian Meade, but it doesn't fool me. It's mostly for show, it's a substitute for things preferred but denied, and its superiority springs not from greener fingers but from a fatter pocketbook. Demeter would linger in theirs, not mine. I'd probably catch that Roman hussy, Flora, on my premises.

Yet gardening has taught me much, mostly about human nature. If you happen to flush me, trowel in hand, over a patch of coco grass, be not deceived: my mind is not on gardening, but on people.

For years I was distressed by the incessant and diversified troubles of a client of mine: she was always in crisis. One day sprinkling the azaleas with aluminum sulphate, the revelation broke over me. Both the plant and the lady required acid soil—they would perish in sweet soil! She needed tragedy and couldn't thrive without it. Ever since the discovery I have taken acid-loving people calmly.

It took years of battle with root-rot to teach me that it does not ravage with equal devastation every variey of iris. The older purer strains seem immune to it, its greatest toll is from the ranks of the hybrids, in which we have learned to fear Mesopotamican blood. But when we cross human beings we give no thought to the racial compatibility of the bloods fused and neglect to observe whether the human hybrids we produce are unhappily subject to rot of one kind or another. In gardening we have learned that death is the best cure for many diseases.

I am always trying to coddle into remaining with me flowers which want to be farther north, such as lilacs, or farther south, such as Indica azaleas. They will exist if I take enough pains with them, but they are not happy and the meagerness of their bloom betrays their incurable nostalgia. The heart too has its climate, without which it is a mere pumping-station.

In roses we demand now the sunset colors of Talisman or the dawn colors of Dainty Bess, and to hold them with us spend our time fighting black spot and mildew. But Aunt Nana has Malmaisons and Maman Cochets, which Père planted fifty years ago and which she has never sprayed or fertilized. They are just roses, not too beautiful, not like sunset or dawn, but heavy with attar, and they don't need coddling: they are so glad of life they fight for it. After all, strength is one of the primary colors.

But the major moral afforded by a garden comes from watching the fight for sunlight waged by those unhappy things rooted against their will in shade. None of them will flower, but by desperate devices, tragic substitutes, some of them will live. They thrust emaciated feelers, gangling and scant of leaf, toward a spot of light. To escape the deeper shadow they twist themselves into ungainliness. Branches die so that the remnant whole may survive. They are bleached as by a sickroom. They seem to have lost not only their beauty but their dignity in straining for the golden warmth that is their source of life. Standing at the post-office corner I recognize my poor sunless plants in the passers-by, sickly, out of shape, ugly with strain, who still search for a sunlight vital to their needs and never found, or found and lost.

However, even these bits of wisdom I pick up from gardening, as a chicken gathers grit for its craw, are not for me the chief reward of a garden. It's a closed and quiet place, the best sort of Ivory Tower, and you can sit in a corner spattered with sunlight and wonder—that's its real function. It's a starting-point for thoughts and backward looks and questionings. It fades easily into other landscapes that seasons do not change. You sit there and think of the trip you have made, fifty-five years of trip, and you wonder what it means and what it totals up to.

Having gone on for half a century, you find to your surprise you have passed the crest and are going down the shady side of the mountain. It is pleasant country and not sad, though tinged with autumn and life in the air deceptively. Down the long easy slope there are no trees, but wideness everywhere and tall seeded grasses that glisten and tremble. To the right great shafts of low sunlight lie benign and quiet, reaching down and down to the tender blue smudge that must be the sea. But in front, near, though down a way, is the cypress grove to which you know you are going. Purple-shadowed, tall, and very still, you see it, but not by looking squarely. You are not afraid to look, but you are not hankering to be there yet, not quite yet. It will not fade out like the sea and the sunlight, no need to hurry. So I rest quietly and at peace on a low bench by the way. I imagine it to be a bench like the one Tom made me for a corner of the garden from a single slab of Sewanee sandstone. Behind his, the real one, are the Cape jessamines he loves, ailing always though heavy bloomers, and in front are the weeping willow and the silver flowering peaches, eager things and, for all their fragility, stout believers in the resurrection. Here is a chance to remember back and count up.

Half a century is a long time, specially in a world as lovely as ours, as starred with brave and pitiful people with honey at their hearts and on their lips. No use remembering the ugly and the evil, they were never very real anyway and nothing came of them. Evil is for the sunny side, to test the strength of the climbers, I suppose. It is easier to remember the good. So I'll think of Tom in the hot summer evenings watering his roses and dousing the screaming children as they tip up behind him, or of Adah serving a cold drink, as Mother used to do, to the golfers as they stop by for more than a julep's refreshment on their way home; or of Rufus hurrying into his soft-ball suit after the hard day and calling out nonsense to his little one. Trifles and little happenings seem dear when you recall you will not be seeing them always.

I know if by chance I joined these twilight doings of my friends my welcome would be unfeigned and tender. Yet I know if I did not join them, if I never joined them, nothing would cease or change. For the place I have won here and there, early and late, though a good place and a proud one, was never first place in any life, and what was mine to possess utterly and sovereignly, without counterclaim, was only the jackdaw pickings of my curious and secret heart. When your heart's a kleptomaniac for bits of color and scraps of god-in-man, its life hoardings make a pile glinting indeed, but of no worth save to the miserly fanatic heart. Now is the time, now when the air is still and the light is going, to spread my treasure out.

The things you like to remember often happen so quickly and simply you are not certain afterwards that they happened at all. It may be in a garden, a simple home garden without landscaping, and you are walking slowly with one you love and understand (as understanding goes between us mortals), one who is self-contained and inarticulate. You pause together and look a long time at an early spring flower, probably a white narcissus with wonder on it, as if the risen Lord had just stepped there, and you hear your companion say: "And some people say there is no God." Looking up quickly, you catch the tail end of a smile, as absorbed and guileless as Adam's when his lids first opened and he beheld Eden, dappled and fresh in the early sunlight. Of course you observe it is time to begin spraying, but actually you are swinging a censer and repeating: "Laus Deo," while the voice goes on: "Let's try Bordeaux mixture this time."

I gaze down the long slope with its grass that bends and shivers and the memories, my very own, drift through me like dim music, like that appeasing heart-broken theme of the *Pathétique* or Gluck's glimpse of the Elysian fields or

the unbearable peace and tears of the Good Friday Spell
or Bach's *Komm', süsser Tod,* only the music is blurred,
with the anguish gone. It has all been good and worth the
tears. I see it as a dream I long to hold, but not to relive. I
hear voices unbelievably soft (whose are they, was it in Rio
or Barcelona or the islands? No matter) that murmur:
Don't go, don't leave me, I love you," and I smile, knowing
I will hear them no more and grateful for their music. I
watch from my balcony the torches of the Capri fishing-
boats far down, sprinkling the deep sea with their stars,
serene under the unpausing divine constellations. I pace
the south portico of the Parthenon in the morning light
across the panels of shadow and glimpse between the luminous columns the misty blue of Salamis, Ægina tremendous
in the glare, and the rose and violet peaks behind Sparta and
Corinth. I see Ætna bathed in sunset, the purple sea at its
feet. I walk the square of Chartres wanting to enter for a
last sight of the Tree of Jesse with its miraculous blue, like
God's very own, but I can't go in because I still can't decide
whether the north or the south spire is the more beautiful.
I tell Timi to paddle from under the hibiscus trees into the
middle of the bay, so I may hear and see the Pacific break
itself to thunder and snowy seethings on the Papatoi reef,
while the mountains watch, and the million palms. The
incredible loveliness of our star! And how well we men
have done by it, having added to its beauty when the gods
who fashioned it could not!

And now I recall, for the mere delight of recalling, scenes
that somehow I can never forget, my very own, bits of my
treasure:

I remember the satyr on the slopes of Parnassus. The
road that traverses those slopes is upland all the way. Above
it to the left hang the gray and golden cliffs, below it to the
right on the broken mountainside stumble the ancient silver

olive trees that grope their way to touch far down the river that has died. Beyond the river-bed a treeless range of peaks joins hands to shut the world out and the Corinthian gulf. Here is a high lost world of its own, austere and primitive, antique and changeless. The silver python of the road, sunning itself on the ledge beneath the cliffs, serves the rough folk of these crumbling times as it served Homer's. The crystal air pours down and pools between the mountains and the cliffs as if caught in a warped and golden bowl. It is like no other air of earth, of autumn purity and life, even when fired with summer, and clothing the planets and their kin with legendary brightness. Were I disengaged spirit, I would haunt there, as I often have in these uneasy trappings of mortality.

When I met the satyr it was past sunset time and I had walked into the splendor. I passed the sacred rubble of the temples, wan in the colorless shadow, and watched the eagles homing to their aeries. By the roadside beneath the Castalian spring women were lifting from the vervain and wild heliotrope the wash where they had spread it out to dry, and other women on their donkeys were returning from the vineyards, children and lambs and kids in their wake and their wooden saddles heaped fore and aft with bundles of furze and babies. Their laughter and hale banter were merely tinklings in the deepening silence. Beyond them, where the road skirted a great rock, I paused on the edge above the olive slopes and looked into the depth of air beneath. It was a limpid evening, the whole broad quarter of the lower sky washed with rose tourmaline and witch's green and lemon, and the vast zenith, silver-blue, flawed with a single star. The obsessed cuckoo had desisted, and deep in the lower olives by the river the first nightingales stammered their faint cold music. Then the moon, winning her mountain climb, floated loose into the heavens, a full moon vast and rosy, with a bruise of purple in the sky around her. Facing the steep I had not heard the patter of climbing hoofs, but suddenly up from the shadows at my feet bounded a prodigious he-goat, with sacrificial spread of twisted horns, long mocking beard, and appraising disillusioned eyes of gold; and behind him a brown boy. He was hardly half as tall as the goat-herd's crook he carried. His shock of straight black hair had never felt a comb. Sandals were on his feet and thongs crisscrossed from his ankles to his knees. His goat-herd's short skirt and nondescript tunic were dirt-colored. From the tight-pulled strand of leather that served for belt glared a conspicuous knife. Over one shoulder was slung a coarse striped haversack to hold his lunch. We were both completely startled. He stared at me as though I were a mortal and I said: "Kala mera." It was all the Greek, modern or classic, I knew, but it wasn't appropriate, for it meant "Good morning." He replied in his language. I observed that the moon was full and his herd, which by this time was pouring into the road, was magnificent. He replied lengthily in his language, and I nodded. He asked to see my watch. He shook it and put it to his ear, but of course did not look at the time. We stood together and watched the moon rise and did not feel like speaking. He returned my watch, crinkled his eyes at me, and stepped to the huge ram. I thought he was leaving. But instead he dropped his crook, held his empty musette bag before him, and shook it. From his throat, not from his mouth, issued animal sounds, half cluck, half guttural bleat, he swayed and bent, and raised one knee. The Pan-faced monster opposite rose to his hind legs, tossed his great horns from side to side, and bellowed. They danced together. The full moon and I saw them dance together. They stopped when the nervous herd started moving on its way. From across the road he frowned on me searchingly a long minute and then, deciding perhaps I really believed in him, he ran across the road and took my hand. So toward the Shining Rocks that Phœbus thrust asunder we walked in silence, hand in hand. But when the great shadow of Agamemnon's plane tree covered us, looking up sideways, he smiled once—but it was like a gale of laughter—and was gone. And the night seemed suddenly bleak.

I remember the sheer Anatolian headland where it reared from the gaudy sea into the blinding sunlight. It was high noon and the sea and the sun were laughing. We climbed to the clump of pine trees on the crest. Among the scented needles in the thin unsteady shade we lay with our lunch on the ground and gazed as from a tower's top across the outspread splendor. The sapphire water shook and glistened, the shallows thrust their fronds of pale green, and farther out a splotch of purple showed where some white-stoled cloud paused absently. We seemed suspended magically at some mid-level, sapphire sky above, sapphire water beneath, and brightness everywhere. In front, very distant, barely scrawled on the horizon, rose the minarets and domes of Constantinople and to the left, palest pink and lavender in the ecstatic light, the bare mountains of Brusa. Except that it was live with rushing air and rustling water it would have seemed a fortunate bright dream. We lay on the ground in the penciled shadow, each in his own burnished reverie. . . . At first we were not sure our ears were hearing; it might be music from some inner isle or some old trick of Pan's. It seemed a voice singing. Without interchange, still unconvinced, we listened separately and heard indeed a human voice that sang. The song rose to us, strong and rude and happy, a Turkish song with the strange Turkish cadences and unexpected intervals. We scrambled to our knees and peered down over the edge. A young man, white and naked, with a mop of gold hair, was swimming beneath us, and as he swam he sang. Oblivious of us, enraptured and alone, brimming with some hale antique happiness not ours to know, he clove the flashing water and sang into the sun. At last the dazzle hid him from us, but still we heard his voice.

I remember the forecastle of the ship that carried us to Rio, where after their watches the crew came up to rest and breathe the night. About the equator the seas are lonely, with no passing ships to hail and no sight of land for unending weeks. The very stars have changed and those we knew lose themselves in our wake like phosphorus. Our ship receded from reality, became a tiny world abandoned to itself, and in the tropic night, despite the appeasing pathos of the moon, it seemed a lonely world, forgotten and adrift, pursuing some mysterious course that might not count a port. Our crew had come together by mere chance, haphazardly, from unrelated shores, Portuguese, Samoan, Finnish, American, Greek, and could speak, but could not communicate. Some of them were old men with sharp or dreamy eyes and some were youngsters, desperate and ensorcelled. Looking down in the semi-night of the mounting moon across the forecastle, I watched them moving like somnambulists, the wind whipping their hair, the moonlight turning their bodies slender and unsubstantial, daubing their cheek-bones and shoulders, the arch of their chests or their buttocks with pallor, and a stillness was on them. They came on deck from the hatches in a sudden glory of light as a door swung open and closed, and for an instant the yellow shaft outlined them, before dimness resumed. They came in all manner of garbs, in work clothes or stripped to the waist; mostly they came alone and kept to themselves. There was always a width of moonlight between them. Some sat on the coils of rope or the winches and smoked. The sparks from their pipes flared wildly across the deck like a midget galaxy rushing to extinction. The wind was too loud for talking or singing, but a few tried one and the other half-heartedly, and the wind took the words and the song. They moved like men who were drugged, slowly and vaguely. Before going below again, each of them walked to the rail and leaned there, staring out into the empty ocean. Leaning there on the rail, waist-deep in moonlight, they gazed a long silent time, as if quite alone, and with their lips parted. Perhaps they were thinking each one of different things, of wives or mothers, of sweethearts or children, of women and liquor, or perhaps they were thinking each one of the same thing. The look on their faces was the same as they gazed beyond the moon's small miracle to the enclosing dimness. The patience of loneliness and the tranquillity of unescapable pain were on their faces like grave beauty. I thought of a lost chart and an unknown port, and I too looked to sea.

Then a great clang shattered the darkness, for the young watch at the bow had crashed the hour from his bell. He cupped his hands, turned to the bridge, and shouted, in a voice piercingly young and full of hope: "The lights are bright, sir!"

I remember the city of Babel on Manhattan when the lights come on in the early winter evening. We leaned from the topmost tower of all the world and gazed on the pride of man, the work of his hands, the miracle of fire and steel that he had fashioned. Like gods we looked down on the apogee of beauty, the race's masterpiece. The solemn buildings, housing imperishable light, soared from the stone earth high and higher till they were standing, massive and at ease, in the bird-lanes of the immaculate air—man's revelation of bulk become passionate, solidity ethereal, and mass a thing of flight. Singly or grouped in brotherhoods, they stood in awful silence, with an air of waiting, and between their ribs their million windows shone. Far as the eye could reach the incredible dark forms stood waiting in the night, silent and breathing, from base to summit beautiful with their own inner light. Above the torment of the dreadful world they brooded, and the ocean sound of its incessant strivings rose like a sea-shell's aimless hum.

Yet the great builders of this unbearable beauty were invisible. We peered into the chasms they had made and saw long files of metal beetles trekking a bare yard when the chains of rubies turned to emeralds. And then we spied the lesser insects on the bottom. We watched their tiny scurryings, their nervous sorties and returns, their feverish small haste, and their bewildered pauses. Unwillingly and rueful to the core, we recognized the poor creating gods of all this majesty. A voice at my side was murmuring to itself: "This is the most touching thing I ever saw." And I was thinking, if Satan, standing where we stood, had offered, not the whole world, but this desperate city in all its piteousness, no Son of God could have had the heart to refuse it.

These memories of mine, these tinsel hoardings, lose nothing of their luster in this time of doom. A tarnish has fallen over the bright world; dishonor and corruption triumph; my own strong people are turned lotus-eaters; defeat is here again, the last, the most abhorrent. But the autumn air is tinged with gold, the spotted sun sleeps in the garden, and the only treasure that's exempt from tarnish is what the jackdaw gathers.

# CHAPTER XXVII

# *Home*

One of the pleasantest places near the home town is the cemetery. It lies along a curve of Rattlesnake Bayou. Across its front used to run the old dirt road to the river-landing down which the raiding Yankees would dash on their forays inland while Holt and the remaining elders of the countryside would snipe them from the bushes. Now the road is of concrete and its unexpected curve often sends motorists in their cups or out of their wits headlong into the well-dredged bayou, which on drainage maps is now called Dredge Ditch No. 4 D. Across the bayou toward the east have grown up new enterprises of which we are proud, a florist's, a nursery, the golf-links, and an exclusive addition full of very old beautiful trees and very new beautiful residences. The cemetery itself was designed during carriage days, with cedar-bordered roads running in parallel semi-circles and too narrow for automobiles. In spite of the neighboring highway with its strident motor-cars it is a quiet spot, eternally green, and from any grave you may look westerly across open fields to the levee and feel the river beyond, deep in its plumy willows. This home of the dead is, quaintly enough, the home of hundreds of mocking-birds, which, mistaking all time for eternal spring, sing the year round. I have heard them append arpeggios and cadenzas to pitiful unreassuring funeral sermons and rain liquid hope while the priest was muttering *in pulverem reverteris.*

Our lot is toward the back and raised a little, as someone hated to think of the river's overflow covering the graves. In the middle of it, backed by a semicircular thicket of ever-greens, stands Malvina Hoffman's bronze figure of a brood-ing knight, sunshine flowing from his body as indicated in low relief on the stone stele behind, and the river at his feet. The one word "Patriot" beneath the statue and Matthew Arnold's "Last Word" on the reverse side of the stele show those who loved him that Father lies near by.

I come here not infrequently because it is restful and comforting. I am with my own people. With them around me I can seem to read the finished manuscripts of their lives, forever unchangeable, and beautiful in the dim way manuscripts have. Here sleep Mother and Father, Mur and Fafar, Mère and Père, the small brother who should be representing and perpetuating the name, Uncle George in one corner, his fishing done, in another under a stone marked "Gentleman" Fafar's brother LeRoy beside Fafar's elder daughter, whose death, caused, he thought, by a quack doctor he himself had chosen, so grieved him he ended his own life. Aunt Fanny is here too, no opiates needed now for her long ills, and close to her her husband, Dr. Walker Percy, who, united and gathered to his own, finds no further need to oppose secession. The latest-comer and the loveliest, Mattie Sue, sleeps to the front, her morn-ing-glory air all gone, but the valor not yet faded from her heart. They are all here, and I am glad there's room to spare. It would be indeed a chilly world without this refuge with its feel of home.

I wish a few others out there, under the cedars, could be in this plot of ours. Miss Carrie's bird-body must by now be a mere pinch of dust and would take no space. Father Koestenbrock, far from his native city and his fathers, might feel less lonely here. Here Judge Griffin might dream of a truer ending for his *Ruin Robed*. And I should like to bring from that far corner where the poor sleep well one brown-eyed lad who sleeps alone there, for he had loved me and gaspingly had told me so while death was choking him and he knew it was death.

I am told that in Arab countries strangers volunteer to carry the coffin of a deceased, and in our cities strangers are hired for this chore. But with us friends are asked to bear their friends to the open grave for the last rites. Far as these white stones reach are graves now closed to which I have carried my friends—poor and well-to-do, obscure and prominent, good and bad, men and women, young and old, Jew and Christian, believer and agnostic. Sometimes with the coffin handle in my grip, staggering heavily toward that angular gash in the curving earth, I forget which one it is this time who is preceding me and wonder absently who will be left to do me a like service. A little while and the living town, this tiny world of mine, will all be here, tucked under the same dark blanket, cosily together. Another little while and the last of us, those I loved and those I disapproved, will be sharing oblivion, for no one will remember any of us. The famous do not share our cedars and our mockingbirds. This is private ground for the lovable obscure. Even Father, who warmed and led and lighted our people—no one will remember him, his name and deeds will be forgotten soon, in another spring, or ten, or a hundred, what matter? Strangers will come and, striving briefly, will join us in our dark, and our mockingbirds, unrecollecting, will sing for them with equal rapture.

While people are still alive we judge them as good or bad, condemn them as failures or praise them as successes, love them or despise them. Only when they are dead do we see them, not with charity, but with understanding. Alive they are remote, even hostile; dead, they join our circle and you see the family likeness. As I loiter among our graves reading the names on the headstones, names that when they identified live men I sometimes hated or scorned as enemies of me and mine and all that we held good, I find myself smiling. How unreal and accidental seem their defects! I know their stories: this one was a whore and this a thief, here lies the town hypocrite and there one who should have died before he was born. I know their stories, but not their hearts. With a little shifting of qualities, with a setting more to their needs, with merely more luck, this woman could have borne children who would have been proud of her, and this thief might have become the father of the poor. Now death has made them only home-folks and I like the sound of their familiar names. They lie there under the grass in the evening light so helplessly, my townsmen, a tiny outpost of the lost tribe of our star. Understanding breaks over my heart and I know that the wickedness and the failures of men are nothing and their valor and pathos and effort everything. Circumscribed and unendowed, ailing in body, derided and beguiled, how well they have done! They have sipped happiness and gulped pain, they have sought God and never found Him, they have found love and never kept him—yet they kept on, they never gave up, they rarely complained. Among these handfuls of misguided dust I am proud to be a man and assuaged for my own defects. I muse on this one small life that it is all I have to show for, the sum of it, the wrong turnings, the weakness of will, the feebleness of spirit, one tiny life with darkness before and after, and it at best a riddle and a wonder. One by one I count the failures—at law undistinguished, at teaching unprepared, at soldiering average, at citizenship unimportant, at love second-best, at poetry forgotten before remembered—and I acknowledge the deficit. I am not proud, but I am not ashamed. What have defeats and failures to do with the good life? But closer lacks, more troubling doubts assail me. Of all the people I have loved, wisely and unwisely, deeply and passingly, I have loved no one so much as myself. Of all the hours of happiness granted me, none has been so keen and holy as a few unpredictable moments alone. I have never walked with God, but I had rather walk with Him through hell than with my heart's elect through heaven. Of the good life I have learned what it is not and I have loved a few who lived it end to end. I have seen the goodness of men and the beauty of things. I have no regrets. I am not contrite. I am grateful.

Here among the graves in the twilight I see one thing only, but I see that thing clear. I see the long wall of a rampart sombre with sunset, a dusty road at its base. On the tower of the rampart stand the glorious high gods, Death and the rest, insolent and watching. Below on the road stream the tribes of men, tired, bent, hurt, and stumbling, and each man alone. As one comes beneath the tower, the High God descends and faces the wayfarer. He speaks three slow words: "Who are you?" The pilgrim I know should be able to straighten his shoulders, to stand his tallest, and to answer defiantly: "I am your son."

3446